HARLEM MOON
BROADWAY

BELOVED HARLEM

<<<<<<<<<<<<<<<<<<<<<<<<<<<

A LITERARY TRIBUTE TO
BLACK AMERICA'S
MOST FAMOUS NEIGHBORHOOD,
FROM THE CLASSICS
TO THE CONTEMPORARY

>>>>>>>>>>>>>>>>>>>>>>>>>>>

EDITED BY

WILLIAM H. BANKS, JR.

EXECUTIVE DIRECTOR OF THE HARLEM WRITERS GUILD

HARLEM MOON

BROADWAY BOOKS / NEW YORK

Published by HARLEM MOON, an imprint of Broadway Books, a division of Random House, Inc.

PRINTED IN THE UNITED STATES OF AMERICA

HARLEM MOON, BROADWAY BOOKS, and the HARLEM MOON logo, depicting a moon and a woman, are trademarks of Random House, Inc. The figure in the Harlem Moon logo is inspired by a graphic design by Aaron Douglas (1899–1979).

Visit our Web site at www.harlemmoon.com

First edition published 2005

Book design by Gretchen Achilles

Library of Congress Cataloging-in-Publication Data

Beloved Harlem : a literary tribute to Black America's most
    famous neighborhood, from the classics to the contemporary /
    edited by William H. Banks, Jr.
      p. cm.
    ISBN 0-7679-1478-3 (tp)
    1. Harlem (New York, N.Y.)—Literary collections. 2. American
literature—New York (State)—New York. 3. American literature—
African American authors. 4. African Americans—Literary
collections. 5. American literature—20th century. 6. Harlem
Renaissance. I. Banks, William, 1946-

PS549.N5B45 2004
810.8'097471—dc22

                                                    2004042512

10 9 8 7 6 5 4 3 2 1

THIS BOOK IS DEDICATED TO OSSIE DAVIS AND ALL LIBRARIANS. THEY ARE GOD'S FIRST AND BEST SEARCH ENGINES.

ACKNOWLEDGMENTS

Special thanks to: The Schomburg Center for Research in Black Culture, The Harlem Writers Guild, New School University, Medgar Evers College, The National Black Writers Conference, The Urban League, The Writers House, Janet Hill, Clarence Haynes, and P. Llanor Alleyne.

IN LOVING MEMORY OF

John Oliver Killens, Dr. John Henrik Clarke, Audre Lorde, Bill Williams Forde, June Jordan, Doris Jean Alston, Lon Elder III, Alice Childress, David Graham Du Bois, Ossie Davis, Warner Guy, James Baldwin, and Gwendolyn Brooks

CONTENTS

II

1940s–1960s:

THE THUNDER ROARS

155

III

1970s–2000s:

AND THEN WE MAKE THE THUNDER

297

IV

NEW STORIES:

NEW VOICES REFLECT, RECOUNT, AND REINVENT

455

INTRODUCTION

Dr. Martin Luther King, Jr., once said: "The arc of the moral universe is long, but it bends toward justice." In terms of the world of writing created about the black experience in America, the arc is also long—certainly longer than the twentieth century—and it bends toward Harlem.

Yet there was a time when black literary expression faced daunting challenges. In 1950, Ralph Ellison and Richard Wright were the only two best-selling black fiction writers of the day, and the major publishing houses were not going out of their way to seek black talent. Worse still, black authors had no forum in which they could hone their craft, showcase their ability, and wait for a break.

Even the New Deal's meager opportunities, such as the writers' branch of the Works Progress Administration, had ended before President Roosevelt's death. Unlike black schoolchildren in the South, black writers could not expect any court decree to swoop in and improve their prospects.

But a group of unheralded black writers based in Harlem came together. They were determined to make the blank pages in their notebooks and ancient typewriters their level playing fields.

These writers found themselves on the fringes of Greenwich Village writing groups led and populated mostly by liberal, and, in some cases, radical white writers. Though Village groups were receptive to the serious writing efforts of black authors, the blacks found little in those groups to nurture themselves spiritually or to appreciate the unique cultural aspects of their work.

To help fill this debilitating void, the Harlem Writers Club (later to become the Harlem Writers Guild) came into being in 1950 in a small, storefront office one flight above the corner of 125th Street and Lenox Avenue.

The first meeting of the group was, according to Dr. Clarke, informal yet profound. He could not remember if any material was even read for consideration. The most important thing that they decided was that there would in fact *be* a group and that they would continue to meet and read and critique each member's work. It was also agreed that vigorous discussions on the state of black affairs in the Americas and the world would be encouraged. In terms of who was present in those early days, Clarke noted that many fine writers, artists, and activists "came and went and visited" their meetings. To the best of his recollection, the ones who became the core of the group were John Oliver Killens, Rosa Guy, Walter Christmas, and Dr. Clarke himself.

About a year before his death in July 1998, John Henrik Clarke, one of the founders of the Guild, shared with me his reflections on the Guild's then-forty-seven-year history and on this anthology.

When I called him in mid-1997, Dr. Clarke was eighty-one years old and quite frail. His sight had left him many years before. On the day we talked, his energies were depleted from the exertion of dictating his eighth book since going blind. I learned of his condition at that time, not from him, but from his housekeeper, who also answered his home phone.

"Try not to keep him on the line too long," she urged. "People keep calling and he insists on talking to just about every serious writer or scholar who wants to talk to him. But he's really not up to it. He needs his rest. He's tired."

Based on what Dr. Clarke's housekeeper said and the fact that he had recently been in and out of the hospital, I was not prepared for what I heard a moment after she had asked me to hold on.

"Hello, Banks!" a strong and resonant voice boomed through the phone. "How's the Guild and that anthology coming along? Somebody just read me portions of Grace Edwards's new mystery novel. Man, that girl can write! And how are the plans coming for getting as many members of the Guild together as possible in 2000?"

His vitality was a complete and much-welcomed surprise. I had called him to get contact information for Daniel H. Watts, editor and publisher of *Liberator*, the magazine that had been the foremost journal of radical black political opinion in the 1960s.

Clarke mused momentarily after my query. Then he readily gave me a lead to use in tracking down Watts. He made quick work of the few other items on my agenda. It was as though he was clearing a somewhat cluttered table so that he could more comfortably sit down for a much anticipated conversation.

Then, for the next several minutes, the same mind that had become a walking repository for much of the knowledge about Africa and African people to be found in public and university libraries in America and abroad soaked up every word I related to him about the current events of the Guild.

"I don't care what you're doing so much as I hope and care that it is being done. Get the work done. That's what it's about," he said. "As to who should be in the anthology? It doesn't matter to me as long as you've got writing from John [Oliver Killens] and Rosa [Guy]. They were there at the beginning. Don't forget Bill Williams Forde. He held things together for so many years. But you know that, Banks." I also knew that he himself belonged on his own short list. When he, Killens, Guy, and a few others formed the Guild in 1950, Clarke was the only one among them who had published his work.

As we conversed, I could imagine him smiling faintly to himself as I had seen him do countless times in various lecture halls after the applause for one of his stirring presentations had ended. I had once asked him, years before, what it was he was thinking about when he seemed to betray a spontaneous smile on those occasions. At first he kidded me and said, "Tired feet, Banks. I'm just thinking about how good it is to sit down after standing up so long." But then he became thoughtful and divulged that in those private moments, he savored the pleasure and satisfaction of knowing that he had imparted knowledge that could be life-enhancing, even life-changing, for those receiving it. "You see, Banks, I love the feeling that others get when they learn something," he'd said.

"Yeah, Banks," he continued in our phone conversation with a gentle sigh. "Let me tell you one last thing now before I get taken off this phone and put back to bed. Whatever you do, when you sit down to put this thing together, don't make it seem that the Guild or other black writing groups were just places to help you get published. Just like *all* the writers who were influenced by Harlem, particularly the ones that came before us, we were also about struggle: The struggle to write, the struggle to get published, but most of all, the struggle of our people to survive in this country and in this world. Now let me go."

Dr. Clarke, of course, was right. I had never thought about it, but the founders of the Guild were in fact the children of the Harlem Renaissance, for struggle, in all of its aspects, is quite familiar to anyone closely associated with the Guild

No one remembers where the rent for the first meeting place came from, or if there was any. It may have been that the first meeting place was simply an unused room in a small office. What is remembered is that from that room the Guild and its meetings moved to libraries, meeting halls, other offices, and finally to the apartments of members. The apartments of Clarke, Killens, Guy, and Forde at one time or another all served as early meeting places. Then, in 1982, the Schomburg Center for Research in Black Culture became and remains the permanent meeting place for the Guild.

As the decades passed, the list of published works by members increased. In 1986, shortly before his death, John Oliver Killens estimated in an interview for *Biographies of American Authors* that members of the Guild had produced over three hundred published works of fiction, nonfiction, and poetry, as well as screen and stage plays.

Even though the struggle to be published showed some positive results, Guild members still found themselves witnesses to continuing injustice in American society. Bearing this witness and reflecting it in writing and activism became an integral part of the Guild's mission. For instance, John Henrik Clarke and his great friend Dr. Ben Yakim, professor emeritus at Cornell University, are widely regarded as two of the cofounders of black studies at the university level. Colleagues of Clarke's such as Amiri Baraka entered traditional politics, helping to elect the new wave of black officials throughout the country, including Kenneth Gibson, who became Newark, New Jersey's first black mayor in 1970.

During the weeks that followed my conversation with Dr. Clarke, I looked over the selections to be included in the anthology with an expanded perspective. I knew that what was needed was a collection that started before the Guild came along and one that would point the way well past our approaching fiftieth anniversary. I could see that the threads of skill, hope, and race consciousness were indeed already there. But because of the collection's diversity, the pattern of human struggle was not readily apparent. A new aspect of my mission therefore became to make known the full context in which these works were created. That is why I have supplemented each contribution with comments that hopefully enhance and sharpen the view of the work and writer. It was during this reexamination that I concluded that the writers who created the work of this anthology are ardent, spirited, but peaceful warriors whose words are, to be sure, like the proverbial pen itself, mightier than any sword.

Several months later, when the outline for the anthology was just about complete, I called Dr. Clarke's home once again to share with him the news of our progress. This time I got no further than his housekeeper. Dr. Clarke was hospitalized again and this time gravely ill. He died two months later.

This book is dedicated to literary giants such as Clarke, Hughes, Baldwin, Hurston, and Killens who have gone before us, but who have left us the broad shoulders of their work to stand upon. They were each first drawn to the promise and sanctuary of Harlem. And once there, they fell in love with it and with the art of putting the African-American experience into words. It then became their beloved Harlem and ours.

—WILLIAM H. BANKS, JR.

PART ONE

1910s–1930s

<<<<<<<<<<<<<<<<<<<<<<<<<<<<

THE DESCENDENTS OF SLAVES
EMANCIPATE A CULTURE

I gnited by a conspiracy of circumstance and opportunity, the Harlem
Renaissance, commonly noted as the decade spanning 1919 to 1929,
stands as a stellar, singular roll of time in which the generations of
blacks born in the wake of the Civil War descended on an unpopular
plot of real estate in upper New York City and commenced to making a
bit of heaven for themselves.

In 1914, with World War I greasing the gears of an industrial boom
across the urban North and the demand for laborers high due to the
stymied influx of European immigrants, thousands of southern
blacks—themselves under the painful peck of Jim Crow segregation
laws and facing the economic devastation of a boll weevil infestation of
the cotton crops—surged upward to Chicago, Detroit, Philadelphia, and
New York.

In these more liberal cities where discrimination and prejudice still
blanketed everyday life, southern African Americans joined blacks from
the Caribbean in taking full advantage of the better jobs, housing, education, and cultural resources (libraries, museums, and theater) made
available to them.

No place was this more true than in New York's Harlem, where the
headquarters of the National Association for the Advancement of Colored People, headed by historian and sociologist W.E.B Du Bois, and the
National Urban League, lead by Dr. George Edmund Haynes, also a sociologist, had established a strong presence. The organizations recog-

nized the economic, political, and social needs of the city's growing black population. To that end, both organizations printed journals (the NAACP's *The Crisis* and NUL's *Opportunity*), which not only addressed the swiftly changing political and social concerns of the day, but provided a space for creative expression.

At the end of World War I, the stream of blacks arriving from all corners of America and the Caribbean was a steady flow. Among their ranks were educated and socially conscious writers carrying with them the heavy bags of racism and the need to continually reshape black identity. By 1917, Caribbean-born Claude McKay had ushered in Harlem as muse with his highly praised poem, "Harlem Dancer."

With the onset of the 1920s, Harlem had become "a city within a city," as noted by novelist and essayist James Weldon Johnson, with many life currents pumping through its streets. Black nationalists like Marcus Garvey were appealing to working-class blacks to invest in back-to-Africa schemes. At the same time, Harlem became the go-to spot for good music and illegal liquor as the rest of the city cowered under strict Prohibition mandates.

But while Harlem's teeming nightlife drew whites uptown, so did its bursting dam of literary voices. In March 1925, Harlem was put on the literati map, when *Survey Graphics,* a progressive magazine that covered social issues across the country, devoted an entire issue to the neighborhood's bourgeoning cache of writers, among them Langston Hughes, Countee Cullen, Charles S. Johnson, and Du Bois. Eight months later, that edition's guest editor, Howard University Philosophy Chair Alain Locke, published an expansion of the issue as the book, *The New Negro,* adding such notables as Zora Neale Hurston and historian J. A. Rogers as contributors. It was the acceleration of a creative and cultural windfall that would last four more years.

Unfortunately, with the stock market crash of 1929 and the nation's rapid decline into an economic crisis, Harlem faced the distinct possibility of becoming a cultural and artistic ghost town. With virtually all white and black financial patronage withdrawn, many of the writers who flourished in the 1920s were forced to leave the city, and in many cases, abandon their craft altogether. But others, like Hurston and Arna Bontemps, continued to work under President Roosevelt's Works Progress Administration, which employed varied artists to produce public works across the country.

Meanwhile, as Harlem continued to feel the devastating effects of the Great Depression, its moniker as the artistic capital of the world was tarnished with the eruption of the Harlem Riot of 1935, which saw a neighborhood frustrated with economic and political inequalities literally burst into flames. Still, a year later, the residents of Harlem peacefully gathered outside the Lafayette Theatre to watch Shakespeare's *Macbeth* performed by the Negro Theatre Unit, itself an outgrowth of the WPA. It was directed by the young, white, volatile director Orson Welles, who had many friends among the black writers, actors, and artists he'd met while working on another federally funded project. Dubbed in the press as "Voodoo *Macbeth*" for its Haitian setting, the play went on to make a triumphant tour of the country.

FROM THE AUTOBIOGRAPHY OF AN EX-COLORED MAN (1912)

JAMES WELDON JOHNSON

Renowned as an author, attorney, activist, poet, songwriter, and diplomat, Johnson was born in Florida to Bahamian parents. He received an undergraduate education at Atlanta University and later took graduate courses at Columbia University after he and his brother moved to Harlem in 1902. While serving in a diplomatic post in Nicaragua, he finished his first novel, *The Autobiography of an Ex-Colored Man,* which followed the journey of an anonymous narrator of mixed ancestry. Johnson also published the book anonymously, hoping that audiences would think it was a true story. The excerpt presented here shows the narrator's total rejection of living to appease whites and his desire to add pride and dignity to the lives of Negroes.

Johnson died in an auto accident in Maine in 1938. His Harlem funeral drew an estimated two thousand mourners.

CHAPTER 1

I know that in writing the following pages I am divulging the great secret of my life, the secret which for some years I have guarded far more carefully than any of my earthly possessions; and it is a curious study to me to analyse the motives which prompt me to do it. I feel that I am led by the same impulse which forces the un-found-out criminal to take somebody into his confidence, although he knows that the act is likely, even almost certain, to lead to his undoing. I know that I am playing with fire, and I feel the thrill which accompanies that most fascinating pastime; and, back of it all, I think I find a sort of savage and diabolical desire to gather up all the little tragedies of my life, and turn them into a practical joke on society.

And, too, I suffer a vague feeling of unsatisfaction, of regret, of almost remorse, from which I am seeking relief, and of which I shall speak in the last paragraph of this account.

I was born in a little town of Georgia a few years after the close of the Civil War. I shall not mention the name of the town, because there are people still living there who could be connected with this narrative. I have only a faint recollection of the place of my birth. At times I can close my eyes and call up in a dreamlike way things that seem to have happened ages ago in some other world. I can see in this half vision a little house—I am quite sure it was not a large one—I can remember that flowers grew in the front yard, and that around each bed of flowers was a hedge of vari-coloured glass bottles stuck in the ground neck down. I remember that once, while playing round in the sand, I became curious to know whether or not the bottles grew as the flowers did, and I proceeded to dig them up to find out; the investigation brought me a terrific spanking, which indelibly fixed the incident in my mind. I can remember, too, that behind the house was a shed under which stood two or three wooden wash-tubs. These tubs were the earliest aversion of my life, for regularly on certain evenings I was plunged into one of them and scrubbed until my skin ached. I can remember to this day the pain caused by the strong, rank soap's getting into my eyes.

Back from the house a vegetable garden ran, perhaps seventy-five or one hundred feet; but to my childish fancy it was an endless territory. I can still recall the thrill of joy, excitement, and wonder it gave me to go on an exploring expedition through it, to find the blackberries, both ripe and green, that grew along the edge of the fence.

I remember with what pleasure I used to arrive at, and stand before, a little enclosure in which stood a patient cow chewing her cud, how I would occasionally offer her through the bars a piece of my bread and molasses, and how I would jerk back my hand in half fright if she made any motion to accept my offer.

I have a dim recollection of several people who moved in and about this little house, but I have a distinct mental image of only two: one, my mother; and the other, a tall man with a small, dark moustache. I remember that his shoes or boots were always shiny, and that he wore a gold chain and a great gold watch with which he was always willing to let me play. My admiration was almost equally divided between the watch and chain and the shoes. He used to come to the house evenings, perhaps two or three times a week; and it became my appointed duty whenever he came to bring him a pair of slippers and to put the shiny shoes in a particular corner; he often gave me in return for this service a bright coin, which my mother taught me to promptly drop in a little tin bank. I remember distinctly the last time this tall man came to the little house in Georgia; that evening before I went to bed he took me up in his arms and squeezed me very tightly; my mother stood behind his chair wiping tears from her eyes. I remember how I sat upon his knee and watched him laboriously drill a hole through a ten-dollar gold piece, and then tie the coin around my neck with a string. I have worn that gold piece around my neck the greater part of my life, and still possess it, but more than once I have wished that some other way had been found of attaching it to me besides putting a hole through it.

On the day after the coin was put around my neck my mother and I started on what seemed to me an endless journey. I knelt on the seat and watched through the train window the corn- and cotton-fields pass swiftly by until I fell asleep. When I fully awoke, we were being driven through the streets of a large city—Savannah. I sat up and blinked at the bright lights. At Savannah we boarded a steamer which finally landed us in New York. From New York we went to a town in Connecticut, which became the home of my boyhood.

My mother and I lived together in a little cottage which seemed to me to be fitted up almost luxuriously; there were horse-hair covered chairs in the parlour, and a little square piano; there was a stairway with red carpet on it leading to a half second story; there were pictures on the walls, and a few books in a glass-doored case. My mother dressed me very neatly, and I developed that pride which well-dressed boys generally have. She was careful about my associates, and I myself was quite particular. As I look back now I can see that I was a perfect little aristocrat. My mother rarely went to anyone's house, but she did sewing, and there were a great many ladies coming to our cottage. If I was round they would generally call me, and ask me my name and age and tell my mother what a pretty boy I was. Some of them would pat me on the head and kiss me.

My mother was kept very busy with her sewing; sometimes she would have another woman helping her. I think she must have derived a fair income from her work. I know, too, that at least once each month she received a letter; I used to watch for the postman, get the letter, and run to her with it; whether she was busy or not, she would take it and instantly thrust it into her bosom. I never saw her read one of these letters. I knew later that they contained money and what was to her more than money. As busy as she generally was, she found time, however, to teach me my letters and figures and how to spell a number of easy words. Always on Sunday evenings she opened the little square piano and picked out hymns. I can recall now that whenever she played hymns from the book her *tempo* was always decidedly *largo*. Sometimes on other evenings, when she was not sewing, she would play simple accompaniments to some old Southern songs which she sang. In these songs she was freer, because she played them by ear. Those evenings on which she opened the little piano were the happiest hours of my childhood. Whenever she started toward the instrument, I used to follow her with all the interest and irrepressible joy that a pampered pet dog shows when a package is opened in which he knows there is a sweet bit for him. I used to stand by her side and often interrupt and annoy her by chiming in with strange harmonies which I found on either the high keys of the treble or the low keys of the bass. I remember that I had a particular fondness for the black keys. Always on such evenings, when the music was over, my mother would sit with me in her arms, often for a very long time. She would hold me close, softly crooning some old melody without words, all the while gently stroking her face against my head; many and many a night I thus fell asleep. I can see her now, her great dark eyes looking into the fire, to where? No one knew but her. The memory of that picture has more than once kept me from straying too far from the place of purity and safety in which her arms held me.

At a very early age I began to thump on the piano alone, and it was not long before I was able to pick out a few tunes. When I was seven years old, I could play by ear all of the hymns and songs that my mother knew. I had also learned the names of the notes in both clefs, but I preferred not to be hampered by notes. About this time several ladies for whom my mother sewed heard me play and they persuaded her that I should at once be put under a teacher; so arrangements were made for me to study the piano with a lady who was a fairly good musician; at the same time arrangements were made for me to study my books with this lady's daughter. My music teacher had no small difficulty at first in pinning me down to the notes. If she played my lesson over for me, I invariably attempted to reproduce the required sounds without the slightest recourse to the written characters. Her daughter, my other teacher, also had her worries. She found that, in reading, whenever I came to words that were difficult or unfamiliar, I was prone to bring my imagination to the rescue and read from the picture. She has laughingly told me, since then, that I would sometimes substitute whole sentences and even paragraphs from what meaning I thought the illustrations conveyed. She said she not only was sometimes amused at the fresh treatment I would give an author's subject, but, when I gave some new and sudden turn to the plot of the story, often grew interested and even excited in listening to hear what kind of a denouement I would bring about. But I am sure this was not due to dullness, for I made rapid progress in both my music and my books.

And so for a couple of years my life was divided between my music and my school-books. Music took up the greater part of my time. I had no playmates, but amused myself with games—some of them my own invention—which could be played alone. I knew a few boys whom I had met at the church which I attended with my mother, but I had formed no close friendships with any of them. Then, when I was nine years old, my mother decided to enter me in the public school, so all at once I found myself thrown among a crowd of boys of all sizes and kinds; some of them seemed to me like savages. I shall never forget the bewilderment, the pain, the heart-sickness, of that first day at school. I seemed to be the only stranger in the place; every other boy seemed to know every other boy. I was fortunate enough, however, to be assigned to a teacher who knew me; my mother made her dresses. She was one of the ladies who used to pat me on the head and kiss me. She had the tact to address a few words directly to me; this gave me a certain sort of standing in the class and put me somewhat at ease.

Within a few days I had made one staunch friend and was on fairly good terms with most of the boys. I was shy of the girls, and remained so; even now a word or look from a pretty woman sets me all a-tremble. This friend I bound to me with hooks of steel in a very simple way. He was a big awkward boy with a face full of freckles and a head full of very red hair. He was perhaps fourteen years of age; that is, four or five years older than any other boy in the class. This seniority was due to the fact that he had spent twice the required amount of time in several of the preceding classes. I had not been at school many hours before I felt that "Red Head"—as I involuntarily called him—and I were to be friends. I do not doubt that this feeling was strengthened by the fact that I had been quick enough to see that a big, strong boy was a friend to be desired at a public school; and, perhaps, in spite of his dullness, "Red Head" had been able to discern that I could be of service to him. At any rate there was a simultaneous mutual attraction.

The teacher had strung the class promiscuously round the walls of the room for a sort of trial heat for places of rank; when the line was straightened out, I found that by skillful maneuvering I had placed myself third and had piloted "Red Head" to the place next to me. The teacher began by giving us to spell the words corresponding to our order in the line. "Spell *first.*" "Spell *second.*" "Spell *third.*" I rattled off: "T-h-i-r-d, third," in a way which said: "Why don't you give us something hard?" As the words went down the line, I could see how lucky I had been to get a good place together with an easy word. As young as I was, I felt impressed with the unfairness of the whole proceeding when I saw the tailenders going down before *twelfth* and *twentieth,* and I felt sorry for those who had to spell such words in order to hold a low position. "Spell *fourth.*" "Red Head," with his hands clutched tightly behind his back, began bravely: "F-o-r-t-h." Like a flash a score of hands went up, and the teacher began saying: "No snapping of fingers, no snapping of fingers." This was the first word missed, and it seemed to me that some of the scholars were about to lose their senses; some were dancing up and down on one foot with a hand above their heads, the fingers working furiously, and joy beaming all over their faces; others stood still, their hands raised not so high, their fingers working less rapidly, and their faces expressing not quite so much happiness; there were still others who did not move or raise their hands, but stood with great wrinkles on their foreheads, looking very thoughtful.

The whole thing was new to me, and I did not raise my hand, but slyly whispered the letter "u" to "Red Head" several times. "Second chance," said the teacher. The hands went down and the class became quiet. "Red Head," his face now red, after looking beseechingly at the ceiling, then pitiably at the floor, began very haltingly: "F-u—" Immediately an impulse to raise hands went through the class, but the teacher checked it, and poor "Red Head," though he knew that each letter he added only took him farther out of the way, went doggedly on and finished: "—r-t-h." The handraising was now repeated with more hubbub and excitement than at first. Those who before had not moved a finger were now waving their hands above their heads. "Red Head" felt that he was lost. He looked very big and foolish, and some of the scholars began to snicker. His helpless condition went straight to my heart, and gripped my sympathies. I felt that if he failed, it would in some way be my failure. I raised my hand, and, under cover of the excitement and the teacher's attempts to regain order, I hurriedly shot up into his ear twice, quite distinctly: "F-o-u-r-t-h, f-o-u-r-t-h." The teacher tapped on her desk and said: "Third and last chance." The hands came down, the silence became oppressive. "Red Head" began: "F—" Since that day I have waited anxiously for many a turn of the wheel of fortune, but never under greater tension than when I watched for the order in which those letters would fall from "Red's" lips "o-u-r-t-h." A sigh of relief and disappointment went up from the class. Afterwards, through all our school-days, "Red Head" shared my wit and quickness and I benefited by his strength and dogged faithfulness.

There were some black and brown boys and girls in the school, and several of them were in my class. One of the boys strongly attracted my attention from the first day I saw him. His face was as black as night, but shone as though it were polished; he had sparkling eyes, and when he opened his mouth, he displayed glistening white teeth. It struck me at once as appropriate to call him "Shiny Face," or "Shiny Eyes," or "Shiny Teeth," and I spoke of him often by one of these names to the other boys. These terms were finally merged into "Shiny," and to that name he answered goodnaturedly during the balance of his public school days.

"Shiny" was considered without question to be the best speller, the best reader, the best penman—in a word, the best scholar, in the class. He was very quick to catch anything, but, nevertheless, studied hard; thus he possessed two powers very rarely combined in one boy. I saw him year after year, on up into the high school, win the majority of the prizes for punctuality, deportment, essay writing, and declamation. Yet it did not take me long to discover that, in spite of his standing as a scholar, he was in some way looked down upon.

The other black boys and girls were still more looked down upon. Some of the boys often spoke of them as "niggers." Sometimes on the way home from school a crowd would walk behind them repeating:

"Nigger, nigger, never die,
Black face and shiny eye."

On one such afternoon one of the black boys turned suddenly on his tormentors and hurled a slate; it struck one of the white boys in the mouth, cutting a slight gash in his lip. At sight of the blood the boy who had thrown the slate ran, and his companions quickly followed. We ran after them pelting them with stones until they separated in several directions. I was very much wrought up over the affair, and went home and told my mother how one of the "niggers" had struck a boy with a slate. I shall never forget how she turned on me. "Don't you ever use that word again," she said, "and don't you ever bother the coloured children at school. You ought to be ashamed of yourself." I did hang my head in shame, not because she had convinced me that I had done wrong, but because I was hurt by the first sharp word she had ever given me.

My school-days ran along very pleasantly. I stood well in my studies, not always so well with regard to my behaviour. I was never guilty of any serious misconduct, but my love of fun sometimes got me into trouble. I remember, however, that my sense of humour was so sly that most of the trouble usually fell on the head of the other fellow. My ability to play on the piano at school exercises was looked upon as little short of marvellous in a boy of my age. I was not chummy with many of my mates, but, on the whole, was about as popular as it is good for a boy to be.

One day near the end of my second term at school the principal came into our room and, after talking to the teacher, for some reason said: "I wish all of the white scholars to stand for a moment." I rose with the others. The teacher looked at me and, calling my name, said: "You sit down for the present, and rise with the others." I did not quite understand her, and questioned: "Ma'm?" She repeated, with a softer tone in her voice: "You sit down now, and rise with the others." I sat down dazed. I saw and heard nothing. When the others were asked to rise, I did not know it. When school was dismissed, I went out in a kind of stupor. A few of the white boys jeered me, saying: "Oh, you're a nigger too." I heard some black children say: "We knew he was coloured." "Shiny" said to them: "Come along, don't tease him," and thereby won my undying gratitude.

I hurried on as fast as I could, and had gone some distance before I perceived that "Red Head" was walking by my side. After a while he said to me: "Le' me carry your books." I gave him my strap without being able to answer. When we got to my gate, he said as he handed me my books: "Say, you know my big red agate? I can't shoot with it any more. I'm going to bring it to school for you tomorrow." I took my books and ran into the house. As I passed through the hallway, I saw that my mother was busy with one of her customers; I rushed up into my own little room, shut the door, and went quickly to where my looking-glass hung on the wall. For an instant I was afraid to look, but when I did, I looked long and earnestly. I had often heard people say to my mother: "What a pretty boy you have!" I was accustomed to hear remarks about my beauty; but now, for the first time, I became conscious of it and recognized it. I noticed the ivory whiteness of my skin, the beauty of my mouth, the size and liquid darkness of my eyes, and how the long, black lashes that fringed and shaded them produced an effect that was strangely fascinating even to me. I noticed the softness and glossiness of my dark hair that fell in waves over my temples, making my forehead appear whiter than it really was. How long I stood there gazing at my image I do not know. When I came out and reached the head of the stairs, I heard the lady who had been with my mother going out. I ran downstairs and rushed to where my mother was sitting, with a piece of work in her hands. I buried my head in her lap and blurted out: "Mother, mother, tell me, am I a nigger?" I could not see her face, but I knew the piece of work dropped to the floor and I felt her hands on my head. I looked up into her face and repeated: "Tell me, mother, am I a nigger?" There were tears in her eyes and I could see that she was suffering for me. And then it was that I looked at her critically for the first time. I had thought of her in a childish way only as the most beautiful woman in the world; now I looked at her searching for defects. I could see that her skin was almost brown, that her hair was not so soft as mine, and that she did differ in some way from the other ladies who came to the house; yet, even so, I could see that she was very beautiful, more beautiful than any of them. She must have felt that I was examining her, for she hid her face in my hair and said with difficulty: "No, my darling, you are not a nigger." She went on: "You are as good as anybody; if anyone calls you a nigger, don't notice them." But the more she talked, the less was I reassured, and I stopped her by asking: "Well, mother. am I white? Are you white?" She answered tremblingly: "No, I am not white, but you—your father is one of the greatest men in the country—the best blood of the South is in you—" This suddenly opened up in my heart a fresh chasm of misgiving and fear, and I almost fiercely demanded: "Who is my father? Where is he?" She stroked my hair and said: "I'll tell you about him some day." I sobbed: "I want to know now." She answered: "No, not now."

Perhaps it had to be done, but I have never forgiven the woman who did it so cruelly. It may be that she never knew that she gave me a sword-thrust that day in school which was years in healing.

CHAPTER II

Since I have grown older I have often gone back and tried to analyse the change that came into my life after that fateful day in school. There did come a radical change, and, young as I was, I felt fully conscious of it, though I did not fully comprehend it. Like my first spanking, it is one of the few incidents in my life that I can remember clearly. In the life of everyone there is a limited number of unhappy experiences which are not written upon the memory, but stamped there with a die; and in long years after, they can be called up in detail, and every emotion that was stirred by them can be lived through anew; these are the tragedies of life. We may grow to include some of them among the trivial incidents of childhood—a broken toy, a promise made to us which was not kept, a harsh, heart-piercing word—but these, too, as well as the bitter experiences and disappointments of mature years, are the tragedies of life.

And so I have often lived through that hour, that day, that week, in which was wrought the miracle of my transition from one world into another; for I did indeed pass into another world. From that time I looked out through other eyes, my thoughts were coloured, my words dictated, my actions limited by one dominating, all-pervading idea which constantly increased in force and weight until I finally realized in it a great, tangible fact.

And this is the dwarfing, warping, distorting influence which operates upon each and every coloured man in the United States. He is forced to take his outlook on all things, not from the view-point of a citizen, or a man, or even a human being, but from the view-point of a *coloured* man. It is wonderful to me that the race has progressed so broadly as it has, since most of its thought and all of its activity must run through the narrow neck of this one funnel.

And it is this, too, which makes the coloured people of this country, in reality, a mystery to the whites. It is a difficult thing for a white man to learn what a coloured man really thinks; because, generally, with the latter an additional and different light must be brought to bear on what he thinks; and his thoughts are often influenced by considerations so delicate and subtle that it would be impossible for him to confess or explain them to one of the opposite race. This gives to every coloured man, in proportion to his intellectuality, a sort of dual personality; there is one phase of him which is disclosed only in the freemasonry of his own race. I have often watched with interest and sometimes with amazement even ignorant coloured men under cover of broad grins and minstrel antics maintain this dualism in the presence of white men.

I believe it to be a fact that the coloured people of this country know and understand the white people better than the white people know and understand them.

I now think that this change which came into my life was at first more subjective than objective. I do not think my friends at school changed so much toward me as I did toward them. I grew reserved, I might say suspicious. I grew constantly more and more afraid of laying myself open to some injury to my feelings or my pride. I frequently saw or fancied some slight where, I am sure, none was intended. On the other hand, my friends and teachers were, if anything different, more considerate of me; but I can remember that it was against this very attitude in particular that my sensitiveness revolted. "Red" was the only one who did not so wound me; up to this day I recall with a swelling heart his clumsy efforts to make me understand that nothing could change his love for me.

I am sure that at this time the majority of my white school-mates did not understand or appreciate any differences between me and themselves; but there were a few who had evidently received instructions at home on the matter, and more than once they displayed their knowledge in word and action. As the years passed, I noticed that the most innocent and ignorant among the others grew in wisdom.

I myself would not have so clearly understood this difference had it not been for the presence of the other coloured children at school; I had learned what their status was, and now I learned that theirs was mine. I had had no particular like or dislike for these black and brown boys and girls; in fact, with the exception of "Shiny," they had occupied very little of my thought; but I do know that when the blow fell, I had a very strong aversion to being classed with them. So I became something of a solitary. "Red" and I remained inseparable, and there was between "Shiny" and me a sort of sympathetic bond, but my intercourse with the others was never entirely free from a feeling of constraint. I must add, however, that this feeling was confined almost entirely to my intercourse with boys and girls of about my own age; I did not experience it with my seniors. And when I grew to manhood, I found myself freer with elderly white people than with those near my own age.

I was now about eleven years old, but these emotions and impressions which I have just described could not have been stronger or more distinct at an older age. There were two immediate results of my forced loneliness: I began to find company in books, and greater pleasure in music. I made the former discovery through a big, gilt-bound, illustrated copy of the Bible, which used to lie in splendid neglect on the centre table in our little parlour. On top of the Bible lay a photograph album. I had often looked at the pictures in the album, and one day, after taking the larger book down and opening it on the floor, I was overjoyed to find that it contained what seemed to be an inexhaustible supply of pictures. I looked at these pictures many times; in fact, so often that I knew the story of each one without having to read the subject, and then, somehow, I picked up the thread of history on which are strung the trials and tribulations of the Hebrew children; this I followed with feverish interest and excitement. For a long time King David, with Samson a close second, stood at the head of my list of heroes; he was not displaced until I came to know Robert the Bruce. I read a good portion of the Old Testament, all that part treating of wars and rumours of wars, and then started in on the New. I became interested in the life of Christ, but became impatient and disappointed when I found that, notwithstanding the great power he possessed, he did not make use of it when, in my judgment, he most needed to do so. And so my first general impression of the Bible was what my later impression has been of a number of modern books, that the authors put their best work in the first part, and grew either exhausted or careless toward the end.

After reading the Bible, or those parts which held my attention, I began to explore the glass-doored bookcase which I have already mentioned. I found there *Pilgrim's Progess*, Peter Parley's *History of the United States*, Grimm's *Household Stories, Tales of a Grandfather*, a bound volume of an old English publication (I think it was called *The Mirror*), a little volume called *Familiar Science,* and somebody's *Natural Theology,* which last, of course, I could not read, but which, nevertheless, I tackled, with the result of gaining a permanent dislike for all kinds of theology. There were several other books of no particular name or merit, such as agents sell to people who know nothing of buying books. How my mother came by this little library which, considering all things, was so well suited to me I never sought to know. But she was far from being an ignorant woman and had herself, very likely, read the majority of these books, though I do not remember ever seeing her with a book in her hand, with the exception of the Episcopal Prayer-book. At any rate she encouraged in me the habit of reading, and when I had about exhausted those books in the little library which interested me, she began to buy books for me. She also regularly gave me money to buy a weekly paper which was then very popular for boys.

At this time I went in for music with an earnestness worthy of maturer years; a change of teachers was largely responsible for this. I began now to take lessons of the organist of the church which I attend with my mother; he was a good teacher and quite a thorough musician. He was so skilful in his instruction and filled me with such enthusiasm that my progress—these are his words—was marvellous. I remember that when I was barely twelve years old I appeared on a program with a number of adults at an entertainment given for some charitable purpose, and carried off the honours. I did more, I brought upon myself through the local newspapers the handicapping title of "infant prodigy."

I can believe that I did astonish my audience, for I never played the piano like a child; that is, in the "one-two-three" style with accelerated motion. Neither did I depend upon mere brilliancy of technique, a trick by which children often surprise their listeners; but I always tried to interpret a piece of music; I always played with feeling. Very early I acquired that knack of using the pedals, which makes the piano a sympathetic, singing instrument, quite a different thing from the source of hard or blurred sounds it so generally is. I think this was due not entirely to natural artistic temperament, but largely to the fact that I did not begin to learn the piano by counting out exercises, but by trying to reproduce the quaint songs which my mother used to sing, with all their pathetic turns and cadences.

Even at a tender age, in playing I helped to express what I felt by some of the mannerisms which I afterwards observed in great performers; I had not copied them. I have often heard people speak of the mannerisms of musicians as affectations adopted for mere effect; in some cases they may be so; but a true artist can no more play upon the piano or violin without putting his whole body in accord with the emotions he is striving to express than a swallow can fly without being graceful. Often when playing I could not keep the tears which formed in my eyes from rolling down my cheeks. Sometimes at the end or even in the midst of a composition, as big a boy as I was, I would jump from the piano, and throw myself sobbing into my mother's arms. She, by her caresses and often her tears, only encouraged these fits of sentimental hysteria. Of course, to counteract this tendency to temperamental excesses I should have been out playing ball or in swimming with other boys of my age; but my mother didn't know that. There was only once when she was really firm with me, making me do what she considered was best; I did not want to return to school after the unpleasant episode which I have related, and she was inflexible.

I began my third term, and the days ran along as I have already indicated. I had been promoted twice, and had managed each time to pull "Red" along with me. I think the teachers came to consider me the only hope of his ever getting through school, and I believe they secretly conspired with me to bring about the desired end. At any rate, I know it became easier in each succeeding examination for me not only to assist "Red," but absolutely to do his work. It is strange how in some things honest people can be dishonest without the slightest compunction. I knew boys at school who were too honourable to tell a fib even when one would have been just the right thing, but could not resist the temptation to assist or receive assistance in an examination. I have long considered it the highest proof of honesty in a man to hand his street-car fare to the conductor who had overlooked it.

One afternoon after school, during my third term, I rushed home in a great hurry to get my dinner and go to my music teacher's. I was never reluctant about going there, but on this particular afternoon I was impetuous. The reason of this was I had been asked to play the accompaniment for a young lady who was to play a violin solo at a concert given by the young people of the church, and on this afternoon we were to have our first rehearsal. At that time playing accompaniments was the only thing in music I did not enjoy; later this feeling grew into positive dislike. I have never been a really good accompanist because my ideas of interpretation were always too strongly individual. I constantly forced my *accelerandos* and *rubatos* upon the soloist, often throwing the duet entirely out of gear.

Perhaps the reader has already guessed why I was so willing and anxious to play the accompaniment to this violin solo; if not—the violinist was a girl of seventeen or eighteen whom I had first heard play a short time before on a Sunday afternoon at a special service of some kind, and who had moved me to a degree which now I can hardly think of as possible. At present I do not think it was due to her wonderful playing, though I judge she must have been a very fair performer, but there was just the proper setting to produce the effect upon a boy such as I was; the half-dim church, the air of devotion on the part of the listeners, the heaving tremor of the organ under the clear wail of the violin, and she, her eyes almost closing, the escaping strands of her dark hair wildly framing her pale face, and her slender body swaying to the tones she called forth, all combined to fire my imagination and my heart with a passion, though boyish, yet strong and, somehow, lasting. I have tried to describe the scene; if I have succeeded, it is only half success, for words can only partially express what I wish to convey. Always in recalling that Sunday afternoon I am subconscious of a faint but distinct fragrance which, like some old memory-awakening perfume, rises and suffuses my whole imagination, inducing a state of reverie so airy as just to evade the powers of expression.

She was my first love, and I loved her as only a boy loves. I dreamed of her, I built air castles for her, she was the incarnation of each beautiful heroine I knew; when I played the piano, it was to her, not even music furnished an adequate outlet for my passion; I bought a new notebook and, to sing her praises, made my first and last attempts at poetry. I remember one day at school, after we had given in our notebooks to have some exercises corrected, the teacher called me to her desk and said: "I couldn't correct your exercises because I found nothing in your book but a rhapsody on somebody's brown eyes." I had passed in the wrong notebook. I don't think I have felt greater embarrassment in my whole life than I did at that moment. I was ashamed not only that my teacher should see this nakedness of my heart, but that she should find out that I had any knowledge of such affairs. It did not then occur to me to be ashamed of the kind of poetry I had written.

Of course, the reader must know that all of this adoration was in secret; next to my great love for this young lady was the dread that in some way she would find it out. I did not know what some men never find out, that the woman who cannot discern when she is loved has never lived. It makes me laugh to think how successful I was in concealing it all; within a short time after our duet all of the friends of my dear one were referring to me as her "little sweetheart," or her "little beau," and she laughingly encouraged it. This did not entirely satisfy me; I wanted to be taken seriously. I had definitely made up my mind that I should never love another woman, and that if she deceived me I should do something desperate—the great difficulty was to think of something sufficiently desperate—and the heartless jade, how she led me on!

So I hurried home that afternoon, humming snatches of the violin part of the duet, my heart beating with pleasurable excitement over the fact that I was going to be near her, to have her attention placed directly upon me; that I was going to be of service to her, and in a way in which I could show myself to advantage—this last consideration has much to do with cheerful service. The anticipation produced in me a sensation somewhat between bliss and fear. I rushed through the gate, took the three steps to the house at one bound, threw open the door, and was about to hang my cap on its accustomed peg of the hall rack when I noticed that that particular peg was occupied by a black derby hat. I stopped suddenly and gazed at this hat as though I had never seen an object of its description. I was still looking at it in open-eyed wonder when my mother, coming out of the parlour into the hallway, called me and said there was someone inside who wanted to see me. Feeling that I was being made a party to some kind of mystery, I went in with her, and there I saw a man standing leaning with one elbow on the mantel, his back partly turned toward the door. As I entered, he turned and I saw a tall, handsome, well-dressed gentleman of perhaps thirty-five; he advanced a step toward me with a smile on his face. I stopped and looked at him with the same feelings with which I had looked at the derby hat, except that they were greatly magnified. I looked at him from head to foot, but he was an absolute blank to me until my eyes rested on his slender, elegant polished shoes; then it seemed that indistinct and partly obliterated films of memory began, at first slowly, then rapidly, to unroll, forming a vague panorama of my childhood days in Georgia.

My mother broke the spell by calling me by name and saying: "This is your father."

"Father, father," that was the word which had been to me a source of doubt and perplexity ever since the interview with my mother on the subject. How often I had wondered about my father, who he was, what he was like, whether alive or dead, and, above all, why she would not tell me about him. More than once I had been on the point of recalling to her the promise she had made me, but I instinctively felt that she was happier for not telling me and that I was happier for not being told; yet I had not the slightest idea what the real truth was. And here he stood before me, just the kind of looking father I had wishfully pictured him to be; but I made no advance toward him; I stood there feeling embarrassed and foolish, not knowing what to say or do. I am not sure but that he felt pretty much the same. My mother stood at my side with one hand on my shoulder, almost pushing me forward, but I did not move. I can well remember the look of disappointment, even pain, on her face; and I can now understand that she could expect nothing else but that at the name "father" I should throw myself into his arms. But I could not rise to this dramatic, or, better, melodramatic, climax. Somehow I could not arouse any considerable feeling of need for a father. He broke the awkward tableau by saying: "Well, boy, aren't you glad to see me?" He evidently meant the words kindly enough, but I don't know what he could have said that would have had a worse effect; however, my good breeding came to my rescue, and I answered: "Yes, sir," and went to him and offered him my hand. He took my hand into one of his, and, with the other, stroked my head, saying that I had grown into a fine youngster. He asked me how old I was; which, of course, he must have done merely to say something more, or perhaps he did so as a test of my intelligence. I replied: "Twelve, sir." He then made the trite observation about the flight of time, and we lapsed into another awkward pause.

My mother was all in smiles; I believe that was one of the happiest moments of her life. Either to put me more at ease or to show me off, she asked me to play something for my father. There is only one thing in the world that can make music, at all times and under all circumstances, up to its general standard; that is a hand-organ, or one of its variations. I went to the piano and played something in a listless, half-hearted way. I simply was not in the mood. I was wondering, while playing, when my mother would dismiss me and let me go; but my father was so enthusiastic in his praise that he touched my vanity—which was great—and more than that; he displayed that sincere appreciation which always arouses an artist to his best effort, and, too, in an unexplainable manner, makes him feel like shedding tears. I showed my gratitude by playing for him a Chopin waltz with all the feeling that was in me. When I had finished, my mother's eyes were glistening with tears; my father stepped across the room, seized me in his arms, and squeezed me to his breast. I am certain that for that moment he was proud to be my father. He sat and held me standing between his knees while he talked to my mother. I, in the mean time, examined him with more curiosity, perhaps, than politeness. I interrupted the conversation by asking: "Mother, is he going to stay with us now?" I found it impossible to frame the word "father"; it was too new to me; so I asked the question through my mother. Without waiting for her to speak, my father answered: "I've got to go back to New York this afternoon, but I'm coming to see you again." I turned abruptly and went over to my mother, and almost in a whisper reminded her that I had an appointment which I should not miss; to my pleasant surprise she said that she would give me something to eat at once so that I might go. She went out of the room and I began to gather from off the piano the music I needed. When I had finished, my father, who had been watching me, asked: "Are you going?" I replied: "Yes, sir, I've got to go to practise for a concert." He spoke some words of advice to me about being a good boy and taking care of my mother when I grew up, and added that he was going to send me something nice from New York. My mother called, and I said good-bye to him and went out. I saw him only once after that.

I quickly swallowed down what my mother had put on the table for me, seized my cap and music, and hurried off to my teacher's house. On the way I could think of nothing but this new father, where he came from, where he had been, why he was here, and why he would not stay. In my mind I ran over the whole list of fathers I had become acquainted with in my reading, but I could not classify him. The thought did not cross my mind that he was different from me, and even if it had, the mystery would not thereby have been explained; for, notwithstanding my changed relations with most of my schoolmates, I had only a faint knowledge of prejudice and no idea at all how it ramified and affected our entire social organism. I felt, however, that there was something about the whole affair which had to be hid.

When I arrived, I found that she of the brown eyes had been re-hearsing with my teacher and was on the point of leaving. My teacher, with some expressions of surprise, asked why I was late, and I stammered out the first deliberate lie of which I have any recollection. I told him that when I reached home from school, I found my mother quite sick, and that I had stayed with her awhile before coming. Then unnecessarily and gratuitously—to give my words force of conviction, I suppose—I added: "I don't think she'll be with us very long." In speaking these words I must have been comical; for I noticed that my teacher, instead of showing signs of anxiety or sorrow, half hid a smile. But how little did I know that in that lie I was speaking a prophecy!

She of the brown eyes unpacked her violin, and we went through the duet several times. I was soon lost to all other thoughts in the delights of music and love. I saw delights of love without reservation; for at no time of life is love so pure, so delicious, so poetic, so romantic, as it is in boyhood. A great deal has been said about the heart of a girl when she stands "where the brook and river meet," but what she feels is negative; more interesting is the heart of a boy when just at the budding dawn of manhood he stands looking wide-eyed into the long vistas opening before him; when he first becomes conscious of the awakening and quickening of strange desires and unknown powers; when what he sees and feels is still shadowy and mystical enough to be intangible, and, so, more beautiful; when his imagination is unsullied, and his faith new and whole—then it is that love wears a halo. The man who has not loved before he was fourteen has missed a foretaste of Elysium.

When I reached home, it was quite dark and I found my mother without a light, sitting rocking in a chair, as she so often used to do in my childhood days, looking into the fire and singing softly to herself. I nestled close to her, and, with her arms round me, she haltingly told me who my father was—a great man, a fine gentleman—he loved me and loved her very much; he was going to make a great man of me. All she said was so limited by reserve and so coloured by her feelings that it was but half truth; and so I did not yet fully understand.

THE NEGRO'S GIFT TO MANKIND (1912)

AND

AN EXCERPT FROM

DARK PRINCESS (1928)

W.E.B. DU BOIS

Du Bois was born in 1868 in Great Barrington, Massachusetts. He is acknowledged as one of the premier scholars of the twentieth century and a defining intellectual forces of the Civil Rights movement. His death, on the of eve of the 1963 March on Washington, moved Dr. Martin Luther King, Jr. to remark, ". . . A long and enormously important chapter in the history of our struggle has just ended."

The year 2003 marked the one hundredth anniversary of the publication of *The Souls of Black Folks.* The passion displayed in those stirring and insightful essays bespoke the soul of an artist. And so, when we learned of his creative works from the late historian Herbert Aptheker and from David Graham Du Bois, a renowned lecturer and the stepson of Dr. Du Bois, we were pleased but not entirely surprised.

Harlem figured prominently in Du Bois's artistic endeavors. It was the locale from which he edited *The Crisis,* a magazine started in 1910 that showcased literature from leading African-American writers. Harlem was also where the pageant "The Negro's Gift to Mankind" was written and first performed. Moreover, even though it is Chicago that is featured in Du Bois's novel *Dark Princess* (1928), he related to Aptheker that the actual physical landscape that he had in mind was New York City, which is why we've selected a chapter from *Dark Princess* for this collection, along with the pageant.

1

THE PEOPLE OF PEOPLES
AND THEIR GIFTS TO MEN

PRELUDE

The lights of the Court of Freedom blaze. A trumpet blast is heard and four heralds, black and of gigantic stature, appear with silver trumpets and standing at the four corners of the temple of beauty cry:

"Hear ye, hear ye! Men of all the Americas, and listen to the tale of the eldest and strongest of the races of mankind, whose faces be black. Hear ye, hear ye, of the gifts of black men to this world, the Iron Gift and Gift of Faith, the Pain of Humility and the Sorrow Song of Pain, the Gift of Freedom and of Laughter, and the undying Gift of Hope. Men of the world, keep silence and hear ye this!"

Four banner bearers come forward and stand along the four walls of the temple. On their banners is written:

"The First Gift of the Negro to the world, being the Gift of Iron. This picture shall tell how, in the deep and beast-bred forests of Africa, mankind first learned the welding of iron, and thus defense against the living and the dead."

What the banners tell the heralds solemnly proclaim.

Whereat comes the

First Episode. The Gift of Iron:
The lights grow dim. The roar of beasts is heard and the crash of the storm. Lightnings flash. The dark figure of an African savage hurries across the foreground, frightened and cowering and dancing. Another follows defying the lightning and is struck down; others come until the space is filled with 100 huddling, crowding savages. Some brave the storm, some pray to their Gods with incantation and imploring dance. Mothers shield their children, and husbands their wives. At last, dimly enhaloed in mysterious light, the Veiled Woman appears, commanding

From The Crisis 6 *(November 1913): 339–341. [This pageant, produced by Charles Burroughs, was shown in October 1913 as part of the National Emancipation Exposition in New York City. A cumulative audience of about 14,000 people were able to see the pageant. Similar pageants by Du Bois were presented in Philadelphia, Washington, and Los Angeles. See H. Aptheker,* Annotated Bibliography of Writings of Du Bois *(Millwood, N.Y.: Kraus-Thomson Organization Limited, 1973), entry nos. 565, 575, 1936, 1937.—ED.]*

in stature and splendid in garment, her dark face faintly visible, and in her right hand Fire, and Iron in her left. As she passes slowly round the Court the rhythmic roll of tomtoms begins. Then music is heard; anvils ring at the four corners. The arts flourish, huts arise, beasts are brought in and there is joy, feasting and dancing.

A trumpet blast calls silence and the heralds proclaim

The Second Episode, saying:

"Hear ye, hear ye! All them that come to know the Truth, and listen to the tale of the wisest and gentlest of the races of men whose faces be black. Hear ye, hear ye, of the Second Gift of black men to this world, the Gift of Civilization in the dark and splendid valley of the Nile. Men of the world, keep silence and hear ye this." The banners of the banner bearers change and read:

"The Second Gift of the Negro to the world, being the Gift of the Nile. This picture tells how the meeting of Negro and Semite in ancient days made the civilization of Egypt the first in the world."

There comes a strain of mighty music, dim in the distance and drawing nearer. The 100 savages thronged round the whole Court rise and stand listening. Slowly there come fifty veiled figures and with them come the Sphinx, Pyramid, the Obelisk and the empty Throne of the Pharoah drawn by oxen. As the cavalcade passes, the savages, wondering, threatening, inquiring, file by it. Suddenly a black chieftain appears in the entrance, with the Uraeus in one hand and the winged Beetle in the other. The Egyptians unveil and display Negroes and mulattoes clothed in the splendor of the Egyptian Court. The savages salaam; all greet him as Ra, the Negro. He mounts the throne and the cavalcade, led by posturing dancers and Ra, and followed by Egyptians and savages, pass in procession around to the right to the thunder of music and tom-toms. As they pass, Ra is crowned as Priest and King. While the Queen of Sheba and Candace of Ethiopia join the procession at intervals.

Slowly all pass out save fifty savages, who linger examining their gifts. The lights grow dim as Egyptian culture dies and the fifty savages compose themselves to sleep. As they sleep the light returns and the heralds proclaim

The Third Episode, saying:

"Hear ye, hear ye! All them that come to see the light and listen to the tale of the bravest and truest of the races of men, whose faces be black. Hear ye, hear ye, of the Third Gift of black men to this world—a Gift of Faith in Righteousness hoped for but unknown; men of the world, keep silence and hear ye this!" The banners change and read:

"The Third Gift of the Negro to the world, being a Gift of Faith. This episode tells how the Negro race spread the faith of Mohammed over half the world and built a new culture thereon."

There is a sound of battle. The savages leap to their feet. Mohammed and fifty followers whirl in and rushing to the right beat the savages back. Fifty Songhay enter and attack the Mohammedans. Fifty other Mohammedans enter and attack the Songhay. Turning, the Songhay bear the last group of Mohammedans back to the left where they clash with the savages. Mohammedan priests strive and exhort among the warriors. At each of the four corners of the temple a priest falls on his face and cries: "God is God! God is God! There is no God but God, and Mohammed is his prophet!" Four more join, others join until gradually all is changed from battle to the one universal cry: "God is God! God is God! There is no God but God, and Mohammed is his prophet!" In each corner, however, some Mohammedans hold slaves in shackles, secretly.

Mansa Musa appears at the entrance with entourage on horseback, followed by black Mohammedan priests and scholars. The procession passes around to the right with music and dancing, and passes out with Mohammedans and Songhay, leaving some Mohammedans and their slaves on the stage.

The herald proclaims

The Fourth Episode, saying:

"Hear ye, hear ye! All them that know the sorrow of the world. Hear ye, hear ye, and listen to the tale of the humblest and the mightiest of the races of men whose faces be black. Hear ye, hear ye, and learn how this race did suffer of Pain, of Death and Slavery and yet of this Humiliation did not die. Men of the world, keep silence and hear ye this!" The banners change again and say:

"The Fourth Gift of the Negro to the world, being a Gift of Humiliation. This gift shows how men can bear even the Hell of Christian slavery and live."

The Mohammedans force their slaves forward as European traders enter. Other Negroes, with captives, enter. The Mohammedans take gold in barter. The Negroes refuse gold, but are seduced by beads and drink. Chains rattle. Christian missionaries enter, but the slave trade increases. The wail of the missionary grows fainter and fainter until all is a scene of carnage and captivity with whip and chain and only a frantic priest, staggering beneath a cross and crowned with bloody thorns, wanders to and fro in dumb despair.

There is silence. Then a confused moaning. Out of the moaning comes the slave song, "Nobody Knows the Trouble I've Seen," and with it and through the chained and bowed forms of the slaves as they pass out is done the Dance of Death and Pain.

The stage is cleared of all its folk. There is a pause, in which comes the Dance of the Ocean, showing the transplantation of the Negro race overseas.

Then the heralds proclaim

The Fifth Episode, saying:

"Hear ye, hear ye! All them that strive and struggle. Hear ye, hear ye, and listen to the tale of the stoutest and the sturdiest of the races of men whose faces be black. Hear ye, hear ye, and learn how this race did rise out of slavery and the valley of the shadow of death. Men of the world, keep silence and hear ye this!" The banners change again and read:

"The Fifth Gift of the Negro to the world, being a Gift of Struggle Toward Freedom. This picture tells of Alonzo, the Negro pilot of Columbus, of Stephen Dorantes who discovered New Mexico, of the brave Maroons and valiant Haytians, of Crispus Attucks, George Lisle and Nat Turner."

Twenty-five Indians enter, circling the Court right and left, stealthily and watchfully. As they sense the coming of the whites, they gather to one side of the temple, watching.

Alonzo, the Negro, enters and after him Columbus and Spaniards, in mail, and one monk. They halt the other side of the temple and look about searchingly, pointing at the Indians. Slaves follow. One of the slaves, Stephen Dorantes, and the monk seek the Indians. The monk is killed and Stephen returns, circling the Court, tells his tale and dies. The Spaniards march on the Indians. Their slaves—the Maroons—revolt and march to the left and meet the Indians on the opposite side. The French, some of the mulattoes and Negroes, enter with more slaves. They march after the Spanish. Their slaves, helped by mulattoes and Toussaint, revolt and start back. The French follow the Spaniards, but the returning Haytians meet oncoming British. The Haytians fight their way through and take their place next to the Maroons. Still more slaves and white Americans follow the British. The British and Americans dispute. Attucks leads the Americans and the British are put to flight. Spanish, French and British, separated by dancing Indians, file around the Court and out, while Maroons, Haytians and slaves file around in the opposite direction and meet the Americans. As they pass the French, by guile induce Toussaint to go with them. There is a period of hesitation. Some slaves are freed, some Haytians resist aggression. George Lisle, a freed Negro, preaches the true religion as the masters listen. Peace ensues and the slaves sing at their tasks. Suddenly King Cotton arrives, followed by Greed, Vice, Luxury and Cruelty. The slave-holders are seduced. The old whips and chains appear. Nat Turner rebels and is killed. The slaves drop into despair and work silently and sullenly. The faint roll of tomtoms is heard.

The heralds proclaim

The Sixth Episode, saying:
"Hear ye, hear ye! Citizens of New York, and learn of the deeds of the eldest and strongest of the races of men whose faces be black. Hear ye, hear ye, of the Sixth and Greatest Gift of black men to the world, the Gift of Freedom for the workers. Men of New York, keep silence and hear ye this." The banners change and say:
"The sixth and last episode, showing how the freedom of black slaves meant freedom for the world. In this episode shall be seen the work of Garrison and John Brown; of Abraham Lincoln and Frederick Douglass, the marching of black soldiers to war and the hope that lies in little children."
The slaves work more and more dejectedly and drivers force them. Slave music comes. The tomtoms grow louder. The Veiled Woman appears with fire and iron. The slaves arise and begin to escape, passing through each other to and fro, confusedly. Benezet, Walker and Garri-

son enter, scattering their writings, and pass slowly to the right, threatened by slave drivers. John Brown enters, gesticulating. A knot of Negroes follow him. The planters seize him and erect a gallows, but the slaves seize his body and begin singing "John Brown's Body."

Frederick Douglass enters and passes to the right. Sojourner Truth enters and passes to the left. Sojourner Truth cries "Frederick, is God dead?" Voices take up the cry, repeating: "Frederick, is God dead?" Douglass answers: "No, and therefore slavery must end in blood." The heralds repeat: "Slavery must end in blood."

The roll of drums is heard and the soldiers enter. First, a company in blue with Colonel Shaw on horseback.

A single voice sings "O Freedom." A soprano chorus takes it up.

The Boy Scouts march in.

Full brasses take up "O Freedom."

Little children enter, and among them symbolic figures of the Laborer, the Artisan, the Servant of Men, the Merchant, the Inventor, the Musician, the Actor, the Teacher, Law, Medicine and Ministry, the All-Mother, formerly the Veiled Woman, now unveiled in her chariot with her dancing brood, and the bust of Lincoln at her side.

With burst of music and blast of trumpets, the pageant ends and the heralds sing:

"Hear ye, hear ye, men of all the Americas, ye who have listened to the tale of the eldest and strongest of the races of mankind, whose faces be black. Hear ye, hear ye, and forget not the gift of black men to this world—the Iron Gift and Gift of Faith, the Pain of Humility and Sorrow Song of Pain, the Gift of Freedom and Laughter and the undying Gift of Hope. Men of America, break silence, for the play is done."

Then shall the banners announce:

"The play is done!"

From The Crisis 7 *(December 1913): 80–82.*

43

THE THREE WISE MEN

The comet was blazing down from the sky on the midnight before Christmas. Three songs were dying away in the East: one from the rich and ornate chapel of the great cathedral on the hills beyond 110th Street—a song of beauty and exquisite finish but coldly and formally sung. Another, a chant from the dim synagogue on the lower East Side—heavy with droning and passionate; the last from West 53rd Street—a minor wail of utter melody. The songs had died away and the three priests, looking at the midnight sky, saw the comet at the same moment. The priest in the ornate chapel, gowned in his silken vestments, paused and stared wonderingly at the star; it seemed drawing near to him and guiding him. Almost before he knew it he had thrown a rich fur cloak about himself and was whirling downtown in a taxicab, watching the star with fascinated gaze. The rabbi on the lower East Side no sooner saw that blaze in the heavens than a low cry of joy left his lips and he followed swiftly, boarding a passing Grand Street car and clanging up Broadway; he hung on the footboard to watch unmindful of the gibes at his white beard and Jewish gabardine. The old black preacher of 53rd Street, with sad and wrinkled face, looked at the moving star thoughtfully and walked slowly with it. So the three men threaded the maze of the Christmas-mad streets, neither looking on the surging crowds nor listening to the shouts of the people, but seeing only the star. The "honk, honk" of the priest's taxicab warned the black priest scarcely too soon, and he staggered with difficulty aside as it whizzed by and made the motorman of the car, which bore the Jew, swear at the carelessness of the chauffeur. One flew, the other whirred swiftly and the third walked slowly; yet because of their differing ways they all came to the steps of the great apartment house at the same moment, and they bowed gravely to each other, yet not without curiosity, as each ascended the steps. The porter was strangely deferential and they rose swiftly to the seventh floor, where a wide hall door flew silently open.

Within and before the wide log fire of the drawing room sat a woman. She was tall and shapely and well gowned. She sat alone. The guests had gone an hour since and the last footsteps of the servants were echoing above; yet she sat there weary, still gazing into the mystery of the fire. She had seen many Christmas Eves and they were growing all to be alike—wretchedly alike. All equally lonely, aimless—almost artificial. She arose once and walked to the window, sweeping aside the heavy curtains, and the brilliancy of the star blazed in upon her. She looked upon it with a start. She remembered how once long, long years ago she had looked upon stars and such things as very real and shining fingers of fate. She remembered especially on a night like this how some such star had told her future. How out of her soul wonderful things were to be born, and she had said unto the star: "How shall this be?" And something had answered: "That holy thing that shall be born of you shall be called the Son of God." And then she had cried in all her maiden faith and mystery: "Behold the handmaiden of the Lord, be it according to thy word." And the angel departed from her, and it never came back again. Here she was reaching the portals of middle age with no prospects and few ambitions; to live and wait and sleep; to work a soulless work, to eat in some great manger like this—that was the life that seemed stretching before her endless and without change, until the End and the Change of Changing. And yet she had dreamed such dreams and fancied such fair destiny! As she thought of these dreams to-night a tear gathered and wandered down her face. It was then that she became suddenly aware of two men standing on either side of her, and she felt, but did not see, a third man, who stood behind. But for the soft voice of the first speaker she would have sprung up in alarm, but he was an old man and deferential with soft ascetic Jewish face, with white-forked beard and gabardine, and he bowed in deep humility as he spoke, saying:

"Where is He that is born King of the Jews, for we have seen His star in the East, and have come to worship Him?"

The other surpliced figure, who stood upon her right hand, said the same thing, only less:

"Where is He who is born King, for we have seen His star in the East, and have come to worship Him?" And scarcely had his voice ceased than the strong low rolling of another voice came from behind, saying:

"Where is He, for we have seen His star in the East, and have come to worship Him?"

She sank back in her chair and smiled. There was evidently some mistake, and she said to the Jew courteously:

"There is no King here."

"But," said the Jew, eagerly, tremulously, "it is a child we seek, and the star has guided us hither; we have brought gifts of gold and frankincense and myrrh." Still the woman shook her head.

"Children are not allowed in these apartments," she said, "and besides, I am unwed."

The face of the Jew grew radiant.

"The Scriptures say He shall be born of a Virgin," he chanted. But the woman smiled bitterly.

"The children of Virgins are not welcome in the twentieth century, even though they be Sons of God!"

"And in a manger," continued the Jew.

"This is, indeed, a manger," laughed the woman, "but He is not here—He is not here—only—cattle feed here."

Then the silk-robed priest on the left interrupted:

"You do not understand," he said, "it is not a child of the body we seek, but of the Word. The Word which was with God and the Word which was God. We seek the illuminating truth which shall settle all our wild gropings and bring light to this blind world." But the woman laughed even more bitterly.

"I was foolish enough once to think," she said, "that out of my brain would leap some wondrous illuminating word which should give light and warmth to the world, but nothing has been born, save here and there an epigram and the smartness of a phrase. No, He is not here."

The surpliced priest drew back with disappointed mien, and then suddenly, in the face of priest and Jew, as they turned toward the unseen figure at her back, she saw the birth of new and wonderful comprehension—Jew and Gentile sank to their knees—and she heard a soft and mighty voice that came up out of the shadows behind her as she bent forward, almost crouching, and it said:

"Him whom we seek is child neither of thy body nor of thy brain, but of thy heart. Strong Son of God, immortal love. We seek not the king of the world nor the light of the world, but the love of the world, and of all men, for all men; and lo! this thou bearest beneath thy heart, O woman of mankind. This night it shall be born!"

Slowly her heart rose and surged within her as she struggled to her feet; a wonderful revelation lighted in her whirling brain. She, of all women; she, the chosen one—the bride of Almighty God; her lips babbled noiselessly searching for that old and saintly hymn: "My soul doth magnify the Lord, and my spirit hath rejoiced in God, my saviour. For he hath regarded the low estate of his hand-maiden, for behold! from henceforth all generations shall call me blessed." A great new strength gripped her limbs. Slowly she arose, and as she rose, the roof rose silently with her—the walls of the vast room widened—the cold wet pavement touched her satined feet, and the pale-blue brilliance of the star rained on her coiled hair and naked shoulders. The shouting, careless, noisy midnight crowds surged by and brushed her gown. Slowly she turned herself, with strange new gladness in her heart, and the last words of the hymn on her lips: "He hath put down the Mighty from their seats and hath exalted them of low degree; he hath filled the hungry with good things and the rich he hath sent empty away." She turned, and lo! before her stood that third figure, an old, bent black man, sad faced and pitiful, and yet with brilliant caverned eyes and mighty wings that curved to Heaven. And suddenly there was with the angel a multitude of the heavenly host praising God and saying:

"Glory to God in the highest; and on earth peace, good will toward men."

SELAH!

DARK PRINCESS

PART I

THE EXILE

AUGUST, 1923

Summer is come with bursting flower and promise of perfect fruit. Rain is rolling down Nile and Niger. Summer sings on the sea where giant ships carry busy worlds, while mermaids swarm the shores. Earth is pregnant. Life is big with pain and evil and hope. Summer in blue New York; summer in gray Berlin; summer in the red heart of the world!

I

Matthew Towns was in a cold white fury. He stood on the deck of the *Orizaba* looking down on the flying sea. In the night America had disappeared and now there was nothing but waters heaving in the bright morning. There were many passengers walking, talking, laughing; but none of them spoke to Matthew. They spoke about him, noting his tall, lean form and dark brown face, the stiff, curled mass of his sinewy hair, and the midnight of his angry eyes.

They spoke about him, and he was acutely conscious of every word. Each word heard and unheard pierced him and quivered in the quick. Yet he leaned stiff and grim, gazing into the sea, his back toward all. He saw the curled grace of the billows, the changing blues and greens; and he saw, there at the edge of the world, certain shining shapes that leapt and played.

Then they changed—always they changed; and there arose the great cool height of the room at the University of Manhattan. Again he stood before the walnut rail that separated student and Dean. Again he felt the bewilderment, the surge of hot surprise.

"I cannot register at all for obstetrics?"

"No," said the Dean quietly, his face growing red. "I'm sorry, but the committee—"

"But—but—why, I'm Towns. I've already finished two years—I've ranked my class. I took honors—why—I— This is my Junior year—I must—"

He was sputtering with amazement.

"I'm sorry."

"Hell! I'm not asking your pity, I'm demanding—"

The Dean's lips grew thin and hard, and he sent the shaft home as if to rid himself quickly of a hateful task.

"Well—what did you expect? Juniors must have obstetrical work. Do you think white women patients are going to have a nigger doctor delivering their babies?"

Then Matthew's fury had burst its bounds; he had thrown his certificates, his marks and commendations straight into the drawn white face of the Dean and stumbled out. He came out on Broadway with its wide expanse, and opposite a little park. He turned and glanced up at the gray piles of tan buildings, threatening the sky, which were the University's great medical center. He stared at them. Then with bowed head he plunged down 165th Street. The gray-blue Hudson lay beneath his feet, and above it piled the Palisades upward in gray and green. He walked and walked: down the curving drive between high homes and the Hudson; by graveyard and palace; tomb and restaurant; beauty and smoke. All the afternoon he walked, all night, and into the gray dawn of another morning.

II

In after years when Matthew looked back upon this first sea voyage, he remembered it chiefly as the time of sleep; of days of long, long rest and thought, after work and hurry and rage. He was indeed very tired. A year of the hardest kind of study had been followed by a summer as clerical assistant in a colored industrial insurance office, in the heat of Washington. Thence he had hurried straight to the university with five hundred dollars of tuition money in his pocket; and now he was sailing to Europe.

He had written his mother—that tall, gaunt, brown mother, hard-sinewed and somber-eyed, carrying her years unbroken, who still toiled on the farm in Prince James County, Virginia—he had written almost curtly: "I'm through. I cannot and will not stand America longer. I'm off. I'll write again soon. Don't worry. I'm well. I love you." Then he had packed his clothes, given away his books and instruments, and sailed in mid-August on the first ship that offered after that long tramp of tears and rage, after days of despair. And so here he was.

Where was he going? He glanced at the pale-faced man who asked him. "I don't know," he answered shortly. The good-natured gentleman stared, nonplused. Matthew turned away. Where *was* he going? The ship was going to Antwerp. But that, to Matthew, was sheer accident. He was going *away* first of all. After that? Well, he had thought of France. There they were at least civilized in their prejudices. But his French was poor. He had studied German because his teachers regarded German medicine as superior to all other. He would then go to Germany. From there? Well, there was Moscow. Perhaps they could use a man in Russia whose heart was hate. Perhaps he would move on to the Near or Far East and find hard work and peace. At any rate he was going somewhere; and suddenly letting his strained nerves go, he dragged his chair to a sheltered nook apart and slept.

To the few who approached him at all, Matthew was boorish and gruff. He knew that he was unfair, but he could not help it. All the little annoyances, which in healthier days he would have laughed away, avoided, or shortly forgotten, now piled themselves on his sore soul. The roommate assigned him discovered that his companion was colored and quickly decamped with his baggage. A Roumanian who spoke little English, and had not learned American customs, replaced him.

Matthew entered the dining-room with nerves a-quiver. Every eye caught him during the meal—some, curiously; some, derisively; some, in half-contemptuous surprise. He felt and measured all, looking steadily into his plate. On one side sat an old and silent man. To the empty seat on the other side he heard acutely a swish of silk approach— a pause and a consultation. The seat remained empty. At the next meal he was placed in a far corner with people too simple or poor or unimportant to protest. He heaved a sigh to have it over and ate thereafter in silence and quickly.

So at last life settled down, soothed by the sea—the rhythm and song of the old, old sea. He slept and read and slept; stared at the water; lived his life again to its wild climax; put down repeatedly the cold, hard memory; and drifting, slept again.

Yet always, as he rose from the deep seas of sleep and reverie, the silent battle with his fellows went on. Now he yearned fiercely for some one to talk to; to talk and talk and explain and prove and disprove. He glimpsed faces at times, intelligent, masterful. They had brains; if they knew him they would choose him as companion, friend; but they did not know him. They did not want to know him. They glanced at him momentarily and then looked away. They were afraid to be noticed noticing him.

And he? He would have killed himself rather than have them dream he would accept a greeting, much less a confidence. He looked past and through and over them with blank unconcern. So much so that a few—simpler souls, themselves wandering alone hither and thither in this aimless haphazard group of a fugitive week—ventured now and then to understand: "I never saw none of you fellers like you—" began one amiable Italian. "No?" answered Matthew briefly and walked away.

"You're not lonesome?" asked a New England merchant, adding hastily, "I've always been interested in your people."

"Yes," said Matthew with an intonation that stopped further conversation along that line.

"No," he growled at an insulted missionary, "I don't believe in God—never did—do you?"

And yet all the time he was sick at heart and yearning. If but one soul with sense, knowledge, and decency had firmly pierced his awkwardly hung armor, he could have helped make these long hard days human. And one did, a moment, now and then—a little tow-haired girl of five or six with great eyes. She came suddenly on him one day: "Won't you play ball with me?" He started, smiled, and looked down. He loved children. Then he saw the mother approaching—typically Middle-West American, smartly dressed and conscious of her social inferiority. Slowly his smile faded; quickly he walked away. Yet nearly every day thereafter the child smiled shyly at him as though they shared a secret, and he smiled slowly back; but he was careful never to see the elaborate and most exclusive mother.

Thus they came to green Plymouth and passed the fortress walls of Cherbourg and, sailing by merry vessels and white cliffs, rode on to the Scheldt. All day they crept past fields and villages, ships and windmills, up to the slender cathedral tower of Antwerp.

III

Sitting in the Viktoria Café, on the Unter den Linden, Berlin, Matthew looked again at the white leviathan—at that mighty organization of white folk against which he felt himself so bitterly in revolt. It was the same vast, remorseless machine in Berlin as in New York. Of course, there were differences—differences which he felt like a tingling pain. He had on the street here no sense of public insult; he was treated as he was dressed, and today he had dressed carefully, wearing the new suit made for the opening school term; he had on his newest dark crimson tie that burned with the red in his smooth brown face; he carried cane and gloves, and he had walked into this fashionable café with an air. He knew that he would be served, politely and without question.

Yes, in Europe he could at least eat where he wished so long as he paid. Yet the very thought made him angry; conceive a man outcast in his own native land! And even here, how long could he pay, he who sat with but two hundred dollars in the world, with no profession, no work, no friends, no country? Yes, these folks treated him as a man—or rather, they did not, on looking at him, treat him as less than a man. But what of it? They were white. What would they say if he asked for work? Or a chance for his brains? Or a daughter in marriage? There was a blonde and blue-eyed girl at the next table catching his eye. Faugh! She was for public sale and thought him a South American, an Egyptian, or a rajah with money. He turned quickly away.

Oh, he was lonesome; lonesome and homesick with a dreadful homesickness. After all, in leaving white, he had also left black America—all that he loved and knew. God! he never dreamed how much he loved that soft, brown world which he had so carelessly, so unregretfully cast away. What would he not give to clasp a dark hand now, to hear a soft Southern roll of speech, to kiss a brown cheek? To see warm, brown, crinkly hair and laughing eyes. God—he was lonesome. So utterly, terribly lonesome. And then—he saw the Princess!

Many, many times in after years he tried to catch and rebuild that first wildly beautiful phantasy which the girl's face stirred in him. He knew well that no human being could be quite as beautiful as she looked to him then. He could never quite recapture the first ecstasy of the picture, and yet always even the memory thrilled and revived him. Never after that first glance was he or the world quite the same.

First and above all came that sense of color: into this world of pale yellowish and pinkish parchment, that absence or negation of color, came, suddenly, a glow of golden brown skin. It was darker than sunlight and gold; it was lighter and livelier than brown. It was a living, glowing crimson, veiled beneath brown flesh. It called for no light and suffered no shadow, but glowed softly of its own inner radiance.

Then came the sense of the woman herself: she was young and tall even when seated, and she bore herself above all with a singularly regal air. She was slim and lithe, gracefully curved. Unseeing, past him and into the struggling, noisy street, she was looking with eyes that were pools of night—liquid, translucent, haunting depths—whose brilliance made her face a glory and a dream.

Matthew pulled himself together and tried to act sensibly. Here—here in Berlin and but a few tables away, actually sat a radiantly beautiful woman, and she was colored. He could see the faultlessness of her dress. There was a hint of something foreign and exotic in her simply draped gown of rich, creamlike silken stuff and in the graceful coil of her hand-fashioned turban. Her gloves were hung carelessly over her arm, and he caught a glimpse of slender-heeled slippers and sheer clinging hosiery. There was a flash of jewels on her hands and a murmur of beads in half-hidden necklaces. His young enthusiasm might overpaint and idealize her, but to the dullest and the oldest she was beautiful, beautiful. Who was she? What was she? How came this princess (for in some sense she must be royal) here in Berlin? Was she American? And how was he—

Then he became conscious that he had been listening to words spoken behind him. He caught a slap of American English from the terrace just back and beyond.

"Look, there's that darky again. See her? Sitting over yonder by the post. Ain't she some pippin? What? Get out! Listen! Bet you a ten-spot I get her number before she leaves this café. You're on! I know niggers, and I don't mean perhaps. Ain't I white. Watch my smoke!"

Matthew gripped the table. All that cold rage which still lay like lead beneath his heart began again to glow and burn. Action, action, it screamed—no running and sulking now—action! There was murder in his mind—murder, riot, and arson. He wanted just once to hit this white American in the jaw—to see him spinning over the tables, and then to walk out with his arm about the princess, through the midst of a gaping, scurrying white throng. He started to rise, and nearly upset his coffee cup.

Then he came to himself. No—no. That would not do. Surely the fellow would not insult the girl. He could count on no public opinion in

Berlin as in New York to shield him in such an adventure. He would simply seek to force his company on her in quite a natural way. After all, the café was filling. There were no empty tables, at least in the forward part of the room, and no one person had a right to a whole table; yet to approach any woman thus, when several tables with men offered seats, was to make a subtle advance; and to approach this woman?—puzzled and apprehensive, Matthew sat quietly and watched while he paid his waiter and slowly pulled on his gloves. He saw a young, smooth-faced American circle carelessly from behind him and saunter toward the door. Then he stopped, and turning, slowly came back toward the girl's table. A cold sweat broke out over Matthew. A sickening fear fought with the fury in his heart. Suppose this girl, this beautiful girl, let the fresh American sit down and talk to her? Suppose? After all, who—what was she? To sit alone at a table in a European café—well, Matthew watched. The American approached, paused, looked about the café, and halted beside her table. He looked down and bowed, with his hand on the back of the empty chair.

The lady did not start nor speak. She glanced at him indifferently, unclasped her hands slowly, and then with no haste gathered up her things; she nodded to the waiter, fumbled in her purse, and without another glance at the American, arose and passed slowly out. Matthew could have shouted.

But the American was not easily rebuffed by this show of indifference. Apparently he interpreted the movement quite another way. Waving covertly to his fellows, he arose leisurely, without ordering, tossed a bill to the waiter, and sauntered out after the lady. Matthew rose impetuously, and he felt that whole terrace table of men arise behind him.

The dark lady had left by the Friedrichstrasse door, and paused for the taxi which the gold-laced porter had summoned. She gave an address and already had her foot on the step. In a moment the American was by her side. Deftly he displaced the porter and bent with lifted hat. She turned on him in surprise and raised her little head. Still the American persisted with a smile, but his hand had hardly touched her elbow when Matthew's fist caught him right between the smile and the ear. The American sat down on the sidewalk very suddenly.

Pedestrians paused. There was a commotion at the restaurant door as several men rushed out, but the imposing porter was too quick; he had caught the eye and pocketed the bill of the lady. In a moment, evidently thinking the couple together, he had handed both her and Matthew into the taxi, slammed the door, and they had whirled away. In a trice they fled down the Friedrichstrasse, left across the Französische, again left to Charlotten, and down the Linden. Matthew glanced anxiously back. They had been too quick, and there was apparently no pursuit. He leaned forward and spoke to the chauffeur, and they drove up to the curb near the Brandenburg Gate and stopped.

"*Mille remerciements, Monsieur!*" said the lady.

Matthew searched his head for the right French answer as he started to step out, but could not remember: "Oh—oh—don't mention it," he stammered.

"Ah—you are English? I thought you were French or Spanish!"

She spoke clear-clipped English with perfect accent, to Matthew's intense relief. Suppose she had spoken only French! He hastened to explain: "I am an American Negro."

"An American Negro?" The lady bent forward in sudden interest and stared at him. "An American Negro!" she repeated. "How singular—how very singular! I have been thinking of American Negroes all day! Please do not leave me yet. Can you spare a moment? Chauffeur, drive on!"

IV

As they sat at tea in the Tiergarten, under the tall black trees, Matthew's story came pouring out:

"I was born in Virginia, Prince James County, where we black folk own most of the land. My mother, now many years a widow, farmed her little forty acres to educate me, her only child. There was a good school there with teachers from Hampton, the great boarding-school not far away. I was young when I finished the course and was sent to Hampton. There I was unhappy. I wanted to study for a profession, and they insisted on making me a farmer. I hated the farm. My mother finally sent me North. I boarded first with a cousin and then with friends in New York and went through high school and through the City College. I specialized on the pre-medical course, and by working nights and summers and playing football (amateur, of course, but paid excellent 'expenses' in fact), I was able to enter the new great medical school of the University of Manhattan, two years ago.

"It was a hard pull, but I plunged the line. I had to have scholarships, and I got them, although one Southern professor gave me the devil of a time."

The lady interrupted. "Southern?" she asked. "What do you mean by 'Southern'?"

"I mean from the former slave States—although the phrase isn't just fair. Some of our most professional Southerners are Northern-born."

The lady still looked puzzled, but Matthew talked on.

"This man didn't mean to be unfair, but he honestly didn't believe 'niggers' had brains, even if he had the evidence before him. He flunked me on principle. I protested and finally had the matter up to the Dean; I showed all my other marks and got a re-examination at an extra cost that deprived me of a new overcoat. I gave him a perfect paper, and he had to acknowledge it was 'good,' although he made careful inquiries to see if I had not in some way cribbed dishonestly.

"At last I got my mark and my scholarship. During my second year there were rumors among the few colored students that we would not be allowed to finish our course, because objection had been made to colored students in the clinical hospital, especially with white women patients. I laughed. It was, I was sure, a put-up rumor to scare us off. I knew black men who had gone through other New York medical schools which had become parts of this great new consolidated school. There had been no real trouble. The patients never objected—only Southern students and the few Southern professors. Some of the trustees had mentioned the matter but had been shamed into silence.

"Then, too, I was firm in my Hampton training; desert and hard work were bound to tell. Prejudice was a miasma that character burned away. I believed this thoroughly. I had literally pounded my triumphant way through school and life. Of course I had met insult and rebuff here and there, but I ignored them, laughed at them, and went my way. Those black people who cringed and cowered, complained of failure and 'no chance,' I despised—weaklings, cowards, fools! Go to work! Make a way! Compel recognition!

"In the medical school there were two other colored men in my class just managing to crawl through. I covertly sneered at them, avoided them. What business had they there with no ability or training? I see differently now. I see there may have been a dozen reasons why Phillips of Mississippi could neither spell nor read correctly and why

Jones of Georgia could not count. They had had no hard-working mother, no Hampton, no happy accidents of fortune to help them on.

"While I? I rose to triumph after triumph. Just as in college I had been the leading athlete and had ridden many a time aloft on white students' shoulders, so now, working until two o'clock in the morning and rising at six, I took prize after prize—the Mitchel Honor in physiology, the Welbright medal in pathology, the Shores Prize for biological chemistry. I ranked the second-year class at last commencement, and at our annual dinner at the Hotel Pennsylvania, sat at the head table with the medal men. I remember one classmate. He was from Atlanta, and he hesitated and whispered when he found his seat was beside me. Then he sat down like a man and held out his hand. 'Towns,' he said, 'I never associated with a Negro before who wasn't a servant or laborer; but I've heard of you, and you've made a damned fine record. I'm proud to sit by you.'

"I shook his hand and choked. He proved my life-theory. Character and brains were too much for prejudice. Then the blow fell. I had slaved all summer. I was worked to a frazzle. Reckon my hard-headedness had a hand there, too. I wouldn't take a menial job—Pullman porter, waiter, bell-boy, boat steward—good money, but I waved them aside. No! Bad for the soul, and I might meet a white fellow student."

The lady smiled. "Meet a fellow student—did none of them work, too?"

"O yes, but seldom as menials, while Negroes in America are always expected to be menials. It's natural, but—no, I couldn't do it. So at last I got a job in Washington in the medical statistics department of the National Benefit. This is one of our big insurance concerns. O yes, we've got a number of them; prosperous, too. It was hard work, indoors, poor light and air; but I was interested—worked overtime, learned the game, and gave my thought and ideas.

"They promoted me and paid me well, and by the middle of August I had my tuition and book money saved. They wanted me to stay with them permanently; at least until fall. But I had other plans. There was a summer school of two terms at the college, and I figured that if I entered the second term I could get a big lead in my obstetrical work and stand a better show for the Junior prizes. I had applied in the spring for admission to the Stern Maternity Hospital, which occupied three floors of our center building. My name had been posted as accepted. I was tired to death, but I rushed back to New York to register. Perhaps if I had been rested, with cool head and nerves—well, I wasn't. I made the office of the professor of obstetrics on a hot afternoon, August 10, I well remember. He looked at me in surprise.

" 'You can't work in the Stern Hospital—the places are all taken.'

" 'I have one of the places,' I pointed out. He seemed puzzled and annoyed.

" 'You'll have to see the Dean,' he said finally.

"I was angry and rushed to the Dean's office. I saw that we had a new Dean—a Southerner.

"Then the blow fell. Seemingly, during the summer the trustees had decided gradually to exclude Negroes from the college. In the case of students already in the course, they were to be kept from graduation by a refusal to admit them to certain courses, particularly in obstetrics. The Dean was to break the news by letter as students applied for these courses. By applying early for the summer course, I had been accepted before the decision; so now he had to tell me. He hated the task, I could see. But I was too surprised, disgusted, furious. He said that I could not enter, and he told me brutally why. I threw my papers in his face and left. All my fine theories of race and prejudice lay in ruins. My life was over-turned. America was impossible—unthinkable. I ran away, and here I am."

V

They had sat an hour drinking tea in the Tiergarten, that mightiest park in Europe with its lofty trees, its cool dark shade, its sense of with-drawal from the world. He had not meant to be so voluble, so self-revealing. Perhaps the lady had deftly encouraged confidences in her high, but gracious way. Perhaps the mere sight of her smooth brown skin had made Matthew assume sympathy. There was something at once inviting and aloof in the young woman who sat opposite him. She had the air and carriage of one used to homage and yet receiving it in-differently as a right. With all her gentle manner and thoughtfulness, she had a certain faint air of haughtiness and was ever slightly remote.

She was "colored" and yet not at all colored in his intimate sense. Her beauty as he saw it near had seemed even more striking; those thin, smooth fingers moving about the silver had known no work; she was carefully groomed from her purple hair to her slim toe-tips, and yet with few accessories; he could not tell whether she used paint or powder. Her features were regular and delicate, and there was a tiny diamond in one nostril. But quite aside from all details of face and jewels—her pearls, her rings, the old gold bracelet—above and beyond and much more than the sum of them all was the luminous radiance of her complete beauty, her glow of youth and strength behind that screen of a grand yet gracious manner. It was overpowering for Matthew, and yet stimulating. So his story came pouring out before he knew or cared to whom he was speaking. All the loneliness of long, lonely days clamored for speech, all the pent-up resentment choked for words.

The lady listened at first with polite but conscious sympathy; then she bent forward more and more eagerly, but always with restraint, with that mastery of body and soul that never for a moment slipped away, and yet with so evident a sympathy and comprehension that it set Matthew's head swimming. She swept him almost imperiously with her eyes—those great wide orbs of darkening light. His own eyes lifted and fell before them; lifted and fell, until at last he looked past them and talked to the tall green and black oaks.

And yet there was never anything personal in her all-sweeping glance or anything self-conscious in the form that bent toward him. She never seemed in the slightest way conscious of herself. She arranged nothing, glanced at no detail of her dress, smoothed no wisp of hair. She seemed at once unconscious of her beauty and charm, and at the same time assuming it as a fact, but of no especial importance. She had no little feminine ways; she used her eyes apparently only for seeing, yet seemed to see all.

Matthew had the feeling that her steady, full, radiant gaze that enveloped and almost burned him, saw not him but the picture he was painting and the thing that the picture meant. He warmed with such an audience and painted with clean, sure lines. Only once or twice did she interrupt, and when he had ended, she still sat full-faced, flooding him with the startling beauty of her eyes. Her hands clasped and unclasped slowly, her lips were slightly parted, the curve of her young bosom rose and fell.

"And you ran away!" she said musingly. Matthew winced and started to explain, but she continued. "Singular," she said. "How singular that I should meet you; and today." There was no coquetry in her tone. It was evidently not of him, the hero, of whom she was thinking, but of him, the group, the fact, the whole drama.

"And you are two—three millions?" she asked.

"Ten or twelve," he answered.

"You ran away," she repeated, half in meditation.

"What else could I do?" he demanded impulsively. "Cringe and crawl?"

"Of course the Negroes have no hospitals?"

"Of course, they have—many, but not attached to the great schools. What can Howard (rated as our best colored school) do with thousands, when whites have millions? And if we come out poorly taught and half equipped, they sneer at 'nigger' doctors."

"And no Negroes are admitted to the hospitals of New York?"

"O yes—hundreds. But if we colored students are confined to colored patients, we surrender a principle."

"What principle?"

"Equality."

"Oh—equality."

She sat for a full moment, frowning and looking at him. Then she fumbled away at her beads and brought out a tiny jeweled box. Absently she took out a cigarette, lighted it, and offered him one. Matthew took it, but he was a little troubled. White women in his experience smoked of course—but colored women? Well—but it was delicious to see her great, somber eyes veiled in hazy blue.

She sighed at last and said: "I do not quite understand. But at any rate I see that you American Negroes are not a mere amorphous handful. You are a nation! I never dreamed—But I must explain. I want you to dine with me and some friends tomorrow night at my apartment. We represent—indeed I may say frankly, we are—a part of a great committee of the darker peoples; of those who suffer under the arrogance and tyranny of the white world."

Matthew leaned forward with an eager thrill. "And you have plans? Some vast emancipation of the world?"

She did not answer directly, but continued: "We have among us spokesmen of nearly all these groups—of them or for them—except American Negroes. Some of us think these former slaves unready for coöperation, but I just returned from Moscow last week. At our last dinner I was telling of a report I read there from America that astounded me and gave me great pleasure—for I almost alone have insisted that your group was worthy of coöperation. In Russia I heard something, and it happened so curiously that—after sharp discussion about your people but last night (for I will not conceal from you that there is still doubt and opposition in our ranks)—that I should meet you today.

"I had gone up to the Palace to see the exhibition of new paintings— you have not seen it? You must. All the time I was thinking absently of Black America, and one picture there intensified and stirred my thoughts—a weird massing of black shepherds and a star. I dropped into the Viktoria, almost unconsciously, because the tea there is good and the muffins quite unequaled. I know that I should not go there unaccompanied, even in the day; white women may, but brown women seem strangely attractive to white men, especially Americans; and this is the open season for them.

"Twice before I have had to put Americans in their place. I went quite unconsciously and noted nothing in particular until that impossible young man sat down at my table. I did not know he had followed me out. Then you knocked him into the gutter quite beautifully. It had never happened before that a stranger of my own color should offer me protection in Europe. I had a curious sense of some great inner meaning to your act—some world movement. It seemed almost that the Powers of Heaven had bent to give me the knowledge which I was groping for; and so I invited you, that I might hear and know more."

She rose, insisted on paying the bill herself. "You are my guest, you see. It is late, and I must go. Then, tomorrow night at eight. My card and address— Oh, I quite forgot. May I have your name?"

Matthew had no card. But he wrote in her tiny memorandum book with its golden filigree, "Matthew Towns, Exile, Hotel Roter Adler."

She held out her hand, half turning to go. Her slenderness made her look taller than she was. The curved line of her flowed sinuously from neck to ankle. She held her right hand high, palm down, the long fingers drooping, and a ruby flamed dark crimson on her forefinger. Matthew reached up and shook the hand heartily. He had, as he did it, a vague feeling that he took her by surprise. Perhaps he shook hands too hard, for her hand was very little and frail. Perhaps she did not mean to shake hands—but then, what did she mean?

She was gone. He took out her card and read it. There was a little coronet and under it, engraved in flowing script, "H.R.H. the Princess Kautilya of Bwodpur, India." Below was written, "Lützower Ufer, No. 12."

VI

Matthew sat in the dining-room of the Princess on Lützower Ufer. Looking about, his heart swelled. For the first time since he had left New York, he felt himself a man, one of those who could help build a world and guide it. He had no regrets. Medicine seemed a far-off, dry-as-dust thing.

The oak paneling of the room went to the ceiling and there broke softly with carven light against white flowers and into long lucent curves. The table below was sheer with lace and linen, sparkling with silver and crystal. The servants moved deftly, and all of them were white save one who stood behind the Princess' high and crimson chair. At her right sat Matthew himself, hardly realizing until long afterward the honor thus done an almost nameless guest.

Fortunately he had the dinner jacket of year before last with him. It was not new, but it fitted his form perfectly, and his was a form worth fitting. He was a bit shocked to note that all the other men but two were in full evening dress. But he did not let this worry him much.

Ten of them sat at the table. On the Princess' left was a Japanese, faultless in dress and manner, evidently a man of importance, as the deference shown him and the orders on his breast indicated. He was quite yellow, short and stocky, with a face which was a delicately handled but perfect mask. There were two Indians, one a man grave, haughty, and old, dressed richly in turban and embroidered tunic, the other, in conventional dress and turban, a young man, handsome and alert, whose eyes were ever on the Princess. There were two Chinese, a young man and a young woman, he in a plain but becoming Chinese costume of heavy blue silk, she in a pretty dress, half Chinese, half European in effect. An Egyptian and his wife came next, he suave, talkative, and polite—just a shade too talkative and a bit too polite, Matthew thought; his wife a big, handsome, silent woman, elegantly jeweled and gowned, with much bare flesh. Beyond them was a cold and rather stiff Arab who spoke seldom, and then abruptly.

Of the food and wine of such dinners, Matthew had read often but never partaken; and the conversation, now floating, now half submerged, gave baffling glimpses of unknown lands, spiritual and physical. It was all something quite new in his experience, the room, the table, the service, the company.

He could not keep his eyes from continually straying sidewise to his hostess. Never had he seen color in human flesh so regally set: the rich and flowing grace of the dress out of which rose so darkly splendid the jeweled flesh. The black and purple hair was heaped up on her little head, and in its depths gleamed a tiny coronet of gold. Her voice and her poise, her self-possession and air of quiet command, kept Matthew staring almost unmannerly, despite the fact that he somehow sensed a shade of resentment in the young and handsome Indian opposite.

They had eaten some delicious tidbits of meat and vegetables and then were served with a delicate soup when the Princess, turning slightly to her right, said:

"You will note, Mr. Towns, that we represent here much of the Darker World. Indeed, when all our circle is present, we represent all of it, save your world of Black Folk."

"All the darker world except the darkest," said the Egyptian.

"A pretty large omission," said Matthew with a smile.

"I agree," said the Chinaman; but the Arab said something abruptly in French. Matthew had said that he knew "some" French. But his French was of the American variety which one excavates from dictionaries and cements with grammar, like bricks. He was astounded at the ease and the fluency with which most of this company used languages, so easily, without groping or hesitation and with light, sure shading. They talked art in French, literature in Italian, politics in German, and everything in clear English.

"M. Ben Ali suggests," said the Princess, "that even you are not black, Mr. Towns."

"My grandfather was, and my soul is. Black blood with us in America is a matter of spirit and not simply of flesh."

"Ah! mixed blood," said the Egyptian.

"Like all of us, especially me," laughed the Princess.

"But, your Royal Highness—not Negro," said the elder Indian in a tone that hinted a protest.

"Essentially," said the Princess lightly, "as our black and curly-haired Lord Buddha testifies in a hundred places. But"—a bit imperiously—

"enough of that. Our point is that Pan-Africa belongs logically with Pan-Asia; and for that reason Mr. Towns is welcomed tonight by you, I am sure, and by me especially. He did me a service as I was returning from the New Palace."

They all looked interested, but the Egyptian broke out:

"Ah, Your Highness, the New Palace, and what is the fad today? What has followed expressionism, cubism, futurism, vorticism? I confess myself at sea. Picasso alarms me. Matisse sets me aflame. But I do not understand them. I prefer the classics."

"The Congo," said the Princess, "is flooding the Acropolis. There is a beautiful Kandinsky on exhibit, and some lovely and startling things by unknown newcomers."

"*Mais,*" replied the Egyptian, dropping into French—and they were all off to the discussion, save the silent Egyptian woman and the taciturn Arab.

Here again Matthew was puzzled. These persons easily penetrated worlds where he was a stranger. Frankly, but for the context he would not have known whether Picasso was a man, a city, or a vegetable. He had never heard of Matisse. Lightly, almost carelessly, as he thought, his companions leapt to unknown subjects. Yet they knew. They knew art, books, and literature, politics of all nations, and not newspaper politics merely, but inner currents and whisperings, unpublished facts.

"Ah, pardon," said the Egyptian, returning to English, "I forgot Monsieur Towns speaks only English and does not interest himself in art."

Perhaps Matthew was sensitive and imagined that the Egyptian and the Indian rather often, if not purposely, strayed to French and subjects beyond him.

"Mr. Towns is a scientist?" asked the Japanese.

"He studies medicine," answered the Princess.

"Ah—a high service," said the Japanese. "I was reading only today of the work on cancer by your Peyton Rous in Carrel's laboratory."

Towns was surprised. "What, has he discovered the etiological factor? I had not heard."

"No, not yet, but he's a step nearer."

For a few moments Matthew was talking eagerly, until a babble of unknown tongues interrupted him across the table.

"Proust is dead, that 'snob of humor'—yes, but his *Recherche du Temps Perdu* is finished and will be published in full. I have only glanced at parts of it. Do you know Gasquet's *Hymnes?*"

"Beraud gets the Prix Goncourt this year. Last year it was the Negro, Maran—"

"I have been reading Croce's *Aesthetic* lately—"

"Yes, I saw the Meyerhold theater in Moscow—gaunt realism—*Howl China* was tremendous."

Then easily, after the crisp brown fowl, the Princess tactfully steered them back to the subject which some seemed willing to avoid.

"And so," she said, "the darker peoples who are dissatisfied—"

She looked at the Japanese and paused as though inviting comment. He bowed courteously.

"If I may presume, your Royal Highness, to suggest," he said slowly, "the two categories are not synonymous. We ourselves know no line of color. Some of us are white, some yellow, some black. Rather, is it not, your Highness, that we have from time to time taken council with the oppressed peoples of the world, many of whom by chance are colored?"

"True, true," said the Princess.

"And yet," said the Chinese lady, "it is dominating Europe which has flung this challenge of the color line, and we cannot avoid it."

"And on either count," said Matthew, "whether we be bound by oppression or by color, surely we Negroes belong in the foremost ranks."

There was a slight pause, a sort of hesitation, and it seemed to Matthew as though all expected the Japanese to speak. He did, slowly and gravely:

"It would be unfair to our guest not to explain with some clarity and precision that the whole question of the Negro race both in Africa and in America is for us not simply a question of suffering and compassion. Need we say that for these peoples we have every human sympathy? But for us here and for the larger company we represent, there is a deeper question—that of the ability, qualifications, and real possibilities of the black race in Africa or elsewhere."

Matthew left the piquant salad and laid down his fork slowly. Up to this moment he had been quite happy. Despite the feeling of being out of it now and then, he had assumed that this was his world, his people, from the high and beautiful lady whom he worshiped more and more, even to the Egyptians, Indians, and Arab who seemed slightly, but very slightly, aloof or misunderstanding.

Suddenly now there loomed plain and clear the shadow of a color line within a color line, a prejudice within prejudice, and he and his again the sacrifice. His eyes became somber and did not lighten even when the Princess spoke.

"I cannot see that it makes great difference what ability Negroes have. Oppression is oppression. It is our privilege to relieve it."

"Yes," answered the Japanese, "but who will do it? Who can do it but those superior races whose necks now bear the yoke of the inferior rabble of Europe?"

"This," said the Princess, "I have always believed; but as I have told your Excellency, I have received impressions in Moscow which have given me very serious thought—first as to our judgment of the ability of the Negro race, and second"—she paused in thought—"as to the relative ability of all classes and peoples."

Matthew stared at her, as she continued:

"You see, Moscow has reports—careful reports of the world's masses. And the report on the Negroes of America was astonishing. At the time, I doubted its truth: their education, their work, their property, their organizations; and the odds, the terrible, crushing odds against which, inch by inch and heartbreak by heartbreak, they have forged their unfaltering way upward. If the report is true, they are a nation today, a modern nation worthy to stand beside any nation here."

"But can we put any faith in Moscow?" asked the Egyptian. "Are we not keeping dangerous company and leaning on broken reeds?"

"Well," said Matthew, "if they are as sound in everything as in this report from America, they'll bear listening to."

The young Indian spoke gently and evenly, but with bright eyes.

"Naturally," he said, "one can see Mr. Towns needs must agree with the Bolshevik estimate of the lower classes."

Matthew felt the slight slur and winced. He thought he saw the lips of the Princess tighten ever so little. He started to answer quickly, with aplomb if not actual swagger.

"I reckon," he began—then something changed within him. It was as if he had faced and made a decision, as though some great voice, crying and reverberating within his soul, spoke for him and yet was him. He had started to say, "I reckon there's as much high-born blood among American Negroes as among any people. We've had our kings, presidents, and judges—" He started to say this, but he did not finish. He found himself saying quite calmly and with slightly lifted chin:

"I reckon you're right. We American blacks are very common people. My grandfather was a whipped and driven slave; my father was never really free and died in jail. My mother plows and washes for a living. We come out of the depths—the blood and mud of battle. And from just such depths, I take it, came most of the worth-while things in this old world. If they didn't—God help us."

The table was very still, save for the very faint clink of china as the servants brought in the creamed and iced fruit.

The Princess turned, and he could feel her dark eyes full upon him.

"I wonder—I wonder," she murmured, almost catching her breath.

The Indian frowned. The Japanese smiled, and the Egyptian whispered to the Arab.

"I believe that is true," said the Chinese lady thoughtfully, "and if it is, this world is glorious."

"And if it is not?" asked the Egyptian icily.

"It is perhaps both true and untrue," the Japanese suggested. "Certainly Mr. Towns has expressed a fine and human hope, although I fear that always blood must tell."

"No, it mustn't," cried Matthew, "unless it is allowed to talk. Its speech is accidental today. There is some weak, thin stuff called blood, which not even a crown can make speak intelligently; and at the same time some of the noblest blood God ever made is dumb with chains and poverty."

The elder Indian straightened, with blazing eyes.

"Surely," he said, slowly and calmly, "surely the gentleman does not mean to reflect on royal blood?"

Matthew started, flushed darkly, and glanced quickly at the Princess. She smiled and said lightly, "Certainly not," and then with a pause and a look straight across the table to the turban and tunic, "nor will royal blood offer insult to him." The Indian bowed to the tablecloth and was silent.

As they rose and sauntered out to coffee in the silk and golden drawing-room, there was a discussion, started of course by the Egyptian, first of the style of the elaborate piano case and then of Schönberg's new and unobtrusive transcription of Bach's triumphant choral Prelude, "Komm, Gott, Schöpfer."

The Princess sat down. Matthew could not take his eyes from her. Her fingers idly caressed the keys as her tiny feet sought the pedals. From white, pearl-embroidered slippers, her young limbs, smooth in pale, dull silk, swept up in long, low lines. Even the delicate curving of her knees he saw as she drew aside her drapery and struck the first warm tones. She played the phrase in dispute—great chords of aspiration and vision that melted to soft melody. The Egyptian acknowledged his fault. "Yes—yes, that was the theme I had forgotten."

Again Matthew felt his lack of culture audible, and not simply of his own culture, but of all the culture in white America which he had unconsciously and foolishly, as he now realized, made his norm. Yet withal Matthew was not unhappy. If he was a bit out of it, if he sensed divided counsels and opposition, yet he still felt almost fiercely that that was his world. Here were culture, wealth, and beauty. Here was power, and here he had some recognized part. God! If he could just do his part, any part! And he waited impatiently for the real talk to begin again.

It began and lasted until after midnight. It started on lines so familiar to Matthew that he had to shut his eyes and stare again at their swarthy faces: Superior races—the right to rule—born to command—inferior breeds—the lower classes—the rabble. How the Egyptian rolled off his tongue his contempt for the "r-r-rabble"! How contemptuous was the young Indian of inferior races! But how humorous it was to Matthew to see all tables turned; the rabble now was the white workers of Europe; the inferior races were the ruling whites of Europe and America. The superior races were yellow and brown.

"You see," said the Japanese, "Mr. Towns, we here are all agreed and not agreed. We are agreed that the present white hegemony of the world is nonsense; that the darker peoples are the best—the natural aristocracy, the makers of art, religion, philosophy, life, everything except brazen machines."

"But why?"

"Because of the longer rule of natural aristocracy among us. We count our millenniums of history where Europe counts her centuries. We have our own carefully thought-out philosophy and civilization, while Europe has sought to adopt an ill-fitting mélange of the cultures of the world."

"But does this not all come out the same gate, with the majority of mankind serving the minority? And if this is the only ideal of civilization, does the tint of a skin matter in the question of who leads?" Thus Matthew summed it up.

"Not a whit—it is the natural inborn superiority that matters," said the Japanese, "and it is that which the present color bar of Europe is holding back."

"And what guarantees, in the future more than in the past and with colored more than with white, the wise rule of the gifted and powerful?"

"Self-interest and the inclusion in their ranks of all really superior men of all colors—the best of Asia together with the best of the British aristocracy, of the German Adel, of the French writers and financiers—of the rulers, artists, and poets of all peoples."

"And suppose we found that ability and talent and art is not entirely or even mainly among the reigning aristocrats of Asia and Europe, but buried among millions of men down in the great sodden masses of all men and even in Black Africa?"

"It would come forth."

"Would it?"

"Yes," said the Princess, "it would come forth, but when and how? In slow and tenderly nourished efflorescence, or in wild and bloody upheaval with all that bitter loss?"

"Pah!" blurted the Egyptian—"pardon, Royal Highness—but what art ever came from the canaille!"

The blood rushed to Matthew's face. He threw back his head and closed his eyes, and with the movement he heard again the Great Song. He saw his father in the old log church by the river, leading the moaning singers in the Great Song of Emancipation. Clearly, plainly he heard that mighty voice and saw the rhythmic swing and beat of the thick brown arm. Matthew swung his arm and beat the table; the silver tinkled. Silence dropped on all, and suddenly Matthew found himself singing. His voice full, untrained but mellow, quivered down the first plaintive bar:

"When Israel was in Egypt land—"

Then it gathered depth:

"Let my people go!"

He forgot his audience and saw only the shining river and the bowed and shouting throng:

"Oppressed so hard, they could not stand,
Let my people go."

Then Matthew let go restraint and sang as his people sang in Virginia, twenty years ago. His great voice, gathered in one long deep breath, rolled the Call of God:

"Go down, Moses!
Way down into the Egypt land,
Tell Old Pharaoh
To let my people go!"

He stopped as quickly as he had begun, ashamed, and beads of sweat gathered on his forehead. Still there was silence—silence almost breathless. The voice of the Chinese woman broke it.

"It was an American slave song! I know it. How—how wonderful."

A chorus of approval poured out, led by the Egyptian.

"That," said Matthew, "came out of the black rabble of America." And he trilled his "r." They all smiled as the tension broke.

"You assume then," said the Princess at last, "that the mass of the workers of the world can rule as well as be ruled?"

"Yes—or rather can work as well as be worked, can live as well as be kept alive. America is teaching the world one thing and only one thing of real value, and that is, that ability and capacity for culture is not the hereditary monopoly of a few, but the widespread possibility for the majority of mankind if they only have a decent chance in life."

The Chinaman spoke: "If Mr. Towns' assumption is true, and I believe it is, and recognized, as some time it must be, it will revolutionize the world."

"It will revolutionize the world," smiled the Japanese, "but not—today."

"Nor this *siècle,*" growled the Arab.

"Nor the next—and so *in saecula saeculorum,*" laughed the Egyptian.

"Well," said the little Chinese lady, "the unexpected happens."

And Matthew added ruefully, "It's about all that does happen!"

He lapsed into blank silence, wondering how he had come to express the astonishing philosophy which had leapt unpremeditated from his lips. Did he himself believe it? As they arose from the table the Princess called him aside.

VII

"I trust you will pardon the interruption at this late hour," said the Japanese. Matthew glanced up in surprise as the Japanese, the two Indians, and the Arab entered his room. "Sure," said he cheerily, "have any seats you can find. Sorry there's so little space."

It was three o'clock in the morning. He was in his shirt sleeves without collar, and he was packing hastily, wondering how on earth all these things had ever come out of his two valises. The little room on the fifth floor of the Roter Adler Hotel did look rather a mess. But his guests smiled and so politely deprecated any excuses or discomfort that he laughed too, and leaned against the window, while they stood about door and bed.

"You had, I believe," continued the Japanese, "an interview with her Royal Highness, the Princess, before you left her home tonight."

"Yes."

"I—er—presume you realize, Mr. Towns, that the Princess of Bwodpur is a lady of very high station—of great wealth and influence."

"I cannot imagine anybody higher."

The elder Indian interrupted. "There are," he said, "of course, some persons of higher hereditary rank than her Royal Highness, but not many. She is of royal blood by many scores of generations of direct descent. She is a ruling potentate in her own right over six millions of loyal subjects and yields to no human being in the ancient splendor of her heritage. Her income, her wealth in treasure and jewels, is uncounted. Sir, there are few people in the world who have the right to touch the hem of her garment." The Indian drew himself to full height and looked at Matthew.

"I'm strongly inclined to agree with you there," said Matthew, smiling genially.

"I had feared," continued the younger Indian, also looking Matthew squarely in the eye, "that perhaps, being American, and unused to the ceremony of countries of rank, you might misunderstand the democratic graciousness of her Royal Highness toward you. We appreciate, sir, more than we can say," and both Indians bowed low, "your inestimable service to the Princess yesterday, in protecting her royal person from insufferable insult. But the very incident illustrates and explains our errand.

"The Princess is young and headstrong. She delights, in her new European independence, to elude her escort, and has given us moments of greatest solicitude and even fright. Meeting her as you did yesterday, it was natural for you to take her graciousness toward you as the camaraderie of an equal, and—quite unconsciously, I am sure—your attitude toward her has caused us grave misgiving."

"You mean that I have not treated the Princess with courtesy?" asked Matthew in consternation. "In what way? Tell me."

"It is nothing—nothing, now that it is past, and since the Princess was gracious enough to allow it. But you may recall that you never addressed her by her rightful title of 'Royal Highness'; you several times interrupted her conversation and addressed her before being addressed; you occupied the seat of honor without even an attempted refusal and actually shook her Highness' hand, which we are taught to regard as unpardonable familiarity."

Matthew grinned cheerfully. "I reckon if the Princess hadn't liked all that she'd have said so—"

The Japanese quickly intervened. "This is, pardon me, beside our main errand," he said. "We realize that you admire and revere the Princess not only as a supremely beautiful woman of high rank, but as one of rare intelligence and high ideals."

"I certainly do."

"And we assume that anything you could do—any way you could coöperate with us for her safety and future, we could count upon your doing?"

"To my very life."

"Good—excellent—you see, my friends," turning to the still disturbed Indians and the silent, sullen Arab, "it is as I rightly divined."

They did not appear wholly convinced, but the Japanese continued:

"In her interview with you she told you a story she had heard in Moscow, of a widespread and carefully planned uprising of the American blacks. She has intrusted you with a letter to the alleged leader of this organization and asked you to report to her your impressions and recommendations; and even to deliver the letter, if you deem it wise.

"Now, my dear Mr. Towns, consider the situation: First of all, our beloved Princess introduces you, a total stranger, into our counsels and tells you some of our general plans. Fortunately, you prove to be a gentleman who can be trusted; and yet you yourself must admit this procedure was not exactly wise. Further than that, through this letter, our reputations, our very lives, are put in danger by this well-meaning but young and undisciplined lady. Her unfortunate visit to Russia has inoculated her with Bolshevism of a mild but dangerous type. The letter contains money to encourage treason. You know perfectly well that the American Negroes will neither rebel nor fight unless put up to it or led like dumb cattle by whites. You have never even heard of the alleged leader, as you acknowledged to the Princess."

"She is evidently well spied upon."

"She is, and will always be, well guarded," answered the elder Indian tensely.

"Except yesterday," said Matthew.

But the Japanese quickly proceeded. "Why then go on this wild goose chase? Why deliver dynamite to children?"

"Thank you."

"I beg your pardon. I may speak harshly, but I speak frankly. You are an exception among your people."

"I've heard that before. Once I believed it. Now I do not."

"You are generous, but you are an exception, and you know you are."

"Most people are exceptions."

"You know that your people are cowards."

"That's a lie; they are the bravest people fighting for justice today."

"I wish it were so, but I do not believe it, and neither do you. Every report from America—and believe me, we have many—contradicts this statement for you. I am not blaming them, poor things, they were slaves and children of slaves. They can not even begin to rise in a century. We Samurai have been lords a thousand years and more; the ancestors of her Royal Highness have ruled for twenty centuries—how can you think to place yourselves beside us as equals? No—no—restrain your natural anger and distaste for such truth. Our situation is too delicate for niceties. We have been almost betrayed by an impulsive woman, high and royal personage though she be. We have come to get that letter and to ask you to write a report now, to be delivered later, thoroughly disenchanting our dear Princess of this black American chimera."

"And if I refuse?"

The Japanese looked pained but patient. The others moved impatiently, and perceptibly narrowed the circle about Matthew. He was thinking rapidly; the letter was in his coat pocket on the bed beyond the Japanese and within easy reach of the Indians if they had known it. If he jumped out the window, he would be dead, and they would eventually secure the letter. If he fought, they were undoubtedly armed, and four to one. The Japanese was elderly and negligible as an opponent, but the young Indian and the Arab were formidable, and the older Indian dangerous. He might perhaps kill one and disable another and raise enough hullabaloo to arouse the hotel, but how would such a course affect the Princess?

The Japanese watched him sadly.

"Why speak of unpleasant things," he said gently, "or contemplate futilities? We are not barbarians. We are men of thought and culture. Be assured our plans have been laid with care. We know the host of this hotel well. Resistance on your part would be absolutely futile. The back stairs opposite your entrance are quite clear and will be kept clear until we go. And when we go, the letter will go with us."

Matthew set his back firmly against the window. His thoughts raced. They were armed, but they would use their arms only as a last resort; pistols were noisy and knives were messy. Oh, they would use them—one look at their hard, set eyes showed that; but not first. Good! Then first, instead of lurching forward to attack as they might expect, he would do a first-base slide and spike the Japanese in the ankles. It was a mean trick, but anything was fair now. He remembered once when they were playing the DeWitt Clinton High— But he jerked his thoughts back. The Japanese was nearest him; the fiery younger Indian just behind him and a bit to the right, bringing him nearer the bed and blocking the aisle. By the door was the elder Indian, and at the foot of the bed, the Arab.

Good! He would, at the very first movement of the young Indian, who, he instinctively knew, would begin the mêlée, slide feet forward into the ankles of the Japanese, catching him a little to the right so that he would fall or lurch between him and the Indian. Then he would with the same movement slide under the low iron bed and rise with the bed as weapon and shield. But he would not keep it. No; he would hurl it sideways and to the left, pinning the young Indian to the wall and the Japanese to the floor. With the same movement he would attempt a football tackle on the Arab. The Arab was a tough customer—tall, sinewy, and hard. If he turned left, got his knife and struck down, quick and sure, Matthew would be done for. But most probably he would, at Matthew's first movement, turn right toward his fellows. If he did, he was done for. He would go down in the heap, knocking the old Indian against the door.

Beside that door was the electric switch. Matthew would turn it and make a last fight for the door. He might get out, and if he did, the stairs were clear. The coat and letter? Leave them, so long as he got his story to the Princess. It was all a last desperate throw. He calculated that he had good chances against the Japanese's shins, about even chances to get under the bed unscathed, and one in two to tackle the Arab. He had not more than one chance in three of making the door unscathed, but this was the only way. If he surrendered without a fight— That was unthinkable. And after all, what had he to lose? Life? Well, his prospects were not brilliant anyhow. And to die for the Princess—silly, of course, but it made his blood race. For the first time he glimpsed the glory of death. Meantime—he said—be sensible! It would not hurt to spar for time.

He pretended to be weighing the matter.

"Suppose you do steal the letter by force, do you think you can make me write a report?"

"No, a voluntary report would be desirable but not necessary. You left with the Princess, you will remember, a page of directions and information about America to guide her in the trip she is preparing to make and from which we hope to dissuade her. You appended your signature and address. From this it will be easy to draft a report in handwriting so similar to yours as to be indistinguishable by ordinary eyes."

"You add forgery to your many accomplishments."

"In the pursuit of our duty, we do not hesitate at theft or forgery."

Still Matthew parried: "Suppose," he said, "I pretended to acquiesce, gave you the letter and reported to the Princess. Suppose even I told the German newspapers of what I have seen and heard tonight."

There was a faraway look in the eyes of the Japanese as he answered slowly: "We must follow Fate, my dear Mr. Towns, even if Fate leads— to murder. We will not let you communicate with the Princess, and you are leaving Berlin tonight."

The Indians gave a low sigh almost like relief.

Matthew straightened and spoke slowly and firmly.

"Very well. I won't surrender that letter to anybody but the Princess—not while I'm alive. And if I go out of here dead I won't be the only corpse."

Every eye was on the Japanese, and Matthew knew his life was in the balance. The pause was tense; then came the patient voice of the Japanese again.

"You—admire the Princess, do you not?"

"With all my heart."

The Indians winced.

"You would do her a service?"

"To the limit of my strength."

"Very well. Let us assume that I am wrong. Assume that the Negroes are worth freedom and ready to fight for it. Can you not see that the name of this young, beautiful, and high-born lady must under no circumstances be mixed up with them, whether they gain or lose? What would not Great Britain give thus to compromise an Indian ruler?"

"That is for the Princess to decide."

"No! She is a mere woman—an inexperienced girl. You are a man of the world. For the last time, will you rescue her Royal Highness from herself?"

"No. The Princess herself must decide."

"Then—"

"Then," said the Princess' full voice, "the Princess will decide."

CARL VAN VECHTEN

Born in Cedar Rapids, Iowa, Van Vechten demonstrated an early interest in music and theater. After attending the University of Chicago, he moved to New York in 1906, where he worked as an assistant music critic for the *New York Times*. He eventually covered dance, as well as music, for the paper. These areas of interest, as well as his marriage to actress Fania Marinoff, led him into the modern art scene of the time and, consequently, into close contact with many black artists. This interest soon grew into a near obsession. He took up photography and photographed, as well as befriended, many of the leading black artists of the day. He soon found himself so taken with black culture that he decided to write a novel that showed the depth of his passion. The result was the controversial book *Nigger Heaven*. With a title that many book buyers deemed scandalous and Van Vechten's status as a white writer of black culture, neither Van Vechten nor the biographers who followed him ever explained away the controversy caused by the book. But the chapter featured here is supposed by many, including Dr. Bruce Kellner, the administrator of the Van Vechten estate, to express the truly affectionate and reverent feeling that he had for blacks who were fortunate enough to live in what he considered the heavenly village of Harlem.

ONE

Mary Love closed the door softly behind her, shutting out the brassy blare of the band playing on the floor below, crossed the room, and hesitated before the open window. Unwontedly, she found herself quite ready to cry and she welcomed the salt breeze that blew in from the ocean. When she had consented to spend the week-end with Adora Boniface she had not taken into consideration, she discovered, all that this acceptance would imply. She had met—she should have known that she would meet—people who, on the whole, were not her kind. Adora, in her earlier life on the stage, and in her later rich marriage, had gathered about her—and tolerated—a set which included individuals who would never have been admitted into certain respectable homes in Harlem. There was, for example, Randolph Pettijohn, the Bolito King. Adora had probably invited him because he was rich and good-natured. Mary conceded the affluence and the good-nature. She even tried not to be a snob when she thought of the manner in which he had accumulated his fortune. Hot-dogs, cabarets, even gambling, all served their purposes in life, no doubt, although the game of Numbers was a deliberate—and somewhat heartless, considering the average winnings—appeal to a weakness in the ignorant members of her race which she could not readily condone. It was not, however, Pettijohn's background which had won Mary's disfavour. Rather, it was his unpleasant habit of stopping her on the landings of the staircases, of pursuing her into the secluded nooks of the garden, behind the fir hedges. Mary's past experience had not been of a nature to fit her to cope easily with these unwelcome advances. Even now, she was perturbed by the reflection that Randolph might dare follow her into Adora's bedroom.

There was, she could perceive, nothing in Adora's attitude, nothing in the attitude of the house-party as a group, which would indicate that any one regarded such conduct with disapproval. Sylvia Hawthorne obviously had come expressly for the purpose of carrying on her more or less clandestine affair with Rumsey Meadows under auspices which would not too completely compromise her either in the eyes of her husband or the eyes of the more formal Harlem world to which she belonged. The others slipped about a good deal in pairs. If you passed a chamber in which two were sitting, you were likely to hear no words spoken. As for Adora herself, it was clear that she had settled her ephemeral fancy on Alcester Parker, but somehow Mary felt that she could forgive Adora anything.

Mary had known all about Adora, and liked her in spite of all she knew, for a long time. Adora's former superior position on the stage, rare for one of her race in the early twentieth century, had awarded her a secure situation even before she married the wealthy real-estate dealer who, through rises in value of Harlem property, had been enabled to turn over to his widow at his death an estate which had few serious rivals in the new community. Frowned upon in many quarters, not actually accepted intimately in others—not accepted in any sense of the word, of course, by the old and exclusive Brooklyn set—Adora nevertheless was a figure not to be ignored. She was too rich, too important, too influential, for that. To be sure, she had never been conspicuous for benefactions to her race. On the other hand, she could be counted on for occasional splurges when a hospital was in need of an endowment or when a riot in some city demanded a call for a defence fund. Also, she was undeniably warm-hearted, amusing, in her outspoken way, and even beautiful, in a queenly African manner that set her apart from the other beauties of her race whose loveliness was more frequently of a Latin than an Ethiopian character. It was her good heart, together with her ready wit, that had won Mary as an adherent, with the additional fact that it suited Adora to be agreeable to Mary. Mary, consequently, really liked her, and often made it a point to seek her out for a chat at one or another of the large parties in Harlem where they met. It was quite reasonable then, when, last week, Adora, encountering Mary in a Lenox Avenue music-shop, remarked that she looked peaked, that too close confinement in the library where she worked was not good for her health, invited her to spend a week-end at her country place on Long Island, for Mary to accept the invitation not only gratefully, but even with alacrity.

She recalled now, however, that certain of her friends, without saying very much, had suggested, perhaps with looks rather than words, that she might find the experiment distasteful. However that might be, Mary, her word once given, had kept it.

She had been here since Friday. It was now Sunday afternoon and several automobiles full of late arrivals had been welcomed with a dance, for which a celebrated jazz-band had been imported from New York. These late-comers had done nothing to dispel the atmosphere of the previous days. Rather, they had enhanced it. One party which had driven down in a great Packard announced its advent by tossing sundry empty gin bottles out into the drive. Another case of this favourite beverage, however, had immediately been opened in their honour. Gin, indeed, flowed as freely as if there had been a natural spring of it, while whisky, Scotch, rye, and Bourbon, was almost equally plentiful. So the petting continued, petting which, in some instances, with the amount of evidence under her eyes, seemed to Mary something which might be called by an uglier name. There were, to be sure, sporadic parties at bridge or pinocle at little tables in several of the rooms in the spacious house, but after a time these were certain to end in a row about money or the desire on the part of some of the gamblers to return to the delights of amorous embraces.

Mary tried to feel that she was not a prig. She tried to assure herself that she might herself enjoy such attentions under more favourable circumstances. She tried to explain to herself that she was selective and not an exhibitionist. However that might be, she was obliged to confess that she was thoroughly out of harmony with her present environment.

At any rate, she mused, it's nobody's fault but my own. I should have had sense enough not to come. Anyway I won't be rude. I suppose I can manage to evade that old satyr for another sixteen hours without being silly or screaming for help—the others would only laugh, in any case, if I did that—and tomorrow I'll be back in my room in Harlem, just as poor as ever, but, thank God, a trifle more intelligent. I won't do just this again in a hurry.

She shook off her sombre mood, almost with a conscious movement of her shoulders, determining to think of impersonal matters. After all, she decided, with a kind of voluntary optimism, the view from this window is superb. In a pool below, shadowed by weeping-willow-trees with spreading boughs which swept the lawn, yellow water-lilies floated and rose lotus blooms nodded on their long, graceful stalks. Beyond, between the trees, across a green sward, lay the sea in which, taking advantage of the splendour of the day, several men were bathing. Two or three of them lay recumbent on the sand, their brown limbs gleaming like bronze in the sun. Others splashed about in the water. Now a youth was mounting the tower in preparation for a dive. He was, she noted, slightly lighter in colour than the others, almost the shade of coffee diluted with rich cream, her preferred tint. At the top of the tower he paused for an instant, arms high over head, long enough for her to catch the symmetrical proportions of his body, the exquisite form of his head, emphasized by his closely cropped, curly, black hair. Now, in a wide, parabolic curve, he dived, cut the water with his hands, and disappeared. Mary emitted an involuntary cry of pleasure: the action was so perfect; *thrilling,* she defined it. It was repeated many times, varied with much laughter and splashing below, and then the young man ran rapidly up the beach and vanished in the bath-house.

Mary turned away from the window and faced the room. Her discontent—disapproval would be a more just word—had vanished. She felt warmer, more understanding and sympathetic. The chamber itself she now found grateful to her eyes, suited to her mood. It was hung in peach-coloured taffeta, expertly draped, the folds held in place by silver coronets, surmounted by plumes of a delicate blue. The bed, innocent of upright pieces, was merely a broad couch hidden beneath a covering of tiger-skins from under which peeped the supports created in the guise of griffins' claws. Magenta and silver cushions were scattered over its expanse. The rest of the furniture was a heavy Bavarian version of Empire, upholstered in dove-hued damask, the arms of the chairs terminating in silver swans' heads. Mary's roving glance included the dressing-table, beneath its canopy of taffeta, laid out with brushes and combs and boxes of tortoise-shell, rows of crystal, ruby, and sapphire bottles and vials, and tiny enamelled receptacles containing rouges and ointments. Loving luxury, all this panoply appealed to Mary's senses, awarded her, in itself, a definite happiness. Had she been alone in this house with Adora, she would have had, she was beginning to believe, a perfect time.

She crossed the room and stood before the dressing-table, regarding her reflection in the mirror, a mirror blessed and consecrated by two hovering silver Cupids. The attentions of Randolph Pettijohn had not augmented her vanity, but she was not displeased by her double. The rich golden-brown colour of her skin was well set off by the simple frock of Pompeian-red crêpe which she wore. Her features were regular, her brown eyes unusually rich. Her hair, parted and smoothed over her forehead, was caught in a low knot just above the nape of her neck. She could not, justifiably, complain about her appearance. Her expression, too, she recognized with pleasure, was lighter, more carefree. What a fool I have been, she assured herself, not to enjoy all this, not to take it for what it is! I may never again be surrounded by such beauty. Mary sighed.

She turned, as she heard the unfastening of the door, to see Adora enter, a languid, fatigued Adora, supported on the one side by Piqua St. Paris, on the other by Arabia Scribner. The group resembled, Mary thought afterwards, Cleopatra, guided by Charmian and Iras.

Perceiving the room to be already occupied, Adora regained a little of her spent vitality.

Why, Mary, she exclaimed, we've missed you. What are you doing off here, all by yourself?

I was tired, Mary explained, and I came up here because you can see the garden better from this window.

I'm tired too, Adora sighed, sinking into a fauteuil, tired to death of all those Niggers[1] downstairs. Sometimes I hate Niggers.

Adora dear, chirped Mrs. St. Paris, in a shrill, sycophantic tone, can't I find something to cover your knees? Looking about she sighted a lemon-yellow dressing-gown hanging over a Coromandel screen. Gathering it in her arms, she spread it over her idol's limbs.

My knees are all right, Adora whined. It's my feet. . . .

Mrs. Scribner was on the floor at once, removing the offending satin shoes.

My feet . . . and those damn Niggers.

Silently, Mary applauded this sentiment.

It isn't you, Mary dear—in making this reservation Adora disregarded the presence of the other two ladies—it isn't you. It's that ink-fingered trash downstairs. Oh, a few of them are all right, but most of them come here to drink my booze and eat my food and raise hell at my expense. If I was poor they wouldn't come near me, not a damn one of them.

Why, Adora, protested Mrs. Scribner, we'd come to you in a hovel.

Um, Adora responded doubtfully, the while she stretched forward her released feet and wriggled her silk-encased toes. Suppose you ring the bell.

Mrs. St. Paris pressed a button in the wall.

Mary was surprised to find herself actually interested in studying Adora. She *was* beautiful, of that there could be no question, beautiful and regal. Her skin was almost black; her nose broad, her lips thick. Her ears were set well on her head; her head was set well on her shoulders. She was a type of pure African majesty. She was garbed in a pansy chiffon robe which matched the pansy lights in her lustrous eyes. Caught by an invisible chain around her ebony forehead gleamed a single pear-shaped emerald.

As, in response to the summons of the bell, a maid entered, Mary noted what she had often observed before in the expression of dependent Negroes in the homes of rich members of her race, a certain sullen mien. We don't like to wait on each other, she reflected bitterly.

---

[1] *While this informal epithet is freely used by Negroes among themselves, not only as a term of opprobrium, but also actually as a term of endearment, its employment by a white person is always fiercely resented. The word Negress is forbidden under all circumstances.*

Nellie, Adora ordered, bring up four champagne-glasses and a bowl of ice.

Without responding, without, indeed, giving any indication that she had heard, the maid shuffled out of the room.

Now, where are my mules?

The sycophants in their haste, each to reach the proper closet first, bumped into each other and exchanged glares.

After she had been shod more comfortably, the former music hall star rose majestically and hobbled towards a chest of drawers. From beneath a heap of filmy chiffon and lace she extracted a bunch of keys. Selecting one, she unlocked a cupboard, the shelves of which, Mary observed, were occupied by rows of reclining bottles bundled in straw. Choosing one, Adora returned to the comfort of her armchair.

I need a drink bad, she averred, and nothing but champagne will do. It always cheers me up.

Presently Nellie returned with the glasses and a silver bowl containing ice. Drawing a small coffee-table near her mistress's chair, she placed her burden upon it and retired as silently as she had approached.

Nellie talks about as much as Coolidge, Adora remarked as she cooled the glasses and poured out the wine. The eyes of Mrs. St. Paris and Mrs. Scribner were greedy, but Adora ignored their message.

Mary, she said, here's yours.

Mary drew nearer and accepted the proffered goblet. Now, somewhat grudgingly, Adora served the other two ladies.

Sit down, Mary.

Mary obeyed her.

I like you, Mary, and I'm going to drink to your success.

Oh, yes, the sycophants echoed, to Mary's success!

Without further preliminary the ladies proceeded to sip their wine.

Thank you, Adora, Mary responded, but I haven't a notion what kind of success I want.

There's only one success for a woman, Adora announced, at least for a coloured woman, and that's a good husband, and a good husband for a coloured woman means a rich husband.

I don't know that I want to be married, Mary protested.

Oh, go on! Now what else can a coloured woman do? You're a librarian, but you'll never get as much pay as the white librarians. They won't even put you in charge of a branch library. Not because you're not as good as the others—probably you're better—but because you're coloured. If you were a trained nurse it would be the same. The only chance a coloured woman has—she can't be a doctor or a lawyer or a preacher or a real-estate agent like a man—is on the stage, and you'd be no good on the stage! Why, probably you can't even dance the Charleston!

I can—a little. Mary laughed grimly.

Well, a little isn't enough. Anyway, they don't want your type on the stage any more, or mine either, for that matter. If I wanted to work to-day I bet I couldn't get a job. The managers, especially the shine managers, are looking for high yallers. Well, I can't say I blame 'em. I'm sick of Niggers myself, damn sick of these black Niggers!

Adora sipped her wine meditatively.

I might open a beauty parlour. Mary essayed a weak attempt at humour.

Yes, you might, but there are forty of those on every street in Harlem already. And you might start another Black Star Line, and peddle snow, or become an undertaker, but you won't do any of these things.

The glasses of Mrs. St. Paris and Mrs. Scribner were conspicuously empty, their expressions eager, their arms all but outstretched. Overlooking this condition, Adora filled her own glass and continued in her rich, steady voice, low and musical, and with the commanding presence she had acquired during her career on the stage: There's an old song which I used to hear when I toured the South: Ain't it hard to be a Nigger? Ever hear it? Without waiting for a reply, Adora lay back in her chair and began to croon:

> Ain't it hard, ain't it hard,
> Ain't it hard to be a Nigger, Nigger, Nigger?
> Ain't it hard, ain't it hard?
> Fo' you can't git yo' money when it's due.

Well, I guess it is, though it partly depends on the way you look at it. It's hard for those who don't face facts. Now, I always do just that. Mary, she went on earnestly, almost pleadingly, I wish you'd get married.

Why, Adora, what can I do if nobody wants me? Mary tried to laugh off her embarrassment.

Well, you know as well as I do there's a certain party round here that's pretty crazy to get you.

Mary regarded her hostess with unfeigned astonishment.

You don't think he wants to *marry* me? she queried, too dumfounded to make any pretence that she was unaware of the identity of the person to whom Adora referred.

In a minute. This afternoon. Neglecting the glasses of her guests—Mary's, as a matter of fact, remained nearly full—she offered herself another libation, whereupon the sycophants scowled.

Mary's conflicting emotions did not permit her to speak at once.

Well, Mary, what do you say?

If you don't mind, Adora. . . . If you don't mind, I'd rather not talk about it.

Nonsense! . . . There came a loud knocking at the door. . . . More of those Niggers! Go see who it is, Piqua, Adora ordered.

It's Ran and Al.

Adora's expression softened. It was even tender. Oh, they can come in, she said.

The fat Bolito King, his smug, brown countenance wreathed in a wrinkled smile, his eyes assisted by a pince-nez, set in gold, entered, followed by a slender tea-coloured youth, in a blue flannel coat, white trousers, and sneakers.

Well, boys, just in time for a little fizz-water, Adora cried.

We was lookin' fo' you an' et, the King admitted.

More particularly for you, Al added.

Well, for that you can both have a drink out of my glass, Adora suggested. Here's yours. She passed the glass to Al who drained the remnant at one gulp. Adora inverted the bottle. Only a few drops trickled out. Get another bottle, Arabia, she commanded, her eyes following Al as he moved towards the window.

The hammering on the portal was repeated.

Let them in, Adora sighed. It's no use trying to be alone in this place. Let them in, but stow away the champagne and bring out the Scotch.

Been looking for you everywhere, Adora, cried Dr. Lister, the handsome and popular young dentist, as the door swung open. Behind him surged Lutie Panola, fat and merry, dressed in violet muslin and resembling an overgrown doll; Sylvia Hawthorne, smart in her shingle-haired, slender, yellow way, in a dress of ecru linen embroidered in bright wools; smiling, smoking a cigarette through an amber holder, she leaned on the arm of Rumsey Meadows; Irwin Latrobe, Lucas Garfield, Guymon Hooker, Carmen Fisher, Hope Rosemount, and finally, the stranger whom Mary had watched diving brought up the rear.

Can we dance in here, 'Dora? Sylvia demanded. We've danced damn near everywhere else.

Her hostess making an impatient gesture of assent, Sylvia set the phonograph which soon was spinning around to the tune of Little Turtle Dove Love!

Roll up the rugs! Sylvia cried.

Rumsey obeyed her and three couples began to dance at once.

Lucas Garfield, who the previous spring had been leading man in a Negro revue called James Crow, Esquire, imitated the strumming of a ukelele with his fingers while he sang:

Oh, how I'm aching for love!
Wish I had a little turtle dove
To coo, coo, coo to me . . .

Lutie Panola had thrown herself on the bed. She lay, a vast violet muslin heap on the tiger-skin covering, kicking up her heels, shivering like a mammoth platter of jelly, and emitting gurgles of joy. Dr. Lister dragged Mary to the floor and she danced with him willingly enough, only too grateful to escape the attentions of Pettijohn for the time being. Adora was beating time with the heel of her mule, while her two satellites and Alcester Parker waved their arms in rhythm with the music.

When the phonograph ran down, the noise increased. The men sought drinks, the women lipsticks. Mary gravitated towards the open window. Suddenly, through the uproar, in a clear undertone that ripped the din like thunder, she heard a voice behind her which unaccountably made her tremble.

You seem out of place here, if you don't mind my saying so, the voice said.

She turned quickly to face the diver, furious that he, a stranger, should take for granted what she felt to be true.

I don't know what you mean, she protested.

Yes, you do too, he went on imperturbably. La Boniface is all right, but apparently she invites a lot of riff-raff to her parties.

I dare say I'm no better than any one else. She could have bitten her tongue out after she had made this priggish remark. What would he think of her?

I dare say none of us is, he responded. It's just a matter of what we like and what we don't like. Now I don't believe you like *this*.

In drunken despair, Lutie was sobbing now. Lucas, still imitating the ukelele, warbled:

What does it matter that
I want you?
What does it matter that
You want me?
Like a sweet lump of sugar
In a hot cup of tea
Love don't last nohow,
Melts away somehow.
What does it matter that . . .

Wow! screamed Sylvia. Bottle it, Lucas, for cryin' out loud.

Mary smiled. I don't believe I've met you, she said.

My name's Byron Kasson: he introduced himself. I'm just graduated from the University of Pennsylvania. Came out here today with a bunch I met in New York. Shall I ask someone to introduce you to me?

No, don't. She spoke quickly. She was less nervous now. My name is Mary Love.

Somehow, Miss Love . . . it was his turn to be embarrassed . . . you stand out in a crowd like this. I couldn't help liking you even before I talked to you.

I saw you first . . . diving.

He smiled. That's the only thing I do well.

You do *that* well. Is it your profession?

I haven't any profession yet. I want to write, he went on.

You're a writer! Mary exclaimed with enthusiasm.

Oh, I haven't published much. I've had a piece or two in *Opportunity*, but that won't keep me alive. At college they said I had promise. I know what they meant, he added, "pretty good for a coloured man." That doesn't satisfy me. I want to be as good as any one. It's frightfully noisy here, he went on. Couldn't we find a quieter spot?

It's noisy all over the place. Downstairs, there's a jazz-band. Anyhow, if we go anywhere else we're sure to be followed. I came up here to get away from the confusion and you can see how successful I've been. Why don't you call on me in New York?

I'm not living in New York. I'm going back to Philadelphia tomorrow. Later, I hope to return.

When?

I don't know. He grinned. You see, I haven't a bean. Got to work at something while I practise writing, and I haven't the faintest notion what I can do.

Interrupted by a terrifying scream, they turned to see Sylvia and Rumsey, one tugging at each ankle, dragging Lutie off the bed. Clinging to the tiger-skin, kicking, shrieking, she fell to the floor.

Here you, be careful of my skins! Adora warned them harshly.

It's all right, 'Dora, Sylvia replied. I'll put it back.

Unwinding the screaming Lutie, Rumsey assisted her to her feet and began to dance with her while he sang ribaldly:

By an' by,
By an' by,
I'm goin' to lay down this heavy load . .

You bum, you! Lutie pummelled him.

Randolph Pettijohn approached the pair in the window.

Ah doan never seem to fin' no chance to speak to you, Miss Mary, he began.

Byron Kasson turned and walked away. Mary realized that she had no right to stop him.

An' Ah got somethin' to say, an' dere ain' much time lef' to say et in, the King continued. Ah knows Ah ain' yo' kin', but you's mine. Ah wants a nice, 'spectable 'ooman for a wife . . . Mary opened her mouth to speak . . . Wait a minute. Ah ain't elegant. Ah ain' got no eddication lak you, but Ah got money, plenty of et, an' Ah got love. Ah'd mek you happy an' you'd give me what Ah wants, a 'spectable 'ooman. Ef you want to, we'd live on Strivers' Row . . .

At last Mary succeeded in stopping him. I'm sorry, Mr. Pettijohn, she said, but it's no use. You see, I don't love you.

Dat doan mek no difference, he whispered softly. Lemme mek you.

I'm afraid it's impossible, Mary asserted more firmly.

The Bolito King regarded her fixedly and with some wonder. You cain' mean no, he said. Ah's willin' to wait, an' to wait some time, but Ah gotta git you. You jes' what Ah desires.

It's impossible, Mary repeated sternly, as she turned away.

The room had now become pandemonium. Singly and in couples the crowd danced the Black Bottom and the Charleston. The phonograph was kept incessantly active. Drinks were poured out lavishly. Guymon Hooker, indeed, playfully emptied a bottle of Scotch through an open window. At last, apparently, Adora had had all she could stand. Rising, she pointed her finger towards the door.

Get out of here, the whole pack of you! she commanded. Go to the garage or the kitchen or the w. c. or the front lawn or go drown yourselves in the ocean. I don't give a damn where you go, just so you get out of here.

The group, aware that Adora, offended, was capable of cutting names off her invitation list, heeded the warning and slunk towards the door. As Mary passed her, Adora held out her hand.

I don't mean you, dearie, she said. You stay here with me.

FROM HOME TO HARLEM (1928)

CLAUDE MCKAY

Born in Jamaica, West Indies, McKay came to America in 1912 and enrolled in the Tuskegee Institute in Alabama. As a result of the quality of his poetry and short stories, he became a charter member of the movement that would become the Harlem Renaissance. He was one of the first of his literary peers to recognize that Harlem itself was a source of inspiration. He saw the locale as a beacon and mecca not just for artists, but for all Negroes who were fortunate enough to get there. With this belief firmly implanted in his heart and mind, he wrote the novel *Home to Harlem*. This is the story of a merchant seaman who, after a long tour of duty at sea, once again approaches the port of New York and, shortly thereafter, his beloved Harlem.

GOING BACK HOME

I

All that Jake knew about the freighter on which he stoked was that it stank between sea and sky. He was working with a dirty Arab crew. The captain signed him on at Cardiff because one of the Arabs had quit the ship. Jake was used to all sorts of rough jobs, but he had never before worked in such a filthy dinghy.

The white sailors who washed the ship would not wash the stokers' water-closet, because they despised the Arabs. And the Arabs themselves made no effort to keep the place clean, although it adjoined their sleeping berth.

The cooks hated the Arabs because they did not eat pork. Whenever there was pork for dinner, something else had to be prepared for the Arabs. The cooks put the stokers' meat, cut in unappetizing chunks, in a broad pan, and the two kinds of vegetables in two other pans. The stoker who carried the food back to the bunks always put one pan inside of the other, and sometimes the bottoms were dirty and bits of potato peelings or egg shells were mixed in with the meat and the vegetables.

The Arabs took up a chunk of meat with their coal-powdered fingers, bit or tore off a piece, and tossed the chunk back into the pan. It was strange to Jake that these Arabs washed themselves after eating and not before. They ate with their clothes stiff-starched to their bodies with coal and sweat. And when they were finished, they stripped and washed and went to sleep in the stinking-dirty bunks. Jake was used to the lowest and hardest sort of life, but even his leather-lined stomach could not endure the Arabs' way of eating. Jake also began to despise the Arabs. He complained to the cooks about the food. He gave the chef a ten-shilling note, and the chef gave him his eats separately.

One of the sailors flattered Jake. "You're the same like us chaps. You ain't like them dirty jabbering coolies."

But Jake smiled and shook his head in a non-committal way. He knew that if he was just like the white sailors, he might have signed on as a deckhand and not as a stoker. He didn't care about the dirty old boat, anyhow. It was taking him back home—that was all he cared about. He made his shift all right, stoking four hours and resting eight. He didn't sleep well. The stokers' bunks were lousy, and fetid with the mingled smell of stale food and water-closet. Jake had attempted to keep the place clean, but to do that was impossible. Apparently the Arabs thought that a sleeping quarters could also serve as a garbage can.

"Nip me all you wanta, Mister Louse," said Jake. "Roll on, Mister Ship, and stinks all the way as you rolls. Jest take me 'long to Harlem is all I pray. I'm crazy to see again the brown-skin chippies 'long Lenox Avenue. Oh boy!"

Jake was tall, brawny, and black. When America declared war upon Germany in 1917 he was a longshoreman. He was working on a Brooklyn pier, with a score of men under him. He was a little boss and a very good friend of his big boss, who was Irish. Jake thought he would like to have a crack at the Germans. . . . And he enlisted.

In the winter he sailed for Brest with a happy chocolate company. Jake had his own daydreams of going over the top. But his company was held at Brest. Jake toted lumber—boards, planks, posts, rafters—for the hundreds of huts that were built around the walls of Brest and along the coast between Brest and Saint-Pierre, to house the United States soldiers.

Jake was disappointed. He had enlisted to fight. For what else had he been sticking a bayonet into the guts of a stuffed man and aiming bullets straight into a bull's-eye? Toting planks and getting into rows with his white comrades at the Bal Musette were not adventure.

Jake obtained leave. He put on civilian clothes and lit out for Havre. He liquored himself up and hung round a low-down café in Havre for a week.

One day an English sailor from a Channel sloop made up to Jake. "Darky," he said, "you 'arvin' a good time 'round 'ere."

Jake thought how strange it was to hear the Englishman say "darky" without being offended. Back home he would have been spoiling for a fight. There he would rather hear "nigger" than "darky," for he knew that when a Yankee said "nigger" he meant hatred for Negroes, whereas when he said "darky" he meant friendly contempt. He preferred white folks' hatred to their friendly contempt. To feel their hatred made him strong and aggressive, while their friendly contempt made him ridiculously angry, even against his own will.

"Sure Ise having a good time, all right," said Jake. He was making a cigarette and growling cusses at French tobacco. "But Ise got to get a move on 'fore very long."

"Where to?" his new companion asked.

"Any place, Buddy. I'm always ready for something new," announced Jake.

"Been in Havre a long time?"

"Week or two," said Jake. "I tooks care of some mules over heah. Twenty, God damn them, days across the pond. And then the boat plows round and run off and leaves me behind. Kain you beat that, Buddy?"

"It wasn't the best o' luck," replied the other. "Ever been to London?"

"Nope, Buddy," said Jake. "France is the only country I've struck yet this side the water."

The Englishman told Jake that there was a sailor wanted on his tug.

"We never 'ave a full crew—since the war," he said.

Jake crossed over to London. He found plenty of work there as a docker. He liked the West India Docks. He liked Limehouse. In the pubs men gave him their friendly paws and called him "darky." He liked how they called him "darky." He made friends. He found a woman. He was happy in the East End.

The Armistice found him there. On New Year's Eve, 1919, Jake went to a monster dance with his woman, and his docker friends and their women, in the Mile End Road.

The Armistice had brought many more black men to the East End of London. Hundreds of them. Some of them found work. Some did not. Many were getting a little pension from the government. The price of sex went up in the East End, and the dignity of it also. And that summer Jake saw a big battle staged between the colored and white men of London's East End. Fisticuffs, razor and knife and gun play. For three days his woman would not let him out-of-doors. And when it was all over he was seized with the awful fever of lonesomeness. He felt all alone in the world. He wanted to run away from the kind-heartedness of his lady of the East End.

"Why did I ever enlist and come over here?" he asked himself. "Why did I want to mix mahself up in a white folks' war? It ain't ever was any of black folks' affair. Niggers am evah always such fools, anyhow. Always thinking they've got something to do with white folks' business."

Jake's woman could do nothing to please him now. She tried hard to get down into his thoughts and share them with him. But for Jake this woman was now only a creature of another race—of another world. He brooded day and night.

It was two years since he had left Harlem. Fifth Avenue, Lenox Avenue, and One Hundred and Thirty-fifth Street, with their chocolate-brown and walnut-brown girls, were calling him.

"Oh, them legs!" Jake thought. "Them tantalizing brown legs! . . . Barron's Cabaret! . . . Leroy's Cabaret! . . . Oh, boy!"

Brown girls rouged and painted like dark pansies. Brown flesh draped in soft colorful clothes. Brown lips full and pouted for sweet kissing. Brown breasts throbbing with love.

"Harlem for mine!" cried Jake. "I was crazy thinkin' I was happy over heah. I wasn't mahself. I was like a man charged up with dope every day. That's what it was. Oh, boy! Harlem for mine!

"Take me home to Harlem, Mister Ship! Take me home to the brown gals waiting for the brown boys that done show their mettle over there. Take me home, Mister Ship. Put your beak right into that water and jest move along." . . .

NEGRO LIFE IN
NEW YORK'S HARLEM (1928)

WALLACE THURMAN

Thurman was born in 1902 in Salt Lake City, Utah. He attended the University of Southern California and later went on to found a magazine called *Outlet*, hoping to duplicate the Harlem Renaissance in Los Angeles. The magazine lasted less then a year and Thurman moved to Harlem in 1925. There, he became managing editor of *The Messenger,* a Renaissance-era publication with a socialist ideology. Thurman later published *FIRE!,* a literary publication that featured his own writing and the works of talents like Arna Bontemps, Countee Cullen, Zora Neale Hurston, and Langston Hughes, and which also caused a stir for its irreverent tone. In addition to his editing work, Thurman wrote and published poems and poetry. He is best known for his satirical 1929 novel dealing with black intraracial prejudice, *The Blacker the Berry.* This essay describes Harlem in the mid-1920s.

I

A LIVELY PICTURE OF A POPULAR
AND INTERESTING SECTION

Harlem has been called the Mecca of the New Negro, the center of black America's cultural renaissance, Nigger Heaven, Pickaninny Paradise, Capitol of Black America, and various other things. It has been surveyed and interpreted, explored and exploited. It has had its day in literature, in the drama, even in the tabloid press. It is considered the most popular and interesting section of contemporary New York. Its fame is international; its personality individual and inimitable. There is no Negro settlement anywhere comparable to Harlem, just as there is no other metropolis comparable to New York. As the great south side black belt of Chicago spreads and smells with the same industrial clumsiness and stock yardish vigor of Chicago, so does the black belt of New York teem and rhyme with the cosmopolitan cross currents of the world's greatest city. Harlem is Harlem because it is part and parcel of greater

New York. Its rhythms are the lackadaisical rhythms of a transplanted minority group caught up and rendered half mad by the more speedy rhythms of the subway, Fifth Avenue, and the Great White Way.

Negro Harlem is located on one of the choice sites of Manhattan Island. It covers the greater portion of the northwestern end, and is more free from grime, smoke, and oceanic dampness than the lower east side where most of the hypenated American groups live. Harlem is a great black city. There are no shanty-filled, mean streets, no antiquated cobblestoned pavement, no flimsy frame fire-traps. Little Africa has fortressed itself behind brick and stone on wide important streets where the air is plentiful and sunshine can be appreciated.

There are six main north and south thoroughfares streaming through Negro Harlem—Fifth Avenue, Lenox Avenue, Seventh Avenue, Eighth Avenue, Edgecombe and St. Nicholas.

Fifth Avenue begins prosperously at 125th Street, becomes a slum district above 131st Street, and finally slithers off into a warehouse-lined, dingy alleyway above 139th Street. The people seen on Fifth Avenue are either sad or nasty looking. The women seem to be drudges or drunkards, the men pugnacious and loud—petty thieves and vicious parasites. The children are pitiful specimens of ugliness and dirt. The tenement houses in this vicinity are darkened dung heaps, festering with poverty-stricken and crime-ridden step-children of nature. This is the edge of Harlem's slum district. Fifth Avenue is its boardwalk. Push-carts line the curbstone, dirty push-carts manned by dirtier hucksters, selling fly-specked vegetables, and other cheap commodities. Evil faces leer at you from doorways and windows. Brutish men elbow you out of their way, dreary looking women scowl at and curse children playing on the sidewalk. This is Harlem's Fifth Avenue.

Lenox Avenue knows the rumble of the subway and the rattle of the crosstown streetcar. It is always crowded, crowded with pedestrians seeking the subway or the streetcar, crowded with idlers from the many pool halls and dives along its line of march, crowded with men and women from the slum district which it borders on the west and Fifth Avenue borders on the east. Lenox Avenue is Harlem's Bowery. It is dirty and noisy, its buildings ill-used, and made shaky by the subway underneath. At 140th Street it makes its one bid for respectability. On one corner there is Tabb's Restaurant and Grill, one of Harlem's most delightful and respectable eating houses; across the street is the Savoy building, housing a first-class dance hall, a motion picture theater and many small business establishments behind its stucco front. But above 141st Street Lenox Avenue gets mean and squalid, deprived of even its crowds of people, and finally peters out into a dirt pile, before leading to a car-barn at 147th Street.

Seventh Avenue—Black Broadway: Harlem's main street, a place to promenade, a place to loiter, an avenue spacious and sleek with wide pavement, modern well-kept buildings, theaters, drug stores, and other businesses. Seventh Avenue, teeming with life and ablaze with color, the most interesting and important street in one of the most interesting and important city sections of greater New York. Negro Harlem is best represented by Seventh Avenue. It is not, like Fifth Avenue, filthy and stark, nor like Lenox, squalid and dirty. It is a great thoroughfare into which every element of Harlem population ventures either for reasons of pleasure or of business. From 125th Street to 145th Street, Seventh Avenue is a stream of dark people going to churches, theaters, restaurants, billiard halls, business offices, food markets, barber shops, and apartment houses. Seventh Avenue is majestic yet warm, and it reflects both the sordid chaos and the rhythmic splendor of Harlem. From five o'clock in the evening until way past midnight, Seventh Avenue is one electric-lit line of brilliance and activity, especially during the spring, summer, and early fall months. Dwelling houses are close, overcrowded, and dark. Seventh Avenue is the place to seek relief. People everywhere: lines of people in front of the box offices of the Lafayette Theatre at 132nd Street, the Renaissance Motion Picture Theatre at 145th Street. Knots of people in front of the Metropolitan Baptist Church at 129th Street, and Salem Methodist Episcopal Church, which dominates the corner at 129th Street. People going into the cabarets. People going into speakeasies and saloons. Groups of boisterous men and boys, congregated on corners and in the middle of the blocks, making remarks about individuals in the passing parade. Adolescent boys and girls flaunting their youth. Street speakers on every corner. A Hindoo fakir here, a loud-voiced Socialist there, a medicine doctor ballyhooing, a corn doctor, a blind musician, serious people, gay people, philanderers, and preachers. Seventh Avenue is filled with deeply rhythmic laughter. It is a civilized lane with primitive traits. Harlem's most representative street.

Eighth Avenue supports the elevated lines. It is noticeably Negroid only from 135th Street to 145th Street. It is packed with dingy, cheap shops owned by Jews. Above 139th Street the curbstone is lined with push-cart merchants selling everything from underwear to foodstuffs. Eighth Avenue is a street for business, a street for people who live west of it to cross hurriedly in order to reach places located east of it.

Edgecombe Avenue, Brandhurst, and St. Nicholas Avenues are strictly thoroughfares of the better variety. Expensive modern apartment houses line these streets. They were once occupied by well-to-do white people who now live on Riverside Drive, West End Avenue, and in Washington Heights. They are luxuriously appointed with imposing entrances, elevator service, disappearing garbage cans, and all the other appurtenances that make a modern apartment house convenient. The Negroes who live in these places are either high-salaried working men or professional folk.

Most of the cross-streets in Harlem, lying between the main north and south thoroughfares, are monotonous and overcrowded. There is little difference between any of them save that some are more dirty and more squalid than others. They are lined with ordinary, undistinguished tenement and apartment houses. Some are well kept, others are run down. There are only four streets that are noticeably different, 136th Street, 137th Street, 138th Street, and 139th Street west of Seventh Avenue, and these are the only blocks in Harlem that can boast of having shade trees. An improvement association organized by people living in these streets, strives to keep them looking respectable.

Between Seventh and Eighth Avenues, is 139th Street, known among Harlemites as "Striver's Row." It is the most aristocratic street in Harlem. Stanford White designed the houses for a wealthy white clientele. Moneyed Negroes now own and inhabit these. When one lives on "Striver's Row" one has supposedly arrived. Harry Willis resides there, as do a number of the leading Babbitts and professional folk of Harlem.

II
200,000 NEGROES IN HARLEM

There are approximately 200,000 Negroes in Harlem. Two hundred thousand Negroes drawn from all sections of America, from Europe, the West Indies, Africa, Asia, or where you will. Two hundred thousand

Negroes living, loving, laughing, crying, procreating, and dying in the segregated city section of Greater New York, about twenty-five blocks long and seven blocks wide. Like all of New York, Harlem is overcrowded. There are as many as 5,000 persons living in some single blocks, living in dark, mephitic tenements, jammed together, brownstone fronts, dingy elevator flats, and modern apartment houses.

Living conditions are ribald and ridiculous. Rents are high and sleeping quarters at a premium. Landlords profiteer and sell bribes, putting out one tenant in order to house another willing to pay more rent. Tenants, in turn, sublet and profiteer on roomers. People rent a five-room apartment, originally planned for a small family, and crowd two oversized families into it. Others lease or buy a private house and partition off spacious front and back rooms in two or three parts. Hallways are curtained off and lined with cots. Living rooms become triplex apartments. Clothes closets and washrooms become kitchenettes. Dining rooms, parlors, libraries, and drawing rooms are all profaned by cots, day beds and snoring sleepers.

There is little privacy, little unused space. The man in the front room of a railroad flat, so called because each room opens into the other like coaches on a train, must pass through three other bedrooms in order to reach the bathroom stuck on the end of the kitchen. He who works nights will sleep by day in the bed of one who works days, and vice versa. Mother and father sleep in a three-quarter bed. Two adolescent children sleep on a portable cot set up in the parents' bedroom. Other cots are dragged by night from closets and corners to be set up in the dining room, in the parlor, or even in the kitchen to accommodate the remaining members of the family. It is all disconcerting, mad. There must be expansion. There is expansion, but it is not rapid enough or continuous enough to keep pace with the ever-growing population of Negro Harlem.

The first place in New York where Negroes had a segregated community was in Greenwich Village, but as the years passed and their numbers increased they soon moved northward into the twenties and lower thirties west of Sixth Avenue until they finally made one big jump and centered around West 53rd Street. About 1900, looking for better housing conditions, a few Negroes moved to Harlem. The Lenox Avenue subway had not yet been built and white landlords were having difficulty in keeping white tenants east of Seventh Avenue because of the poor transportation facilities. Being good businessmen they eagerly accepted the suggestion of a Negro real estate agent that these properties be opened to color tenants. Then it was discovered that the few houses available would not be sufficient to accommodate the sudden influx. Negroes began to creep west of Lenox Avenue. White property owners and residents began to protest and tried to find means of checking or evicting unwelcome black neighbors. Negroes kept pouring in. Negro capital, belligerently organized, began to buy all available properties.

Then, to quote James Weldon Johnson, "the whole movement, in the eyes of the whites, took on the aspect of an 'invasion'; they became panic stricken and began fleeing as from a plague. The presence of one colored family in a block, no matter how well-bred and orderly, was sufficient to precipitate a flight. House after house and block after block was actually deserted. It was a great demonstration of human beings running amuck. None of them stopped to reason why they were doing it or what would happen if they didn't. The banks and the lending companies holding mortgages on these deserted houses were compelled to take them over. For some time they held these houses vacant, preferring to do that and carry the charges than to rent or sell them to colored people, but values dropped and continued to drop until at the outbreak of the war in Europe property in the northern part of Harlem had reached the nadir."

With the war came a critical shortage of common labor and the introduction of thousands of southern Negroes into northern industrial and civic centers. A great migration took place. Negroes were in search of a holy grail. Southern Negroes, tired of moral and financial blue days, struck out for the promised land, to seek adventure among factories, subways, and skyscrapers. New York, of course, has always been a magnet for ambitious and adventurous Americans and foreigners. New York to the Negro meant Harlem, and the great influx included not only thousands of Negroes from every state in the union, but also over thirty thousand immigrants from the West Indian Islands and the Caribbean regions. Harlem was the promised land.

Thanks to New York's many and varied industries, Harlem Negroes have been able to demand and find much work. There is a welcome and profitable diversity of employment. Unlike Negroes in Chicago, or in Pittsburgh, or in Detroit, no one industry is called upon to employ the great part of their population. Negroes have made money in New York;

Negroes have brought money to New York with them, and with this money they have bought property, built certain civic institutions and increased their business activities until their real estate holdings are now valued at more than sixty million dollars.

III
THE SOCIAL LIFE OF HARLEM

The social life of Harlem is both complex and diversified. Here you have two hundred thousand people collectively known as Negroes. You have pure-blooded Africans, British Negroes, Spanish Negroes, Danish Negroes, Cubans, Puerto Ricans, Arabians, East Indians and black Abyssinian Jews in addition to the racially well-mixed American Negro. You have persons of every conceivable shade and color. Persons speaking all languages, persons representative of many cultures and civilizations. Harlem is a magic melting pot, a modern Babel mocking the gods with its cosmopolitan uniqueness.

The American Negro predominates and, having adopted all of white America's prejudices and manners, is inclined to look askance at his little dark-skinned brothers from across the sea. The Spanish Negro, i.e., those Negroes hailing from Spanish possessions, stays to himself and has little traffic with the other racial groups in his environment. The other foreigners, with the exception of the British West Indians, are not large enough to form a separate social group and generally become quickly identified with the regulation social life of the community.

It is the Negro from the British West Indies who creates and has to face a disagreeable problem. Being the second largest Negro group in Harlem, and being less susceptible to American manners and customs than others, he is frowned upon and berated by the American Negro. This intraracial prejudice is an amazing though natural thing. Imagine a community made up of people universally known as oppressed, wasting time and energy trying to oppress others of their kind, more recently transplanted from a foreign clime. It is easy to explain. All people seem subject to prejudice, even those who suffer from it most, and all people seem inherently to dislike other folk who are characterized by cultural and lingual differences. It is a failing of man, a curse of humanity, and if these differences are accompanied, as they usually are, by quarrels concerning economic matters, there is bound to be an intensifying of the bitter antagonism existent between the two groups. Such has been the case with the British West Indian in Harlem. Because of his numerical strength, because of his cockney English inflections and accent, because of his unwillingness to submit to certain American do's and don'ts, and because he, like most foreigners, has seemed willing to work for low wages, he has been hated and abused by his fellow-Harlemites. And, as a matter of protection, he has learned to fight back.

It has been said that West Indians are comparable to Jews in that they are "both ambitious, eager for education, willing to engage in business, argumentative, aggressive, and posses a great proselytizing zeal for any cause they espouse." Most of the retail business in Harlem is owned and controlled by West Indians. They are also well represented and often officiate as provocative agents and leaders in racial movements among Harlem Negroes. And it is obvious that the average American Negro, in manifesting a dislike for the West Indian Negro, is being victimized by that same delusion which he claims blinds the American white man; namely, that all Negroes are alike. There are some West Indians who are distasteful; there are some of all people about whom one could easily say the same thing. It is to be seen then that all this widely diversified population would erect an elaborate social structure. For instance, there are thousands of Negroes in New York from Georgia. These have organized themselves into many clubs, such as the Georgia Circle or the Sons of Georgia. People from Virginia, South Carolina, Florida, and other states do likewise. The foreign contingents also seem to have a mania for social organization. Social clubs and secret lodges are legion. And all of them vie with one another in giving dances, parties, entertainments, and benefits, in addition to public turnouts and parades.

Speaking of parades, one must mention Marcus Garvey. Garvey, a Jamaican, is one of the most widely known Negroes in contemporary life. He became notorious because of his Back-to-Africa campaign. With the West Indian population of Harlem as a nucleus, he enlisted the aid of thousands of Negroes all over America in launching the Black Star Line, the purpose of which was to establish a trade and travel route between America and Africa by and for Negroes. He also planned to establish a black empire in Africa of which he was to be emperor. The man's imagination and influence were colossal; his manifestations of these qualities often ridiculous and adolescent, though they seldom lacked color and interest.

Garvey added much to the gaiety and life of Harlem with his parades. Garmented in a royal purple robe with crimson trimmings and an elaborate headdress, he would ride in state down Seventh Avenue in an open limousine, surrounded and followed by his personal cabinet of high chieftains, ladies in waiting, and protective legion. Since his incarceration in Atlanta Federal Prison on a charge of having used the mails to defraud, Harlem knows no more such spectacles. The street parades held now are uninteresting and pallid when compared to the Garvey turnouts, brilliant primitive as they were.

In addition to the racial and territorial divisions of the social structure there are also minor divisions determined by color and wealth. First there are the "dictys," that class of Negroes who constitute themselves as the upper strata and have lately done much wailing in the public places because white and black writers have seemingly overlooked them in their delineations of Negro life in Harlem. This upper strata is composed of the more successful and more socially inclined professional folk—lawyers, doctors, dentists, druggists, politicians, beauty parlor proprietors, and real estate dealers. They are for the most part mulattoes of light brown skin and have succeeded in absorbing all the social mannerisms of the white American middle class. They live in the stately rows of houses on 138th and 139th Streets between Seventh and Eighth Avenue, or else in the "high-tone" apartment houses on Edgecombe and St. Nicholas. They are both stupid and snobbish as is their class in any race. Their most compelling if sometimes unconscious ambition is to be as near white as possible, and their greatest expenditure of energy is concentrated on eradicating any trait or characteristic commonly known as Negroid.

Their homes are expensively appointed and comfortable. Most of them are furnished in good taste, thanks to the interior decorator who was hired to do the job. Their existence is one of smug complacency. They are well satisfied with themselves and with their class. They are without a doubt the basic element from which the Negro aristocracy of the future will evolve. They are also good illustrations, mentally, sartorially, and socially, of what the American standardizing machine can do to susceptible material.

These people have a social life of their own. They attend formal dinners and dances, resplendent in chic expensive replicas of Fifth Avenue finery. They arrange suitable inter-coterie nuptial showers, wedding breakfasts and the like. They attend church socials, fraternity dances and sorority gatherings. They frequent the downtown theaters, and occasionally, quite occasionally, drop into one of the Harlem night clubs which certain of their lower cast brethren frequent and white downtown excursionists make wealthy.

Despite this upper strata which is quite small, social barriers among Negroes are not as strict and well regulated in Harlem as they are in other Negro communities. Like all cosmopolitan centers, Harlem is democratic. People associate with all types should chance happen to throw them together. There are a few aristocrats, a plethora of striving bourgeoisie, a few artistic spirits, and a great proletarian mass, which constitutes the most interesting and important element in Harlem, for it is this latter class and their institutions that give the community its color and fascination.

IV
NIGHT LIFE IN HARLEM

Much has been written and said about night life in Harlem. It has become the *leit motif* of sophisticated conversation and shop girl intimacies. To call yourself a New Yorker you must have been to Harlem at least once. Every up-to-date person knows Harlem, and knowing Harlem generally means that one has visited a night club or two. These night clubs are now enjoying much publicity along with the New Negro and Negro art. They are the shrines to which white sophisticates, Greenwich Village artists, Broadway revellers, and provincial commuters make eager pilgrimage. In fact, the white patronage is so profitable and so abundant that Negroes find themselves crowded out and even segregated in their own places of jazz.

There are, at the present time, about one dozen of these night clubs in Harlem—Bamville, Connie's Inn, Baron Wilkins, the Nest, Small's Paradise, the Capitol, the Cotton Club, the Green Cat, the Sugar Cane Club, Happy Rhone's, the Hoofers Club and the Little Savoy. Most of these generally have from two to ten white persons for every black one.

Only the Hoofers, the Little Savoy, and the Sugar Cane Club seem to cater almost exclusively to Negro trade.

At Bamville and at Small's Paradise, one finds smart white patrons, the type that read the ultra-sophisticated *New Yorker*. Indeed, that journal says in its catalogue of places to go: "Small's and Bamville are the show places of Harlem for downtowners on their first excursion. Go late. Better not to dress." And so the younger generation of Broadway, Park Avenue, Riverside Drive, Third Avenue, and the Bronx go late, take their own gin, applaud the raucous vulgarity of the entertainers, dance with abandon and go home with a headache. They have seen Harlem.

The Cotton Club and Connie's Inn make a bid for theatrical performers and well-to-do folk around town. The Nest and Happy Rhone's attract travelling salesmen, store clerks, and commuters from Jersey and Yonkers. The Green Cat has a large Latin clientele. Baron Wilkins draws glittering ladies from Broadway with their sleek gentlemen friends. Because of these conditions of invasion, Harlem's far-famed night clubs have become merely side shows staged for sensation-seeking whites.

Nevertheless, they are still an egregious something to experience. Their smoking cavernous depths are eerie and ecstatic. Patrons enter, shiver involuntarily, then settle down to be shoved about and scared by the intangible rhythms that surge all around them. White night clubs are noisy. White night clubs affect weird music, soft light, Negro entertainers, and dancing waiters, but, even with all these contributing elements, they cannot approximate the infectious rhythm and joy always found in a Negro cabaret.

Take the Sugar Cane Club on Fifth Avenue near 135th Street, located on the border of the most "low-down" section of Harlem. This place is visited by few whites or few "dicty" Negroes. Its customers are the rough-and-ready, happy-go-lucky more primitive type—street walkers, petty gamblers, and pimps, with an occasional adventurer from other strata of society.

The Sugar Cane Club is a narrow subterranean passageway about twenty-five feet wide and 125 feet long. Rough wooden chairs, and the orchestra stands, jammed into the right wall center, use up about three-quarters of the space. The remaining rectangular area is bared for dancing. With a capacity for seating about one hundred people, it usually finds room on gala nights for twice that many. The orchestra weeps and moans and groans as only an unsophisticated Negro jazz orchestra can.

A blues singer croons vulgar ditties over the tables to individual parties or else wah-wahs husky syncopated blues songs from the center of the floor. Her act over, the white lights are extinguished, red and blue spot lights are centered on the diminutive dancing space, couples push back their chairs, squeeze out from behind the tables and from against the wall, then finding one another's bodies, sweat gloriously together, with shoulders hunched, limbs obscenely intertwined, and hips wiggling: animal beings urged on by liquor and music and physical contact.

Small's Paradise, on Seventh Avenue near 135th Street, is just the opposite of the Sugar Cane Club. It caters almost exclusively to white trade with just enough Negroes present to give the necessary atmosphere and "difference." Yet even in Small's with its symphonic orchestra, full-dress appearance and dignified onlookers, there is a great deal of that unexplainable, intangible rhythmic presence so characteristic of a Negro.

In addition to the well-known cabarets, which are largely show places to curious whites, there are innumerable places—really speakeasies—which are open only to the initiate. These places are far more colorful and more full of spontaneous joy than the larger places to which one has ready access. They also furnish more thrills to the spectator. This is possible because the crowd is more select, the liquor more fiery, the atmosphere more intimate and the activities of the patrons not subject to being watched by open-mouthed white people from downtown and the Bronx.

One particular place known as the Glory Hole is hidden in a musty damp basement behind an express and trucking office. It is a single room about ten feet square and remains an unembellished basement except for a planed-down plank floor, a piano, three chairs, and a liberty table. The Glory Hole is typical of its class. It is a social club, commonly called a dive, convenient for the high times of a certain group. The men are unskilled laborers during the day, and in the evenings they round up their girls or else meet them at the rendezvous in order to have what they consider and enjoy as a good time. The women, like the men, swear, drink, and dance as much as vulgarly as they please. Yet they do not strike the observer as being vulgar. They are merely being and doing what their environment and their desire for pleasure suggest.

Such places as the Glory Hole can be found all over the so-called "bad-lands" of Harlem. They are not always confined to basement rooms. They can be found in apartment flats, in the rear of barber shops, lunch counters, pool halls, and other such conveniently blind places. Each one has its regular quota of customers with just enough new patrons introduced from time to time to keep the place alive and prosperous. These intimate, lowdown civic centers are occasionally misjudged. Social service reports damn them with the phrase "breeding places of vice and crime." They may be. They are also good training grounds for prospective pugilists. Fights are staged with regularity and with vigor. And most of the regular customers have some mark on their faces or bodies that can be displayed as having been received during a battle in one of the glory holes.

The other extreme of amusement places in Harlem is exemplified by the Bamboo Inn, a Chinese-American restaurant that features Oriental cuisine, a jazz band, and dancing. It is the place for select Negroes' Harlem night life, the place where debutantes have their coming-out parties, where college lads take their coeds and society sweethearts, and where dignified matrons entertain. It is a beautifully decorated establishment, glorified by a balcony with booths, and a large gyroflector, suspending from the center of the ceiling, on which colored spotlights play, flecking the room with triangular bits of vari-colored light. The Bamboo Inn is *the* place to see "high Harlem," just like the Glory Hole is *the* place to see "low Harlem": Well-dressed men escorting expensively garbed women and girls; models from *Vanity Fair* with brown, yellow, and black skins; doctors and lawyers, Babbitts and their ladies with fine manners (not necessarily learned through Emily Post); fine clothes and fine homes to return to when the night's fun has ended. The music plays. The gyroflector revolves. The well bred, polite dancers mingle on the dance floor. There are a few silver hip flasks. There is an occasional burst of too spontaneous-for-the-environment laughter. The Chinese waiters slip around, quiet and bored. A big black-face bouncer, arrayed in tuxedo, watches eagerly for some too boisterous, too unconventional person to put out. The Bamboo Inn has only one blemishing feature. It is also the rendezvous for a set of Oriental men who favor white women, and who, with their pale-face partners, mingle with Harlem's four hundred.

When Harlem people wish to dance, without attending a cabaret, they go to the Renaissance Casino or to the Savoy, Harlem's two most famous public dance halls. The Savoy is the pioneer in the field of giving dance-loving Harlemites some place to gather nightly. It is an elaborate ensemble with a Chinese garden (Negroes seem to have a penchant for Chinese food—there are innumerable Chinese restaurants all over Harlem), two orchestras that work in relays, and hostesses provided at twenty-five cents per dance for partnerless young men. The Savoy opens at three in the afternoon and closes at three in the morning. One can spend twelve hours in this jazz palace for sixty-five cents and the price of a dinner or an occasional sustaining sandwich or drink. The music is good, the dancers are gay, and the setting is conducive to joy.

The Renaissance Casino was formerly a dance hall, rented out only for social affairs, but when the Savoy began to flourish, the Renaissance, after closing awhile for redecorations, changed its policy and reopened as a public dance hall. It has no lounging room or Chinese garden, but it stages a basketball game every Sunday night that is one of the most popular amusement institutions in Harlem, and it has an exceptionally good orchestra, comfortable sitting-out places, and a packed dance floor nightly. Then, when any social club wishes to give a dance at the Renaissance, the name of the organization is flashed from the electric signboard that hangs above the entrance and in return for the additional and assured crowd, some division of the door receipts is made. The Renaissance is, I believe, in good Harlemese, considered more "dicty" than the Savoy. It has a more regulated and more dignified clientele, and almost every night in the week the dances are sponsored by some well-known social group.

In addition to the above two places, the Manhattan Casino, an elaborate dance palace, is always available for the more deluxe gatherings. It is at the Manhattan Casino that the National Association for the Advancement of Colored People has its yearly whist tournament and dance, that Harlem society folk have their charity balls and select formals, and that the notorious Hamilton Lodge holds its spectacular masquerade each year. All of the dances held in this Casino are occasions never to be forgotten. Hundreds of well-dressed couples dancing on the floor, hundreds of Negroes of all types and colors mingling together on the dance floor, gathering in the boxes, meeting and conversing on the promenade. And here and there are occasional white persons, or is it a Negro who can "pass"?

Negroes love to dance, and in Harlem where the struggle to live is so intensely complex, the dance serves as a welcome and feverish outlet. Yet it is strange that none of these dance palaces are owned or operated by Negroes. The Renaissance Casino was formerly owned by a syndicate of West Indians and has now fallen into the hands of a Jewish group. And despite the thousands of dollars Negroes spend in order to dance, the only monetary returns in their own community are the salaries paid to the Negro musicians, ushers, janitors, and doormen. The rest of the profits are spent and exploited outside of Harlem.

This is true of most Harlem establishments. The Negro in Harlem is not, like the Negro in Chicago or other metropolitan centers, in charge of the commercial enterprises located in his community. South State Street in Chicago's great Black belt, is studded with Negro banks, Negro office buildings, housing Negro insurance companies, manufacturing concerns, and other major enterprises. There are no Negro-controlled banks in Harlem. There are only branches of downtown Manhattan's financial institutions, manned solely by whites and patronized almost exclusively by Negroes. Harlem has no outstanding manufacturing concern like the Overton enterprises in Chicago, the Poro school and factory in St. Louis, or the Madame Walker combine in Indianapolis. Harlem Negroes own over sixty million dollars worth of real estate, but they neither own nor operate one first-class grocery store, butcher shop, dance hall, theater, clothing store, or saloon. They do have their money in barber shops, beauty parlors, pool halls, tailor shops, restaurants, and lunch counters.

V

THE AMUSEMENT LIFE OF HARLEM

Like most good American communities, the movies hold a primary position in the amusement life of Harlem. There are seven neighborhood motion picture houses in Negro Harlem proper, and about six big time cinema palaces on 125th Street that have more white patronage than black, yet whose audiences are swelled by movie fans from downtown.

The picture emporiums of Harlem are comparable to those in any residential neighborhood. They present second and third run features with supporting bills of comedies, novelties, and an occasional special performance when the management presents a bathing beauties contest, a plantation jubilee, an amateur ensemble, and other vaudeville students.

The Renaissance Theatre, in the same building with Renaissance

Casino, is the cream of Harlem motion picture houses. It, too, was formerly owned and operated by Negroes, the only one of its kind in Harlem. Now Negroes only operate it. The Renaissance attracts the more select movie audiences; it has a reputable symphony orchestra, a Wurlitzer organ, and presents straight movies without vaudeville flapdoodle. It is spacious and clean and free from disagreeable odors.

The Roosevelt Theatre, the New Douglas, and the Savoy are less aristocratic competitors. They show the same pictures as the Renaissance, but seem to be patronized by an entirely different set of people, and, although their interiors are more spacious, they are not as well decorated or as clean as the Renaissance. They attract a set of fresh youngsters, smart aleck youths, and lecherous adult males who attend, not so much to see the picture as to pick up a susceptible female or to spoon with some girl they have picked up elsewhere. The places are also frequented by family groups, poor but honest folk, who cannot afford other forms or places of amusement.

The Franklin and the Gem are the social outcasts of the group. Their audiences are composed almost entirely of loafers from the low-grade pool rooms and dives in their vicinity, and tenement-trained drudges from the slums. The stench in these two places is nauseating. The Board of Health rules are posted conspicuously, admonishing patrons not to spit on the floor or to smoke in the auditorium, but the aisle is slippery with tobacco spew and cigarette smoke adds to the density of the foul air. The movies flicker on the screen, some wild west picture three or four years old, dirty babies cry in time with the electric piano that furnishes the music, men talk out loud, smoke, spit, and drop empty gin or whiskey bottles on the floor when emptied. All of these places from the Renaissance to the Gem are open daily from two in the afternoon until eleven at night, and save for a lean audience during the supper hour are usually filled to capacity. Saturdays, Sundays, and holidays are harvest times, and the Jewish representatives of the chain to which a theater belongs walk around excitedly and are exceedingly gracious, thinking no doubt of the quarters that are being deposited at the box office.

The Lafayette and Lincoln theaters are three-a-day combination movie and music comedy revue houses. The Lafayette used to house a local stock company composed of all Negro players, but it has now fallen into less dignified hands. Each week it presents a new revue. These revues are generally weak-kneed, water variations on downtown productions. If Earl Carroll is presenting *Artists and Models on Broadway*, the Lafayette presents *Brown Skin Models in Harlem* soon afterwards. Week after week one sees the same type of "high yaller" chorus, hears the same blues songs, and applauds different dancers doing the same dance steps. There is little originality on the part of the performers and seldom any change of fare. Cheap imitations of Broadway successes, nudity, vulgar dances, and vulgar jokes are the box office attractions.

On Friday nights there is a midnight show, which is one of the most interesting spectacles in Harlem. The performance begins some time after midnight and lasts until four or four-thirty the next morning. The audience is as much if not more interesting and amusing than the performers on the stage. Gin bottles are carried and passed among groups of friends. Cat calls and hisses attend any dull bit. Outspoken comments punctuate the lines, songs and dances of the performers. Impromptu acts are staged in the orchestra and in the gallery. The performers themselves are at their best and leave the stage to make the audience a part of their act. There are no conventions considered, no reserve is manifested. Everyone has a jolly good time, and after the theater there are parties or work according to the wealth and inclinations of the individual.

The Lincoln Theatre is smaller and more smelly than the Lafayette, and most people who attend the latter will turn up their noses at the Lincoln. It too has revues and movies, and its only distinguishing feature is that its shows are even worse than those staged at the Lafayette. They are so bad that they are ludicrously funny. The audience is comparable to that found in the Lafayette on Friday nights at the midnight jamboree. Performers are razzed. Chorus girls are openly courted or damned, and the spontaneous utterances of the patrons are far more funny than any joke the comedians ever tell. If one can stand the stench, one can have a good time for three hours or more just by watching the unpredictable and surprising reactions of the audience to what is being presented on the stage.

VI
HOUSE RENT PARTIES, NUMBERS, AND HOT MEN

The Harlem institutions that intrigue the imagination and stimulate the most interest on the part of investigators are House Rent Parties, Numbers, and Hot Men. House rent parties are the result of high rents. Private houses containing nine or ten or twelve rooms rent from $185 up to $250 per room or more, according to the newness of the building and the conveniences therein. Five-room flats, located in walk-up tenements, with inside rooms, dark hallways, and dirty stairs, rent for $10 per room or more. It can be seen then that when the average Negro working man's salary is considered (he is often paid less for his labors than a white man engaged in the same sort of work), and when it is also considered that he and his family must eat, dress, and have some amusements and petty luxuries, these rents assume a criminal enormity. And even though every available bit of unused space is sublet at exorbitant rates to roomers, some other source of revenue is needed when the time comes to meet the landlord.

Hence we have hundreds of people opening their apartments and houses to the public, their only stipulation being that the public pay twenty-five cents admission fee and buy plentifully of the food and drinks offered for sale. Although one of these parties can be found any time during the week, Saturday night is favored. The reasons are obvious: folk don't have to get up early on Sunday morning and most of them have had a pay day. Of course the commercialization of spontaneous pleasure in order to pay the landlord has been abused, and now there are folk who make their living altogether by giving alleged house rent parties. This is possible because there are in Harlem thousands of people with no place to go, thousands of people lonesome, unattached, and cramped, who stroll the streets, eager for a chance to form momentary contacts, to dance, to drink, and make merry. They willingly part with more of the week's pay than they should just to enjoy an oasis in the desert of their existence and a joyful intimate party, open to the public yet held in a private home, is, as they say, "their meat."

So elaborate has the technique of these parties and their promotion become that great competition has sprung up between prospective party givers. Private advertising stunts are resorted to, and done quietly so as not to attract too much attention from the police, who might want to collect a license fee or else drop in and search for liquor. Cards are passed out in pool halls, subway stations, cigar stores, and on the street. This is an example:

> *Hey! Hey!*
> *Come on boys and girls let's shake*
> *that thing*
> *Where?*
> *At Hot Poppa Sam's*
> *West 134th Street, three flights up.*
> *Jelly Roll Smith at the piano*
> *Saturday night, May 7, 1927*
> *Hey! Hey!*

Saturday night comes. There may be only piano music, there may be a piano and drums, or a three- or four-piece ensemble. Red lights, dim and suggestive, are in order. The parlor and the dining room are cleared for the dance, and one bedroom is utilized for hats and coats. In the kitchen will be found boiled pigs' feet, ham hock and cabbage, Hopping John (a combination of peas and rice), and other proletarian dishes.

The music will be barbarous and slow. The dancers will use their bodies and the bodies of their partners without regard to the conventions. There will be little restraint. Happy individuals will do solo specialties, will sing, dance—have Charleston and Black Bottom contests and breakdowns. Hard little tenement girls will flirt and make dates with Pool Hall Johnnies and drug store cowboys. Prostitutes will drop in and slink out. And in addition to the liquor sold by the house, flasks of gin and corn and rye will be passed around and emptied. Here "low" Harlem is in its glory, primitive and unashamed.

I have counted as many as twelve such parties in one block, five in one apartment house containing forty flats. They are held all over Harlem with the possible exception of 137th, 138th, and 139th Streets between Seventh and Eighth Avenues where the bulk of Harlem's upper class lives. Yet the house rent party is not on the whole a vicious institution. It serves a real and vital purpose, and it is as essential to "low Harlem" as the cultured receptions and soirees held on "Strivers' Row" are to "high Harlem."

House rent parties have their evils; it is an economic evil and a social evil that makes them necessary, but they also have their virtues. Like all over institutions of man it depends upon what perspective you view them from. But regardless of abstract matters, house rent parties do provide a source of revenue to those in difficult financial straits, and they also give lonesome Harlemites, caged in by intangible bars, some place to have their fun and forget problems of color, civilization, and economics.

Numbers, unlike house rent parties, is not an institution confined to any one class of Harlem folk. Almost everybody plays the numbers, a universal and illegal gambling pastime, which has become Harlem's favorite indoor sport. Numbers is one of the most elaborate, big-scale lottery games in America. It is based on the digits listed in the daily reports of the New York Stock Exchange. A person wishing to play the game places a certain sum of money, from one penny up, on a number composed of three digits. This number must be placed in the hands of a runner before ten o'clock in the morning as the reports are printed in the early editions of the afternoon papers. The clearing house reports are like this:

Exchanges...$1,023,000,000
Balances 128,000,000
Credit Balance...98,000,000

The winning number is composed from the second and third digits in the millionth figures opposite exchanges and from the third figure in the millionth place opposite the balances. Thus if the report is like the example above, the winning number for that day will be 238.

An elaborate system of placement and paying off has grown around this game. Hundreds of persons known as runners make their rounds daily collecting number slips and cash placements from their clients. These runners are the middle men between the public and the banker, who pays the runner a commission on all collections, reimburses winners, if there are any, and also gives the runner a percentage of his clients' winnings.

These bankers and runners can well afford to be and often are rogues. Since numbers is an illegal pastime, they can easily disappear when the receipts are heavy or a number of people have chosen the correct three digits and wish their winnings. The police are supposed to make some effort to enforce the law and check the game. Occasionally a runner or a banker is arrested, but this generally occurs only when some irate player notifies the police that he "ain't been done right by." Numbers can be placed in innumerable ways: the grocer, the butcher, the confectioner, the waitress at the lunch counter, the soda clerk, and the choir leader all collect slips for the numbers bankers.

People look everywhere for a number to play. The postman passes, some addict notes the number on his cap and puts ten cents on it for that day. A hymn is announced by the pastor in church and all the members in the congregation will note the number for future reference. People dream, each dream is a symbol for a number that can be ascertained by looking in a dream book for sale at all Harlem newsstands. Street car numbers, house numbers, street numbers, chance calculations—anything that has figures on it or connected with it will give some player a good number and inspire him to place much money on it.

There is slight chance to win, it is a thousand to one shot, and yet this game and its possible awards have such a hold on the community that it is often the cause for divorce, murder, scanty meals, dispossess notices, and other misfortunes. Some player makes a "hit" for one dollar and receives five hundred and forty dollars. Immediately his acquaintances and neighbors are in a frenzy and begin staking large sums on any number their winning friend happens to suggest. It is all a game of chance. There is no way to figure out scientifically or otherwise that digits will be listed in the clearing house reports. Few people placing fifty cents on No. 238 stop to realize how many other combinations of three digits are liable to win. One can become familiar with the market's slump days and fat days, but even then the digits which determine the winning number could be almost anything. People who are moral in every other respect, church-going folk, who damn drinking, dancing, or gambling in any other form, will play the numbers. For some vague reason this game is not considered as gambling, and its illegality gives little concern to anyone—even to the Harlem police, who can be seen slipping into a corner cigar store to place their number for the day with an obliging and secretive clerk.

As I write, a friend of mine comes in with a big roll of money, $540. He has made a "hit." I guess I will play fifty cents on the number I found stamped inside the band of my last year's straw hat.

Stroll down Seventh Avenue on a spring Sunday afternoon. Everybody seems to be well dressed. The latest fashions prevail, and though there are the usual number of folk attired in outlandish color combinations and queer styles, the majority of the promenaders are dressed in good taste. In the winter, expensive fur coats swathe the women of Harlem's Seventh Avenue as they swathe the pale face fashion plates on Fifth Avenue downtown, while the men escorting them are usually sartorially perfect.

How is all this well-ordered finery possible? Most of these people are employed as menials—dish washers, elevator operators, porters, waiters, red caps, longshoremen, and factory hands. Their salaries are notoriously low; not many men picked at random on Seventh Avenue can truthfully say that they regularly earn more than $100 per month, and from this salary must come room rent, food, and other of life's necessities and luxuries. How can they dress so well? There are, of course, installment houses, considered by many authorities one of the main economic curses of our present-day civilization, and there are numerous people who run accounts at such places just to keep up a front, but these folk have little money to jingle in their pockets. All of it must be dribbled out to the installment collectors. There was even one chap I knew, who had to pawn a suit he had bought on the installment plan in order to make the final ten dollar payment and prevent the credit house collector from garnisheing his wages. And it will be found that the majority of the Harlemites, who must dress well on a small salary, run the installment house leechers and patronize the "hot men."

"Hot men" sell "hot stuff," which when translated from Harlemese into English, means merchandise supposedly obtained illegally and sold on the Q.T. far below par. "Hot men" do a big business in Harlem. Some have apartments fitted out as showrooms, but the majority peddle their goods piece by piece from person to person. "Hot stuff" is supposedly stolen by shop lifters or by store employees or by organized gangs, who run warehouses and freight yards. Actually, most of the "hot stuff" sold in Harlem originally comes from bankrupt stores. Some ingenious group of people make a practice of attending bankruptcy sales and by buying blocks of merchandise get a great deal for a small sum of money. This merchandise is then given in small lots to various agents in Harlem, who secretly dispose of it.

There is a certain glamour about buying stolen goods aside from their cheapness. Realizing this, "hot men" and their agents maintain that their goods are stolen whether they are or not. People like to feel that they are breaking the law, and when they are getting undeniable bargains at the same time, the temptation becomes twofold. Of course, one never really knows whether what they are buying has been stolen from a neighbor next door or bought from a defunct merchant. There have been many instances when a gentleman, strolling down the avenue in a newly acquired overcoat, has had it recognized by a former owner, and found himself either beaten up or behind the bars. However, such happenings are rare, for the experienced Harlemite will buy only that "hot stuff" which is obviously not secondhand.

One evening I happened to be sitting in one of the private receptions rooms of the Harlem Y.W.C.A. There was a great commotion in the adjoining room, a great coming in and going out. It seemed as if every girl in the Y.W.C.A. was trying to crowd into that little room. Finally the young lady I was visiting went to investigate. She was gone for about fifteen minutes. When she returned she had on a new hat, which she informed me, between laughs at the bewildered expression on my face, she had obtained from a "hot man" for two dollars. This same hat, according to her, would cost $10 downtown and $12 on 125th Street. I placed my chair near the door and watched the procession of young women entering the room bareheaded and leaving with new headgear. Finally the supply was exhausted and a perspiring little Jew emerged, his pockets filled with dollar bills. I discovered later that this man was a store keeper in Harlem, who had picked up a large supply of spring hats at a bankruptcy sale and stating that it was "hot stuff" had proceeded to sell it not openly in his store but sub-rosa in private places.

There is no limit to the "hot man's" supply or the variety of goods he offers. One can, if one knows the ropes, buy any article of wearing apparel from him. And in addition to the professional "hot man" there are always the shoplifters and thieving store clerks, who accost you secretly and eagerly place at your disposal what they have stolen.

Hence, low-salaried folk in Harlem dress well, and Seventh Avenue is a fashionable street crowded with expensively dressed people, parading around in all their "hot" finery. A cartoonist in a recent issue of one of the Negro monthlies depicted the following scene: A number of people at a fashionable dance are informed that the police have come to search for some individual known to be wearing stolen goods. Immediately there is a confused and hurried exodus from the room because all of the dancers present were arrayed in "hot stuff."

This, of course, is exaggerated. There are thousands of well-dressed people in Harlem able to be well-dressed not because they patronize a "hot man" but because their incomes make it possible. But there are a mass of people, working for small wages, who make good use of the "hot man," for not only can they buy their much wanted finery cheaply but, thanks to the obliging "hot man," can buy it on the installment plan. Under the circumstances, who cares about breaking the law?

VII
THE NEGRO AND THE CHURCH

The Negro in America has always supported his religious institutions even though he would not support his schools or business enterprises. Migrating to the city has not lessened his devotion to religious institutions even if it has lessened his religious fervor. He still donates a portion of his income to the church, and the church is still a major social center in all Negro communities.

Harlem is not an exception to this rule, and its finest buildings are the churches. Their attendance is large, their prosperity amazing. Baptist, Methodist, Episcopal, Catholic, Presbyterian, Seventh Day Adventist, Spiritualist, Holly Roller, and Abyssinian Jew—every sect and every creed with all their innumerable subdivisions can be found in Harlem.

There are few new church buildings, most of them having been bought from white congregations when the Negro invaded Harlem and claimed it for his own. The most notable of the second-hand churches are the Metropolitan Baptist Church at 128th Street and Seventh Avenue, and Mt. Olive Baptist Church at 120th Street and Lenox Avenue. This latter church has had a varied career. It was first a synagogue, then it was sold to white Seventh Day Adventists, and finally fell into its present hands.

The most notable new churches are the Abyssinian Baptist Church on 138th Street, Mother Zion on 137th Street, and St. Mark's. The latter church has just recently been finished. It is a dignified and colossal structure occupying a triangular block on Edgecombe and St. Nicholas Avenues between 137th and 138th Streets. It is the latest thing in churches, with many modern attachments—gymnasium, swimming pool, club rooms, Sunday school quarters, and other sub-auditoriums. When it was formally opened, there was a gala dedication week to celebrate the occasion. Each night, services were held by the various secret societies, the Elks, the Masons, the Knights of Pythias, the Odd Fellows, and others. The members of every local chapter of the various orders turned out to do homage to the new edifice. The collection proceeds were donated to the church.

St. Mark's goes in for elaborate ceremony quite reminiscent of the Episcopal or Roman Catholic service. The choir is regaled in flowing robes and chants hymns by Handel. The pulpit is a triumph of carving and wood decoration. There is more ceremony than sermon.

The better class of Harlemites attends the larger churches. Most of the so-called "dictys" are registered as "Episcopalians at St. Phillip's," which is the religious sanctum of the socially elect and wealthy Negroes of Harlem. The congregation at St. Phillip's is largely mulatto. This church has a Parish House that serves as one of the most ambitious and important social centers in Harlem. It supports a gymnasium that produces annually a first-class basketball team, an art sketch class that is both large and promising, and other activities of interest and benefit to the community.

Every Sunday all of the churches are packed, and were they run entirely on the theatrical plan they would hang out the S.R.O. sign. No matter how large they are they do not seem to be large enough. And in addition to these large denominational churches there are many smaller ones also crowded, and a plethora of outlaw sects, ranging from Holy Rollers to Black Jews and Moslems.

The Holy Rollers collect in small groups of from twenty-five to one hundred and call themselves various things. Some are known as the Saints of God in Christ, others call themselves members of the Church of God, and still others call themselves Sanctified Children of the Holy Ghost. Their meetings are primitive performances. Their songs and chants are lashing to the emotions. They also practice healing, and, during the course of their services, shout and dance as erotically and sincerely as savages around a jungle fire.

The Black Jews are a sect migrated from Abyssinia. Their services are similar to those in a Jewish synagogue, only they are of a lower order, for these people still believe in alchemy and practice polygamy when they can get away with it. Just recently a group of them were apprehended by agents from the Department of Justice for establishing a free love farm in the State of New Jersey. They were all citizens of Harlem and had induced many young Negro girls to join them.

The Mohammedans are beginning to send missionaries to work among Negroes in America. Already they have succeeded in getting enough converts in Harlem, Chicago, St. Louis, and Detroit to establish mosques in these cities. There are about one hundred and twenty-five active members of the Mohammedan church in Harlem, practicing the precepts of the Koran under the leadership of an Islamic missionary.

The Spiritualist churches also thrive in Harlem. There are about twenty-five or more of their little chapels scattered about. They enjoy an enormous patronage from the more superstitious, ignorant classes. The leaders of the larger ones make most of their money from white clients, who drop in regularly for private sessions.

VIII
NEGRO JOURNALISTS IN HARLEM

The Harlem Negro owns, publishes, and supports five local weekly newspapers. These papers are just beginning to influence Harlem thought and opinion. For a long time they were merely purveyors of local gossip and scandal. Now some of them actually have begun to support certain issues for the benefit of the community and to cry out for reforms in the regulation journalistic manner.

For instance, *The New York Age,* which is the oldest Negro weekly in New York, has been conducting a publicity campaign against numbers and saloons. These saloons are to this paper as unwelcome a Harlem institution as the numbers. Each block along the main streets has at least one saloon, maybe two or three. They are open affairs, save instead of calling themselves saloons, they call themselves cafes. To get in is an easy matter. One has only to approach the door and look at a man seated on a box behind the front window, who acknowledges your look by pulling a chain which releases a bolt on the door. Once in, you order what you wish from an old fashioned bartender and stand before an old fashioned bar with a brass rail, mirrors, pictures, spittoons, and everything. What is more, they even have a ladies' room in the rear.

The editor of *The New York Age* is in the process of conducting his crusade and published the addresses of all these saloons and urged that they be closed. The result of his campaign was that they are still open and doing more business than ever, thanks to his having informed people where they were located.

At first glance, any of the Harlem newspapers give one the impression that Harlem is a hot-bed of vice and crime. They smack of the tabloid in this respect and should be considered accordingly. True, there is vice and crime in Harlem as there is in any community where living conditions are chaotic and crowded. For instance, there are 110 Negro women in Harlem for every 100 Negro men. Sixty and six tenths percent of them are regularly employed. This, according to social service reports, makes women cheap, and conversely I suppose makes men expensive. Anyway, there are a great number of youths and men who are either wholly or partially supported by single or married women. These male parasites, known as sweetbacks, dress well and spend their days standing on street corners, playing pool, gambling, and looking for some other "fish" to aid in their support. This is considered by some an alarming condition, in as much as many immigrant youths from foreign countries and rural southern American districts naturally inclined to be lazy, think that it is smart and citified to be a parasite and do almost anything in order to live without working.

The newspapers of Harlem seldom speak of this condition, but their headlines give eloquent testimony to the results, with their reports of gun play, divorce actions (and in New York State there is only one ground for divorce), and brick-throwing parties. These conditions are magnified, of course, by proximity and really are not important at all when the whole vice and crime situation in greater New York is taken under consideration.

To return to the newspapers, *The Negro World* is the official organ of the Garvey Movement. At one time it was one of the most forceful weeklies among Negroes. Now it has little life or power, its life-giving mentor, Marcus Garvey, being in Atlanta Federal Prison. Its only interesting feature is the weekly manifesto Garvey issues from his prison sanctum, urging his followers to remain faithful to the cause and not fight among themselves while he is kept away from them.

The Amsterdam News is the largest and most progressive Negro weekly published in Harlem. It, like all of its contemporaries, is conservative in politics and policy, but it does feature the work of many of the leading Negro journalists and has the most forceful editorial page of the group, even if it does believe that most of the younger Negro artists are "bad New Negroes."

The New York News is a political sheet, affecting the tabloid form. *The Tattler* is a scandal sheet. It specializes in personalities and theatrical and sports news.

IX
THE NEW NEGRO

Harlem has been called the center of the American Negro's cultural renaissance and the mecca of the New Negro. If this is so, it is so only because Harlem is a part of New York, the cultural and literary capital of America. And Harlem becomes the mecca of the so-called New Negro only because he imagines that once there he can enjoy the cultural contact and intellectual stimulation necessary for his growth. This includes the young Negro writer who comes to Harlem in order to be near both patrons and publishers of literature, and the young Negro artist and musician who comes to Harlem in order to be near the most reputable artistic and musical institutions in the country.

These folk, along with the librarians employed at the Harlem Branch of the New York Public Library, a few of the younger, more cultured professional men and women, and the school teachers, who can be found in the grammar and high schools all over the city, constitute the Negro intelligentsia. This group is sophisticated and small and more a part of New York's life than of Harlem's. Its members are accepted as social and intellectual equals among whites downtown and can be found at informal and formal gatherings in any of the five boroughs that compose greater New York. Harlem, to most of them, is just a place of residence; they are not "fixed" there as are the majority of Harlem's inhabitants.

Then there are the college youngsters and local intellectuals, whose prototypes can be found in any community. These people plan to attend lectures and concerts, given under the auspices of the Y.M.C.A., Y.W.C.A., churches, and public school civic centers. They are the people who form intercollegiate societies, who stage fraternity go-to-school campaigns, who attend the course of lectures presented by the Harlem Branch of the

New York Public Library, during the winter months, and who frequent the many musical and literary entertainments given by local talent in Harlem auditoriums.

Harlem is crowded with such folk. The three great major educational institutions of New York, Columbia, New York University, and the College of the City of New York, have a large Negro student attendance. Then there are many never-to-be-top-notch literary, artistic, and intellectual strivers in Harlem as there are all over New York. Since the well advertised "literary renaissance," it is almost a Negro Greenwich Village in this respect. Every other person one meets is writing a novel, a poem, or a drama. And there is seemingly no end to artists who do oils, pianists who pound out Rachmaninoff's Prelude in C Sharp Minor, and singers with long faces and rolling eyes who sing spirituals.

X
HARLEM—MECCA OF THE NEW NEGRO

Harlem, the so-called citadel of Negro achievement in the New World, the alleged mecca of the New Negro, and the advertised center of colored America's cultural renaissance. Harlem, a thriving black city, pulsing with vivid passions, alive with colorful personalities, and packed with many types and classes of people.

Harlem is a dream city pregnant with wide-awake realities. It is a masterpiece of contradictory elements and surprising types. There is no end to its versatile presentation of people, personalities, and institutions. It is a mad medley.

There seems to be no end to its numerical and geographical growth. It is spreading north, east, south, and west. It is slowly pushing beyond the barriers imposed by white people. It is slowly uprooting them from their present homes in the near vicinity of Negro Harlem as it has uprooted them before. There must be expansion, and Negro Harlem is too much a part of New York to remain sluggish and still while all around is activity and expansion. As New York grows, so will Harlem grow. As Negro America progresses, so will Negro Harlem progress.

New York is now most liberal. There is little racial conflict, and there have been no interracial riots since the San Juan Hill days. The question is, will the relations between New York Negro and New York white man always remain as tranquil as they are today? No one knows, and once in Harlem one seldom cares, for the sight of Harlem gives any Negro a feeling of great security. It is too large and too complex to seem to be affected in any way by such a futile thing as race prejudice.

There is no typical Harlem Negro as there is no typical American Negro. There are too many different types and classes. White, yellow, brown, and black, and all the intervening shades. North American, South American, African, and Asian; Northerner and Southerner; high and low; seer and fool—Harlem holds them all and strives to become a homogeneous community despite it motley hodge-podge of incompatible elements, and its self-nurtured or outwardly imposed limitations.

SPUNK (1935)

AND

ART AND SUCH (1938)

ZORA NEALE HURSTON

Hurston was born in Eatonville, Florida, in 1892. She was one of the youngest artists who made up the Harlem Renaissance and one of the few women. She studied anthropology at both Howard University and Barnard College. Her interest in art and creative writing came as much from her scientific study of Negro life and culture as it did from the personal experiences she shared with others in the community. Hurston's life and work influenced and inspired such important modern writers as Alice Walker, who virtually rescued her legacy from obscurity, and Marita Golden, who has further immortalized Hurston's career with the Hurston Wright Foundation. Her short story "Spunk" was written while she was a member of the Harlem branch of the WPA writers' workshop, and her essay "Art and Such" gives her view of the artist's responsibility.

SPUNK

A giant of a brown skinned man sauntered up the one street of the Village and out into the palmetto thickets with a small pretty woman clinging lovingly to his arm.

"Looka theah, folkses!" cried Elijah Mosley, slapping his leg gleefully. "Theah they go, big as life an' brassy as tacks."

All the loungers in the store tried to walk to the door with an air of nonchalance but with small success.

"Now pee-eople!" Walter Thomas gasped, "Will you look at 'em!"

"But that's one thing Ah likes about Spunk Banks—he ain't skeered of nothin' on God's green footstool—*nothin'!* He rides that log down at saw-mill jus' like he struts 'round wid another man's wife—jus' don't give a kitty. When Tes' Miller got cut to giblets on that circle-saw, Spunk steps right up and starts ridin'. The rest of us was skeered to go near it."

A round shouldered figure in overalls much too large, came nervously in the door and the talking ceased. The men looked at each other and winked.

"Gimme some soda-water. Sasspirilla Ah reckon," the new-comer ordered, and stood far down the counter near the open pickled pig-feet tub to drink it.

Elijah nudged Walter and turned with mock gravity to the new-comer.

"Say Joe, how's everything up yo' way? How's yo' wife?"

Joe started and all but dropped the bottle he held in his hands. He swallowed several times painfully and his lips trembled.

"Aw 'Lige, you oughtn't to do nothin' like that," Walter grumbled. Elijah ignored him.

"She jus' passed heah a few minutes ago goin' thata way," with a wave of his hand in the direction of the woods.

Now Joe knew his wife had passed that way. He knew that the men lounging in the general store had seen her, moreover, he knew that the men knew *he* knew. He stood there silent for a long moment staring blankly, with his Adam's apple twitching nervously up and down his throat. One could actually *see* the pain he was suffering, his eyes, his face, his hands and even the dejected slump of his shoulders. He set the bottle down upon the counter. He didn't bang it, just eased it out of his hand silently and fiddled with his suspender buckle.

"Well, Ah'm goin' after her today. Ah'm goin' an' fetch her back. Spunk's done gone too fur."

He reached deep down into his trouser pocket and drew out a hollow ground razor, large and shiny, and passed his moistened thumb back and forth over the edge.

"Talkin' like a man, Joe. Course that's *yo'* fambly affairs, but Ah like to see grit in anybody."

Joe Kanty laid down a nickel and stumbled out into the street.

Dusk crept in from the woods. Ike Clarke lit the swinging oil lamp that was almost immediately surrounded by candle-flies. The men laughed boisterously behind Joe's back as they watched him shamble woodward.

"You oughtn't to said whut you did to him, Lige,—look how it worked him up," Walter chided.

"And Ah hope it did work him up. Tain't even decent for a man to take and take like he do."

"Spunk will sho' kill him."

"Aw, Ah doan't know. You never kin tell. He might turn him up an' spank him fur gettin' in the way, but Spunk wouldn't shoot no unarmed man. Dat razor he carried outa heah ain't gonna run Spunk down an' cut him, an' Joe ain't got the nerve to go up to Spunk with it knowing he totes that Army 45. He makes that break outa heah to bluff us. He's gonna hide that razor behind the first likely palmetto root an' sneak back home to bed. Don't tell me nothin' 'bout that rabbit-foot colored man. Didn't he meet Spunk an' Lena face to face one day las' week an' mumble sumthin' to Spunk 'bout lettin' his wife alone?"

"What did Spunk say?" Walter broke in—"Ah like him fine but tain't right the way he carries on wid Lena Kanty, jus' cause Joe's timid 'bout fightin'."

"You wrong theah, Walter. 'Tain't cause Joe's timid at all, it's cause Spunk wants Lena. If Joe was a passle of wile cats Spunk would tackle the job just the same. He'd go after *anything* he wanted the same way. As Ah wuz sayin' a minute ago, he tole Joe right to his face that Lena was his. 'Call her,' he says to Joe. 'Call her and see if she'll come. A woman knows her boss an' she answers when he calls.' 'Lena, ain't I yo' husband?' Joe sorter whines out. Lena looked at him real disgusted but she don't answer and she don't move outa her tracks. Then Spunk reaches out an' takes hold of her arm an' says: 'Lena, youse mine. From now on Ah works for you an' fights for you an' Ah never wants you to look to nobody for a crumb of bread, a stitch of close or a shingle to go over yo' head, but *me* long as Ah live. Ah'll git the lumber foh owah house tomorrow. Go home an' git yo' things together!'

" 'Thass mah house' Lena speaks up. 'Papa gimme that.'

" 'Well,' says Spunk, 'doan give up whut's yours, but when youse inside don't forgit youse mine, an' let no other man git outa his place wid you!'

"Lena looked up at him with her eyes so full of love that they wuz runnin' over an' Spunk seen it an' Joe seen it too, and his lip started to tremblin' and his Adam's apple was galloping up and down his neck like a race horse. Ah bet he's wore out half a dozen Adam's apples since Spunk's been on the job with Lena. That's all he'll do. He'll be back heah after while swallowin' an' workin' his lips like he wants to say somethin' an' can't."

"But didn't he do *nothin'* to stop 'em?"

"Nope, not a frazzlin' thing—jus' stood there. Spunk took Lena's arm and walked off jus' like nothin' ain't happened and he stood there gazin' after them till they was outa sight. Now you know a woman don't want no man like that. I'm jus' waitin' to see whut he's goin' to say when he gits back."

II

But Joe Kanty never came back, never. The men in the store heard the sharp report of a pistol somewhere distant in the palmetto thicket and soon Spunk came walking leisurely, with his big black Stetson set at the same rakish angle and Lena clinging to his arm, came walking right into the general store. Lena wept in a frightened manner.

"Well," Spunk announced calmly, "Joe come out there wid a meatax an' made me kill him."

He sent Lena home and led the men back to Joe—Joe crumple and limp with his right hand still clutching his razor.

"See mah back? Mah cloes cut clear through. He sneaked up an' tried to kill me from the back, but Ah got him, an' got him good, first shot," Spunk said.

The men glared at Elijah, accusingly.

"Take him up an' plant him in 'Stoney lonesome'," Spunk said in a careless voice. "Ah didn't wanna shoot him but he made me do it. He's a dirty coward, jumpin' on a man from behind."

Spunk turned on his heel and sauntered away to where he knew his love wept in fear for him and no man stopped him. At the general store later on, they all talked of locking him up until the sheriff should come from Orlando, but no one did anything but talk.

A clear case of self-defense, the trial was a short one, and Spunk walked out of the court house to freedom again. He could work again, ride the dangerous log-carriage that fed the singing, snarling, biting, circle-saw; he could stroll the soft dark lanes with his guitar. He was free to roam the woods again; he was free to return to Lena. He did all of these things.

III

"Whut you reckon, Walt?" Elijah asked one night later. "Spunk's gittin' ready to marry Lena!"

"Naw! Why Joe ain't had time to git cold yit. Nohow Ah didn't figger Spunk was the marryin' kind."

"Well, he is," rejoined Elijah. "He done moved most of Lena's things—and her along wid 'em—over to the Bradley house. He's buying it. Jus' like Ah told yo' all right in heah the night Joe wuz kilt. Spunk's crazy 'bout Lena. He don't want folks to keep on talkin' 'bout her— thass reason he's rushin' so. Funny thing 'bout that bob-cat, wan't it?"

"Whut bob-cat, 'Lige? Ah ain't heered 'bout none."

"Ain't cher? Well, night befo' las' was the fust night Spunk an' Lena moved together an' jus' as they was goin' to bed, a big black bob-cat, black all over, you hear me, *black,* walked round and round that house and howled like forty, an' when Spunk got his gun an' went to the winder to shoot it, he says it stood right still an' looked him in the eye, an' howled right at him. The thing got Spunk so nervoused up he couldn't shoot. But Spunk says twan't no bob-cat nohow. He says it was Joe done sneaked back from Hell!"

"Humph!" sniffed Walter, "he oughter be nervous after what he done. Ah reckon Joe come back to dare him to marry Lena, or to come out an' fight. Ah bet he'll be back time and agin, too. Know what Ah think? Joe wuz a braver man than Spunk."

There was a general shout of derision from the group.

"Thass a fact," went on Walter. "Lookit whut he done; took a razor an' went out to fight a man he knowed toted a gun an' wuz a crack shot, too; 'nother thing Joe wuz skeered of Spunk, skeered plumb stiff! But he went jes' the same. It took him a long time to get his nerve up. 'Tain't nothin' for Spunk to fight when he ain't skeered of nothin'. Now, Joe's done come back to have it out wid the man that's got all he ever had. Y'll know Joe ain't never had nothin' nor wanted nothin' besides Lena. It musta been a h'ant cause ain' nobody never seen no black bob-cat."

" 'Nother thing," cut in one of the men, "Spunk waz cussin' a blue streak today 'cause he 'lowed dat saw wuz wobblin'—almos' got 'im once. The machinist come, looked it over an' said it wuz alright. Spunk musta been leanin' t'wards it some. Den he claimed somebody pushed 'im but 'twant nobody close to 'im. Ah wuz glad when knockin' off time come. I'm skeered of dat man when he gits hot. He'd beat you full of button holes as quick as he's look atcher."

IV

The men gathered the next evening in a different mood, no laughter. No badinage this time.

"Look 'Lige, you goin' to set up wid Spunk?"

"Naw, Ah reckon not, Walter. Tell yuh the truth, Ah'm a lil bit skittish. Spunk died too wicket—died cussin' he did. You know he thought he wuz done outa life."

"Good Lawd, who'd he think done it?"

"Joe."

"Joe Kanty? How come?"

"Walter, Ah b'leeve Ah will walk up thata way an' set. Lena would like it Ah reckon."

"But whut did he say, 'Lige?"

Elijah did not answer until they had left the lighted store and were strolling down the dark street.

"Ah wuz loadin' a wagon wid scantlin' right near the saw when Spunk fell on the carriage but 'fore Ah could git to him the saw got him in the body—awful sight. Me an' Skint Miller got him off but it was too late. Anybody could see that. The fust thing he said wuz: 'He pushed me, 'Lige—the dirty hound pushed me in the back!'—He was spittin' blood at ev'ry breath. We laid him on the sawdust pile with his face to the East so's he could die easy. He helt mah han' till the last, Walter, and said: 'It was Joe, 'Lige—the dirty sneak shoved me . . . he didn't dare come to mah face . . . but Ah'll git the son-of-a-wood louse soon's Ah get there an' make hell too hot for him. . . . Ah felt him shove me. . . !' Thass how he died."

"If spirits kin fight, there's a powerful tussle goin' on somewhere ovah Jordan 'cause Ah b'leeve Joe's ready for Spunk an' ain't skeered anymore—yas, Ah b'leeve Joe pushed 'im mahself."

They had arrived at the house. Lena's lamentations were deep and loud. She had filled the room with magnolia blossoms that gave off a heavy sweet odor. The keepers of the wake tipped about whispering in frightened tones. Everyone in the Village was there, even old Jeff Kanty, Joe's father, who a few hours before would have been afraid to come within ten feet of him, stood leering triumphantly down upon the fallen giant as if his fingers had been the teeth of steel that laid him low.

The cooling board consisted of three sixteen-inch boards on saw horses, a dingy sheet was his shroud.

The women ate heartily of the funeral baked meats and wondered who would be Lena's next. The men whispered coarse conjectures between guzzles of whiskey.

ART AND SUCH

When the scope of American art is viewed as a whole, the contribution of the Negro is found to be small, that is, if we exclude the anonymous folk creations of music, tales, and dances. One immediately takes into consideration that only three generations separate the Negro from the muteness of slavery, and recognizes that creation is in its stumbling infancy.

Taking things as time goes we have first the long mute period of slavery during which many undreamed-of geniuses must have lived and died. Folk tales and music tell us this much. Then the hurly-burly of the Reconstruction and what followed when the black mouth became vocal. But nothing creative came out of this period because this new man, this first talking black man, was necessarily concerned with its newness. The old world he used to know had been turned upside down and so made new for him, [and it] naturally engaged his wonder and attention. Therefore, and in consequence, he had to spend some time, a generation or two, talking out his thoughts and feelings he had during centuries of silence.

He rejoiced with the realization of old dreams and he cried new cries for wounds that had become scars. It was the age of cries. If it seems monotonous one remembers the ex-slave had the pitying ear of the world. He had the encouragement of Northern sympathizers.

In spite of the fact that no creative artist who means anything to the arts of Florida, the United States, [or] the world came out of this period, those first twenty-five years are of tremendous importance no matter which way you look at it. What went on inside the Negro was of more importance than the turbulent doings going on external of him. This postwar generation time was a matrix from which certain ideas came that have seriously affected art creation as well as every other form of Negro expression, including the economic.

Out of this period of sound and emotion came the Race Man and Race Woman; that great horde of individuals known as "Race Champions." The great Frederick Douglass was the original pattern, no doubt, for these people who went up and down the land making speeches so fixed in type as to become a folk pattern. But Douglass had the combination of a great cause and the propitious moment as a setting for his talents and he became a famous man. These others had the wish to be heard and a set of phrases as they became Race Men or Women as the case might be. It was the era of tongue and lung. The "leaders" loved to speak and the new-freed field hands loved gatherings and brave words, so the tribe increased.

It was so easy to become a Race Leader in those days. So few Negroes knew how to read and write that any black man who was proficient in these arts was something to be wondered at. What had been looked upon as something that only the brains of the master-kind could cope with was done by a black person! Astonishing! He must be exceptional to do all that! He was a leader, and went north to his life work of talking the race problem. He could and did teach school like white folks. If he was not "called to preach" he most certainly was made a teacher and either of these positions made him a local leader. The idea grew and traveled. When the first Negroes entered Northern colleges even the Northern whites were tremendously impressed. It was apparent that while setting the slaves free they had declared the equality of men, they did not actually believe any such thing except as voting power. To see a Negro enter Yale to attempt to master the same courses as the whites was something to marvel over. To see one actually take a degree at Harvard, let us say, was a miracle. The phenomenon was made over and pampered. He was told so often that his mentality stood him alone among his kind and that it was a tragic accident that made him a Negro that he came to believe it himself and struck the tragic pose. Naturally he became a leader. Any Negro who graduated from a white school automatically became a national leader and as such could give opinions on anything at all in which the word Negro occurred. But it had to be sad. Any Negro who had all that brains to be taking a degree at a white college was bound to know every thought and feeling of every other Negro in America, however remote from him, and he was bound to feel sad. It was assumed that no Negro brain could ever grasp the curriculum of a white college, so the black man who did had come by some white folks' brain by accident and there was bound to be conflict between his dark body and his white mind. Hence the stultifying doctrine that has not altogether been laughed out of existence at the present. In spite of the thousands and thousands of Negro graduates of good colleges, in spite of hundreds of graduates of New England and Western colleges, there are gray-haired graduates of New England colleges still clutching at the vapors of uniqueness. Despite the fact that Negroes have distinguished themselves in every major field of activity in the nation some of the leftovers still grab at the mantle of Race Leader. Just let them hear that white people have curiosity about some activity among Negroes, and these "leaders" will not let their shirttails touch them (i.e., sit down) until they have rushed forward and offered themselves as an authority on the subject whether they have ever heard of it before or not. In the very face of a situation as different from the 1880s as chalk is from cheese, they stand around and mouth the same trite phrases, and try their practiced best to look sad. They call spirituals "Our Sorrow Songs" and other such tomfoolery in an effort to get into the spotlight if possible without having ever done anything to improve education, industry, invention, art and never having uttered a quotable line. Though he is being jostled about these days and paid scant attention, the Race Man is still with us—he and his Reconstruction pulings. His job today is to rush around seeking for something he can "resent."

How has this Race attitude affected the arts in Florida? In Florida as elsewhere in America this background has worked the mind of the creator. Can the black poet sing a song to the morning? Up springs the song to his lips but it is fought back. He says to himself, "Ah, this is a beautiful song inside me. I feel the morning star in my throat. I will sing of the star and the morning." Then his background thrusts itself between his lips and the star and he mutters, "Ought I not to be singing of our sorrows? That is what is expected of me and I shall be considered forgetful of our past and present. If I do not some will even call me a coward. The one subject for a Negro is the Race and its sufferings and so the song of the morning must be choked back. I will write of a lynching instead." So the same old theme, the same old phrases, get done again to the detriment of art. To him no Negro exists as an individual—he exists only as another tragic unit of the Race. This in spite of the obvious fact that Negroes love and hate and fight and play and strive and travel and have a thousand and one interests in life like other humans. When his baby cuts a new tooth he brags as shamelessly as anyone else without once weeping over the prospect of some Klansman knocking it out when and if the child ever gets grown. The Negro artist knows all this but he conceives that a Negro can do nothing but weave something in his particular art form about the Race problem. The writer thinks that he has been brave in following in the groove of the Race Champions, when the truth is, it is the line of least resistance and least originality—certain to be approved of by the "champions" who want to hear the same thing over and over again even though they already know it by heart, and certain to be unread by everybody else. It is the same thing as waving the American flag in a poorly constructed play. Anyway, the effect of the whole period has been to fix activities in a mold that precluded originality and denied creation in the arts.

Results:

In painting one artist, O. Richard Reid of Fernandina, who at one time created a stir in New York art circles with his portraits of Fannie Hurst, John Barrymore, and H. L. Mencken. Of his recent works we hear nothing.

In sculpture, Augusta Savage of Green Cove Springs is making greater and greater contributions to what is significant in American art. Her subjects are Negroid for the most part but any sort of preachment is absent from her art. She seems striving to reach out to the rimbones of nothing and in so doing she touches a responsive chord in the universe and grows in stature.

The world of music has been enriched by the talents of J. Rosamond Johnson, a Jacksonville Negro. His range has been from light and frivolous tunes of musical comedy designed to merely entertain to some beautiful arrangements of spirituals which have been sung all over the world in concert halls. His truly great composition is the air which accompanies the words of the so-called "Negro National Anthem." The bittersweet poem is by his brother James Weldon Johnson.

Though it is not widely known, there is a house in Fernandina, Florida, whose interior is beautifully decorated in original wood carving. It is the work of the late Brooks Thompson, who was born a slave. Without ever having known anything about African art, he has achieved something very close to African concepts on the walls, doors, and ceilings of three rooms. His doors are things of wondrous beauty. The greater part of the work was done after he was in his seventies. "The feeling just came and I did it" is his explanation of how the carpenter turned wood-carver in his old age.

In literature Florida has two names: James Weldon Johnson, of many talents, and Zora Neale Hurston. As a poet Johnson wrote scattered bits of verse, and he wrote lyrics for the music of his brother Rosamond. Then he wrote the campaign song for Theodore Roosevelt's campaign, "You're Alright Teddy," which swept the nation. After Theodore Roosevelt was safe in the White House he appointed the poet as consul to Venezuela. The time came when Johnson published volumes of verse and collected a volume of Negro sermons which he published under the title of *God's Trombones*. Among his most noted prose works are *The Autobiography of an Ex-Colored Man*, *Black Manhattan*, and his story of his own life, *Along This Way*.

Zora Neale Hurston won critical acclaim for two new things in Negro fiction. The first was an objective point of view. The subjective view was so universal that it had come to be taken for granted. When her first book, *Jonah's Gourd Vine*, a novel, appeared in 1934, the critics announced across the nation: "Here at last is a Negro story without bias. The characters live and move. The story is about Negroes but it could be anybody. It is the first time that a Negro story has been offered without special pleading. The characters in the story are seen in relation to themselves and not in relation to the whites as has been the rule. To watch these people one would conclude that there were not white people in the world. The author is an artist that will go far."

The second element that attracted attention was the telling of the story in the idiom—not the dialect—of the Negro. The Negro's poetical flow of language, his thinking in images and figures, was called to the attention of the outside world. Zora Hurston is the author of three other books, *Mules and Men*, *Their Eyes Were Watching God* (published also in England; translated into the Italian by Ada Prospero and published in Rome), and *Tell My Horse*.

It is not to be concluded from these meager offerings in the arts that Negro talent is lacking. There has been a cruel waste of genius during the long generations of slavery. There has been a squandering of genius during the three generations since Surrender on Race.

So the Negro begins feeling with his fingers to find himself in the plastic arts. He is well established in music, but [there is] still a long way to go to overtake his possibilities. In literature the first writings have been little more than putting into writing the sayings of the Race Men and Women and champions of "Race Consciousness." So that what was produced was a self-conscious document lacking in drama, analysis, characterization, and the universal oneness necessary to literature. But

the idea was not to produce literature—it was to "champion the Race."
The Fourteenth and Fifteenth Amendments got some pretty hard wear,
and that sentence "You have made the *greatest* progress in so and so
many years" was all the art in the literature in the purpose and period.

But one finds on all hands the weakening of race consciousness, impatience with Race Champions, and a growing taste for literature as
such. The wedge has entered the great mass and one may expect some
noble things from the Florida Negro in art in the next decade.

from THE NEGRO VERSION OF *MACBETH* (1936)

WILLIAM SHAKESPEARE AND
ORSON WELLES

In 1936, William Shakespeare was a seventeenth-century icon and a young, struggling director named Orson Welles was virtually unknown. Welles knew that to survive and achieve the fame and success that he craved and would later obtain, he would have to distinguish himself from other artists who were also barely getting by during the depths of the Depression. While living on a small stipend from a federally funded writers' project, he met many fine black writers, artists, and actors. He also noticed that Harlem afforded some of the lowest production costs in the city and was part of a transit system that could easily bring whites from downtown.

Soon, Welles hit upon the idea of producing an all-Negro version of *Macbeth* in Harlem, and eventually did in 1936. Welles and his stage manager, John Houseman, added drums, gunfire, and a chorus of black witches to the original version. The results were overwhelming: There were overflow (mostly white) crowds every night, and even though the production was dubbed "Voodoo *Macbeth*" in the press, it sustained and launched the careers of several black performers. The production helped to keep Harlem alive and viable as an artistic and cultural community, and it gave Welles the reputation that he needed to get a chance to produce his radio drama *The War of the Worlds*.

FEDERAL THEATRE
Hallie Flanagan
Philip W. Barber

Complete Working Script of

"MACBETH"

BY WILLIAM SHAKESPEARE

NEGRO VERSION

Conceived • Arranged • Staged

BY ORSON WELLES

opened on April 14, 1936
at Lafayette Theatre

Manuscript assembled by Elsa Ryan of Federal Theatre

1936

"MACBETH"
CAST OF CHARACTERS

DUNCAN (The King)	*Service Bell*
MALCOLM (Son to the King)	*Wardell Saunders*
MACDUFF	*Maurice Ellis*
BANQUO	*Cananda Lee*
MACBETH Nobles	*Jack Carter*
ROSS	*Frank David*
LENNOX	*Thomas Anderson*
SIWARD	*Archie Savage*
FIRST MURDERER	*George Nixon*
SECOND MURDERER	*Kenneth Renwick*
THE DOCTOR	*Lawrence Chenault*
THE PRIEST	*Al Watts*
FIRST MESSENGER	*Philandre Thomas*
SECOND MESSENGER	*Herbert Glynn*
THE PORTER	*J. Lewis Johnson*
SEYTON	*Larrie Lauria*
A LORD	*Charles Collins*
FIRST CAPTAIN	*Lisle Grenidge*
SECOND CAPTAIN	*Ollie Simmons*
FIRST CHAMBERLAIN	*Wm. Cumberbatch*
SECOND CHAMBERLAIN	*Benny Tattnall*
FIRST COURT ATTENDANT	*Chauncey Worrell*
SECOND COURT ATTENDANT	*George Thomas*
FIRST PAGE BOY	*Sarah Turner*
SECOND PAGE BOY	*Beryle Banfield*
LADY MACDUFF	*Marie Young*
LADY MACBETH Noble Ladies	*Edna Thomas*
THE DUCHESS	*Alma Dickson*
THE NURSE	*Virginia Girvin*
YOUNG MACDUFF	*Bertram Holmes*
DAUGHTER TO MACDUFF	*Wanda Macy*
FLEANCE	*Carl Crawford*
HECATE	*Eric Burroughs*
FIRST WITCH	*Wilhelmina Williams*

SECOND WITCH	*Josephine Williams*
THIRD WITCH	*Zola King*
WITCH DOCTOR	*Abdul*

COURT LADIES *Helen Carter, Carolyn Crosby, Evelyn Davis, Ethel Drayton, Helen Brown, Aurelia Lawson, Margaret Howard, Olive Wanamaker, Evelyn Skipworth, Aslean Lynch*

COURT GENTLEMEN *Herbert Glynn, Jose Miralda, Jimmy Wright, Otis Morse, Merritt Smith, Walter Brogsdale, Harry George Grant*

SOLDIERS *Benny Tattnall, Herman Patton, Ernest Brown, Ivan Lewis, Richard Ming, George Spelvin, Albert Patrick, Chauncey Worrell, Albert McCoy, William Clayton, Jr., Allen Williams, William Cumberbatch, Henry J. Williams, Amos Laing, Louis Gilbert, Theodore Howard, Leonardo Barros, Ollie Simmons, Ernest Brown, Merritt Smith, Harry George Grant, Herbert Glynn, Jimmy Wright, George Thomas, Richard Ming, Clifford Davis, Frederick Gibson*

WITCH WOMEN *Juanita Baker, Beryle Banfield, Sybil Moore, Nancy Hunt, Ollie Burgoyne, Jacqueline Ghant Martin, Fannie Suber, Ethel Milner, Dorothy Jones*

WITCH MEN *Archie Savage, Charles Hill, Leonardo Barros, Howard Taylor, Amos Laing, Allen Williams, Ollie Simmons, Theodore Howard*

CRIPPLES *Clyde Gooden, Clarence Potter, Milton Lacey, Hudson Prince, Theodore Howard*

VOODOO WOMEN *Lena Halsey, Jean Cutler, Effie McDowell, Irene Ellington, Marguerite Perry, Essie Frierson, Ella Emanuel, Ethel Drayton, Evelyn Davis*

VOODO MEN *Ernest Brown, Howard Taylor, Henry J. Williams, Louis Gilbert, William Clayton, Jr., Albert McCoy, Merritt Smith, Richard Ming*

DRUMMERS *James Cabon, James Martha, Jay Daniel*

SYNOPSIS OF SCENES

ACT I
Scene 1—The Jungle
Scene 2—The Palace
Intermission (Ten Minutes)

ACT II
Scene 1—The Palace
Scene 2—The Jungle
Intermission (Eight Minutes)

ACT III
Scene 1—The Palace
Scene 2—The Coast
Scene 3—The Jungle
Scene 4—The Palace

MUSIC

JOE JORDAN   **CONDUCTOR**

OVERTURE (Yamekraw)   *James P. Johnson*
"YAMEKRAW" is a genuine Negro treatise on spiritual, syncopated, and blues melodies, expressing the religious fervor and happy moods of the natives of Yamekraw, a Negro settlement situated on the outskirts of Savannah, Georgia. It is believed to be the first Negro rhapsody.)

INTERMEZZO (Adagio Aframerique)   *Porter Grainger*
INTERMEZZO (River)   *Arranged by Joe Jordon*

STAFF OF THE NEGRO UNIT

MANAGING PRODUCER   *John Houseman*
CASTING DIRECTOR   *Edward G. Perry*

MUSICAL DIRECTOR	Joe Jordon
STAGE MANAGER	Leroy Willis
ASSISTANT STAGE MANAGERS	Edw. Dudley, Jr. &
	Gordon Roberts

FOR "MACBETH"

GENERAL MANAGER	Chandos Sweet
TREASURER	Sheppard Chartor
ADVANCE REPRESENTATIVES	Harold Lane &
	Matt Meeker
ADVANCE AGENT	John Silvera

CREDITS

ASSISTANT DIRECTOR	Thomas Anderson
Musical arrangements under direction of	Virgil Thomson
Voodoo Chants and Dances under direction of	Asadata Dafora Horton
Dances under direction of	Clarence Yates
Chorus under direction of	Leonard de Paur
Costumes, Painting & Properties executed by	Federal Theatre Workshop

Building by the Construction Staff of the Negro Unit
Masks executed by James Cochran
"Yamekraw"—courtesy of Alfred Music Co., Inc.

| COSTUMES AND SETTINGS | Nat Karson |

| LIGHTING | Feder |

ACT TWO

SCENE 2

THE JUNGLE—A cauldron is smoking, over a blazing fire which is masked by a double half circle of the Voodoo women; squatting, as the scene begins. The three witches, raised somewhat above the stage level, are already in a state of ecstacy from the fumes rising out of the cauldron.

SECOND WITCH: By the pricking of my thumbs,

*CUE I—WORD CUE (*HECATE *LIGHT)*

Something wicked this way comes.

(The leaves part and MACBETH *enters, followed by* HECATE. *All rise.)*

HECATE: Say, if thou'dst rather hear it from their mouths,

Or from their masters?

MACBETH: Call 'em.

(Drums. MACBETH *to one side)*

HECATE: Round about the cauldron go.

(The half circle becomes a full one, moves around the cauldron in time to the drums and the chanting.)

In the poison'd entrails throw

Toad, that under cold stone

Days and nights has thirty one.

FIRST VOICE: *(Each item is chanted by a different voice among the celebrants.)*

Fillet of a foony snake

In the cauldron bail and bake;

SECOND VOICE: Eye of newt and toe of frog.

THIRD VOICE: Wool of bat.

FOURTH VOICE: And tongue of dog.

FIFTH VOICE: Adder fork.

SIXTH VOICE: And blind-worm's sting.

SEVENTH VOICE: Lizard's leg.

EIGHTH VOICE: And howlet's wing.

ALL: Double, double, toil and trouble

Fire burn and cauldron bubble.

Scales of dragon.

Tooth of wolf.

Witches' mummy.

WARNING FOR CUE 2

Naw and gulf of the ravin's salt-sea shark
Finger of birth-strangled babe,
Ditch-deliver'd by a drab.

ALL: Double, double, toil and trouble,
Fire burn, and cauldron bubble,
For a charm of powerful trouble
Like a hell-broth boil and bubble.

CUE 2 1 PAGE FADE HECATE *LIGHT BRING UP 8*

HECATE: Pour in sow's blood, that hath eaten
Her nine farrow; grease that's sweeten
From the murderer's gibbet throw
Into the flame.
Cool it with a baboon's blood
Then the charm is firm and good.

ALL: Double, double, toil and trouble;
Fire burn, and cauldron bubble.

MACBETH: What is't you do?

HECATE: A deed without a name.

FIRST WITCH: (*Screaming out his name. Speaking through her teeth in the queer voice of her "control"*)
Macbeth! Macbeth! Macbeth!
Beware Macduff!
Beware the Thame of Fife. Dismiss me. Enough.

SECOND WITCH: (*As the first witch—possessed*)
Macbeth! Macbeth! Macbeth!
Be bloody, bold, and resolute; laugh to scorn
The power of man, for none of woman born
Shall harm Macbeth.

MACBETH: Then live, Macduff; what need I fear of thee?
But yet I'll make assurance double sure.
And take a bond of fate; thou shalt not live;
That I may tell pale-hearted fear it lies
And sleep in spite of thunder.

THIRD WITCH: (*As with the other two his name violently screamed, the rest of the messaged pronounced*)
Macbeth! Macbeth! Macbeth!

Be lion-mettled, proud; and take no care

Who chafes, who frets, or where conspirers are;

Macbeth shall never vanquished be until

Great Birnam wood to high Dunsinane hill

Shall come against him.

MACBETH: *(To himself, and partly to* HECATE*)*

That will never be;

Who can impress the forest, bid the tree

Unfix his ear-bound root? Sweet Bodements! Good!

    (To the witches, raising his voice)

Yet my heart

Throbs to know one thing; tell me, if your art

Can tell so much; shall Banquo's issue never

Reign in this kingdom?

    *(*WITHCES *hysterical)*

HECATE: Seek to know no more.

    (General panic)

MACBETH: *WARNING FOR CUE 3*

I will be satisfied.

    (Silence)

Deny me this,

And an eternal curse fall on you!

    (General derisive laughter)

HECATE: *(Silencing the laughter)*

Show his eyes, and grieve his heart;

Come like shadows, so depart!

                        CUE 3—1 PAGE (STROBILE LIGHT FADE OUTS)

    (Drums—first apparition rises)

MACBETH: *(Terrified)*

Thou art too like the spirit of Banquo;

Down!

    (Second apparition)

Thy crown does scar mine eyeballs. And thy hair

Thou other gold-bound brow, is like the first.

    (Third apparition)

A third is like the former. Filthy hags!

Why do you show me this?

    (Fourth apparition)

                                          BELOVED HARLEM

A fourth! Start, eyes!

(*Fifth and sixth apparition*)

What, will the line stretch out to the crack of doom?

(*Seventh apparition*)

A seventh! I'll see no more.

Horrible sight! Now, I see, 'tis true;

For the blood bolter'd Banquo smiles upon me,

And points at them for this.

(*Turning to* HECATE)

What, is this so?

½ WAY THRU CUE 3

HECATE: Ay, sir, all this is so.

(MACBETH *turns back, but the devils have vanished.*)

MACBETH: Blood hath been shed ere now, i' the olden time,

Ere human status purged the gentle weal;

Ay, and since too, murders have been perform'd

Too terrible for the ear. The times have been,

That, when the brains were out, the man would die

And there an end; but now, they rise again,

With twenty mortal murders on their crowns.

HECATE: But why stands Macbeth thus amazedly?

CUE 3 ENDS

MACBETH: Let this pernicious hour

Stand aya accursed in the calendar!

(*With determination*)

From this moment

The very firstlings of my heart

Shall be the firstlings of my hand!

(*There is the first light of dawn.*)

HECATE: No boasting like a fool

Seize on Macduff, give to the edge o' the sword

His wife, his babes, and all unfortunate souls

That trace him in his lice.

MACBETH: This deed I'll do before this purpose cool

(*Suddenly fearful again*)

But no more sights!

CUE 4—WORD CUE—FAST

(*He runs out. All laugh wildly.*

HECATE *holds up his arm in a gesture he uses always for cursing*
MACBETH. *Absolute and sudden silence)*

HECATE: He shall spurn fate, scorn death, and bear
His hopes 'bove wisdom, grace and fear;
(*To the celebrants*)
And you all know, security
Is mortal's chiefest enemy.

END OF SCENE II

ACT III

SCENE 3

This scene is entirely incomplete. Its setting and arrangement depend on physical production decision.

(**LADY MACBETH** *enters.*)

THREE WITCHES: Here eyes are open
Their sense is shut.

LADY MACBETH: Out, damned spot! out, I say!—One:
Two; why, then't is time to do't.
Hell is murky!—Fie, my lord, fie! a soldier and afeard?
What need we fear who knows it, when none can call our
power to account?
Yet who would have thought the old man to have so
much blood in him.
The Thane of Fife had a wife; where is she now?
What, will these hands ne'er be clean? mar all with this
starting.
Here's the smell of the blood still; all the
Perfumes of Arabia will not sweeten this little hand.
Oh, oh, oh;
Wash your hands, put on your night-gown;
I tell you yet again
Bancuo's buried; he cannot come out on's grave.
Even so?

To bed, to bed! There's knocking at the gate!

Come, come, come, come, give me your hand.

What's done cannot be undone.—To bed, to bed, to bed.

   (*Exit*)

CUE I—WORD CUE

WITCHES: Unnatural deed do breed unnatural troubles;

   Infected minds keep eyes upon her.

   (*Enter* MACDUFF, MALCOLM, ROSS *and forces*)

MALCOLM: We learn no other but the confident tyrant

   Keeps still in Dunsinane, and will endure

   Our setting down befor't,

   Some say he's mad; others that lesser hate him

   Do call it valiant fury.

MACDUFF: How does he feel

   His secret murders sticking on his hands;

   Those he commands move only in command,

   Nothing, in love; now does he feel his title

   Hang loose upon him, like a giant's robe

   Upon a dwarfish thief.

MALCOLM: What wood is this before us?

HECATE: The wood of Birnam,

   Let every soldier hew him down a bough

   And bear't before him; thereby shall you shadow

   The numbers of your host and make discovery

   Err in report of you.

MACDUFF: It shall be done.

   FADE OUT COMPLETELY

END OF SCENE III

ACT THREE

SCENE 4

CHECK: CASTLE WINDOW OPEN

THE PALACE MACBETH, *wild-eyed, dressed only in his trousers and shirt, on the throne, five or six runners on their faces before him.*

MACBETH: Bring me no more reports; let them fly all;

CUE 2—1½ PAGES

    Till Birnam wood remove to Dunsinane.
      (Sits)
    What's the boy Malcolm? Was he not born of woman?
    The spirits that know
    All mortal consequences have pronounced me thus;
    "Fear not, Macbeth; no man that's born of woman
    Shall e'er have power upon thee"
      (Enter SERVANT, *running up to throne throwing himself*
      at MACBETH'*s feet)*
    Where got'st thou that goose look?
SERVANT: *(Breathlessly)*
    There is ten thousand—
MACBETH: Geese, villain?
SERVANT: Soldiers, sir.
MACBETH: *(Striking him violently across the face)*
    What soldiers, patch?
SERVANT: *(Covering his face with his hands. After a moment terrified)*
    The English force, so please you.
MACBETH: Take thy face hence.
      (Exit SERVANT—*the rest remain on their knees)*
    Seyton! I am sick of heart,
    I have loved long enough; my way of life

½ WAY THRU CUE I

    Is fall'n into the sear, the yellow leaf;
    And that which should accompany old age,

As honour, love, obedience, troops of friends,

I must not look to have! Seyton!

(Still no answer. HE *turns to one of the kneeling figures.)*

How does your patient, doctor?

DOCTOR: *(looking up)*

Not so sick, my lord;

As she is troubled with thick-coming fancies

That keep her from her rest.

MACBETH: *(turning away)*

Cure her of that.

DOCTOR: Therein the patient must minister to himself.

*(*MACBETH *wheels on him; he bows his head to the ground again*
quietly.)

MACBETH: Throw physic to the dogs; I'll have none of it.

WARNING TO END CUE I

Seyton! Seyton! I say!

(Enter SEYTON, *running)*

SEYTON: What is your gracious pleasure?

MACBETH: What news more?

SEYTON: *(Prostrating himself)*

All is confirmed, my lord, which was reported.

CUE I ENDS

MACBETH: Hang our banners on the outward walls;

CUE 2—2 PAGES

(All but three of four, the messengers, rise at this, and a couple exit.)

The cry is still "They come"; Our castle's strength

Will laugh a siege to scorn; here let them lie

Till famine and the plague eat them up.

(Some of the servants have MACBETH'*s coat, sword and plumed hat.*
They hurry over to him and help to dress him.)

Hang those that talk of fear!

Come, put my belt on now! Give me my sword!

Come sir, dispatch! Put on, I say!

Seyton, send out.

*(*MACBETH *stands up, fully dressed, brave in his shining regalia. Proudly*
to the DOCTOR, *who stands near the throne.)*

Doctor, the thanes fly from me.

(From outside the palace comes a strange sound, high-pitched chorus of

*wails. It is heard very suddenly and the effect should be startling. All
jump to their feet, frightened, stand waiting, listening—silence.)*
What is that noise?

(After this last line of Macbeth's, the sound again, more reaction)

SEYTON: It is the cry of women, my good lord.

½ WAY THRU CUE 2

*(General relaxation, relief, but all still very mystified. The sound again,
and now it continues, growing louder.)*

MACBETH: I have almost forgot the taste of fears,
The time has been, my senses would have cool'd
To hear a night-shried; and my fell of hair
Would at a dismal treatise rouse and stir
As life were in't; I have supp'd full with horrors;
Direness, familiar to my slaughterous thoughts
Cannot once start me. Wherefore was that cry?

DOCTOR: The queen, my lord, is dead.

*(They bring the crown and get it before MACBETH. He stares at it.
Chanting stops.)*

MACBETH: She should have died hereafter;
There would have been a time for such a word.
Tomorrow, and tomorrow, and tomorrow,
Creeps in this petty pace from day to day
To the last syllable of recorded time,
And all our yesterdays have lighted fools.

WARNING TO END CUE 2

The way to dusty death. Out, out, brief candle!
Life's but a walking shadow, a poor player
That struts and frets his hour upon the stage
And then is heard no more; it is a tale
Told by an idiot, full of sound and fury!
Signifying nothing.

CUE 2 ENDS

(The PORTER runs down from his watch on the battlements.)
Thou comest to use thy tongue; the story quickly.

PORTER: *WARNING FOR CUE 3*

Gracious, my lord.
I should report that which I say I saw

But know not how to do it.

MACBETH: Well, say, sir.

PORTER: As I did stand my watch upon the wall.

I look's toward Birnam, and anon, me thought

The wood began to move!

> *(Sensation; screams. All exit in confusion except* PORTER *and* MACBETH,
> *who has jumped on the former and holds him by the throat.)*

MACBETH: Liar and slave!

PORTER: Let me endure your wrath, if't be not so;

I say, a moving grove.

> *(The tops of palm trees begin slowly to rise over the battlements, jungle
> creeps in the gates—slowly, slowly.)*

MACBETH: If thou speak'st false

CUE 3—WORD CUE

Upon the next tree shalt thou hang alive,

Till famine cling thee;

> *(The jungle grows.* MACBETH *suddenly sees it.* HE *lets the* PORTER *drop.
> Stares at it)*

I care not if thou dost for me as much.

CUE 4—WORD CUE

> *(The trees rise, the leaves move in. Drums. The* PORTER *picks himself up
> and scrambles off. At length* MACBETH *speaks.)*

"Fear not, till Birnam wood

Do come to Dunsinane." Arm, arm, and out!

CUE 5—WORD CUE

There is nor flying hence nor tarrying here.

I gin to be aweary of the sun,

And wish the estate of the world were now undone.

CUE 6—WORD CUE

> *(Cries, shots from within the foliage)*

Ring the alarm-bell! Blow! Wind, come, wrack!

At least we'll die with harness on our back.

CUE 7—WORD CUE

> *(Bell begins to clang, shot and cries up.* MACBETH *starts
> up the battlements.)*

What's he

That was not born of woman. Such a one

Am I to fear, or none.

(*Enter* YOUNG SIWARD *from the mass of still leaves. Pistol in hand, he confronts* MACBETH.)

YOUNG SIWARD: What is thy name?

MACBETH: Thou'lt be afraid to hear it.

YOUNG SIWARD: No; though thou call'st thyself a hotter name
Than any is in hell.

CUE 8—WARNING

(MACBETH *shoots him.*)

MACBETH: My name's Macbeth.

(*Siward falls.*)

Thou wast born of woman!

(HE *turns and continues up the wall. Enter* MACDUFF *below the gates.*)

But sword I smile at, and weapons laugh to scorn
Brandish'd by man that's of woman born.

MACDUFF: Let me find him, fortune! Tyrant, show thy face!

CUE 8—½ PAGE

(MACBETH *on the wall above, hears his voice, and stands frozen with horror.* MACDUFF *is moving toward the wall, looking at him.*)

I cannot strike at wretched kerns, whose arms
Are hired to bear their staves.

My wife and children's ghosts will haunt me still!

(MACDUFF *has started up the battlements.* MACBETH *wheels and starts running madly over the bridge.* MACDUFF *sees him.*)

Turn, hell-hound, turn!

(*The last turn stops* MACBETH, *who wheels to face him.*)

MACBETH: Of all men else I have avoided thee;
But get thee back; my soul is too much charged
With blood of thine already.

CUE 8 ENDS

WARNING FOR CUE 9

MACDUFF: Then yield thee, coward,
And love to be the show and gaze o' the time;
We'll have thee, as our rarer monsters are,
Fainted upon a pole, and underwrite,
"Here may you see the tyrant."

MACBETH: I will not yield
Though Birnam wood be come to Dunsinane,

Yet I will try thee last.

MACDUFF: I have no words.

(HE fires at MACBETH, *who shoots back.* HE *fires his other gun. All aims have missed.* MACDUFF *draws his sword and runs up to* MACBETH. THEY *fight—the lower stage is completely filled*

CUE 10—WORD CUE

with the leaves the army is bearing. All sound way down here. Even the drums very low.)

MACBETH: Thou losest labour

I bear a charmed life, which must not yield

To one of a woman born.

MACDUFF: Despair thy charm;

(On "Charm" sudden complete silence)

And let the angel whom thou still hast served

Tell thee, Macduff was from his mother's womb

Untimely ripp'd.

(MACBETH is off his guard, MACDUFF *runs him through.* MACBETH *stands, teetering, clutching his wound. The silence is filled weirdly with the witches chant: "All hail Macbeth! Hail, King of Scotland.")*

MACBETH: Accursed be the tongue that tell me so

WARNING FOR CUE 11

And he these juggling fiends no more believed!

(MACBETH falls dead. The derisive cackle of the witches is heard, MAC-BETH *has fallen so his body is hidden behind the battlements at the top of the tower.* MACDUFF *kneels behind this during the laughter and rises to silence it, holding in his hand,* MACBETH's *bloody head.* MACDUFF *throws the head into the mass of waving leaves below.)*

MACDUFF: Hail, king!

CUE 11—WORD CUE

(At this the army drops the branches and jungle collapses; revealing a stage full of people. MALCOLM *is on the throne, crowned. All bow before him—all but* HECATE *and the* THREE WITCHES *who stand above the body of* LADY MACBETH. *They have caught* MACBETH's *head and they hold it high, triumphantly.)*

For so thou art! Behold,

Where stands

The usurper's cursed head;

THE NEGRO VERSION OF *MACBETH*   141

(The WITCHES *gleefully raise the head above them.)*
The time is free!

CUE 12—WORD CUE

Hail, King of Scotland!

VOICES OF VOODOO WOMEN: All Hail Malcolm—

*(*THEY *are interrupted by the thunderous chorus of the* ARMY.*)*

ARMY: Hail, King of Scotland.

CUE 13—WORD CUE

VOODOO WOMEN: Thrice to mine and thrice to thine;
And thrice again to make up nine.

HECATE: Peace!

(Drums, army, music, voodoo voices, all are instantly silent.)
The charm's wound up!

CURTAIN

142BELOVED HARLEM

FROM DRUMS AT DUSK (1939)

BY ARNA BONTEMPS

Originally from Louisiana, Bontemps was a stellar student who started college at the age of fourteen. He graduated from Pacific Union College (now UCLA) three years later. His first published works were poems in the NAACP-sponsored magazine *The Crisis*. His first poem published was entitled "Hope," and the editor was W.E.B. Du Bois.

Bontemps also wrote nonfiction, short stories, and children's books and in 1949 won the Newbery Award for his book for children, *The Story of the Negro.* Presented here is a chapter from an adult novel *Drums at Dusk,* a story about a massive slave insurrection in Saint Dominique, which he wrote while in the Harlem branch of the WPA writers' workshop.

CHAPTER ONE

I

Only ghosts walked on that pathway now. Ghosts—and people so old they were about to become ghosts. Captain Frounier sometimes came that way when paying his weekly respects to M. Bayou de Libertas in the other's counting house behind the magnificent colonial mansion at Bréda, for the captain was ninety-one, as toothless as a sparrow, as wobbly in the joints as the spars of his own sailing vessels and as violently profane of tongue as any man this side of torment. Mme Jacques Juvet, once indentured as a house servant at this same Bréda, was also attached to the path. In her case too the reason was simple. Mme Juvet was eighty if she was a day. Her teeth had become fangs. Snuff left a nasty smudge around her old mouth. She walked with a cane that resembled a corkscrew, and the slaves had already begun to shun her as a witch. Mars Plasair liked the path not because he was old but because he was coughing his lungs out and was perhaps as near his ghosthood as the others who walked there. Moreover he was a slave and had been badly used.

Partly, it may have been the trees that gave the path its character.

DRUMS AT DUSK   **143**

Elsewhere on the vast acres of Bréda there was the lofty murmur of long-necked coconut palms and the refined swish of banana leaves. Here a row of naked cottonwoods, blighted long since by a mysterious plague, stood like giant skeletons along the path.

Others than the ghosts found the path as unsatisfactory as it was unattractive. The footing was exceedingly bad. Some broken rocks had been scattered there once and covered with gravel. Subsequent rains had taken the gravel. This was not a circumstance to dismay a ghost, but it was the last straw where young Diron Desautels was concerned. And now, having beguiled himself into trying it, he cursed every foot of the way.

Yet, thank heaven, he was not obliged to continue as he had started. He might cut across the slope behind the slave quarters, come out on the carriage road and follow it till he reached the wooded sections of the hills. On second thought, that was precisely what he would do. As well as Diron loved to hunt, he was not willing to crack his shins in the pursuit of a few game birds while there was another way. It was still night, of course, the dark land still sleeping in lemon moonlight, but Diron knew that his seedy old falcon was alert only at daybreak, and he was determined to reach the hillside before the sun appeared. Furthermore he had promised to meet his uncle at the edge of the wood, and he did not propose to keep the older man waiting.

The clear slope was in reality a reaped grain field. It was bounded by a black hedge; and beyond that the level acres, dim miles of them, supported a remarkably heavy crop of sugar cane. Diron walked briskly now, the fowler sitting placidly on his left wrist. In his right hand he carried a stick, his only weapon aside from the pistol worn inside his sash-like belt. He was dressed in apple-green breeches and jacket, and his heavy mane, neatly gathered at the neck and tied with a silver cord, gave back to the moon a lacquered shine.

The sound of horses halted his steps before he reached the coach road, however, and Diron found a friendly shadow and waited. A coach at that hour? A slave-driven ox cart would have been nothing unusual. Neither would a carriage have surprised him had it been headed for Cap Français before daybreak. Plantation masters in the northern department of Saint Domingue were in the habit of making early business errands to the seat of their colonial government. But this present affair was not the same. Here was a coach drawn by fast horses coming out from the city at an hour when planters were generally expected to be asleep. Diron saw it come into view dimly and then flash by in a maze of dust and shadows. The clatter was enormous.

He came out upon the road and tried to imagine what fresh unrest this thing heralded. Of course, a peaceful mission was conceivable, but it was much easier to account for the presence of the coach in other ways. There was little enough of harmony between the Paris-appointed officials in Cap Français and their landed constituents, not to mention the turmoil among local classes and the tendency of sparks from the Revolution in faraway France to land unexpectedly now and again on this island possession in the Caribbean Sea. So Diron Desautels, a young man who had taken a very decided stand on more than one of the questions that helped to cause the bloody confusion, felt a shiver of excitement.

Before the carriage vanished completely, he assured himself that it was headed for Bréda, which meant that if anything unusual brewed, he would—as a neighbor and friend of the overseer—hear more about it. Satisfied of this, he turned again toward the wooded hillside half a mile beyond. A smile twisted the corners of his mouth suddenly, distorted the thin, neatly trimmed but immature mustache on his lip. There was also another source of information available to him, if his curiosity demanded it, another means of finding out some of the things that went on at Bréda. But he refrained from calling her name at the moment, even silently to himself. He was not always as bold as he might have been.

The son of a naturalist who had made the Caribbean islands his field, Diron had spent most of his life in Saint Domingue, the French half of the island which Spanish explorers had at first been in the habit of calling *Haiti* or high land. At the moment both the young man's parents were in Paris again while the father, patient old scholar, was dutifully seeing a large volume of his observations of tropical flora through the press. But this serious occupation, if the whole truth must be known, did not completely explain the son's separation from his parents.

Neither did Diron's attachment to his uncle, M. Philippe Desautels, tell the real motive. While his affection for that elderly gentleman was genuine, as his haste to join him this morning on a fowling jaunt indicated, it was definitely secondary. M. Philippe Desautels, lately relieved of his post as naval commissioner of the colony and still in political disfavor in Cap Français as well as in Paris, remained an aristocrat. He hadn't yet gone over to the other side as had his nephew. Still his own adversities had rendered him tolerant of the opposition. He knew perfectly well what dangerous considerations had helped to speed the rash boy's return from France after a short stay during the previous year.

Diron had joined *Les Amis des Noirs.* This exuberant society of violent anti-slavery partisans, counting among its members such gaudy lights as La Rochefoucauld, Lafayette, Danton and Robespierre, had fascinated him from the start. Brissot, its founder, was an old acquaintance of the family. The writings of Abbé Grégoire stirred the young Diron like lyric poetry. Beside these he had placed Abbé Raynal's *Histoire Philosophique des deux Indes,* and his destiny had been sealed. Two or three ringing, eloquent phrases, the touchstones of their movement, echoed in his mind continually. . . . *No part of the French nation shall demand its rights at the hands of the Assembly in vain. . . . All men are born and continue free and equal as to their rights. . . .*

Even now hastening to overtake the soft-voiced uncle who had preceded him on horseback to the hillside, Diron was sure that his tingling excitement owed as much to these slogans as to the danger of his position in the local scheme. His friend Sylvestre Viard had paid a price for holding just such views. Would that be a lesson to Diron? The boy stretched his legs in the open road and began to feel as tall as two men. Never. Never would he turn from his convictions. No matter what the consequences he intended to stand his ground. Fear and the shadow of fear both left him promptly. Hearing the dim tock-tock of a horse in the distance, he filled his lungs with air and whistled loudly. A moment later there was an answer. He had overtaken his uncle.

"Did you see it?" he asked when he was near enough to speak.

"I recognized the coachmen of M. de Libertas," the other answered. "Guests, perhaps."

"Guests, at this hour? After all, *Oncle* Philippe, Bréda is not an inn."

They had paused, but now they were walking again, the boy at the left and a step in advance of the horse. The uncle, wearing long gloves and an orange scarf, sat slim and erect on his saddle.

"No, Bréda is certainly not an inn, but I dare say it entertains as many guests as an inn during the course of a year. Shall we turn off the road here?"

"This is as good a place as any. We can tie the horse in the clump there."

On the ground, the older man adjusted his jacket, inspected his well-oiled fowling piece.

"A few more men at Bréda wouldn't hurt," he reflected. "It's overrun with women."

Diron laughed.

"In that I agree heartily."

"And I accept your agreement with salt. You might not be so ready to agree if the women at Bréda were as beautiful, say, as the dark-haired wife of your young friend."

"Mme Sylvestre Viard?"

M. Philippe Desautels clearly had not meant to have that name spoken in just that way. He was in a pleasant mood, and he certainly had not hoped to call up morbid associations.

"I refer to her type," he added quickly. "Not necessarily herself."

"It's hard for me to think of Paulette as a type," Diron said slowly.

"Of course, there aren't many as beautiful as Paulette Viard."

"And few as unreliable," the boy added.

"I once knew one as unreliable," M. Philippe Desautels insisted. "Oh, quite as unreliable. Consequently I've never married."

"And I know one as beautiful," Diron said, repeating his uncle's tone. "Quite as beautiful. Consequently—"

"I know. Consequently you're between two fires."

"It's not as bad as you think. But about that coach. I have a feeling it wasn't bringing guests. No ordinary guests, at least."

"If our curiosity holds up," the uncle smiled, "we'll eventually know all that is to be known about their affairs at Bréda. I suggest we get on with the *houchiba*."

Their object being the hunting of birds, Diron was as willing as the uncle to get on with the business. They separated, walking several yards apart, and became silent as they climbed a dewy slope covered with *tchia-tchia* trees and thickets. Almost immediately a gray paleness came to the eastern sky. The place was alive with twittering. Long dry pods rattled on the lacy trees. Doves drummed sadly. Striding alone now, a stone's throw from his uncle, Diron unhooded his falcon.

But even as the bird sprang from his wrist, he assured himself that his interest in the Bréda household and its guests was not the sort of curiosity his uncle playfully imagined it to be. Perhaps if *Oncle* Philippe had not been away from Paris so long he would not feel so far removed from the terrible business that was still drenching her streets with blood. In that case, perhaps, the arrival of strangers might tend to suggest things to his mind. But then, unfortunately, he'd have to suffer the same restless discomfort that troubled Diron at this very moment.

2

Céleste Juvet, sleeping in a maid-servant's room overlooking the driveway, was awakened by the first blast from the coachman's horn. Her presence did not mean that she was connected with this household. She was there because for days there had been great expectancy at the Bréda plantation; and Céleste, who at fifteen was not to be left at home alone in that wanton paradise called Saint Domingue, had come along when her gnarled old grandmother was summoned to help with the preparations. Now, aroused suddenly, the girl sat erect beneath a canopy of mosquito netting. A hushed silence followed the shrill announcement below, but in the next instant there was a scurrying in the yard and busy activity at the ovens and cook stoves behind the great French mansion. Then something that suggested a gust of wind flung the door open, and two shadowy, near-nude women rushed through the room to get a view of the driveway from Céleste's window. Both of them wore negligible, weblike night dresses and night caps, and neither had bothered to find slippers or dressing gown. Neither paid the slightest attention to the girl in the bed.

Céleste flushed momentarily with embarrassment. Prematurely ripened in a warm tropical climate, she seemed at times a trifle more than her age; but as she watched the women, childishness was written clearly on her face.

"Yes, it's the count," the older one chuckled.

"Curse his old bones."

They had about them, as they snickered together, the air of two who shared a secret that was almost too rich to keep. Yet their merriment was clearly tinged with a certain dark resentment. There was malice in every tone they uttered. The first one bent forward, resting her hand on the window frame.

"The triumphal return," she said sarcastically.

She was a statuesque old person, far above average height, but her teeth were bad, and her large bones showed unpleasantly at the elbows, the wrists, and the ankles.

"I'm dying to see who he's brought this time," the other giggled.

"Mind what you say," the older woman cautioned, pointing her thumb at Céleste's bed without turning. "Big ears, you know."

The second woman, apparently a dozen years younger than her companion, was broad of hip and shoulder and had the muscles of a man. She was perhaps forty, but she had been overfed and already her eyes were becoming beady. It was impossible to distinguish her smile from her frown, her lips making an identical pattern for each. Heeding the other woman's caution, she lowered her voice and commenced to whisper.

Céleste didn't mind. She had heard enough. Mme Juvet had already told her what this perfectly irrelevant old couple was doing at Bréda, and knowing that, Céleste could well understand why they scampered through her room to get a first view of the Count Armand de Sacy on this latest of his very infrequent visits from Paris to his cousin's colonial estate in the new world. Céleste had at first regarded the two females, whose names were Claire and Annette, as simply a part of Bréda like the hundreds of slaves or perhaps her friend Mme Bayou de Libertas, the overseer's wife. But Mme Juvet would have her know they didn't really belong. The slaves had their place. M. Bayou de Libertas was employed. But these two—no, they didn't belong.

The Count de Sacy, it seemed, was a man of means who could afford to indulge a taste for variety and change in his mistresses. He had found it convenient (and stimulating) when his ardor flagged, to personally escort his former favorites across the sea for a vacation at this magnificent island plantation in the northern department of Saint Domingue. He had tried it first with Claire, the statuesque one, some twenty years earlier. Surrounding her with ebony servants, locating her in an elegantly appointed room, just down the hall from the one Céleste now occupied, he had assured her that she would be divinely happy till he returned—at the moment he was compelled to make a most urgent business call at Jamaica—and that they could later return to Paris together. Of course, "circumstances" delayed his return, so he wrote two or three soothing and reassuring letters, then took ship directly to France and forgot about her entirely.

Ten years later, with much the same guile, he brought Annette to Bréda. Much younger than the woman she had supplanted in his affections, plump where the other was gaunt, richly dressed, wildly perfumed, she had at first shown only scorn for the strange, pale Claire. But time put the boot on the other foot. When the count left Bréda and returned to his respectable family in Paris, Claire ridiculed the other woman openly. Mme Juvet recalled that the two fading courtesans had called each other vile names, hurling *bitch* and *strumpet* back and forth till the words lost their mordant and satisfactory flavor; then they had entered upon actual hostilities. Claire spat in Annette's face; the latter retaliated with a smart open palm across the older woman's mouth. But Claire got along tolerably well without the front tooth she lost in the encounter, and Annette eventually forgave the slimy insult. By the time Céleste began noticing things at Bréda in her occasional visits there, the two were as intimate as sisters. Every day they put on brilliant afternoon dresses and lunched together on the leaf-fringed terrace. In the mornings they donned riding habits and rode horses through the banana grove. In the afternoons they drank a bottle of wine each, smoked black cigars, then slept till the supper hour.

Ten years having elapsed since the arrival of Annette, the two had become bitterly philosophical about the whole business. They giggled a great deal as they stood at the window of Céleste's room and tried to speculate whether the newest arrival would be fair like Claire or dark like Annette. Would she be good company after the count had left her, or would there be unpleasantness before she became resigned to her lot?

Céleste, unnoticed in the excitement, slipped out of her bed and took her place at another window as the tumult increased downstairs. A half-dozen blacks were prancing around the gaudy coach, swinging traveling boxes and bags to the ground, hustling them around to a side entrance. The dreamy-eyed Toussaint, down from the driver's seat, stood at rigid attention beside the coach door, his head tied in a madras handkerchief, a wiry pigtail hanging out, while a half-grown black boy held the bits of the team. At length the count emerged, a man as tiny as a woman, his immense curls only partly hidden by his hat, and began scratching himself like an aged dog, now stroking his sea-legs, now digging at his crotch. He spent a moment finding his snuff box and filling his lip. During the pause a spot of light, the first of the morning, revealed a wine-colored coat with wide skirt and white lapels, gray silk stockings and shoes with large paste buckles. Presently he turned and extended a diffident hand to the woman inside the coach.

"There," Claire said. "She's going to get out now."

"He probably won't even bother to lie to her as he did to us," Annette said.

"She's a neat little trick, though. You wouldn't think . . . so soon. Nice walk, too."

"She may have bad breath."

"*He* seems to have piles."

"But he still looks fit—considering everything."

"Fit? Yes, but he's lost a lot."

A moment later both of them left the room, disregarding its young occupant to the last. Céleste did not mind. At no time had she ever been made to feel too utterly at home at Bréda, and never before had she been more pleased to regard herself as a stranger on that rich estate. The aristocracy, such as she had seen of it, did not entice her, even at fifteen.

Whether or not she had anything to fear at the hands of the élite she had never considered. She was pretty, uncommonly pretty, despite an early hint of plumpness, and men already noticed her—a few men, at any rate. If at Bréda she was out of her depth, she did not mind. Mme Bayou de Libertas was a sweet character, plumper than Céleste would ever be, and thoughtfully kind whenever the girl was on the place. Gratitude for this was the only tenderness Céleste felt for the gaudy, feudal Bréda and its patrician elegance.

When the newcomers passed out of sight below, she left the window and commenced dressing.

3

M. Bayou de Libertas whistled in his kettle of warm suds as three grinning blacks in loin cloths doused and splashed and mauled him gleefully in what he regarded as his special-occasion bath. In the deep wooden vessel that served the quality at Bréda for ablutions he squatted wretchedly, his knees propped higher than his chin. A fourth slave stood near by with additional pots of hot and cold water. M. Bayou de Libertas was a fool about bathing and he didn't care who knew it. Why, if it had been left to his own discretion—and if it had not been a shame to take up so much of the slaves' time, considering all the really urgent work—he might have taken a complete scrubbing every day of his life. He just naturally liked it, and he didn't mind how much other people laughed at him.

Today, alas, he was compelled to cut short the pleasant operations. The coachman's horn, blown a moment or two earlier by the reliable Toussaint, had indicated the arrival of the count; and M. de Libertas certainly did not hope to have that high-born gentleman find him wedged in a wooden kettle, covered with snowy suds.

"There now, we'll have to leave off with that," he said loudly, one eye shut fast, the other perfectly round and blinking like a pigeon's eye. "You'll have to get me out of here now."

The African beside the door put down his pots. At a nod from one of the other three he joined them in the complicated chore of extricating M. de Libertas, one leg at a time, from his bath. With feet on the floor, arms resting on the sides of the kettle, aided by the expert and painstaking help of the four blacks, M. de Libertas gradually rose. Through it all he fairly shrieked with pleasure.

But there would be no more whistling at present where he was concerned, he told himself soberly as he gained his feet. As overseer at Bréda and master of that estate in the absence of its true owner, he had much to think about even at this hour of the morning. There were always a few important considerations—apart from the social rites so cherished by the tiny nobleman—when the Count de Noé's cousin and representative returned for one of his rare visits, just as there were when M. de Libertas made his yearly trip to Paris. And this year problems were multiplied due to the bloody business in Paris and all the local complications that grew out of it. The overseer's mind at this hour, however, was chiefly perplexed over a batch of half-sick slaves, drooping, vomiting, and fainting at their work.

The morning clothes of M. de Libertas were neatly arranged on a sofa and chair in his bedroom, a slim black valet waiting ceremoniously beside them. But first there was the somewhat hurried business of shaving. Then when the barber had retired with his razors and mug and towels, the hair-dresser, tall and mincing, a willowy African with a woman's hands and a woman's puckered mouth, came in for his session. An hour had elapsed since M. de Libertas had roused from sleep in his net-canopied bed in the adjoining room, but the overseer was still in his underdrawers and Madame had not yet blinked an eye. Presently, however, the inquisition of hot curling irons, stiff brushes and jerking combs over, the slim, ghost-like Mars stepped from his place between the chair and the sofa and began dusting his master's neck and shoulders with powder, preparatory to slipping a freshly ruffled shirt over the gentleman's head.

"Well, Mars, today's another day. How are you doing?"

M. de Libertas was genuinely kindly, and nowhere did his good humor show itself more than in his dealings with the slaves of Bréda. His smile was always ready, despite a mouth which could show some of the worst dental work in the French colonies.

"I can still get around," the valet said.

"But you're not well."

"I *have* felt better, monsieur."

"Yes, I can see that you have. How about the others?"

"Toussaint looked at us this morning while the boys were hitching the carriage. Felt our foreheads. Said he took it to be some kind of fever."

"How many of you are complaining now?"

"Eight, monsieur. Three down and out—five of us dragging our tails around."

"With the four that died, that makes twelve who've had it."

"Yes, monsieur."

"When you finish with me, Mars, get the other four and bring them with you to the counting house."

"Yes, monsieur."

"I'm going to have the count look you over before breakfast and see what he makes of it."

Supporting himself by placing one hand on the back of a chair, Mars finished his work, brushed a speck of lint from M. de Libertas's shoulder. The gentleman overseer stepped to a mirror and inspected himself. He had a comedian's face, a pock-marked nose, no eyebrows, absurd wrinkles; but he was, as ever, well got up in his clothes. That is, well got up above the waist. M. de Libertas never looked at his own legs. They were travesties on the fashion of knee breeches, and he knew it. They were no more than broomsticks with gross knots for knees. But this circumstance notwithstanding, they were this morning encased in silk. And now, in silver breeches and flowered waistcoat, sky blue coat and dark hat, M. de Libertas felt that he was ready to greet the rising sun as well as a nobleman from Paris.

"Mars—my stick and snuff box."

"H'm."

Sniffing gingerly as he went, M. de Libertas started down the hall. At the head of the stair he discovered that he had developed a little hiccough—curse the luck. After all his care here he was hiccoughing like a bumpkin as he went to meet the cousin and personal representative of the Count de Noé, owner of Bréda. He was startled presently, however, by women's voices and the abrupt opening of a door; suddenly, thanks to Claire and Annette, his hiccough vanished. There in the door frame stood the two half-dressed women, their long stockings pinned to their corsets, their cheeks spotted with round dabs of rouge.

"Was that a neigh I heard?" the overseer asked soberly.

Claire showed her teeth.

"Just a little misguided whinny," she said. "Annette heard your footsteps and thought you were the count."

Two ebony slave women stood behind the pair, clinging to the strings of their half-laced corsets. A third black woman left the room carrying a chamber pot and passed down the hall toward a rear stair. The door closed; the overseer continued down the steps, one hand sliding on the carved rail.

PART TWO
1940s–1960s

<<<<<<<<<<<<<<<<<<<<<<<<<<<

THE THUNDER ROARS

As the Harlem Renaissance sank under the weight of the Great Depression, the Great Migration was still underway. With the approach of World War II, the revived economy again demanded manpower to push forward the war effort, and Harlem continued to be a primary destination for blacks from the South and the Caribbean.

The NAACP now had offices and a large membership in the South. Meanwhile, the president of the Brotherhood of Sleeping Car Porters, A. Philip Randolph, called for a 1943 March on Washington, the threat of which spurred the demise of prohibitions that excluded blacks from defense and military labor jobs. As Harlem's attention turned to the Civil Rights Movement, the spirit of the Harlem Renaissance thrived in writers like Richard Wright, James Baldwin (himself a native Harlemite), and Ann Petry. Their works zeroed in on the social and economic problems many urban black families faced in light of the informal segregation of the North.

As the Civil Rights Movement burrowed further into the South during the post-World War II years, Harlem managed to maintain its literary legacy with the formation of the Harlem Writers Guild in 1950. Founding members John Henrik Clarke, Rosa Guy, John O. Killens, and Walter Christmas initially met to discuss not only their writing, but the heavy political atmosphere that would only get thicker with the arrival of Malcolm X at Harlem's Mosque No. 7 and the meteoric rise of Dr. Martin Luther King, Jr., during the start of the 1950s. The Guild soon outgrew its small gathering spot as it attracted a wider membership, including Caribbean author Paule Marshall and actor and playwright Ossie Davis.

The radical dawn of the 1960s once again shifted the creative focus of writers who lived in Harlem or employed the neighborhood as muse. In 1965, the nascent Black Arts Movement (BAM)—considered the creative arm of the militant Black Power Movement that spawned organizations like the Black Panther Party—lead by playwright, poet, and publisher Leroi Jones (later known as Amiri Baraka), began to take root in Harlem, Chicago, Detroit, and San Francisco. While the political allegiances of those who followed BAM varied, its belief that black art should be in service to the self-determination and empowerment of blacks brought some overlapping membership with the Harlem Writers Guild. It was through efforts initiated by BAM and its affiliate organizations that several universities across the country instituted black studies departments, including Harlem's own City College of New York.

MAMMY (1940)

DOROTHY WEST

Born in Boston in 1908, the daughter of an emancipated slave, Dorothy West's family moved to Harlem when she was a teenager. In 1926, she joined a group of writers known as the New Negro Movement, which became one of the signature organizations of the Harlem Renaissance. Though she was the youngest member of the group when she joined, her first story, "The Typewriter," won second place in a national contest sponsored by *Opportunity* magazine. A film project sponsored by the Communist Party took her to Russia in 1932. When she returned a year later, the Great Depression's impact had forced many artists to leave Harlem. Yet West stayed, and founded a journal called *Challenge.* Then, in 1937, she and Richard Wright founded *New Challenge.* Like the earlier journal, it was short-lived, but became the launching platform for many writers. Her later work as a social worker brought her close to much of the pain in Harlem life. This was contrasted by her personal life, much of which she spent in Oak Bluffs, a section of Martha's Vineyard. The contrasts that intrigued her in African-American life are to be found in *The Richer, The Poorer: Stories, Sketches and Reminiscences.* "Mammy" is a short story from that collection.

The young Negro welfare investigator, carrying her briefcase, entered the ornate foyer of the Central Park West apartment house. She was making a collateral call. Earlier in the day she had visited an aging colored woman in a rented room in Harlem. Investigation had proved that the woman was not quite old enough for Old Age Assistance, and yet no longer young enough to be classified as employable. Nothing, therefore, stood in the way of her eligibility for relief. Hers was a clear case of need. This collateral call on her former employer was merely routine.

The investigator walked toward the elevator, close on the heels of a well-dressed woman with a dog. She felt shy. Most of her collaterals were to housewives in the Bronx or supervisors of maintenance workers in office buildings. Such calls were never embarrassing. A moment ago as she neared the doorway, the doorman had regarded her intently.

The service entrance was plainly to her left, and she was walking past it. He had been on the point of approaching when a tenant emerged and dispatched him for a taxi. He had stood for a moment torn between his immediate duty and his sense of outrage. Then he had gone away dolefully, blowing his whistle.

The woman with the dog reached the elevator just as the doors slid open. The dog bounded in, and the elevator boy bent and roughhoused with him. The boy's agreeable face was black, and the investigator felt a flood of relief.

The woman entered the elevator and smilingly faced front. Instantly the smile left her face, and her eyes hardened. The boy straightened, faced front, too, and gaped in surprise. Quickly he glanced at the set face of his passenger.

"Service entrance's outside," he said sullenly.

The investigator said steadily, "I am not employed here. I am here to see Mrs. Coleman on business."

"If you're here on an errand or somethin' like that," he argued doggedly, "you still got to use the service entrance."

She stared at him with open hate, despising him for humiliating her before and because of a woman of an alien race.

"I am here as a representative of the Department of Welfare. If you refuse me the use of this elevator, my office will take it up with the management."

She did not know if this was true, but the elevator boy would not know either.

"Get in, then," he said rudely, and rolled his eyes at his white passenger as if to convey his regret at the discomfort he was causing her.

The doors shut and the three shot upward, without speaking to or looking at each other. The woman with the dog, in a far corner, very pointedly held her small harmless animal on a tight leash.

The car stopped at the fourth floor, and the doors slid open. No one moved. There was a ten-second wait.

"You getting out or not?" the boy asked savagely.

There was no need to ask whom he was addressing.

"Is this my floor?" asked the investigator.

His sarcasm rippled. "You want Mrs. Coleman, don't you?"

"Which is her apartment?" she asked thickly.

"Ten-A. You're holding up my passenger."

When the door closed, she leaned against it, feeling sick, and trying to control her trembling. She was young and vulnerable. Her contact with Negroes was confined to frightened relief folks who did everything possible to stay in her good graces, and the members of her own set, among whom she was a favorite because of her two degrees and her civil service appointment. She had almost never run into Negroes who did not treat her with respect.

In a moment or two she walked down the hall to Ten-A. She rang, and after a little wait a handsome middle-aged woman opened the door.

"How do you do?" the woman said in a soft drawl. She smiled. "You're from the relief office, aren't you? Do come in."

"Thank you," said the investigator, smiling, too, relievedly.

"Right this way," said Mrs. Coleman, leading the way into a charming living room. She indicated an upholstered chair. "Please sit down."

The investigator, who never sat in overstuffed chairs in the homes of her relief clients, plumped down and smiled again at Mrs. Coleman. Such a pleasant woman, such a pleasant room. It was going to be a quick and easy interview. She let her briefcase slide to the floor beside her.

Mrs. Coleman sat down in a straight chair and looked searchingly at the investigator. Then she said somewhat breathlessly, "You gave me to understand that Mammy has applied for relief."

The odious title sent a little flicker of dislike across the investigator's face. She answered stiffly, "I had just left Mrs. Mason when I telephoned you for this appointment."

Mrs. Coleman smiled disarmingly, though she colored a little.

"She has been with us ever since I can remember. I call her Mammy, and so does my daughter."

"That's a sort of nurse, isn't it?" the investigator asked coldly. "I had thought Mrs. Mason was a general maid."

"Is that what she said?"

"Why, I understood she was discharged because she was no longer physically able to perform her duties."

"She wasn't discharged."

The investigator looked dismayed. She had not anticipated complications. She felt for her briefcase.

"I'm very confused, Mrs. Coleman. Will you tell me just exactly what happened, then? I had no idea Mrs. Mason was—was misstating the situation." She opened her briefcase.

Mrs. Coleman eyed her severely. "There's nothing to write down. Do you have to write down things? It makes me feel as if I were being investigated."

"I'm sorry," said the investigator quickly, snapping shut her briefcase. "If it would be distasteful . . . I apologize again. Please go on."

"Well, there's little to tell. It all happened so quickly. My daughter was ill. My nerves were on edge. I may have said something that upset Mammy. One night she was here. The next morning she wasn't. I've been worried sick about her."

"Did you report her disappearance?"

"Her clothes were gone, too. It didn't seem a matter for the police. It was obvious that she had left of her own accord. Believe me, young woman, I was very relieved when you telephoned me." Her voice shook a little.

"I'm glad I can assure you that Mrs. Mason appears quite well. She only said she worked for you. She didn't mention your daughter. I hope she has recovered."

"My daughter is married," Mrs. Coleman said slowly. "She had a child. It was stillborn. We have not seen Mammy since. For months she had looked forward to nursing it."

"I'm sure it was a sad loss to all of you," the investigator said gently. "And old Mrs. Mason, perhaps she felt you had no further use for her. It may have unsettled her mind. Temporarily," she added hastily. "She seems quite sane."

"Of course, she is," said Mrs. Coleman with a touch of bitterness. "She's just old and contrary. She knew we would worry about her. She did it deliberately."

This was not in the investigator's province. She cleared her throat delicately.

"Would you take her back, Mrs. Coleman?"

"I want her back," cried Mrs. Coleman. "She has no one but us. She is just like one of the family."

"You're very kind," the investigator murmured. "Most people feel no responsibility for their aging servants."

"You do not know how dear a mammy is to a Southerner. I nursed at Mammy's breast. I cannot remember a day in my life without her."

The investigator reached for her briefcase and rose.

"Then it is settled that she may return?"

A few hours ago there had been no doubt in her mind of old Mrs. Mason's eligibility for relief. With this surprising turn there was nothing to do but reject the case for inadequate proof of need. It was always a feather in a field worker's cap to reject a case that had been accepted for home investigation by a higher-paid office worker.

Mrs. Coleman looked at the investigator almost beseechingly.

"My child, I cannot tell you how much I will be in your debt if you can persuade Mammy to return. Can't you refuse to give her relief? She really is in need of nothing as long as I am living. Poor thing, what has she been doing for money? How has she been eating? In what sort of place is she staying?"

"She's very comfortable, really. She had three dollars when she came uptown to Harlem. She rented a room, explained her circumstances to her landlady, and is getting her meals there. I know that landlady. She has other roomers who are on relief. She trusts them until they get their relief checks. They never cheat her."

"Oh, thank God! I must give you something to give to that woman. How good Negroes are. I am so glad it was you who came. You are so sympathetic. I could not have talked so freely to a white investigator. She would not have understood."

The investigator's smile was wintry. She resented this well-meant restatement of the trusted position of the good darky.

She said civilly, however, "I'm going back to Mrs. Mason's as soon as I leave here. I hope I can persuade her to return to you tonight."

"Thank you! Mammy was happy here, believe me. She had nothing to do but a little dusting. We are a small family, myself, my daughter, and her husband. I have a girl who comes every day to do the hard work. She preferred to sleep in, but I wanted Mammy to have the maid's room. It's a lovely room with a private bath. It's next to the kitchen, which is nice for Mammy. Old people potter about so. I've lost girl after girl who felt she was meddlesome. But I've always thought of Mammy's comfort first."

"I'm sure you have," said the investigator politely, wanting to end the interview. She made a move toward departure. "Thank you again for being so cooperative."

Mrs. Coleman rose and crossed to the doorway.

"I must get my purse. Will you wait a moment?"

Shortly she reappeared. She opened her purse.

"It's been ten days. Please give that woman this twenty dollars. No, it isn't too much. And here is a dollar for Mammy's cab fare. Please put her in the cab yourself."

"I'll do what I can." The investigator smiled candidly. "It must be nearly four, and my working day ends at five."

"Yes, of course," Mrs. Coleman said distractedly. "And now I just want you to peep in at my daughter. Mammy will want to know how she is. She's far from well, poor lambie."

The investigator followed Mrs. Coleman down the hall. At an open door they paused. A pale young girl lay on the edge of a big tossed bed. One hand was in her tangled hair, the other clutched an empty bassinet. The wheels rolled down and back, down and back. The girl glanced briefly and without interest at her mother and the investigator, then turned her face away.

"It tears my heart," Mrs. Coleman whispered in a choked voice. "Her baby, and then Mammy. She has lost all desire to live. But she is young and she will have other children. If she would only let me take away that bassinet! I am not the nurse that Mammy is. You can see how much Mammy is needed here."

They turned away and walked in silence to the outer door. The investigator was genuinely touched, and eager to be off on her errand of mercy.

Mrs. Coleman opened the door, and for a moment seemed at a loss as to how to say good-bye. Then she said quickly, "Thank you for coming," and shut the door.

The investigator stood in indecision at the elevator, half persuaded to walk down three flights of stairs. But this she felt was turning tail, and pressed the elevator button.

The doors opened. The boy looked at her sheepishly. He swallowed and said ingratiatingly, "Step in, miss. Find your party all right?"

She faced front, staring stonily ahead of her, and felt herself trembling with indignation at this new insolence.

He went on whiningly, "That woman was in my car is mean as hell. I was just puttin' on to please her. She hates niggers 'cept when they're bowin' and scrapin'. She was the one had the old doorman fired. You see for yourself they got a white one now. With white folks needin' jobs, us niggers got to eat dirt to hang on."

The investigator's face was expressionless except for a barely perceptible wincing at his careless use of a hated word.

He pleaded, "You're colored like me. You ought to understand. I was only doing my job. I got to eat same as white folks, same as you."

They rode the rest of the way in a silence interrupted only by his heavy sighs. When they reached the ground floor, and the doors slid open, he said sorrowfully, "Good-bye, miss."

She walked down the hall and out into the street, past the glowering doorman, with her face stern, and her stomach slightly sick.

The investigator rode uptown on a northbound bus. At One Hundred and Eighteenth Street she alighted and walked east. Presently she entered a well-kept apartment house. The elevator operator deferentially greeted her and whisked her upward.

She rang the bell of number fifty-four, and visited briefly with the landlady, who was quite overcome by the unexpected payment of twenty dollars. When she could escape her profuse thanks, the investigator went to knock at Mrs. Mason's door.

"Come in," called Mrs. Mason. The investigator entered the small, square room. "Oh, it's you, dear," said Mrs. Mason, her lined brown face lighting up.

She was sitting by the window in a wide rocker. In her black, with a clean white apron tied about her waist, and a white bandana bound around her head, she looked ageless and full of remembering.

Mrs. Mason grasped her rocker by the arms and twisted around until she faced the investigator.

She explained shyly, "I just sit here for hours lookin' out at the people. I ain' seen so many colored folks at one time since I left down home. Sit down, child, on the side of the bed. Hit's softer than that straight chair yonder."

The investigator sat down on the straight chair, not because the bedspread was not scrupulously clean, but because what she had come to say needed stiff decorum.

"I'm all right here, Mrs. Mason. I won't be long."

"I was hopin' you could set awhile. My landlady's good, but she's got this big flat. Don't give her time for much settin'.'"

The investigator, seeing an opening, nodded understandingly.

"Yes, it must be pretty lonely for you here after being so long an intimate part of the Coleman family."

The old woman's face darkened. "Shut back in that bedroom behin' the kitchen? This here's what I like. My own kind and color. I'm too old a dog to be learnin' new tricks."

"Your duties with Mrs. Coleman were very slight. I know you are getting on in years, but you are not too feeble for light employment. You were not entirely truthful with me. I was led to believe you did all the housework."

The old woman looked furtively at the investigator. "How come you know diff'rent now?"

"I've just left Mrs. Coleman's."

Bafflement veiled the old woman's eyes. "You didn't believe what all I tol' you?"

"We always visit former employers. It's part of our job, Mrs. Mason. Sometimes an employer will rehire our applicants. Mrs. Coleman is good enough to want you back. Isn't that preferable to being a public charge?"

"I ain't-a goin' back," said the old woman vehemently.

The investigator was very exasperated. "Why, Mrs. Mason?" she asked gently.

"That's an ungodly woman," the old lady snapped. "And I'm God-fearin'. Tain't no room in one house for God and the devil. I'm too near the grave to be servin' two masters."

To the young investigator this was evasion by superstitious mutterings.

"You don't make yourself very clear, Mrs. Mason. Surely Mrs. Coleman didn't interfere with your religious convictions. You left her home the night after her daughter's child was born dead. Until then, apparently you had no religious scruples."

The old woman looked at the investigator wearily. Then her head sank forward on her breast.

"That child warn't born dead."

The investigator said impatiently, "But surely the hospital—?"

"T'warn't born in no hospital."

"But the doctor—?"

"Little sly man. Looked like he'd cut his own throat for a dollar."

"Was the child deformed?" the investigator asked helplessly.

"Hit was a beautiful baby," said the old woman bitterly.

"Why, no one would destroy a healthy child," the investigator cried indignantly. "Mrs. Coleman hopes her daughter will have more children." She paused, then asked anxiously, "Her daughter is really married, isn't she? I mean, the baby wasn't . . . illegitimate?"

"It's ma and pa were married down home. A church weddin'. They went to school together. They was all right till they come up North. Then *she* started workin' on 'em. Old ways wasn't good enough for her."

The investigator looked at her watch. It was nearly five. This last speech had been rambling gossip. Here was an old woman clearly disoriented in her Northern transplanting. Her position as mammy made her part of the family. Evidently she felt that gave her a matriarchal right to arbitrate its destinies. Her small grievances against Mrs. Coleman had magnified themselves in her mind until she could make this illogical accusation of infanticide as compensation for her homesickness for the folkways of the South. Her move to Harlem bore this out. To explain her reason for establishing a separate residence, she had told a fantastic story that could not be checked, and would not be recorded, unless the welfare office was prepared to face a libel suit.

"Mrs. Mason," said the investigator, "please listen carefully. Mrs. Coleman has told me that you are not only wanted, but very much needed in her home. There you will be given food and shelter in return for small services. Please understand that I sympathize with your imaginings, but you cannot remain here without public assistance, and I cannot recommend to my superiors that public assistance be given you."

The old woman, who had listened worriedly, now said blankly, "You mean I ain't-a gonna get it?"

"No, Mrs. Mason, I'm sorry. And now it's ten to five. I'll be glad to help you pack your things, and put you in a taxi."

The old woman looked helplessly around the room as if seeking a hiding place. Then she looked back at the investigator, her mouth trembling.

"You're my own people, child. Can' you fix up a story for them white folks at the relief, so's I could get to stay here where it's nice?"

"That would be collusion, Mrs. Mason. And that would cost me my job."

The investigator rose. She was going to pack the old woman's things herself. She was heartily sick of her contrariness, and determined to see her settled once and for all.

"Now where is your bag?" she asked with forced cheerfulness. "First I'll empty these bureau drawers." She began to do so, laying things neatly on the bed. "Mrs. Coleman's daughter will be so glad to see you. She's very ill, and needs your nursing."

The old woman showed no interest. Her head had sunk forward on her breast again. She said listlessly, "Let her ma finish what she started. I won't have no time for nursin'. I'll be down on my knees rasslin' with the devil, I done tol' you the devil's done eased out God in that house."

The investigator nodded indulgently, and picked up a framed photograph that was lying face down in the drawer. She turned it over and involuntarily smiled at the smiling child in old-fashioned dress.

"This little girl," she said, "it's Mrs. Coleman, isn't it?"

The old woman did not look up. Her voice was still listless.

"That was my daughter."

The investigator dropped the photograph on the bed as if it were a hot coal. Blindly she went back to the bureau, gathered up the rest of the things, and dumped them over the photograph.

She was a young investigator, and it was two minutes to five. Her job was to give or withhold relief. That was all.

"Mrs. Mason," she said, "please, please understand. This is my job."

The old woman gave no sign of having heard.

THE STREET (1946)

ANN PETRY

Born in Old Saybrook, Connecticut, to middle-class parents, Petry lived comfortably in a predominantly white community for most of her early years. But her parents' status shielded her from racial realities only until she was about seven years old, the age at which she was surprised by racist taunts from white children that were hurled at her while she walked to Sunday school. Her parents did their best to heal those wounds and protect her from more of the same by instilling pride in her about their free black New England heritage, which dated back four generations. They also gave her the best education that they could afford. This culminated in her earning a Ph.D. from the Connecticut College of Pharmacy in 1931. She found her way to professional writing by way of marrying mystery writer George Petry in 1938. She published her first story in the *Amsterdam News* in 1939 under the name Arnold Petry and her first novel, *The Street,* was published seven years later. John Henrik Clarke said that it showed the most profound understanding of Harlem life as it really was in the time that she lived, more so than in any other book that he had ever read.

CHAPTER I

There was a cold November wind blowing through 116th Street. It rattled the tops of garbage cans, sucked window shades out through the top of opened windows and set them flapping back against the windows; and it drove most of the people off the street in the block between Seventh and Eighth Avenues except for a few hurried pedestrians who bent double in an effort to offer the least possible exposed surface to its violent assault.

It found every scrap of paper along the street—theater throwaways, announcements of dances and lodge meetings, the heavy waxed paper that loaves of bread had been wrapped in, the thinner waxed paper that had enclosed sandwiches, old envelopes, newspapers. Fingering its way along the curb, the wind set the bits of paper to dancing high in the air, so that a barrage of paper swirled into the faces of the people on the street. It even took time to rush into doorways and areaways and find chicken bones and pork-chop bones and pushed them along the curb.

It did everything it could to discourage the people walking along the street. It found all the dirt and dust and grime on the sidewalk and lifted it up so that the dirt got into their noses, making it difficult to breathe; the dust got into their eyes and blinded them; and the grit stung their skins. It wrapped newspaper around their feet entangling them until the people cursed deep in their throats, stamped their feet, kicked at the paper. The wind blew it back again and again until they were forced to stoop and dislodge the paper with their hands. And then the wind grabbed their hats, pried their scarves from around their necks, stuck its fingers inside their coat collars, blew their coats away from their bodies.

The wind lifted Lutie Johnson's hair away from the back of her neck so that she felt suddenly naked and bald, for her hair had been resting softly and warmly against her skin. She shivered as the cold fingers of the wind touched the back of her neck, explored the sides of her head. It even blew her eyelashes away from her eyes so that her eyeballs were bathed in a rush of coldness and she had to blink in order to read the words on the sign swaying back and forth over her head.

Each time she thought she had the sign in focus, the wind pushed it away from her so that she wasn't certain whether it said three rooms or two rooms. If it was three, why, she would go in and ask to see it, but if it said two—why, there wasn't any point. Even with the wind twisting the sign away from her, she could see that it had been there for a long time because its original coat of white paint was streaked with rust where years of rain and snow had finally eaten the paint off down to the metal and the metal had slowly rusted, making a dark red stain like blood.

It was three rooms. The wind held it still for an instant in front of her and then swooped it away until it was standing at an impossible angle on the rod that suspended it from the building. She read it rapidly. Three rooms, steam heat, parquet floors, respectable tenants. Reasonable.

She looked at the outside of the building. Parquet floors here meant that the wood was so old and so discolored no amount of varnish or shellac would conceal the scars and the old scraped places, the years of dragging furniture across the floors, the hammer blows of time and children and drunks and dirty, slovenly women. Steam heat meant a rattling, clanging noise in radiators early in the morning and then a hissing that went on all day.

Respectable tenants in these houses where colored people were allowed to live included anyone who could pay the rent, so some of them would be drunk and loud-mouthed and quarrelsome; given to fits of depression when they would curse and cry violently, given to fits of equally violent elation. And, she thought, because the walls would be flimsy, why, the good people, the bad people, the children, the dogs, and the godawful smells would all be wrapped up together in one big package— the package that was called respectable tenants.

The wind pried at the red skullcap on her head, and as though angered because it couldn't tear it loose from its firm anchorage of bobby pins, the wind blew a great cloud of dust and ashes and bits of paper into her face, her eyes, her nose. It smacked against her ears as though it were giving her a final, exasperated blow as proof of its displeasure in not being able to make her move on.

Lutie braced her body against the wind's attack determined to finish thinking about the apartment before she went in to look at it. Reasonable—now that could mean almost anything. On Eighth Avenue it meant tenements—ghastly places not fit for humans. On St. Nicholas Avenue it meant high rents for small apartments; and on Seventh Avenue it meant great big apartments where you had to take in roomers in order to pay the rent. On this street it could mean almost anything.

She turned and faced the wind in order to estimate the street. The buildings were old with small slit-like windows, which meant the rooms were small and dark. In a street running in this direction there wouldn't be any sunlight in the apartments. Not ever. It would be hot as hell in summer and cold in winter. 'Reasonable' here in this dark, crowded street ought to be about twenty-eight dollars, provided it was on a top floor.

The hallways here would be dark and narrow. Then she shrugged her shoulders, for getting an apartment where she and Bub would be alone was more important than dark hallways. The thing that really mattered was getting away from Pop and his raddled women, and anything was better than that. Dark hallways, dirty stairs, even roaches on the walls. Anything. Anything. Anything.

Anything? Well, almost anything. So she turned toward the entrance of the building and as she turned, she heard someone clear his or her throat. It was so distinct—done as it was on two notes, the first one high and then the grunting expiration of breath on a lower note—that it came to her ears quite clearly under the sound of the wind rattling the garbage cans and slapping at the curtains. It was as though someone had said 'hello,' and she looked up at the window over her head.

There was a faint light somewhere in the room she was looking into and the enormous bulk of a woman was silhouetted against the light. She half-closed her eyes in order to see better. The woman was very black, she had a bandanna knotted tightly around her head, and Lutie saw, with some surprise, that the window was open. She began to wonder how the woman could sit by an open window on a cold, windy night like this one. And she didn't have on a coat, but a kind of loose-looking cotton dress—or at least it must be cotton, she thought, for it had a clumsy look—bulky and wrinkled.

'Nice little place, dearie. Just ring the Super's bell and he'll show it to you.'

The woman's voice was rich. Pleasant. Yet the longer Lutie looked at her, the less she liked her. It wasn't that the woman had been sitting there all along staring at her, reading her thoughts, pushing her way into her very mind, for that was merely annoying. But it was understandable. She probably didn't have anything else to do; perhaps she was sick and the only pleasure she got out of life was in watching what went on in the street outside her window. It wasn't that. It was the woman's eyes. They were as still and as malignant as the eyes of a snake. She could see them quite plainly—flat eyes that stared at her—wandering over her body, inspecting and appraising her from head to foot.

'Just ring the Super's bell, dearie,' the woman repeated.

Lutie turned toward the entrance of the building without answering, thinking about the woman's eyes. She pushed the door open and walked inside and stood there nodding her head. The hall was dark. The low-wattage bulb in the ceiling shed just enough light so that you wouldn't actually fall over—well, a piano that someone had carelessly left at the foot of the stairs; so that you could see the outlines of—oh, possibly an elephant if it were dragged in from the street by some enterprising tenant.

However, if you dropped a penny, she thought, you'd have to get down on your hands and knees and scrabble around on the cracked tile floor before you could ever hope to find it. And she was wrong about being able to see an elephant or a piano because the hallway really wasn't wide enough to admit either one. The stairs went up steeply—dark high narrow steps. She stared at them fascinated. Going up stairs like those you ought to find a newer and more intricate—a much-involved and perfected kind of hell at the top—the very top.

She leaned over to look at the names on the mail boxes. Henry Lincoln Johnson lived here, too, just as he did in all the other houses she'd looked at. Either he or his blood brother. The Johnsons and the Jacksons were mighty prolific. Then she grinned, thinking who am I to talk, for I, too, belong to that great tribe, that mighty mighty tribe of Johnsons. The bells revealed that the Johnsons had roomers—Smith, Roach, Anderson—holy smoke! even Rosenberg. Most of the names were inked in over the mail boxes in scrawling handwriting—the letters were big and bold on some of them. Others were written in pencil; some printed in uneven scraggling letters where names had been scratched out and other names substituted.

There were only two apartments on the first floor. And if the Super didn't live in the basement, why, he would live on the first floor. There it was printed over One A. One A must be the darkest apartment, the smallest, most unrentable apartment, and the landlord would feel mighty proud that he'd given the Super a first-floor apartment.

She stood there thinking that it was really a pity they couldn't somehow manage to rent the halls, too. Single beds. No. Old army cots would do. It would bring in so much more money. If she were a landlord, she'd rent out the hallways. It would make it so much more entertaining for the tenants. Mr. Jones and wife could have cots number one and two; Jackson and girl friend could occupy number three. And Rinaldi, who drove a cab nights, could sublet the one occupied by Jackson and girl friend.

She would fill up all the cots—row after row of them. And when the tenants who had apartments came in late at night, they would have the added pleasure of checking up on the occupants. Jackson not home yet but girl friend lying in the cot alone—all curled up. A second look, because the lack of light wouldn't show all the details, would reveal—ye gods, why, what's Rinaldi doing home at night! Doggone if he ain't tucked up cozily in Jackson's cot with Jackson's girl friend. No wonder she looked contented. And the tenants who had apartments would sit on the stairs just as though the hall were a theater and the performance about to start—they'd sit there waiting until Jackson came home to see what he'd do when he found Rinaldi tucked into his cot with his girl friend. Rinaldi might explain that he thought the cot was his for sleeping and if the cot had blankets on it did not he, too, sleep under blankets; and if the cot had girl friend on it, why should not he, too, sleep with girl friend?

Instead of laughing, she found herself sighing. Then it occurred to her that if there were only two apartments on the first floor and the Super occupied one of them, then the occupant of the other apartment would be the lady with the snake's eyes. She looked at the names on the mail boxes. Yes. A Mrs. Hedges lived in One B. The name was printed on the card—a very professional-looking card. Obviously an extraordinary woman with her bandanna on her head and her sweet, sweet voice. Perhaps she was a snake charmer and she sat in her window in order to charm away at the snakes, the wolves, the foxes, the bears that prowled and loped and crawled on their bellies through the jungle of 116th Street.

Lutie reached out and rang the Super's bell. It made a shrill sound that echoed and re-echoed inside the apartment and came back out into the hall. Immediately a dog started a furious barking that came closer and closer as he ran toward the door of the apartment. Then the weight of his body landed against the door and she drew back as he threw himself against the door. Again and again until the door began to shiver from the impact of his weight. There was the horrid sound of his nose snuffing up air, trying to get her scent. And then his weight hurled against the door again. She retreated toward the street door, pausing there with her hand on the knob. Then she heard heavy footsteps, the sound of a man's voice threatening the dog, and she walked back toward the apartment.

She knew instantly by his faded blue overalls that the man who opened the door was the Super. The hot fetid air from the apartment in back of him came out into the hall. She could hear the faint sound of steam hissing in the radiators. Then the dog tried to plunge past the man and the man kicked the dog back into the apartment. Kicked him in the side until the dog cringed away from him with its tail between its legs.

She heard the dog whine deep in its throat and then the murmur of a woman's voice—a whispering voice talking to the dog.

'I came to see about the apartment—the three-room apartment that's vacant,' she said.

'It's on the top floor. You wanta look at it?'

The light in the hall was dim. Dim like that light in Mrs. Hedges' apartment. She pulled her coat around her a little tighter. It's this bad light, she thought. Somehow the man's eyes were worse than the eyes of the woman sitting in the window. And she told herself that it was because she was so tired; that was the reason she was seeing things, building up pretty pictures in people's eyes.

He was a tall, gaunt man and he towered in the doorway, looking at her. It isn't the bad light, she thought. It isn't my imagination. For after his first quick furtive glance, his eyes had filled with a hunger so urgent that she was instantly afraid of him and afraid to show her fear.

But the apartment—did she want the apartment? Not in this house where he was super; not in this house where Mrs. Hedges lived. No. She didn't want to see the apartment—the dark, dirty three rooms called an apartment. Then she thought of where she lived now. Those seven rooms where Pop lived with Lil, his girl friend. A place filled with roomers. A place spilling over with Lil.

There seemed to be no part of it that wasn't full of Lil. She was always swallowing coffee in the kitchen; trailing through all seven rooms in housecoats that didn't quite meet across her lush, loose bosom; drinking beer in tall glasses and leaving the glasses in the kitchen sink so the foam dried in a crust around the rim—the dark red of her lipstick like an accent mark on the crust; lounging on the wide bed she shared with Pop and only God knows who else; drinking gin with the roomers until late at night.

And what was far more terrifying giving Bub a drink on the sly; getting Bub to light her cigarettes for her. Bub at eight with smoke curling out of his mouth.

Only last night Lutie slapped him so hard that Lil cringed away from her dismayed; her housecoat slipping even farther away from the fat curve of her breasts. 'Jesus!' she said. 'That's enough to make him deaf. What's the matter with you?'

But did she want to look at the apartment? Night after night she'd come home from work and gone out right after supper to peer up at the signs in front of the apartment houses in the neighborhood, looking for a place just big enough for her and Bub. A place where the rent was low enough so that she wouldn't come home from work some night to find a long sheet of white paper stuck under the door: 'These premises must be vacated by—' better known as an eviction notice. Get out in five days or be tossed out. Stand by and watch your furniture pile up on the side-walk. If you could call those broken beds, worn-out springs, old chairs with the stuffing crawling out from under, chipped porcelain-topped kitchen table, flimsy kitchen chairs with broken rungs—if you could call those things furniture. That was an important point—now could you call fire-cracked china from the five-and-dime, and red-handled knives and forks and spoons that were bent and coming apart, could you really call those things furniture?

'Yes,' she said firmly. 'I want to look at the apartment.'

'I'll get a flashlight,' he said and went back into his apartment, clos-ing the door behind him so that it made a soft, sucking sound. He said something, but she couldn't hear what it was. The whispering voice in-side the apartment stopped and the dog was suddenly quiet.

Then he was back at the door, closing it behind him so it made the same soft, sucking sound. He had a long black flashlight in his hand. And she went up the stairs ahead of him thinking that the rod of its length was almost as black as his hands. The flashlight was a shiny black—smooth and gleaming faintly as the light lay along its length. Whereas the hand that held it was flesh—dull, scarred, worn flesh—no smooth-ness there. The knuckles were knobs that stood out under the skin, pulled out from hauling ashes, shoveling coal.

But not apparently from using a mop or a broom, for, as she went up and up the steep flight of stairs, she saw that they were filthy, with wastepaper, cigarette butts, the discarded wrappings from packages of snuff, pink ticket stubs from the movie houses. On the landings there were empty gin and whiskey bottles.

She stopped looking at the stairs, stopped peering into the corners of the long hallways, for it was cold, and she began walking faster try-ing to keep warm. As they completed a flight of stairs and turned to walk up another hall, and then started climbing another flight of stairs, she was aware that the cold increased. The farther up they went, the colder it got. And in summer she supposed it would get hotter and hotter as you went up until when you reached the top floor your breath would be cut off completely.

The halls were so narrow that she could reach out and touch them on either side without having to stretch her arms any distance. When they reached the fourth floor, she thought, instead of her reaching out for the walls, the walls were reaching out for her—bending and swaying toward her in an effort to envelop her. The Super's footsteps behind her were slow, even, steady. She walked a little faster and apparently without hurrying, without even increasing his pace, he was exactly the same distance behind her. In fact his heavy footsteps were a little nearer than before.

She began to wonder how it was that she had gone up the stairs first, why was she leading the way? It was all wrong. He was the one who knew the place, the one who lived here. He should have gone up first. How had he got her to go up the stairs in front of him? She wanted to turn around and see the expression on his face, but she knew if she turned on the stairs like this, her face would be on a level with his; and she wouldn't want to be that close to him.

She didn't need to turn around, anyway; he was staring at her back, her legs, her thighs. She could feel his eyes traveling over her—estimating her, summing her up, wondering about her. As she climbed up the last flight of stairs, she was aware that the skin on her back was crawling with fear. Fear of what? she asked herself. Fear of him, fear of the dark, of the smells in the halls, the high steep stairs, of yourself? She didn't know, and even as she admitted that she didn't know, she felt sweat start pouring from her armpits, dampening her forehead, breaking out in beads on her nose.

The apartment was in the back of the house. The Super fished another flashlight from his pocket which he handed to her before he bent over to unlock the door very quietly. And she thought, everything he does, he does quietly.

She played the beam of the flashlight on the walls. The rooms were small. There was no window in the bedroom. At least she supposed it was the bedroom. She walked over to look at it, and then went inside for a better look. There wasn't a window—just an air shaft and a narrow one at that. She looked around the room, thinking that by the time there was a bed and a chest of drawers in it there'd be barely space enough to walk around in. At that she'd probably bump her knees every time she went past the corner of the bed. She tried to visualize how the room would look and began to wonder why she had already decided to take this room for herself.

It might be better to give it to Bub, let him have a real bedroom to himself for once. No, that wouldn't do. He would swelter in this room in summer. It would be better to have him sleep on the couch in the living room, at least he'd get some air, for there was a window out there, though it wasn't a very big one. She looked out into the living room, trying again to see the window, to see just how much air would come through, how much light there would be for Bub to study by when he came home from school, to determine, too, the amount of air that would reach into the room at night when the window was open, and he was sleeping curled up on the studio couch.

The Super was standing in the middle of the living room. Waiting for her. It wasn't anything that she had to wonder about or figure out. It wasn't by any stretch of the imagination something she had conjured up out of thin air. It was a simple fact. He was waiting for her. She knew it just as she knew she was standing there in that small room. He was holding his flashlight so the beam fell down at his feet. It turned him into a figure of never-ending tallness. And his silent waiting and his appearance of incredible height appalled her.

With the light at his feet like that, he looked as though his head must end somewhere in the ceiling. He simply went up and up into darkness. And he radiated such desire for her that she could feel it. She told herself she was a fool, an idiot, drunk on fear, on fatigue and gnawing worry. Even while she thought it, the hot, choking awfulness of his desire for her pinioned her there so that she couldn't move. It was an aching yearning that filled the apartment, pushed against the walls, plucked at her arms.

She forced herself to start walking toward the kitchen. As she went past him, it seemed to her that he actually did reach one long arm out toward her, his body swaying so that its exaggerated length almost brushed against her. She really couldn't be certain of it, she decided, and resolutely turned the beam of her flashlight on the kitchen walls.

It isn't possible to read people's minds, she argued. Now the Super was probably not even thinking about her when he was standing there like that. He probably wanted to get back downstairs to read his paper. Don't kid yourself, she thought, he probably can't read, or if he can, he probably doesn't spend any time at it. Well—listen to the radio. That was it, he probably wanted to hear his favorite program and she had thought he was filled with the desire to leap upon her. She was as bad as Granny. Which just went on to prove you couldn't be brought up by someone like Granny without absorbing a lot of nonsense that would spring at you out of nowhere, so to speak, and when you least expected it. All those tales about things that people sensed before they actually happened. Tales that had been handed down and down and down until, if you tried to trace them back, you'd end up God knows where—probably Africa. And Granny had them all at the tip of her tongue.

Yet would wanting to hear a radio program make a man look quite like that? Impatiently she forced herself to inspect the kitchen; holding the light on first one wall, then another. It was no better and no worse than she had anticipated. The sink was battered; and the gas stove was a little rusted. The faint smell of gas that hovered about it suggested a slow, incurable leak somewhere in its connections.

Peering into the bathroom, she saw that the fixtures were old-fashioned and deeply chipped. She thought Methuselah himself might well have taken baths in the tub. Certainly it looked ancient enough, though he'd have had to stick his beard out in the hall while he washed himself, for the place was far too small for a man with a full-grown beard to turn around in. She presumed because there was no window that the vent pipe would serve as a source of nice, fresh, clean air.

One thing about it the rent wouldn't be very much. It couldn't be for a place like this. Tiny hall. Bathroom on the right, kitchen straight ahead; living room to the left of the hall and you had to go through the living room to get to the bedroom. The whole apartment would fit very neatly into just one good-sized room.

She was conscious that all the little rooms smelt exactly alike. It was a mixture that contained the faint persistent odor of gas, of old walls, dusty plaster, and over it all the heavy, sour smell of garbage—a smell that seeped through the dumb-waiter shaft. She started humming under her breath, not realizing she was doing it. It was an old song that Granny used to sing. 'Ain't no restin' place for a sinner like me. Like me. Like me.' It had a nice recurrent rhythm. 'Like me. Like me.' The humming increased in volume as she stood there thinking about the apartment.

There was a queer, muffled sound from the Super in the living room. It startled her so she nearly dropped the flashlight. 'What was that?' she said sharply, thinking, My God, suppose I'd dropped it, suppose I'd been left standing here in the dark of this little room, and he'd turned out his light. Suppose he'd started walking toward me, nearer and nearer in the dark. And I could only hear his footsteps, couldn't see him, but could hear him coming closer until I started reaching out in the dark trying to keep him away from me, trying to keep him from touching me—and then—then my hands found him right in front of me— At the thought she gripped the flashlight so tightly that the long beam of light from it started wavering and dancing over the walls so that the shadows moved—shadow from the light fixture overhead, shadow from the tub, shadow from the very doorway itself—shifting, moving back and forth.

'I cleared my throat,' the Super said. His voice had a choked, unnatural sound as though something had gone wrong with his breathing.

She walked out into the hall, not looking at him; opened the door of the apartment and stepping over the threshold, still not looking at him, said, 'I've finished looking.'

He came out and turned the key in the lock. He kept his back turned toward her so that she couldn't have seen the expression on his face even if she'd looked at him. The lock clicked into place, smoothly. Quietly. She stood there not moving, waiting for him to start down the hall toward the stairs, thinking, Never, so help me, will he walk down those stairs in back of me.

When he didn't move, she said, 'You go first.' Then he made a slight motion toward the stairs with his flashlight indicating that she was to precede him. She shook her head very firmly.

'Think you'll take it?' he asked.

'I don't know yet. I'll think about it going down.'

When he finally started down the hall, it seemed to her that he had stood there beside her for days, weeks, months, willing her to go down the stairs first. She followed him, thinking, It wasn't my imagination when I got that feeling at the sight of him standing there in the living room; otherwise, why did he have to go through all that rigamarole of my going down the stairs ahead of him? Like going through the motions of a dance; you first; no, you first; but you see, you'll spoil the pattern if you don't go first; but I won't go first, you go first; but no, it'll spoil the—

She was aware that they'd come up the stairs much faster than they were going down. Was she going to take the apartment? The price wouldn't be too high from the looks of it and by being careful she and Bub could manage—by being very, very careful. White paint would fix the inside of it up; not exactly fix it up, but keep it from being too gloomy, shove the darkness back a little.

Then she thought, Layers and layers of paint won't fix that apartment. It would always smell; finger marks and old stains would come through the paint; the very smell of the wood itself would eventually win out over the paint. Scrubbing wouldn't help any. Then there were these dark, narrow halls, the long flights of stairs, the Super himself, that woman on the first floor.

Or she could go on living with Pop. And Lil. Bub would learn to like the taste of gin, would learn to smoke, would learn in fact a lot of other things that Lil could teach him—things that Lil would think it amusing to teach him. Bub at eight could get a liberal education from Lil, for she was home all day and Bub got home from school a little after three.

You've got a choice a yard wide and ten miles long. You can sit down and twiddle your thumbs while your kid gets a free education from your father's blowsy girl friend. Or you can take this apartment. The tall gentleman who is the superintendent is supposed to rent apartments, fire the furnace, sweep the halls, and that's as far as he's supposed to go. If he tries to include making love to the female tenants, why, this is New York City in the year 1944, and as yet there's no grass growing in the streets and the police force still functions. Certainly you can holler loud enough so that if the gentleman has some kind of dark designs on you and tries to carry them out, a cop will eventually rescue you. That's that.

As for the lady with the snake eyes, you're supposed to be renting the top-floor apartment and if she went with the apartment the sign out in front would say so. Three rooms and snake charmer for respectable tenant. No extra charge for the snake charmer. Seeing as the sign didn't say so, it stood to reason if the snake charmer tried to move in, she could take steps—whatever the hell that meant.

Her high-heeled shoes made a clicking noise as she went down the stairs, and she thought, Yes, take steps like these. It was all very well to reason lightheartedly like that; to kid herself along—there was no explaining away the instinctive, immediate fear she had felt when she first saw the Super. Granny would have said, 'Nothin' but evil, child. Some folks so full of it you can feel it comin' at you—oozin' right out of their skins.'

She didn't believe things like that and yet, looking at his tall, gaunt figure going down that last flight of stairs ahead of her, she half-expected to see horns sprouting from behind his ears; she wouldn't have been greatly surprised if, in place of one of the heavy work shoes on his feet, there had been a cloven hoof that twitched and jumped as he walked so slowly down the stairs.

Outside the door of his apartment, he stopped and turned toward her.

'What's the rent?' she asked, not looking at him, but looking past him at the One A printed on the door of his apartment. The gold letters were filled with tiny cracks, and she thought that in a few more years they wouldn't be distinguishable from the dark brown of the door itself. She hoped the rent would be so high she couldn't possibly take it.

'Twenty-nine fifty.'

He wants me to take it, she thought. He wants it so badly that he's bursting with it. She didn't have to look at him to know it; she could feel him willing it. What difference does it make to him? Yet it was of such obvious importance that if she hesitated just a little longer, he'd be trembling. No, she decided, not that apartment. Then she thought Bub would look cute learning to drink gin at eight.

'I'll take it,' she said grimly.

'You wanta leave a deposit?' he asked.

She nodded, and he opened his door, standing aside to let her go past him. There was a dim light burning in the small hall inside and she saw that the hall led into a living room. She didn't wait for an invitation, but walked on into the living room. The dog had been lying near the radio that stood under a window at the far side of the room. He got up when he saw her, walking toward her with his head down, his tail between his legs; walking as though he were drawn toward her irresistibly, even though he knew that at any moment he would be forced to stop. Though he was a police dog, his hair had such a worn, rusty look that he resembled a wolf more than a dog. She saw that he was so thin, his great haunches and the small bones of his ribs were sharply outlined against his skin. As he got nearer to her, he got excited and she could hear his breathing.

'Lie down,' the Super said.

The dog moved back to the window, shrinking and walking in such a way that she thought if he were human he'd walk backward in order to see and be able to dodge any unexpected blow. He lay down calmly enough and looked at her, but he couldn't control the twitching of his nose; he looked, too, at the Super as though he were wondering if he could possibly cross the room and get over to her without being seen.

The Super sat down in front of an old office desk, found a receipt pad, picked up a fountain pen and, carefully placing a blotter in front of him, turned toward her. 'Name?' he asked.

She swallowed an impulse to laugh. There was something so solemn about the way he'd seated himself, grasping the pen firmly, moving the pad in front of him to exactly the right angle, opening a big ledger book whose pages were filled with line after line of heavily inked writing that she thought he's acting like a big businessman about to transact a major deal.

'Mrs. Lutie Johnson. Present address 2370 Seventh Avenue.' Opening her pocketbook she took out a ten-dollar bill and handed it to him. Ten whole dollars that it had taken a good many weeks to save. By the time she had moved in here and paid the balance which would be due on the rent, her savings would have disappeared. But it would be worth it to be living in a place of her own.

He wrote with a painful slowness, concentrating on each letter, having difficulty with the numbers twenty-three seventy. He crossed it out and bit his lip. 'What was that number?' he asked.

'Twenty-three seventy,' she repeated, thinking perhaps it would be simpler to write it down for him. At the rate he was going, it would take him all of fifteen minutes to write ten dollars and then figure out the difference between ten dollars and twenty-nine dollars which would in this case constitute that innocuous looking phrase, 'the balance due.' She shouldn't be making fun of him, very likely he had taught himself to read and write after spending a couple of years in grammar school where he undoubtedly didn't learn anything. He looked to be in his fifties, but it was hard to tell.

It irritated her to stand there and watch him go through the slow, painful process of forming the letters. She wanted to get out of the place, to get back to Pop's house, plan the packing, get hold of a moving man. She looked around the room idly. The floor was uncarpeted—

a terrible-looking floor. Rough and splintered. There was a sofa against the long wall; its upholstery marked by a greasy line along the back. All the people who had sat on it from the time it was new until the time it had passed through so many hands it finally ended up here must have ground their heads along the back of it.

Next to the sofa there was an overstuffed chair and she drew her breath in sharply as she looked at it, for there was a woman sitting in it, and she had thought that she and the dog and the Super were the only occupants of the room. How could anyone sit in a chair and melt into it like that? As she looked, the shapeless small dark woman in the chair got up and bowed to her without speaking.

Lutie nodded her head in acknowledgment of the bow, thinking, That must be the woman I heard whispering. The woman sat down in the chair again. Melting into it. Because the dark brown dress she wore was almost the exact shade of the dark brown of the upholstery and because the overstuffed chair swallowed her up until she was scarcely distinguishable from the chair itself. Because, too, of a shrinking withdrawal in her way of sitting as though she were trying to take up the least possible amount of space. So that after bowing to her Lutie completely forgot the woman was in the room, while she went on studying its furnishings.

No pictures, no rugs, no newspapers, no magazines, nothing to suggest anyone had ever tried to make it look homelike. Not quite true, for there was a canary huddled in an ornate birdcage in the corner. Looking at it, she thought, Everything in the room shrinks: the dog, the woman, even the canary, for it had only one eye open as it perched on one leg. Opposite the sofa an overornate table shone with varnish. It was a very large table with intricately carved claw feet and looking at it she thought, That's the kind of big ugly furniture white women love to give to their maids. She turned to look at the shapeless little woman because she was almost certain the table was hers.

The woman must have been looking at her, for when Lutie turned the woman smiled; a toothless smile that lingered while she looked from Lutie to the table.

'When you want to move in?' the Super asked, holding out the receipt.

'This is Tuesday—do you think you could have the place ready by Friday?'

'Easy,' he said. 'Some special color you want it painted?'

'White. Make all the rooms white,' she said, studying the receipt. Yes, he had it figured out correctly—balance due, nineteen fifty. He had crossed out his first attempt at the figures. Evidently nines were hard for him to make. And his name was William Jones. A perfectly ordinary name. A highly suitable name for a superintendent. Nice and normal. Easy to remember. Easy to spell. Only the name didn't fit him. For he was obviously unusual, extraordinary, abnormal. Everything about him was the exact opposite of his name. He was standing up now looking at her, eating her up with his eyes.

She took a final look around the room. The whispering woman seemed to be holding her breath; the dog was dying with the desire to growl or whine, for his throat was working. The canary, too, ought to be animated with some desperate emotion, she thought, but he had gone quietly to sleep. Then she forced herself to look directly at the Super. A long hard look, malignant, steady, continued. Thinking, That'll fix you, Mister William Jones, but, of course, if it was only my imagination upstairs, it isn't fair to look at you like this. But just in case some dark leftover instinct warned me of what was on your mind—just in case it made me know you were snuffing on my trail, slathering, slobbering after me like some dark hound of hell seeking me out, tonguing along in back of me, this look, my fine feathered friend, should give you much food for thought.

She closed her pocketbook with a sharp, clicking final sound that made the Super's eyes shift suddenly to the ceiling as though seeking out some pattern in the cracked plaster. The dog's ears straightened into sharp points; the canary opened one eye and the whispering woman almost showed her gums again, for her mouth curved as though she were about to smile.

Lutie walked quickly out of the apartment, pushed the street door open and shivered as the cold air touched her. It had been hot in the Super's apartment, and she paused a second to push her coat collar tight around her neck in an effort to make a barrier against the wind howling in the street outside. Now that she had this apartment, she was just one step farther up on the ladder of success. With the apartment Bub would be standing a better chance, for he'd be away from Lil.

Inside the building the dog let out a high shrill yelp. Immediately she headed for the street, thinking he must have kicked it again. She paused for a moment at the corner of the building, bracing herself for the full blast of the wind that would hit her head-on when she turned the corner.

'Get fixed up, dearie?' Mrs. Hedges' rich voice asked from the street-floor window.

She nodded at the bandannaed head in the window and flung herself into the wind, welcoming its attack, aware as she walked along that the woman's hard flat eyes were measuring her progress up the street.

FROM GO TELL IT ON THE MOUNTAIN (1952)

JAMES BALDWIN

Born in Harlem, Baldwin was an avid reader as a child, but his only preadult writing was in a high school literary journal called *The Magpie*. Even while writing his early stories as an adult, which were all set in Harlem and often about dysfunctional families and religion, he was getting his essays published in prominent journals such as *The New Leader, The Nation* and the *Partisan Review*. With the help of Richard Wright, he won a Rosenwald Fellowship in 1948. *Go Tell It on the Mountain* was his first novel. It is set in Harlem and it tells of the experiences of a young Negro boy, who, like Baldwin himself, converted to the Pentecostal church at age fourteen.

PART ONE

THE SEVENTH DAY

And the Spirit and the bride say, Come.
And let him that heareth say, Come.
And let him that is athirst come.
And whosoever will, let him take
the water of life freely.

I looked down the line,
And I wondered.

Everyone had always said that John would be a preacher when he grew up, just like his father. It had been said so often that John, without ever thinking about it, had come to believe it himself. Not until the morning of his fourteenth birthday did he really begin to think about it, and by then it was already too late.

His earliest memories—which were in a way, his only memories—

were of the hurry and brightness of Sunday mornings. They all rose together on that day; his father, who did not have to go to work, and led them in prayer before breakfast; his mother, who dressed up on that day, and looked almost young, with her hair straightened, and on her head the close-fitting white cap that was the uniform of holy women; his younger brother, Roy, who was silent that day because his father was home. Sarah, who wore a red ribbon in her hair that day, and was fondled by her father. And the baby, Ruth, who was dressed in pink and white, and rode in her mother's arms to church.

The church was not very far away, four blocks up Lenox Avenue, on a corner not far from the hospital. It was to this hospital that his mother had gone when Roy, and Sarah, and Ruth were born. John did not remember very clearly the first time she had gone, to have Roy; folks said that he had cried and carried on the whole time his mother was away; he remembered only enough to be afraid every time her belly began to swell, knowing that each time the swelling began it would not end until she was taken from him, to come back with a stranger. Each time this happened she became a little more of a stranger herself. She would soon be going away again, Roy said—he knew much more about such things than John. John had observed his mother closely, seeing no swelling yet, but his father had prayed one morning for the "little voyager soon to be among them," and so John knew that Roy spoke the truth.

Every Sunday morning, then, since John could remember, they had taken to the streets, the Grimes family on their way to church. Sinners along the avenue watched them—men still wearing their Saturday-night clothes, wrinkled and dusty now, muddy-eyed and muddy-faced; and women with harsh voices and tight, bright dresses, cigarettes between their fingers or held tightly in the corners of their mouths. They talked, and laughed, and fought together, and the women fought like the men. John and Roy, passing these men and women, looked at one another briefly, John embarrassed and Roy amused. Roy would be like them when he grew up, if the Lord did not change his heart. These men and women they passed on Sunday mornings had spent the night in bars, or in cat houses, or on the streets, or on rooftops, or under the stairs. They had been drinking. They had gone from cursing to laughter, to anger, to lust. Once he and Roy had watched a man and woman in the basement of a condemned house. They did it standing up. The woman had wanted fifty cents, and the man had flashed a razor.

John had never watched again; he had been afraid. But Roy had watched them many times, and he told John he had done it with some girls down the block.

And his mother and father, who went to church on Sundays, they did it too, and sometimes John heard them in the bedroom behind him, over the sound of rats' feet, and rat screams, and the music and cursing from the harlot's house downstairs.

Their church was called the Temple of the Fire Baptized. It was not the biggest church in Harlem, nor yet the smallest, but John had been brought up to believe it was the holiest and best. His father was head deacon in this church—there were only two, the other a round, black man named Deacon Braithwaite—and he took up the collection, and sometimes he preached. The pastor, Father James, was a genial, well-fed man with a face like a darker moon. It was he who preached on Pentecost Sundays, and led revivals in the summertime, and anointed and healed the sick.

On Sunday mornings and Sunday nights the church was always full; on special Sundays it was full all day. The Grimes family arrived in a body, always a little late, usually in the middle of Sunday school, which began at nine o'clock. This lateness was always their mother's fault—at least in the eyes of their father; she could not seem to get herself and the children ready on time, ever, and sometimes she actually remained behind, not to appear until the morning service. When they all arrived together, they separated upon entering the doors, father and mother going to sit in the Adult Class, which was taught by Sister McCandless, Sarah going to the Infant's Class, John and Roy sitting in the Intermediate, which was taught by Brother Elisha.

When he was young, John had paid no attention in Sunday school, and always forgot the golden text, which earned him the wrath of his father. Around the time of his fourteenth birthday, with all the pressures of church and home uniting to drive him to the altar, he strove to appear more serious and therefore less conspicuous. But he was distracted by his new teacher, Elisha, who was the pastor's nephew and who had but lately arrived from Georgia. He was not much older than John, only seventeen, and he was already saved and was a preacher. John stared at Elisha all during the lesson, admiring the timbre of Elisha's voice, much deeper and manlier than his own, admiring the leanness, and grace, and strength, and darkness of Elisha in his Sunday suit, wondering if he would ever be holy as Elisha was holy. But he did not follow the lesson, and when, sometimes, Elisha paused to ask John a question, John was ashamed and confused, feeling the palms of his hands become wet and his heart pound like a hammer. Elisha would smile and reprimand him gently, and the lesson would go on.

Roy never knew his Sunday school lesson either, but it was different with Roy—no one really expected of Roy what was expected of John. Everyone was always praying that the Lord would change Roy's heart, but it was John who was expected to be good, to be a good example.

When Sunday school service ended there was a short pause before morning service began. In this pause, if it was good weather, the old folks might step outside a moment to talk among themselves. The sisters would almost always be dressed in white from crown to toe. The small children, on this day, in this place, and oppressed by their elders, tried hard to play without seeming to be disrespectful of God's house. But sometimes, nervous or perverse, they shouted, or threw hymnbooks, or began to cry, putting their parents, men or women of God, under the necessity of proving—by harsh means or tender—who, in a sanctified household, ruled. The older children, like John or Roy, might wander down the avenue, but not too far. Their father never let John and Roy out of his sight, for Roy had often disappeared between Sunday school and morning service and had not come back all day.

The Sunday morning service began when Brother Elisha sat down at the piano and raised a song. This moment and this music had been with John, so it seemed, since he had first drawn breath. It seemed that there had never been a time when he had not known this moment of waiting while the packed church paused—the sisters in white, heads raised, the brothers in blue, heads back; the white caps of the women seeming to glow in the charged air like crowns, the kinky, gleaming heads of the men seeming to be lifted up—and the rustling and the whispering ceased and the children were quiet; perhaps someone coughed, or the sound of a car horn, or a curse from the streets came in; then Elisha hit the keys, beginning at once to sing, and everybody joined him, clapping their hands, and rising, and beating the tambourines.

The song might be: *Down at the cross where my Saviour died!*
Or: *Jesus, I'll never forget how you set me free!*
Or: *Lord, hold my hand while I run this race!*

They sang with all the strength that was in them, and clapped their hands for joy. There had never been a time when John had not sat watching the saints rejoice with terror in his heart, and wonder. Their singing caused him to believe in the presence of the Lord; indeed, it was no longer a question of belief, because they made that presence real. He did not feel it himself, the joy they felt, yet he could not doubt that it was, for them, the very bread of life—could not doubt it, that is, until it was too late to doubt. Something happened to their faces and their voices, the rhythm of their bodies, and to the air they breathed; it was as though wherever they might be became the upper room, and the Holy Ghost were riding on the air. His father's face, always awful, became more awful now; his father's daily anger was transformed into prophetic wrath. His mother, her eyes raised to heaven, hands arced before her, moving, made real for John that patience, that endurance, that long suffering, which he had read of in the Bible and found so hard to imagine.

On Sunday mornings the women all seemed patient, all the men seemed mighty. While John watched, the Power struck someone, a man or woman; they cried out, a long, wordless crying, and, arms outstretched like wings, they began the Shout. Someone moved a chair a little to give them room, the rhythm paused, the singing stopped, only the pounding feet and the clapping hands were heard; then another cry, another dancer; then the tambourines began again, and the voices rose again, and the music swept on again, like fire, or flood, or judgment. Then the church seemed to swell with the Power it held, and, like a planet rocking in space, the temple rocked with the Power of God. John watched, watched the faces, and the weightless bodies, and listened to the timeless cries. One day, so everyone said, this Power would possess him; he would sing and cry as they did now, and dance before his King. He watched young Ella Mae Washington, the seventeen-year-old granddaughter of Praying Mother Washington, as she began to dance. And then Elisha danced.

At one moment, head thrown back, eyes closed, sweat standing on his brow, he sat at the piano, singing and playing; and then, like a great, black cat in trouble in the jungle, he stiffened and trembled, and cried out. *Jesus, Jesus, oh Lord Jesus!* He struck on the piano one last, wild note, and threw up his hands, palms upward, stretched wide apart. The tambourines raced to fill the vacuum left by his silent piano, and his cry drew answering cries. Then he was on his feet, turning, blind, his face congested, contorted with this rage, and the muscles leaping and swelling in his long, dark neck. It seemed that he could not breathe, that his body could not contain this passion, that he would be, before their eyes, dispersed into the waiting air. His hands, rigid to the very fingertips, moved outward and back against his hips, his sightless eyes looked upward, and he began to dance. Then his hands closed into fists, and his head snapped downward, his sweat loosening the grease that slicked down his hair; and the rhythm of all the others quickened to match Elisha's rhythm; his thighs moved terribly against the cloth of his suit, his heels beat on the floor, and his fists moved beside his body as though he were beating his own drum. And so, for a while, in the center of the dancers, head down, fists beating, on, on, unbearably, until it seemed the walls of the church would fall for very sound; and then, in a moment, with a cry, head up, arms high in the air, sweat pouring from his forehead, and all his body dancing as though it would never stop. Sometimes he did not stop until he fell—until he dropped like some animal felled by a hammer—moaning, on his face. And then a great moaning filled the church.

There was sin among them. One Sunday, when regular service was over, Father James had uncovered sin in the congregation of the righteous. He had uncovered Elisha and Ella Mae. They had been "walking disorderly"; they were in danger of straying from the truth. And as Father James spoke of the sin that he knew they had not committed yet, of the unripe fig plucked too early from the tree—to set the children's teeth on edge—John felt himself grow dizzy in his seat and could not look at Elisha where he stood, beside Ella Mae, before the altar. Elisha hung his head as Father James spoke, and the congregation murmured. And Ella Mae was not so beautiful now as she was when she was singing and testifying, but looked like a sullen, ordinary girl. Her full lips were loose and her eyes were black—with shame, or rage, or both. Her grandmother, who had raised her, sat watching quietly, with folded hands. She was one of the pillars of the church, a powerful evangelist and very widely known. She said nothing in Ella Mae's defense, for she must have felt, as the congregation felt, that Father James was only exercising his clear and painful duty; he was responsible, after all, for Elisha, as Praying Mother Washington was responsible for Ella Mae. It was not an easy thing, said Father James, to be the pastor of a flock. It might look easy to just sit up there in the pulpit night after night, year in, year out, but let them remember the awful responsibility placed on his shoulders by almighty God—let them remember that God would ask an accounting of him one day for every soul in his flock. Let them remember this when they thought he was hard, let them remember that the Word was hard, that the way of holiness was a hard way. There was no room in God's army for the coward heart, no crown awaiting him who put mother, or father, sister, or brother, sweetheart, or friend above God's will. Let the church cry amen to this! And they cried: "Amen! Amen!"

The Lord had led him, said Father James, looking down on the boy and girl before him, to give them a public warning before it was too late. For he knew them to be sincere young people, dedicated to the service of the Lord—it was only that, since they were young, they did not know the pitfalls Satan laid for the unwary. He knew that sin was not in their minds—not yet; yet sin was in the flesh; and should they continue with their walking out alone together, their secrets and laughter, and touching of hands, they would surely sin a sin beyond all forgiveness. And John wondered what Elisha was thinking—Elisha, who was tall and handsome, who played basketball, and who had been saved at the age of eleven in the improbable fields down south. *Had* he sinned? Had he been tempted? And the girl beside him, whose white robes now seemed the merest, thinnest covering for the nakedness of breasts and insistent thighs—what was her face like when she was alone with Elisha, with no singing, when they were not surrounded by the saints? He was afraid to think of it, yet he could think of nothing else; and the fever of which they stood accused began also to rage in him.

After this Sunday Elisha and Ella Mae no longer met each other each day after school, no longer spent Saturday afternoons wandering through Central Park, or lying on the beach. All that was over for them. If they came together again it would be in wedlock. They would have children and raise them in the church.

This was what was meant by a holy life, this was what the way of the cross demanded. It was somehow on that Sunday, a Sunday shortly before his birthday, that John first realized that this was the life awaiting him—realized it consciously, as something no longer far off, but imminent, coming closer day by day.

<<<<<

John's birthday fell on a Saturday in March, in 1935. He awoke on this birthday morning with the feeling that there was menace in the air around him—that something irrevocable had occurred in him. He stared at a yellow stain on the ceiling just above his head. Roy was still smothered in the bedclothes, and his breath came and went with a small, whistling sound. There was no other sound anywhere; no one in the house was up. The neighbors' radios were all silent, and his mother hadn't yet risen to fix his father's breakfast. John wondered at his panic, then wondered about the time; and then (while the yellow stain on the ceiling slowly transformed itself into a woman's nakedness) he remembered that it was his fourteenth birthday and that he had sinned.

His first thought, nevertheless, was: "Will anyone remember?" For it had happened, once or twice, that his birthday had passed entirely unnoticed, and no one had said "Happy Birthday, Johnny," or given him anything—not even his mother.

Roy stirred again and John pushed him away, listening to the silence. On other mornings he awoke hearing his mother singing in the kitchen, hearing his father in the bedroom behind him grunting and muttering prayers to himself as he put on his clothes; hearing, perhaps, the chatter of Sarah and the squalling of Ruth, and the radios, the clatter of pots and pans, and the voices of all the folk nearby. This morning not even the cry of a bed-spring disturbed the silence, and John seemed, therefore, to be listening to his own unspeaking doom. He could believe, almost, that he had awakened late on that great getting-up morning; that all the saved had been transformed in the twinkling of an eye, and had risen to meet Jesus in the clouds, and that he was left, with his sinful body, to be bound in hell a thousand years.

He had sinned. In spite of the saints, his mother and his father, the warnings he had heard from his earliest beginnings, he had sinned with his hands a sin that was hard to forgive. In the school lavatory, alone, thinking of the boys, older, bigger, braver, who made bets with each other as to whose urine could arch higher, he had watched in himself a transformation of which he would never dare to speak.

And the darkness of John's sin was like the darkness of the church on Saturday evenings; like the silence of the church while he was there alone, sweeping, and running water into the great bucket, and overturning chairs, long before the saints arrived. It was like his thoughts as he moved about the tabernacle in which his life had been spent; the tabernacle that he hated, yet loved and feared. It was like Roy's curses, like the echoes these curses raised in John: he remembered Roy, on some rare Saturday when he had come to help John clean the church, cursing in the house of God, and making obscene gestures before the eyes of Jesus. It was like all this, and it was like the walls that witnessed and the placards on the walls which testified that the wages of sin was death. The darkness of his sin was in the hardheartedness with which he resisted God's power; in the scorn that was often his while he listened to the crying, breaking voices, and watched the black skin glisten while they lifted up their arms and fell on their faces before the Lord. For he had made his decision. He would not be like his father, or his father's fathers. He would have another life.

For John excelled in school, though not, like Elisha, in mathematics or basketball, and it was said that he had a Great Future. He might become a Great Leader of His People. John was not much interested in his people and still less in leading them anywhere, but the phrase so often repeated rose in his mind like a great brass gate, opening outward for him on a world where people did not live in the darkness of his father's house, did not pray to Jesus in the darkness of his father's church, where he would eat good food, and wear fine clothes, and go to the movies as often as he wished. In this world John, who was, his father said, ugly, who was always the smallest boy in his class, and who had no friends, became immediately beautiful, tall, and popular. People fell all over themselves to meet John Grimes. He was a poet, or a college president, or a movie star; he drank expensive whisky, and he smoked Lucky Strike cigarettes in the green package.

It was not only colored people who praised John, since they could not, John felt, in any case really know; but white people also said it, in fact had said it first and said it still. It was when John was five years old and in the first grade that he was first noticed; and since he was noticed by an eye altogether alien and impersonal, he began to perceive, in wild uneasiness, his individual existence.

They were learning the alphabet that day, and six children at a time were sent to the blackboard to write the letters they had memorized. Six had finished and were waiting for the teacher's judgment when the back door opened and the school principal, of whom everyone was terrified, entered the room. No one spoke or moved. In the silence the principal's voice said:

"Which child is that?"

She was pointing at the blackboard, at John's letters. The possibility of being distinguished by her notice did not enter John's mind, and so he simply stared at her. Then he realized, by the immobility of the other children and by the way they avoided looking at him, that it was he who was selected for punishment.

"Speak up, John," said the teacher, gently.

On the edge of tears, he mumbled his name and waited. The principal, a woman with white hair and an iron face, looked down at him.

"You're a very bright boy, John Grimes," she said. "Keep up the good work."

Then she walked out of the room.

That moment gave him, from that time on, if not a weapon at least a shield; he apprehended totally, without belief or understanding, that he had in himself a power that other people lacked; that he could use this to save himself, to raise himself; and that, perhaps, with this power he might one day win that love which he so longed for. This was not, in John, a faith subject to death or alteration, nor yet a hope subject to destruction; it was his identity, and part, therefore, of that wickedness for which his father beat him and to which he clung in order to withstand his father. His father's arm, rising and falling, might make him cry, and that voice might cause him to tremble; yet his father could never be entirely the victor, for John cherished something that his father could not reach. It was his hatred and his intelligence that he cherished, the one feeding the other. He lived for the day when his father would be dying and he, John, would curse him on his deathbed. And this was why, though he had been born in the faith and had been surrounded all his life by the saints and by their prayers and their rejoicing, and though the tabernacle in which they worshipped was more completely real to him than the several precarious homes in which he and his family had lived, John's heart was hardened against the Lord. His father was God's minister, the ambassador of the King of Heaven, and John could not bow before the throne of grace without first kneeling to his father. On his refusal to do this had his life depended, and John's secret heart had flourished in its wickedness until the day his sin first overtook him.

< < < < <

In the midst of all his wonderings he fell asleep again, and when he woke up this time and got out of his bed his father had gone to the factory, where he would work for half a day. Roy was sitting in the kitchen, quarreling with their mother. The baby, Ruth, sat in her high chair banging on the tray with an oatmeal-covered spoon. This meant that she was in a good mood; she would not spend the day howling, for reasons known only to herself, allowing no one but her mother to touch her. Sarah was quiet, not chattering today, or at any rate not yet, and stood near the stove, arms folded, staring at Roy with the flat black eyes, her father's eyes, that made her look so old.

Their mother, her head tied up in an old rag, sipped black coffee and watched Roy. The pale end-of-winter sunlight filled the room and yellowed all their faces; and John, drugged and morbid and wondering how it was that he had slept again and had been allowed to sleep so long, saw them for a moment like figures on a screen, an effect that the yellow light intensified. The room was narrow and dirty; nothing could alter its dimensions, no labor could ever make it clean. Dirt was in the walls and the floorboards, and triumphed beneath the sink where roaches spawned; was in the fine ridges of the pots and pans, scoured daily, burnt black on the bottom, hanging above the stove; was in the wall against which they hung, and revealed itself where the paint had cracked and leaned outward in stiff squares and fragments, the paper-thin underside webbed with black. Dirt was in every corner, angle, crevice of the monstrous stove, and lived behind it in delirious communion with the corrupted wall. Dirt was in the baseboard that John scrubbed every Saturday, and roughened the cupboard shelves that held the cracked and gleaming dishes. Under this dark weight the walls leaned, under it the ceiling, with a great crack like lightning in its center, sagged. The windows gleamed like beaten gold or silver, but now John saw, in the yellow light, how fine dust veiled their doubtful glory. Dirt crawled in the gray mop hung out of the windows to dry. John thought with shame and horror, yet in angry hardness of heart: *He who is filthy, let him be filthy still.* Then he looked at his mother, seeing, as though she were someone else, the dark, hard lines running downward from her eyes, and the deep, perpetual scowl in her forehead, and the downturned, tightened mouth, and the strong, thin, brown, and bony hands; and the phrase turned against him like a two-edged sword, for was it not he, in his false pride and his evil imagination, who was filthy? Through a storm of tears that did not reach his eyes, he stared at the yellow room; and the room shifted, the light of the sun darkened, and his mother's face changed. Her face became the face that he gave her in his dreams, the face that had been hers in a photograph he had seen once, long ago, a photograph taken before he was born. This face was young and proud, uplifted, with a smile that made the wide mouth beautiful and glowed in the enormous eyes. It was the face of a girl who knew that no evil could undo her, and who could laugh, surely, as his mother did not laugh now. Between the two faces there stretched a darkness and a mystery that John feared, and that sometimes caused him to hate her.

Now she saw him and she asked, breaking off her conversation with Roy: "You hungry, little sleepyhead?"

"Well! About time you was getting up," said Sarah.

He moved to the table and sat down, feeling the most bewildering panic of his life, a need to touch things, the table and chairs and the walls of the room, to make certain that the room existed and that he was in the room. He did not look at his mother, who stood up and went to the stove to heat his breakfast. But he asked, in order to say something to her, and to hear his own voice:

"What we got for breakfast?"

He realized, with some shame, that he was hoping she had prepared a special breakfast for him on his birthday.

"What you *think* we got for breakfast?" Roy asked scornfully. "You got a special craving for something?"

John looked at him. Roy was not in a good mood.

"I ain't said nothing to you," he said.

"Oh, I *beg* your pardon," said Roy, in the shrill, little-girl tone he knew John hated.

"What's the *matter* with you today?" John asked, angry, and trying at the same time to lend his voice as husky a pitch as possible.

"Don't you let Roy bother you," said their mother. "He cross as two sticks this morning."

"Yeah," said John, "I reckon." He and Roy watched each other. Then his plate was put before him: hominy grits and a scrap of bacon. He wanted to cry, like a child: "But, Mama, it's my birthday!" He kept his eyes on his plate and began to eat.

"You can *talk* about your Daddy all you want to," said his mother, picking up her battle with Roy, "but *one* thing you can't say—you can't say he ain't always done his best to be a father to you and to see to it that you ain't never gone hungry."

"I been hungry plenty of times," Roy said, proud to be able to score this point against his mother.

"Wasn't *his* fault, then. Wasn't because he wasn't *trying* to feed you. That man shoveled snow in zero weather when he ought've been in bed just to put food in your belly."

"Wasn't just *my* belly," said Roy indignantly. "He got a belly, too, I *know* it's a *shame* the way that man eats. I sure ain't asked him to shovel no snow for me." But he dropped his eyes, suspecting a flaw in his argument. "I just don't want him beating on me all the time," he said at last. "I ain't no dog."

She sighed, and turned slightly away, looking out of the window. "Your Daddy beats you," she said, "because he loves you."

Roy laughed. "That ain't the kind of love I understand, old lady. What you reckon he'd do if he didn't love me?"

"He'd let you go right on," she flashed, "right on down to hell where it looks like you is just determined to go anyhow! Right on, Mister Man, till somebody puts a knife in you, or takes you off to jail!"

"Mama," John asked suddenly, "is Daddy a good man?"

He had not known that he was going to ask the question, and he watched in astonishment as her mouth tightened and her eyes grew dark.

"That ain't no kind of question," she said mildly. "You don't know no better man, do you?"

"Looks to me like he's a mighty good man," said Sarah. "He sure is praying all the time."

"You children is young," their mother said, ignoring Sarah and sitting down again at the table, "and you don't know how lucky you is to have a father what worries about you and tries to see to it that you come up right."

"Yeah," said Roy, "we don't know how lucky we *is* to have a father what don't want you to go to movies, and don't want you to play in the streets, and don't want you to have no friends, and he don't want this and he don't want that, and he don't want you to do *nothing*. We so *lucky* to have a father who just wants us to go to church and read the Bible and beller like a fool in front of the altar and stay home all nice and quiet, like a little mouse. Boy, we sure is lucky, all right. Don't know what I done to be so lucky."

She laughed. "You going to find out one day," she said, "you mark my words."

"Yeah," said Roy.

"But it'll be too late, then," she said. "It'll be too late when you come to be . . . sorry." Her voice had changed. For a moment her eyes met John's eyes, and John was frightened. He felt that her words, after the strange fashion God sometimes chose to speak to men, were dictated by Heaven and were meant for him. He was fourteen—was it too late? And this uneasiness was reinforced by the impression, which at that moment he realized had been his all along, that his mother was not saying everything she meant. What, he wondered, did she say to Aunt Florence when they talked together? Or to his father? What were her thoughts? Her face would never tell. And yet, looking down at him in a moment that was like a secret, passing sign, her face did tell him. Her thoughts were bitter.

"I don't care," Roy said, rising. "When *I* have children I ain't going to treat them like this." John watched his mother; she watched Roy. "I'm *sure* this ain't no way to be. Ain't got no right to have a houseful of children if you don't know how to treat them."

"You mighty grown up this morning," his mother said. "You be careful."

"And tell me something else," Roy said, suddenly leaning over his mother, "tell me how come he don't never let me talk to him like I talk to you? He's my father, ain't he? But he don't never listen to me—no, I all the time got to listen to him."

"Your father," she said, watching him, "knows best. You listen to your father, I guarantee you, you won't end up in no jail."

Roy sucked his teeth in fury. "I ain't looking to go to no *jail*. You think that's all that's in the world is jails and churches? You ought to know better than that, Ma."

"I know," she said, "there ain't no safety except you walk humble before the Lord. You going to find it out, too, one day. You go on, hardhead. You going to come to grief."

And suddenly Roy grinned. "But you be there, won't you, Ma—when I'm in trouble?"

"You don't know," she said, trying not to smile, "how long the Lord's going to let me stay with you."

Roy turned and did a dance step. "That's all right," he said. "I know the Lord ain't as hard as Daddy. Is he, boy?" he demanded of John, and struck him lightly on the forehead.

"Boy, let me eat my breakfast," John muttered—though his plate had long been empty, and he was pleased that Roy had turned to him.

"That sure is a crazy boy," ventured Sarah, soberly.

"Just listen," cried Roy, "to the little saint! Daddy ain't never going to have no trouble with her—*that* one, she was born holy. I bet the first words she ever said was: 'Thank you, Jesus.' Ain't that so, Ma?"

"You stop this foolishness," she said, laughing, "and go on about your work. Can't nobody play the fool with you all morning."

"Oh, is you got work for me to do this morning? Well, I declare," said Roy, "what you got for me to do?"

"I got the woodwork in the dining-room for you to do. And you going to do it, too, before you set foot out of *this* house."

"Now, why you want to talk like that, Ma? Is I said I wouldn't do it? You know I'm a right good worker when I got a mind. After I do it, can I go?"

"You go ahead and do it, and we'll see. You better do it right."

"I *always* do it right," said Roy. "You won't know your old woodwork when *I* get through."

"John," said his mother, "you sweep the front room for me like a good boy, and dust the furniture. I'm going to clean up in here."

"Yes'm," he said, and rose. She *had* forgotten about his birthday. He swore he would not mention it. He would not think about it any more.

To sweep the front room meant, principally, to sweep the heavy red and green and purple Oriental-style carpet that had once been that room's glory, but was now so faded that it was all one swimming color, and so frayed in places that it tangled with the broom. John hated sweeping this carpet, for dust rose, clogging his nose and sticking to his sweaty skin, and he felt that should he sweep it forever, the clouds of dust would not diminish, the rug would not be clean. It became in his imagination his impossible, lifelong task, his hard trial, like that of a man he had read about somewhere, whose curse it was to push a boulder up a steep hill, only to have the giant who guarded the hill roll the boulder down again—and so on, forever, throughout eternity; he was still out there, that hapless man, somewhere at the other end of the earth, pushing his boulder up the hill. He had John's entire sympathy, for the longest and hardest part of his Saturday mornings was his voyage with the broom across this endless rug; and, coming to the French doors that ended the living-room and stopped the rug, he felt like an indescribably weary traveler who sees his home at last. Yet for each dustpan he so laboriously filled at the doorsill demons added to the rug twenty more; he saw in the expanse behind him the dust that he had raised settling again into the carpet; and he gritted his teeth, already on edge because of the dust that filled his mouth, and nearly wept to think that so much labor brought so little reward.

Nor was this the end of John's labor; for, having put away the broom and the dustpan, he took from the small bucket under the sink the dust-rag and the furniture oil and a damp cloth, and returned to the living-room to excavate, as it were, from the dust that threatened to bury them, his family's goods and gear. Thinking bitterly of his birthday, he attacked the mirror with the cloth, watching his face appear as out of a cloud. With a shock he saw that his face had not changed, that the hand of Satan was as yet invisible. His father had always said that his face was the face of Satan—and was there not something—in the lift of the eyebrow, in the way his rough hair formed a V on his brow—that bore witness to his father's words? In the eye there was a light that was not the light of Heaven, and the mouth trembled, lustful and lewd, to drink deep of the wines of Hell. He stared at his face as though it were, as indeed it soon appeared to be, the face of a stranger, a stranger who held secrets that John could never know. And, having thought of it as the face of a stranger, he tried to look at it as a stranger might, and tried to discover what other people saw. But he saw only details: two great eyes, and a broad, low forehead, and the triangle of his nose, and his enormous mouth, and the barely perceptible cleft in his chin, which was, his father said, the mark of the devil's little finger. These details did not help him, for the principle of their unity was undiscoverable, and he could not tell what he most passionately desired to know: whether his face was ugly or not.

And he dropped his eyes to the mantelpiece, lifting one by one the objects that adorned it. The mantelpiece held, in brave confusion, photographs, greeting cards, flowered mottoes, two silver candlesticks that held no candles, and a green metal serpent, poised to strike. Today in his apathy John stared at them, not seeing; he began to dust them with the exaggerated care of the profoundly preoccupied. One of the mottoes was pink and blue, and proclaimed in raised letters, which made the work of dusting harder:

Come in the evening, or come in the morning,
Come when you're looked for, or come without
    warning,
A thousand welcomes you'll find here before you,
And the oftener you come here, the more we'll
    adore you.

And the other, in letters of fire against a background of gold, stated:

For God so loved the world, that He gave His only begotten Son, that whosoever should believe in Him should not perish, but have everlasting life.

                                                    John iii, 16

These somewhat unrelated sentiments decorated either side of the mantelpiece, obscured a little by the silver candlesticks. Between these two extremes, the greeting cards, received year after year, on Christmas, or Easter, or birthdays, trumpeted their glad tidings; while the green metal serpent, perpetually malevolent, raised its head proudly in the midst of these trophies, biding the time to strike. Against the mirror, like a procession, the photographs were arranged.

These photographs were the true antiques of the family, which seemed to feel that a photograph should commemorate only the most distant past. The photographs of John and Roy, and of the two girls, which seemed to violate this unspoken law, served only in fact to prove it most iron-hard: they had all been taken in infancy, a time and a condition that the children could not remember. John, in his photograph lay naked on a white counterpane, and people laughed and said that it was cunning. But John could never look at it without feeling shame and anger that his nakedness should be here so unkindly revealed. None of the other children was naked; no, Roy lay in his crib in a white gown and grinned toothlessly into the camera, and Sarah, somber at the age of six months, wore a white bonnet, and Ruth was held in her mother's arms.

When people looked at these photographs and laughed, their laughter differed from the laughter with which they greeted the naked John. For this reason, when visitors tried to make advances to John he was sullen, and they, feeling that for some reason he disliked them, retaliated by deciding that he was a "funny" child.

Among the other photographs there was one of Aunt Florence, his father's sister, in which her hair, in the old-fashioned way, was worn high and tied with a ribbon; she had been very young when this photograph was taken, and had just come North. Sometimes, when she came to visit, she called the photograph to witness that she had indeed been beautiful in her youth. There was a photograph of his mother, not the one John liked and had seen only once, but one taken immediately after her marriage. And there was a photograph of his father, dressed in black, sitting on a country porch with his hands folded heavily in his lap. The photograph had been taken on a sunny day, and the sunlight brutally exaggerated the planes of his father's face. He stared into the sun, head raised, unbearable, and though it had been taken when he was young, it was not the face of a young man; only something archaic in the dress indicated that this photograph had been taken long ago. At the time this picture was taken, Aunt Florence said, he was already a preacher, and had a wife who was now in Heaven. That he had been a preacher at that time was not astonishing, for it was impossible to imagine that he had ever been anything else; but that he had had a wife in the so distant past who was now dead filled John with a wonder by no means pleasant. If she had lived, John thought, then he would never have been born; his father would never have come North and met his mother. And this shadowy woman, dead so many years, whose name he knew had been Deborah, held in the fastness of her tomb, it seemed to John, the key to all those mysteries he so longed to unlock. It was she who had known his father in a life where John was not, and in a country John had never seen. When he was nothing, nowhere, dust, cloud, air, and sun, and falling rain, *not even thought of,* said his mother, *in Heaven with the angels,* said his aunt, she had known his father, and shared his father's house. She had loved his father. She had known his father when lightning flashed and thunder rolled through Heaven, and his father said: "Listen. God is talking." She had known him in the mornings of that far-off country when his father turned on his bed and opened his eyes, and she had looked into those eyes, seeing what they held, and she had not been afraid. She had seen him baptized, *kicking like a mule and howling,* and she had seen him weep when his mother died; *he was a right young man then,* Florence said. Because she had looked into those eyes before they had looked on John, she knew what John would never know—the purity of his father's eyes when John was not reflected in their depths. She could have told him—had he but been able from his hiding-place to ask!—how to make his father love him. But now it was too late. She would not speak before the judgment day. And among those many voices, and stammering with his own, John would care no longer for her testimony.

When he had finished and the room was ready for Sunday, John felt dusty and weary and sat down beside the window in his father's easy chair. A glacial sun filled the streets, and a high wind filled the air with scraps of paper and frosty dust, and banged the banging signs of stores and storefront churches. It was the end of winter, and the garbage-filled snow that had been banked along the edges of sidewalks was melting now and filling the gutters. Boys were playing stickball in the damp, cold streets; dressed in heavy woolen sweaters and heavy pants, they danced and shouted, and the ball went *crack!* as the stick struck it and sent it speeding through the air. One of them wore a bright-red stocking cap with a great ball of wool hanging down behind that bounced as he jumped, like a bright omen above his head. The cold sun made their faces like copper and brass, and through the closed window John heard their coarse, irreverent voices. And he wanted to be one of them, playing in the streets, unfrightened, moving with such grace and power, but he knew this could not be. Yet, if he could not play their games, he could do something they could not do; he was able, as one of his teachers said, to think. But this brought him little in the way of consolation, for today he was terrified of his thoughts. He wanted to be with these boys in the street, heedless and thoughtless, wearing out his treacherous and bewildering body.

But now it was eleven o'clock, and in two hours his father would be home. And then they might eat, and then his father would lead them in prayer, and then he would give them a Bible lesson. By and by it would be evening and he would go to clean the church, and remain for tarry service. Suddenly, sitting at the window, and with a violence unprecedented, there arose in John a flood of fury and tears, and he bowed his head, fists clenched against the windowpane, crying, with teeth on edge: "What shall I do? What shall I do?"

Then his mother called him; and he remembered that she was in the kitchen washing clothes and probably had something for him to do. He rose sullenly and walked into the kitchen. She stood over the washtub, her arms wet and soapy to the elbows and sweat standing on her brow. Her apron, improvised from an old sheet, was wet where she had been leaning over the scrubbing-board. As he came in, she straightened, drying her hands on the edge of the apron.

"You finish your work, John?" she asked.

He said: "Yes'm," and thought how oddly she looked at him; as though she were looking at someone else's child.

"That's a good boy," she said. She smiled a shy, strained smile. "You know you your mother's right-hand man?"

He said nothing, and he did not smile, but watched her, wondering to what task this preamble led.

She turned away, passing one damp hand across her forehead, and went to the cupboard. Her back was to him, and he watched her while she took down a bright, figured vase, filled with flowers only on the most special occasions, and emptied the contents into her palm. He heard the chink of money, which meant that she was going to send him to the store. She put the vase back and turned to face him, her palm loosely folded before her.

"I didn't never ask you," she said, "what you wanted for your birthday. But you take this, son, and go out and get yourself something you think you want."

And she opened his palm and put the money into it, warm and wet from her hand. In the moment that he felt the warm, smooth coins and her hand on his, John stared blindly at her face, so far above him. His heart broke and he wanted to put his head on her belly where the wet spot was, and cry. But he dropped his eyes and looked at his palm, at the small pile of coins.

"It ain't much there," she said.

"That's all right." Then he looked up, and she bent down and kissed him on the forehead.

"You getting to be," she said, putting her hand beneath his chin and holding his face away from her, "a right big boy. You going to be a mighty fine man, you know that? Your mama's counting on you."

And he knew again that she was not saying everything she meant; in a kind of secret language she was telling him today something that he must remember and understand tomorrow. He watched her face, his heart swollen with love for her and with an anguish, not yet his own, that he did not understand and that frightened him.

SPANISH BLOOD (1959)

LANGSTON HUGHES

Born in 1902, Hughes was selected best poet in his eighth-grade class in Joplin, Missouri; his literary passion grew steadily from there. His father didn't agree with young Langston's sensibilities and sent him east to attend engineering school at Columbia University. Hughes left with a B average and descended from Morningside Heights to live and work in Harlem, where his first poem, "The Negro Speaks of Rivers," was published in a children's publication, *The Brownie Book*. He later earned a B.A. from Lincoln University in 1929. In his forty-year career, he wrote two novels, sixteen volumes of poetry, and twenty plays and edited three collections of short stories, and seven anthologies. "Spanish Blood" is a story set in East Harlem in the 1950s.

In that amazing city of Manhattan where people are forever building things anew, during prohibition times there lived a young Negro called Valerio Gutierrez whose mother was a Harlem laundress, but whose father was a Puerto Rican sailor. Valerio grew up in the streets. He was never much good at school, but he was swell at selling papers, pitching pennies, or shooting pool. In his teens he became one of the smoothest dancers in the Latin-American quarter north of Central Park. Long before the rhumba became popular, he knew how to do it in the real Cuban way that made all the girls afraid to dance with him. Besides, he was very good looking.

At seventeen, an elderly Chilean lady who owned a beauty parlor called La Flor began to buy his neckties. At eighteen, she kept him in pocket money and let him drive her car. At nineteen, younger and prettier women—a certain comely Spanish widow, also one Dr. Barrios' pale wife—began to see that he kept well dressed.

"You'll never amount to nothin'," Hattie, his brownskin mother, said. "Why don't you get a job and work? It's that foreign blood in you, that's what it is. Just like your father."

"*¿Qué va?*" Valerio replied, grinning.

"Don't you speak Spanish to me," his mama said. "You know I don't understand it."

"O.K., Mama," Valerio said. *"Yo voy a trabajar."*

"You better *trabajar,*" his mama answered. "And I mean work, too! I'm tired o' comin' home every night from that Chinee laundry and findin' you gone to the dogs. I'm gonna move out o' this here Spanish neighborhood anyhow, way up into Harlem where some real *colored* people is, I mean American Negroes. There ain't nobody settin' a decent example for you down here 'mongst all these Cubans and Puerto Ricans and things. I don't care if your father was one of 'em, I never did like 'em real well."

"Aw, Ma, why didn't you ever learn Spanish and stop talking like a spook?"

"Don't you spook me, you young hound, you! I won't stand it. Just because you're straight-haired and yellow and got that foreign blood in you, don't you spook me. I'm your mother and I won't stand for it. You hear me?"

"Yes, ma'am. But you know what I mean. I mean stop talking like most colored folks—just because you're not white you don't have to get back in a corner and stay there. Can't we live nowhere else but way up in Harlem, for instance? Down here in 106th Street, white and colored families live in the same house—Spanish-speaking families, some white and some black. What do you want to move further up in Harlem for, where everybody's all black? Lots of my friends down here are Spanish and Italian, and we get along swell."

"That's just what I'm talkin' about," said his mother. "That's just why I'm gonna move. I can't keep track of you, runnin' around with a fast foreign crowd, all mixed up with every what-cha-ma-call-it, lettin' all shades o' women give you money. Besides, no matter where you move, or what language you speak, you're still colored less'n your skin is white."

"Well, I won't be," said Valerio. "I'm American, Latin-American."

"Huh!" said his mama. "It's just by luck that you even got good hair."

"What's that got to do with being American?"

"A mighty lot," said his mama, "in America."

< < < < < <

They moved. They moved up to 143rd Street, in the very middle of "American" Harlem. There Hattie Gutierrez was happier—for in her youth her name had been Jones, not Gutierrez, just plain colored Jones. She had come from Virginia, not Latin America. She had met the Puerto Rican seaman in Norfolk, had lived with him there and in New York for some ten or twelve years and borne him a son, meanwhile working hard to keep him and their house in style. Then one winter he just disappeared, probably missed his boat in some far-off port town, settled down with another woman, and went on dancing rhumbas and drinking rum without worry.

Valerio, whom Gutierrez left behind, was a handsome child, not quite as light as his father, but with olive-yellow skin and Spanish-black hair, more foreign than Negro. As he grew up, he became steadily taller and better looking. Most of his friends were Spanish-speaking, so he possessed their language as well as English. He was smart and amusing out of school. But he wouldn't work. That was what worried his mother, he just wouldn't work. The long hours and low wages most colored fellows received during depression times never appealed to him. He could live without struggling, so he did.

He liked to dance and play billiards. He hung out near the Cuban theater at 110th Street, around the pool halls and gambling places, in the taxi dance emporiums. He was all for getting the good things out of life. His mother's moving up to black 143rd Street didn't improve conditions any. Indeed, it just started the ball rolling faster, for here Valerio became what is known in Harlem as a big-timer, a young sport, a hep cat. In other words, a man-about-town.

His sleek-haired yellow star rose in a chocolate sky. He was seen at all the formal invitational affairs given by the exclusive clubs of Harlem's younger set, although he belonged to no clubs. He was seen at midnight shows stretching into the dawn. He was even asked to Florita Sutton's famous Thursday midnight-at-homes, where visiting dukes, English authors, colored tap dancers, and dinner-coated downtowners vied for elbow room in her small Sugar Hill apartment. Hattie, Valerio's mama, still kept her job ironing in the Chinese laundry—but nobody bothered about his mama.

Valerio was a nice enough boy, though, about sharing his income with her, about pawning a ring or something someone would give him to help her out on the rent or the insurance policies. And maybe, once or twice a week, Mama might see her son coming in as she went out in the morning or leaving as she came in at night, for Valerio often slept all day. And she would mutter, "The Lord knows, 'cause I don't, what will become of you, boy! You're just like your father!"

Then, strangely enough, one day Valerio got a job. A good job, too—at least, it paid him well. A friend of his ran an after-hours nightclub on upper St. Nicholas Avenue. Gangsters owned the place, but they let a Negro run it. They had a red-hot jazz band, a high-yellow revue, and bootleg liquor. When the Cuban music began to hit Harlem, they hired Valerio to introduce the rhumba. That was something he was really cut out to do, the rhumba. That wasn't work. Not at all, *hombre!* But it was a job, and his mama was glad.

Attired in a yellow silk shirt, white satin trousers, and a bright red sash, Valerio danced nightly to the throbbing drums and seed-filled rattles of the tropics—accompanied by the orchestra's usual instruments of joy. Valerio danced with a little brown Cuban girl in a red dress, Concha, whose hair was a mat of darkness and whose hips were nobody's business.

Their dance became the talk of the town—at least, of that part of the town composed of nightlifers—for Valerio danced the rhumba as his father had taught him to dance it in Norfolk when he was ten years old, innocently—unexpurgated, happy, funny, but beautiful, too—like a gay, sweet longing for something that might be had, sometime, maybe, someplace or other.

Anyhow, business boomed. Ringside tables filled with people who came expressly to see Valerio dance.

"He's marvelous," gasped ladies who ate at the Ritz any time they wanted to.

"That boy can dance," said portly gentlemen with offices full of lawyers to keep track of their income tax. "He can dance!" And they wished they could, too.

"Hot stuff," said young rumrunners, smoking reefers and drinking gin—for these were prohibition days.

"A natural-born eastman," cried a tan-skin lady with a diamond wristwatch. "He can have anything I got."

That was the trouble! Too many people felt that Valerio could have anything they had, so he lived on the fat of the land without making half an effort. He began to be invited to fashionable cocktail parties down-town. He often went out to dinner in the East Fifties with white folks. But his mama still kept her job in the Chinese laundry.

Perhaps it was a good thing she did in view of what finally hap-pened, for to Valerio the world was nothing but a swagger world tingling with lights, music, drinks, money, and people who had every-thing—or thought they had. Each night, at the club, the orchestra beat out its astounding songs, shook its rattles, fingered its drums. Valerio put on his satin trousers with the fiery red sash to dance with the little Cuban girl who always had a look of pleased surprise on her face, as though amazed to find dancing so good. Somehow she and Valerio made their rhumba, for all their hip shaking, clean as a summer sun.

Offers began to come in from other nightclubs, and from small pro-ducers as well. "Wait for something big, kid," said the man who ran the cabaret. "Wait till the Winter Garden calls you."

Valerio waited. Meanwhile, a dark young rounder named Sonny, who wrote number bets for a living, had an idea for making money off of Valerio. They would open an apartment together where people could come after the nightclubs closed—come and drink and dance—and love a little if they wanted to. The money would be made from the sale of drinks—charging very high prices to keep the riffraff out. With Valerio as host, a lot of good spenders would surely call. They could get rich.

"O.K. by me," said Valerio.

"I'll run the place," said Sonny, "and all you gotta do is just be there and dance a little, maybe—you know—and make people feel at home."

"O.K.," said Valerio.

"And we'll split the profit two ways—me and you."

"O.K."

So they got a big Seventh Avenue apartment, furnished it with deep, soft sofas and lots of little tables and a huge icebox, and opened up. They paid off the police every week. They had good whisky. They sent out cards to a hundred downtown people who didn't care about money. They informed the best patrons of the cabaret where Valerio danced— the white folks who thrilled at becoming real Harlem initiates going home with Valerio.

From the opening night on, Valerio's flat filled with white people from midnight till the sun came up. Mostly a sporty crowd, young blades accompanied by ladies of the chorus, racetrack gentlemen, white cabaret entertainers out for amusement after their own places closed, musical-comedy stars in search of new dance steps—and perhaps three or four brownskin ladies-of-the-evening and a couple of chocolate gigolos, to add color.

There was a piano player. Valerio danced. There was impromptu entertaining by the guests. Often famous radio stars would get up and croon. Expensive nightclub names might rise to do a number—or several numbers if they were tight enough. And sometimes it would be hard to stop them when they really got going.

Occasionally guests would get very drunk and stay all night, sleeping well into the day. Sometimes one might sleep with Valerio.

Shortly all Harlem began to talk about the big red roadster Valerio drove up and down Seventh Avenue. It was all nickel-plated—and a little blond revue star known on two continents had given it to him, so folks said. Valerio was on his way to becoming a gigolo deluxe.

"That boy sure don't draw no color lines," Harlem commented. "No, sir!"

"And why should he?" Harlem then asked itself rhetorically. "Colored folks ain't got no money—and money's what he's after, ain't it?"

But Harlem was wrong. Valerio seldom gave a thought to money—he was having too good a time. That's why it was well his mama kept her job in the Chinese laundry, for one day Sonny received a warning, "Close up that flat of yours, and close it damn quick!"

Gangsters!

"What the hell?" Sonny answered the racketeers. "We're payin' off, ain't we—you and the police, both? So what's wrong?"

"Close up, or we'll break you up," the warning came back. "We don't like the way you're running things, black boy. And tell Valerio to send that white chick's car back to her—and quick!"

"Aw, nuts!" said Sonny. "We're paying the police! You guys lay off."

But Sonny wasn't wise. He knew very well how little the police count when gangsters give orders, yet he kept right on. The profits had gone to his head. He didn't even tell Valerio they had been warned, for Sonny, who was trying to make enough money to start a number bank of his own, was afraid the boy might quit. Sonny should have known better.

<<<<<

One Sunday night about three-thirty a.m., the piano was going like mad. Fourteen couples packed the front room, dancing close and warm. There were at least a dozen folks whose names you'd know if you saw them in any paper, famous from Hollywood to Westport.

They were feeling good.

Sonny was busy at the door, and a brown bar boy was collecting highball glasses, as Valerio came in from the club where he still worked. He went in the bedroom to change his dancing shoes, for it was snowing and his feet were cold.

O, rock me, pretty mama, till the cows come home . . .

sang a sleek-haired Harlemite at the piano.

Rock me, rock me, baby, from night to morn . . .

when, just then, a crash like the wreck of the Hesperus resounded through the hall and shook the whole house, as five Italian gentlemen in evening clothes who looked exactly like gangsters walked in. They had broken down the door.

Without a word they began to smash up the place with long axes each of them carried. Women began to scream, men to shout, and the piano vibrated, not from jazz-playing fingers, but from axes breaking its hidden heart.

"Lemme out," the piano player yelled. "Lemme out!" But there was panic at the door.

"I can't leave without my wrap," a woman cried. "Where is my wrap? Sonny, my ermine coat!"

"Don't move," one of the gangsters said to Sonny.

A big white fist flattened his brown nose.

"I ought to kill you," said a second gangster. "You was warned. Take this!"

Sonny spit out two teeth.

Crash went the axes on furniture and bar. Splintered glass flew, wood cracked. Guests fled, hatless and coatless. About that time the police arrived.

Strangely enough, the police, instead of helping protect the place from the gangsters, began themselves to break, not only the furniture, but also the *heads* of every Negro in sight. They started with Sonny. They laid the barman and the waiter low. They grabbed Valerio as he emerged from the bedroom. They beat his face to a pulp. They whacked the piano player twice across the buttocks. They had a grand time with their nightsticks. Then they arrested all the colored fellows (and no whites) as the gangsters took their axes and left. That was the end of Valerio's apartment.

In jail Valerio learned that the woman who gave him the red roadster was being kept by a gangster who controlled prohibition's whole champagne racket and owned dozens of rum-running boats.

"No wonder!" said Sonny, through his bandages. "He got them guys to break up our place! He probably told the police to beat hell out of us, too!"

"Wonder how he knew she gave me that car?" asked Valerio innocently.

"White folks know everything," said Sonny.

"Aw, stop talking like a spook," said Valerio.

When he got out of jail, Valerio's face had a long nightstick scar across it that would never disappear. He still felt weak and sick and hungry. The gangsters had forbidden any of the nightclubs to employ him again, so he went back home to Mama.

"Umm-huh!" she told him. "Good thing I kept my job in that Chinee laundry. It's a good thing . . . Sit down and eat, son . . . What you gonnan do now?"

"Start practicing dancing again. I got an offer to go to Brazil—a big club in Rio."

"Who's gonna pay your fare way down yonder to Brazil?"

"Concha," Valerio answered—the name of his Cuban rhumba partner whose hair was a mat of darkness. "Concha."

"A woman!" cried his mother. "I might a-knowed it! We're weak that way. My God, I don't know, boy! I don't know!"

"You don't know what?" asked Valerio, grinning.

"How women can help it," said his mama. "The Lord knows you're *just* like your father—and I took care o' him for ten years. I reckon it's that Spanish blood."

"*¡Qué va!*" said Valerio.

FROM PURLIE VICTORIOUS (1961)

OSSIE DAVIS

Like his friend John Henrik Clarke, Davis routinely inhabited libraries. But Davis would be quick to tell you that, unlike Dr. Clarke, he would very often find himself in libraries because he was sleeping there. The years after World War II were not easy for struggling young black actors such as Davis and his friends, like Harry Belafonte, Canada Lee, and Sidney Poitier. But Davis, a World War II veteran, was sure of two things: First, he was sure of the love of his beautiful and equally talented wife, Ruby Dee, and second, he was absolutely sure that he wanted to write and direct, as well as act. And so when he heard that a group of writers was meeting and reading their work up in Harlem, he went there. He listened and within a year, he read the first act of his comedic, southern-based play *Purlie Victorious* for the members of the Guild. The play was produced and staged in 1961, and Davis and Dee went on to long and fruitful careers in movies and television and on the stage. The first act of *Victorious* appears in this section.

ACT I

SCENE 1

Scene: The setting is the plain and simple interior of an antiquated, run-down farmhouse such as Negro sharecroppers still live in, in South Georgia. Threadbare but warm-hearted, shabby but clean. In the Center is a large, rough-hewn table with three homemade chairs and a small bench. This table is the center of all family activities. The main entrance is a door in the Upstage Right corner, which leads in from a rickety porch which we cannot see. There is a small archway in the opposite corner, with some long strips of gunny-sacking hanging down to serve as a door, which leads off to the kitchen. In the center of the Right wall is a window that is wooden, which opens outward on hinges. Downstage Right is a small door leading off to a bedroom, and opposite, Downstage Left, another door leads out into the backyard, and on into the cotton fields beyond. There is also a smaller table and a cupboard against the wall. An old dresser stands against the Right wall, between the window and the Downstage door. There is a shelf on the Left wall with a pail of drinking water, and a large tin dipper. Various cooking utensils, and items like salt and pepper are scattered about in appropriate places.

At Rise: The CURTAIN rises on a stage in semi-darkness. After a moment, when the LIGHTS have come up, the door in the Up Right corner bursts open: Enter PURLIE JUDSON. PURLIE JUDSON is tall, restless, and commanding. In his middle or late thirties, he wears a wide-brim, ministerial black hat, a string tie, and a claw hammer coat, which, though far from new, does not fit him too badly. His arms are loaded with large boxes and parcels, which must have come fresh from a department store. PURLIE is a man consumed with that divine impatience, without which nothing truly good, or truly bad, or even truly ridiculous, is ever accomplished in this world—with rhetoric and flourish to match.

PURLIE: (Calling out loudly.) Missy! (No answer.) Gitlow!—It's me—Purlie Victorious! (Still no answer. PURLIE empties his overloaded arms, with obvious relief, on top of the big Center table. He stands, mops his brow, and blows.) Nobody home it seems. (This last he says to someone he assumes has come in with him. When there is no answer he hurries to the door through which he entered.) Come on—come on in!

(Enter LUTIEBELLE JENKINS, slowly, as if bemused. Young, eager, well-built: though we cannot tell it at the moment. Clearly a girl from the backwoods, she carries a suitcase tied up with a rope in one hand, and a greasy shoebox with what's left of her lunch, together with an outmoded, out-sized handbag, in the other. Obviously she has traveled a great distance, but she still manages to look fresh and healthy. Her hat is a horror with feathers, but she wears it like a banner. Her shoes are flat-heeled and plain white, such as a good servant girl in the white folks' kitchen who knows her place absolutely is bound to wear. Her fall coat is dowdy, but well-intentioned with a stingy strip of rabbit fur around the neck. LUTIEBELLE is like thousands of Negro girls you might know. Eager, desirous—even anxious, keenly in search for life and for love, trembling on the brink of self-confident and vigorous young womanhood—but afraid to take the final leap: because no one has *ever told her it is no longer necessary to be white in order to be virtuous, charming, or beautiful.)*

LUTIEBELLE: *(Looking around as if at a museum of great importance.)* Nobody home it seems.

PURLIE: *(Annoyed to find himself so exactly echoed, looks at her sharply. He takes his watch from his vest pocket, where he wears it on a chain.)* Cotton-picking time in Georgia it's against the law to be home. Come in—unload yourself. *(Crosses and looks out into the kitchen.* LUTIEBELLE *is so enthralled, she still stands with all her bags and parcels in her arms.)* Set your suitcase down.

LUTIEBELLE: What?

PURLIE: It's making you lopsided.

LUTIEBELLE: *(Snapping out of it.)* It is? I didn't even notice. *(Sets suitcase, lunch box, and parcels down.)*

PURLIE: *(Studies her for a moment; goes and gently takes off her hat.)* Tired?

LUTIEBELLE: Not stepping high as I am!

PURLIE: *(Takes the rest of her things and sets them on the table.)* Hungry?

LUTIEBELLE: No, sir. But there's still some of my lunch left if you—

PURLIE: *(Quickly.)* No, thank you. Two ham-hock sandwiches in one day is my limit. *(Sits down and fans himself with his hat.)* Sorry I had to walk you so far so fast.

LUTIEBELLE: *(Dreamily.)* Oh, I didn't mind, sir. Walking's good for you, Miz Emmylou sez—

PURLIE: Miz Emmylou can afford to say that: Miz Emmylou got a car. While all the transportation we got in the world is tied up in second-hand shoe leather. But never mind, my sister, never-you-mind! *(Rises, almost as if to dance, exaltation glowing in his eyes.)* And toll the bell, Big Bethel—toll that big, black, fat and sassy liberty bell! Tell Freedom the bridegroom cometh; the day of her deliverance is now at hand! *(*PURLIE *catches sight of* MISSY *through door Down Left.)* Oh, there she is. *(Crosses to door and calls out.)* Missy!—Oh, Missy!

MISSY: *(From a distance.)* Yes-s-s-s!

PURLIE: It's me!—Purlie!

MISSY: Purlie Victorious?

PURLIE: Yes. Put that battling stick down and come on in here!

MISSY: All right!

PURLIE: *(Crosses hurriedly back to above table at Center.)* That's Missy, my sister-in-law I was telling you about. *(Clears the table of everything but one of the large cartons, which he proceeds to open.)*

LUTIEBELLE: *(Not hearing him. Still awe-struck to be in the very house, in perhaps the very same room that* PURLIE *might have been born in.)* So this is the house where you was born and bred at.

PURLIE: Yep! Better'n being born outdoors.

LUTIEBELLE: What a lovely background for your homelife.

PURLIE: I wouldn't give it to my dog to raise fleas in!

LUTIEBELLE: So clean—and nice—and warm hearted!

PURLIE: The first chance I get I'ma burn the damn thing down!

LUTIEBELLE: But—Reb'n Purlie!—It's yours, and that's what counts. Like Miz Emmylou sez—

PURLIE: Come here! *(Pulls her across to the window, flings it open.)* You see that big white house, perched on top of that hill with them two windows looking right down at us like two eyeballs: that's where Ol' Cap'n lives.

LUTIEBELLE: Ol' Cap'n?

PURLIE: Stonewall Jackson Cotchipee. He owns this dump, not me.

LUTIEBELLE: Oh—

PURLIE: And that ain't all: hill and dale, field and farm, truck and tractor, horse and mule, bird and bee and bush and tree—and cotton!—cotton by bole and by bale—every bit o' cotton you see in this county!—Everything and everybody he owns!

LUTIEBELLE: Everybody? You mean he owns people?

PURLIE: *(Bridling his impatience.)* Well—look!—ain't a man, woman or child working in this valley that ain't in debt to that ol' bastard!—*(Catches himself.)* bustard!—*(This still won't do.)* buzzard!—And that includes Gitlow and Missy—everybody—except me.—

LUTIEBELLE: But folks can't own people no more, Reb'n Purlie. Miz Emmylou sez that—

PURLIE: *(Verging on explosion.)* You ain't working for Miz Emmylou no more, you're working for me—Purlie Victorious. Freedom is my business, and I say that ol' man runs this plantation on debt: the longer you work for Ol' Cap'n Cotchipee, the more you owe at the commissary; and if you don't pay up, you can't leave. And I don't give a damn what Miz Emmylou nor nobody else sez—that's slavery!

LUTIEBELLE: I'm sorry, Reb'n Purlie—

PURLIE: Don't apologize, wait!—Just wait!—til I get my church;—wait til I buy Big Bethel back—*(Crosses to window and looks out.)* Wait til I stand once again in the pulpit of Grandpaw Kinkaid, and call upon my people—and talk to my people—About Ol' Cap'n, that miserable son-of-a—

LUTIEBELLE: *(Just in time to save him.)* Wait—!

PURLIE: Wait, I say! And we'll see who's gonna dominize this valley!—him or me! *(Turns and sees* MISSY *through door Down Left.)* Missy—!

(Enter MISSY, *ageless, benign, and smiling. She wears a ragged old straw hat, a big house apron over her faded gingham, and low-cut, dragged-out tennis shoes on her feet. She is strong and of good cheer—of a certain shrewdness, yet full of the desire to believe. Her eyes light on* LUTIEBELLE, *and her arms go up and outward automatically.)*

MISSY: Purlie!

PURLIE: *(Thinks she is reaching for him.)* Missy!

MISSY: *(Ignoring him, clutching* LUTIEBELLE, *laughing and crying.)* Well—well—well!

PURLIE: *(Breaking the stranglehold.)* For God's sake, Missy, don't choke her to death!

MISSY: All my life—all my life I been praying for me a daughter just like you. My prayers is been answered at last. Welcome to our home, whoever you is!

LUTIEBELLE: *(Deeply moved.)* Thank you, m'am.

MISSY: "M'am—m'am." Listen to the child, Purlie. Everybody down here calls me Aunt Missy, and I'd be much obliged if you would, too.

LUTIEBELLE: It would make me very glad to do so—Aunt Missy.

MISSY: Uhmmmmmm! Pretty as a pan of buttermilk biscuits. Where on earth did you find her, Purlie? (PURLIE *starts to answer.)* Let me take your things—now, you just make yourself at home—Are you hungry?

LUTIEBELLE: No, m'am, but cheap as water is, I sure ain't got no business being this thirsty!

MISSY: *(Starts forward.)* I'll get some for you—

PURLIE: *(Intercepts her; directs* LUTIEBELLE.) There's the dipper. And right out yonder by the fence just this side of that great big live oak tree you'll find the well—sweetest water in Cotchipee county.

LUTIEBELLE: Thank you, Reb'n Purlie. I'm very much obliged. (Takes dipper from water pail and exits Down Left.)

MISSY: Reb'n who?

PURLIE: (Looking off after LUTIEBELLE.) Perfection—absolute Ethiopian perfect. Hah, Missy?

MISSY: (Looking off after LUTIEBELLE.) Oh, I don't know about that.

PURLIE: What you mean you don't know? This girl looks more like Cousin Bee than Cousin Bee ever did.

MISSY: No resemblance to me.

PURLIE: Don't be ridiculous; she's the spitting image—

MISSY: No resemblance whatsoever!

PURLIE: I ought to know how my own cousin looked—

MISSY: But I was the last one to see her alive—

PURLIE: Twins, if not closer!

MISSY: Are you crazy? Bee was more lean, loose, and leggy—

PURLIE: Maybe so, but this girl makes it up in—

MISSY: With no chin to speak of—her eyes: sort of fickle one to another—

PURLIE: I know, but even so—

MISSY: (Pointing off in LUTIEBELLE's direction.) Look at her head—it ain't nearly as built like a rutabaga as Bee's own was!

PURLIE: (Exasperated.) What's the difference! White folks can't tell one of us from another by the head!

MISSY: Twenty years ago it was, Purlie, Ol' Cap'n laid bull whip to your natural behind—

PURLIE: Twenty years ago I swore I'd see his soul in hell!

MISSY: And I don't think you come full back to your senses yet—That ol' man ain't no fool!

PURLIE: That makes it one "no fool" against another.

MISSY: He's dangerous, Purlie. We could get killed if that old man was to find out what we was trying to do to get that church back.

PURLIE: How can he find out? Missy, how many times must I tell you, if it's one thing I am foolproof in it's white folks' psychology.

MISSY: That's exactly what I'm afraid of.

PURLIE: Freedom, Missy, that's what Big Bethel means. For you, me and Gitlow. And we can buy it for five hundred dollars, Missy. Freedom!—You want it, or don't you?

MISSY: Of course I want it, but—after all, Purlie, that rich ol' lady didn't exactly leave that $500 to us—

PURLIE: She left it to Aunt Henrietta—

MISSY: Aunt Henrietta is dead—

PURLIE: Exactly—

MISSY: And Henrietta's daughter Cousin Bee is dead, too.

PURLIE: Which makes us next in line to inherit the money by law!

MISSY: All right, then, why don't we just go on up that hill man-to-man and tell Ol' Cap'n we want our money?

PURLIE: Missy! You have been black as long as I have—

MISSY: (Not above having her own little joke.) Hell, boy, we could make him give it to us.

PURLIE: Make him—how? He's a white man, Missy. What you plan to do, sue him?

MISSY: (Drops her teasing; thinks seriously for a moment.) After all, it is our money. And it was our church.

PURLIE: And can you think of a better way to get it back than that girl out there?

MISSY: But you think it'll work, Purlie? You really think she can fool Ol' Cap'n?

PURLIE: He'll never know what hit him.

MISSY: Maybe—but there's still the question of Gitlow.

PURLIE: What about Gitlow?

MISSY: Gitlow has changed his mind.

PURLIE: Then you'll have to change it back.

GITLOW: (Offstage.) Help, Missy; help, Missy; help, Missy; help, Missy! (GITLOW runs on.)

MISSY: What the devil's the matter this time?

GITLOW: There I was, Missy, picking in the high cotton, twice as fast as the human eye could see. All of a sudden I missed a bole and it fell—it fell on the ground, Missy! I stooped as fast as I could to pick it up and—(He stoops to illustrate. There is a loud tearing of cloth.) ripped the seat of my britches. There I was, Missy, exposed from stem to stern.

MISSY: What's so awful about that? It's only cotton.

GITLOW: But cotton is white, Missy. We must maintain respect. Bring me my Sunday School britches.

MISSY: What!

GITLOW: Ol' Cap'n is coming down into the cotton patch today, and I know you want your Gitlow to look his level best. (MISSY *starts to answer.*) Hurry, Missy, hurry! (GITLOW *hurries her off.*)

PURLIE: Gitlow—have I got the girl!

GITLOW: Is that so—what girl?

PURLIE: *(Taking him to the door.)* See? There she is! Well?

GITLOW: Well what?

PURLIE: What do you think?

GITLOW: Nope; she'll never do.

PURLIE: What you mean, she'll never do?

GITLOW: My advice to you is to take that girl back to Florida as fast as you can!

PURLIE: I can't take her back to Florida.

GITLOW: Why can't you take her back to Florida?

PURLIE: 'Cause she comes from Alabama. Gitlow, look at her: she's just the size—just the type—just the style.

GITLOW: And just the girl to get us all in jail. The answer is no! *(Crosses to kitchen door.)* MISSY! *(Back to* PURLIE.*)* Girl or no girl, I ain't getting mixed up in no more of your nightmares—I got my own. Dammit, Missy, I said let's go!

MISSY: *(Entering with trousers.)* You want me to take my bat to you again?

GITLOW: No, Missy, control yourself. It's just that every second Gitlow's off the firing line-up, seven pounds of Ol' Cap'n's cotton don't git gotten. *(Snatches pants from* MISSY *but is in too much of a hurry to put them on—starts off.)*

PURLIE: Wait a minute, Gitlow. . . . Wait! (GITLOW *is off in a flash.*) Missy! Stop him!

MISSY: He ain't as easy to stop as he used to be. Especially now Ol' Cap'n's made him Deputy-For-The-Colored.

PURLIE: Deputy-For-The-Colored? What the devil is that?

MISSY: Who knows? All I know is Gitlow's changed his mind.

PURLIE: But Gitlow can't change his mind!

MISSY: Oh, it's easy enough when you ain't got much to start with. I warned you. You don't know how shifty ol' Git can git. He's the hardest man to convince and keep convinced I ever seen in my life.

PURLIE: Missy, you've got to make him go up that hill, he's got to identify this girl—Ol' Cap'n won't believe nobody else.

MISSY: I know—

PURLIE: He's got to swear before Ol' Cap'n that this girl is the real Cousin Bee—

MISSY: I know.

PURLIE: Missy, you're the only person in this world ol' Git'll really listen to.

MISSY: I know.

PURLIE: And what if you do have to hit him a time or two—it's for his own good!

MISSY: I know.

PURLIE: He'll recover from it, Missy. He always does—

MISSY: I know.

PURLIE: Freedom, Missy—Big Bethel; for you; me; and Gitlow—!

MISSY: Freedom—and a little something left over—that's all I ever wanted all my life. (*Looks out into the* yard.) She do look a little somewhat like Cousin Bee—about the feet!

PURLIE: Of course she does—

MISSY: I won't guarantee nothing, Purlie—but I'll try.

PURLIE: (*Grabbing her and dancing her around.*) Everytime I see you, Missy, you get prettier by the pound!

(LUTIEBELLE *enters.* MISSY *sees her.*)

MISSY: Stop it, Purlie, stop it! Stop it. Quit cutting the fool in front of company!

PURLIE: (*Sees* LUTIEBELLE, *crosses to her, grabs her about the waist and swings her around too.*)

How wondrous are the daughters of my people,
Yet knoweth not the glories of themselves!

(*Spins her around for* MISSY'S *inspection. She does look better with her coat off, in her immaculate blue and white maid's uniform.*)

Where do you suppose I found her, Missy—
This Ibo prize—this Zulu Pearl—
This long lost lily of the black Mandingo—

Kikuyu maid, beneath whose brown embrace
Hot suns of Africa are burning still: where—where?
A drudge; a serving wench; a feudal fetch-pot:
A common scullion in the white man's kitchen.
Drowned is her youth in thankless Southern dishpans;
Her beauty spilt for Dixiecratic pigs!
This brown-skinned grape! this wine of Negro vintage—

MISSY: (Interrupting.) I know all that, Purlie, but what's her name?

(PURLIE *looks at* LUTIEBELLE *and turns abruptly away.*)

LUTIEBELLE: I don't think he likes my name so much—it's Lutiebelle,
ma'am—Lutiebelle Gussiemae Jenkins!

MISSY: (Gushing with motherly reassurance.) Lutiebelle Gussiemae Jenkins! My, that's nice.

PURLIE: Nice! It's an insult to the Negro people!

MISSY: Purlie, behave yourself!

PURLIE: A previous condition of servitude, a badge of inferiority, and I
refuse to have it in my organization!—change it!

MISSY: You want me to box your mouth for you!

PURLIE: Lutiebelle Gussiemae Jenkins! What does it mean in Swahili?
Cheap labor!

LUTIEBELLE: Swahili?

PURLIE: One of the thirteen silver tongues of Africa: Swahili,
Bushengo, Ashanti, Baganda, Herero, Yoruba, Bambora, Mpongwe,
Swahili: a language of moons, of velvet drums; hot days of rivers,
red-splashed, and birdsong bright!, black fingers in rice white at
sunset red!—ten thousand Queens of Sheba—

MISSY: (Having to interrupt.) Just where did Purlie find you, honey?

LUTIEBELLE: It was in Dothan, Alabama, last Sunday, Aunt Missy, right
in the junior choir!

MISSY: The junior choir—my, my, my!

PURLIE: (Still carried away.)
Behold! I said, this dark and holy vessel,
In whom should burn that golden nut-brown joy
Which Negro womanhood was meant to be.
Ten thousand queens, ten thousand Queens of Sheba:
(Pointing at LUTIEBELLE.)

Ethiopia herself—in all her beauteous wonder,

Come to restore the ancient thrones of Cush!

MISSY: Great Gawdamighty, Purlie, I can't hear myself think—!

LUTIEBELLE: That's just what I said last Sunday, Aunt Missy, when Reb'n Purlie started preaching that thing in the pulpit.

MISSY: Preaching it!?

LUTIEBELLE: Lord, Aunt Missy, I shouted clear down to the Mourners' Bench.

MISSY: (To PURLIE.) But last time you was a professor of Negro Philosophy.

PURLIE: I told you, Missy: my intention is to buy Big Bethel back; to reclaim the ancient pulpit of Grandpaw Kincaid, and preach freedom in the cotton patch—I told you!

MISSY: Maybe you did, Purlie, maybe you did. You got yourself a license?

PURLIE: Naw!—but—

MISSY: (Looking him over.) Purlie Victorious Judson: Self-made minister of the gospel-claw-hammer coattail, shoe-string tie and all.

PURLIE: (Quietly but firmly holding his ground.) How else can you lead the Negro people?

MISSY: Is that what you got in your mind: leading the Negro people?

PURLIE: Who else is they got?

MISSY: God help the race.

LUTIEBELLE: It was a sermon, I mean, Aunt Missy, the likes of which has never been heard before.

MISSY: Oh, I bet that. Tell me about it, son. What did you preach?

PURLIE: I preached the New Baptism of Freedom for all mankind, according to the Declaration of Independence, taking as my text the Constitution of the United States of America, Amendments First through Fifteenth, which readeth as follows: "Congress shall make no law—"

MISSY: Enough—that's enough, son—I'm converted. But it is confusing, all the changes you keep going through. (To LUTIEBELLE.) Honey, every time I see Purlie he's somebody else.

PURLIE: Not any more, Missy; and if I'm lying may the good Lord put me down in the book of bad names: Purlie is put forever!

MISSY: Yes. But will he stay put forever?

PURLIE: There is in every man a finger of iron that points him what he must and must not do—

MISSY: And your finger points up the hill to that five hundred dollars with which you'll buy Big Bethel back, preach freedom in the cotton patch, and live happily ever after!

PURLIE: The soul-consuming passion of my life! *(Draws out watch.)* It's 2:15, Missy, and Gitlow's waiting. Missy, I suggest you get a move on.

MISSY: I already got a move on. Had it since four o'clock this morning!

PURLIE: Time, Missy—exactly what the colored man in this country ain't got, and you're wasting it!

MISSY: *(Looks at* PURLIE, *and decides not to strike him dead.)* Purlie, would you mind stepping out into the cotton patch and telling your brother Gitlow I'd like a few words with him? *(*PURLIE, *overjoyed, leaps at* MISSY *as if to hug and dance her around again, but she is too fast.)* Do like I tell you now—go on! *(*PURLIE *exits singing.* MISSY *turns to* LUTIEBELLE *to begin the important task of sizing her up.)* Besides, it wouldn't be hospitable not to set and visit a spell with our distinguished guest over from Dothan, Alabama.

LUTIEBELLE: *(This is the first time she has been called anything of importance by anybody.)* Thank you, ma'am.

MISSY: Now. Let's you and me just set back and enjoy a piece of my potato pie. You like potato pie, don't you?

LUTIEBELLE: Oh, yes, ma'am, I like it very much.

MISSY: And get real acquainted. *(Offers her a saucer with a slice of pie on it.)*

LUTIEBELLE: I'm ever so much obliged. My, this looks nice! Uhm, uhn, uhn!

MISSY: *(Takes a slice for herself and sits down.)* You know—ever since that ol' man—*(Indicates up the hill.)* took after Purlie so unmerciful with that bull whip twenty years ago—he fidgets! Always on the go; rattling around from place to place all over the country: one step ahead of the white folks—something about Purlie always did irritate the white folks.

LUTIEBELLE: Is that the truth!

MISSY: Oh, my yes. Finally wound up being locked up a time or two for safekeeping—*(*LUTIEBELLE *parts with a loud, sympathetic grunt. Changing her tack a bit.)* Always kept up his schooling, though. In fact that boy's got one of the best second-hand educations in this country.

LUTIEBELLE: *(Brightening considerably.)* Is that a fact!

MISSY: Used to read everything he could get his hands on.

LUTIEBELLE: He did? Ain't that wonderful!

MISSY: Till one day he finally got tired, and throwed all his books to the hogs—not enough "Negro" in them, he said. After that he puttered around with first one thing then another. Remember that big bus boycott they had in Montgomery? Well, we don't travel by bus in the cotton patch, so Purlie boycotted mules!

LUTIEBELLE: You don't say so?

MISSY: Another time he invented a secret language, that Negroes could understand but white folks couldn't.

LUTIEBELLE: Oh, my goodness gracious!

MISSY: He sent it C.O.D. to the NAACP but they never answered his letter.

LUTIEBELLE: Oh, they will, Aunt Missy; you can just bet your life they will.

MISSY: I don't mind it so much. Great leaders are bound to pop up from time to time 'mongst our people—in fact we sort of look forward to it. But Purlie's in such a hurry I'm afraid he'll lose his mind.

LUTIEBELLE: Lose his mind—no! Oh, no!

MISSY: That is unless you and me can do something about it.

LUTIEBELLE: You and me? Do what, Aunt Missy? You tell me—I'll do anything!

MISSY: *(Having found all she needs to know.)* Well, now; ain't nothing ever all that peculiar about a man a good wife—and a family—and some steady home cooking won't cure. Don't you think so?

LUTIEBELLE: *(Immensely relieved.)* Oh, yes, Aunt Missy, yes. *(But still not getting* MISSY's *intent.)* You'd be surprised how many tall, good-looking, great big, ol' handsome looking mens—just like Reb'n Purlie—walking around, starving theyselves to death! Oh, I just wish I had one to aim my pot at!

MISSY: Well, Purlie Judson is the uncrowned appetite of the age.

LUTIEBELLE: He is! What's his favorite?

MISSY: Anything! Anything a fine-looking, strong and healthy—girl like you could put on the table.

LUTIEBELLE: Like me? Like ME! Oh, Aunt Missy—!

MISSY: *(*PURLIE's *future is settled.)* Honey, I mind once at the Sunday School picnic Purlie et a whole sack o' pullets!

LUTIEBELLE: Oh, I just knowed there was something—something—just reeks about that man. He puts me in the mind of all the good things I ever had in my life. Picnics, fish-fries, corn-shuckings, and love-feasts, and gospel-singings—picking huckleberries, roasting groundpeas, quilting-bee parties and barbecues; that certain kind of—welcome—you can't get nowhere else in all this world. Aunt Missy, life is so good to us—sometimes!

MISSY: Oh, child, being colored can be a lotta fun when ain't nobody looking.

LUTIEBELLE: Ain't it the truth! I always said I'd never pass for white, no matter how much they offered me, unless the things I love could pass, too.

MISSY: Ain't it the beautiful truth!

(PURLIE *enters again; agitated.*)

PURLIE: Missy—Gitlow says if you want him come and get him!

MISSY: *(Rises, crosses to door Down Left; looks out.)* Lawd, that man do take his cotton picking seriously. *(Comes back to* LUTIEBELLE *and takes her saucer.)* Did you get enough to eat, honey?

LUTIEBELLE: Indeed I did. And Aunt Missy, I haven't had potato pie like that since the senior choir give—

MISSY: *(Still ignoring him.)* That's where I met Gitlow, you know. On the senior choir.

LUTIEBELLE: Aunt Missy! I didn't know you could sing!

MISSY: Like a brown-skin nightingale. Well, it was a Sunday afternoon—Big Bethel had just been—

PURLIE: Dammit, Missy! The white man is five hundred years ahead of us in this country, and we ain't gonna ever gonna catch up with him sitting around on our non-Caucasian rumps talking about the senior choir!

MISSY: *(Starts to bridle at this sudden display of passion, but changes her mind.)* Right this way, honey. *(Heads for door Down Right.)* Where Cousin Bee used to sleep at.

LUTIEBELLE: Yes, ma'am. *(Starts to follow* MISSY.)

PURLIE: *(Stopping her.)* Wait a minute—don't forget your clothes! *(Gives her a large carton.)*

MISSY: It ain't much, the roof leaks, and you can get as much September inside as you can outside any time; but I try to keep it clean.

PURLIE: Cousin Bee was known for her clothes!

MISSY: Stop nagging, Purlie—*(To* LUTIEBELLE.*)* There's plenty to eat in the kitchen.

LUTIEBELLE: Thank you, Aunt Missy. *(Exits Down Right.)*

PURLIE: *(Following after her.)* And hurry! We want to leave as soon as Missy gets Gitlow in from the cotton patch!

MISSY: *(Blocking his path.)* Mr. Preacher—*(She pulls him out of earshot.)* If we do pull this thing off—*(Studying him a moment.)* what do you plan to do with her after that—send her back where she came from?

PURLIE: Dothan, Alabama? Never! Missy, there a million things I can do with a girl like that, right here in Big Bethel!

MISSY: Yeah! Just make sure they're all legitimate. Anyway, marriage is still cheap, and we can always use another cook in the family!

*(*PURLIE *hasn't the slightest idea what* MISSY *is talking about.)*

LUTIEBELLE: *(From Offstage.)* Aunt Missy.

MISSY: Yes, honey.

LUTIEBELLE: *(Offstage.)* Whose picture is this on the dresser?

MISSY: Why, that's Cousin Bee.

LUTIEBELLE: *(A moment's silence. Then she enters hastily, carrying a large photograph in her hand.)* Cousin Bee!

MISSY: Yes, poor thing. She's the one the whole thing is all about.

LUTIEBELLE: *(The edge of panic.)* Cousin Bee—Oh, my!—Oh, my goodness! My goodness gracious!

MISSY: What's the matter?

LUTIEBELLE: But she's pretty—she's so pretty!

MISSY: *(Takes photograph; looks at it tenderly.)* Yes—she was pretty. I guess they took this shortly before she died.

LUTIEBELLE: And you mean—you want me to look like her?

PURLIE: That's the idea. Now go and get into your clothes. *(Starts to push her off.)*

MISSY: They sent it down to us from the college. Don't she look smart? I'll bet she was a good student when she was living.

LUTIEBELLE: *(Evading* PURLIE.*)* Good student!

MISSY: Yes. One more year and she'd have finished.

LUTIEBELLE: Oh, my gracious Lord have mercy upon my poor soul!

PURLIE: *(Not appreciating her distress or its causes.)* Awake, awake! Put on they strength, O, Zion—put on thy beautiful garments. *(Hurries her*

Offstage.) And hurry! *(Turning to* MISSY.) Missy, Big Bethel and Gitlow is waiting. Grandpaw Kincaid gave his life. *(Gently places the bat into her hand.)* It is a far greater thing you do now, than you've ever done before—and Gitlow ain't never got his head knocked off in a better cause. (MISSY *nods her head in sad agreement, and accepts the bat.* PURLIE *helps her to the door Down Left, where she exits, a most reluctant executioner.* PURLIE *stands and watches her off from the depth of his satisfaction. The door Down Right eases open, and* LUTIEBELLE, *her suitcase, handbag, fall coat and lunch box firmly in hand, tries to sneak out the front door.* PURLIE *hears her, and turns just in time.)* Where do you think you're going?

LUTIEBELLE: Did you see that, Reb'n Purlie? *(Indicating bedroom from which she just came.)* Did you see all them beautiful clothes—slips, hats, shoes, stockings? I mean nylon stockings like Miz Emmylou wears—and a dress, like even Miz Emmylou don't wear. Did you look at what was in that big box?

PURLIE: Of course I looked at what was in that big box—I bought it—all of it—for you.

LUTIEBELLE: For me!

PURLIE: Of course! I told you! And as soon as we finish you can have it!

LUTIEBELLE: Reb'n Purlie, I'm a good girl. I ain't never done nothing in all this world, white, colored or otherwise, to hurt nobody!

PURLIE: I know that.

LUTIEBELLE: I work hard; I mop, I scrub, I iron; I'm clean and polite, and I know how to get along with white folks' children better'n they do. I pay my church dues every second and fourth Sunday the Lord sends; and I can cook catfish—and hushpuppies—You like hushpuppies, don't you, Reb'n Purlie?

PURLIE: I love hushpuppies!

LUTIEBELLE: Hushpuppies—and corn dodgers; I can cook you a corn dodger would give you the swimming in the head!

PURLIE: I'm sure you can, but—

LUTIEBELLE: But I ain't never been in a mess like this in all my life!

PURLIE: Mess—what mess?

LUTIEBELLE: You mean go up that hill, in all them pretty clothes, and pretend—in front of white folks—that—that I'm your Cousin Bee—somebody I ain't never seen or heard of before in my whole life!

PURLIE: Why not? Some of the best pretending in the world is done in front of white folks.

LUTIEBELLE: But Reb'n Purlie, I didn't know your Cousin Bee was a student at the college; I thought she worked there!

PURLIE: But I told you on the train—

LUTIEBELLE: Don't do no good to tell ME nothing, Reb'n Purlie! I never listen. Ask Miz Emmylou and 'em, they'll tell you I never listen. I didn't know it was a college lady you wanted me to make like. I thought it was for a sleep-in like me. I thought all that stuff you bought in them boxes was stuff for maids and cooks and—Why, I ain't never even been near a college!

PURLIE: So what? College ain't so much where you been as how you talk when you get back. Anybody can do it; look at me.

LUTIEBELLE: Nawsir, I think you better look at me like Miz Emmylou sez—

PURLIE: *(Taking her by the shoulders, tenderly.)* Calm down—just take it easy, and calm down. *(She subsides a little, her chills banished by the warmth of him.)* Now—don't tell me, after all that big talking you done on the train about white folks, you're scared.

LUTIEBELLE: Talking big is easy—from the proper distance.

PURLIE: Why—don't you believe in yourself?

LUTIEBELLE: Some.

PURLIE: Don't you believe in your own race of people?

LUTIEBELLE: Oh, yessir—a little.

PURLIE: Don't you believe the black man is coming to power some day?

LUTIEBELLE: Almost.

PURLIE: Ten thousand Queens of Sheba! What kind of a Negro are you! Where's your race pride?

LUTIEBELLE: Oh, I'm a great one for race pride, sir, believe me—it's just that I don't need it much in my line of work! Miz Emmylou sez—

PURLIE: Damn Miz Emmylou! Does her blond hair and blue eyes make her any more of a woman in the sight of her men folks than your black hair and brown eyes in mine?

LUTIEBELLE: No, sir!

PURLIE: Is her lily-white skin any more money-under-the-mattress than your fine fair brown? And if so, why does she spend half her life at the beach trying to get a sun tan?

LUTIEBELLE: I never thought of that!

PURLIE: There's a whole lotta things about the Negro question you ain't thought of! The South is split like a fat man's underwear; and somebody beside the Supreme Court has got to make a stand for the everlasting glory of our people!

LUTIEBELLE: Yessir.

PURLIE: Snatch Freedom from the jaws of force and filibuster!

LUTIEBELLE: Amen to that!

PURLIE: Put thunder in the Senate—!

LUTIEBELLE: Yes, Lord!

PURLIE: And righteous indignation back in the halls of Congress!

LUTIEBELLE: Ain't it the truth!

PURLIE: Make Civil Rights from Civil Wrongs; and bring that ol' Civil War to a fair and a just conclusion!

LUTIEBELLE: Help him, Lord!

PURLIE: Remind this white and wicked world there ain't been more'n a dime's worth of difference twixt one man and another'n, irregardless of race, gender, creed, or color—since God Himself Almighty set the first batch out to dry before the chimneys of Zion got hot! The eyes and ears of the world is on Big Bethel!

LUTIEBELLE: Amen and hallelujah!

PURLIE: And whose side are you fighting on this evening, sister?

LUTIEBELLE: Great Gawdamighty, Reb'n Purlie, on the Lord's side! But Miss Emmylou sez—

PURLIE: (Blowing up.) This is outrageous—this is a catastrophe! You're a disgrace to the Negro profession!

LUTIEBELLE: That's just what she said all right—her exactly words.

PURLIE: Who's responsible for this? Where's your Maw and Paw at?

LUTIEBELLE: I reckon I ain't rightly got no Maw and Paw, wherever they at.

PURLIE: What!

LUTIEBELLE: And nobody else that I knows of. You see, sir—I been on the go from one white folks' kitchen to another since before I can remember. How I got there in the first place—whatever became of my Maw and Paw, and my kinfolks—even what my real name is— nobody is ever rightly said.

PURLIE: (Genuinely touched.) Oh. A motherless child—

LUTIEBELLE: That's what Miz Emmylou always sez—

PURLIE: But—who cared for you—like a mother? Who brung you up—who raised you?

LUTIEBELLE: Nobody in particular—just whoever happened to be in charge of the kitchen that day.

PURLIE: That explains the whole thing—no wonder; you've missed the most important part of being somebody.

LUTIEBELLE: I have? What part is that?

PURLIE: Love—being appreciated, and sought out, and looked after; being fought to the bitter end over even.

LUTIEBELLE: Oh, I have missed that, Reb'n Purlie, I really have. Take mens—all my life they never looked at me the way other girls get looked at!

PURLIE: That's not so. The very first time I saw you—right up there in the junior choir—I give you that look!

LUTIEBELLE: *(Turning to him in absolute ecstasy.)* You did! Oh, I thought so!—I prayed so. All through your sermon I thought I would faint from hoping so hard so. Oh, Reb'n Purlie—I think that's the finest look a person could ever give a person—Oh, Reb'n Purlie! *(She closes her eyes and points her lips at him.)*

PURLIE: *(Starts to kiss her, but draws back shyly.)* Lutiebelle—

LUTIEBELLE: *(Dreamily, her eyes still closed.)* Yes, Reb'n Purlie—

PURLIE: There's something I want to ask you—something I never—in all my life—thought I'd be asking a woman—Would you—I don't know exactly how to say it—would you—

LUTIEBELLE: Yes, Reb'n Purlie?

PURLIE: Would you be my disciple?

LUTIEBELLE: *(Rushing into his arms.)* Oh, yes, Reb'n Purlie, yes!

(They start to kiss, but are interrupted by a NOISE coming from Off-stage.)

GITLOW: *(Offstage; in the extremity of death.)* No, Missy. No—no!—NO!—(This last plea is choked off by the sound of some solid object brought smartly into contact with sudden flesh. "CLUNK!" PURLIE and LU-TIEBELLE stand looking off Left, frozen for the moment.)*

LUTIEBELLE: *(Finally daring to speak.)* Oh, my Lord, Reb'n Purlie, what happened?

PURLIE: Gitlow has changed his mind. (*Grabs her and swings her around bodily.*) Toll the bell, Big Bethel!—toll that big, fat, black and sassy liberty bell. Tell Freedom—(LUTIEBELLE *suddenly leaps from the floor into his arms and plants her lips squarely on his. When finally he can come up for air.*) Tell Freedom—tell Freedom—WOW!

CURTAIN

ACT I

SCENE 2

Time: It is a little later the same afternoon.

Scene: We are now in the little business office off from the commissary, where all the inhabitants of Cotchipee Valley buy food, clothing, and supplies. In the back a traveler has been drawn with just enough of an opening left to serve as the door to the main part of the store. On Stage Left and on Stage Right are simulated shelves where various items of reserve stock are kept: A wash tub, an axe, sacks of peas, and flour; bolts of gingham and calico, etc. Downstage Right is a small desk, on which an ancient typewriter, and an adding machine, with various papers and necessary books and records of commerce are placed. There is a small chair at this desk. Downstage Left is a table, with a large cash register, that has a functioning drawer. Below this is an entrance from the street.

At Rise: As the CURTAIN rises, a young white Man of 25 or 30, but still gawky, awkward, and adolescent in outlook and behavior, is sitting on a high stool Downstage Right Center. His face is held in the hands of IDELLA, *a Negro cook and woman of all work, who has been in the family since time immemorial. She is the only mother* CHARLIE, *who is very much oversized even for his age, has ever known.* IDELLA *is as little as she is old and as tough as she is tiny, and is busily applying medication to* CHARLIE'S *black eye.*

CHARLIE: Ow, Idella, ow!—Ow!
IDELLA: Hold still, boy.
CHARLIE: But it hurts, Idella.

IDELLA: I know it hurts. Whoever done this to you musta meant to knock your natural brains out.

CHARLIE: I already told you who done it—OW!

IDELLA: Charlie Cotchipee, if you don't hold still and let me put this hot poultice on your eye, you better! (CHARLIE *subsides and meekly accepts her ministrations.*) First the milking, then the breakfast, then the dishes, then the washing, then the scrubbing, then the lunch time, next the dishes, then the ironing—and now; just where the picking and plucking for supper ought to be—you!

CHARLIE: You didn't tell Paw?

IDELLA: Of course I didn't—but the sheriff did.

CHARLIE: *(Leaping up.)* The sheriff!

IDELLA: *(Pushing him back down.)* Him and the deputy come to the house less than an hour ago.

CHARLIE: *(Leaping up again.)* Are they coming over here!

IDELLA: Of course they're coming over here—sooner or later.

CHARLIE: But what will I do, Idella, what will I say?

IDELLA: *(Pushing him down.* CHARLIE *subsides.)* "He that keepeth his mouth keepeth his life—"

CHARLIE: Did they ask for me?

IDELLA: Of course they asked for you.

CHARLIE: What did they say?

IDELLA: I couldn't hear too well; your father took them into the study and locked the door behind them.

CHARLIE: Maybe it was about something else.

IDELLA: It was about YOU: that much I could hear! Charlie—you want to get us both killed!

CHARLIE: I'm sorry, Idella, but—

IDELLA: *(Overriding; finishing proverb she had begun.)* "But he that openeth wide his lips shall have destruction!"

CHARLIE: But it was you who said it was the law of the land—

IDELLA: I know I did—

CHARLIE: It was you who said it's got to be obeyed—

IDELLA: I know it was me, but—

CHARLIE: It was you who said everybody had to stand up and take a stand against—

IDELLA: I know it was me, dammit! But I didn't say take a stand in no barroom!

CHARLIE: Ben started it, not me. And you always said never to take low from the likes of him!

IDELLA: Not so loud; they may be out there in the commissary! *(Goes quickly to door Up Center and peers out; satisfied no one has overheard them she crosses back down to CHARLIE.)* Look, boy, everybody down here don't feel as friendly towards the Supreme Court as you and me do—you big enough to know that! And don't you ever go outta here and pull a fool trick like you done last night again and not let me know about it in advance. You hear me!

CHARLIE: I'm sorry.

IDELLA: When you didn't come to breakfast this morning, and I went upstairs looking for you, and you just setting there, looking at me with your big eyes, and I seen that they had done hurt you—my, my, my! Whatever happens to you happens to me—you big enough to know that!

CHARLIE: I didn't mean to make trouble, Idella.

IDELLA: I know that, son, I know it. *(Makes final adjustments to the poultice.)* Now. No matter what happens when they do come I'll be right behind you. Keep your nerves calm and your mouth shut. Understand?

CHARLIE: Yes.

IDELLA: And as soon as you get a free minute come over to the house and let me put another hot poultice on that eye.

CHARLIE: Thank you, I'm very much obliged to you. Idella—

IDELLA: What is it, son?

CHARLIE: Sometimes I think I ought to run away from home.

IDELLA: I know, but you already tried that, honey.

CHARLIE: Sometimes I think I ought to run away from home—again!

(OL' CAP'N has entered from the Commissary just in time to hear this last remark.)

OL' CAP'N: Why don't you, boy—why don't you? (OL' CAP'N COTCHIPEE *is aged and withered a bit, but by no mans infirm. Dressed in traditional southern linen, the wide hat, the shoestring tie, the long coat, the twirling moustache of the Ol' Southern Colonel. In his left hand he carries a cane, and in his right a coiled bull whip: his last line of defense. He stops long enough to establish the fact that he means business, threatens them both* with a mean cantankerous eye, then hangs his whip—the definitive answer to all who might foolishly question his Confederate power and glory—upon a peg. CHARLIE *freezes at the sound of his voice.* IDELLA *tenses but keeps working on* CHARLIE's *eye.* OL' CAP'N *crosses down, rudely pushes her hand aside, lifts up* CHARLIE's *chin so that he may examine the damage, shakes his head in disgust.)* You don't know, boy, what a strong stomach it takes to stomach you. Just look at you, sitting there—all slopped over like something the horses dropped; steam, stink and all!

IDELLA: Don't you dare talk like that to this child!

OL' CAP'N: *(This stops him—momentarily.)* When I think of his grandpaw, God rest his Confederate soul, hero of the battle of Chicamauga— *(It's too much.)* Get outta my sight! (CHARLIE *gets up to leave.)* Not you—you! *(Indicates* IDELLA. *She gathers up her things in silence and starts to leave.)* Wait a minute—(IDELLA *stops.)* You been closer to this boy than I have, even before his ma died—ain't a thought ever entered his head you didn't know 'bout it first. You got anything to do with what my boy's been thinking lately?

IDELLA: I didn't know he had been thinking lately.

OL' CAP'N: Don't play with me, Idella—and you know what I mean! Who's been putting these integrationary ideas in my boy's head? Was it you—I'm asking you a question, dammit! Was it you?

IDELLA: Why don't you ask him?

OL' CAP'N: *(Snorts.)* Ask him! ASK HIM! He ain't gonna say a word unless you tell him to, and you know it. I'm asking you again, Idella Landy, have you been talking integration to my boy!?

IDELLA: I can't rightly answer you any more on that than he did.

OL' CAP'N: By God, you will answer me. I'll make you stand right there—right there!—all day and all night long, till you do answer me!

IDELLA: That's just fine.

OL' CAP'N: What's that! What's that you say?

IDELLA: I mean I ain't got nothing else to do—supper's on the stove; rice is ready, okra's fried, turnip's simmered, biscuits' baked, and stew is stewed. In fact them lemon pies you wanted special for supper are in the oven right now, just getting ready to burn—

OL' CAP'N: Get outta here!

IDELLA: Oh—no hurry, Ol' Cap'n—

OL' CAP'N: Get the hell out of here! (IDELLA *deliberately takes all the time in the world to pick up her things. Following her around trying to make his point.)* I'm warning both of you; that little lick over the eye is a small skimption compared to what I'm gonna do. (IDELLA *pretends not to listen.)* I won't stop till I get to the bottom of this! (IDELLA *still ignores him.)* Get outta here, Idella Landy, before I take my cane and—*(he raises his cane but* IDELLA *insists on moving at her own pace to exit Down Left.)* And save me some buttermilk to go with them lemon pies, you hear me! *(Turns to* CHARLIE; *not knowing how to approach him.)* The sheriff was here this morning.

CHARLIE: Yessir.

OL' CAP'N: Is that all you got to say to me: "Yessir"?

CHARLIE: Yessir.

OL' CAP'N: You are a disgrace to the southland!

CHARLIE: Yessir.

OL' CAP'N: Shut up! I could kill you, boy, you understand that? Kill you with my own two hands!

CHARLIE: Yessir.

OL' CAP'N: Shut up! I could beat you to death with that bull whip—put my pistol to your good-for-nothing head—my own flesh and blood—and blow your blasted brains all over this valley! *(Fighting to retain his control.)* If—if you wasn't the last living drop of Cotchipee blood in Cotchipee County, I'd—I'd—

CHARLIE: Yessir. *(This is too much.* OL' CAP'N *snatches* CHARLIE *to his feet. But* CHARLIE *does not resist.)*

OL' CAP'N: You trying to get non-violent with me, boy? (CHARLIE *does not answer, just dangles there.)*

CHARLIE: *(Finally.)* I'm ready with the books, sir—that is—whenever you're ready.

OL' CAP'N: *(Flinging* CHARLIE *into a chair.)* Thank you—thank you! What with your Yankee propaganda, your barroom brawls, and all your other non-Confederate activities, I didn't think you had the time.

CHARLIE: *(Picks up account book; reads.)* "Cotton report. Fifteen bales picked yesterday and sent to the cotton gin; bringing our total to 357 bales to date."

OL' CAP'N: *(Impressed.)* 357—boy, that's some picking. Who's ahead?

CHARLIE: Gitlow Judson, with seventeen bales up to now.

OL' CAP'N: Gitlow Judson; well I'll be damned; did you ever see a cotton-pickinger darky in your whole life?!

CHARLIE: Commissary report—

OL' CAP'N: Did you ever look down into the valley and watch ol' Git a-picking his way through that cotton patch? Holy Saint Mother's Day! I'll bet you—

CHARLIE: Commissary report!

OL' CAP'N: All right!—commissary report.

CHARLIE: Yessir—well, first, sir, there's been some complaints: the flour is spoiled, the beans are rotten, and the meat is tainted.

OL' CAP'N: Cut the price on it.

CHARLIE: But it's also a little wormy—

OL' CAP'N: Then sell it to the Negras—Is something wrong?

CHARLIE: No, sir—I mean, sir . . . , we can't go on doing that, sir.

OL' CAP'N: Why not? It's traditional.

CHARLIE: Yessir, but times are changing—all this debt—*(Indicates book.)* According to this book every family in this valley owes money they'll never be able to pay back.

OL' CAP'N: Of course—it's the only way to keep 'em working. Didn't they teach you nothin' at school?

CHARLIE: We're cheating them—and they know we're cheating them. How long do you expect them to stand for it?

OL' CAP'N: As long as they're Negras—

CHARLIE: How long before they start a-rearing up on their hind legs, and saying: "Enough, white folks—now that's enough! Either you start treating me like I'm somebody in this world, or I'll blow your brains out"?

OL' CAP'N: *(Shaken to the core.)* Stop it—stop it! You're tampering with the economic foundation of the southland! Are you trying to ruin me? One more word like that and I'll kill—I'll shoot—(CHARLIE *attempts to answer.)* Shut up! One more world and I'll—I'll fling myself on your Maw's grave and die of apoplexy. I'll—! I'll—! Shut up, do you hear me? Shut up! *(Enter* GITLOW, *hat in hand, grin on face, more obsequious today than ever.)* Now what the hell *you* want?

GITLOW: *(Taken aback.)* Nothing, sir, nothing!—That is—Missy, my ol' 'oman—well, suh, to git to the truth of the matter, I got a little business—

OL' CAP'N: Negras ain't got no business. And if you don't get the hell back into that cotton patch you better. Git, I said! (GITLOW *starts to beat a hasty retreat.)* Oh, no—don't go. Uncle Gitlow—good ol' faithful ol' Gitlow. Don't go—don't go.

GITLOW: *(Not quite sure.)* Well—you're the boss, boss.

OL' CAP'N: *(Shoving a cigar into GITLOW's mouth.)* Just the other day, I was talking to the Senator about you—What's that great big knot on your head?

GITLOW: Missy—I mean, a mosquito!

OL' CAP'N: *(In all seriousness, examining the bump.)* Uh! Musta been wearin' brass knuck—And he was telling me, the Senator was, how hard it was—impossible, he said, to find the old-fashioned, solid, hard-earned, Uncle Tom type Negra nowadays. I laughed in his face.

GITLOW: Yassuh. By the grace of God, there's still a few of us left.

OL' CAP'N: I told him how you and me growed up together. Had the same mammy—my mammy was your mother.

GITLOW: Yessir! Bosom buddies!

OL' CAP'N: And how you used to sing that favorite ol' speritual of mine: *(Sings.)* "I'm a-coming . . . I'm a-coming, For my head is bending low," (GITLOW *joins in on harmony.)* "I hear the gentle voices calling, Ol' Black Joe. . . ." *(This proves too much for* CHARLIE; *he starts out.)* Where you going?

CHARLIE: Maybe they need me in the front of the store.

OL' CAP'N: Come back here! (CHARLIE *returns.)* Turn around—show Gitlow that eye. (CHARLIE *reluctantly exposes black eye to view.)*

GITLOW: Gret Gawdamighty, somebody done cold cocked this child! Who hit Mr. Charlie, tell Uncle Gitlow who hit you? (CHARLIE *does not answer.)*

OL' CAP'N: Would you believe it? All of a sudden he can't say a word. And just last night, the boys was telling me, this son of mine made hisself a full-fledged speech.

GITLOW: You don't say.

OL' CAP'N: All about Negras—NeGROES he called 'em—four years of college, and he still can't say the word right—seems he's quite a specialist on the subject.

GITLOW: Well, shut my hard-luck mouth!

OL' CAP'N: Yessireebob. Told the boys over at Ben's bar in town, that he was all for mixing the races together.

GITLOW: You go on 'way from hyeah!

OL' CAP'N: Said white children and darky children ought to go the same schoolhouse together!

GITLOW: Tell me the truth, Ol' Cap'n!

OL' CAP'N: Got hisself so worked up some of 'em had to cool him down with a co-cola bottle!

GITLOW: Tell me the truth—again!

CHARLIE: That wasn't what I said!

OL' CAP'N: You calling me a liar, boy!

CHARLIE: No, sir, but I just said, that since it was the law of the land—

OL' CAP'N: It is not the law of the land no sucha thing!

CHARLIE: I didn't think it would do any harm if they went to school together—that's all.

OL' CAP'N: That's all—that's enough!

CHARLIE: They do it up North—

OL' CAP'N: This is down South. Down here they'll go to school together over me and Gitlow's dead body. Right, Git?!

GITLOW: Er, you the boss, boss!

CHARLIE: But this is the law of the—

OL' CAP'N: Never mind the law! Boy—look! You like Gitlow, you trust him, you always did—didn't you?

CHARLIE: Yessir.

OL' CAP'N: And Gitlow here, would cut off his right arm for you if you was to ask him. Wouldn't you, Git?

GITLOW: (Gulping.) You the boss, boss.

OL' CAP'N: Now Gitlow ain't nothing if he ain't a Negra!—Ain't you, Git?

GITLOW: Oh—two-three hundred percent, I calculate.

OL' CAP'N: Now, if you really want to know what the Negra thinks about this here integration and all lacka-that, don't ask the Supreme Court—ask Gitlow. Go ahead—ask him!

CHARLIE: I don't need to ask him.

OL' CAP'N: Then I'll ask him. Raise your right hand, Git. You solemnly swear to tell the truth, whole truth, nothing else but, so help you God?

GITLOW: (Raising hand.) I do.

OL' CAP'N: Gitlow Judson, as God is your judge and maker, do you believe in your heart that God intended white folks and Negra children to go to school together?

GITLOW: Nawsuh, I do not!

OL' CAP'N: Do you, so help you God, think that white folks and black should mix and 'sociate in street cars, buses, and railroad stations, in any way, shape, form, or fashion?

GITLOW: Absolutely not!

OL' CAP'N: And is it not your considered opinion, God strike you dead if you lie, that all my Negras are happy with things in the southland just the way they are?

GITLOW: Indeed I do!

OL' CAP'N: Do you think ary single darky on my place would ever think of changing a single thing about the South, and to hell with the Supreme Court as God is your judge and maker?

GITLOW: As God is my judge and maker and you are my boss, I do not!

OL' CAP'N: *(Turning in triumph to* CHARLIE.*)* The voice of the Negra himself! What more proof do you want!

CHARLIE: I don't care whose voice it is—it's still the law of the land, and I intend to obey it!

OL' CAP'N: *(Losing control.)* Get outta my face, boy—get outta my face, before I kill you! Before I—

*(*CHARLIE *escapes into the commissary.* OL' CAP'N *collapses.)*

GITLOW: Easy, Ol' Cap'n, easy, suh, easy! *(*OL' CAP'N *gives out a groan.* GIT-LOW *goes to shelf and comes back with a small bottle and a small box.)* Some aspirins, suh . . . , some asaphoetida? *(*PURLIE *and* LUTIEBELLE *appear at door Left.)* Not now—later—later! *(Holds bottle to* OL' CAP'N'S *nose.)*

OL' CAP'N: Gitlow—Gitlow!

GITLOW: Yassuh, Ol' Cap'n—Gitlow is here, suh; right here!

OL' CAP'N: Quick, ol' friend—my heart. It's—quick! A few passels, if you please—of that ol' speritual.

GITLOW: *(Sings most tenderly.)* "Gone are the days, when my heart was young and gay . . ."

OL' CAP'N: I can't tell you, Gitlow—how much it eases the pain—*(*GIT-LOW *and* OL' CAP'N *sing a phrase together.)* Why can't he see what they're doing to the southland, Gitlow? Why can't he see it, like you and me? If there's one responsibility you got, boy, above all others, I said to him, it's these Negras—your Negras, boy. Good, honest, hard-working cotton choppers. If you keep after 'em.

GITLOW: Yes, Lawd. (Continues to sing.)

OL' CAP'N: Something between you and them no Supreme Court in the world can understand—and wasn't for me they'd starve to death. What's gonna become of 'em, boy, after I'm gone—?

GITLOW: Dass a good question, Lawd—you answer him. (Continues to sing.)

OL' CAP'N: They belong to you, boy—to you, evah one of 'em! My ol' Confederate father told me on his deathbed: feed the Negras first— after the horses and cattle—and I've done it evah time! (By now OL' CAP'N is sheltered in GITLOW's arms. The LIGHTS begin slowly to fade away. GITLOW sings a little more.) Ah, Gitlow ol' friend—something, absolutely sacred 'bout that speritual—I live for the day you'll sing that thing over my grave.

GITLOW: Me, too, Ol' Cap'n, me, too! (GITLOW's voice rises to a slow, gentle, yet triumphant crescendo, as our LIGHTS fade away.)

BLACKOUT

CURTAIN

ROSA GUY

Guy was the youngest cofounder of the Harlem Writers Guild. But, like Dorothy West in the New Negro Movement a generation before, Rosa Guy made her place for herself in the Harlem Writers Guild with her talent and activism, and would be recognized as an important part of the Black Art Movement of the sixties and seventies. She became the first woman in the Harlem Writers Guild to publish a book when *Bird at My Window* appeared in 1966 to critical acclaim. Maya Angelou described the book, which is set in Harlem, as a "brave examination of a loving, yet painful, relationship between a black mother and her son." Guy went on to author ten books for adults and young adults, and her play *Once on This Island* was a hit musical on Broadway.

3

This was the street that Big Willie had brought them to when he blew into Harlem in all his fury, and Big Willie was mad when he hit into town. There was no getting away from that. He knew because he had grown up in the white heat of Big Willie's anger, had been nurtured by it, up to the day Big Willie dropped dead and even long after. It was a way of life with him, something he never bothered to question.

The way Wade had it figured, without anyone ever explaining, was that Big Willie never wanted to run. Big Willie wanted to stay down there and take on those peck-o-woods, but it was on account of his family that he didn't. He didn't care about dying. He could just as soon go as long as he was taking some of those crackers along with him. Big Willie didn't, and it caused a big hate in him until his dying day. That hate was a part of Wade's smell and taste and sight, as long as he could remember.

It always seemed to Wade that that was the reason why Big Willie didn't ever pay them much attention as he went about his way of doing things. As if they were the barrier between him and his self-respect. . . . As if he was ashamed of loving them, hated it, because it was that love that stopped him from acting like the man he wanted to be. Wade never knew how that feeling came about. It was nothing that he thought out, but it was there, a part of his knowledge just as his nose was part of his face.

Just as he could never figure out how he came about remembering Mumma's face, all through that long ride from the South, first by car and then by train and then by car again, all funny and strained-looking, her eyes never blinking or closing as though sleep was a far distant thing and the only way she could catch up to it was for them to get where they were going. They all slept and got up and went to sleep again, but Mumma sat stiff and unbending as a board, looking out of the window with her staring eyes, until they came into Harlem and into the little kitchenette that a friend of Big Willie had rented for them. Then they all realized that she had been afraid, because she crumbled to her knees and cried:

"Thank you, Lord, for delivering us from your just wrath, and leading us into safety. Oh, Lord, I will ever be grateful."

Big Willie stood over her and said in a voice so terrible that it touched fear to the center of each of their hearts, "Get up from your knees, Evelyn. Get up from your goddamn knees."

Mumma looked stricken. "Willie Earl, as God is my witness, I must have laid with the devil the day I laid with you."

"If you laid with the devil, Evelyn, then all your children are misbegotten. I am a man. There are them that would forget that, but don't you never. I am a man."

It had been the beginning of a strange conflict for Wade because Mumma never really got off her knees and Big Willie never got finished with his anger. Little as Wade was, he understood them both. Never once did he doubt their feelings for him, even though they had a hard time understanding each other.

Wade remembered Mumma taking off on Big Willie one day, calling him all kinds of names because he didn't come home nights, didn't do a thing in the house, and in general acted as though he didn't give a damn.

"You got three children in this house, and you don't do nothing for them. You don't as much as take them around the corner. What kind of man are you, anyhow? You don't care one bit about them. I declare, you don't care one bit."

She said it loud enough for Wade to hear because she wanted to set him against Pappa. It was like a regular game with her, trying to set them against Pappa because he stayed out so many nights gambling and sometimes went for days and nights without sleeping. Mumma even tried to make out at times that Pappa had a girl friend, although she never came right out with it. But Wade would have dug his eyes and tongue out before he believed it. Yet she tried to turn them against Pappa and Pappa knew it.

"Come here, boy," he called Wade roughly after Mumma said that. Wade went up to him and Big Willie looked him hard in the eye. "Go get my slippers." Wade went and got his slippers and that was all that was said. But Wade knew that man loved him—loved him as he would his foot or even his heart. And since he wasn't the kind of man who would forgive his foot or his hand if they had to be cut off, making him less of a man, he had never forgiven that love that had started him running and making him less a man.

Sure, they had made up jokes about it through the years—belly-busting jokes; even Big Willie used to laugh, loud, long bitter belly laughs, laughs that didn't change anything, not even a man's opinion of himself. But Wade had whittled his laughter down through the years. Somehow the sense of Big Willie's hurt had got bigger after Big Willie's death and had grown as his memory had dimmed.

Yes, this was the street, with Sam's Barbershop at the corner, the oversized barbershop pole with its red and white peppermint stripes spiraling up; the Father Devine shoe-shine parlor that operated year after year even though the "Father" had faded into the past; the rooming house where Mabel used to live with her whore of a mother, the room-to-let sign forever hanging by one ring, always seeming about to but never falling; the long row of brownstone private houses that the West Indians had bought from the Jewish people, giving a semblance of decent living in the midst of squalor.

That was the reason Mumma remained in the neighborhood, even though they had always lived squeezed together in one or one-and-a-half rooms with kitchen. Here you did not have to worry about the heat or hot water. True, sharing the bathroom could sometimes be dangerous, but they were kept reasonably clean because the Barbadian or Trinidadian woman, and it usually was a woman, lived in the building. Their kitchenette was usually furnished, making it easy to buy only a few things to call it "home."

This was the street. And right in the middle of those brownstones was the house that Big Willie had fallen over in. Dead.

The men had all been crowded into the front part of the room near the kitchenette playing blackjack; and the children were crowded into the bed behind the curtain, with Mumma. It never bothered the children. They usually fell asleep trying to stay awake, listening to what was happening on the other side of the curtain. But Mumma usually lay praying and damning Big Willie, never understanding that there was nothing else Big Willie wanted, nothing he could do to make a living except gambling.

The men usually played until late in the morning or sometimes to midday. Not that they always played at Big Willie's. There were six of them playing regularly and they all got the chance to disturb their families. But although there were six regulars, every game had at least twenty players, coming and going, standing around, whispering, going broke and going home.

It was at one of the big games that it happened. They had been sleeping to the quiet laughter and cussing, when suddenly Wade found himself wide awake. Not so much because of the noise as for the lack of it.

Mumma, who had been sitting bolt upright, slipped out of bed, quietly moving toward the curtain, and Wade wiggled past the sleeping form of Willie Earl and hit the floor as he heard Big Willie say, "I ain't never cheated a man in my life but I killed a-many."

"But I ain't cheated," a voice answered, quivering the way the man himself must have been quivering. "I swear to God, I ain't known how that card got there."

Wade peeped into the room and saw the men sitting around the table, silent, watchful, grim, made unreal, like a ten-cent mystery or weird tale, by the thick smoke drifting over and around the players.

Big Willie had pushed his chair back so that it had fallen, and he moved toward a skinny little fellow who was shaking as if he had caught a real bad chill or something. Uncle Dan, who never played cards, sat near the wall all boozed up, trying to fight through the haze over his mind to what was happening.

The little fellow really wanted to run, but he was too scared. He was hemmed in by sitting near the wall instead of the door and all he could do was sit and look as Big Willie approached, but when Big Willie was almost upon him, the stud stuck his hand in his pocket and came out with a gun. He fired right at Big Willie's chest.

Big Willie never stopped walking toward the man. Big Willie grabbed him and he let the gun drop to the floor as he covered his face with his hands and cried. It didn't do a bit of good. By the time Big Willie was finished, the man's jaw was broken in three places and they carried him out, more dead than alive.

Uncle Dan struggled to his feet. "Willie boy, Willie boy, looks as though that son-of-a-bitch shot you. Let me see. Let me see." They opened his shirt, and sure enough, there was a bullet hole clean as anything right through his chest.

Uncle Dan and a couple of the other men took him to the hospital while Mumma sat in a chair waiting. By that time Faith had got up and sat beside Wade. They silently watched Mumma rubbing her hands together, rocking back and forth, but never saying a word, just waiting. Willie Earl never even turned over in bed.

They came in about noon, Uncle Dan and Pappa. Uncle Dan's face was ashen with worry. "That man is dead, Evelyn. Big Willie is dead. That bullet took him right in the heart. Doc couldn't take it out so he just closed the hole up, but Big Willie is just about dead."

They all looked at Big Willie, towering over the room, a cigarette stuck in the corner of his mouth, the smoke drifting up over his face so that his eyes narrowed, and they did not know if they were narrowed from the smoke, or from the pain they thought he must be feeling. He didn't crack a smile over what Uncle Dan said, but went to answering that stunned question in Mumma's eyes.

"I got unfinished business, Evelyn. Ain't no man got a right to die if he ain't finished up his business."

Wade and Faith nodded in agreement. And Uncle Dan, catching a look at them, nodded too, only he was kind of bewildered. But Mumma sat rubbing her hands together for a long time before she came out with what was on her mind.

"It's the devil's doing, that's what it is. Ain't no man got no call to live with a bullet in his heart, if it ain't the devil's doings."

Faith and Wade stared at each other in downright surprise. Mumma knew better than that. It was no secret that Big Willie was sworn to go back South and have his revenge on those crackers. They never spoke about it but everybody knew it, so it was sort of natural to him and Faith that Pappa just couldn't die until he had got them all back home.

Mumma went to church every day now, taking them and trying to force them to pray for the deliverance of Pappa's soul into the hands of God. Little as he was, Wade refused to pray. He didn't want Big Willie delivered into anybody's hands. Still she kept after him wanting him to pray so hard that one day he stood up in church and shouted, "I don't want God to have Pappa's soul. I hate God. I hate Him, I hate Him, I hate Him." He raised so much fuss and shamed Mumma so badly that she took him home telling him that he was Big Willie's son in the soul, as he was in the flesh, and she would never take him to church again.

Wade never knew what Big Willie did toward finishing his business. Pappa kept right on with that hard gambling, sitting around a table full of people playing cards, while Uncle Dan sat behind him boozing. Later, Wade had it figured that Pappa had been trying to make enough money gambling to do what he wanted.

One day, almost a year to the day he was shot, a game started in the house. It was an early game. Willie Earl was still in the streets playing and Faith had not come home from Aunt Julie's. Wade sat in the big chair in the front part of the room, glad to be around Pappa and Uncle Dan and their rough-talking friends, who rubbed his hair or pushed his head, or made boxing jabs at him. This was something he liked doing, sitting in a hot, crowded room, surrounded by rough voices, until he nodded, and then Mumma picked him up and put him to bed.

It was just about the time he got to nodding that he heard Pappa say in a funny voice, "Evelyn—get me the . . ." Pappa never finished the sentence, just doubled over and died.

Mumma rushed to get all of the brothers and sisters from her church to come over to the house to pray all of that night and into the next day and the next night. Pray and sing . . .

"It's me, it's me, it's me, Oh Lord
Standing in the need of prayer.
It's me, it's me, it's me, Oh Lord
Standing in the need of prayer. . . ."

Mumma might not have been happy, but she looked right contented. Wade heard her say to one of the sisters in a grave but satisfied voice, "He said he wouldn't die unless he finished his business, but he died before he could even finish his last sentence." It suited Mumma that way. Things fitting into place. She was happy, not so much that Pappa died, as that nobody dictated to God. He took you when He wanted to and you hadn't one earthly thing to say about it. It relieved her that, after all, she had been living with a mortal, and that made her thankful.

But it shook Wade to his very soul and when Mama and Faith and Willie Earl stood up singing with the rest of the brothers and sisters, he sat in Uncle Dan's lap and cried, rubbing his thick fat fists into his eyes until they were red and swollen. Uncle Dan cried too, but for different reasons. He had lost his brother and only pal, and he didn't know who would take care of him when he got boozed up. Wade cried, running from the house and from the pious, religious sisters, beating his fists against the stoop until they were bruised and bloody. When Uncle Dan pulled him away, he flung his arms around his uncle's neck and cried harder than ever. Folks thought it was strange that one so young—that lil' bit of a thing—would take on so over anybody's death. But it was not Big Willie's death so much as it was that he had no right dying if he hadn't finished his business.

Maybe the reason Mumma turned, from the very beginning, to Willie Earl instead of to him was because of the way he took on over Pappa. That, and of course the fact that Willie Earl was much older. Older and more able to get around her prayers, tears and fears. Mumma's praying doubled instead of lessening after Big Willie died. It seemed to her even more the work of the devil, that she had to be crucified in the bowels of a city like New York with three children as her cross.

Mumma was afraid about everything, not only for herself but for them. She refused to let them go out of the neighborhood, setting their limits between 116th Street and 125th Street. She wouldn't go downtown shopping, afraid to tangle with the white folks, buying instead at the higher-priced stores of 125th Street, saying that what she put out in money, she made up in peace of mind.

Willie Earl listened to everything she said, nodded his head and went about his own way of doing things. But once when someone saw him go past 116th Street and Mumma got after him, he pleaded and cried, argued and got excited, angry and then repentant, saying that he was not a baby to be confined to a ten-block limit. He carried on in such a way that Mumma, tired and worn, unable to endure such persistence, gave in, extending his boundaries to most of Harlem.

Faith and Wade listened to everything Mumma had to say, never questioned her, never went past the limits she set for them, except for that one time when Wade went with Willie Earl. That one time was enough and he never did it again.

After Big Willie died, Willie Earl had taken to hustling shoe shines to help Mumma out. And one morning, after months of listening and ignoring Wade's pleas, Willie agreed to make Wade a shoe-shine box and take him along.

Mumma helped them dress, kissed them, sending them on their way. He was proud as anything to be going out with his big brother. Willie was six years older and tall for his age. Folks said he was just like Pappa. But Wade, ever since he could remember, clung to the idea that he was the one like his father, and the idea of bringing home money and throwing it in Mumma's lap casually the way Pappa used to, saying, "Here, Evelyn, see what you can do with this," pleased him.

Willie walked him right past 116th Street to 110th. It was the first time he had been that far from home, but before he could get used to the excitement, Willie Earl had grabbed his arm and was pulling him into the subway. "Listen, Wade," he whispered as though Mumma might have been right behind them. "I'm going to take you where we can make a lot of money, but if you tell, I'm going to knock the hell outa you and I ain't never going to take you with me again." That was always Willie Earl. Nothing but a bag of secrets.

Willie Earl waited until the train rushed into the station and had almost closed its doors before pushing Wade under the turnstile, dragging him across the platform, shoving him through the closing door, and wiggling in after him. They were off, making it to "Willie's" corner in a place that Willie called "wop-town," and all the while they were riding, Willie Earl kept giving instructions: "Keep your eyes peeled for the kids on the block. Never set up when you see a kid around. If he ain't seen you, hide until he passes. If he catches one glimpse of you, we can just call it a day, understand? Cause if you see one, you'll see a dozen."

Wade nodded to every instruction. He didn't understand anything, but he was puzzled more than a little at Willie's running battle with Mumma for a 110th Street limit, when the whole city was already his stomping ground. That was the way with Willie Earl, he had a natural knack of fighting over a little bone to hide a whole *side* of meat he had stored up somewhere.

Willie's corner was near a broken-down tenement on the Lower East Side, where people came and went as if it was a train station. Fine cars stopped here and well-dressed men flashing big diamond rings jumped out to disappear into the interior of the broken-down house, coming out in a very few minutes to drive away. But many, seeing a shoe-shine box, decided on a shine. The boys started making money right away. These men didn't mind paying twenty-five cents or fifty cents, and sometimes as much as a dollar for a five-cent shine. Of course, Willie made the big tips because he knew how to shine. He could have made even more, except that he had to stop every few minutes to give Wade pointers, and even to finish some of the shoes Wade started. But he still made money, and Wade did too.

It was because of Wade taking so long to finish one pair of shoes that they got caught. Willie looked up in the middle of a shine, saw one of the neighborhood kids and said under his breath, "Psst, chicky Wade, let's cut." He gave the shoe he had been working on a lick and a promise, then he was ready. Wade, stuck with too much of the thick liquid over his customer's shoe, was afraid to stop, and by the time Willie Earl had run to the corner, to look around, come back and grabbed his arm, pulling him away from the unfinished shoe, they were surrounded.

"Hey," one big boy, the leader, called. "Don't you know we don't let no spooks around here? How you get out of nigger town?" That was the first instant when Wade realized that he had not seen one black face since they started. The very thought made him shake inside.

Slick Willie Earl wasted no words, he just kept looking around for a way out, holding on to Wade's arm, because he knew he could talk his way out of anything with Mumma, except leaving his little brother in another part of town. Willie Earl tried to inch toward the corner, but they were locked in. The leader was a boy much older than Willie Earl; and the youngest, much older than Wade, who was hardly rid of his baby fat.

The kids called them black sons-of-bitches and dirty niggers and coons. Told them that they would show them what they did to dirty bastards when they caught them where they didn't belong. Willie Earl never wasted a breath, he just kept looking around and thinking.

Wade later heard Willie Earl often say, "When you know all you can do is talk, start working your mouth so that nobody gets in a word. But when talking ain't gon' do it, save your breath and use your head." That was what he was doing then, because when the leader of the group took a long switchblade knife and started playing with it, touching the blade as though he saw it already disappearing into their guts, Willie's hand left Wade's arm and before anyone knew what was happening, he had brought the shoe-shine box down on the boy's head. The crack of bones sounded in the air and at the same time, Wade felt himself flying, his feet not even touching the ground.

The surprise attack upset the white boys, giving Willie and Wade a good head start. They had almost reached the subway when two of the bigger ones caught up with them—and the fight was on.

A policeman broke it up and took them down the steps into the station, paid their fares and said, "Look, this part of town ain't no place for you little niggers. Stay uptown where you belong because the next time I catch you guys around here, I'll run you in myself."

Wade remembered looking at this giant of a man with his big pistol bulging at his hip, and promised himself and Mumma that he would never go around where white folks were again. He had never been so afraid, not before, not since.

All the way uptown on the train he was terrified and he thought Willie Earl must be too, that is, until Willie started talking. "How many pairs did you do, Wade?"

"What?"

"Shoes, Wade. How many pairs did you do?"

"I dunno." Shoes were the farthest thing from his mind. He had left his shoe-shine box along with the unfinished pair of shoes and had not given it another thought.

"Count how much money you got." Wade dug into his pocket and came out with four quarters. "Good. Now you give Mumma fifty cents and keep the rest."

Willie Earl dug into his pockets and counted his money aloud. Wade, self-conscious, looked around noticing the people looking at them with their noses pulled down, their eyes pointed and accusing, those sitting next to them pulling their clothes away not wanting to touch the two dirty, badly beaten-up boys.

He and Willie might as well have been stink from a garbage can placed into the subway for the prime purpose of disturbing the gentle noses of the fine white people there. Wade caught a glimpse of a couple of well-dressed colored men. Unlike the white folks, they pulled their gaze away and were busy looking out the windows, pretending those two dirty colored boys did not exist. For Willie, it was the people around who didn't exist. He talked loud, counting his money, never noticing them.

"I got seven dollars and fifty cents," he said. "Now I'll give her two dollars. I'll keep the fifty cents on account of I don't want to have to break into the five. . . ."

"You can't do that to Mumma," Wade whispered, horrified.

"Do what to Mumma?" Surprised, Willie raised his voice even louder. Wade's face burned because he knew that all of the white folks in this silent car were looking and listening, and he knew he couldn't shut Willie's mouth.

"We ain't doing nothing to Mumma. You better wake up, boy, and get some skin on your simple head. Number one, if we give her all the money, she's going to want to know how we made so much. Number two, if we tell her we been downtown, she going to cry and carry on and turn us every way but loose. Number three, if we had stayed where she wanted us to stay, let me see—you did about four pairs—you would have got one nickel a pair and *no* tip cause you slow. I did about ten and I would have got one nickel a pair, and maybe a nickel tip from some studs trying to play big. That would have been twenty cents from you and less than a dollar from me. Now, you tell me, what we doing wrong to Mumma?"

Wade pulled his mouth together and didn't care what kind of figuring Willie Earl did. They had gone out to work to help Mumma and all the money rightly belonged to her and he was going to tell.

And sure enough the minute Mumma opened the door and gave one look at their faces, she got to crying. "Lord, where in the world you-all been?"

"Oh, we just been in a scramble with some guys around . . ." Willie Earl began, but Wade wouldn't have it.

"No, Mumma, we been downtown and them white boys jumped on us and . . ."

He didn't go any further because Mumma grabbed Willie Earl just the way Willie said she would and started to beat him as if she had taken leave of her senses.

Willie Earl got to yelling and screaming as though he was being killed, and people from upstairs came down and people passing in the streets crowded around the window, but Mumma didn't let up her beating or Willie Earl his hollering.

"You fool. You fool. They could have killed you-all. They could have killed you-all." And every time she repeated this she would start on him again as though she intended to do just that, and Willie Earl would go into his hell-raising scene.

Wade sat in a chair quietly waiting his turn but she never touched him. She didn't have the strength. After she had finished, she sat down and cried. "You don't know white folks, Willie Earl. You don't know them. They ain't no different up here than they are down home. They'll kill you and leave you in the streets and ain't nobody know where you come from. They could string you up on one of them lamp posts and set fire to you and leave you in the street and don't nobody know what you even look like. And we all the way up here not even knowing where you been. Ain't you got no sense at all?"

Her love for Willie Earl, her fear, all came out in that cry. But it passed right over Willie's hard head and fastened into Wade. He knew it had no effect on Willie because later that night, when everything was quiet, Willie said he was sorry and he wouldn't do it again, and gave Mumma just what he said he would, not one penny more. Anybody who knew Willie knew he'd sooner die than leave that money downtown.

But to Wade sitting there quietly, filled with shame at what they had done, the terror in her voice and in her face as she cried got right to him, the very center of him, and he remembered the first night in the city, when she fell to her knees and prayed; then he had not known whether to go to her or stay away, and he sat very much as he was doing now, hurt and sorry, only now he bore the guilt of her fear. What the policeman standing with his big red face, his gun bulging at his hip, had started, she had sealed with her fears. His limits, his boundaries, forever.

WILLIAM MELVIN KELLEY

Born in 1937, Kelley attended Fieldston School and Harvard University. He has taught literature and writing at New School University, SUNY at Geneseo, the University of Paris at Nanterre, and Sarah Lawrence College. A noted novelist and short-story writer, critics found his episodic and symbolic novel *dem,* which continued his focus on race relations, angrier than his earlier work.

To find this Cooley, the Black baby's father, he knew he would have to contact Opal Simmons. After dressing, he began to search for her address and number. Tam, very organized for a woman, saved everything. Among the envelopes containing the sports-clothes receipts, a letter from her dressmaker asking for payment, old airline tickets, the nursery school bill, the canceled checks, and deposit slips, he finally found Opal's address.

He went to the phone and dialed her number, knowing that this conversation would not be pleasant, for either of them. He could only remind Opal that Tam had taken from her a man she may have loved. And then there was the whole business of her stealing. Though he had never asked her, she must have had good reason to risk job and reputation. And she must have sold everything quickly, for cash; he had never found any of it in her possession, had never even been certain what she had taken. But for good reason or no, he knew she would not enjoy speaking again to the person who had exposed her.

Opal picked up her phone after the third ring. "Hello?"

He did not know where to begin. He tried to announce himself, but could not. Before he realized it, he had quietly slipped the receiver back into its cradle. "Hell—"

He sat at the phone table wondering why he had been unable to give even his name. After all, he and Opal were not strangers; she had worked for them eighteen months. Suddenly—her name and number in front of him—he remembered that once he had driven her home, to a project in the north Bronx, countless tall red buildings, surrounded by patches of yellow grass. He had been unable to speak on that drive, though, hating silence, he always tried to fill it. In his apartment, they had talked about hundreds of things, what Jake had done during the day, or how well she cooked, or whether one of his suits had been returned from the cleaners. But that night in the car, just as a few minutes before on the phone, he could not speak.

He stood up, finally convincing himself that it did not really matter. It was probably better not to have spoken to her. She might have refused to see him. Now he knew she was at home. He would drive to the Bronx and speak to her in person.

It was nearly six when he reached the highway; there were few cars. Even so, after a moment or two, he found himself being pursued through the November dusk by two white headlights, could feel their heat on his neck. He tried to look for a face, a cloth hat with a wire frame, but the car was almost invisible above the lights. He sped up, but the lights stayed with him, exploding in his mirror.

Then the road ahead was filled with small red lights, which spread across his windshield. The cars, bunched now, began to move to the right. He passed a splintered wooden pole, then the aluminum lamp shades, mashed and wrinkled like foil. He had to swerve to avoid an arm, and the steering wheel its hand still clutched. The first car rested partly on the grass divide, a wheel quiet beside it. The second car was on its back. A Black man sat in the driver's seat of the third car.

A Black woman sat beside it, on the grass, her feet in the highway. She must have weighed two hundred pounds, one huge breast in a white bra hanging through a rip in her flowered dress. She had not tried to cover it; her hands lay palms up on her thighs. She wore only one shoe; a large yellow hat, crushed now, the cloth flowers torn, rested in the grass next to her. She was shaking her head.

Once he had passed it all, the road again open before him, Mitchell too shook his head. Some people, he thought, ought not to be allowed to get licenses. It was too easy for the reckless to get them. It was that way with many things. Some people worked very hard, earning their way; others hitched rides—holding up those who had been nice enough to pick them up. As he turned off the highway, and passed a large ceme- tery, he thought he was beginning to understand what Tam's mother had been trying to tell him.

10

In twenty more minutes, he parked his car. On the sidewalk, three young Black men stopped talking as he climbed out. They watched him roll up his windows, lock and check his doors, securing his car against theft. He made a wide circle around them, started up a walk leading to four buildings. He stayed to the side of the walk, his knee grazing the chain which protected the dead yellow grass from children.

In front of the first building, a group of small Black girls were arguing in high little voices. One had a long rope. "It's your turn to hold, Gail."

"No, it ain't. It's Wanda's turn."

"See that? See that? I ain't your friend if you don't hold."

Gail, head divided into neat squares of hair, took the rope. Another girl held the other end. Just before Mitchell reached them, the girls began to jump, over two strands, each looping in opposite directions. He could not get by them, and had to wait.

> *Sitting in a teepee, smoking a pipe.*
> *Polar bear come with a great big knife.*
> *Polar bear take and put us in a boat.*
> *So many children, thing couldn't float.*
> *Sitting in a boat, with a necklace of iron.*
> *Bear come down and say, "You're mine."*
> *Children started crying, raise up a noise.*
> *Everybody's crying, even the boys.*

The jumping girl sang the loudest, her skirt billowing around thin black legs, the ribbons in her hair following her up and down. All the girls looked cold, their dark skin filmed with ashes.

> *Sitting in a cabin, smoking a pipe.*
> *The polar bear say I his wife.*
> *Take me by the hand and lead me out.*
> *Bear in the grass with a big cold snout.*
> *Sitting in a cabin, apron up high.*
> *So homesick I wish I could die. . . .*

The jumping girl tripped on the ropes, and the other girls began to laugh. Then they were all staring at Mitchell, mouths poked out.

"You a child molasses?" the girl called Gail asked.

He took a step backward and asked for Opal's building.

They held a short conference, then pointed toward the last building in the row, and permitted him to pass. His neck muscles did not relax until the ropes began again to slap the pavement and he heard them chanting.

By then he had reached the lobby, was wading through the contents of a broken bag of garbage, avoiding a gravy-filled grapefruit shell, fat oozing from a green soda bottle. He pressed the elevator button.

"Sure you got the right place?" A brown man in a blue imitation policeman's uniform tapped him on the shoulder with his club. He was shorter than Mitchell, graying around the ears, with a neat little mustache.

Mitchell nodded, his back against the elevator door.

"For your own protection, you know. Better make sure you mean to be here." He struck his palm lightly.

"I'm visiting Miss Opal Simmons."

The imitation policeman smiled. "I ain't going to ask what for. You got business here, all right. I'm just thinking about people come around making trouble." He paused. "The people I work for pays me to keep things calm, nice and calm."

"I'm calm. Really."

"Sure." He nodded. "I can see that. It's for your own protection. When you go back put in a good word for me. Tell them I'm keeping things calm." Mitchell started to ask where the imitation policeman thought he was returning to, but was cut off: "Your elevator's here." And bowing slightly, the imitation policeman opened the door for him.

11

The elevator banged up the shaft, and Mitchell stepped out into a long gray hall, lit by one bulb in a broken glass globe. He found Opal's apartment, rang the bell, and, after a moment, a small barred hole opened in the door. "Yes?"

He put his mouth close to the bars. "Opal, it's Mr. Pierce."

The little round hole closed, locks clicked, the big door opened. Opal's eyes seemed as large as the door-hole. "Mr. Pierce?"

"Hello, Opal. How are you?"

"Fine, Mr. Pierce." She pulled the door wider, asked him to come in, please, as if once again she were answering his door. He crossed the doorsill, wondering why she was being so nice.

The living room was small, strangely familiar. The sofa was green, plastic-covered. A light brown coffee table squatted in front of it. On the wall was one picture, a reproduction of a painting by a famous modern Spanish artist. Opal asked him to sit down. He did, under the reproduction; she sat across from him, in a red chair, also plastic-covered, also familiar.

He cleared his throat. "How've you been, Opal?"

"Fine. And you, Mr. Pierce?" She had gained a great deal of weight. Her legs, pressed tightly together at the knee, were still shapely. But her shoulders had taken on a thick padding of fat, which spilled down her arms as far as her elbows. He remembered he had always worried about her eating too much rice.

"Fine." He tried to think of something more to say, but could not. It did not matter. She seemed so nervous it put him at ease. "Listen, Opal, I want you to do me a favor."

She leaned forward, a smile pulling at her lips. "Sure, Mr. Pierce."

He took a deep breath. "I'd like to find your friend Cooley." He watched closely for her reaction, saw a tear pop into her eye. "Opal?"

"He cause you more trouble, Mr. Pierce? I'm sorry I ever brought him to your house. Of all the men I ever met, he was the most trouble-causing . . ." She shook her head.

"Wait a minute, Opal."

"That man was a jinx." She looked at him, a tear stalled on her cheek, like brown wax. "Why'd you fire me, Mr. Pierce? It was for going around with men like Cooley, wasn't it."

"Now, Opal . . ."

"The best job I ever had and I lost it because of a common, ordinary nigger. Excuse me, Mr. Pierce, but we both know what he was." She wiped her tears with a chubby hand. "A nigger."

"No, Opal." Mitchell shook his head. "We fired you because you were stealing. That's why I went through your purse. Don't you remember?"

"Me?" She sat up, snorted. "I never stole from you, Mr. Pierce. Not even leftover food. My pay check was always enough."

Mitchell suddenly realized that at very least she believed what she was telling. Either she had forgotten or had gone insane. He was certain he would know if she was lying. "No, Opal, you were stealing from us."

"What kind of person would I be to steal from you, as good as you was to me?"

He had often wondered that himself. "But, Opal . . ." He stopped because he knew now why the living room seemed so familiar; it was a poor copy of his own—designed by Tam—even to the reproduction.

"What did I steal, Mr. Pierce?"

He hesitated. "Well, Opal, I don't really know." That too seemed strange; they had never really missed anything. He tried to remember why he had even believed Opal to be a thief.

"You see?" She was triumphant, but not angry. "It was because of that Cooley. You were right to fire me, Mr. Pierce. I never should've had that nigger come to your house. I didn't even like him. I only went out with him three times." She stopped. "What you want him for, Mr. Pierce?"

The idea that Opal had not stolen from them had, for the moment, pushed Cooley from his head. "I want him to do a favor for me."

"He won't do nothing for you, Mr. Pierce. He's too evil. You stay away from him."

"No. I have to see him." He looked at her, saw her old thin face encased in fat, like one balloon inside another. "Listen, Opal, I guess I made a mistake about firing you." He nodded. "How would you like to come work for us again?"

Her mouth became the top of a brown jar. "Me? Work for you again? Even after what I done?"

"We'll forget that." He smiled. "We want you to work for us. I can give you, oh say, twenty dollars more a month than you were making before. You see, Mrs. Pierce just had a baby, and she'll need help."

"A new baby? And how's my old baby, Jakie? I'd love to work for you. And I promise never to go out with any nigger like Cooley again."

"Good." He paused. "Now, where can I find him? By the way, Opal, what's his last name?"

"God, Mr. Pierce, I don't know. He never told me. I ain't even seen him in a year and a half. Like I tell you, I didn't go out with him but three times. But I met him by my nephew. His name's Carlyle . . . Bedlow. He may know where Cooley's at." She got up, and, bending over a small desk, huge buttocks filling the room, wrote down her nephew's address. "He only lives a few blocks from here."

He told her to come to work in two days—enough time for him to dismiss the German woman, whom he had never liked. If Tam did not approve, he could say he was following her mother's advice. Besides, Opal was no longer attractive.

Downstairs, walking to his car, he felt so good that he was not even nervous when he passed the jumping, chanting Black girls.

12

It was full dark now. Steering his car around great holes in the tattered streets, it was hard for Mitchell to believe he was still in New York City. He passed shadowed swamplike lots, glimpsed a goat in his headlights. In places, there were no sidewalks.

Opal's nephew lived in one of a row of attached, three-story brick houses. Each owner had tried to make his house distinctive. One had a white picket fence and green awnings, another an iron fence and red awnings. But still, it remained one long building, with four or five entrances.

Mitchell pressed the button under the name—BEdLow. The buzzer rang; he pushed open the door, stepped into a dark, cold hallway, and crept forward until he came to a stairway—then light.

"How do you go, Brother?" A young man's voice.

"Hello?" Mitchell shouted. "What did you say?" He started climbing clean rubber-covered stairs, heard footsteps coming to meet him. He had almost gained a small landing, when the young man appeared around a corner.

"A devil?" The young man, in his late teens, was short, heavy eyebrows over brown eyes, embedded in an otherwise hairless dark-brown head. "What you want, devil?"

Mitchell stopped. "Are you Carlyle Bedlow?"

The young man did not answer, turned, and started back up the stairs. "A devil for you, Carlyle!"

Mitchell followed timidly, turned the corner, found another young man standing in a doorway, staring down at him. He was older than the first, his skin as dark, a mustache hiding his upper lip, his hair long—and straight? "What you want?"

Clearing his throat, Mitchell gave his name. "Your aunt, Opal Simmons, sent me over."

The young man nodded. "Yeah?"

"I'm trying to find a friend of hers, and yours? named Cooley." Looking up was making his neck ache.

"Cooley? Cooley what? Sorry, Mr. Pierce. I don't think I know no Cooley." The young man was wearing a knit sport shirt, tight pants. "What're you to my A'nt Opal?"

Mitchell explained that some two years before Opal had worked for him, and, beginning Monday, would work for him again.

While he talked, the young man lit a cigaret. "Yeah, I remember being told about you. You fired her for stealing, right? Yeah. A'nt Opal stealing, that's funny as all shit."

Mitchell nodded. "It was a misunderstanding. That's why I rehired her."

"Oh, I see it now. That's real nice. Cooley. I think I know him after all. So you want to find Cooley, huh?" He stepped back into the apartment. "Come on up. I ain't seen him in a while, but . . ."

Mitchell reached the top step, climbed into the apartment. The young man reached out his hand. "Carlyle Bedlow, Junior. Carlyle."

"Nice to know you." Mitchell took his hand.

"Come on in my room." Carlyle closed the door and started toward the front of the apartment. Mitchell followed, looking over his shoulder, where a lighted doorway had attracted his attention. The first young man was sitting at a desk in a little room, reading. On the floor were piles of books and magazines, on the wall, a portrait, in color, of a black, fat-faced man with long kinky hair, his eyes hidden by blue, gold-rimmed sunglasses.

"That's Mance, my brother." Carlyle had not turned his head. "He trying to find a way to kill you." They entered a room, lit only by an orange bulb.

Mitchell felt a pain in his chest. "Me?"

"White people, man. He's a Jesuit. You know, a Black Jesuit?" He sat down, sighing, in the room's only chair. "Reads all the time. Looking for a way." He laughed, a snort. "May find it too. Close the door." Mitchell did—after one more look at Mance, bent over his studies.

Mitchell came from the door; the room was too small. "But why does he want to kill all white people?"

Carlyle watched him a moment, then motioned for him to sit on the bed. "I guess because you need it; he's an idealist. You want some Smoke?"

"No, thanks. I have some cigarets."

"Yeah, okay." He blinked, rubbed his eyes. "So, why you want to find Cooley, Mr. Pierce?"

"Well, if you don't mind I'd rather not say." Then to put Carlyle at ease. "But it's not anything illegal, if you're worried about that."

Carlyle sat up straighter. "I'm glad you said that, Mr. Pierce. I sure don't like to get involved in nothing E-legal."

Mitchell, still wearing his overcoat, was beginning to sweat. "Can you help me?"

"That's hard to say, Mr. Pierce. Like I say, I ain't seen Cooley for a while and he moves around a lot." He opened a drawer in a little table beside his chair, took out a package of cigaret paper and a bottle filled with greenish tobacco. "It's imported, man. Very strong, smells like hell. How soon you want to find him?"

"As soon as I can."

Carlyle poured some of the green tobacco into the paper, rolled a thin cigaret, and lit it. It did smell bad. "You see, that's the thing. Could cost some money."

Mitchell was becoming suspicious. He had read about white men swindled by Black. He would be cautious, careful. "How do you mean?"

"You got a car?" Mitchell nodded. "Well, we could get in your car, drive to Harlem, and go some places he might be. But we might have to pay admission and like that. And . . . I think I should warn you, man, Cooley's kind of an underworld figure. A lot of people'd look at you and think you was a cop, and we'd have to give them some money to get them to talk. You understand?"

"I see." This seemed reasonable enough. "I think I have money for that."

Carlyle shrugged. "I want to be honest with you." He patted his chest. "I mean, there a lot of bad feelings between the races. Like with my brother. But me? I don't go for it. A man is a man, and I don't kid no man. So I got to warn you: we might spend some money and never find him or anything about him."

Mitchell was moved by Carlyle's honesty. "Well, I hope we do find him, but if we don't, I'll know you tried to help me."

Carlyle stood up. "You a good man, Mr. Pierce. I guess I should've known that by the way you took A'nt Opal back after that misunderstanding." He went to his closet and put on a wine-colored sport coat. "So, I guess we better start."

"Good."

They left the room; Carlyle stopped at the front door. "Say, Mance, I'm cutting. I'll catch you later."

Mance looked up from his book, nodded.

Mitchell smiled. "Good-bye, now."

"Devil."

13

Outside, under a streetlamp, Carlyle suggested it might be easier if he drove; he would not have to direct Mitchell through the Harlem streets. "Besides, man, there's this race business." He winked. "They won't wreck your car if they see me get from behind the wheel." Mitchell asked to see his license, and, satisfied they would not be breaking the law, surrendered the keys.

Because Carlyle knew the Bronx streets, they were soon on the highway. They passed the place where, not three hours before, Mitchell had seen the accident. The cars and people were gone; only the splintered pole marked the spot. They climbed a short hill and in front of him, Mitchell saw the tall, light-barnacled shadows of the city.

He was beginning to relax now, growing accustomed to the way Carlyle drove his car. He felt certain he would find Cooley and be rid of the baby before the evening was over. He slid down, his head on the seat, and tried to remember how Cooley had looked that night eighteen months before, the only time Mitchell had ever seen him.

He had been sitting at the kitchen table, enjoying the smell of the apple pie Opal had baked for him. She had just left the room, Jake in her arms, his hand inside the neck of her dress, his fingers tugging on the strap of her bra. Then the buzzer, and he had opened the door.

First, Mitchell had noticed Cooley's nose, as if the heel of a hand had jammed the end of it back and up toward his small, red eyes, and held it there, stretching the nostrils to the size of black quarters. The upper lip had been three fingers wide, the lower lip drooping, pink—all this packed onto a head no larger, it almost seemed, than a softball, and that sitting, neckless, on shoulders the width of the door. The shoulders and chest had been covered by a chartreuse jacket, with the name—Cooley—in gold thread over the heart. He had looked down at Mitchell almost from the top of the doorway. "Who are you?"

He had not allowed Cooley to intimidate him. "Mitchell Pierce," he had answered deliberately. "And just who are you?"

"Cooley." Challenged, he seemed to shrink a bit. "I come for Opal."

Already, Mitchell had begun to get angry, but before he could answer, Opal had entered the kitchen. And then the rest of it. He had demanded that Cooley wait outside, had begun to reprimand her, had called her a thief, had dismissed her. It was clear now what had happened; anger had confused him. He had attacked Opal because of Cooley's rudeness . . .

They crossed a bridge, the tires howling on hivelike steel, and stopped next to a big, new car carrying a Black man and two brown girls, one of them under blond, almost white hair. Carlyle elbowed him. "Roll down the window."

Mitchell did, and Carlyle lay across his lap, that straight, oily hair, sweet-smelling just under his nose. The roots were not at all straight. "Hey, baby, where you going?"

The blond turned toward him, scowled. The man smiled. "Sorry, bubba, all for me."

"Go on, man, she don't need no translator."

The blond smiled, but turned away.

"Listen, I'll tell you what—you meet me at the Apple-O at midnight, I'll take you to the show. You can get rid of them people."

The blond was still smiling. "I seen it already, baby. Besides, I meet you and my man'll beat hell out of me. Won't you, honey?" She leaned over and kissed the man. Behind them, horns started, and the car disappeared up a ramp, its back red with lights.

"Okay, Mr. Pierce, roll up." Carlyle stepped on the gas, and they started down Seventh Avenue.

"Isn't it dangerous to talk like that to another man's wife?"

"Ain't no other man; that's my Brother."

Mitchell did not understand, but did not dwell on it. Cooley still loomed in his mind. He wondered now, as the dead trees on the narrow center strip whipped by, how Tam had ever met him. Someday, but not soon, he would ask her. Opal had said she had gone out with him only three times. Probably the night of the misunderstanding had been the last time.

Cooley had probably come to the house before that, seen Tam, and had decided he loved her.

Perhaps he had come late one morning, after the German woman had taken Jake to the park. Tam would have been in bed, napping, reading, watching television, when the doorbell rang:

The German woman, Tam thinks, has forgotten her key. She gets up and goes to the door, not bothering to cover her pink, freckled shoulders, the white lace. She opens the door.

Cooley stands in the hall, his large black hands buried in dark pockets. "I like to see Opal for a minute. I'm Cooley."

At first Tam is frightened, but if Cooley knows Opal, it is probably safe. "Opal doesn't work here anymore."

His eyes blink. "Oh . . ."

Now Tam realizes he is looking through the lace, but he does not leer; there is an innocence about him. He has been expecting to see Opal. Now he is a disappointed child. She asks him in, runs to get a robe.

When she returns to the living room, he is on the edge of the small antique chair, afraid to put his full weight on the twisted legs, awed by the tranquillity of the room she has designed.

She sits across from him on the sofa. "Do you know Opal well?"

"No, ma'am, I only been out with her three times." He finds it hard to look at her.

"So she didn't tell you she's not working here anymore?"

He shakes his tiny black head. He cannot sustain it, cannot lie to her; he must look at her, confess. "I seen you before, Mrs. Pierce, one time when I come for Opal. I ain't been able to think of nothing else. I can't work; I can't sleep. And now today I come down here and asks for Opal. I know Opal don't work here no more." He drops from the chair to his knees. "But I figured I'd come to the door and ask for her, just on the chance of seeing you." The knuckles of his black hands sink into the rug; he begins to crawl toward her, the chartreuse satin, like skin across his shoulders. "Just to see you. But then you was kind enough to ask me into your house. I ain't never seen a house this nice."

Tam slides back onto the sofa. "Please, Cooley."

"I ain't going to hurt you, Mrs. Pierce. I wouldn't do that." Over her knees, she can see only his small red eyes. His hands grip her ankles. "I loves you, Mrs. Pierce." Her feet are growing numb, cold, even so, she can feel his lips just behind her toes.

She should jump up, scream, but does not. She thinks of Mitchell, who no longer loves her, who does not appreciate her. They are arguing. And now Opal's Cooley has come to her, and, demanding nothing, has confessed honest, childlike love for her. She begins to unbutton her robe.

But she never finishes. By her ankles, he pulls her off the sofa, bouncing her soft buttocks to the rug. He tears at the robe. Pink, cloth-covered buttons pop and fly. And now the freckles under white lace seem to madden him. He pulls at the lace, destroys the knitted cobwebs.

She lies still, beginning to cry, thinking, Mitchell, Mitchell, see what you've driven me to do . . .

"First stop, Mr. Pierce." Carlyle had parked in a dark, litter-strewn street. Down at the corner were the lights of an avenue, a bar window turning the gray pavement yellow. The houses were old, Victorian, their entrances guarded by stone dragons, angels with chipped noses. "There's a party here he might be at."

Mitchell continued to see Tam, as still as rags, spread under Cooley's shadow. He tried to shake them out of his head.

"You still want to find him?" The streetlamp caught the hard wave in Carlyle's hair.

Mitchell sat up, reached for the door handle. "Of course I do. More than ever."

14

They descended steps to a cellar doorway, passed rows of steel garbage cans. Already Mitchell could hear music. Carlyle pushed open a door into a stone hallway. "Listen, Mr. Pierce, don't say nothing. You let me talk." He winked. "This race business." They stopped and Carlyle rang the bell. "And if you don't mind, I'd better call you Mitchell."

The door opened a crack, then all the way. "Hiya, Carlyle!" Mitchell could not see her face, only tight pink slacks, a yellow turtleneck sweater, red hair, and plump arms, each with a charm bracelet, rushing to embrace Carlyle. "How you doing?"

"All right." His hand stroked the pink slacks. "You miss me?"

"Sure did." She pulled back from him, gold teeth smiling in a copper face. "And just where you been?"

"Around." Carlyle's forehead was greasy.

The gold disappeared behind lavender lips, her face serious now. "You ain't been up state, has you?"

"Nothing like that, Glora." He smiled. "Just hustling."

"Well, come in and party." From behind a hard face, she looked at Mitchell. "What's this?" scolding Carlyle with her eyes.

"You see that, Mitchell?" Carlyle shook his head. "White skin and she act like a red skin." He sucked his tongue. "This my cousin, Mitchell, from Canada. From a small, snowy-ass town where the underground railway left his granddaddy's butt. Had to integrate to keep the blood moving."

She smiled at Mitchell now, gold teeth in the dim light. "Cousin!" He felt her arms around him, red hair in his face, high breasts just above his stomach. "Welcome home. I'm sorry I took you for Sir Charles, the White Knight."

"That's all right." Mitchell did not know if he liked being . . . colored.

"What we standing out here for when they partying inside?" She hugged Mitchell's arm, pulled him over the marble doorsill, and took his coat.

"You got a cover, man," Carlyle whispered. "Just don't dance. They know you a phoney for sure if you get on that floor."

Mitchell nodded, slightly offended. He had always considered himself a good dancer, especially when he was drunk.

Carlyle was still at his ear. "Listen, they trying to pay the Jew, so lay something on them."

"What?" The hallway was dark, a door at the end, lit red. The music came from the doorway, and inside the room, Mitchell could see shadows weaving.

"It's a rent party, so drop two dollars in the basket. A dollar a drink, and if you hungry, she got her mama making chicken and potato salad, a dollar a plate."

Glora was back, hugging his arm again. "I'm taking over your cousin, Carlyle." As if to consolidate her claim, she put her hand on Carlyle's stomach, and pushed him away.

"I'll see you later, man." Before Mitchell could protest, Carlyle winked and left them.

Glora pulled him into the room where Black people danced, nodding heads, jerking hips, feet scraping on the wooden floor. Some of the men were sweating under the red light, patting their faces with neatly folded handkerchiefs. The women's faces were stern above their dancing bodies. Mitchell had never seen a group of Black people dance before, and was surprised to find no one writhing on the floor, none of the women with skirts hitched to their waist. Everyone did the same step, moved the same way in time to the music. Even so, they seemed to be having a good time.

Around the dancers, at the edges of the room, others stood talking. In the closest group to him, a half-dozen men, and a few women stood listening, their eyes downcast, but no one seemed to be talking. Glora led him toward them.

"Well look what the cat drug in," one of the women said. "What's that, Glora?"

"This is Carlyle Bedlow's cousin from Canada. Mitchell. Don't he look white though?" She introduced him around, ". . . and down there is Shorty."

Out of the shadows in the center of their small circle reached a yellow hand. Mitchell looked down at a pinched face under a pile of straight yellow hair. The midget wore a tuxedo, a lace-front shirt. "Glad to meet you." He mashed Mitchell's knuckles. "Where from in Canada?" His voice was high, forced through tiny nostrils.

Mitchell answered that he was from a small town near Ottawa.

"That's a long way from home. I ain't never worked there." He stared at Mitchell a moment longer, almost suspiciously, then turned to the others. "Anyway, like I say, I didn't really want to join, but I like testing them. So I look up the name in the phone book: The Little Folks Club, downtown, and walks in there one day, with my Great Dane and my two-foot cane. They had like kindergarten furniture, everything low down on the floor. There's this blond at the reception desk, maybe two-six, nice body on her. I asks if I could join up. She look at me like she ain't never seen a midget before, then at my dog, and runs on into the inner sanctum and in a minute she comes out with this official-looking cat. He wearing a little Ivy League suit with a vest and these big glasses. He tried all kinds of ways to tell me they didn't allow no niggers to join, and I play it dumb, asking questions, twisting his mind around, letting my dog lick his face. Finally I asks him how short you got to be to join. He say they didn't let no one in who taller than three feet. I look him in the eye, calm and quiet as you please, then shouts, 'Three feet? Why, man, that's discrimination! I'm afraid I couldn't join no club with such an unfair policy. Some of the best midgets I know is three-foot-one!' And I jumps up on my dog's back and rides out of there. That's Charles for you!"

Only Mitchell did not laugh. Bigotry was not to him a laughing matter. The rest spun with laughter, hiding their faces on each other's shoulders.

"Say, you is out of it," Glora whispered, then kissed his ear. "Come on, I'll teach you the New York way." She embraced him.

The music had turned slow—a high tenor over a rumble. Couples stood still on the floor, their arms around each other. Mitchell wanted to pull away, but knew he had to pretend; anything to find Cooley.

"Tell me about Canada." He could just hear her above the music. Her breasts were not at all hard. He began to sweat.

"It's cold and there's a lot of snow."

"Ooooh." She squeezed him tighter. There was perfume in her hair. Suddenly, he wanted to bury his face in it, kiss her scalp, but was afraid. And now he could feel himself getting excited, was afraid of that too.

"Listen, before I forget, I want to pay." He pushed her away.

She shook her head. "Mitchell, you been with white people too damn long. You don't even know how to relax—all tied up in knots, thinking about money. This the weekend, man."

She took his hand and led him to the door, pointed: "My mama's in the kitchen. Pay her." She was angry. "And while you're there, get a couple drinks in you. That's the way white folks do, ain't it? Can't have a good time until they get drunk and start breaking things." She shook her head again. "Sometimes I think the Jesuits is right. I seen more good niggers ruined by integration!"

15

It was only a few steps to the kitchen. Just inside the door, a table blocked the way, a money-filled saucepan in the center. Behind the table, the kitchen was a high-ceilinged room. At one time it had been some bright color. Now it was impossible to tell what color; no one would have chosen the gray which covered the walls.

At the far end was a spattered white stove, crouching hidden behind a Black woman at least as tall and twice as wide as Mitchell. She wore a black dress decorated with large yellow sunflowers, one of which stretched across her broad back, like the picture on a team jacket.

"Is this where I pay?"

"No place else, baby." She turned now, smoke rising from an iron kettle behind her. She was the woman he had seen sitting beside the highway.

"Well?" She moved toward the table. "Ain't you got change?" She stood behind the table, large hands hanging at her sides. "It's in the pan there. Go on, I trust you."

"Didn't I see you a few hours ago on the highway?"

She wrinkled her tiny nose. "Highway?"

Perhaps he was mistaken. But . . . "You look very familiar to me."

"I ain't never been to Canada."

Mitchell was confused, decided to let the matter drop. "Is this where I pay?"

"That's what I said. Don't you light-skinned niggers never listen to anybody but white folks?"

"Why, yes." He took a five-dollar bill from his wallet. "And could I have three drinks. Do you have bourbon?"

"Course I do." She bent into a cabinet, brought out the bottle. "Three?" She squinted at him.

Perhaps three drinks were too many. "Yes." He wanted them all himself; they might relax him. "One's a double."

She poured the drinks, using a jigger glass with a thick bottom. "What's wrong now?"

"Not a thing."

"What's wrong with you, boy? You a *retard*?" She did not wait for his answer, but returned to the stove, picked up a two-pronged fork, began to spear each piece of chicken, bringing it close to her face for inspection.

He choked down a large swallow. "It's just that I think I've seen you before."

Her back to him: "I probably look like your mama."

Mitchell smiled, almost laughed. His mother, dead now eight years, had been small and dry. "No, that's not it." He took another swallow. The alcohol could not possibly be in his arteries yet, but knowing it was on its way made him feel better. "But—"

"I get one of you at every party Glora gives." She spun around. "You light-skinned, educated boys! Young Black girls scare you, so you come out and talk to mammy."

Mitchell tried not to laugh. "Really, that's not—"

"Well, mammy's a girl too and she ain't got time for scared boys." She smiled suddenly. "Unless you want to come on in the kitchen with me." She shook her head. "No, you don't want that. Go on away from here. Mammy ain't got no time no more for scared boys. Mammy wants men!"

Mitchell finished the double bourbon. "I'm not afraid."

"Then why you hanging around the kitchen?" She advanced on him, pointing the prongs of her fork at his eyes. "Go on now."

He backed away, into the darkness of the hall, and wandered, paper cup in hand, toward the dancing room. Glora was on the floor, moving inside her pink slacks. He stared at her, growing more confident all the time, certain that even across the room she would be able to feel what he was thinking about her. But she did not turn from her partner.

He stepped onto the floor, to cut in, but at that moment, saw Carlyle in a far corner talking to another man, their foreheads nearly touching. He came up behind them. "Hi, Carlyle."

"We was just talking about you." He put his arm around the other man's shoulder. "Here's a man who knows where you can find Cooley. Ain't that right, Calvin."

Calvin nodded. He was Mitchell's height and very dark, with pouches under his eyes, a thin mustache below his sharp nose. His hair was short, neatly parted. He was wearing a dark suit and white shirt. He too looked familiar, but Mitchell had to admit now that he did not know enough Black people to be able to tell them apart. He had always considered this a cliché, but realized now that it was at least partly true.

Carlyle told him that Calvin's last name was Johnson. Mitchell shook his hand, rough and cracked, but with a weak grip. "So what's happening?"

"Happening? Oh, nothing. You know Cooley?"

Calvin nodded. "I ain't seen him in about a week, but I'm pretty sure I know where he is. Carlyle says you ain't telling why you want to see him."

Mitchell realized now that, given Black people's fear and suspicion, his not telling his reasons could make it difficult to find Cooley. "You see, it's kind of private. I . . ."

"Ain't planning to kill him, are you?"

"Me?" Calvin was not joking. "No. I just want to talk to him."

"You understand my position, don't you? I wouldn't want to set up a friend of mine for a killing."

This talk of murder made Mitchell uneasy. "Sure, I know that."

"Good." He turned to Carlyle, smiled, then his tired eyes were on Mitchell again. "But I hope you won't be offended if I don't trust you for a while. I seen squarer-looking killers than you. So we'll just hang out and if you seem like you telling the truth, then maybe I'll take you to see Cooley. That sound all right to you?"

"Sure, but I really don't want to hurt him." He did not like the pleading in his voice, tried to harden it. "There may be some money in it for him."

"Okay. But if the deal's a good one, it'll keep, now won't it."

"I guess so." Mitchell was beginning to wonder whether it might be better just to forget about finding Cooley. He could force Tam to give the baby to an adoption agency. Her mother would help him. He did not at all like the people he was meeting.

Calvin smiled at him. "I know you want to find him. And I'll help you. But Coley and me is close, and got to stick together. The business we in, can't take no chances."

Mitchell nodded.

"Carlyle tells me you like Glora a little bit." He leaned closer. "What say you take Glora; Carlyle and me'll get us some ladies, and we can go over to a place I know of and drink up some liquor and . . . see what happens. It got lots of guest rooms."

Mitchell was about to refuse, but Calvin turned him around so that he could see Glora's pink slacks. He watched for a few moments, then agreed. It was important that he win Calvin's confidence.

16

Carlyle drove, Gerri-Ann (his girl?), in a light blue coat with some kind of fur collar, beside him. Calvin sat in the death seat, his arm lying on the seat, his hand, one finger ringed, just behind Carlyle's wine-colored shoulder. Glora and Rochelle (who seemed to be Calvin's girl) flanked Mitchell in the back. He could feel Glora's soft hip through slacks and outer coat. Rochelle's legs were crossed, and something—perhaps the clasp of her garter belt—was digging into him. They were leaving Harlem.

"How you doing there?" He could see Calvin's face in profile, the darkness equalizing his color, his hooked nose making him a Jew.

Glora rested her red head on his shoulder. "He doing fine. Ain't you?" Her fingers were making their way through the spaces between the buttons of his overcoat, through his suitcoat, to his shirt. Sharp nails caught in the bandagelike material of his undershirt.

"Yes." The street sign told him he was on Eighth Avenue. Then the neon signs ended and he saw the low stone wall of the park, behind it trees.

The back seat was shrinking. Rochelle seemed constantly to cross, uncross her legs. He glanced at her, found her staring at him, nodding her head. She uncrossed, recrossed her legs again, then suddenly turned away; he was looking at the back of her head, the hair in the kitchen cut into a V.

He sank down into the seat, enjoying Glora's hand massaging his stomach. So this was how Black people were by themselves. He had often seen carloads of them, had wondered where they were going, what they would do when they got there. Now he was finding out.

Then Carlyle had stopped, was parking the car. They climbed out onto the pavement, cold even through his shoes. Mitchell was still wedged between the two girls.

He dozed in the elevator, the three bourbons and two more besides, pressing his eyes shut. They woke him, made him walk—down the marble-floored hall, into Calvin's apartment, dropped him onto a large white leather sofa, put a drink into his hand.

He opened his eyes, the glass half-empty now, and watched Glora dance with Carlyle—too close, and he wondered if she was really his girl. He struggled to his feet, pushed Carlyle away, glimpsed her lavender lips before she rested her head on his chest; his hands slipped between the waistband of her pink slacks, his fingers pinched the elastic on her underpants.

The music stopped; he opened his eyes. Carlyle and Gerri-Ann were gone. So was Rochelle. Calvin sat in the middle of the sofa, rather small, looking uncomfortable. But he raised his glass to Mitchell, then pointed past him, nodding. Mitchell danced Glora in a circle until he could look down a hallway, where he knew he would find Calvin's guest rooms. He completed the circle, to signal Calvin he understood, but Calvin had disappeared.

Of course, Glora wanted to make love to him, had been flirting with him all evening, but he was not quite sure how to introduce the topic. With Tam, he had waited politely until she showed him that she would not reject him. She had been working as a reader in a publishing house then, had invited him to her apartment for dinner. They had finished a bottle of good wine, listened to some Brahms, talked, necked. Then she had guided his hand to her breast.

But this was a Black woman. He tried to remember what the Southerners he had known in the Service had told him about Black women. But even their experiences had been somewhat different. Glora was not a prostitute, and he was not planning to rape her.

The answer was simple enough—so simple in fact that he realized he must be quite drunk not to have found it immediately. Glora thought he was Black. He would simply do and say what he thought Carlyle, Calvin, or perhaps even Cooley, would do and say in the same circumstances. There was even some justice in it. Cooley had taken advantage of Tam's unhappiness. Now he, Mitchell, would take advantage of one of their women. He would convince Glora to help him find Cooley.

He began by sitting her on the sofa, his arm around her. "You never told me where you work."

"Huh?" She had been leaning, snuggling against him. She sat up slowly, blinking.

He smiled, tried to relax his face. "I asked you where you work?"

"Why you want to know that?" Before he could answer, she asked him for a cigaret. He gave her one, held a light for her, staring at her over the flame.

"I want to know as much as I can about you."

She took a drag, her lips leaving lavender on the white filter. "Why?"

He shrugged. "I think I'll be moving to New York soon and I want to see you again."

She gave him her golden smile. "Your wife won't like that a bit." Before he could ask how she knew he was married, she answered him: "Carlyle told me. He say you got a little boy." She leaned toward him, put her arms around his neck, smeared lipstick from one side of his mouth to the other. "But what I care! Maybe you'll give me a baby too, and have to come visit me."

His plan seemed to be working. He put his hand under her sweater, whispered. "Why don't"—clearing his throat—"why don't we find an empty room."

She stood up, took his hand and pulled him to his feet, smiling, and led him down the hallway, past several closed doors, where he guessed he would find Carlyle, Calvin, and their girls. They entered the last room. She closed the door, walked to a low dresser, and looked at herself in the mirror.

Then she placed her fingers to her temples, as if to hold a headache, and lifted away her red hair. Underneath, her hair was black, kinky, a round lamb hat.

For some reason, it frightened him, and he took a step backward, trying to recover himself. "I wouldn't have guessed that."

She was proud. "I know. It's a good one. I saved for six months." She crossed her arms over her breasts, grabbed the bottom of the yellow sweater. Her head popped from the neckband. Her bra, against copper skin, was light green.

Lurking near the door, he watched her go to the bed, fold back the spread. The light green straps blinked like neon. When she had finished preparing the bed, she sat down, looked at him. "Anything wrong?"

He was trying to think of what Cooley would say, but the Cooley of his imagination remained silent. "I want to tell you about my wife." He wished immediately that he had not said that.

"Now?" She reached for the button on her pink slacks.

"Only that she's a bitch." He enjoyed saying it, even if it was a lie.

"I know that." She stood up, slid the slacks down over her thighs. "If she wasn't, you wouldn't be here, right?"

"Why, yes." Her underpants were lemon yellow. He closed his eyes. Opening them, he found her no more than a foot away, her arms spread to him. "I'll make up for that."

He backed up, but she kept coming. "Wait." She put her hands on his waist, began to pull his shirt out of his pants. "Do you know Cooley?"

She stopped, his shirttail between her fingers. "Cooley? Why . . . yeah, I know him." She looked confused, retreated to the bed, and sat down. Cooley certainly had a profound effect on people.

Sensing that he had thrown her off guard, he followed her. "Do you know where I can find him?"

"Look, honey, I don't want to get myself in no mess."

He sat down beside her, put his arm around her, speaking softly. "There won't be any mess. I just want to talk to him."

"About what?"

Perhaps he could tell her the truth, not that he was white, which, after the way he had completely deceived her would be too much for her, but everything else. Of course, he did not trust her. But after all she was sitting beside him almost naked, obviously had some feeling for him. He searched her face, realizing suddenly that he had seen it before, many times. The Black girl who worked in the file room at his office had the same face, and all of the girls he saw on the subway. They were all stupid, simple girls. Each wanted only a good job, a nice home, some bright clothes. And they were willing to do almost anything to get them. He need only give her a glimpse into his world and she would tell him everything he wanted to know. "I asked you before, where do you work?"

She bit her lip. "I ain't got a job."

"How would you like a nice job in a good company?" He was stroking her plump, soft arm.

"I couldn't get no job like that." Already her dark eyes could see herself riding the subway downtown.

"Yes, you could, with my help." He kissed her ear; she tried to move away, but he held her. "I want to tell you a secret, Glora. Originally, I'm from Canada, but now I live in New York." She did not seem surprised. "And I work in a big company downtown." He remembered a movie he had seen a long time before. "I'm passing for white."

"Really?" She smiled.

"Now, I'll get you a good job in my company and all you have to do is tell me where I can find Cooley."

He saw fear in her eyes now. "Why you want to find him?"

"If I tell you, you have to promise not to tell anyone, except Cooley. You do want that good job, don't you?"

She nodded.

He sighed, hating to mouth the words, especially to someone like this. "My wife just had his baby."

"She really is a bitch, ain't she?"

He did not reply, knowing she would never understand all that had happened between him and Tam. "And I want Cooley to take the baby."

"Bye-bye job." She shook her head. "Cooley won't want no baby."

"I think he'll want this one." He decided not to tell her why. Then she would know he was not Black. Cooley might not want just any woman's baby, but this was Tam's baby—half-white. Of course he would want the baby. "It's a good job." And it would be nice to have her indebted to him, close at hand. "Well, what d'you say?"

"What you think, honey?" She tossed herself into his arms, pushed him down onto the bed, began to kiss his face. "And I'll be good to you too." She was on top of him. He inhaled her perfume, smiling, and reaching around her back, unhooked her bra. She began to undress him.

Both naked, they slid under the covers. He could not take his hands out of her hair; it pushed against his fingers like sponge. At first he found it distasteful, but then began to enjoy it. Between kisses, she kept talking. "So you ain't from Canada. You had me fooled. I bet you really fool those white folks downtown. You so cool. And you wait until I get there. All you got to do is call me in your office. 'Glora, will you bring me them letters from so-and-so company?' I'll have my pants down before you can close the door. One time, I was working downtown, in a mail-order house, for a little white man. He looking at me all the time. So I figured maybe it'd be good for a raise and I ran into him one night, accidentally." She winked down at him. "He took me up to his place and made his play for me. You thank God you never had to make it with no pasty-faced white man." She laughed so hard she rolled off him, and almost off the bed. She crawled back to him, rested her spongy head on his chest. "Let me tell you, honey, going over, he squeal like a little fat pig: eeee eeee eeee!" She started to laugh again. "That was the last time. I bet if any white man even get close to me, I'd know it. Eeee eeee eeee! You sure you ain't passing for colored, Mitchell?"

He denied it, trying to joke, but felt as if she had thrown ice water on his stomach and thighs. For the next fifteen minutes, he tried to recover. It was hopeless. Finally, he sat up.

She looked at him from the pillow, bewildered, perhaps a little angry.

He knew that unless he gave her a reason, she would not help him, might even turn against him. "It's an old war wound," he explained. "I never know when it's going to hit me."

She sat up, her face softer, and hugged him. "Sure is terrible the sacrifices a man got to make for his country." She kissed his shoulder. "You call me when you get over it."

He dressed, took her phone number, kissed her good-bye, all the while trying to avoid her dark eyes. "I'll be all right. I'll call you tomorrow, about Cooley."

"You do that, honey." She smiled, but suddenly buried her face in the pillow. Her back began to shake, short quick little shakes as if she was giggling. He had really disappointed her.

Outside, the sky was gray, the trees in the park black. He found his car and drove home, surprised to discover that the distance between Calvin's house and his own was less than a mile.

THIS CHILD'S GONNA LIVE
(1969)

SARAH ELIZABETH WRIGHT

Born on Maryland's Eastern Shore, Sarah Elizabeth Wright brought her
memory of her early years there to the Harlem Writers Guild in the form
of a manuscript entitled *This Child's Gonna Live,* which told the story of
Mariah Upshur, an inhabitant of a Maryland fishing village, who remains
hopeful despite her life's harsh circumstances. After it was published in
1969, the *New York Times* proclaimed it as one of the year's ten best
books.

1

Sometimes the sun will come in making a bright yellow day. But then
again, sometimes it won't.

Mariah Upshur couldn't see herself waiting to know which way it
was coming as she fretted to see through the sagging windows squeezed
between her upstairs roofs. The bed with Jacob's legs sprawled all over
her was a hard thing to stay put in.

Strain cut in her face in such a heavy way, she thought, "My skin
must be sliced up with the wrinkles the same as an old black walnut."
She touched it and found not a single line.

She had the same tight skin, the same turned-up nose that people
used to say went with her "high-minded gallop" when she wasn't doing
a thing but marking time on Tangierneck's slowing-up roads. Pyorrhea
in the gums had taken all of her back teeth, but her jaws stayed firm and
slanty—pretty as a picture of any white girl's she ever saw on those
Christmas candy boxes that her mamma used to cut out and hang on the
cedar tree and the walls. Little "star light, star bright" twinkling angels,
that's what Mamma Effie always hung on that tree. And she told Mariah,
"You got to be *that* good and pure before the Lord's gonna bless you
with anything."

"But I got a different set of eyes in this night, Jesus. If you'll spare me, me and my children getting out of this Neck."

Such a chilliness crept over Mariah, and she cried all down in herself, for she couldn't wake her children. She'd been dosing them up all through the night with the paregoric so they could get some easement from their coughing.

"Done promised you me and the children getting out of here so many times, Jesus, you must think I'm crazy. But you ain't sent many pretty days this way lately."

With a start Mariah caught herself criticizing the Lord and said, "Excuse me, Jesus. I'm willing to do my part. Just make this a pretty day so I can haul myself out of this house and make me some money. Jesus, I thanks you for whatever you do give to me. I ain't meant to say nothing harsh to you. Jesus, you know I thanks you. I thanks you. I thanks you."

Then it felt to Mariah as if the comforts of the Lord's blessing spread all over her.

Soft sleep rested so lightly on her eyes, and she was home safe in a harbor warm, just a-rocking in the arms of Jesus. And the spirit of the Lamb became a mighty fire prevailing in the woman's eyes sunk now to dreaming, and she could just about see how this new day's sun was gonna come in.

It was gonna sail up blazing and red and hoe a steady path on up to the middle parts of the sky. Clouds get in the way? It was just gonna bust on through them and keep on sailing until it rolled on up easy over the crest of those worrisome waves.

Then it was gonna rock awhile—all unsteady like—until it made up its mind that it was on high and it hadn't sailed through anything but some feathery nuisances. Rock awhile and then turn all yellow and golden as it smiled at the cloud waves turned to nothing but some washed-out soapsuds foaming on the treetops of what Mariah liked to call this Maryland side of the long-tailed Dismal Swamp.

It was gonna sit there a long time grinning and spilling those fields full of itself, making every potato digger—leastwise herself—feel good down to the quick same as if it was summer still.

And she could dig a-many a potato on a day like this. Just scramble down those rows and flip potato after potato into those four-eight baskets. Dirt flying in her face? Well, honies, she wasn't even gonna mind.

She'd eat that dirt and hustle on. She wouldn't even mind how the dirt got packed under whatever fingernails she had left—not even mind when the hurting from the dirt pressure made her shoulder blades cleave all up to themselves. She was just gonna suck her fingers every now and then—dirt and all—and keep on tearing down those rows. And when Bannie Upshire Dudley's hired man wrinkled his old pokey face in consternation from handing her "that many!" tokens for all those solid loaded baskets she got such a shortness of the breath from lugging up to the field shanty, and when he snickered to her, "Mariah, ain't you done stole some baskets from Martha from on Back-of-the-Creek?" she was gonna sic her big bad word doggies on him. Gonna sound worse than a starved-out bloodhound baying at the teasing smell of fresh-killed meat, ten thousand times worse than the menfolks do when they're away from the white-man bosses—all except that no-talking Jacob she was stuck with.

"Jam your dick up your turd hole, cracker, and bust from the hot air you bloated with. You believe every colored person that's getting a-hold of something's stealing. I believes in working for my money. Give me my money, man. I ain't no thief like the woman you working for. *That's* the thief!"

If he said half a word back to her she was gonna grab his squelched-down, corn-colored head and twist it to the east and the west and the north and the south so he could get a good look at all the scores of acres that used to be in Jacob's papa's hands. Didn't care if she rang it off like she'd do a chicken. "See, see, you ass-licking poor white. See how Miss Bannie done glutted up our land. Now you want to talk about a thief, you talk about her. She knowed most of the colored was renting land off of Pop Percy. She knowed it just as good as anything when she went and lent him all that money to get his affairs straightened out. Then she come charging him interest on top of interest with things as hard as they is. Knows we ain't able to pay it. And selling food for the hogs and things as high as mighty. She knows good and well we ain't got no way into Calvertown to buy it cheap since the steamboat stop running. I ain't like the rest of the niggers you and Miss Bannie got, saying your shit don't smell bad when you use them for a toilet. I ain't saying tiddely-toe and grinning when you fart in my face no more, when I know good and well that tiddely ain't got no toes and your fart don't smell like perfume."

Then she was gonna tell him where his old bleached-out papa come from and his weak-behinded mamma too, if she could stomach herself getting down that low. She was gonna stomp his ass good, buddies. Set it on fire. Gonna send him popping across those fields the same as if he was a never-ending firecracker. Wishing she had a razor on her like most white people thought colored carried, so she could catch up with him and cut his old woman-beating fists off and then slice out his dick so he wouldn't plug up that simple-minded Anna of his anymore with his corn-colored bastards to tease her little Skeeter and Rabbit about the way they looked. But she wasn't gonna waste any time dwelling on that, for the old fart-bloated cracker wasn't worth her getting a murder charge laid against her name. She was just gonna be glad she sent him running.

And then in the plain light of day—yes, yes, my God, on that pretty day! She was gonna reach up to that culling board where he had a habit of spreading out a pile of tokens to glisten in the sun so as to entice the colored people's eyes as they scrambled up those potato rows. Gonna scoop herself up a handful of tokens, just a-singing to the world. "No more short change for me, my Lordy. No more shitting on me and then telling me I smell bad 'cause you won't let me wash it off. No more! No more mocking my children when they come down to this field to help me out, calling the little naps on their heads 'gun bullets' and making them feel bad. No more!"

And all around here there was gonna be such a commotion. With people running up from the rows to the field shanty, crying, "Glory Hallelujah, Mariah done chased the money changers out of the temple." And black working hands looking so pretty next to those gold-colored tokens were just gonna be scooping them up. But most and especially there was gonna be little old hickory-nutty Aunt Saro Jane with all those little winning airs she put on even though she must be going on a hundred, saying, "Mariah, now you know you ought not to have done that white man that way. We colored in Tangierneck have to depend on those people!"

"Look like they the ones been depending on us, Aunt Saro Jane. We built up this Tangierneck and now they taking it away from us."

"Can't help that, Mariah. They got the money. They got the banks."

"But we doing the work for to make that money, Aunt Saro Jane."

That's the way Mariah was gonna talk back to her. Then she was gonna stroll on off. No, she was gonna stomp on off, and run. Head thrown back the same as if she were a wild mare filly. If anybody stopped her to ask where she was going, she was gonna just holler back, "I'm on my way to the North. Going to the city where me and my children can act in some kind of a dignified way."

As she ran she wasn't gonna worry about a thing except maybe whether or not she'd scooped up enough tokens to pay for Skeeter and them to get some good clothes instead of having to wear those tow sacks she sewed into garments for them, and some medicine for the colds in their chests and things like that.

She might give a thought or two to giving Jacob a little piece of the money she'd have, for after all it was Jacob that put in all of that time last year pulling out the crabgrass and the jimson weeds from around those potato plants. He tended that field so good when those potatoes weren't anything but some little old twigs and promises. My, how he sprinkled that nitrate of soda over that low ground so as to give those little brown potato babies something worth eating for to suck on. Spent a whole heap of time plowing that ground so it would be soft and tender for those things to nestle down in and nurse until they got good and fat and ready for the harvesttime. And now Miss Bannie done claimed that field for herself, too.

She wasn't gonna take up too much time with Jacob though, for he wasn't going one step to save his own life. And when she grabbed her children and headed for the road going North, she wasn't even gonna look back at Jacob standing in the yard telling her that her talk about the children needing this and that for to grow on was nothing but a whole lot of "horse manure."

Even in that last minute, I mean buddies, in that very last minute, he wouldn't have the spine to grow an inch taller on. He never could so much as say the word "shit" when he meant it. He was just weak, weak, weak, that's all there was to it—and always hiding behind the Lord. If the crops failed, it was the Lord's will. If the children stayed sick with the colds, it was the Lord's will. And she never was able to tell him anything, honies, about those little corn-colored children of Bannie's field man calling Skeeter and them out of their names when they came down to the fields to help her out. All of that was the "Lord's will."

She used to say to him, "Jacob, everything ain't the Lord's will. Some of these things happening is these Maryland type of white people's will. I don't care how much they go to the church, they ain't living by the word of the Lord. They living by their greedy pocketbooks. They got a different set of white people in them cities up North. Your brothers done gone, Jacob. You the only one sticking to this land."

In spite of the devil, Jacob would answer her with something like, "But they'll be back, Mariah. They ain't doing nothing up there in them cities but getting pushed around. Trying to do some fancy singing they got on them radios up there, but there ain't nothing to it. They don't own nothing, Mariah. Ain't a cent they got they can call their own. Paying off furniture on some time plans and all of that kind of foolishness. A man is his land. In other words, what he owns that he paid for outright. A man is his land."

Then he'd quote from some old simple-assed poem he learned from his father:

I am master over all I survey
My rights there are none to dispute
From the land all around to the sea
I am Lord o'er fowl and brute

Said to him a-many a time, "My children ain't no fowl and brute. I wants my children to live. They human beings just like anybody else." But if he thought she was gonna stop and whine those words to him now, he had another thought coming, for she was running, honies, running. And it wouldn't be worthwhile for her to turn around and say one thing at all, for all he was gonna do was call her a nag.

Nag, shit, the woman panted in the dreams of morning. All I ever been trying to do was tell him something in an easy way of speaking, so as not to hurt his feelings. Just run now, that's all she was gonna do.

Littlest one of her children, Gezee, weighed heavily in her arms, and her stomach was so swolled up with the gas, his sleepy weight just caused her to ache so much.

"Skeeter, Rabbit, you all come along here! Skeeter, what you doing letting Rabbit drag you along? You the oldest. Don't be trying to hang back with your daddy. Skeeter, stop that coughing, child. We can't slow down for you to catch your breath. I got a heavy enough aching on me as it is."

She couldn't let Skeeter's lagging and waving his arms back for his daddy hold her up one bit as she went sailing over those sand dunes going down the hill past blabbermouth. Tillie's house, past those distant-acting in-laws of hers high-and-mighty-looking house.

It's a long stretch of road when you're running with such a weight bearing down on you. Renting-people's little shanty houses stretch a good ten-minute run along that sandy road when you're in good shape. But Lord help you when you're heavy. Children linking themselves around Mariah's arms and legs felt just like chains in the running. They weighed heavy on her when she tried to run past her own mamma and papa's house. Slowed her down to a standstill, and she couldn't fight her way past her papa standing there in the road.

Papa was something to fight. The only man in Tangierneck who ever paid off his land entirely to Percy Upshur. He liked to broke his back doing it, but then Pop Harmon was a mighty man. If you measured him by inches he wasn't so tall. She'd give him five feet and seven inches, but she couldn't measure Pop Harmon by the inches. She had to measure him by the squall in his face and his shoulders all flung back. He was a deep mustard kind of yellow, but he called himself black. It wouldn't do for anything frail to be getting in his path. He'd just mow it down.

"You too high-minded, woman, too busy gazing for the stars to see the storm clouds right around us. Folks have to navigate their ways through the rough seas of life before they can set back and feast their eyes on the stars. You think you seeing some stars now that you're running up to them cities? Well, honies, I'm here to tell you you can't see no stars anywhere at any time with your naked eye in the time of a storm. It's the time of a storm all over for the colored man. They lynching colored men every day by the wholesale lot just south of this swamp, and up there in them cities, too. But in a different sort of way."

"But what about the colored *woman?*" Mariah tried to answer him back. "All I keep hearing is you all talking about the hard times a colored *man's* got."

"See my scars! See my scars! Colored woman's always been more privileged than the man. You ain't got no hard time in this community." He roared against her terrible screaming of "Papa, let me go!"

But his powerful shoulders pushed her back, flail out against them all she pleased. He almost knocked her down in the shifting sand. She came back at him like a foaming-mouthed terrier. But nothing came out of her mouth except a moan.

"Don't talk to me about the colored woman, gal, until you see my scars." In a split second he was naked, standing in a blazing sun. Bleeding all over his back. "See my scars, woman, see my scars!"

And all Mariah could see to him was his scars. Even as naked as he was, she couldn't make out a thing else about him except his scars.

"White men up there to Baltimore Harbor liked to beat my as off when I landed in this 'land of the free.' They said to me, 'Horace, you come here all the way from Barbados hid down in the hold of our ship. You ain't paid a cent for the passage. You ain't worked for us, you ain't done nothing. Now what you gonna do, you little monkey?' I says to 'em, 'Monkey your Goddamned self. Let me go!' Now heifer, I want you to know they let me go 'cause I went into them for the kill. See my scars. . . ."

Last shades of night hung on for Mariah, and deeper into sleep she sank. The dream kept coming: her papa pushing her down in the sand, in the choking sand while he called up to that little squeezy house she was born and reared in for her mamma, Effie, to come to the road.

"Effie, Effie, this gal of yours is getting out of control. Bring your switch out here and beat this gal, Effie. Whip her ass good!"

Mamma Effie always was a good beating-stick for Papa. He did the talking but Mamma did the beating. Her whole body was like a whipping switch, thin and lean and crackling. Her great dark eyes were always filled with lightning, and most of the time she never said a word to her children except something like, "I'll beat the living daylights out of you if you don't listen to your papa."

There was but one of those children left now, and that was Mariah. Mariah tossing under the quilts Mamma Effie made for the times of her giving birth. Mariah heavy with a sleep that wouldn't let her go. Mariah groaning in her sleep from the beating. A switch can draw blood, but getting beat up with a stove-lid lifter can make a person cry for her own death. Those things are made of iron. A beating on your back and legs with one will make a person's soul cave in.

As her mamma beat her, her papa talked on.

"Stop that running, gal. You ain't getting past me. You can't run your way through the brambles and the bushes of life. You got to chop down those vines and creepers first before you go headlong through them. Old rattlers are coiled up in them. Pretty flowers on them vines is just there to entice you out of your senses. Rattler's going to sink his fangs in you on this road.

"All of this talk about you going away to the cities to make something of yourself don't mean a thing 'cause you still don't see nothing but the flowers on the bushes. Ain't a decent woman *enough* for you to be? You'd better pray for God to send us a pretty day tomorrow so we can get out of here and pull some holly out of this swamp. We got to pay off this land."

Mariah couldn't wiggle out of her papa's hands. He had some big, strong hands. Just holding her. "Effie, beat her, beat her. Beat her ass good. Make her work. A child is the servant of the parent."

A violent wrenching of herself got Mariah free to hobble, broken, on up that road. Saying to her papa, "I ain't no more child, Papa. What you all holding me up for? You ain't suppose to be talking to me like when I was a child. I got my own children." Moaning, "Come on, Rabbit. Come on, Skeeter. Help me to carry Gezee. . . ."

Mamma Effie tore after her, hollering, "Come back here, slut! Look a-here, here comes Jacob bringing that little near-white affliction you done bore to him. If you gonna leave, take 'em all. The thing ain't Jacob's. Why you leave that burden on him?"

"I ain't got no other child, Mamma! Why you always trying to accuse me of something!"

With a jolting start Mariah sat up in the bed. She cried, "Jesus!"

Her eyes groped in the darkness for something to hold on to. A bit of light from the kerosene lamp she kept in the hallway helped her out some. The woman prayed, "Jesus, it ain't dawn yet."

The little attic type of a room took shape. Little by little the chest of drawers with the blue paint peeling off it, and the wallpaper gone limp and nipply from the damp and the winds easing their ways in between the boards of her upstairs roof sank into her head. She thought she heard Jacob mumbling from under the quilts, "Woman, go on back to sleep." And maybe she did, but she couldn't be quite for sure, for his legs were such heavy weights on her. He must be sound asleep.

She inched herself toward the edge of the bed as much as Jacob's warmed-up, pinning-down feet would let her. A fearful sickness rolled through every inch of her lumpish body. She tried to get free, but every time she tried to move, the way Jacob had of throwing himself any which a-way in the bed so he got the quilt tangled up and locking her in wouldn't let her.

Teeth wiggled in her gums so bad they hurt. Gritting her teeth too much. Gums hurt her. Head was just a-pounding, but she couldn't feel a thing else. Just her gums aching and the pounding in her head.

She hissed into the night that looked like it was never gonna go away, "Move!"

But Jacob did not move.

Outside in the nearly-about-morning world, the wind growled and hawked and spit the same as if it had a throat. Wind wasn't doing a thing except messing up everything in God's creation, spitting in the face of hopes for a pretty day, moaning nothing but more of what Tangierneck mostly was these days—a place of standing still and death.

"Death!" Mariah could hardly say the word, for it seemed the thing was creeping its way into her soul-case. She had seen a naked man in her dream!

"No, he wasn't naked! He wasn't naked, God Jesus! I ain't seen it, have I?"

A stillness came over her. Jaws became solid frozen. Her elbows cracked as she let her hands go trembling over the mound rising up from her middle parts. She could hardly ease her body down to wait for the coming of dawn. A shudder started in her shoulders—locked her neck to the pillow.

"Why, the child hadn't moved in a good while! Dreams are a sign. . . . Oh my God, my God, I done killed it! It can't be dead!" She drummed on the skin stretched tight on her belly. Tried to sound out life, but no matter which combination of taps she drummed, life wouldn't sound back. "Must be lazy this morning. Bet you's a girl. Girls is lazy." Terror scalded her eyes. The dream flooded over her—the running into her papa naked, and Mamma Effie's accusation.

"Jacob's your daddy, honey. I talked it over with Jesus. Know he wouldn't lead me wrong." She pleaded softly to the unborn child, but the child didn't make a single move.

A loathsome sickness wormed in her throat. Shame for everything washed all over her. The cussing and the anger of her dream. Maybe if she prayed to God to wash her sinful dream away the child would move!

She opened her mouth to scream, but no sound came. A whisper jerked its way out. "My child's all right, ain't it, Lord?"

"Woman, what in the name of God you doing, pulling all the covers off of me?" Jacob's voice came over the thundering in her skull.

Mariah let go of the covers. Didn't realize she was pulling them. There was nothing eviler and more contrary than Jacob if the cold air got to him when he was sleeping.

"Woman, lay on back down will you, or stay still or something unless there's something the matter with you?"

Mariah froze. Couldn't answer Jacob to save her life.

The man said no more.

Humble yourself to the Lord, Mariah. Apologize one more time. If she could only speak. If she could only run. Get on that speeding-up Route 391 and run. Wished she'd kept on running when she went to see that Dr. Grene. Run right past him. Gone on to the Calvertown Hospital clinic.

"Didn't believe they'd treat me right though, Lord. Thought it'd be easier to talk to that new colored doctor about my headache—tell him about the screaming that backed up in my head when Mary died . . . Jesus!" The woman cringed in startled panic.

"Jesus!" Her lips moved without a sound. She fixed her eyes on the little white lambs flocking around the white-robed figure on the Jamison Funeral Home calendar.

"You know that's over with, Jesus. You ain't gonna punish me no more. You ain't let me kill this young'un, has you?

"I know I ain't nothing but a woman filled with sins. But I cares for my children. Remember, you said to me, 'Now Mariah, you're on the side of life. You're a mother. Two sins don't make a right.' I know you had to talk to me right smart, Jesus, because I was scared. But you know how people do when they get scared. Do anything. But you snatched that other bottle of Febrilline out of my hands before I had a chance to pour it down my throat when my head was wobbling from that first bottle of quinine mess like it was fit to roll off in one of those oyster buckets. . . ."

Her head filled now, tighter than a skin drum full of water. "Let the child kick. Let the day come in nice. Spare the child, Lord, and I promise you, if I use every last bit of strength I got, we getting out of this place."

She closed her eyes, for a little voice far back in her head said, "Jesus is just testing you out, Mariah, Jesus just testing you out." And right along with the voice came a movement around her navel, soft as a little spring breeze.

She smiled to the Lord. "Gonna stop thinking about death. Ain't gonna cry no more."

Later in the dawn she cracked her eyes again, and a little light did come in. October sun comes so late. She dug her chapped knuckles into the deep, warm places her eyes made, and lifted her heavy lids.

She wondered sometimes how the sun ever made it at all coming from the easternmost part of God-knows-where down to low-laying Tangierneck. Lowest place on the whole Eastern Shore of Maryland, she did believe. Wonder was that it hadn't been washed away, the way that big, wide, bossy, ocean-going Nighaskin River keeps pouring water down into the mouth of the Neck until Deep Gut swallows all it can hold and backs the rest of it out for the ocean. Orange ball bouncing on the Nighaskin Sound, heaving and setting and hardly climbing up at all. Oyster boats tossing helplessly.

She balled her hands up until they hurt. "Jacob, I swamp it, Deep Gut's filled up with wind again. Spewing out ponds all over the fields. There's not gonna be a cent made today."

Every muscle swoll in her craning neck. She swallowed hard. Last night's terror left a nasty morning taste. "Nothing here, Jacob, but death. Nothing down here but nothing."

Jacob stirred. "Death coming sooner or later, woman. What you all the time harping on it for?"

"Children ain't had no milk in the longest kind of time. I ain't neither. I was thinking to myself I'd send Skeeter down to Bannie's to get us some. . . ."

Jacob flew right into her. "Don't send Skeeter nor nobody else down to Bannie's for nothing. I done told you once. I ain't gonna tell you no more. And another thing, woman, I don't want to catch you digging no more potatoes for Bannie."

"Tell me the Welfare people's giving out cans of Pet milk by the case full. . . ."

"Shut up, woman. I done told you now. I provides for my family."

Silence hung between them like the deep maroon drapes in Jimmy Jamison's funeral home parlor. She might have known he'd act like that. But there used to be a different kind of time, the woman thought. There used to be a time when she could really tackle Jacob. She'd tell him in a minute about picking up his own trash behind himself, or about throwing his money down on the table for her to keep them and the children halfway going like he was throwing a bone to a worrisome pet dog. He'd throw the money down and stroll on out of the house, not even saying as much as "Dog"—that was the least he could call her—"here's the money for this or that."

In one day and time she'd go in to Jacob like lightning with, "Man, why don't you change your drawers a little more often and wipe yourself good? Any dog gets tired sometimes of scrubbing out somebody else's shit from their drawers."

That kind of thing would set him on fire, but she'd go on. "Sparrow, they tell me that Uncle Marsh Harper's about the cleanest man on the oyster rocks. Tell me when he gets through doing his business, he wipes himself good with his glove, then leans over in the Gut and washes himself off and his glove."

"He's about the purest fool we got on the boats, woman!" Jacob would thunder back. "Fool's gonna catch the pneumonia first and last splashing that cold water on himself."

And Mariah, she used to play a little bit, too. "Did you say first in the ass, Jacob?"

Then he'd have to break down and laugh himself. But then he'd go on and give her a lecture about cussing and how sinful it was in the eyes of the Lord. But those times were all over with now. . . .

There was no sense in her mentioning the Welfare to him anymore, because he wasn't gonna answer. But somehow she couldn't help herself from wishing that they had some milk. How many times had she wished the milk in her breasts could flow by the gallon—enough for all of them to drink. She could almost see herself pulling Jacob's bony, hurtful-looking face to her breasts. . . . But she was leaving Tangierneck. Talked it over with God. Taking her children and leaving death. And she wanted to take Jacob, too.

"Death's so close to you now, Jacob, you can reach out and touch it."

But Jacob did not answer, nor move his reddish, tight-faced head one single inch. He just rubbed his teeth together over and over again, making a terrible grating sound.

"It's been a bad October, Rah. November's almost here. There's a time in the land."

Sounded almost like a cry. Mariah moved closer to him. Tears worked around in her eyes. "Stop gritting your teeth, Jacob. Stop it. You hear me. Don't, I'm gonna give you a dose of Bumpstead's Worm Syrup to work those worms out of you."

"Cut out the foolishness, Rah. Getting too near your time for you to be carrying on like that." Covers fell away from his bony shoulders and he sat bolt upright in the bed.

"My time, Jacob?" If she could only get the sight of him out of her eyes. "My time! And what you done about it?"

"Rah, I done told you. . . ."

"Don't want no Lettie Cartwright, nor no other midwife killing another child of mine. Mary would've been here today if she'd been born in the hospital. . . ."

Jacob didn't take his red, wind-eaten eyes off of her. Tired, beaten-looking eyes with a little bit of stubble for eyelashes jiggling on his sunken cheeks.

"May as well cut out the foolishness, Rah. We ain't got no hospital money, and we ain't getting on no Welfare."

He turned his back to her, mumbling from under the quilts where he buried his head, "You done took all the teas in the world, and some of that Dr. Grene's medicine, too. How come you always harping on death? You need to pray, Mariah. Have a good talk with God."

"You must think you the holiest thing out, Mr. Jacob. Let me tell you how I talked things over with God!"

But the man didn't move. "Rah, I'm going to want my breakfast now and in a few minutes" was all he raised the quilt to say.

"That's all you got to say. That's all you got to say?" Her heart pounded. She was gonna break down and holler at him in a minute.

But he didn't answer.

"Well, let me tell you something, Mr. Jacob. I got something to say."

And all the horror of the night just gone flooded out of her.

"Me and my children getting out of this death trap, Tangierneck, and you can stay here, buddies, 'cause we don't want you with us."

He threw back the quilts. Mariah tried to catch something that happened in her husband's face. It wasn't tight anymore. It fell all to pieces. And though her hands wanted to reach for him, she couldn't bring herself to touch him.

His lips hardly moved. "Cut out the foolishness, Rah."

She wanted to gather up the pieces. If only she could do something nice for him. Get up and fry some oyster fritters, open a can of corn—if she could put her hands on one—set his breakfast on the table, snappy and hot, with some milk to go along with it. Fool ought to know he needed milk. It would clear up the rattling in his chest, make him feel like singing. And she could call him Sparrow once more, for he really was a regular song sparrow before his mouth got clamped down with hunger and worriation. But there were no oysters, for wind had bossed the rocks for two whole days, and there was no corn—just a single can left for Sunday—and there was no milk.

The salt of tears burned through the chapped crust on her lips, and she turned her eyes from Jacob's twitching face. "Ain't nothing down here but nothing."

"Yes, it is too, Rah."

Looked as if his bony hand was going to make it across the quilt hills to touch her. "Why don't you tell it like it is, Mr. Jacob?"

She couldn't bear to look at his torn-up face. "Let go my legs, man!" She jerked herself free. "You'd stay down here until the year 2000 if you could live for seventy more. You gonna pay off the land, huh, Mr. Jacob? Gonna collect all the money that's due on your pappy's land. Pay off Miss Bannie. Gonna make the County give a schoolhouse to your children."

"Woman!"

But she couldn't stop. "And if this child dies, gonna be your fault! So sorry you were when the last one died, you gonna see to it this one comes here in the hospital. . . ."

"Woman!" He shoved a swollen-jointed finger up to her eyes. "Just lift one finger to take either one of my children out of Tangierneck, and I s'pect that'll be the last finger you'll ever lift. . . . And another thing, woman. Child dies, gonna be your fault for lifting and lugging them potato baskets. Told you to stay out of them fields. Never thought you wanted this young'un no way. Sometimes I get the feeling that if you had your way you'd a-killed it."

All over her it was cold. Nothing in her moved. But she stepped out of bed, snatched her hair free of its pins. "I'm going, Jacob." And the trembling-faced man said no more.

Her head was nothing but a throbbing hunk of mostly hair with a little bitty brown face screwed down under it. *Heavy head to tote in the morning, Lord. Heaviest head I ever had.* Almost had a mind to go downstairs and run a straightening comb through that mess of hair so it would flow long and wavy like Jacob used to say he liked it. "But I'm going, Lord."

For a moment she stared at the wall of her husband's back. Wanted to tell him so badly how sluggish the child was acting. *But it ain't his,* evil mind wanted to tell her. Nerves felt like they were about to give out on her. Jacob's back was a hunk of stone. She twisted her hair tightly into a bun again, pulling her face and mind and everything in her tight. "Done talked it over with the Lord," she muttered, and straightened herself on up.

She bounded down the steps, pulling the big, secondhand robe over her stiffened shoulders. Worried to craziness by the stillness, sniffling angrily at the morning mustiness of her body and the thought of the man. Hitting her soles on the bottom steps to stir up warmth, she announced to the early morning darkness of the kitchen, and the wind that crept in between the baseboards, and the wallboards and the places she'd chinked and chinked until she wasn't gonna chink no more, and the sounds of rats and mice gnawing in the molding: "I'm gonna make me a fire. Ought to burn down this place. . . ."

She rubbed her bare feet, one on top of the other, screwed them around on the cold linoleum. Kindling wood bent in her toughened hands, some so damp it would hardly splinter. She took the front lids off the big, black kitchen stove and filled it with wood. The oil that was left in the coal oil can wasn't enough, so she went back up the stairs and got the night lamp burning in the hallway. Blew the flame out and dumped all the kerosene in the oil chamber on to the soggy pinewood.

"Gonna make me a good fire!" And she struck a match. In the gray morning a flame shot up. Up the chimney roaring, out of the sides of the stove, through the cracks between the other stove lids, out of the bottom grating, shooting last night's ashes all over her feet.

There was an orange pain in her eyes and her arm was on fire and she almost cried "Jacob" but she didn't. She smothered her burning arm in the cavity between her breast and her belly, and with her free hand she crushed the last embers in the smoldering sleeve.

Such a kicking went on inside of her!

She stood still while her hands burnt and the lashes of her eyes fell down over her half-fried cheeks. She grinned real wide in the smoked-up morning light. Grinned real wide at the sounds of rats and mice a-gnawing in the molding.

"That's right, baby, kick. Kick all you want to." The bony ribs under her heart hurt. Hurt all the way through her heart and . . . "Kick, you contrary thing. Don't care if you kick my guts out. . . ."

She cried as she greased her face down with Vaseline. "That's right, baby, kick . . . thank the Lord, thank the Lord, thank the Lord." And the grease wouldn't stay around her smarting eyes, she cried so hard. "Jesus, God, and all your little angels, thank you, Lord." She choked up and swore in the light of the quieting-down flame. "Ain't gonna say no more to Jacob about it. Just make this a pretty day, Jesus, and I'll go out of this house and make the hospital money my ownself. Gonna get my children out of this Tangierneck."

Her greasy lips pursed in determination as she went out to the corn-house to slice off the last slab of fatback, not even wrapping herself up good from the wind.

PART THREE

1970s–2000s

<<<<<<<<<<<<<<<<<<<<<<<<<<<<<

AND THEN WE MADE THE THUNDER

It is unquestionable that by the beginning of the 1970s, African Americans had established a creative visibility evident not only in their literary canon, but also in music, theater, television, and radio. Running parallel, and at times within, this prolific output were the active voices of the Black Arts Movement, the Black Power Movement, Pan-Africanism, and Cultural Nationalism. In the first five years of the decade, several members of the Harlem Writers Guild, including John A. Williams and poets Audre Lorde and Maya Angelou, published works that reflected the timbre of the times.

John A. Williams, already critically acclaimed for his fictional portrayal of the black American experience in 1967's *The Man Who Cried I Am* and 1969's *Sons of Darkness, Sons of Light: A Novel of Some Probability*, issued *Captain Blackman* (1974), a narrative of a wounded black United States soldier in Vietnam; openly gay poet Audre Lorde, dispatched *Cables to Rage* (1970), *From a Place Where Other People Live* (1973), and *New York Head Shop and Museum* (1974), notable for its fixed poetic and political gaze on the titular city's poverty and decay; and fellow poet and memoirist Maya Angelou began a prolific career with the autobiographical *I Know Why the Caged Bird Sings* (1970) and the Pulitzer Prize–nominated collection of poetry *Just Give Me a Cool Drink of Water 'fore I Diiie* (1971).

But outside the constructs of literature, Harlem by the mid-1970s was a neighborhood seriously in trouble. Middle-class flight to the suburbs and national inflation, coupled with the ever-present afflictions of crime and poverty, forced much of New York City, including Harlem, to succumb to urban decay. On a hot July night in 1977, the neighborhood boiled over when a citywide blackout ignited looting and violence, actions many observers would later blame on the fiscal and social crises that held New York City in a vise grip. Little would change during the monstrously decadent 1980s, when the twin epidemics of crack and AIDS infiltrated the collective American psyche.

Yet, throughout Harlem's physical decline, the Guild continued to nurture writers, and in 1987, five years after finding a permanent home at the Schomburg Center for Research in Black Culture, the Guild found a breakout star in member Terry McMillan, whose first novel, *Mama*, was published to critical praise. She would follow that first success with four more best-sellers, including 1992's *Waiting to Exhale*, which helped create a publishing boom for black modern fiction writers.

The reawakened interest of publishers in works by black authors in the mid-1990s ironically mirrored the economic and creative rebirth happening uptown in Harlem. In a different kind of migration, New Yorkers priced out of ritzier parts of the city set their sights on the abandoned, windowless, boarded-up brownstones that littered much of Harlem. Economic incentives from the city, state, and federal government, the arrival of corporate giants such as Starbucks and HMV, as well as the high-profile presence of former President Bill Clinton, who opened a legal office on West 125th Street in 2001, have all fueled Harlem's revitalization, prompting many observers to predict the coming of a "second Renaissance."

FROM DADDY WAS A NUMBER RUNNER (1970)

LOUISE MERIWETHER

Meriwether joined the Harlem Writers Guild in 1970, and was also a member of the Watts Writers Workshop. *Daddy Was a Number Runner,* about a twelve-year-old in 1930s Harlem, became her best-known novel. In his foreword for the book, James Baldwin called it "stunning" and "filled with a strong and authentic sense of Harlem and its people."

ONE

"I dreamed about fish last night, Francie," Mrs. Mackey said, sliding back the chain and opening the door to admit me. "What number does Madame Zora's dream book give for fish?"

"I dreamed about fish last night, too," I said, excited. Maybe that number was gonna play today. "I dreamed a big catfish jumped off the plate and bit me. Madame Zora gives five fourteen for fish."

I smiled happily at Mrs. Mackey, ignoring the fact that if I stood here exchanging dreams with her, I'd be late getting back to school and Mrs. Oliver would keep me in again.

"What more hunch could a body want," Mrs. Mackey grinned, "us both dreaming about fish. Last night I dreamed I was going under the Bridge to buy some porgies and it started to rain. Not raindrops, Francie, but fish. Porgies. So I just opened up my shopping bag and caught me a bagful. Ain't that some dream?"

She laughed, her cheeks puffing up like black plums, and I laughed with her. You had to laugh with Mrs. Mackey, she was that jolly and fat. She waddled to the dining-room table and I couldn't keep my eyes off her bouncing, big behind. When she passed by in the street, the boys would holler, "Must be jelly 'cause jam don't shake," and she would laugh with them. They were right. Her behind was a quivering, shivering delight and I hoped when I grew up I would have enough meat on my skinny butt to shimmy like that.

Mrs. Mackey sat at the dining-room table and began writing her number slip.

"Mrs. Mackey," I said timidly, "my father asks would you please have your numbers ready when I get here so I won't have to wait. I'm always late getting back to school."

"They's ready, lil darlin'. I just wanna add five fourteen to my slip. I'm gonna play it for a quarter straight and sixty cents combination. How is your daddy and your mama, too?"

"They're both fine."

She handed me her number slip and two dollar bills which I slipped into my middy blouse pocket.

"Them's my last two dollars, Francie, so you bring me back a hit tonight, you hear? I didn't mean to spend so much but I couldn't play our fishy dreams cheap, right?"

We both giggled and I left. I raced down the stairs, holding my breath. Lord, but this hallway was funky, all of those Harlem smells bumping together. Garbage rotting in the dumbwaiter mingled with the smell of frying fish. Some drunk had vomited wine in one corner and peed in another, and a foulness oozing up from the basement meant a dead rat was down there somewhere.

The air outside wasn't much better. It was a hot, stifling day, June 2, 1934. The curbs were lined with garbage cans overflowing into the gutters, and a droopy horse pulling a vegetable wagon down the avenue had just deposited a steaming pile of manure in the middle of the street.

The sudden heat had emptied the tenements. Kids too young for school played on the sidewalks while their mamas leaned out of their windows searching for a cool breeze or sat for a moment on the fire escapes.

Knots of men, doping out their numbers, sat on the stoops or stood wide-legged in front of the storefronts, their black ribs shining through shirts limp with sweat. They spent most of their time playing the single action—betting on each number as it came out—and they stayed in the street all day until the last figure was out. I was glad Daddy was a number runner and not just hanging around the corners like these men. People were always asking me if I knew what number was out, like I was somebody special, and I guess I was. Everybody liked an honest runner like Daddy who paid off promptly the same night of the hit. A number runner is something like Santa Claus and any day you hit the number is Christmas.

I turned the corner and raced down forbidden 118th Street because I was late and didn't have time to go around the block. Daddy didn't want me in this street because of the prostitutes, but I knew all about them anyway. Sukie had told me and she ought to know. Her sister, China Doll, was a whore on this very same street. Anyway, it was too early for them to be out hustling, so Daddy didn't have to worry that I might see something I shouldn't.

A half-dozen boys standing in front of the drugstore were acting the fool, as usual, pretending they were razor fighting, their knickers hanging loose below their knees to look like long pants. Three of them were Ebony Earls, for sure, I thought. I tried to squeak past them but they saw me.

"Hey, skinny mama," one of them yelled. "When you put a little pork chops on those spareribs I'm gonna make love to you."

The other boys folded up laughing and I scooted past, ignoring them. I always hated to pass a crowd of boys because they felt called upon to make some remark, usually nasty, especially now that I was almost twelve. So I was skinny and black and bad looking with my short hair and long neck and all that naked space in between. I looked just like a plucked chicken.

"Hey, there goes that yellow bastard," one of the boys yelled. They turned their attention away from me to a skinny light kid who took off like the Seventh Avenue Express when he saw them. With a wild whoop the gang lit out after him, running over everybody who didn't move out of their way.

"Damn tramps," a woman muttered, nursing her foot that had been trampled on.

I held my breath, hoping the light kid would escape. The howling boys rounded Lenox Avenue and their yells died down.

I ran down the street and turned the corner of Fifth Avenue, but ducked back when I saw Sukie playing hopscotch by herself in front of my house, not caring whether she was late for school or not. That Sukie. She was a year older than me, but much bigger. I waited until her back was turned to me, then with a burst of energy I ran toward my stoop. But she saw me and her moriney face turned pinker and she took out after me like a red witch. I was galloping around the first landing when I heard her below me in the vestibule.

"Ya gotta come downstairs sometime, ya bastard, and the first time I catch ya I'm gonna beat the shit out of ya."

That Sukie. We were best friends but she picked a fight whenever she felt evil, which was often, and if she said she was going to beat the shit out of me, that's just what she would do.

I kept on running until I reached the top floor and then I collapsed on the last step, leaning my head against the rusty iron railing. I heard someone on the stairs leading up to the roof and my heart began that crazy tap dancing it does when I get scared.

Somebody whispered: "Hey, little girl."

I tiptoed around the railing and peaked up into the face of that white man who had followed me to the movies last Monday. He had tried to feel my legs and I changed my seat. He found me and sat next to me again, giving me a dime. His hands fumbled under my skirt and when he got to the elastic in my bloomers, I moved again. It was the same man, all right, short and bald with a fringe of fuzzy hair around the back of his head. He was standing in the roof doorway.

"Come on up for a minute, little girl," he whispered.

I shook my head.

"I've got a dime for you."

"Throw it down."

"Come and get it. I won't hurt you. I just want you to touch this."

He fumbled with the front of his pants and took out his pee-pee. It certainly was ugly, purple and wet looking. Sukie said that everybody did it. Fucked. That's how babies were made, she said. I believed the whores did it but not my own mother and father. But Sukie insisted everybody did it, and she was usually right.

"Come on up, little girl. I won't hurt you."

"I don't wanna."

"I'll give you a dime."

"Throw it down."

"Come on up and get it."

"I'm gonna tell my Daddy."

He threw the dime down. I picked it up and the man disappeared through the roof door. I went back around the railing and leaned on our door and the lock sprang open. Daddy was always promising to fix that lock but he never did.

Our apartment was a railroad flat, each small room set flush in front of the other. The door opened into the dining room, so junky with heavy furniture that the room seemed tinier than it was. In the middle of the room a heavy, round mahogany table squatted on dragon-head legs. Against the wall was a long matching buffet with dragon heads on the sideboards. Scattered about were four straight-back chairs with the slats falling out, their tall backs also carved with ugly dragons. The furniture, scratched with scars, was a gift from the Jewish plumber downstairs, and was one year older than God.

"Mother," I yelled. "I'm home."

"Stop screaming, Francie," Mother said from the kitchen, "and put the numbers up."

I took the drawer out of the buffet, and reaching to the ledge on the side, pulled out an envelope filled with number slips. I put in Mrs. Mackey's numbers and the money, replaced the envelope on the ledge, and slid the drawer back on its runners. It stuck. I took it out again and shoved the envelope farther to the side. Now the drawer closed smoothly.

"Did you push that envelope way back so the drawer closes good?" Mother asked as I went into the kitchen.

"Yes, Mother."

I sat down at the chipped porcelain table, tilting crazily on uneven legs. Absentmindedly I knocked a scurrying roach off the table top to the floor and crunched it under my sneaker.

"If you don't stop racing up those stairs like that, one of these days you gonna drop dead."

"Yes, Mother."

I wanted to tell her that Sukie had promised to beat me up again, but Mother would only repeat that Sukie would stop bullying me when I stopped running away from her.

Mother was short and dumpy, her long breasts and wide hips all sort of running together. Her best feature was her skin, a smooth light brown, with a cluster of freckles over her nose. Her hair was short and thin, and she had rotting yellow teeth, what was left of them. In truth, she had more empty spaces in her mouth than she had teeth, but you would never know she was sensitive about it except for the fact that she seldom smiled. It was hard to know what Mother was sensitive about. Daddy shouted and cursed when he was mad, and danced around and hugged you when he was feeling good. But you just couldn't tell about Mother. She didn't curse you but she didn't kiss you either.

She placed a sandwich before me, potted meat stretched from here to yonder with mayonnaise, which I eyed with suspicion.

"I don't like potted meat."

"You don't like nothing. That's why you're so skinny. If you don't want it, don't eat it. There ain't nothing else."

She gave me a weak cup of tea.

"We got any sugar?"

"Borrow some from Mrs. Caldwell."

I got a chipped cup from the cupboard and going to the dining-room window, I knocked on our neighbor's windowpane. The Caldwells lived in the apartment building next door and our dining rooms faced each other. They were West Indians and Maude was my best friend, next to Sukie. We were the same age, but where my legs were long, Maude's were bowed just like an O. Maude's father had died last year, and Pee Wee, her oldest brother, had just gone off to jail again, which was his second home. Maude came to the window.

"Can I borrow a half cup of sugar?" I asked.

She took the cup and disappeared, returning in a few minutes with it almost full. "Y'all got any bread?" she asked. "I need one more piece to make a sandwich."

"Maude wants to borrow a piece of bread," I told Mother.

"Give her two slices," Mother said.

I gave Maude two pieces of whole wheat.

"Elizabeth's coming back home today with her kids and Robert," she said. "Their furniture got put out in the street."

Elizabeth was her oldest sister and Robert her husband. He used to be a tailor but wasn't working now.

"Y'all gonna be crowded," I said.

"Yep," she answered, her head disappearing from the window.

I returned to the kitchen and told Mother Elizabeth was coming home.

"Lord, where they all gonna sleep?" she asked.

Maude and her sister, Rebecca, sixteen, had one bedroom, their mother the other, and their brother, Vallie, slept in the front room.

I sat down at the table and began to sip my tea, looking at the greasy walls lumpy with layers of paint over cracked plaster. Vomit-green, that's what Daddy called its color. The ceiling was dotted with brown and yellow water stains. Daddy had patched up the big leaks but it didn't do much good and when it rained outside it rained inside, too. The last time the landlord had been there to collect the rent Daddy told him the roof needed fixing and that if the ceiling fell down and hurt one of his kids he was going to pitch the landlord headfirst down the stairs. The landlord left in a hurry but that didn't get our leaks fixed.

The outside door slammed and my brother Sterling came into the kitchen and slumped down at the table. He was fourteen, brown-skinned, and lanky, his long, tight face always bunched into a frown, and today was no exception.

"Where's James Junior?" Mother asked.

"I'm not his keeper," Sterling grumbled. "I didn't see him at recess."

James Junior, my oldest brother, was a year older than Sterling, and good looking like Daddy. He was nicer than Sterling, too, but slow in his studies, always getting left back, and Sterling had already passed him in school and was going to graduate this month.

The door slammed shut again and I could tell from the heavy foot-steps that it was Daddy. I jumped up and ran into the dining room hurling myself against him. He laughed and scooped me up in his arms, swinging me off the floor. Mother was always telling me that men were handsome, not beautiful, but she just didn't understand. Handsome meant one thing and beautiful something else and I knew for sure what Daddy was. Beautiful. In the first place he was a giant of a man, wide and thick and hard. He was dark brown, black really, with thick crinkly hair and a wide laughing beautiful mouth. I loved Daddy's mouth.

He sat down at the dining-room table and began pulling number slips from his pocket.

"Get the envelope for me, sugar."

I removed the drawer and handed him the envelope, smiling. "I dreamed a big catfish jumped off the plate and bit me, Daddy. The dream book gives five fourteen for fish. And Mrs. Mackey dreamed it was raining fish."

"Great God and Jim," Daddy cried, and we grinned at each other. "My chart gives a five to lead today. I'm gonna play a'dollar on five fourteen straight and sixty cents combination."

Daddy said that of all the family my dreams hit the most. If 514 came out today we'd be rich, which would be a good thing 'cause Mother was always grumbling that we were playing all of our commission back on the numbers.

From force of habit I huddled close to the radiator, which was cold now. The green and red checkerboard linoleum around it was worn so thin you couldn't even see its pattern and there was a jagged hole in the floor near the pipe almost big enough to get your foot through. Daddy was always nailing cardboard and linoleum over that hole but it kept wearing out.

"Henrietta," Daddy called, "where are the boys?"

Mother came to the kitchen door. "Sterling's here eating, but James Junior ain't come home yet."

Daddy's fist hit the table with a suddenness which made me jump. "If that boy's stayed out of school again it's gonna be me and his behind. Sterling," he shouted, "where's your brother?"

"I ain't seen him since this morning," Sterling answered from the kitchen.

Daddy turned on Mother. "If that boy gets into any trouble I'm gonna let his butt rot in jail, you hear? I'm warning you. I've done told him time and time again to stop hanging out with those Ebony Earls, but his head is damned hard. All of them's gonna end up in Sing Sing, you mark my words, and ain't no Coffin ever been to jail before. Do you know that?"

Mother nodded. She also knew, as I did, that Daddy would be the first one downtown to see about Junior if anything happened to him.

Junior had started hanging around with the Ebony Earls a few months ago, together with his buddies Sonny and Maude's brother Vallejo. Sterling didn't belong to the gang. He said gangs were stupid and boys who hung out together like that were morons.

Daddy started adding up the amounts of his number slips and counting the money. Mother sat down at the table beside him and said nervously that she heard Slim Jim had been arrested. He was a number runner like Daddy.

"Slim Jim is a fool," Daddy said. "His banker thinks he can operate outside the syndicate but nobody can buck Dutch Schultz. The cops will arrest anybody his boys finger, and they did just that. Fingered Slim Jim and his banker."

"Maybe you'd better stop collecting numbers now before . . ." Mother began nervously, but Daddy cut her off.

"For christsakes, Henrietta, let's not go through that again. How many times I gotta tell you it ain't much more dangerous collecting numbers than playing them. As long as the cops are paid off, which they are, they ain't gonna bother me. Schultz even pays off that stupid ass, Dodge, we've got for a district attorney, so stop worrying."

Mother played the numbers like everyone else in Harlem but she was scared about Daddy being a number runner. Daddy started working for Jocko on commission about six months ago when he lost his house-painting job, which hadn't been none too steady to begin with.

Jocko's name was really Jacques and he was a tall Creole from Haiti. He wore a blue beret cocked on the side of his head and had curly black hair and olive skin. Now, Jocko was handsome but he wasn't beautiful. He ran a candy store on Fifth Avenue and 117th Street as a front and everybody said he was real close to Big Boy Donatelli, his banker, who was real close to Dutch Schultz. Daddy said Jocko was as big a man in the syndicate as a colored man could get since the gangsters took over the numbers. Daddy said the gangsters controlled everything in Harlem—the numbers, the whores, and the pimps who brought them their white trade.

Mother grumbled: "I thought Mayor La Guardia say he was gonna clean up all this mess."

"If they really wanted to clean up this town," Daddy said, "they would stop picking on the poor niggers trying to hit a number for a dime so they won't starve to death. Where else a colored man gonna get six hundred dollars for one? What they need to do is snatch the gangsters banking the numbers, they're the ones raking in the big money. But the cops ain't about to cut off their gravy train. But you stop worrying now, Henrietta. Ain't nothing gonna happen to me, you hear?"

Mother nodded slowly. Then she looked at me. "Francie, get up from there and go on back to school before you be late again. Sterling," she yelled.

"Okay," he answered from the kitchen. "I'm comin'."

"Francie! Don't let me have to tell you again."

"Okay, Mother. I'm goin'. 'Bye, Daddy."

" 'Bye, sugar."

When I got downstairs I peaked outside but Sukie was nowhere in sight. I ran most of the way back to school but was good and late anyhow.

FROM THE COTILLION, OR ONE GOOD BULL IS HALF THE HERD
(1971)

JOHN OLIVER KILLENS

As cofounder of the Harlem Writers Guild in 1950, Killens knew the political importance of writing. He and other Guild cofounders guided and shaped the organization and their careers to embrace writing as craft, human rights, the empowerment of the oppressed, and the notion that true art is a reflection of struggle. His first novel, *Youngblood,* was published in 1954 and his second novel, *And Then We Heard the Thunder,* was published in 1963. His novel *The Cotillion, or One Good Bull Is Half the Herd,* takes place in Harlem and Brooklyn, New York, as it follows the beautiful Yoruba's plans to shake up high society. The book was nominated for a Pulitzer Prize.

Over the course of his career, Killens was a writer-in-residence at a variety of universities, including Fisk University, Howard University, and Bronx Community College. Killens created the world-renowned Black Writers Conference at Medgar Evers College in Brooklyn a year before he died in 1987.

1

YORUBA

Hey!

CALL HER YORUBA, RIGHT?

High priestess of the Nation!

You ready for that?

Negritude? Okay?

African queen!

Black and comely was this Harlem princess.

Yoruba, her father named her.

And Yoruba she would always be—praise Allah from whom all blessings flow. Would you believe—GreatGodAlmighty!?

She was Yoruba Evelyn Lovejoy, a working girl that summer, and a queen she was among all working girls. Hell yes! Say it plain—Yoruba! Dig it! And named she was, proudly, from her Georgia father's Black and wondrously angry and terribly frustrated nationalism.

Pure, beautiful, untampered-by-the-white-man Yoruba. Black and princessly Yoruba, as if she'd just got off the boat from Yoruba-land in the western region of the then Nigeria. Sometimes, when her father got into one of his rare and whiskeyed moods, he would trace his father's father's father back to Ogshogbo, then further eastward, to Benin City, then clear across the mighty Niger, at Asaba and Onitsha, south by southeast, by ferry, foot and mammywagon, all the way to Arachuku, that land of fable of the long juju.

Now—she—the girl—Yoruba—walked westward through the jungle to Eighth Avenue and went down into Manhattan's man-made earth and took the "A" Train. Her middle name was Evelyn, the first syllable pronounced, Britishly, like the woman made from Adam's ribs and like Christmas Eve and the night before the New Year. Spell it E-V-E-L-Y-N— pronounce it Eve-lyn, was her mother's contribution. Her strong, proud, West Indian mother from the small and windward island of Barbados.

The "A" Train almost leaped the tracks, as it thundered underneath the city, reeling and rocking and screeching, like it had blown its natural stack. Winging nonstop from Fifty-ninth all the way to the main stem at One Hundred and Twenty-fifth. Vacuum-packed with perspiring, dehydrated, Black and white humanity of all sizes and denominations. An air-swindled concoction of sound and sweat and soap and perfume and beaucoup talk, Afro-Americanese, West Indianese, Italianese, Jewishese, Puerto-Ricanese, all screwed up with New Yorkese. Africa—Europe— Caribbean. East to West, the twain was met. And it was a mess to listen to. And hot air, baby, by the ton, hot air was blown, stirred together by the whirligig electric fans overhead and shaken up by this St. Vitus-dancing, boogalooing, epileptic "A" Train. Funky Broadway all the time. Funky! Oooh! Yeah! Dig it! Creating one overwhelming impact which rendered Yoruba's senses numb, and the dear child almost senseless. She felt a total assault upon her mouth, nostrils, eyes, ears, throat. Her Black and brown and righteous body. It happened every week-day that memorable summer, after she finished high school and took a job downtown in the garment wilderness.

FIVE P.M. And people erupted out of the monstrous buildings like missiles catapulted from great guns, onto the streets, and flowed in floodtide through the jungle toward those insatiable subways, which, like great carnivorous beasts, starved, and from another age, swallowed men and women whole; then, belching and breaking wind and regurgitating, threw them up again onto the overflowing streets uptown. Every evening it was—

TAKE THE "A" TRAIN
Every day. Every day.
Hurry—Hurry—Hurry—
TAKE THE "A" TRAIN

She—the girl—Yoruba closed her eyes, as she held onto the subway strap, closed her large eyes, dark and wide ones, and she could hear the Duke of Ellington's immortal music, feel it pouring through her senses like cascades of clear branch water, oooweee! Hear it, feel it, in all its varied and varying movements, in a stormy crescendo now, surging ever onward, upward, swelling, gathering its forces as it went, sweeping all and everything before it, even as the train itself went clackety-clack, slapping the rails with its own peculiar Afro rhythm, amassing speed and sound and frenzy, as it moved toward its conclusion. Destination Harlem. It was the Soul Train. Dig it, mother—brother—sister—

It was no accident, the girl, Yoruba, thought, that a Black man had composed this great song, this tribute to New York's regal train. A train whose soul was as Black and beautiful as burnished ebony. It had rhythm. It had heart. It had Negritude. Right? And it was not the "B" or "G" Train, but the "A" Train.

With her left hand Yoruba clung to the subway strap with a kind of final desperation, as the train roared past the local stop at One Hundred and Third Street, wailing, moaning, groaning, making with the beat and the righteous sounds and taking care of business. At the same time the Black girl jabbed, accidentally-on-purpose, her right elbow into a cushiony overstuffed belly of a fortyish-year-old manchild, who stood behind her much too close to her for comfort (Yoruba's blessed comfort), and was trying his best to maneuver himself into an even cozier situation. She had a violent, well-trained right elbow for mashers. Sometimes she carried a hatpin for such overfriendly straphangers.

The famous train was moving now past the local stop at One Hundred and Sixteenth Street, and braking, shaking, screaming, rocking, screeching like a jet airliner coming in for landing. A case of pure and sweet hysteria. The sound, the smell of burning black-eyed peas and fresh coffee cooking, the shakes, the dance, the rock-the-roll, the sweat, the vacuum-packed homo sapiens were too much for Yoruba sometimes, and today, this day, she knew a giddiness in her head and a feeling like seasickness at rock-bottom in her stomach. She thought she might faint standing up, and she panicked for a moment. She would not faint though, she knew she could not faint, for there was no space for such bourgeois self-indulgences here on this jam-packed subway train.

She was Yoruba (sometimes her father called her Ruba, with affection). Eve and Ruby to her mother. Yo-roo-ba to some. She was a burnished-Black-brown slightly burnt toast of a girl; her skin was like it had been scrubbed with fine stones from the River Niger (her father used to say); scrubbed till her dear dark skin cried out in hurt and protest. She had her mother's thin nose; the tip was turned up ever so slightly like her mother's disposition. She had her father's wide thick, curving generous lips, sensitive and sensuous. Life—love—anguish. Her mouth told you so many things. Compassion, tears, laughter. Her mouth was soul music, brothers. Listen to the sounds come out. The bottom lip perhaps slightly smaller than the top. Her eyes were Black on Black. Oooh! so deeply black were they, and wide in the middle and narrow at the outer edges. And slanting like the Orient. The girl thought, here on this train there is no room to faint, as smilingly she remembered an old blues fragment she had heard the great Odetta do the one time Ruba had been down to the Village Gate. She thought:

AIN'T IT HARD TO STUMBLE
WHEN YOU GOT NO PLACE TO FALL?

As the train came reeling squealing screaming to a lurching stop, throwing bodies against bodies, in an orgy of crazy off-time dancing, and various and varied familiarities, Yoruba thought she knew how Jonah must have felt in the belly of Moby Dick's great-great-grand-poppa. She thought, Jonah never had it so good. Grandpop's stomach could not possibly have been as congested as the "A" Train. First and foremost, the great train was Billy Strayhorn and Duke Ellington. So it was Blood. Right? It was sound and frenzy, the thunder and the lightning. The train was folks. Right? The train was also happenings. Always and forever happening. Every day—every day. Hurry! Hurry! Hurry!

Halfway between One Hundred and Sixteenth and One Hundred and Twenty-fifth Street, the people fell away from each other, the waves of people parted like the Red Sea must have parted when old Moses waved his famous rod. This time, instead of Moses, here on this train was a tall, powerfully constructed Black woman, weighing in at about two hundred and twenty pounds and nearing forty years of sojourn on this planet. This time, instead of a rod, it was an umbrella that the lady brandished. And she waved it above her head and brought it down again and again upon the blond head of a sawed-off, undernourished, red-faced white man, as she drove him before her, and beat him out of the train onto the platform. She outweighed the pale-faced culprit by seventy pounds or more. A clear-cut case of overmatching, or undermatching, depending on your point of view or how you placed your bets this evening.

As the dangerous and dastardly molester (you ready?) pulled himself, with difficulty, slowly up from the platform, Miss Heavyweight of Nineteen-Sixty-Something shook her umbrella down at him, and told him, with enormous dignity: "I bet you'll think twice about it the next time you git it into your rotten mind to git fresh with a poor helpless Black lady like me, you goddamn no-good peckerwood trash. It's gittin so it ain't safe for a lady to be by herself in broad open daylight. I don't know what's gonna 'come of us poor defenseless womenfolks. I declare before the Lord I don't."

The four-eyed, bug-eyed, cross-eyed desperado looked like an accident on the lookout for a place to make the scene. He mumbled his apologies and dragged himself away down toward the other end of the platform, limping along pathetically, as if his life depended on it. Miss Poor Defenseless Womanhood brandished her umbrella after the hapless hoodlum. Then she turned and walked proudly, and with righteous indignation, up the stairway to the street.

Some of the Black folk (including Yoruba) cracked up with laughter, when a brother amongst them raised his arm and pumped his right fist up and down, and shouted softly: "Black Power, mother! Black Power! Keep the mammy-hunching faith!"

Up topside on the street it was summertime and the breathing was easier than down there in that underworld underneath the city. Are you ready for Yoruba? Yoruba Evelyn Lovejoy? She, the girl, the princess, felt good walking along her street (One Hundred and Twenty-fifth) in the middle September of her eighteenth year, and the dear fox knew she looked good walking; moreover she was a child who loved to walk. She always walked in a hurry, like she was late for an appointment. Long-legged Black girl, she was aware of the men along the main drag and the eyes they had for her and the shaking of their heads in honest admiration. She strolled like she was used to carrying bundles on her lovely head, as if somehow she conjured up from the depths of some dark mysterious whirlpool of sweet remembrance deep inside of her, she called up memories of the roads her great ancestors used to travel on their way to Lagos and Accra. Enugu, Bamako, Ouagadougou. Her distant cousins still strolled down those distant highways. Uhuru! Skin-givers—plank-spankers. Ujamaa!

She was Yoruba and she was pretty poetry set to rhythm. Proud she was and princessly. Her long legs were not skinny, neither were they fat. Slimly round—roundly slim. Her ample hips were built a trifle high up from the sidewalk. That was the only thing. Some of her friends in high school used to call the girl "High Pockets." One old fresh big-head boy always called the child "Long Goodie."

But behind all that and notwithstanding, she was Yoruba of the long strides and the swaying hips and the black heavy hair down to her shoulders, of the dark staring eyes, now laughing, now brimming-full with sorrow. She walked along the street of dreams. Past the Baby Grand Club, where Nipsey Russell used to call the question nightly, before he got "discovered." Walked past Frank's Restaurant, and across Eighth Avenue.

One Hundred and Twenty-fifth Street was also the street of sounds. Magnificent sounds. Jukeboxes all along the main stem blasting out the classics. Serious music by serious musicians. Max Roach, Ray Charles, Lou Rawls, Etta Jones, Archie Shepp, John Coltrane, horn-blowing horn-blowers. Abbey Lincoln wailing freedom. Nina's Mississippi Goddamn! And always there was the aristocracy. The Duke of Ellington, the Count of Basie and the Earl of Hines, Lester Young, the late lamented President. Yoruba loved the street of sounds. This child dug the aristocracy. And she was an aristocrat. Dig it! She was clean! Black *and* comely! Understand?

The marquee at the Apollo told her James Brown was holding

court. And Pigmeat Markham. George Wiltshire—yeah! All right! Well! Folks were lined up almost half the block. New York's riot squad stood at the everloving ready. Three young jiving signifying cats, standing outside the theater away from the line, eyeballed her as she flowed along the main stem. Amongst all these strolling people, she stood out like Lew Alcindor.

As she passed, she heard one of them say, in a kind of singsong, "Hi do, Miss Foxy Youngblood, please m'am!"

Another said, "Walk pretty for the people!"

The third one said, "Lord, make me truly thankful for what I'm about to perceive!"

Yoruba took it all in stride (and this father's child could truly stride). Her head held aloft, she always walked three inches taller than her actual height. (Did you ever dig Miriam, on stage, Makeba?) Yoruba's face did not give away the fact that she had heard the brothers sounding on her, signifying, but all the same she felt a nervous giggle in the bottom of her stomach.

"Walk that walk, Miss Sweet Chocolate Fox!"

"Miss Fine Brown-Black Frame!"

"Come on home, Miss Youngblood!"

Across the street and down the block was the Black and Beautiful Burlesque (the B.B.B. as it was called with fond affection), a famous girlie house, newly founded, where Afro-naturalized Black beauties did a dignified striptease, by the numbers, every day and thrice on Sunday. Long lines of voyeurs clear around the block. And there were pickets picketing pickets picketing pickets, who were picketing. After a while you had to be some kind of a genius to figure who was picketing whom and how come and what for. There was a Black Nationalist group picketing the theater against the whole idea of Black nudity. *"A pure disgrace!"* There was another group of Black picketeers against the admission of white voyeurs.

"Keep the Hunkie's eyes off our Beautiful Black women!"

There was a group of integrated picketeers who came out forthright for integrated burlesque queens. White queens had filed complaints against B.B.B. with the Human Rights Commission. B.B.B. was where the action was, and there were fist fights every other night.

Across Seventh Avenue almost a hundred folks were gathered. In the midst of them a Black man stood on a ladder beside a ragged Star-Spangled Banner, which flapped lifelessly and indifferently in a soft September breeze. A reddish-brown smog hung over the city, ominous and brooding, as if it might fling fire and brimstone down upon the Black and true believers any minute. The man on the ladder was waving his arms back and forth and up and down, as if he were directing traffic. He was working up a perspiration. But Yoruba could not make out what he was saying until she crossed over the beautiful wide parkway of an avenue.

Now she stood on the outskirts of the group of Black folk and half listened to Billy "Bad Mouth" Williams. Self-styled Black nationalist leader. Self-appointed. Self-anointed. Mayor of Black nationalist Harlem. God's and/or Allah's most precious gift to the lucky Harlem masses. Don't take anybody else's word for it. Check it out with Bad Mouth himself. He'd tell you he was the last of the great Black Nationalists. Uncrowned prime minister of the Black government in exile. Hey! There was Garvey, Malcolm, Bad Mouth Williams. After that—well, Armageddon.

Yoruba overheard one man in the crowd running down the action to another. "Bad Mouth's here every damn day the Good Lord sends, running his game, just as often as goose go barefooted. He's the biggest bullshitter on the Avenue."

He was a man of medium height, was Bad Mouth, powerfully gotten together, especially through his massive shoulders. Coal-black was his skin, his eyes aflame like burning coals. And he could talk that talk. He could really blow. He never drew large crowds like Malcolm used to draw. And Yoruba remembered Malcolm. Oh my, yes, yes, yes! Yes! Yes! Yes! Praise Allah—she remembered Malcolm. A Salaam Alaikum! Tall and fire-haired, manhood oozing from every pore of him, fiery in his oratory, lightning fast of wit, uncompromising in his integrity, tough and tender with his people. She remembered Malcolm. She had been helplessly and hopelessly in love with him, like a thousand other girls her age who were of the Black persuasion, and she had cried continuously and for four weeks running after that February Sunday of the fatal infamy.

But like the man said, Bad Mouth was consistent. Every day. Every day. And he was a natural-born champeen at haranguing and cajoling. Yoruba had heard most of his spiel it seemed, a hundred times and more, and in many variations. Bad Mouth could phrase like Louis Armstrong, could orchestrate like Cootie Williams.

"I was born in North Carolina." Bad Mouth paused and let this great revelation sink in. "I lived in a house that I could lay on my pallet and look up through the roof and dig the stars, and look down through the floor and count the chickens. It was built-in ventilation."

Behind this statement came a chuckling kind of laughter from his audience. Yoruba laughed, notwithstanding she had heard it all before. She laughed almost unknowingly.

"We got so damn much fresh air we could hardly catch our breath. Almost choked ourselves to death."

They laughed more loudly now. Warming up. And gathering.

"Go on, Bad Mouth."

"Tell it like it i-s is!"

"You oughta be shame of yourself telling them all them bogus lies!"

A four-eyed bearded young man shouted, "Check that shit out, Bad Mouth! Run it down, baby brother! Run it down!"

"Watch your language, young man," another man said to the bearded young man.

"You ain't got nothing to laugh about," Bad Mouth told his audience. "Down home we did at least breathe fresh air, but up here you don't do nothing but fill your lungs with poison. Damn white man so greedy behind them Yankee dollars, he has polluted the air you breathe and poisoned the water you need to drink. Charlie so greedy he'll wipe out his own race including his own self just to make some more of that bread. And you niggers running around here following them hustling preachers teaching you to love the white man. You gon pray for him that spitefully use you."

"Put bad mouth on 'em, Bad Mouth!" one tall, skinny Black cat shouted softly. He sported the baddest Afro-natural hairdo Yoruba had ever seen, standing underneath that wild black bush so thick and so way out the sun could never touch his face, and he was slowly going pale from the lack of sunlight. He wore a truly bad dashiki, long earrings flapping from his hound-dog ears like jingle bells. Everybody on the street knew him to be a plainclothesman in the hire of New York's Finest, even though his clothes were hardly plain. Sometimes he wore a long flowing yellow boubou. He made all the meetings, the greatest shouter in the crowd. Every day. Every day. Old Plainclothes always made the scene.

Bad Mouth continued. "These jackleg preachers telling you when Charlie kick your ass on one cheek, you supposed to turn the other one. You supposed to bend over and to tell him, 'Be my guest.' That's how come some of you walk bent over all the time. You done turned them cheeks so many times you can't hardly sit 'em down to rest."

"Blow, Bad Mouth! Blow, baby! You bad-mouth motherfucker!"

"Rap, brother!"

"Sit down—sit down—you can't sit down—"

Bad Mouth paused and asked his people, "Am I right or wrong?"

"Right!" Plainclothes was jumping up and down. "Rap your Black thing, baby!" He was working himself into a lather. Sometimes he wore a red, black and green African robe, one shoulder bare, the hem of the garment sweeping the street, as if he were from the sanitation department instead of the police.

"Check it, Bad Mouth. Check that shit out!"

"Blow, baby, blow!"

"Do your thing, baby!" The dashiki-ed plainclothesman was screaming now at the top of his voice. Some of the brothers called him Maxwell Smart. Some brothers called him less affectionate names.

"Run it down—run it down!"

"Them hustling preachers telling you to love the man that kicks your Black ass, and you ain't got no better sense than to follow what the hustlers tell you. They the biggest shuckers God ever put breath in."

"Blow, baby, blow!"

"Takes a shucker to know a shucker!" From a lady in the crowd.

"One more time!"

Bad Mouth continued. "I know hustling when I see it. I used to be a hustler my own damn self."

"Used to be?" From a brother in the audience.

"My daddy was a stone hustler. Taught me all the fine points of shucking and hustling. That's right. My daddy was one of them big fat greasy Black and burly chicken-eating Baptist preachers down in Peckerwood, North Carolina."

"Peckerwood, North Carolina? Come on, Bad Mouth!"

One brother in the crowd said, "You a lying ass and a tinkling symbol!"

"That's right," Bad Mouth answered. "That's where my daddy used to preach. That's where I come from. Peckerwood, North Carolina. My daddy was a stone jackleg. Picked cotton all week long and talked shit all day Sunday."

The crowd was laughing now, without restraint. A toothless old lady shouted merrily, "Mind your langwitch, son, else I'll pull you down off that ladder and wash your mouth out with lye soap. Don't think you so big, I won't take you down a peg or two."

"Uh-uh!" From a chuckling brother in the crowd.

"Go on, Mother," Bad Mouth said, good-naturedly. "Go sell your papers on another corner."

"I ain't your mother," the old lady fired right back at Bad Mouth. Both of them were speaking louder now, almost shouting, competing with the fire trucks that came clanging down the avenue past the meeting, piercing eardrums with their sirens blasting. Every evening about this time the fire trucks paid their respects to Bad Mouth's meetings, or to any other meeting on this corner of all corners. The speaker's ladder stood in front of Michaux's famous Black and nationalistic bookstore.

Diagonally across the avenue stood the famous Hotel Theresa, where the great Joe Louis used to hang out in the late thirties and early forties, and where history was made in the early sixties, when Fidel took up lodging there and people stood outside in the chilly rain and shouted:

"Viva Castro!"

"Viva Fidel!"

"I ain't your mother," the old lady repeated, shouting even louder this time. "If your mother hadda brung you up right, I wouldn't have to be putting your backside down this late in life."

"OOOoo-weeeee! You ready for that?"

"Grandma putting old Bad Mouth in the natural dozens—damn!"

"Blow, grandma! Blow, baby!"

"Old Bad Mouth do not play the two-time-sixes!"

"Let him pat his big bad feet then. Miles Davis plays it!"

Everybody was laughing now, including Yoruba. And more folks were gathering now, attracted by the laughter. It was as if Bad Mouth and the old lady had learned their lines and rehearsed them well ahead of time.

Well?

Would you believe?

"Go along, old lady," Bad Mouth said tolerantly. "I want to talk to my people about some serious matters. If you can't listen quietly, get yourself your own corner and draw your own crowd. I pay weekly rent for this here corner."

Yoruba walked away from the gathering crowd, away from the scattered laughter. Behind her she could hear Bad Mouth's froggy voice croaking to his people.

"Black brothers and sisters, it's time we chased the Bible-toting money-changers out of the holy places of our worship. Am I right or wrong? It's time we got some healthy-sized buggy whips and kicked some big fat rusty-dusties and took some names. We got to get our own houses clean before we can worry about taking care of Whitey's. Am I right or wrong?"

Yoruba thought, It's preachers today. Yesterday it was "Negro" leaders. The day before that it was the "white Communist liberals." Tomorrow he would be doing a putdown on something else. The labor movement. The NAACP. The President. It was always something, or somebody. Bad Mouth was the World's champeen putdowner. He'd tell anybody: "Not a living ass is sacred, when Bad Mouth begins to blow. The best you can do is batten down the hatches, send out hurricane warnings and pray to Allah for a rainbow."

Behind her, she could hear him carrying on. "Take this city! Take it! Take it! It belongs to you. And it's just right here for the taking. Between the spooks and the spicks, we can take this valuable piece of real estate known as New York City. All we got to do is get together. But you wanna chase the great and glorious white folks all over the mother-loving suburbs!" He paused. "And you don't want no power. You just want to intergrate."

She walked a few blocks up the avenue, as the applause and laughter ebbed behind her, walked past a half dozen bars and liquor stores, and people, and just about as many funeral parlors and store-front churches, and people, and she turned right off Seventh Avenue into the block where she had spent most of the eighteen years of her life. She, the girl, Yoruba, was, at long last, home.

This evening, somehow, when she reached the block, she felt an overwhelming relief coursing through all of her senses, as if she had been on a long long journey into a foreign land, a hostile country, and now she had come home at last. It was not the first time she had had this feeling after she had spent all day downtown in Manhattan in that jungle that some people called the garment center. Today, as she walked toward the other end of the block, warm memories poured over her with the coolness of a sweet summer shower. And she was a little girl again. Romping rope (double dutch) and hopscotch (potsy) and tag and ten-ten-double-ten and follow-the-leader. Tag was a game that went on and on and on and never ended. Playing with Enrique and Ernie and Claudie and Lloyd and Susan and Cheryl and all the rest of that ragtag group (her mother's term for the gone friends of her yesteryears). All of the times that came back to her now from that faraway age were good times to her. It seemed a million years ago. But Yoruba remembered.

Remembered skinny, big-eyed, snotty-nosed Ernie when they were both about six and seven and eight years old (he was always two or three years older), and they were puppy-lovers, and he, her ragged Black prince, would come and sit on her stoop with her for hours and pick his nose and sometimes suck his thumb, and stare at her in a kind of wordless admiration. His father was a seaman and was away from home much of the time. His mother did days work away up somewhere in the Bronx. Remembered the day she invited Ernie to dinner, much to her mother's great annoyance. She had told Yoruba a million times: "I ain't want you playing with them common low-class Southern niggers on this block, and I particularly ain't want them in my house."

But at the dinner table she pumped the boy with questions like she was from the FBI or something.

"How many rooms in your apartment, Ernest?"

"Two rooms and a bath, Miss Daphne."

"Is that exclusive of a kitchen?"

"Exwho-sive?"

Yoruba's father said, "If you're so interested, why don't you pay Mrs. Billings a visit sometimes? You are the nosiest woman God ever made."

Mrs. Lovejoy ignored her husband, as she had a way of doing—sometimes. "You mean your mother has one room, one kitchen and a bath, ain't you, Ernest?"

"Yessum, that's what I meant to say. And the toilet is down on the next floor. We use it with the Williamses. Sometimes we have to stand in line. Sometimes we have to use the pot."

"Where do you sleep, Ernest?"

He picked his nose and stared at his finger. "With my mother most of the time, excepting when my uncle spends the night, he sleep with Mama, and I sleep on the cot in the kitchen. Course when my daddy is home, he sleep with Mama—"

Ernie was usually a quiet boy, but when he got turned on, it was hard to turn him off again.

During those days, Yoruba's folks were more "well-off" than Ernie's. They afforded all of two rooms and a kitchen. All this and a private bath. The girl slept in the living room on a great Bistro convertible. It was after midnight when she was awakened by her parents' voices from the bedroom. She lay there between sleep and wake trying to get herself together.

Her mother with her clipped British-Barbadian accent. She talked twice as fast as her father.

"One of these days you'll listen to me, damn your Black soul. I tell you a million times these damn low-class darkies on this block is no damn good! Nothing but a bunch of wort'less vagabunds. I ain't blame the white man for not wanting to live around them."

"Shut up, woman," Matt Lovejoy harshly whispered. "You wanna wake up Ruba?"

"That's why I try to teach my daughter to stay away from these wort'less pickaninnies on the block. But the more I try to culturize her, the more you pull the other way. You're enough the vex the devil himself."

She—the girl—Yoruba—sitting up in bed and staring through the darkness toward the bedroom. She had been dreaming, and she had trouble now figuring out whether this was part of the dream or not, or was the dream the real thing and was this a nightmare she had stumbled into? Lie back on your bed and close your eyes and try to catch up with your dream again. Shut out the sound of battle from the other room. Put your fingers in your ears. Still you hear the battle raging.

"Quiet, woman, goddamnit! Keep your mouth shut and people'll just think you a fool. Keep opening it and there ain't gon be no doubt about it."

Yoruba pulled the sheet up over her head and tried in vain to shut out the sound of her mother's weeping. "You ain't appreciate me!" Crying—sobbing—choking. "You ain't love me!"

Her father's rough and tender voice. "Come on now, Daphne—

come on now. You know better than that. Come on now, lil ole crybaby."
In the eyes of Yoruba's imagination, she could see her mother, still shaking with sobs, cuddling up to her father now. "You ain't appreciate nothing I try to do." She had seen it happen before—the times they'd fought
in front of her. "Crybaby—crybaby—crybaby." Her mother was in her
father's arms now, and Yoruba was wide awake, and it would be hours
before she fell asleep again. She would never catch up with her dream.
She could not even remember what her dream had been about.

Ernie's mother had died a few years back, and Yoruba had no idea
where Ernie was now or whether he was living or dead. Maybe he was
at sea like his father used to be most of the time. It seemed centuries ago
when they romped innocent and heedless up and down these streets,
this turf, this block. And ripped their dresses and tore their pants. And
laughed just for the sheer joy that came from laughter. It didn't have to
be funny, whatever it was they laughed about. Her mother wanted her
to be a lady and never run and sweat and play or swear or rassle with the
hoi polloi. "Never get your face dirty. Never ever soil your dresses." But
her mother fought a losing battle.

She remembered how she would be playing in the streets with her
friends and she would look down the street and see her father turn the
corner coming home from work, and she would take off down the block
like jet propulsion and race toward him and leap into his arms. It was the
happiest moment in the day for both of them. Her father would put her
on his shoulders with her legs around his neck and ride her all the way
up the block and into the house.

Her mother would scold the two of them. "Take that child from
around your neck. How can I ever teach her to be a lady? Both of you're
just as common as all the other no-good darkies in this ratty neighborhood."

And it was indeed a ratty neighborhood. The rat inhabitants made
their presence felt all over. Always they were in evidence. Walked along
the streets, worshiped in the churches, dug the movies in the theaters,
especially the cowboy pictures. Put up light housekeeping in the tenements. But refused to chip in on the rent. The rat population was ever
on the increase. Wherever people of the neighborhood were, rats were
always very close by. They had a fond affection for the folks of Harlem.
Notwithstanding, it was a case of unrequited love. Loveless love. Yoruba
would always remember her father's desperate lifelong battle with the

rodent citizenry. Big rats, little rats, in-between. "There gon be more of them than Black folks one of these days. They gon take over Harlem before we do." He would put down big steel traps all over the apartment and bait the traps with bread or cheese. But these rats were city-slick and hip to everything and everybody. Next morning, the food would be gone, the traps sprung, but not a single rat in any of the deadly traps. Her father tried to figure it out, and after months of great puzzling frustration, he concluded: "These damn rats so hip they put broom straws in their mouths to spring the traps and get the cheese."

Yoruba remembered sleepless nights, with the sound of rats playing in the kitchen, in the oven, and rattling the pots and pans. Some nights she would awaken and hear them scratching and romping around inside the walls. One night about three o'clock in the morning, a trap went off (bang!) and they all jumped out of bed and her father switched on the lights, and before they could get to the place of execution, bread, rat and trap had already split the scene.

A couple of rats got so bold and familiar, the Lovejoys knew them by sight. They would walk out in broad open daylight. And stake their claims. Her father named them Pretty Boy Floyd and John Dillinger. He said they had more sense than their namesakes, seeing as how they never got caught.

One night when Yoruba was about five years old, a great big rat got real affectionate and jumped into her bed and bit her on the jaw. Left a scar on her face that was still with her. Her father said it was her tribal mark. People thought it was a birthmark. Said it was her beauty spot. Her father battled the rat for more than half an hour all over the kitchen. Quietly swearing and swinging the broom, he must have struck the rat more than fifty times, blood splattering all over the place, till the rat ran out of steam and let himself get cornered, and Yoruba's father swung away at him till the blood flew all over the kitchen floor and all of the poor rat's insides had come outside.

All in all they were good days though, rats and all, the way the girl remembered them. And some days in this new time, she wished desperately she could turn back the clock and be her father's baby again. Dirty-faced, dress-torn, snotty-nosed tomboy. But she could not turn back the clock. She never really wanted to. And she was Yoruba, gentle Yoruba, and she had grown to be a gentlewoman, despite her mother's dedication and determination that this dear child should achieve ladyship. "Lady Eve-lyn."

In front of her house now, three-storied-and-basement brownstone. They lived on the parlor floor. She hoped her father had come home from work by now. Particularly this night, she hoped Matt Lovejoy was already home. She did not feel like facing her mother alone this evening in the very very middle of her eighteenth September.

She turned and stared back down the street past the children skipping rope, playing potsy, a few of them calling playful pleasant mother-fuckers, past the winos on a stoop, and the junkies, past the forever double-parked cars, stared longingly toward the corner at the other end of the block trying to look Matt Lovejoy around the corner coming home from work. She felt that if her father did materialize in the deep glow of the Harlem sunset she would break into a run like in the old days when she was six and seven and eight and believed in a jolly, old, fat white man by the name of Santa Claus, and thought the whole world was right there on her block in Harlem, and God was great and God was good and everything was for the best, because He worked mysteriously, the Grand Magician of them all. Cars honking, racing motors, fumes belching, children screaming, cursing, squealing, laughing. She stared past the busy intersection clear across Seventh Avenue all the way west to the river where the sun was a blazing disk of fire and washing the streets with a million colors and descending slowly down between the buildings at the very end of the street, down down it was sinking slowly sinking to set afire the Hudson River. Her eyes filled up and almost over-flowed at the beauty of the Harlem sunset. The tenements bathed in soft sweet tender shadows now. She took one long last look down toward the other end of her block. Come around the corner, Daddy! Come around the corner! And I will run again to meet you. She turned toward the house. Maybe he was already home. Silently she prayed he was already in the house.

She was in no mood this day to hear her mother carry on and on about the grandest of all the Grand Cotillions. "You are indeed a lucky one, Eve-lyn. And of all the scrumptious places, it will be held down-town at the Waldorf, where few white folks get a chance to go and de-cidedly no niggers at all. You'll be one of those selected too. The grand magnificent Cotillion. It's everything I've worked to give you, dearie.

The opportunity of a lifetime. My own dear baby is going to be a debutante!"

The girl walked wearily up the steps. Suddenly she was of the aged ones. And heavy-limbed. As if great iron weights hung from her arms, her legs. Her body tired; her soul weary; her mind exhausted.

Be home, Daddy!

Be home, Daddy!

Be home, Daddy!

Please!

Be home.

CRYING FOR HER MAN (1971)

ANN ALLEN SHOCKLEY

Trained as a librarian and eventually appointed head of Fisk University's Special Collections, Ms. Shockley wrote this story for a 1971 issue of *Liberator* magazine. It shows the strong, clear, and—unfortunately—comparatively rare voice of a woman in the Blacks Arts Movement.

Br-r-ring!

The alarm clock shrilled like a screaming cat, tearing into her uneasy sleep. She struggled awake, reaching out numbly to shut off the sound. Gray light filtered through the closed blinds, splaying the room with early shadows.

Now the man beside her groaned, turning on the pillow to half open dark eyes to her. "Why you have to set that damn thing every night?" he grumbled sleepily. "Can't you wake without it?"

Fully awake now, she sat up quickly, slinging back the covers. "Sorry to disturb you, dear," she said in mock sweetness, getting out of the bed. "But I set that alarm to get up in time to go to work. *Work*. You ever heard of *that?* To pay *bills*. You ever heard of *them?*"

"Aw, hell. Nag, nag, nag. First thing in the morning, last thing at night. Why you wanna nag all the time?"

"Because I think it's time you got off your ass in the morning and looked for a job."

Suddenly he sprang up, standing glowering across the room at her. "All right! See, I'm up. Up! Off my ass! You satisfied now?" He reached shakily for a crumpled pack of cigarettes on the nightstand.

She glared back at him for a moment, standing there and dragging heavily on the cigarette in his T-shirt and shorts. He was tall, brown, and strong-muscled with a head shaped with soft black curls. His sex protruded obscenely at her through his underwear, and she looked away, wondering why he didn't go to the bathroom.

"I been lookin' for a job. You know that, Bonnie," he said, the words softer now. "But what chance I got being Black? 'Sorry, we'll call *you.*' Shit! I'm sick of holding my hat in my hand for a bunch of nigger-hating white bastards."

"You could go back to that cab driver's job with the *colored* company," she struck back, jaws tightening.

"In *what?* I told you I need a *new* cab. But no-o-o. You won't sign the note."

"An Impala to drive a cab? Flash, don't be ridiculous."

"OK, OK, so you don't see it," he retorted sullenly, watching her go to the bureau mirror. "It really don't make no difference anyhow. I got another deal on. Me and Tex."

The words were there, but she did not listen, having heard them all before. Instead, she looked carefully at herself in the mirror. There were new dark lines encircling her eyes. But the ginger-colored skin remained clear and the soft pert mouth had not yet hardened with telling creases. She still looked young and attractive. She reached for the shower cap, pulling it tightly over the mound of curlers.

"This is a sure thing," he went on, voice louder, as if her unspoken thoughts had challenged him.

Sure thing, she reflected to herself. *That means another gamble ending on a sour note with Tex. Why doesn't he try to find a job with a steady income? Anything to help pay for this too-big apartment lined with expensive furniture still smelling new.*

"If you wanna git someplace big in the white man's world, you got to be in the *know.* You got to know how to git in and 'round Mista Charlie. How to git some of that *all* he's got. And I can tell you, he sure ain't going to let me git it through no job."

She wheeled around, facing him stormily. "Why don't you stop? You make me sick always talking about you can't find this or do that because of the white man. I'm beginning to think that's a good old excuse for plain laziness."

He snorted. "Oh yeah, I forgot. *You* got an ed-u-ca-shon. You can walk out of here every day and be Miss Ann. Go to *teach.* My folks didn't have the money to put *me* through no college. Nor any high school either. I had to git the hell out on the damn dirt-filled people-stinking streets and *hustle.* Morning, noon, and night."

She sighed, for here it was again. "I told you, Flash, my folks didn't have all that much. They were just hard working people."

"Hah!" he sneered, rummaging noisily through his chest of drawers searching for clean underwear.

She felt the ache anew, climbing painfully up her neck to twist sharply around in her head. Slowly she began to massage the back of her neck, thinking of him and the first time she came to this town to teach. She had been fresh out of college, and there was Flash, who drove a cab and was the handsomest man she had ever seen—white or Black. He had all the women crazy about him, but somehow, she had won out over the other myriad paint-colored shadows that always seemed to surround him. Only, no sooner had they married when two months later, he quit his job. The cab wasn't any good, he said. He didn't make enough money. He wanted something bigger.

He came up behind her, scattering her thoughts. His arms went around her waist, drawing her back into him. "Why you worry 'bout bills so much all the time, baby? Let the Man worry 'bout them."

"You realize those weekend parties you like to throw cost money? And—" she stopped, deciding not to add the expensive suits and shirts he liked too. Always the dresser. Thomas "Flash" Jackson. Sharp, neat, cool. Even in the cab.

"You have fun those times too!" he said accusingly. Then slowly he began to push suggestively against her breasts, caressing them lightly. "Aw, honey, I just want you to have fun. Live it up!"

"I would if I didn't have to *pay* for it."

"But, baby, it ain't going to be this way *all* the time."

Ain't, ain't, ain't. The simple lesson in grammar for which she had to correct her students. Sometimes she felt like screaming at him: *Isn't, please say isn't!* She tried to move away, but his arms tightened around her.

"Let me git that Impala, baby," he whispered, muzzling her ear with his nose. "Man can't make no good deals unless he looks like he already got money. Hum-m-m, you'd sure look good sitting in one."

His hands slid over her stomach and down, stayed there, and began a slow movement. "My sweet baby. Let's git a lil bit."

As his warm lips made a path down her neck, the familiar surge of weakness flooded her, warm, deadening, separating her from time and space and eternity itself.

"You know I love you, baby. Just give me time. Come on. Be nice to Daddy. Daddy'll make you feel real good. You got time . . ."

When she arrived at school, she felt drained and spent. All morning the students unnerved her, and in between the impromptu busy work she assigned them, she managed to slip out to the lounge.

Evelyn, the music teacher, was there doing her nails on her free period. "Well," she smiled, "behold the bride. Or do they still call you that after six months?"

Bonnie sank wearily on the couch, wishing she could look as relaxed and urbanely sophisticated as the lanky mustard-colored woman opposite her. Evelyn invariably made her feel younger than she was.

"You aren't in the family way *yet,* are you?" the woman continued, raising neat eyebrows. "Aren't you aware of the new scientific aid for women—the pill?"

"Oh, Evelyn, stop being sarcastic."

"Not sarcastic—helpful. Didn't you know? I'm the original brown Ann Landers. You do look like something the cat brought in."

Bonnie reached for a cigarette someone had left in a pack on the table. She leaned back, blowing streams of curling smoke in the air. She wished the day was over, thinking of the afternoon classes—recitations and papers to grade.

"How's married life?" Evelyn asked, buffing her nails to a high polished sheen. "From this end, it looks tiring."

"Why don't you try it and find out?" she replied crossly, then regretted it. She liked Evelyn better than the others with whom she worked. Only Evelyn had an uncanny way of fully comprehending people. Like advising her about Flash before she married him. "He's too good-looking, has too many women after him, and not in your league," she had warned half seriously, half in jest.

Evelyn stopped her motions for a moment to look steadily at her. "My dear child, it just dawned on me what you asked. You want *me* to give up my Black independence to be tied down to a man? Honey, hardly any Black man makes enough money to take care of himself, not including wife and children—particularly in the way I want to be supported. It takes *two* to tango with the work for Black folks to do that. So, why should I get married and still have to get out of my warm bed mornings and have a frustrated man run me crazy along with it? I've seen too many of our women go through *that* bit."

"Evelyn—" she hesitated, embarrassed, thinking of Flash and herself. "It's—it's better than being alone."

"Alone? Honey, I'd rather have peace with loneliness than war with company."

"Oh, stop being so hard."

"Hard? Bonnie, face it. The Black man gets stepped on by the white man, and he in turn gets mad and takes it out on his Black woman. Most of those little Black faces staring out at me in class are hits and runs of Black men. They stay long enough to make the women happy, drop babies for the welfare rolls and leave." Evelyn yawned, stretching her arms. "Well, in a way, you can't blame the men. The women let them do it, and that's *one* sure way the men can prove they haven't been completely castrated by the white race."

Bonnie put out the cigarette as a knock sounded at the door. A small ribboned head peered in. "Miz Jackson, you wanted on the phone in the principal's office."

"Thank you." She got up, reaching for her handbag.

"Yes, you're still on your honeymoon. Must be the Mister calling to say sweet nothings," Evelyn chuckled.

When she got to the office, she found out it was the Ajax Furniture Company wanting payment on a past due note. Softly she tried to assure the man that the money would be sent on the next day without the principal's sharp ears hearing. He had warned them against collectors calling at the school. When she left, he did not look up, but she knew he had guessed.

That evening, upon arriving home, she could hear the loud music even before she reached the second floor landing. Unlocking the door, she saw Flash sitting in the living room, tie loosened and leg flung over a chair arm. A half-filled bottle of scotch was on the coffee table.

"Hi, baby. Here's Tex." He motioned toward a paunchy, dark balding man seated on the sofa puffing heavily on a cigar.

"Hello there, Miz Jackson," Tex greeted in a hoarse rasping voice. "Good to see you again." When she did not answer, he asked smirkingly: "Have a hard day? Aw-w-w, guess I shouldn't ask a pro-fessi-nal lady that." He grinned at Flash, exposing two gold front teeth.

Silently she went to the hi-fi and turned down the volume, then hung up her coat in the closet. For a long moment, she looked at the expensive bottle of scotch. "Who's treating this time?"

Flash cleared his throat and smiled. "We are, baby. This man's got a tip to end all tips. We'll be up there in no time. I'll have my baby dressed in a mink coat come Sunday. She'll sure look good in a mink coat, won't she, Tex?"

"Sure will. I like my high brown women in fur coats."

Deliberately she turned away and went to the kitchen, noticing the bed hadn't been made. The sink was filled with dirty glasses and a smudge of lipstick grazed one.

"Want a drink, baby?" She heard Flash call to her.

His words were slightly thick, and she knew he had been drinking a long time. "No—" she replied listlessly, opening the refrigerator. The chops hadn't been taken out of the freezer even though she had reminded him to before leaving. She ran a pan of warm water and set the meat in it to thaw.

"Baby—" he began, coming into the kitchen holding a fresh drink, "Tex and me are going out for a while. Going to work on this deal with a couple of guys. Can you let me have twenty?"

Impatiently she started prying the chops apart. "I don't have twenty, fifteen, ten, or five. I'm broke until payday. I even had to charge my lunch."

"Now, baby, I know you got *some* bread stashed away."

"Well, I don't," she snapped, setting the skillet down hard on the stove.

"Look, we can clinch this thing tonight."

"Go on and clinch it. Don't let me stop you." *Lord*, she thought, *I'm tired. What's come over me—us? I'm tired of being man, wife, and mother!*

"I *need* the twenty." His tone was pleading.

"And, Flash, I don't have it," she insisted, sounding as if she was sorry and a little glad too.

"It's a sure hit, baby. 250."

"No!" she shrieked, tired of him and his pleading.

He scowled at her, mouth drawn in a hard straight line. Abruptly he swerved back into the living room. She could hear him whispering to Tex, and the man's low answering laugh drifted back to her.

She dried and floured the chops, afterwards dropping them in the hot grease. The hi-fi sound had been turned up again, and she recognized the Ramsey Lewis Trio with its soft off-beat rhythm. She set the table for one, knowing he wasn't going to eat. It would be nice if he ate regular meals with her. The only time he appeared hungry or seemed to enjoy a meal was when they were out to a restaurant. Even then, he looked as if he relished the waitresses more than the food.

When he entered the kitchen again, she could tell he was more than slightly drunk. His eyes were red and he swayed a little. "Tex has to go."

"So?" She turned the fire down low under the pan and put a lid over it.

"You ain't going to let me have the bread?"

Tacitly she brushed past him going into the living room. She stood over the coffee table reading the label on the bottle. *Chivas Regal. Bigtime Flash with high ideas on a beer budget.* Shrugging, she reached for a glass and poured herself a drink. *I might as well,* she thought. *I'm paying for it.*

"See my sweet wife, Tex?" he murmured, moving beside her. "Got me an ed-u-ca-ted gal."

"Sure did. And lookin' *good!*"

His arms enclosed around her, drawing her near.

"But there's *one* department *I'm* real good at you don't need no schooling for. Ain't there, baby?" He winked at the man on the sofa. Tex laughed loudly, slapping his knee.

Flushing, she sipped the drink, feeling it ease some of the tightness within her. She was tired and hungry and wished she was alone.

"I ain't no fool, even though I ain't been to school—"

"Tell it like it is, man," Tex sniggered.

She shifted out of the circle of his arms, put down her glass, and walked stiffly back to the sanctuary of the kitchen. The chops were almost done, and she turned them over.

Within a few minutes, he yelled again to her, this time from the bedroom. "Bonnie!"

Taking a deep breath, she went to him. He was in the center of the room peeling off his shirt and throwing it on a chair filled with others. "You going to let me have that money?"

"I don't have it," she said wearily, wondering how many times she would have to repeat it before he understood. But she knew he wouldn't. He never tried to understand anything he didn't want to.

"You got it," he said petulantly. Then: "Plenty of women 'round here'd be more'n glad to let me have that. And then some!"

"I don't doubt it," she rejoined, remembering the glass.

"Baby, I *know* you can let me have it. You refusing *me?* Flash?"

She watched him half bend his knees in his favorite stance for peering in the mirror to slick down his hair. Putting down the brush and buttoning his shirt, he walked to the door. "Hey, Tex, meet me downstairs in a minute."

"Sure, man, sure. You got bizness?"

"I got bizness."

When the door closed, he faced her. "Baby, I'm telling you all I need is twenty bucks."

Ignoring him, she returned to the kitchen where she turned off the stove. Suddenly like a springing cat, he was behind her, spinning her around. "Where's the money, goddammit!"

"No! We're two months behind now in the rent."

"I'll git it tonight. Enough for *six* months' rent!"

"Like all the nights you were going to *git* it?"

His eyes half closed into glassy pinpoints. The hands holding her clamped her arms so tightly they felt numb, without flesh and bone and blood. "I ain't one of your damn school kids. Now git me that money—"

"No—Flash. I can't. We need—"

His hand whipped across her face, sounding like a sharp pistol crack, knocking her head sharply to the side. The pain was so intense that at first she couldn't feel it at all.

"Give me that money before I beat the living shit out of you!"

The thoughts rose like foam in her head, soaring to the top in one gushing fountain. *It has come to this! But, of course, it had to. He doesn't know anything else. He was born and brought up in the squalid slums of this, and it's the only way he knows how to act and think and be.*

Feeling his hand move again, she murmured quickly: "The mattress. Under the mattress." At the words, she almost giggled. *How unoriginal of me to hide it under the mattress.*

A weight lifted from her as his hands released her. The pressure was gone—the pain and anguish still there. She sank weakly against the wall, tasting the blood at the corners of her mouth, closing her eyes until he was beside her again.

"Still my baby?" His voice was softly wheedling.

She opened her eyes to see him smiling at her while jerking a tie beneath his shirt collar.

"Sure you are," he said soothingly, taking her in his arms now and kissing her. His hands grasped each rounded buttock and slowly began to rotate them in a circular motion. The hardness of his manhood was thrust against her and held there.

And for her, there it was once again. The heady, sensual flowing weakness of being caught in fire and smoke and ice until she couldn't breathe or see—only feel. A dizziness overpowered her, causing her to choke and hate the lack of strength in her femininity. She shut her eyes to him, succumbing to the tremorlike ache in her body, breathing with many rapid timeless breaths while he slowly lifted her dress. Hands smoothed her thighs like hard crawling spiders and tucked into the elastic of her panties to pull them down. The wall was the only thing supporting her now. She heard him laugh low and sure deep in his throat.

The sensation this time as he entered her was intense and new and thundering. She heard the remote groan in her throat and felt the top of his head brushing her chin. Then the explosion. A roaring in her head and a painful blackness drawing an ecstatic curtain over her mind.

Hours, minutes, seconds passed and she stayed there prostrate against the wall after he had gone. Distantly she made out a record playing over and over, and she tried to bring herself together by listening to it. A blues—it was a blues sung by a moaning Black woman:

Oh, the blues ain't nothin',
    but a woman cryin' for her man,
Oh, the blues ain't nothin',
    but a woman cryin' for her man

The man had gone. And she thought about all the dark specters of men—Black in skin, spirit, and life, kept alive by the phallic symbol. He and all the other disembodied shadows caught in an entangling web spun at birth. She pitied them and all those like herself who could not help the Cimmerian ghosts to become alive except above the murky span of their loins.

Lord, she cried silently, Lord. Then she went to turn off the wailing Black woman singer crying like herself for her man.

JOHN A. WILLIAMS

Born in 1925 in Jackson, Mississippi, Williams served in World War II as a pharmacist's mate. He earned a B.A. from Syracuse University in 1950 and later worked as a journalist for CBS, *Ebony, Jet,* and *Newsweek.* He has also taught at the City University of New York, University of Hawaii, Boston University, and Rutgers University where, in 1990, he was named the Paul Robeson Professor of English. He is the author of twelve novels, and is perhaps best known for *The Man Who Cried I Am,* which appeared in 1967. *Captain Blackman,* his 1972 novel set in Harlem, is about the life of an injured army soldier who, as he falls in and out of a coma, goes back through time to experience various wars as a black soldier.

17

CADENCES

The windows were open, there were no fans. After all, the boys were out there in the far-flung jungles of the world without relief from the heat, why couldn't they suffer a little in here?

The uniformed men sat somewhat stiffly in the heavy chairs that had been placed around the great table. A slender, youngish four-star General entered and everyone stood; he waved them back to their seats and ran a thin hand through a shock of flaxen hair.

"Gentlemen," he said. "We have got ourselves some problems. Real problems." He patted his papers into a neat pile. "First off, these people want to fly."

"What!"

"Incredible!"

"Why? Why they can't even walk. All they do is dance."

The young General raised his hand. "The politicians say they will fly."

A groan went up.

"Next, they're complaining about not having their own chaplains. To tell you the truth, I don't see too much wrong with letting them have a few chap-

lains. They're a church-going people, when they're not knifing each other to death. I mean, chaplains have a place in war."

"All right, all right. A few."

"A few, you mean. We aren't going to have that many combat troops that're colored. We don't have them in brigade strength in any single town in the country, except at Huachuca, a division, but they're sixty miles from nowhere. Let's be big and say five, General."

The General said, "Looks like we've got to have a dozen."

"Is that what the politicians say?"

"They say at least a dozen."

Several new cigarettes were lit during the silence that followed. There was no real need to argue points here; they were all after the same thing. And they were really one big family, white, Protestant, Scotch-Irish, German-Irish. Many had relatives who had fought during the Revolution, 1812, the Civil War, the Spanish-American War. A number of the men in this room had themselves fought in World War I. One or two had designed his own uniform. Most were from southern or border states.

"General Whittman, sir?"

"Yes, Smitty."

"The er—uh—morale, is it as bad as we've heard?"

"Worse, Smitty. That's our major problem." He shifted his feet to a wide stance. "Now, we've had riots at Murfreesboro, Gurdon—"

"Fort Dix," someone said.

"Huachuca," said another.

"Tuskegee, Polk, Livingston—"

"—Beauregard, Claiborne, Alexandria, Pollock, Esler, Bragg—"

"—Van Horn, Stewart, Lake Charles, March Field, Luis Obispo, Bliss, Phillips, Breckinridge, Shenango—"

An Admiral spoke up. "We've had them at Sampson, Great Lakes, Shoemaker, Treasure Island, Norfolk, San Diego, Pendleton, Gulfport, St. Albans, Brooklyn, Hueneme, Pearl Harbor, Boston—"

A voice heavily accented with the South blustered, "Now, goddammit, you just cain't take northern nigras and station 'em in the South—"

"But we did because you wanted the bases there to give your economy a boost. Government installations and all that—"

The four-star General raised both hands. "All right. We've got a long agenda. The rest of that problem is overseas deployment. Where do we send them? Had that little ruckus in Australia and the Aussies are nervous. Queried

MacArthur and he says he can handle the black troops there now and those be-ing sent, so that situation seems stable."

"But Gruening in Alaska doesn't think the Negroes ought to be sent up there to mix with the Indians and Eskimos. Undesirable, I think he said. What's he think they're going to do, overthrow the government?"

"Panama wants us to remove a company of Negroes—"

"Isn't that something! That damned canal was built by niggers!"

The General went on. "—Chile and Venezuela will not, repeat, will not, ac-cept Negro coast artillery units, and Colonel McBride tells me that colored troops will not be satisfactory in Liberia, South Africa, no; New Zealand looks okay; some political reservations in China. The Belgian Congo and French West Africa look sticky; the Belgians even in exile insist on no Negro troops in the Congo. . . ."

Abraham Blackman heard a noise, a noise with a pattern, and he thought it was someone snoring. But it was a voice, droning in prayer:

"—and Lord God Almighty, some of us may never see home again, or our loved ones, having this week entered the training of the soldier. Dear God, we implore you to watch over us, guide us safely through the hail of bullets, bombs, and hand grenades to come, and return us home safely, whole in our devotion to you. We ask it in the name of Him who taught us to say when we pray:

"Our Father—"

Blackman trailed the voice to its source. The man they called Big Tim was leading the prayer. He was from Texas, a nice-looking cat, some white in him, a little Mexican, but mostly spade. Big Tim was on his knees; five older men who'd come in a couple of days ago were also on their knees, looking very pious, like the trustees or elders of the church Blackman was raised in when they were about to take up a spe-cial collection.

Now someone at the far end of the barracks spoke sleepily, "What the fuck is you niggers doin? You ain't hardly got here, talkin about some goddamn bombs and bullets. They gonna send you old cats back home, anyhow. Ain't that a bitch, layin around here prayin an hour before time to get up. Boy, I tell you, a nigger ain't shit."

"—as we forgive those who trespass against us, for Thine is the king-dom and the power and the glory. Amen."

Big Tim sprang clumsily to his feet and lunged down to the end of the barracks.

"You sacrilegious, no-count, zoot-suit-wearin motherfucker, how the hell you gonna innerup a *prayer* service, man? Didn't your momma teach you nuthin?"

Now Blackman recognized the complainant's voice. A guy they called Flash, from Philly. "Okay, okay, man. I'm sorry. You just broke in on my sleep. You right, man, that sure wasn't cool. Okay, Big Tim? You a man of God, I know you're gonna forgive me."

Big Tim bellowed, "You right about that. I'ma let you slide this time, Flash, but the next time I'ma be on your ass like stink on shit."

Blackman heard Big Tim striding away, grumbling. Then Flash's voice came again. "Hey, Big Tim."

"Now whatchew want, Flash?"

"Fuck you, Big Tim."

There came the sound of running feet and Flash's laughter riding hard in the corridor. Big Tim came back in, breathing hard. "I'ma break that nigguh's neck yet, you watch I don't."

For the next half hour Blackman lay in his cot, thinking. He'd been here two days now and seen almost every kind of black male come in— youths wearing sweaters with high school block letters on them; farmering young men up from the Deep South, still reeking of animal dung and their own sweat that'd crawled into the very fabric of their faded blue coveralls; hipsters in their zoot suits and hippie-dips trying to be as sharp as the hipsters, but failing; there were one or two college freshmen; and several about whom he could discover nothing.

Later, dressed and back from mess, he felt a tap on his shoulder and turned. It was the man they called Benjy, outa Chicago. Zoot-suit type, but unlike the other hipsters, he was a funny cat. "Where you from, man, standin around pickin up on these clowns comin in here like you was a camera or somethin?"

The observer observed, Blackman thought. He'd always thought of himself as the guy who watched the guys watching the broad with the fine legs. Now he was caught. He laughed down at Benjy and wondered what he'd look like after the Army got rid of his conk.

"The Apple, man." He could see Benjy thinking, Maybe this is another type cat, slicker n slick in them ol square clothes.

Benjy pressed.

"Where at in the Apple?"

"Eighth Avenue and Hunnert n Forty-fifth. What you know about it?"

Benjy grinned, yellow teeth bucking. "Jim, you'd be surprised what I know."

"You know so fuckin much, how come you're in the Army?"

"I had to cut out. Some people fuckin over me. So I cut out from the turf. Give time for things to cool off, y dig?"

All the hipsters had some answer for being in. Babes givin 'em trouble, The Man lookin for 'em. A choice between jail and heavyfootin it—Blackman was sure that most of them just weren't as slick or cunning as they pretended to be. "Yeah," he said to Benjy. "If that's what you say."

"Well, damn, Big Man, why I got to lie about saving my neck?"

Blackman shrugged. He wasn't going to get dragged into any prolonged argument or discussion about something that didn't matter to him. He laughed at Benjy because he desperately wanted Blackman to believe his story.

They both turned to watch Felson pass; he was one of the college freshmen. He was a short, fat, light-skinned youth, and he spoke in a soft voice. His long eyelashes were startling in his altogether ugly face. Parts of Felson jiggled when he walked. Benjy cut his eyes back to Blackman's. "Sho hope times don't git hard," he said.

At the end of that week, although everyone said they despised the Army, Blackman noticed that they were glad, even eager enough to get their uniforms, and as if that were not enough, when they began company drill, they strutted, Blackman with them, as if every simple drill on the stubbled field was being attended by a thousand girls, parents, and guys who were too sick, from one thing or another, to have been drafted. Like the man before him on the pivot, Blackman camel-walked, shot forward like a flash. He pitied the old guys who couldn't do the push-ups, and scrambled through the obstacle course like a young god, hardly breathing at the end of it, laughing at the men like Big Tim, who almost always quit midway through or got hung up on the ropes or barriers.

As the weeks shot by, the company dissolved after training hours into groups; the last names became as familiar as the first names they'd been known by before the Army. Now came the teasing of Felson with his jello-ish buttocks; Benjy's head was lumpy with the conk gone; Flash had teamed with another youth named Tisdale and they became known (among the more bold) as the Gold Dust Twins; Big Dick was from Bamberg, South Carolina, and he had one and would throw it upon one of the tables at the slightest provocation; he claimed he couldn't shoot straight on the firing range because it got in his way.

By now, when the troops gathered in the rec hall or in a corner of the barracks, the talk was of the Army General Classification Test. This was going to separate the men from the boys, the geniuses from the dummies, the slicksters from the squares.

Benjy announced, "I don't much care if I wind up in a service out-fit. I don't wanna be shot at. All you cats talkin about how cool you was on the infiltration course with live ammo, you all can have it."

Blackman listened to it. He hoped he did well on the tests; he was ready to meet whatever came head on. No stuff about being slick and staying alive; hell, he was going to do that anyway, but he was going to do it as a full-fledged man. Being slick was the easy way out; you didn't even have to challenge yourself. Maybe he'd even wind up in Officers' Candidate School and get himself some bars. Wouldn't that look great on Eighth Avenue and Hundred Forty-fifth! He saw himself in summer-lightweight tans striding through Harlem, his name and picture in the *Amsterdam News* and the *Afro-American;* the chicks would sure dig that. Be into that stuff *every* night, jack! Maybe he could even transfer into the Air Force then; they'd told him that the quota was full. Quota, he wondered. Why would they have a quota on the number of guys who wanted to fly planes and blow the Nazis and the Japs outa the sky? Thought they needed every flier they could get their hands on.

It didn't bother him that this was an all-black company. Like the others, he accepted it as the way things were without question, because that was the way he'd lived for all of his young life, and living that way, he couldn't see any value in certain aspects of living or soldiering with whites.

Whites. They were, if not a favorite, a constant topic of the talk, and each man was grateful they were not training in a southern camp from which, nearly every day, news of riots reached them. This was good news, for the Negroes were fighting back. More often and with far more frequency they heard of lynchings, shootings, and beatings, all apparently condoned by the Army, which did nothing about them.

"Sometimes," Benjy said, "I'm not even sure I'm in the same Army with them bastards. It sure don't seem like it."

It all seemed far away to Blackman. Fort Sheridan, hard by Lake Michigan, was miles away from the shootings, the humiliations suffered by other, less fortunate black soldiers. So far away that he could not conceive of these things happening to him. Emboldened, he said, "That crap couldn't happen here. The guys from the North wouldn't take it."

Big Dick, stroking his penis, still inside his pants, looked up and said, "You Harlem and Chicago niggers really think you're somethin special, doncha? It's all you cats what's gittin blowed away Down Home. Y'git sent there and right away you gonna change things cause they ain't like they was at home. Been livin in Harlem all your life, or Southside Chicago, or some other nigger neighborhood, without makin a peep. All of a sudden they can't do it to you down South. You niggers make me sick."

"Man, how you sound?"

"Goddamn burrhead. That's the first time in your life that cracker down there ever let you get away, Big Dick."

But the responses were not answers, Blackman noticed. Perhaps there were none.

Blackman scored in Grade I in the AGCT. So did Benjy, who tried to conceal his elation by declaring that he hadn't tried, that he guessed at the answers, not knowing them, of course, and that there'd been some mistake. Felson had made Grade III.

I beat that college boy, Blackman kept thinking. How often had he walked through the Convent Avenue gate of City College, waiting for the day when he could leave off helping to support the family and enroll there. When he enlisted, he was driving a freight elevator in a factory in Queens. Still, he smiled to himself, I ain't so dumb. I wasted that college boy. Me and Benjy both. Shi-it.

Still elated, he went on furlough; he'd return to Sheridan for training in the Medical Corps, to which he and Benjy had been assigned on the basis of their grades. There would be WACS, too, when school began. He was anxious to go home and get back, for he knew that officers were selected from Grade I of the AGCT.

18

They left the barracks with a drummer and marched through the camp roads that led to the hospital compound. The drummer got cute when they came down the main hospital road, and the contingent, Blackman in the front rank, put 'em down and picked 'em up. Blackman almost laughed; if black folks couldn't do anything else, they could sure march; he hadn't seen any white boys who could match the worst Negro training company in drill. The more the white soldiers and WACs paused to watch them, the more they swaggered, until, at last, they stopped before their new barracks.

There was a roll call and a formal welcome by the Exec of the hospital and the Commander of the Medical Corps Training School. As they spoke, Blackman was noticing that the barracks was at the end of the street, hard against the eight-foot barbed wire fence, behind which an armed guard was visible. The mess hall was directly across the street; seeing it, the smells seemed to grow more intense to Blackman. Cooking, waste, garbage cans; they'd smell this for six weeks. And then they were inside, choosing the best-located bunks, for others were due in for that particular class.

Later that evening, a corporal named Gummidge, who'd been placed in charge of the contingent, called an impromptu meeting. Blackman looked at Gummidge and wondered why he was in the Army at all. He was a fat man who spoke with a soft voice, and his eyes were soft.

Blackman knew none of the others except Benjy; they'd all come from other camps in other parts of the country. They focused their attention on Gummidge, a man, Blackman guessed, over thirty. This, Gummidge said, moving his hands languidly on air, was the first class of Army medical corpsmen in this war. The *Chicago Defender* has already broken the news to colored people. They expected the class to do well. Hanging on our every endeavor, Gummidge said, were thirteen million Negroes. Ours, therefore, was a grave and great responsibility, but he knew every man would succeed. He had felt so much pride watching the march into the hospital. Gummidge paused and his gentle, compassionate eyes wandered over the group. "That's all I wanted to say," he said.

"Except, when we're finished here, we just don't know where we'll be headed. Some to service outfits"—and here Blackman saw Benjy smile—"and some to the combat outfits. There's just no telling."

The meeting broke up quietly. Blackman went outside and sat on the steps. The guard outside the fence passed slowly, like a shred of dirty brown fog, and moved out of sight. Down the street the barracks lights were all on, and Blackman could hear radios and phonographs playing. How long, he wondered, would it take him to make T-5; how long to get to OCS? He had to do well here, maybe move up quickly, into another branch, even, where the promos came quicker. He heard footsteps on the porch behind him but didn't turn.

"You sure lookin' evil," the voice said, and then Blackman recognized Linkey, who'd just come in that afternoon.

"Am I?"

"Real evil. You Blackman, aincha?"

"Yeah."

Still behind him, Linkey said, "This looks like a solid, good deal, don't it?"

"This school?"

"Yeah, man," he said sounding impatient. "Well, it's cool for me, cause I just married the most gorgeous well-put-together chick in the *world!*" Blackman turned just as Linkey stomped a foot and clapped his hands. "And this give me another six weeks to be close to that fine, brown frame, jack, another month and a half!"

Momentarily Blackman envied him. "Enjoy it while you can," he said, and felt the air become suddenly charged.

Linkey bent down over him. "What do you mean by that, man? You signifyin or somethin?"

"No. Forget it, man," and Blackman shut up and turned his back to Linkey, busied himself staring at the barracks lights. Linkey moved away slowly. His movements seemed to say, You may be evil, but you fuck with me and I'll kick your ass. I'm just lightenin up on you cause you're in your mood.

Blackman heard him open the door and said, "Hey, man. I know she's fine as wine. Good luck. Don't pay me no mind."

Linkey chuckled. "Yeah, champ. Everything's solid."

<<<<<

The days began to unwind, to slip by in a mélange of classes, meals, conversations, leaves into Waukegan, where the boogey-bears hung out, women who snapped off dicks as fast as they could come from behind buttons; or into Chicago, haunting Parkway Ballroom, the Pershing, the Black Cat, the Rhumboogie, the DuSable. Blackman caught the trains into Waukegan or Chicago; he caught the last cars back to the hospital, just in time for reveille, and walked about all day, his penis half hard from thinking how he got it in the backseat of a jitney while the driver prowled up and down South Parkway, sighing in the front seat and peeking in at his rearview mirror; or how he got some under the stone steps of the Black Cat, pants down around his ankles, his hands protecting the girl's bottom from the Chicago night while the El passed overhead, casting a long sliver of nervous light; he didn't hear the lectures on materia medica or physiology or anatomy and the rest; his ears still rang with the sound of Johnny Hodges or the Duke; Lucky Millinder, Fatha Hines, Billy Eckstine singing "Stormy Monday Blues."

Basie's "One o'Clock Jump" throbbed in his head; Al Hibbler's hip voice echoed over talk of rib cages, GSW's, and morphine Syrettes; Erskine Hawkins and Dash and Bascomb. Blackman thought he smelled perfume at various times of the day, and at evening colors, when he stood looking toward the flag, he thought of their faces and bodies. There was so much of it out there, and from time to time, with the WACs, in here.

Just past the midway point, Benjy and Blackman, on leave together, drifted into a USO dance in Waukegan, having failed everywhere else. The record playing was a Lucky Millinder side, Sister Rosetta Tharpe singing. He saw her from across the room and began circling, sidling, getting close. Blackman looked over his shoulder; Benjy was watching: Go on, man. Work out. If you can.

Blackman was close to her when "Sophisticated Lady" started and he held out his hand; she took it. He didn't release her when the record was over, and they moved to "The Skater's Waltz." She flowed out from him and returned, like a wave, gently, splashing over him; she had a way of caressing his neck before she slid her arm down to his waist. Blackman didn't want to stop dancing with her, and whenever he saw someone ready to cut in, he moved her across the floor.

"I could dance with you all night," he said, and immediately felt foolish.

"All right, let's."

Later, when he knew her name was Osa and she knew his, they walked around watching the other dancers; the long, lean cats from Down Home, who had more steps, more grace and moves than should've been allowed, and the city cats with their studied nonchalance, that Savoy-Regal cool. Downstairs at the Coke machine, the room empty, they listened to the old building creaking to the dance steps, heard two hundred feet slipping along the waxed floor in unison, *shoom, shoom, shoom-shoom-shoom; shoom, shoom, shoom-shoom-shoom.* Goddamn, Blackman thought, listen to them niggers go! Osa tilted her head backward as if she'd read his thoughts. "I like to come down here and listen to them," she said. "I didn't think anyone else in the world could be so moved by the sound. My husband wasn't."

"Married?" Blackman tried to sound casual, but he felt strangely and suddenly deprived, and inexplicably jealous. Why, he wondered. All he wanted was some pussy.

She laughed and now he could see that she was perhaps twenty-five or close to it. A grown woman. "Sure. Isn't nearly everybody?" She became coy. "Thought you had a chippie, did you, Abraham?"

"Well, I—uh—ah—," pointing to her finger as she placed her hand in his and looked, too.

"Don't wear one, baby."

"Where's he?"

"North Africa. Ninety-ninth."

A pilot, Blackman thought. "Well, since I can't take you home—"

That smile again. Warm. Teasing. Interested. "Why can't you? I live in Evanston."

"Evanston!" Blackman blurted. That meant going back past the fort, almost into Chicago, and then returning. For a moment Osa didn't look worth all the trouble, but in the next, she did; worth it and more.

They sat together on a seat facing Benjy, who slept all the way to the fort. He got off shaking his head at them, but Osa smiled warmly and moved closer to Blackman when the train continued. They talked in whispers, close to each other's ears. She was from Evanston, born and raised; had gone to Drake, in Iowa. Married a year. Not sure about it.

When they'd given each other their pasts briefly, he said, "Osa," then whispered it. "Osa."

"You say it pretty, baby." She stroked his cheek and studied him.

"It's a pretty name."

"Say it again?"

"Osa."

"Ummm." She moved closer to him and said, "Strange, strange."

It's gonna be cool, Blackman thought. This trim is gonna be mine. He wondered what time it was; he didn't want to get caught sneaking a look at his watch. And then he thought, Hey, I could really go for this chick. Older, but—I'm gonna be detailed out before long, to somewhere, and I'd better cut on into this good thing while I got the chance. But, lord, why does she have to live in Evanston?

At last the train slowed and stopped. Blackman hesitated on the platform. "Listen," he said. "It's late and I'd better catch the next train back. I'll call you," he said with a rush, "I'll really call you, I want to call—" He stopped and listened to his voice burbling around the deserted platform, the rushing train now a low rumble in the distance. Another train, the express, blasted out of the north and roared after the local. During the moments they couldn't speak, they looked at each other. Then she took his hand and led him down the stairs inside the station. "We'll call a cab here," she said. "And go home. I'll drive you to the fort."

She answered the question in his eyes. "Doesn't look so good at a USO thing. I've even managed to do with Coke at those dances."

They sat in the cab and held hands. The streets were empty, quiet. Suddenly they both spoke at the same time.

"Do you ever have the feeling that you're the only person alive in the world when it's early like this?"

"Jesus Christ," she whispered, and turned to look out the window.

Then they were inside her flat, the morning struggling hard to come up, and later, roaring up to Fort Sheridan in her car, sharing a quart of bitterly cold milk and a pack of cigarettes, he thought of what she had on under her coat. Nothing. He wanted her to stop, but said nothing; he placed his hand in her crotch and slid his finger in. She drove back and forth across the road, her mouth wide, her legs opening and closing, the long, brown thighs he'd mounted in so much haste earlier trembling. She gasped, pulled over, and lay her head on the wheel when she stopped. "You drive."

Before he started, she loosened his belt, and he himself slid down his pants and drawers. As he drove back onto the road, he felt her grasping it; it was already hard and steaming. She was on the floor now, her breasts quivering on the seat, and then she was making love to it. With clenched teeth, Blackman was driving straight enough, but every time he glanced at the speedometer, he was doing eighty.

He called her that night and the night after, suddenly conscious of time left, the talk of places where they might be sent, filling every spare moment. He found that Benjy was forever tapping him out of a day-dream, and he had no energy; he just wanted to think of Osa. Blackman sought out Linkey, and they talked of good women, of beautiful women, and of women who were good in bed, and he knew he was thinking of Osa, while Linkey was thinking of his wife.

Suddenly all leaves were canceled and Blackman panicked. The course had been shortened; assignments would be drawn within the next three or four days. Osa, he thought. I've got to see Osa! Desperate, he called her and told her to park on the road outside the hospital, that he'd find her. Benjy, against his wishes, distracted the guard for him, and Blackman went over the fence. She was there, waiting, and to save time, they drove at top speed into Waukegan and rented a room above a bar. They made love on the sagging, spring-sprung bed; on the gritty linoleum floor, in a creaking wicker chair, and then they drove back to the fort, Osa crying all the way and Blackman promising he'd do his best to see her again before he left.

He came back through the tall grass, crouching, hearing Benjy's voice, for Blackman's return time had been set. Benjy was already at work, distracting the guard again. "Hey, you crazy motherfucker. How's your momma today? You got a momma, white boy? I bet that's the only pussy you *ever* got next to. Does your momma wear drawers, boy? She do?"

Red in the face, the guard was walking slowly but steadily away from Benjy's voice. "Say, boy, you passed here and I didn't see nothin hangin heavy in your pants. What you got down there, a pussy? You gon far in the Army if that's what you got, man. I like a little round eye my-self once in a while, specially on tender, lil ol white boys."

Benjy was signaling Blackman and Blackman was up and over the fence and onto the ground. He was so tired he just lay there. Benjy grasped for his arm. "Get up, man. I got that boy so mad he's liable to start shootin any minute. Abe, you better get the hell up from there."

Blackman got up, staggered into the barracks, and got a Coke. Benjy came in and looked at him. "This nigger's in love," he said. "You a little tender for that babe, man. She got five years on you—"

Blackman glared at him. He knew all that. How many times had he gone over it in his own mind, trying to see Osa the way his father would see her, or his mother; what would it be like, being married to her?

Blackman finished at the top of his class and made some discreet inquiries about applying to OCS and, failing that, where he was going to be sent. The officers he asked smiled, admitted he'd done well, but he'd have to wait and see what happened because no orders had come in yet. When the orders did come in, they were all assigned to Services of Supply; some were going east and some west. Benjy was happy, Blackman and Linkey glum. They were going to Fort Ord; the next stop would be the Pacific. Europe seemed the more civilized place; there were famous towns and cities, and everyone knew, from the last war, that European women were especially grateful to American rescuers. They were envious of Benjy.

The railroad station was a big, noisy catacomb. Linkey and Blackman had two hours between trains. Now Linkey was somewhere in the station with his wife, and Blackman and Osa were drinking coffee and sitting in long silences. When they were tired of that, they walked around the station. "I'm coming to California," Osa said. "I'm going to try. If you want me to. Maybe you're glad you're going away from an old woman like me."

"No. You know I'm not. But I don't know how long I'll be at Ord."

"I'll come for as long as you're there."

He didn't ask about her husband; he never asked about him except for the first time.

The panic came when his train was announced; then he wondered why they hadn't found a room. Had they enjoyed being sad, holding hands, and showing their sadness to the world, the way the soldier and the girl did in the movies?

"Call as soon as you get settled," she said, stretching up to him, clutching the sleeve of his coat.

"Yes, I will. I will."

She stayed on the platform beneath his window, alternately crying and smiling. Linkey's wife, next to her, smiled little smiles to Linkey, who leaned over Blackman to press his lips to the window. The train jerked and Blackman saw Osa's mouth fall open; bumping into Linkey's wife, she took a few tentative steps in the direction the train was moving, then stopped, giving up; her head seemed to sink beneath her shoulders. She raised her gloved hand once and bent the fingers down to the palm, and the train rushed forward.

CADENCES

"If we can get it into a bomb that a plane can carry, who'll we drop it on, the Germans or the Japs?"

"We got the plane coming. They call it the Superfort."

"Good, but where do we dump the goddamn thing?"

"Doctor, do you have relatives in Japan?"

"Of course, not, Doctor. Do I look like it?"

"Were the Japs on the Mayflower? Did they settle St. Augustine? Did they carve out the West?"

"Doctor, if you'll excuse me, those are silly fucking questions."

"Think of all the words in your vocabulary that're Japanese. Know any?"

"None, Doctor, as you well know, except for menus—"

"Ever heard of anyone going to the Japanese Riviera?"

"No."

"Are the Louvre, Prado, Rijksmuseum, British Museum in Japan?"

"Goddamn it, no."

"Where did this business start, anyway?"

"Why, in Germany, and then there's—"

"You bet your sweet ass, Doctor. You've answered your own question. Now let's get back to work. This fission is a pain in the ass. Fusion, that's the answer, more power, less space. Boom! You hear me, Doctor, BA—roOM!"

At their aid station at Ord they passed the days playing touch football, cards, or shooting craps. They didn't have to fight the mess lines; they simply ordered enough food for the patients in the station and themselves and drew lots to see who would go get the mess cart and return it. Blackman spent some of his nights waiting on line at the communications center to call Osa, others in the movies or talking about getting to San Francisco. There were no furloughs; they were all on standby.

Gnawing at Blackman was his assignment to a Services of Supply unit. Why, with his grades? He was officer material! Right now someone somewhere should be processing his papers and discovering him. Then all would be put right. But Christ, let him get detailed out to one of those miserable islands, they'd never find him, never. Linkey was his only consolation, he being even more glum than Blackman. When Blackman greeted him during the day, Linkey would invariably answer: "Man, I just ain't doin no good." Each night he wrote to his wife while on duty in the ward, and when he came out, the calls would begin for him to do "The Signifyin Monkey."

"Hey, Linkey. Do 'The Signifyin Monkey.' "

"No, man, do 'Shine.' "

"You jokers're a pain in the ass," he'd say, taking his time getting undressed, not saying yes or no. Once in bed, he cleared his throat loudly and the barracks fell silent, waiting. Linkey had a big, basso pro-fundo voice, and he could recite with all the nuances; it was easy to laugh, night after night.

But this night Linkey prefaced his recital. "I might as well go on and do it, cause I ain't gonna be with you motherfuckers much longer. I'm cuttin out to the Windy City. Big Chi. And I'm gonna think about you. For about five minutes."

A chorus of voices rose in derision.

"Nigger, shut up and recite."

"That cat supposed to be slick."

"Joadie Grinder," Linkey shouted. "And I'ma be sharp, too. Touch me and bleed to death, square cocksuckers." He laughed.

Pfc. called Scovall, out of Baltimore, called out: "Stop the shit, Linkey. You gonna be just like the rest of us, over there on them goddamn beaches beggin the Japs not to shoot you in the mouth and pleadin for the infantry not to shoot you in the ass. Who you jivin?"

"Money!" Linkey shouted.

"Twenty dollars," Scovall laughed back.

"Fool, that ain't no money," Linkey retorted. *"Fifty* dollars!!"

"I'ma call your bluff, nigger!" Scovall was out of his bunk, sliding down the barrack floor, his finger jabbing the air toward Linkey.

"Hey, Abe," Linkey said. "Collect the gelt in the morning, okay?"

Blackman said, "All right, man, now will you do " 'The Signifyin Monkey?' "

"In a minute. I wanna tell you." Linkey's voice sounded joyful. "First thing, I'ma get outa this nasty-ass khaki. Get me some three or four reee-al sharp fronts, and some of them loafers that's the style now. Then me and my old lady gonna hit South Parkway, jim; we gonna cool it from Sixty-third Street down to Forty-seventh, just tippin, jim. Naturally, we gonna fall by a few joints; take some top-shelf to the Rhumboogie, take in a show at the Regal, taste us some ribs. Then we gonna cool it back home and come outa them vines . . ."

Goddamn him, Blackman thought. Linkey's voice was so filled with confidence, and they were all listening to him, *seeing* him do what he said he was going to do. Hey, Blackman thought. Maybe the cat does have something up his sleeve.

Scovall's voice came out of the darkness, a little shakily, Blackman thought. "Yeah, and I'ma walk on the Pacific Ocean tomorrow."

Linkey's voice, still confident and happy; "Okay, sucker. You gonna make me fifty dollars richer. You niggers ready?"

"Oh, go on, man."

"Wait. This poem is dedicated to Scovall." Linkey laughed.

Said the monkey to the lion, one bright sunny day,
There's a big burly mothafucka down the jungle way,
An the way he's talkin bout you, he can't be your friend,
An when you two lock asses, one of you's bound to been;
He say, you king of the beasts with your shaggy-ass mane?
He gon stomp your ass till you feels no pain;
Say, you growlin and roarin, keepin up fuss?
Well, he gon kick your ass, jack, till you shittin pus;
He say you got a momma what's a two-bit whore,
What don't do nothin but suck, shit, and snore.
Now, up jumped ol lion in a helluva rage,
His tail a-twitchin like he'd blown him some gage.
Say, which way's that mothafucka, I'll stop his shit,
And he shot through the jungle hot as a bitch.
Ol elephant was munchin some tall collard greens,

When the king of the jungle stomped out mean.
Say, now, jack, gonna beat yo ass to death;
Gon stomp you till you ain't got no breath left.
Soundin on me, mighty king of all beasts,
I'll show your fat ass just who is the chief.
Elephant say, man, what the hell's wrong with you?
Better find you some broad you can lay down and screw;
I don know what you talkin about,
So don start no shit's gonna git you punched out.
Ol lion jumped back and threw up his paws,
Just as elephant went BAM! upside his jaw;
Then grabbed lion's tail, turned im ever'way but loose;
Stomped him, beat him, pure mashed him to juice.
Lion saw stars and the sun and the moon,
Lay on his ass thinkin, shit, I have been ruined.
From up high in a tree the monkey looked down,
Say to the lion, man, what you doin on the ground?
You s'posed to be king of the jungle, just look at your ass;
Elephant done fucked over you from friss to frass
Monkey waxed bold and he jumped up and down,
Say to the lion, you ol jive-ass clown,
If I wasn't cool, I'd beat your ass, too—
Turkey mothafucka, you jive through and through.
Monkey was 'cited, jumpin all around,
Then his big foot slipped and his ass hit the ground.
Like a flash of lightning and a bolt of white heat,
Lion was on his ass with all four feet.
Say, Signifyin Monkey, your goddamn time has come,
That big mouth of yours no more will run.
Monkey say, now look, mighty king,
I didn't mean nothing, you the best of everything.
No, monkey, no, said the lion, drawing back,
Your nasty-assed mouth done got you in a crack.
Please, mighty lion, have pity on me—
Stomp! Stomp! say lion, fuckin wid me.
Now, needless to say, the monkey's no more,
And the jungle's quiet cause the lion don't roar.

19

Morning spilled over the mountains, pitted with fast-moving gray clouds and specks of sun trying to break through. Blackman couldn't concentrate on anything as he lay in his bunk. He had the duty; he'd have to get the mess cart. Why hadn't he heard from Osa, after all those calls? What did Linkey have in mind? He swung his legs to the floor and looked at his shoes.

"Everybody in there's running a temperature," he heard one of the duty medics saying to somebody.

Tough, Blackman thought. Now he glanced at the others starting to come awake. He didn't feel like talking to anybody this morning. Dress and get the fuck outa here, he thought, and then he paused. What's wrong with today? Why does it feel, already, so sharp, so dangerous? Ah, Osa, he thought, don't do it. Please, don't do it, baby. I love you.

But Linkey was already up and waiting for him in the latrine.

"Gotta talk to you, Abe."

Grunting, sprinkling drops of urine all over the wall and floor.

"I got the duty this morning, man."

"Okay. I'll go with you."

Shit, Blackman thought.

Within minutes they were taking long strides along dirt paths and roads toward the main mess hall, where the lines were already impossibly long, but moving at a brisk clip past the armed guards. Armed guards because of mess hall trouble—riots—wholesale battles between black and white. Armed guards kept the peace, more or less.

"How's Osa?"

"Okay." Now he'd have to ask after Linkey's wife. "How's your wife?"

"Okay. But that's what I wanted to talk to you about, Abe. I need your help."

They cut through one of the lines.

"I need your help," Linkey said again.

"For what?"

"I'ma get outa this motherfucker."

"You said that last night."

"And I meant it. Now here's what—"

The sounds around them had been growing louder; now they positively exploded. Out of the corner of his searching eye, Blackman saw a sudden, violent movement, and told himself he hadn't seen it. But he had, blurs. Three white soldiers in fatigues pummeling to the ground a black soldier who even now was struggling to get up from the ground, his face in an appeal mixed with anger. Now bouncing off Blackman and Linkey came a swarm of black soldiers. Another movement in the lines and a cluster of whites broke through, then more and more involved, yet apart; it was like watching an amoeba gone wild, stretching to break itself and form anew. Blackman started throwing punches, at first measured and with snap, at every white face he saw cresting the billowing bodies. Then, in self-defense, he threw faster and faster, ducked, spun, and began to feel a growing fear as he felt the weight of all those bodies writhing and pummeling. The mass opened suddenly and Blackman found himself in its center, blows raining on his face, body, and legs. He went low, but stayed on his feet. Don't go down, he told himself. He grabbed a waist above which pink and white skin was visible, and came up with his knee.

"Jesus, Jesus," the man said, and melted out of his grip.

Still in his crouch, Blackman turned and eagerly sought another. This was a race riot! The middle of it! No guns. Flesh on flesh.

"Motherfuckers!" he heard Linkey bellowing. "Here's some more!" Linkey bellowed not in pain but in some primitive triumph. Above the grunts, groans, yells, shrieks, and sounds of blows being landed, voices snarled, "Niggercrackercocksuckerblacksonofabitchfaggotpeckerwood stinkinniggerdicklickinpaddiekickyoassripthatbigprickoffyoukillkillkill."

Before Blackman could complete his turn, something hit his back, and his arms and legs flew out and a group already on the ground jerked up and pounded him in the face and neck; one bit him. Flashes of silver and gold raced past Blackman's eyes; then they stopped, leaving in their places a sharp pain growing sharper. He covered his head with his arms and worked himself to his knees. Bam! Another sharp pain, this one in the face. Blackman slipped to one side and went down again. His fear was now turgid; he wanted to be angry. Anger. The fear was implacable and it was coming on. He felt it and suddenly began to flail out, and the more he did, the less he felt the fear. He was coming erect, growling; the more he moved and flailed, the louder he growled, then started to bellow. (Holler when you throw that bayonet in, HOLLER!) All over the plain before the mess hall, men were down, about to go down, or knocking each other down.

Unmistakably a BAR, Blackman thought when he heard it banging nearby. Then there were whistles and shouts of authority. "You men! You people! Break it up! Attention! On your feet, you hear me, on your feet! Get your hands up. Up, I said, UP." More gunfire. The movement slowed, like a sea settling before a dying wind. Hands went up, as in a mass prayer. Blackman saw the trucks with machine-guns mounted on the roofs of the cabins, foot soldiers with M-IS held at the ready. These last began to move into the mass, herding the whites into one group, the blacks into another. A soldier next to Blackman, his face split and bleeding, shouted, "Cracker bastards tried to cut in on me on the line, three of 'em, like I wasn't nothin—"

"Shut up in there!" a lieutenant shouted.

From nearby Blackman—he thought it was Linkey: "Fuck you, peckerwood."

"How's that?" Moving in threateningly, but not too far. "How's that again?"

Prodded with rifle barrels, they started to climb into the two-and-a-half-ton trucks, now rolling up in a cloud of dust, the blacks into one group, the whites into another. Now ambulances came careening up, and medics spilled out to look after the wounded. The trucks drove through the fort on the way to the stockade. Black soldiers were trotting in small groups toward the mess hall. "What happened?" one said, addressing Blackman.

"Paddy boys jumped us on the mess line."

"Oh oh. Some more of that lame shit, huh? Anybody hurt?"

"Don't know, but there're lotsa cats layin back there."

Linkey wasn't in Blackman's truck; he hoped he wasn't back there on the ground.

The stockade was far too small to hold all the men charged with grievous assault. Lists of names were compiled; these men would go up for courts-martial. Blackman was released for evening mess.

There was an uneasy silence in the station when he arrived. It was on a street where the black and white sections merged. Scovall met him at the door, baseball bat in hand. He grinned. "Now we're all present and accounted for."

Looking around, Blackman saw Linkey sprawled on his bunk. "You okay, Abe? What took you so long, man? What they gonna do with you? You get assault, too?"

For the first time Blackman realized this would go on his record; he'd never make OCS now. While he compared notes with Linkey, the four men who'd gone for the mess cart returned. Safely. After the meal (the cart wasn't being returned until morning), the lights were turned off and a chair propped against the door. Scovall said hoarsely, "I think it's gonna be cool tonight."

"I don't give a damn if it *ain't* cool; I *got* my shit." Linkey said.

Blackman heard a tiny, rushing sound that terminated in a loud, metallic clack. Switchblade. No one asked if he'd used it earlier at the mess hall. Two white soldiers had been badly cut.

"You're going to ruin the spring," Blackman said.

"Oh, yeah, Abe. There's some mail for you."

Blackman's heart tumbled. "Yeah, where?"

"Nigger sounds like he don't want it," someone snickered.

Reluctantly, while sitting in the latrine in a corner, Blackman ripped open the letter. He read it once and trembled with rage. He took a deep breath and reread it, looking for clues that would make it all right again. There were none. It was over. This time, "a wonderful sailor from Great Lakes." Slowly, he ripped up the letter and stuck the pieces under him into the bowl.

He didn't sleep well that night. He thought of the sailor riding his woman, of the smiles she was turning on him, of his eyes wide at the sight of those breasts that fitted his hands so nicely.

The next morning Linkey and Blackman stood outside the station.

"We didn't have a chance to talk yesterday. We were, what you might call, rudely interrupted." Linkey chuckled.

"Yeah. What were you going to talk about?"

"I want you to puncture my eardrum."

A wind swept through the street, scattering surface dust and candy wrappers. Blackman turned from Linkey. "Shit."

"C'mon, man."

"Do it yourself."

"Can't. Tried."

"Get Scovall to do it. He'll bust your head while he's at it, too."

"No. You, Abe."

"Why me?"

Linkey grinned. "Don't exactly know why. A hunch."

"What's that supposed to mean?"

"I told you. I don't know. You'll do it, won't you? Don't worry about hurting me. Got to hurt a little, but so what?"

Today Blackman wanted to hurt, and he knew it. He said, "I might hurt you bad, Linkey."

"Goddamn it, man, just do it. Don't nobody have to know about it but me and you."

Blackman stared out over the brown hills over which some infantrymen were running and said again, "I might hurt you."

"Oh, nigger, that's what it's all about? What's the matter with you?" He was getting angry now. "Let's stop the shit. You gonna do it or not?"

Blackman shrugged. "Sure. How do you want it?"

"First, let's try concussion."

Later, after the others crept out to play touch football, Linkey and Blackman went into the latrine. Linkey talked nervously. "I keep thinkin about all those guys with bad eardrums. They ain't in. Got to get back to my old lady, man. They really gonna do us in at the court-martial." He paused and looked at Blackman. "Okay, lay it on, jack."

They agreed on the left ear. "You ready?" Blackman asked.

"Go head."

Blackman's first blow was short and measuring, with the palm of his hand, but it jolted Linkey. "You okay?"

Linkey said, "Yeah."

Blackman got more leverage with the next. Between blows he asked, "You okay?" and Linkey would answer through clenched teeth, "Shit, yeah. Git it on, man, git it on." Blackman laid it on until his hand grew sore, until his palm was as red as Linkey's ear.

"It's singin like a bitch," Linkey said. "Like a volcano going off, like Niagara Falls all rolled into one. Good God Almighty. If this ain't it—"

He waited a day, then went to see a doctor. There was nothing wrong with the ear.

When they returned to the latrine, Linkey handed Blackman a 20-CC syringe with a needle attached. Blackman took it without comment, swabbed the needle with a piece of alcohol-soaked cotton. Linkey bent down so Blackman could get more light. He said, "Git it, man."

Holding the needle poised, Blackman said, "You sure you want it this way?"

Linkey exploded. *"Stick* that motherfucker, man. We ain't playin no games here."

Lightly, Blackman went into the ear. He felt the needle point bouncing ever so lightly against the membrane.

"Am I there, man?"

"That's it, that's it, go on, go on—" He sucked in his breath, closed his eyes, and ground his teeth.

Blackman went in, pressed, felt resistance, and then he was through. Linkey gasped, shuddered, and then moaned. "Goddamn it, man," Blackman hissed. "Don't jump like that! You want this fucking thing in your brain?" He withdrew the needle; there was a neat, thin stream of blood on it.

"Let's see."

Blackman handed him the works.

"That ought to get it," Linkey said with a smile. Then he leaned over a toilet and vomited.

"You okay?"

"Shit, yeah. You a crazy cat, Blackman. Thanks."

"Any time, Linkey."

Linkey didn't return to the station after he saw the doctor. He called and asked Blackman to get his clothes and bring the money, and Scovall went to the hospital with Blackman and even talked to the doctor, who said it was very likely that Private Linkey would be discharged after treatment. Did Private Scovall know anything about the injury, which seemed to be fresh, although one couldn't always tell about the eardrums?

Blackman didn't have time to miss Linkey or grieve any further over Osa. Like every other black soldier in the mess hall riot, he was going overseas on the next boat.

The engines on the ship stopped, then started up again, slowly. Blackman, who'd been laying in his bunk, twisted suddenly, and his eyes caught the startled stare of the man in the next bunk.

"We stoppin," he said. Then, "Oh shit."

A stink, sharper than usual, seemed to billow up in the hold, and everyone started to move at once, climbing slowly down from their bunks, checking and rechecking packs, nervously fitting on the helmets. The men who had weapons checked them stoically; most didn't have them. What did a stevedore require a weapon for? Some of the men were evil and snarled and cursed whenever someone approached them; others were quiet, as if in reflection, or perhaps, prayer. And they were considerate; this might count toward saving their lives.

Blackman watched. There was no need to check his pack or his kit; he knew exactly what was in both. In the latter, tags, sulfa powders, morphine Syrettes, bandages. Blackman's bowels tightened. He had to fart, and tried to, turning himself up on one haunch, but he quit; he couldn't tell which would come, the gas or the feces. The PA was issuing orders, hold by hold. Lines were forming in the passageway to the latrine, each man seeming to be unaware of the many others with the same problem.

Blackman kept attuned to the noises he could hear outside the ship. Planes, he guessed from Guadalcanal, and big guns from the few ships that'd come up the channel with them. Those, he thought, must be bombs.

The slow throbbing in the belly of the ship stopped again. Blackman closed his eyes to slow his racing stomach. The engines were the technological stimuli; they ran panting to his senses, shouting to him what the absence of the sound of those engines meant.

"They're going!" came a shout.

The white soldiers of the Thirty-seventh and the marines of the First were hitting the nets. They'd have to secure the beach and adjacent areas; Blackman's group would then go in and begin handling cargo— ammo, ammo, and more ammo, and then, perhaps, food. If they lost the beach?

Naw. They'd said Bougainville was easy.

Soon, too soon, Blackman found himself moving in a line, climbing the steep steps to the upper deck, where the cool sea air whipped around wisps of cordite.

As in a daze, Blackman watched the line of heaving barges dip into the sea and out of it. Some started to pull away; others were already returning from the beach. Strange, fluttering sounds rushed through the air to explode against the steep hillsides, and planes, roaring in low from the 'Canal, passed mast-high overhead, pulled up, and their bombs exploded, too, as if there was no connection between the planes, already flying away, and the noise of their missiles. Pushed from behind, Blackman moved ahead to the bulkhead, found the start of the browned, wet, rope net and started to climb down. There was water in the barges.

"Shit," Blackman said.

"Get down, get down," said the young sailor at the wheel at the rear of the craft. He sounded bored.

Feeling foolish, Blackman tucked his head below the gunwales; the brave cats, he thought, can leave them up. In times past, when men were so tightly packed together, the jokes came: "Man, you sure got some fine, soft buns."

"Baby, you feelin mighty good around the hindparts there."

"Turn my ass loose, motherfucker, and take hold to my dick. You know that's what you tryin to git to."

But now, nothing.

Blackman looked back at the life-jacketed coxswain. Young. White. Defiant. He'd laid aside his helmet and his hair sprayed out in the wind. Somehow Blackman found that reassuring. The engine of the boat began to boil and gurgle; the craft sought a deeper seat in the water. It seemed to slide out from behind the ship and was now unprotected from the sweep of wind. They swung wide under the bow of the ship and Blackman saw the island again. It looked different from the barge, larger, more menacing.

They headed straight in, the barge taking the waves head on, then shuddering, skidding, continued on its course through barbed wire that'd been cut. The planes kept coming, and Blackman could now see the ships firing. The barge line was crooked, Blackman saw, unable to keep below the gunwale. The explosions on the island were becoming louder. Blackman glanced behind him at the coxswain, saw that he'd put on his helmet, and grew nervous. Then he heard the first sibilant whisper of sand on the keel, just as the coxswain was reversing his engines, spinning his wheel furiously. The ramp plopped into the water without ceremony and bunched up; they ran out, crouching.

"Hit it!" someone shouted. "Spread out, spread out and dig in, what're you, the Twenty-fourth?"

"Yeah," a sergeant shouted back.

"Okay, dig in till I get back to you." The man ran heavily across the sand, hailing other incoming barges, a .45 held in one hand.

Downshore, a disabled barge, upended, lunged futilely at the sky. Marines fired from behind it. Three leaped from the cover of the barge, splattered through the water, and gained the beach, which now seemed vast to Blackman. The marines started across to the area where the kunai grass formed the start of land, the end of beach. Two ran abreast, grenades in their hands. The third marine ran straight up, clutching a BAR. A sharp, light rattle, like seasoned bamboo sticks knocking in the wind, came from the grass.

Was that a Nambu? Blackman wondered.

The two front marines, their momentum carrying them forward, pitched to their faces and lay still. The third marine stopped suddenly, as if he'd run into a chest-high wall, and fell hard on his back. He, too, lay still. Blackman began to sweat.

By midmorning they'd been waved off the beach and into the grass. Blackman was still sweating and wondering what he'd do if someone shouted, "Medic! I'm hit!" But the sounds of battle seemed to be bulging deeper into the island. He told himself, again, I'm gonna be cool in just another few minutes; I'm gonna be all right then. If they— the marines he now saw walking with apparent unconcern back and forth across the beach—could do it, damned if he couldn't. Even as he was watching, one marine clapped his hands to his face, blood like syrup oozing from between the fingers, and fell. Blackman wasn't sure he'd heard a shot; there were so many. But the other marines were shouting now and pointing toward a tall palm tree. Now they were firing at it, and others were calling, "Sniper! Sniper!" and they ran up to join in the firing. In the tree Blackman thought he saw an alien presence, one that did not conform to the color of the palms or the trunk. Something black fell from the tree, then a rifle, and then something familiar, splotched with red. The marines stopped firing and closed in; Blackman saw the flash of a knife and a marine swung around, holding something that could've been his own penis. Another tucked the sniper's helmet under his arm, another hoisted the rifle, stock up, on his shoulder.

They were walking away laughing when the first two mortar shells hit, without warning, shattering the cluster of souvenir hunters. All save one went down, and he, the marine with the penis, started to run in the deep sand, slid, fell, crawled, got up, and ran again. Blackman turned away from them; he wasn't going to hear them if they were alive; he wasn't going out into that shit, not for those guys. Medic all they wanted to, but none of this medic would they see.

Like the marines, Blackman didn't hear or see the next mortar rounds come in. In the middle of a moment of horror, when the first round blew apart two men in his company lying in front of him, the second came and he felt himself flying through the air and slammed down on the sand.

The steam was all the way up and the master of USS *President Adams* was anxious to get under way. He was under orders first to clear the beach of the wounded—an extra roster of doctors, both Army and Navy, and medics and corpsmen were aboard—and head for the port of San Francisco. On this trip the sick bay would be a virtual hospital. The seriously and critically wounded would be, the calculations said, small, and the *Adams* could handle them.

The *Adams* had left San Francisco several months ago with a division bound for Australia. From there to New Zealand, then New Caledonia and Guadalcanal, carrying troops to augment both the Army and the Navy's Fleet Marine Forces. Bougainville was the last SoPac stop this trip.

From the bridge, the master could see the first barges of the wounded making for his ship. He glanced at his watch; they'd get away in good time. Good time. He made his way down to the sick bay, to give an official presence, a kind of ranking welcome, to the wounded. The first casualty brought in was a huge black soldier, completely out, small clots of blood in his ears and nose. Nothing else as far as he could see. He patted the shoulder of a marine who held tightly to a Japanese rifle that lay beside him on his stretcher. "Don't let anybody take my souvenir, hear? It's mine, mine." The master patted him reassuringly again, then with a nod at the doctors, left and returned to the bridge; it was time to check the radio room and see if the escorts and whatever other convoy was going would be at Mutupina Point. There were times when the Slot could still be a very tough place to cross, not that he had any real fear of it any longer; hell, half the Jap Navy was at the bottom of the Slot. He began to hum "California, Here I Come."

20

CADENCES

"Here's a boy made Grade I in AGCT."

"What? Let me see? Jesus, you're right. And these boogies been screaming for officers."

"Been overseas, too. Bogie."

"Yeah, a medic, though . . ."

"Hell, he can be a sanitation, supply, morale, or infantry officer. That little old six weeks of training."

"Abraham Blackman. Humm. Purple Heart for the Bogie action—"

"Oh, you know how that one goes. Some one- or two-star goes to a hospital, walks up and down the wards, handing out Purple Hearts—"

"I know, I know, but if this kicks back, we at least had good reasons for putting it through in the first place. Overseas. Bogie. Purple Heart and Grade I. Maybe we better go back over this stack, Ralph, and see if we can't find some more nigger second-lieutenant material; we got some quotas to fill, man."

"Yeah. Where we gonna send this man?"

"The Ninety-second is the only boogie outfit I know of that's getting ready for transfer overseas. We can give this man some training—he's already had combat infantry—and have him ready by the time those boys leave Huachuca."

"Where's the Ninety-second on that priority list?"

"They're number two."

"Okay. We done created ourselves a second looey named Abraham Blackman, in the image of man."

"Better not let anybody else hear you say that last thing."

"Can't you take a joke?"

"Niggers ain't no joke, Ralph."

"So you like Florence and Italy very much," he said she'd asked him.

He'd answered, "Yes."

They walked without touching, although he wanted very much to touch her, glancing across the Arno at the old section, allowing their eyes to skip quickly over the bridges that'd been blown up. He liked the way the sun touched the old houses and walls and made them look like gold.

"Up there," she said, "is the Uffizi Gallery. Of course, the paintings are not there now. The war," she finished softly.

Now he took her hand without looking at her, afraid to read a No in them. When he did look at her, saying, "This is a lovely country, and you're lovely," he was relieved to see her smile.

"The war," she said again.

"No. Not the war."

He said he'd stiffened when he saw the pair of MPs. She must've felt it, for she gripped his hand harder. Then he thought, What had they to fear? This was her country; her family, Tuscans all, had lived here for uncounted generations. When the soldiers were gone, they'd be here for perhaps another thousand generations. Still, as they drew near the staring MPs, they communicated their uneasiness to each other. He squared his shoulders and said something jolly to her as they moved out to go around the soldiers.

"Hold it, soldier," one of the MPs said.

He had stopped, and feeling the girl tremble beside him, smiled and said, "It's all right."

"Let's see your pass."

He fished it out and was relieved that they both seemed to be studying it so intensely they were not looking at the girl. One of the MPs, with a gesture meant to assure that the pass would be returned, stuck it in his pocket. The other said to the girl, "Let's see your ID."

He had felt frightened and helpless. "She has no ID," he said. IDs were carried by prostitutes, and he knew they knew it.

"Card? Card?" she said, backing up. She knew what they meant. "What is it you're doing? I'm not a prostitute."

The MPs looked at each other and one said, "Jim, she ain't got no ID."

"Aw, she just don't want this boy to know she's a whore. No decent Eyetalian women goes out with these boys—"

"—C'mon, you guys, you—"

"Quiet, soldier! Not talkin to you!"

He had crumbled in his silence. What could he do? One moment he owned the world and the next he was crawling over it. She didn't know them; she didn't know what they would and could do to him. How in the hell had he got in this mess, anyway? For three months they'd sat in her parents' small apartment, not touching, hardly talking, just looking at each other, while her parents smiled at them, blessed them with an unspoken benevolence. This, this, was their first time away from her parents, their first time alone.

He felt ashamed because he was afraid. Trembling himself now, he put an arm around the girl. At first she stiffened at the touch of his arm, and his fear momentarily opened on a pit of horror. He saw the flicker in the MPs' eyes. Then she relaxed against his arm.

"Look," he had said. "She's not a whore. She's a nice girl. You've got it all wrong." He probed deeply for assurance that all would be well; he walked into the pale blue eyes he looked into, seeking, and therefore never saw the club that came down on his head.

He came to in the annex of a pro station. The girl was sitting beside him. "They said we can go now," she said. She tried to smile. "They said your head would be all right."

Outside they walked quickly, but he stopped suddenly when, after a long silence, she began to moan, and he turned and saw that she was crying.

"What is it?"

She did not want to be too close to him; she resisted his gentle pressure to put her head on his shoulder.

"They gave me an examination. They put me on the table where they put the whores and they—examined me." He heard her grind her teeth. She fished in her bag and took out a yellow card. She held it out to him. "Then they gave me this and said I should never be without it, or I'd go to jail."

The kid—Blackman thought of him as a kid, although he was only a year, maybe less, younger than Blackman—started to cry again. Blackman didn't want to say "Tough luck, kid," or "Look, soldier, don't make a martyr out of yourself." He touched the kid on the shoulder, but he didn't want to look up with tears in his eyes again. He shook his head and Blackman understood; he'd wait. That was his job, as Morale Officer.

Blackman stared at the kid's bobbing head. Why hadn't he just gone ahead and got the pussy, like most guys, instead of parading around with that bitch holding his hand? Christ, how many complaints like this had he already fired off? Fifth Army couldn't care less about cracker MPs busting black boys seen with white babes. And even if it did, the crackers from Down Home and Up Home both would keep on doing the same thing. Pussy, who's getting it, sure worries the white man to death, he thought.

A LOVE SO FINE (1974)

WILLIAM H. BANKS, JR.

Over thirty years ago, because of mutual friends, I was fortunate enough to have one of the greatest writers who ever lived review the first draft of the novel from which this excerpt is taken. I remember the writer saying, while tapping a well-used red pencil on my would-be first novel: "Well, there's a story in there somewhere. . . . You just have to decide which one you want to tell and be prepared for a lot of hard work. Get to know your characters intimately. Listen to them! When they're as good as you can make them, they'll tell the story that should be written. Above all, do a lot of drafts."

The writer was correct, of course. I took the advice and about three years later, *A Love So Fine* was published. This excerpt is what the main characters, Andy and Vivian, told me to write about campus turmoil in the 1960s. It was inspired by real-life conflicts (now long since resolved) between Columbia University and activists who were both students and Harlem residents. Though reviews of *A Love So Fine* were very good (*Publishers Weekly* called it "a beautiful depiction of the young, gifted and black in the 1960s"), it went out of print after a couple of years. In the year 2000, as a part of the Harlem Writers Guild fiftieth anniversary celebration, we started the Harlem Writers Guild Press and thereby gave new life to titles such as *A Love So Fine.* Who was the writer who advised me on the manuscript? Toni Morrison.

CHAPTER 5

The back pages of the next year and a half do not reoccur to me as chapters in our lives. Instead they seem more like captioned pictures. The memory of Vivian's first visit to my home on Thanksgiving of 1966 is framed in my mind as the four of us gathered around one of my mother's traditionally grand Thanksgiving tables. Christmas of the same year, I went to Birmingham and the picture is one of Vivian, her sisters, her mother, and myself trying to squeeze all of our grinning faces into the first photograph of Reverend Reed's new Polaroid.

Elsewhere, the memories are just as clear, but not as happy. President Johnson had cranked up the economy to almost a trillion dollars. Inflation accompanied this growth, but unemployment was low. Regrettably, however, Johnson had put more than half a million men to work in Vietnam. Virtually every third or fourth letter I received from my mother told me of the death of some young black man that I knew.

The collective head of young white Americans was turning away from the paths which had been appointed to them. They read their books, but they listened to their music. Dylan told them that the Old World, though dead, was killing them. The Rolling Stones told them that tomorrow was not a promise, but a lie. The Beatles made them grow their hair long and laid them down in Strawberry Fields to smoke the grass.

Young black Americans were beginning to see Dr. King's Nobel Peace Prize as a gilded shackle; there could be no peace without power. Many young blacks began to burn exploitative merchants as well as much-needed housing out of the urban ghetto. This was the "turf" that their older brothers had fought and died for in the mock feudalism of gang warfare. The blacks on college campuses saw this turmoil as revolution and, while still within the relative safety of the campus, they struggled with the values which they thought had deprived them of their blackness and, therefore, their power.

The three-piece suit became a straitjacket imposed by the insanity of middle classness. Brushed and straightened hair became the denial of black reality. Dashikis and Afros bloomed, and clenched fists waved above proud black heads like pennants in the winds of change.

CHAPTER 6

The tremors of the April 1968 eruption at Columbia could be felt as early as January. Columbia's SDS was being isolated from campus life both by its own design and by the smoldering impatience of the rest of the university. SDS became the only campus group which had the categorical hatred of all other campus groups, including the most radical blacks. (An early sign that even the "revolution" could not deal with racial antagonism.)

In response to this, the SDS began to inflict themselves upon the Columbia community. As their isolation grew, so then did their presence. Besides harassing Columbia's ROTC and Institute of Defense Analysis, the group blockaded and disrupted classes and dining halls. They picketed and shouted rhetoric everywhere. The boredom of the campus climate was being supplanted by the screams of radicals.

By late February 1968, our phone bills were so large from frequent long-distance calls that Vivian and I began writing each other a great deal. In one of her letters she described the scene at Columbia like this: ". . . Andy, I'm scared. These kids are crazy here. The white ones (mostly the SDS creeps) are everywhere touting that communist trash and taking away everyone else's rights at the same time.

"The athletes and white fraternity guys are starting to push the radicals around. It's the same old ethnic antagonism, of course—the all-American-boy types against the grubby New York Jews. But violent beatings and stuff can't be far away.

"The blacks here are almost as bad. The Students' Afro-American Society is in a shambles. The militants won the leadership of SAS in the last election. But, of course, that only proves they're the best showmen. To prove themselves as leaders and men, they're mimicking Rap, Stokely, etc. Anyone who doesn't go along with them is branded an Uncle Tom. That's the real danger, Andy, the manhood thing. If the leadership question is reduced to which group of guys has the real men then they may fight, too.

"But it seems that this thing about the new Columbia gym in Morningside Park is becoming bigger than all of SAS. A number of Harlem community groups want either a lot of free access to the gym or for it not to be built.

"This issue might give the rival 'leadership' (ha-ha) groups something they can both attack, either together or individually.

"The black women will continue to watch the guys and we'll go wherever the men go, I guess.

"By the way, when can I come to New Haven? I don't want you to come here, we won't have any peace. . . ."

CHAPTER 13

At 12:15 A.M. on the morning of April 30, 1968, the water flowing into the occupied buildings was shut off, as were the phones. Hours earlier the trustees at Columbia had decided to remove the students from the buildings. They had weighed the safety of the students in the balance with the value of order. And order was to prevail. All that remained was to wait for the deepest part of the night to catch the rebels in a nod.

Hamilton Hall's bust was to be different from the reclamation of the other buildings. The blacks had wisely negotiated their own safety, which the administration was glad to guarantee with Harlem sleeping only blocks away. The whites who had professed the communist affections as well as their disaffections with the university were to go down under the billy clubs. Their roots were miles away from the campus in different cities and states. And between them and their homes was a vast unsympathetic Middle America which would revel in having the rebels brought to their knees.

The rumors of the imminent bust led Orson and myself to a small second-story apartment across the street from Hamilton Hall. The apartment had been converted into a lounge by a disaffected but nonpolitical campus group called Warmth. The lounge was strewn with donated books, records, and clothes to which visitors could help themselves. From the front window we watched the rallies come and go with the tides of police harassment. By midnight, the last of the rallies and most of our strength had gone. And so we slept.

At 1:00 A.M. we were awakened by screams from the campus. There had been a lot of shouting and screaming that night, but this time the proverbial wolf had really come.

Below us we saw dozens of New York City buses crawl down Amsterdam in an almost perfect single-file procession. One by one they parked behind each other and waited. The insides of the buses were unlighted, but not nearly empty. We could see the orange glow of cigarettes whirl in the buses' darkness with the occasional flashes from shiny visored helmets, badges, and buttons.

"The armies of the night," Orson said sullenly. "This is it, Anderson. The end," he said, turning away.

The cops filed out of the buses, some forming preassigned details for the operation. Some squadrons poured down College Walk, which connected Amsterdam Avenue with Broadway. The rest of the police surrounded Hamilton Hall.

Screams were growing louder from the direction of Low Plaza, which was out of our view. But we could only think of the blacks directly across the street in Hamilton Hall. Many of the windows were lit and open, but the rooms appeared to be empty.

A group of about twenty white kids formed on our side of Amsterdam and started calling the police "fascist pigs." Half-hearted shouts of "commie punks" and "faggots" were returned by the police, but they stayed across the street in formation. A window was broken somewhere in the vicinity. With that, half of the cops broke their ranks and charged the scattering kids. The largely unathletic Ivy Leaguers were no match for the policemen, many of whom may have been star high-school athletes too poor to go to college. At least five of the kids were caught and either flung to the ground or clubbed. The sound of clubs on the bodies of the kids was heavy and low-pitched like the slam of a massive safe. But the sound of clubs against flesh carried up to us from the street as clearly as the shrill screams. The blood that puddled on the pavement had a bluish metallic tint under the neon streetlights. The police would wipe the kids' blood from the helmet visors as if it were sweat or dust and then continue the beating as if keeping time to a rhythm. Finally, a chunky helmeted cop with a gold badge ran to the center of the street from the Hamilton Hall side, yelling, "Never mind them! We got the colored kids! We're bringing them out! Come on, let's go!"

The police turned from the beaten kids without another stroke and joined the mass of cops swarming around the entrance to College Walk. Police buses with barred windows sped down Amsterdam Avenue to the entrance and rumbled to a halt.

The beaten kids had been rejoined by those who had gotten away and scores of others who had come to help and watch. Instead of taking the beaten students down the street to St. Luke's Hospital, their limp bodies were propped against buildings and cars. There they waited for the removal of the blacks.

Moments later unhelmeted black cops with gold badges and no clubs led the blacks out of the entrance to College Walk to the waiting police buses. Hoarse and shrill cheers rose from the crowd as the blacks walked the short distance from the entrance gates to the waiting buses.

By twos and threes they came. Weary, but erect. Visibly unafraid, but not defiant. They did not look for cameras to perform for, but few of them shielded their eyes from the floodlights and flashbulbs of the media.

Suddenly there was Vivian. Orson strained to see Lucy; she was just behind Vivian. Their steel handcuffs reflected the light in stark cold flashes, but their eyes were like summer stars. A moment later they stepped into the darkness of the bus.

FROM IN THE SHADOW OF THE PEACOCK (1988)

GRACE F. EDWARDS

Edwards joined the Harlem Writers Guild in 1970. *In the Shadow of the Peacock* was her first novel. Dr. John Henrik Clarke wrote of her in a review of the book, "She has the finest appreciation and expression of Harlem that I have seen since the great writing that Ann Petry showed us in her novel, *The Street.*" This collection contains the novel's vivid and moving prelude. (The Peacock is actually a fictional Harlem bar.)

Edwards went on to created the critically acclaimed Mali Anderson mystery series, and from there she has moved on to the writing of thrillers with her 2003 novel *The Viaduct.* Born and raised in Harlem, Edwards now resides in the Crown Heights section of Brooklyn, New York.

PROLOGUE

HARLEM 1943

Frieda heard the sound and ignored it. When she heard it again, she opened the window and leaned out. The noise had come from the direction of the avenue and was faint, barely distinguishable from the other, ordinary, night summer sounds. She strained for a better view but, as usual, was blocked by the fire escape.

She listened intently for the sound of a motorcade. Perhaps it was another Negro Freedom rally organized by Paul Robeson, or it might be Mayor LaGuardia again, touring Harlem as he had done a few weeks ago with the Liberian president. But those motorcades always came up Seventh Avenue and this sound, this noise, was different.

Directly below, she noticed that the loungers had given up top positions on the stoop, and strollers, in frozen attitudes, appeared to be listening for some extraordinary signal. Across the street, flowered, striped, and gauzy curtains were torn aside and windows were suddenly filled with wide-eyed, frightened faces.

She thought of climbing outside but wondered what Noel would say if he came in and found her on the fire escape in her condition. The thought was broken again by the sound, no longer an undercurrent but elevated high on the hot night wind.

It was heavy and pulsating, a roar rolling before the measured tread of an army on the march. It poured up the avenue, preceding the mob by several minutes. It engulfed the strollers and loungers, sucked them in and swelled the dimensions of the sound and the mob.

Fragments:

"Whut?? Whut happened, man?"

"Cop kill a Gee-Eye . . . outside the Braddock!"

"Naw!!"

"If I'm lyin', I'm flyin'."

It happened in Chicago, Texas, and Alabama, where a colored man in uniform, momentarily confused by the heady breath of patriotism, might forget himself and then pay for the lapse. But this was New York. Harlem. Where there was safety in collective anger.

"Mmm . . . uhm! Cats gon' raise some hell tonight, betcha that!!"

At first the bricks connected only with the streetlights and glass rained down in darkness. All but invisible, the mob, a solid sea of blackness, surged up the wide avenue. Their familiar badges of mops and brooms now transformed into torches that winked dangerously in the blackness. Then came the sound of heavy glass. Storefront glass. Pawnshop glass.

Frieda listened, thought of Noel, and left the window where she had crouched.

"Don't let nuthin' happen to him . . . don't let him be in the middle of this, whatever it is . . ."

She had abandoned prayer as comfort years ago, but her mouth moved anyway as she made her way down the stairs. At the bottom of the landing, she paused, breathing heavily, and realized that she had not run this fast in a long time. She sat on the third step from the bottom, feeling her breath leave and enter, leave and enter in fitful bursts, burning her nostrils and drying her mouth.

. . . calm . . . calm . . . quiet . . . don't . . . don't get too excited . . . not now, not now . . .

The lobby door swung open and she recognized Sam and Dan as they slipped out of the darkness of the street into the dim hallway. They moved toward the steps, huge, handsome young men burdened with the weight of several large cartons. Despite their size, they had the quick, quiet grace of street cats. They stopped when they saw her.

"Frieda! Outside ain't no place for you. Not tonight anyway!"

Sam turned to his twin. "Where this girl think she goin'?"

"He's right, Frieda. Things is jumpin' off out there . . ." said Dan as he surveyed the dim hallway for a place to stash his take. It was going to be a long night and he didn't plan to make more than one trip up four flights, no matter how much he stole.

The only available space was the shallow alcove behind the stairs. Anything placed there would be visible from the lobby, easy pickings for any common thief who had no respect for another person's hard labor.

"Hell with it," he sighed, turning again to Frieda. "Looka here now, you can't go outside. Not in your condition . . ." Frieda instinctively put her hand to her swollen stomach.

"Dan . . . I didn't mean . . . what's goin' on . . . you seen Noel?"

"Ain't seen nobody 'cept wall-to-wall busted heads. The bulls is swingin' and we swingin' right back . . ."

"But why? What happened . . . ?"

"Gee-Eye took a bullet," said Dan as he started up the stairs, "right here on his own turf. Didn't even git overseas and he a casualty. And they don't be dealin' no purple hearts for the Braddock."

Frieda was surprised. The Braddock restaurant had always been a lively, crowded place where people waited hours to taste Miss Beryl's West Indian cooking, but there had never been any trouble.

"Listen," said Dan, pausing as he passed her, "don't go out there. Them people'll run right over you, pregnant or not. You won't stand a chance . . ."

"Besides," said Sam, "we goin' back out. Give us a list. We'll git anything you want. . . ."

Frieda, silent, stared toward the door with wide eyes, trying, all at once, to absorb what she had just heard, and listening for some new sound.

"Girl, stop worryin'. Noel, he all right. Now look, you place your order while the gittin's good. We deliver. No money down and no monthly payments. Not even a slight installation charge. You name it, you got it—basins, bowls, basinettes, bottles, brooms, everything and anything for the pretty little mama . . ."

His sales pitch was interrupted by a howling scream outside which caused the three of them to recoil.

A woman was running, crying. "Help me git 'im to the hospital. His hand is nearly off!! Help me . . . !!"

"Who tol' 'im to put his fist through the goddamn window in the first place," someone yelled back. "Everybody else usin' garbage cans and this nigger wanna play King Kong. Oughtta bleed to death on gee-pee. Come on . . . but dammit, don't bleed all over my car!!"

The screaming continued down the block in a long, unbroken wail. Sam shook his head and started up the stairs after his brother. At the top, he leaned over the railing. "Don't you worry 'bout Noel. He all right. You just sit tight. Things is too hot out there. Just sit tight."

As soon as their footsteps faded, Frieda opened the door. The streets had gone from wartime brownout to total darkness. Only the lights from the hallways sliced the night at measured intervals. Broken glass covered every inch of sidewalk, and runners, heading for the avenue, performed strange arabesques as they slid and skated in and out of the dim yellow pools.

She left the stoop. Where was she going? Suppose Noel came from another direction . . . no . . . he always came this way . . . from the avenue . . . I know . . . I know . . .

She stayed near the buildings, clinging to the handrails as she crept along. The roar by now had become so sustained that she felt it had always been there, as part of the background. Except for the futile howl of a burglar alarm and an occasional scream louder than the rest, the noise reminded her of the waterfall back home in the south.

She remembered a night like this. A different kind of mob running wild. Heavy, sweating faces staring down the barrel of a shotgun. Retreating, retreating . . .

She shook her head . . . calm . . . calm . . . once I see Noel . . . calm . . . calm . . .

At the corner, two men carrying a huge orange sofa blocked her way. "You be careful out here, little girl . . ." They maneuvered their cargo around her with a series of grunts and groans and were gone. A woman followed in their wake with a portable sewing machine balanced delicately on her head. Graceful as a ballerina, she stepped lightly over the shards of glass and disappeared in the dark.

Eighth Avenue was devastated. Windows were smashed and locks and gates were bent into intricate curlicues. Broken furniture spilled from discarded cartons, and headless mannequins, stripped of clothing, lay amid the debris, their stark plaster limbs spread at impossibly obscene angles.

Frieda crept past Johnson's meat market and Clark's grocery store, two places where she shopped every chance she got because the mysteriously abundant displays of food reassured her and she didn't have to think about the war and shortages and red and blue ration stamps. Now, both places, side by side, appeared to have been sucked out by a giant vacuum. Even the refrigeration systems had been destroyed.

. . . how could this happen . . . they say somebody shot a soldier . . . what did he do . . . is he dead . . . what could've happened to cause all this . . .

She concentrated on the devastation to keep from thinking about Noel, but that was impossible. Somehow the two were intermixed. She felt cold standing there trying to think and not think.

The siren clanging above the roar distracted her and she saw, four blocks away, the faint glow as it spread in the dark, small at first, then seconds later, leaping in long orange tongues up the side of the building from the store below, bursting windows and buckling frames.

Frieda could hear the screams from where she stood. The tide, which had been flowing away from the wreckage, stopped in wonder. "Who the hell set that fire?? Don't they know there's people upstairs over that store? Who set the fire??"

The question shot out of the darkness, and the tide reversed itself. People began to run toward the building, careless of the glassy pavement, as the screams of the trapped rose above the roar.

Frieda was overcome with confusion, and the terror which had crept up her back by inches now immobilized her.

"What's goin' on?? What's goin' on??"

There was no answer as the mob pressed in. That is, she heard no distinct answer. Only the hollow scream that rolled out of the darkness as she was swept like flotsam into the tide that enveloped her.

<<<<<

A few blocks away, the "A" train pulled into the 145th Street station and Noel was asleep as usual. He slept with his head thrown back, but the rest of his six-foot frame was curled into itself protectively.

Al glanced at him. He did not understand how Noel could have accustomed himself so quickly to the fast pace of the city and, worst of all, the grinding noise of the subway.

Damn, he thought, dude in the city less than a year and he cattin' like he born here. Probably sleep right on through a Jap attack . . .

He poked Noel lightly with his elbow. "Rise and shine, man. This is it."

Noel was awake, instantly alert although his eyes retained a sleepy, languid look. He rose from his seat and suppressed an urge to stretch. Several women in the crowded car looked up from knitting and newspapers and put a smile on the edge of their lips just in case he glanced their way. But Noel was too tired to notice. He yawned and waited impatiently for the train to stop.

"Tell me somethin'," Al said, "what you gonna do when I catch my digit and quit this job? You liable to ride all the way up to the yards some nights . . ."

"You can hit the number all you want to," Noel replied, "but you ain't quittin' this job. This the most and steadiest money you seen in your life."

"That's only 'cause of the war," Al said as they made their way to the door with the crowd. "only 'cause of the war. And how long can it last? Six months? A year at most? Sam got a B-24 rollin' off the assembly line every hour. What them Japs got? They just a dot in some ocean nobody never heard of. How long can they last? This war could be over tomorrow, then what? Where we gonna be? Worse off than ever, that's where. . . . They singin' that stuff 'bout 'praise the lord, pass the ammunition and we'll stay free' don't mean us, you know."

They headed for the exit, both feeling the weight of the twelve-hour, six-day work shift. Noel only half listened as Al spoke. He was too tired to argue.

He thought: That's what happens when a man been catchin' hell too long. He never forget it. Then again, he ain't supposed to . . . keep 'im prepared for whatever comes up . . . but hell, he ain't the only one seen a bad time . . .

He knew what was coming and with effort tried to rechannel his thoughts. He had promised himself, once he and Frieda had gotten safely away, that he would live only in the now and think only of the future. But sometimes, in that hour of the night when the mind exercises the least control over the body, Noel would waken out of a deep sleep, bolt upright in the bed, arms and legs twitching frightfully as he saw the flames, smelled the terrible odor, and tried to close his ears to the screaming that never stopped.

Sometimes, Frieda would wake him. And they would wrap themselves into each other, silently, and remain like that until dawn.

. . . I'm tired, he thought, I'm just tired, that's all. Got enough grit on me to weigh a ton. Nobody'd believe that Navy Yard could be so dirty. They don't show that on them posters. A slip of the lip might sink a ship. Pitch in for democracy. Shit. They hired the women, old men, even the crippled folks, then they hire us. Give us the dirtiest jobs left over and swear to God they doin' us a favor. Ah, hell with 'em. Right now, the first thing I'm gonna do when I git home is hit the tub. Nice . . . warm . . . let Frieda rub my back a little.

But it wasn't his back that was bothering him. He relaxed, slackening his pace as he imagined the touch of her hands, soft and gentle, on his back, neck, and shoulders and, finally, sliding between his thighs in the warm, soapy water.

. . . sure be glad when the baby finally git here, awh, Jesus . . .

"Hey Noel! Man, you sailin' 'long like you in a trance," said Al, "bet you didn't hear a word I said. If I'd a known the dream was that good, I'd a left you on the train. Didn't mean to disturb you."

"Naw, man, naw. It ain't like that. Just thinking . . ." said Noel. He did not remember coming through the turnstile or passing the change booth. They had come to the stairs, and he was surprised to find the exit blocked, jammed with people.

"What's goin' on?" yelled Al, "come on, let's move. I'm tired and wanna git home . . ."

Al was short and powerfully built and had a scar near his ear which he had never spoken of to Noel. They had both arrived in the city on the same bus a little less than a year ago and wound up working on the same job and living in the same building.

Noel seemed quiet and easygoing, and it puzzled Al when he noticed that Noel never smiled and never talked about home, wherever that was. But, on reflection, he realized that he himself said very little.

"Come on," Al yelled again, "what's goin' on up there?"

"We trottin' fast as we can," someone shot back, "keep your drawers on, for chrissakes."

Outside, on the avenue, they stared in open-mouthed surprise.

"What the hell happened?"

"Look like the japs got us . . ."

"Man, where in hell alla these people come from . . . ?"

". . . and lookit all that smoke . . ."

They heard the story on the run—in distorted, disjointed chapters.

". . . they say she wasn't nuthin' but a trick . . ."

"So what? That don't give no wop cop no right to be beatin' on her . . ."

"Braddock'll never be the same . . ."

"Sho' won't. They done crisped the joint . . ."

". . . poor Miss Beryl . . . work so hard . . ."

"Heard the Gee-Eye come from uptown. Ex-Jolly Stomper . . ."

"Good God amighty. No wonder he so bad . . ."

"Took that cop's billy an' made 'im eat it. Them uptown cats 'bout the baddes' things on two feet . . ."

"He still alive? Heard he took three bullets . . ."

"In Sydenham, they say . . ."

"Naw, took the cop to Sydenham. The Gee-Eye up at Harlem . . ."

"Hell . . . make it to Harlem breathin', he make it all the way. They say 'what come in, if it's still squawkin', guaranteed it'll go out walkin'.'"

The crowd flowed in all directions, its members imagining in the dark confusion that anyone or anything flowing against them was a mortal enemy. The thick, wet smell and taste of blood was in the air and on the tongue.

"Hell gon' pay tonight . . ."

Al and Noel were out of breath when they approached the burning building. The heat radiated out and over the scene. Fire engines and yards of tangled hose cluttered the area. The crowd, uncontrolled by the few police still present, milled around the blaze. The flames had reached the third floor, and one by one the windows bulged from the intense heat, burst outward, and sprayed shards of hot glass on the crowd below. The people retreated momentarily, regrouped, and surged in again.

Noel pulled at Al's sleeve. "I'm cuttin' out man . . . wanna see 'bout Frieda."

He turned and nearly fell over the small boy standing directly behind him.

"Jim-Boy!"

"Please, Mistuh Noel . . ." The rest was lost in the uproar.

Noel crouched down, gathering the child in his arms. "Whut you doin' out here in all this mess??"

For answer, the boy clung to Noel so tightly that Noel could feel, almost hear, the wild beating of the child's heart.

Jim-Boy and Noel had a special friendship, begun last summer, when Noel had retrieved a ball thrown wild. "Better be careful with that traffic, sonny," Noel said, "them cars don't stop on a dime, you know . . ."

"—name ain't Sonny, it's Jonrobert but Granma call me Jim-Boy . . ."

"Well, it don't matter who calls you what, you go after that ball and traffic catch you the wrong way, you won't have no name at all, understand?"

Every evening after that, Jim-Boy sat on the stoop and waited, his small, round face dark and expressionless except for the lemon-yellow mark above his eyelid. When Noel appeared, Jim-Boy smiled, waved, and disappeared into the house. The house was now on fire.

"Where's your mama?"

"She down south, but Grandma . . . she . . . she . . ."

"Where's your grandma—"

The boy was pointing to the top floor. "—in'er wheelchair . . ."

Noel could not bring himself to look at the building. He concentrated on the boy's shaking finger instead and fought the urge to run, to push Jim-Boy away from him and run, screaming, from this nightmare.

. . . here it is all over again, he thought. All over again. He wanted to rock back on his heels and laugh and shout and demand of God how something like this could happen twice in the lifetime of one man.

But the crowd milled around him, pressing him in the awkward crouching position. He felt the boy's heart beating against his own and, unbidden, the nightmare memory flashed in, obliterating present sight and sound. He heard his father's cry, strange and strangled behind the sheet of flame.

. . . curse all you . . . curse all your . . . children's children . . . and the cursing dissolving into a screaming, gurgling sound, then nothing save the crackling flames. And he, unobserved, creeping upon that scene too late, not knowing it was his own father until one of the mob laughed.

. . . this'll teach 'im . . . this'll teach 'im. Wavin' that shotgun . . . Now. We gotta git that no count nigger gal . . ."

That no count nigger gal. Frieda.

The yellow flames tore at the body against the tree, until the man no longer looked like a man and even the tree turned a dull crimson in the dark.

. . . daddy . . . daddy . . . daddy . . . He had shut his eyes to keep from screaming, and the flames leaped orange against his closed lids.

. . . daddy . . . daddy . . . daddy . . .

"Noel!! For God's sake, you okay? You gonna squeeze the life outta that kid!" Al's hand shook him, and Noel blinked Jim-Boy back into focus.

"Your grandma—she in there and you ain't said nuthin' . . . ?"

"But I did, I did . . . oh! . . . I tol' 'em . . ." The child pointed to the firemen and his voice, drained by fright, sank to a whisper.

Noel felt the constriction in his own voice and spoke rapidly. "Now listen, boy. You sure nobody got her out . . ."

"She's still there, Mistuh Noel, I know she is . . ."

"Top floor?"

"Top floor . . . near the roof. Sometimes I go play on the roof but Grandma don't like it. She like for me to be in the street where she can watch me . . . but the roof . . ."

"How you git down—"

"Over the roof . . . I tol' you—"

Al followed Noel as he pushed his way through the crowd.

"What you gonna do, man? You can't do nuthin' . . . come back!"

Noel reached the core of the crowd, and a fireman working the pump yelled, "Keep outta the way!"

"There's a woman up there!" Noel shouted, "on the top floor!"

"No there ain't," another fireman replied. "They're all out. Out stealin' . . ."

The firemen's laughter was heavy and their movements, though co-ordinated from years of routine, were extremely slow. Noel was per-plexed. Then he realized that they were all drunk. Without another thought, he left the crowd, skipped over the scattered hose, and raced into the adjoining building.

"Where you goin', you crazy nigger??" yelled another fireman at Noel's retreating figure.

Al, who had been behind Noel, grabbed the man by his throat and lifted him off the ground. "Who you callin' nigger, motherfucker?"

His arm shot out like a piston and the fireman went down under the blows. The crowd had heard the word, and the roar reached a deafening level as the people surged forward. The remaining firemen grabbed hatchets, pikes, and picks and crowded together in a tight circle to de-fend themselves. The few policemen at the scene joined the firemen.

"Get back! Back, or we open fire!"

The order came from a red-faced sergeant, frightened into sobriety and frightened beyond reason.

Inside was black with smoke. Noel reached the third floor, smashed a rear window, and leaned out. On the fifth floor, he tripped over some de-bris and lost his footing. He went down and continued on his hands and knees until he reached the roof.

The two buildings were separated by a brick hedgelike barrier three feet high. He swung his legs over and the tar stuck to his shoes as he moved.

"Stairway's out," he said aloud to himself, surprised by the calm in his voice. "She watched him on the street, so she gotta be in the front . . ."

The smoke was thick and smelled of old rugs. He could not see in front of him but knew that he had reached the edge when he felt the sharp rise under his foot. The railing leading down the fire escape was warm. As he descended, the metal felt hotter. The entire right side of the building was now enveloped, and the heat hit Noel in the face like a hammer, taking his breath away.

He was suddenly fatigued and thought of turning back, when a loud roar went up from the crowd below. They had seen him and, not knowing his mission, shouted for him to come down.

Al looked up with tears in his eyes. "Noel!! You damn fool! Noooeelll . . ."

The name buzzed in circles.

"Noel . . ."

"Who . . . ?"

"Some damn fool name Noel . . ."

It reached the ears of a pregnant girl who had been caught in the crowd.

She began to scream and claw her way to the front. Two big men, who stood head and shoulders above the rest, spotted her and plowed forward, shouting her name.

Inside the burning building, the heat was not half as intense as it had been outside, but the smoke was worse. Noel crawled only a few inches before he touched the wheel of the overturned chair. The woman lay beside it.

"Lady . . ." He barely whispered. He wondered what he would do if she were dead. Bring her out anyway. Leave her. He could move faster if he left her. He wondered if he could leave another body burning. Smell the smell again. And who was to blame now. Last time, it was different.

"Lady," he called again.

With great effort, he placed his hand on her chest. His fingers touched a double-strand rope of pearls, rising up and down in slow, laborious rhythm. He found her shoulders and began to pull her toward the window. From the ease with which she moved, he knew that she didn't weigh more than a hundred pounds.

Out on the fire escape, he saw that he was right. She hung in his arms like a frail gray doll, eyes closed, breath coming in shallow, irregular impulses.

The ladder had grown hotter, and he wrapped the hem of the woman's dress around his hands before climbing up. On the roof, his shoes sank deeper into the tar and he noticed that it had begun to bubble in some places.

He made it to the second floor of the adjoining building before the flames spread laterally and engulfed the stairwell above him. The intensity of the heat staggered him so that the old woman nearly slipped from his grasp. He clawed at her shoulders and drew her up again.

A terrible crackling roar filled his ears, and he began to run blindly down the last flight of stairs. He did not know where he was. He felt the heat behind and around him. A tight band squeezed against his chest, emptying his lungs.

Suddenly, he felt the flow of air. Through the smoke and tears, he could make out a doorway and the street beyond. It was only a glimpse before he was blinded again by the smoke. He moved forward by sheer force of will.

A keen eye in the crowd noticed that the sergeant's arm was shaking.

"Hey sucker, whyn't you rest that piece?"

"Mebbe he need a little help . . ."

"He gonna need a lotta help . . ."

"Get back, I'm telling you!!"

". . . *been* gittin' back, motherfucker. All our lives, matta fact . . ."

The crowd, bold, pressed nearer. The white man was in their territory now. Familiar ground and strange circumstance. His uniform, soaked and stained, smelled of a mouth-drying, gut-turning, ball-shrinking fear. The smell floated out and touched those in the crowd nearest him and they were amazed. It was no different from the way they had felt every minute of every day of their lives as they floundered in unfamiliar, dangerous, downtown territory, their only protection being a flimsy waiter's apron or doorman's uniform.

The shouts and threats melted into thick, ominous silence. Everyone was waiting, but no one saw the bottle sail out of the darkness until it actually hit the sergeant in the eye. He got off a single, wild shot before he went down; the crowd, hungry in its hatred, seized the moment and closed in screaming.

"Git 'em, git 'em, giii . . ."

The roar reached a pitch too high to hear.

Switchblades and straight razors flashed open as axes and picks swung in wide, furious arcs. Fighters grappled and grunted and slipped in their own blood. Two firemen grabbed a high-powered hose and focused, scatter-shot fashion, on anything that moved.

The tremendous force of the water hit Noel as he staggered from the building, the flames at his back. The force struck him, catapulting him back into the heart of the inferno where the wall collapsed on him and his frail burden.

Frieda fell to the ground screaming. The twins leaped over her, tore the two men from the hose and tossed them, like sticks of kindling, into the flames. They watched as the flames licked at the rubber slickers, the bodies inside performing grotesque gyrations, snapping and jerking like dancers in a film gone awry.

"We oughtta fry all these motherfuckers . . ."

"Later . . . we gotta git this girl to a hospital quick."

Halfway from the scene, halfway to the hospital, the twins stopped. Frieda had made no outcry—she was beyond that—but there was a sudden convulsion. They laid her down in the shattered street, but before they could summon help, they heard a crying so faint they might have imagined it.

The twins looked at each other.

"How could she—how could anybody—bring a kid into this—this goddamn mess," Sam cried.

Dan turned away from him to kneel beside Frieda. He did not want to see his brother's tears. "She didn't know, man. She just didn't know it was gonna turn out this way . . ."

A CHRISTMAS STORY (1990)

ANDREA BROADWATER

Broadwater has been a member of the Harlem Writers Guild since 1993. Her critically acclaimed biography of Marion Anderson for young people appeared in 1999. Her short story, "A Christmas Story," published in 1990 in *Catalyst* magazine, was developed in the Guild.

Where *is* Melanie? I told her to meet me on the corner of Spring Street and Liberty. Spring and Liberty. I don't have much time. I have to make it back before Leotha misses me. Leotha is my mother but since I'm almost fourteen "Mama" is too babyish for me so I call her Leotha, behind her back. Leotha believes you should be with your family on the holidays, so hanging around with friends is strictly forbidden. We can't ice skate, go to the movies or do any fun things like that. On any big holiday, Jeff, Sissie and I are locked up in the house with a whole bunch of aunts and uncles and first cousins and second cousins and third—well, you get the picture. But I just had to break out today and show Melanie, my best friend, what I got for Christmas. This morning, under our tree, wrapped in gold paper and green felt ribbon was my new leather jacket. It's dark brown with pockets on the sides and on the sleeves and snaps up the front. It is *bad*. When I asked Leotha if I could leave for just a few minutes to show it to Melanie, she got all huffy and said no. "You can show it to her tomorrow," she said. "What's the point of getting a leather jacket for Christmas if you can't show it to anybody on Christmas day?" I asked her. "Jessica," Leotha said, "Christmas is more than presents."

Yeah, right, explain the Three Wise Men to me. I'm not supposed to get excited about a jacket I've been waiting months for. Well, I couldn't take it anymore so when she was busy basting her turkey and Jeff was making a lot of noise with his Nintendo games, I sneaked out the back door. I'm risking two weeks of being grounded here but some things are just too important to wait.

For a while I was even afraid that I wouldn't get a leather for Christmas. When I asked Leotha for one she told me that she just bought a jacket last year. Like I'm supposed to wear last year's jacket when all the kids got leathers this year. Well, not all the kids. Just the *real* ones. The play-doughs like Donna and Janet have the fake ones. The other day they tried to strut around in the cafeteria in their imitation leathers and Carl shouted out, "Hey Rudy, what do you buy play leather with?" Rudy shouted back, "Play dough." And we rolled. Melanie didn't get one yet but I told her it's better to wait and get a real one than to get a fake.

It's a good thing Christmas is here because Leotha doesn't buy anything between September and December. What we don't get during back-to-school shopping we won't get until it's sitting under our tree all wrapped up in Leotha's fancy gift wrapping. Last year she took a course at night just to learn how to gift wrap. Leotha goes all out for the holidays. Paper skeletons on Halloween. Heart shaped cakes on Valentine's Day. Even pistachio ice cream on St. Patrick's (and believe me, we are no way Irish). But Christmas is when she really goes off. Spray painted snowflakes. A big, fat Santa propped on our roof. And lights! Uncle Lemon said that if we put any more lights around the house, pilots will land in our back yard thinking it's the airport. It used to be fun when I was little but now it's all a bit embarrassing.

And you would think that the parties she throws at the Sunnyside Nursing Home would be enough. Every month she bakes or sews something for her patients there. "It's a shame," she's always saying, "no one comes to see Mr. So-and-so, no one visits Mrs. So-and-so. And they have children," she says. One time I said, "Maybe they're busy." Well, why did I say that. "They're so busy, Jessica, that they can't see their own parents," she snapped. "They're off on the holidays. Holidays are for families."

I never said anything else after that. I don't need her mad at me for what those people are doing. I get into enough trouble on my own. Like what I'm going to be in today if I don't get back soon. Uh oh, it's almost six. If I'm late for Christmas dinner, Leotha will kill me. But I don't see Melanie anywhere. Maybe I better head towards her house and catch her coming. I really don't want to leave after I told her to come and see my jacket. I am sure glad I got it. Can you imagine everybody with a leather jacket and not me? Everybody. You have to be careful with that word around Leotha. *"Everybody's* going?" she says. "There are a thousand students in your school and Mrs. Gregory is letting one thousand kids come to Sherry's birthday party?" Of course when I say everybody I mean the *real* kids. But I always have to watch what I say around Leotha because for somebody who's always in the holiday spirit, she can turn into a Scrooge in no time when it comes to me:

No R Rated movies
No spiked punch
No loud music
No TV during homework
No phone calls after ten
No blue eye shadow or purple or green

Believe me, she can really squeeze the juice out of life.

I still don't see Melanie but no sense turning back now. Her house is on Cherry Road, not much farther away. I've only been there a few times. Seems as if her father doesn't like people over too much. Her mother seemed nice though. Smiled a lot when I met her. Melanie's always saying her father did this or did that for her. Maybe he's just too tired for company. I wish I were wearing my sneakers. Since Leotha makes us dress up for Christmas, I got my Sunday pumps on which are hard to run in. But if I don't, I'll be late for dinner *and* the Christmas story. Every year, while he's carving the turkey, my father tells the Christmas story. Not the one with the manger and the star. The story he tells is about the Christmas his mother had pneumonia and he had to walk ten miles in the snow to the white lady's house his mother worked for just to get some old clothes and a half cooked goose that the lady had tried to cook herself but they had to cook it again when he got home and they all laughed about it but was glad to get it because it was all they had for Christmas, and if I miss that story my goose will be cooked.

Uh oh, that looks like Mrs. Douglas. I can't stop to talk to her now. She always wants to ask a million questions about my family as if she doesn't see us in church every Sunday. Sometimes I think she likes to use me as a double check. She can be so—Hello Mrs. Douglas. Merry Christmas to you too. Bye.—I know she's going to tell my mother she saw me but I can't worry about that now.

At last, Melanie's house. The gray and white one. Undecorated and unblinking. Just a plain old house which doesn't say, like ours, look at me, I'm weird. Hmm, I can hear talking inside. Wait, it sounds more like fussing. Maybe I shouldn't ring the bell now. If I tiptoe around the bushes, I can see through the window. *There's* Melanie. Uh oh, looks like her parents are having an argument. Melanie is just sitting there on the couch, though, with a strange look on her face. She looks bored or tired or both. Her mother seems to be doing most of the fussing. I can hear her but I can't understand a word she is saying. Melanie's father looks strange also. Although he's talking back, he doesn't seem mad or angry at all. He looks more disgusted than anything. Now her mother is waving her hand and moving towards him, only she's wobbling as if she's sick or something. Oh no! Her mother just fell out like somebody hit her but I know nobody touched her because I'm looking straight at them. Melanie and her father are just staring at her. They're not calling 911 or anything. Now her father is walking away like she's not even lying there on the floor. He's saying something to Melanie. Oh sweat. "She's drunk, *again,*" he said. "Merry Christmas." Melanie hasn't moved from the couch. She's just gazing at her mother like she's really not her mother at all but a stranger who just stumbled in from the street. Finally she's getting up and is going over to her. Oh sweat. She has her by the waist and is dragging her across the floor. It's a good thing her mother is small, I guess. Now she's laying her across the couch the best way she can.

She's looking at the clock now and is reaching for her coat. Oh, no, she's coming to meet me! I've got to do something fast. I can't let her find me here. I don't want her to know that I know. Melanie is zipping up her jacket. I've got to get out of here. I'm thinking fast forward but my feet are on pause. Come on Jessica, move! I'm racing down Cherry Road now as fast as I can. With or without sneakers, I've got to beat her to the corner. I can't look back to see if she sees me cause I can't lose the time. Come on, Jessica, you can do it. Just a few more houses.

Whew! I made it. My heart is beating triple time. I never ran so fast in my life. Oh here she comes now jogging up the street. I have to catch my breath and be cool. Can't let on what I just saw.

"Hi Jess," she says when she sees me.

"Hey Melanie. What took you so long?" I ask with fake annoyance.

She shrugs her shoulders. "I had to do something at home." Her eyes are blank behind her glasses.

"Oh," I say.

"I like your leather," Melanie says, rubbing my sleeve. "It's *bad*."

"Oh, thanks." I had to look down. I had forgotten that I was wearing my new jacket. Somehow it doesn't feel as good as it did this morning. And neither do I. "Well, I've got to hurry back," I tell her. No use asking what she got for Christmas.

"Okay. See ya."

I turn to leave but I can't. I can't just leave her there alone. "Say Mel, why don't you come and have dinner with us," I ask her.

She looks surprised. She has heard all of my Leotha stories. "Come for Christmas dinner?" she asks.

"Sure. I forgot Leotha said I could invite a friend." I am really lying now but what else can I do. I can't send her back home.

"Well, okay," she says.

"Great. It'll be fun." I look at my watch. It's after six! "Come on Mel, we're already late." I grab her arm and we start running down Liberty to my house. "You can see what else I got. Jeff and Sissie will bug you with their new toys but you can just ignore them. Also you'll have to meet dozens of cousins but don't even try to remember their names because I can't." I'm really babbling now, trying to sound glad that she's coming and I am glad that she's coming although I don't know what's going to happen when we get there. Leotha is probably laying for me now. I snuck out of the house after she said no and now I'm coming back late for dinner with a girlfriend to boot. I don't care what happens to me right now. I just don't know what I'm going to do with Melanie.

When I open the door the whole family is sitting around the dining table. All eyes leave the huge turkey and turn to us. Leotha jumps up when she sees me and marches towards us with her just-where-have-you-been look on her face. I wish I could tell her what happened but I can't. Melanie is standing right behind me.

"Hello, Mrs. Dunbar," Melanie says.

"Hello, Melanie."

"Mama," I say, trying to speak low so Melanie can't hear the begging in my voice, "I invited Melanie to have dinner with us. It's Christmas, Mama," I whisper.

She looks at Melanie and then back at me. "It sure is Christmas, Jessica, and Christmas is for family," she says. I feel really rotten. I've got to send Melanie home. I turn to tell her when Leotha says, "And how can I have Christmas dinner without my other daughter," and winks at

Melanie. "Sissie, put another setting on the table," she calls across the room. "You two hurry and wash up. Your father is starting the story."

"Come on, Melanie," I yell. We throw off our jackets and rush down the hallway. As we wash our hands with reindeer shaped soap, I am suddenly in the holiday spirit. Right now, I am very proud of Leotha, I mean Mama. Underneath the fake snow, elf hats and fancy wrapped presents, Mama really knows that there is more than that to Christmas. Today, right after Melanie, Mama is my very best friend. And that you can't put under a tree.

Merry Christmas.

FROM VOICES OF THE SELF (1991)

KEITH GILYARD

Keith Gilyard was born in Lutheran Hospital at 144th Street and Convent Avenue on February 24, 1952. He attended P.S. 90 before his family moved to Queens, when he was almost seven years old. However, for several years afterward, the family regularly came back to the neighborhood to attend Convent Avenue Baptist Church. Gilyard, a graduate of the City University of New York and a recipient of graduate degrees from Columbia and NYU, is a professor of English at Penn State. He received the American Book Award in 1992 for his educational memoir *Voices of the Self*, and he is the author or editor of eleven other books, including the anthology *African American Literature*. The following excerpt from *Voices* captures some of his memories—all crucial to his development—of his early childhood locale.

2

FIRST LESSONS

Some events come before the memory. Completely beyond the veil of vagueness. Just no way to recall. The only knowledge I have of the times came through eavesdropping. I could not deal with direct questioning because it was clear that made me a bug. Try to open up the past and I would get shrugged off with stares like roach spray. So I just kept listening and observing and drawing my own conclusions, trying to get a sense of what the pre-memory was all about. That's important to me because it's a part of life too and it's a lot like the wind, you know, you can't see it but it can kick your rump pretty good if it blows hard enough.

I hit the scene uptown in 1952 on a Sunday afternoon. I think I started out as a good reason for all to be happy, but there was a curious error on the take-home copy of my birth certificate. In the space where the name of the father belongs my own name was written in. His was left off the document altogether. That error, however committed, was my first omen.

I hadn't yet cut a tooth when I received omen number two. A fire broke out in our apartment. Started in back of the refrigerator. My mother detected it first, yanked my one-year-old sister out of her bed, snatched me up from the crib, and hustled on outdoors. She didn't bother to arouse her husband/my dad. It's a blessing he managed to get out on his own. I've always thought that was a horrible thing for her to do although by the time I heard the story, with the influence I was under, I felt he probably deserved it. And I have chuckled about the event on numerous occasions since. But at other times I have pictured my father lying dead in a robe of bright yellow flames and felt my own palms moisten with fear. There was no doubt something cruel going on in our little world.

The signs persisted like ragweed. Sad events that would be revealed to me in tale. The tale of the perfectly thrown frying pan, you know, it's more feistiness than I would like to see in a woman of mine. Sherry and I were, in one sense, beneath it all. Down on the floor knocking over and spilling everything. But we also assumed a role in the power play as it was we who became its center. Mama took that battle also; as far back as we can remember we had the distinct impression that we belonged to her exclusively. We were her objects of adornment and possession, always dressed for compliments. Pops could get no primary billing in that setup. When I think back now to my earliest remembrances I sense him only as a haze in the background. And even as I reel forward again and he begins to crystallize for me, it's quite some time before he appears essential. Moms, on the other hand, was ranked up there next to sunlight from the beginning.

That's a long way to come from Ashford, Alabama. Way down by the Chipola River. Little Margie, with stubbornness her most celebrated trait. Might as well whip a tree, they would say, if you were figuring on whipping her for a confession. At least you spare your own self some pain. And she was real close to her few chosen friends. If she liked you she could bring you loyalty in a million wheelbarrows. Labeled "good potential," she worked far below it. Skated her way through school. Folks have camped just outside her earshot for years whispering, "She's smart so she could do better if. . . ."

Ammaziah, though bright, didn't have a chance to skate through school. He had to work on a farm northeast of Ashford, going up toward the Chattahoochee. "He's just a plain nice man" is the worst thing I have ever heard anybody outside of our own household say about him. And I guess it would be hard not to like a big and gentle Baptist with a basic decency who could hold his liquor and had a name you could make fun of.

He liked to watch all the horses run and all the New York women too. Couldn't lick either gamble. He hadn't developed enough finesse for the big town. I know he tried hard at times but whenever he put together two really good steps irresponsibility would rear up and knock him back three. He couldn't be any Gibraltar for you.

All this going on around our heads. The big folks. Both destined to be enshrined in the best-friend-you-could-possibly-have hall of fame, provided they could keep each other off the selection committee. But they still hung out together. Hadn't fully understood the peace that can crop up here and there amid the greatest confusion. And right in the middle of 1954 came daughter number two. Judy ate well and slept a lot, then less, and grew to be a good partner to knock around with as we caromed off the walls of the Harlem flat and tumbled forward.

In the early reaches of memory events swirl about like batches of stirred leaves. No order or sequence. I remember we had two pet turtles. One had a yellow shell. The other's was red. We kept them in a bowl with a little plastic palm tree and tiny cream-colored pebbles. Sherry fed them and I poured in the fresh water. Well the turtles were a bit frisky. They often climbed out of the bowl and we had to overturn tables and cushions and chairs to find them. I don't recall how many times we went on this chase but it was all over one morning when they were found under the sofa with their bellies ripped open by rats. For a long time afterward I would associate rats with turtlemeat first, rather than cheese, which I guess isn't exactly a good start toward a high IQ.

So the turtles died early on. But I can't tell you whether that was before the back of my head was split open on the front stoop. There was a bunch of us out there preparing to run a dash down 146th Street. Victory wasn't the main thing in these races. Just please don't come in last or you would be the first one to get your mother talked about and everything. I had poor position inside along the rail next to this chubby girl, but as we came thundering past the front of the building I began to pull away from her. I was getting away from the last spot for sure when she reached out and pushed me down. My head banged hard into the edge of a concrete step and the blood started dripping down the back of my neck and I started screaming like crazy. Then I had to get shaven bald in one spot and look like a jerk so I could get patched up right. But that was better still than being last. I mean I had heard Pee Wee Thomas, who was in school already, tell Tyrone that the reason he was so slow was because whoever Tyrone's father was had to be slow too not to have been able to get away from Tyrone's ugly damn mama.

There was a babysitter we went to sometimes down on Seventh Avenue. Her name was Janine and she had boy-girl twins, Diane and Darnell, who were a few months older than Sherry. She was real nice and let us drag our toys all over the house, but whenever her husband, Butch, would come home early in the afternoon she would round us up quickly and herd us into the kids' room. We were under strict orders not to come out and of course we didn't. But she never said anything about peeping. The first time was at Darnell's suggestion. We crept up to the door and cracked it with the stealth of cat burglars. I couldn't see over Sherry and the twins so I crouched to the floor and never did get a look at the action. Darnell almost burst out laughing and we retreated to the farthest corner of the room. We sent Judy off to play with some blocks.

"What is they doin Sherry?" I whispered as I took a seat atop Darnell's wagon.

"Oh you so stupid Keith."

"Well I ain't see so good."

"Oh you just so stupid. Tell him Darnell." She and Diane were giggling.

"No you Sherry."

"No Darnell you."

"It's your brother. You 'pose to."

"I can't. I don't know for real."

"You know for real."

"No I don't."

"Then why you laughin?"

"I was laughin at you." And they all started laughing at each other. Then Darnell came and whispered in my ear: "They doin nasty."

"NASTY OOOOHNAS—." Darnell clamped his hand over my mouth. "You gotta be quiet Keith or we can't go no more."

I was quiet. And got to go many times before I decided, or was it Diane who decided, that we could do some nasty of our own. But we announced our intentions first and Sherry squealed and Janine gave both of us a spanking. Barely five, I was mad I had to wait.

I remember one Saturday we were coming home from the beauty parlor with my mother. I had on my cowboy get up, six-shooters at my sides. We were walking well up in front of her as usual, trained to stop at the corner. That morning, however, I took it into my head to go dashing across Eighth Avenue on my own. I think I saw my father but I'm not sure. I know I didn't look for any traffic lights. I tripped about halfway across and couldn't get to my feet again. I was struggling hard but my coordination had deserted me. Like scrambling on ice. There was a screeching of brakes and then the most gigantic bus imaginable was hovering over me. I still couldn't get the feet to work together. I was somehow yanked from under the bus, dragged the rest of the way across the street and, with my own pistols, beaten all the way up the block. It was a fierce thrashing and there were folks out there imploring my mother to stop. But verbal support was all I received. Wasn't anybody out there going to risk tangling with Moms. I have never fallen in any roadway, nor been pistol-whipped, since.

One evening we were digging into some fruit cocktail after dinner and heard a great ruckus out in the hallway. The cops were chasing these two drug addicts and they were headed for the roof. "They's junkies I know" said a man across the hall. Sherry had mentioned something about junkies to me before, but when the police paraded them down the stairs stark naked with their hands cuffed behind their backs it was the first time I had a good opportunity to see what they actually looked like. It was somewhat disappointing, however, for they looked just about like everybody else.

I was bringing a loaf of bread home from the store when I saw this gray dog getting his neck chewed off in a dogfight on the corner. I dropped my bag to go save him and was trying to push my way through the circle of gamblers and spectators when this huge man hoisted me up onto his shoulder. He thought I merely wanted a better view. Before I could figure a way to get down another man rescued the dog, though he was cursing the poor animal, and green bills changed hands around the circle.

Sherry had gone off to kindergarten and I decided to give Judy a sex change operation while our mother was asleep. I slipped her into a change of my clothing as I kept reassuring her. "You know it gon be more fun. You know it right?" She was properly willing. We had to roll the pants up at the bottom and her feet couldn't make it down into the toes of my sneakers but we could live with that. But we were dissatisfied with her hair. Such soft long braids. Boys get away with that now but not in '57.

"You gotta cut it."

"Then I be a boy Keith? I finish that I be a boy?"

"Yeah you'll be one. It gon be more fun too."

Scissors please. She wouldn't cut it in one fell swoop like I wanted her to do. She started nibbling at the edges. Tiny dark patches falling gently to the floor. As she became more relaxed, however, she began to clip at a faster pace and made a clearing on one side all the way to the scalp. I was urging her to clip even faster, "go head Judy go head," when Sherry came charging into the apartment, saw what was taking place, let out a long and soulful "Oooooooooh I'm gonna tell Ma," and ran into the other room to awaken her. I began to sweat.

"You made me" Judy accused.

"No I didn't and you gon git in trouble and git a beatin too."

"You made me."

"I did not."

"Yes you did."

"I DID NOT." I had to get loud to prove my innocence. Moms was already approaching fast like an enraged lioness and I wanted no part of her fury. She slashed me across the legs with her strap and cast me aside. I was getting off light. Unbelievably so. But Judy got it all.

Maybe I could have stood up for Judy, but by then I was taking the vast majority of the whippings in the household. So I guess I figured what the heck, Judy could stand to share some of the weight. She may have become a trifle less eager to pursue my ideas of fun but I was sort of growing bored with running around the house with her all morning anyway. I mean Sherry was bringing home books and fingerpaintings all the time and making kindergarten seem like the hip thing.

It was all right I suppose. Artwork and musical chairs and fairy tales. The biggest kindergarten thrill for me, however, was the chance to come home along Eighth Avenue unescorted. Sherry didn't get out until three o'clock and my mother didn't embarrass me by picking me up like I was a baby, so every day I had a three-and-a-half-block distance to negotiate as I pleased. Or at least I took it that way.

Some of us would go scampering along the Avenue. Anything could happen out there. The side streets were tall and narrow with hallways no more interesting than our own. But Eighth Avenue, well, that was the real world. We stuck our noses into the barber shop, the shoe repair shop, the fish market, the bars. The conversation was mostly baseball and whores. Willie Mays was clearly the Prince of Uptown, and the next best thing you could be was a pimp. We threw stones at sleeping winos and followed the vegetable wagon all the way down to 140th Street waiting for the horse to move his bowels in the middle of the street. Then we'd stay and watch the cars run over the large piles of dung. Every time a tire scored a bull's eye we'd shout "Squish" and spin about with glee. Don't let it be a truck that scored. Ecstasy. Sometimes we would run straight across 148th Street to Colonial Park to play tag and rock fight and climb the hill until the guilt snuck up on us one by one and then, each according to his conscience, we would begin to head for home.

From the very beginning my mother couldn't understand why it should take me over an hour to walk less than four blocks, especially when it meant showing up with my new jacket all muddy or my pants ripped at the knee, you know, the kinds of things you never notice until your mother points them out. And she made all her points clear with that belt. I tried telling her that the clock on the kitchen wall must be broken or something because I always ran straight home, but she wouldn't buy it. I eventually had to come around. And that's when I really got jammed.

There was a substitute teacher for our class one day and she didn't know the proper time to dismiss us. It must have been going on 12:30 and she was still reading us a story about Curious George. Our class was at the end of the hall, so when the other classes let out we couldn't hear them. There was no impatient parent to rescue us. The substitute just kept on and on about this wonderful monkey.

Finally she sensed something was wrong and asked us what time we were supposed to let out.

"Twelve o'clock" we chorused.

"Oh no" she exclaimed. "Are you sure?"

"We get out twelve o'clock" some of us repeated, as general chatter erupted about the room. Louis went up to her and said, "We get out when the two hands is straight up. That's twelve o'clock right?" She ran out of the room. When she returned a few moments later she was shouting "Hats and coats everybody. Hats and coats now. We're late."

Late was the last word I needed to hear. She couldn't let us out of there fast enough to suit me. I sprinted home as swiftly as possible, scaled the six flights of stairs in record time, and as I burst into the apartment out of breath my mother, as I knew she would be, was waiting for me belt in hand. She backed me up against the door with her stern voice.

"Haven't I told you about not coming straight home from school?" I caught my breath. I was sure glad I was armed with the truth.

"Ma we had a substitute. We had a substitute Ma and she didn't know what time to let us out. I ran all the way home."

"Boy don't tell that barefaced lie. I'll take the skin off your backside for lying to me."

"But I ain't lyin Ma. I ain't."

"Shut up boy! Ain't no teacher can keep no class late like that."

"But she was readin us a story."

"Shut up I said. Don't be standin there and givin me no cold-ass argument." She drew back the strap and I cringed in terror. I sidestepped her, as the first blow crashed against my thigh, and took off for the living room. She was right behind me. I dove to my knees and stuck my head under the couch. It was one of the several defensive maneuvers I had developed by then. I was always mortgaging my rear to save my head. Wasn't going to let anybody beat me in the head. Which was all right with Moms.

"You ain't accomplishin nothing by stickin that behind up there like that boy. That's the part I want any old how. I'll teach you yet about not payin me no mind." She had that talking-beating rhythm in high gear. You know how you had to receive a lecture to go along with your whipping. And can't anyone on earth hand out a more artistic ass whipping than a Black woman can. Syncopated whippings: Boy didn't I lash lash tell you about lash lash lying to me? Lash lash lash lash hunh? Lash hunh boy? Lash lash lash hunh boy? Hunh? I was always supposed to answer these questions although my answering them never stopped anything and sometimes made matters worse, especially if I was giving the wrong answers as I was that day. Although I was hollering my head off

I still managed to insist upon my innocence. To no avail. Lash lash lash I will break your behind lash if necessary lash boy. Do you hear me? Do you lash lash hear me?

I heard and I felt and it hurt both ways. After the beating I continued to proclaim my innocence. Only stopped when she became angry all over again and threatened me with more punishment. Afterwards I complained to my sisters on occasion, but it was weeks before I mentioned the incident to my mother again. She just gave me a warm smile and said, "I'll tell you something Keith. It all evens out."

Sibling rivalry stalked me from behind. I was getting intensive reading lessons from Sherry and had made progress to the point where I was ready to show off for Moms. We had her cornered on the sofa and I was holding the book out in front of me. Sherry was on my right, ready to help if I faltered, so I started reading something like:

"See here," said Don. "Here are blue flowers. We want blue flowers. Let us get blue flowers."

It was something along those lines, you know, and I was performing well. My mother was beaming and I had her undivided attention until Judy came out of somewhere, slid the edge of a razor blade into the side of my face clear to the bone, narrowly missing my eye, and ripped a deep diagonal clean past my ear.

Blood popped out everywhere. I spent what seemed like hours with my head ducked under a running faucet. Towels. Compresses. Mercurochrome. Bandages. Then my mother seized a high-heeled shoe and beat Judy worse than she had beaten me for almost getting myself killed out on the Avenue.

My little sister never apologized. In fact she used to taunt me about this incident as she was later becoming a favorite target for my aggression. No matter what I did to her. Kick her, trip her, whatever. She would just keep repeating, "So I cut you in the face."

"Do it again" I would retort most angrily.

"I did it already."

"I dare you to do it again. I'll push you out the window."

"No you won't."

"Yes I will."

"No you won't."

"I will so."

"Then I'll cut you in your face again."

"Then come on. Come on if you still think you so big and bad."

"I ain't scared."

"Come on then sucker."

"I'll cut you right in the face again."

"What you waitin for then fraidy cat?"

"I did it already."

She was about as mean a three year old as you will ever find.

Actually I had my hardest battles with Sherry. She was good for teaching me things but when her mood shifted I had to watch out. She gave me my next permanent scar by pressing a hot steam iron to the back of my hand. Burned off a circle of flesh. I later shattered a light bulb against the bridge of her nose but she escaped unharmed. I think you can say we were taking this rivalry thing a bit too seriously.

At times my sisters would double-team me. We were heavily into words now and when my sisters discovered that to stifle mine was the best weapon they could use against me, it led to some of the unhappiest moments I can recall. They had found my fledgling sensitivity, clutched it about the windpipe, and squeezed. They teased me and baited me but whenever I began to reply they would shout as loudly as they could to obscure what I was saying. Their favorite lines were "Am sam sam sam sam. Am sam sam sam sam." As soon as I parted my lips they would start chanting and send me straight to tears. I would wipe aside the water, swallow hard to compose myself, and fall apart all over again. I could rumble and accept insults but I couldn't ever deal with not being allowed to speak. Their am sam curse was too devastating. I had neither the sense to ignore nor the strength to attack.

I don't recall much about a whole pregnancy, but when my mother left for the hospital one night in June of '58 there was only a single wish ringing in my consciousness: BOY. And I knew I would get a brother because it was the only thing that could even the score. He would be my guarantee to be heard because wasn't anybody going to brainwash little brother but me. I alone would teach him how to bound down the stairs two at a time and sneak to the park. And he'd be the real thing. No imitation like Judy. No turncoat like Sherry. I knew I would have to handle his fights for him but that was fine as long as he listened to me and helped me beat the am sam curse. We'd start our own "Ooma booma booma booma" or something like that. Fix them good.

When the phone rang my grandmother, who was up from Alabama, reached it first. I watched her smile as she spoke. As she turned toward me she was saying, "Yeah he standin right here. You know he can't wait to hear the news." She handed me the receiver.

"Hi Ma."

"Hi" she answered dreamily. "You finally have another sister."

I was condemned. I dropped the receiver and walked out of the room in a daze. Debra Lynn showed up a few days later with a head full of wild hair. She was a beauty, and from that day to this she has never been out of my heart. But she couldn't be a brother.

I had just one more summer to pass on 146th Street. Farmer Gray cartoons in the morning. The Jocko Show in the afternoon. Sit down and rock Debra Lynn for a spell or jump up and go wild to the rhythm of my first favorite record, "Tequila," by the Champs. And I was beginning to tread more lightly about the apartment, trying to avoid all scars and bruised feelings, overjoyed at any opportunity to go outside. Just give me the playground or send me to the corner grocery so I can squeeze in as much Eighth Avenue as possible before I have to hurry back. I couldn't shoot a basketball high enough to make a goal but I began learning how to dribble and saw my first pair of dead wide open eyes on a fat man lying amid a crowd in front of the fish market with a thin jagged line of blood across the width of his throat.

On Sundays, for religion, we went up on the hill. Skipping along the hexagon-shaped tile in Colonial Park. Darting up the steps to Edgecomb Avenue. Stopping in the candy store on St. Nicholas to load up. Leaning forward for leverage to finish the climb up to the church. I was always impressed by this particular house of the Lord. Tremendous gray and white cinder blocks. Polished maple pews in the main service room. Red carpet, stained windows, and gigantic organ pipes. And the Lord, he owned the best singers available. There was nothing like a gorgeous soprano wailing and sweating under influence of the spirit and a hot wig. There were always old women with blue dye in their hair shrieking and swooning during the sermon as folks around them grabbed hold of them while exclaiming, "Yes Lord. I see you done come to us." With women like that falling out in droves you had to believe. And Pops was up in the front row with the rest of the deacons. A broad-shouldered frame in a gray or blue suit. Sometimes wore white gloves to serve communion. He always winked at us when he passed by.

The first grade brought a teacher, Miss Novick, who we thought was the top genius on the planet. She was going to turn us all into little scientists she would say. And there was invariably one experiment or another for us to observe.

She placed a glass jar, two small candles in holders, and a box of matches on her desk. She raised the jar and candles over her head and waved them slowly for all to see.

"I have here a glass jar and two simple candles. Can everyone see them?"

"Yes Miss Novick" we replied, speaking as everyone.

"See them James?"

"Yeah."

"See them Karen?"

"Uh hunh."

"See them John?"

"I sees it."

"Okay." She returned the objects to her desk, lit the candles and held them overhead. Our eyes were transfixed with magic show expectations.

"Now the candles are lit. You see? Rosanne? Ryan? Keith?" I gave a nod of affirmation. Then she lowered the candles to the desk and lifted the jar, upside down, as we inched forward in our seats.

"Now who can tell me what will happen if I set this jar down over one of these flames? Can anyone tell me? James?" He could not. He was smart but stumped. Sat looking dumb with his face greased and his eyes bulged and his index finger glued to his chin.

"How about you Barbara?"

"You gonna catch the des' on fire Miss Novick."

"YEAAHHHHHHHH. . . ."

"No, little scientists. No. No. No. We will not harm the desk. Anyone else? . . . No? . . . Well let us observe."

She placed the jar over one of the candles and we stared eagerly at both flames until the one inside the jar died out. Miss Novick surveyed our puzzled faces and smiled.

"Now why did that happen class?"

"You mean why it went out?"

"Yes Harold. Can you tell me why?"

"Because you put that jar on there. You made it go out Miss Novick. You did it."

"Sure Harold. But how could I do it with only the jar?"

"I don't know. Was there some water in there?"

"There wasn't Harold. We all looked at the jar together, remember?"

"Oh yeah."

"Anyone else?" Miss Novick was extremely patient and thoroughly flustered us all before giving us our first formal explanation concerning oxygen.

I liked the prospect of becoming a resident scientist up at P.S. 90 (strange what faith I had in the public school system up there), and when the announcement came later that fall that we were moving into a house out in Queens I was, at first, a bit disheartened. I knew there were scientific experiments elsewhere but I wasn't so sure I could get another Miss Novick or even more important, in a related field, another Eighth Avenue.

I wasn't anti-Queens; all I knew about the place was that it was over a bridge somewhere. But I surely had no beef with Harlem. I didn't recoil at the sight of its streets as I would at other times later in life. I had no sense of society being so terrible. I was there and I fit.

On another level, however, I guess I did welcome a chance to leave the apartment I was associating more and more with misunderstanding and pain. *House* sounded like more space to stay out of the way of others.

So at the age of six it was time for a crossing. My young mind poised for any game that came along. Could play the middle or skirt the fringe as I saw fit. Just come out stepping light and easy, you know, and if it gets hectic remember to cover in the clinch. The point was to hold the defense together while all about me from complex fabrics of frustration and rejection and sensitivity and conflict and hope and loneliness and resignation and reticence and wonderment and bewilderment and romantic notions and romantic disappointments, from all this and more, the imposing offense was being woven.

And the bridge bowed gracefully and beckoned. Bore me upon its majestic back and arched me high above the cold and swirling dark waters of that November toward another shore, and another truth, which all should know: Most times a bridge is just another two-way street.

TONI MORRISON

An internationally revered writer and Noble Prize winner, Morrison con-
siders *Jazz* and her latest book, *Love,* to be her most perfect novels. Set
in Harlem in the 1940s, *Jazz* has improvisation and rhythm, as well as
intense emotional volume and pitch. Ms. Morrison herself selected this
chapter for inclusion in *Beloved Harlem.*

Sth, I know that woman. She used to live with a flock of birds on Lenox
Avenue. Know her husband, too. He fell for an eighteen-year-old girl
with one of those deepdown, spooky loves that made him so sad and
happy he shot her just to keep the feeling going. When the woman, her
name is Violet, went to the funeral to see the girl and to cut her dead
face they threw her to the floor and out of the church. She ran, then,
through all that snow, and when she got back to her apartment she took
the birds from their cages and set them out the windows to freeze or fly,
including the parrot that said, "I love you."

The snow she ran through was so windswept she left no footprints
in it, so for a time nobody knew exactly where on Lenox Avenue she
lived. But, like me, they knew who she was, who she had to be, because
they knew that her husband, Joe Trace, was the one who shot the girl.
There was never anyone to prosecute him because nobody actually saw
him do it, and the dead girl's aunt didn't want to throw money to helpless lawyers or laughing cops when she knew the expense wouldn't improve anything. Besides, she found out that the man who killed her
niece cried all day and for him and for Violet that is as bad as jail.

Regardless of the grief Violet caused, her name was brought up at
the January meeting of the Salem Women's Club as someone needing
assistance, but it was voted down because only prayer—not money—
could help her now, because she had a more or less able husband (who
needed to stop feeling sorry for himself), and because a man and his
family on 134th Street had lost everything in a fire. The Club mobilized

itself to come to the burnt-out family's aid and left Violet to figure out on her own what the matter was and how to fix it.

She is awfully skinny, Violet; fifty, but still good looking when she broke up the funeral. You'd think that being thrown out the church would be the end of it—the shame and all—but it wasn't. Violet is mean enough and good looking enough to think that even without hips or youth she could punish Joe by getting herself a boyfriend and letting him visit in her own house. She thought it would dry his tears up and give her some satisfaction as well. It could have worked, I suppose, but the children of suicides are hard to please and quick to believe no one loves them because they are not really here.

Anyway, Joe didn't pay Violet or her friend any notice. Whether she sent the boyfriend away or whether he quit her, I can't say. He may have come to feel that Violet's gifts were poor measured against his sympathy for the brokenhearted man in the next room. But I do know that mess didn't last two weeks. Violet's next plan—to fall back in love with her husband—whipped her before it got on a good footing. Washing his handkerchiefs and putting food on the table before him was the most she could manage. A poisoned silence floated through the rooms like a big fishnet that Violet alone slashed through with loud recriminations. Joe's daytime listlessness and both their worrying nights must have wore her down. So she decided to love—well, find out about—the eighteen-year-old whose creamy little face she tried to cut open even though nothing would have come out but straw.

Violet didn't know anything about the girl at first except her name, her age, and that she was very well thought of in the legally licensed beauty parlor. So she commenced to gather the rest of the information. Maybe she thought she could solve the mystery of love that way. Good luck and let me know.

She questioned everybody, starting with Malvonne, an upstairs neighbor—the one who told her about Joe's dirt in the first place and whose apartment he and the girl used as a love nest. From Malvonne she learned the girl's address and whose child she was. From the legally licensed beauticians she found out what kind of lip rouge the girl wore; the marcelling iron they used on her (though I suspect that girl didn't need to straighten her hair); the band the girl liked best (Slim Bates' Ebony Keys which is pretty good except for his vocalist who must be his woman since why else would he let her insult his band). And when she was shown how, Violet did the dance steps the dead girl used to do. All that. When she had the steps down pat—her knees just so—everybody, including the ex-boyfriend, got disgusted with her and I can see why. It was like watching an old street pigeon pecking the crust of a sardine sandwich the cats left behind. But Violet was nothing but persistent and no wisecrack or ugly look stopped her. She haunted PS-89 to talk to teachers who knew the girl. JHS-139 too because the girl went there before trudging way over to Wadleigh, since there were no high schools in her district a colored girl could attend. And for a long time she pestered the girl's aunt, a dignified lady who did fine work off and on in the garment district, until the aunt broke down and began to look forward to Violet's visits for a chat about youth and misbehavior. The aunt showed all the dead girl's things to Violet and it became clear to her (as it was to me) that this niece had been hardheaded as well as sly.

One particular thing the aunt showed her, and eventually let Violet keep for a few weeks, was a picture of the girl's face. Not smiling, but alive at least and very bold. Violet had the nerve to put it on the fireplace mantel in her own parlor and both she and Joe looked at it in bewilderment.

It promised to be a mighty bleak household, what with the birds gone and the two of them wiping their cheeks all day, but when spring came to the City Violet saw, coming into the building with an Okeh record under her arm and carrying some stewmeat wrapped in butcher paper, another girl with four marcelled waves on each side of her head. Violet invited her in to examine the record and that's how that scandalizing threesome on Lenox Avenue began. What turned out different was who shot whom.

I'm crazy about this City.

Daylight slants like a razor cutting the buildings in half. In the top half I see looking faces and it's not easy to tell which are people, which the work of stonemasons. Below is shadow where any blasé thing takes place: clarinets and lovemaking, fists and the voices of sorrowful women. A city like this one makes me dream tall and feel in on things. Hep. It's the bright steel rocking above the shade below that does it. When I look over strips of green grass lining the river, at church steeples and into the cream-and-copper halls of apartment buildings, I'm strong.

Alone, yes, but top-notch and indestructible—like the City in 1926 when all the wars are over and there will never be another one. The people down there in the shadow are happy about that. At last, at last, everything's ahead. The smart ones say so and people listening to them and reading what they write down agree: Here comes the new. Look out. There goes the sad stuff. The bad stuff. The things-nobody-could-help stuff. The way everybody was then and there. Forget that. History is over, you all, and everything's ahead at last. In halls and offices people are sitting around thinking future thoughts about projects and bridges and fast-clicking trains underneath. The A&P hires a colored clerk. Big-legged women with pink kitty tongues roll money into green tubes for later on; then they laugh and put their arms around each other. Regular people corner thieves in alleys for quick retribution and, if he is stupid and has robbed wrong, thieves corner him too. Hoodlums hand out goodies, do their best to stay interesting, and since they are being watched for excitement, they pay attention to their clothes and the carving out of insults. Nobody wants to be an emergency at Harlem Hospital but if the Negro surgeon is visiting, pride cuts down the pain. And although the hair of the first class of colored nurses was declared unseemly for the official Bellevue nurse's cap, there are thirty-five of them now—all dedicated and superb in their profession.

Nobody says it's pretty here; nobody says it's easy either. What it is is decisive, and if you pay attention to the street plans, all laid out, the City can't hurt you.

I haven't got any muscles, so I can't really be expected to defend myself. But I do know how to take precaution. Mostly it's making sure no one knows all there is to know about me. Second, I watch everything and everyone and try to figure out their plans, their reasonings, long before they do. You have to understand what it's like, taking on a big city: I'm exposed to all sorts of ignorance and criminality. Still, this is the only life for me. I like the way the City makes people think they can do what they want and get away with it. I see them all over the place: wealthy whites, and plain ones too, pile into mansions decorated and redecorated by black women richer than they are, and both are pleased with the spectacle of the other. I've seen the eyes of black Jews, brimful of pity for everyone not themselves, graze the food stalls and the ankles of loose women, while a breeze stirs the white plumes on the helmets of the UNIA men. A colored man floats down out of the sky blowing a saxophone, and below him, in the space between two buildings, a girl talks earnestly to a man in a straw hat. He touches her lip to remove a bit of something there. Suddenly she is quiet. He tilts her chin up. They stand there. Her grip on her purse slackens and her neck makes a nice curve. The man puts his hand on the stone wall above her head. By the way his jaw moves and the turn of his head I know he has a golden tongue. The sun sneaks into the alley behind them. It makes a pretty picture on its way down.

Do what you please in the City, it is there to back and frame you no matter what you do. And what goes on on its blocks and lots and side streets is anything the strong can think of and the weak will admire. All you have to do is heed the design—the way it's laid out for you, considerate, mindful of where you want to go and what you might need tomorrow.

I lived a long time, maybe too much, in my own mind. People say I should come out more. Mix. I agree that I close off in places, but if you have been left standing, as I have, while your partner overstays at another appointment, or promises to give you exclusive attention after supper, but is falling asleep just as you have begun to speak—well, it can make you inhospitable if you aren't careful, the last thing I want to be.

Hospitality is gold in this City; you have to be clever to figure out how to be welcoming and defensive at the same time. When to love something and when to quit. If you don't know how, you can end up out of control or controlled by some outside thing like that hard case last winter. Word was that underneath the good times and the easy money something evil ran the streets and nothing was safe—not even the dead. Proof of this being Violet's outright attack on the very subject of a funeral ceremony. Barely three days into 1926. A host of thoughtful people looked at the signs (the weather, the number, their own dreams) and believed it was the commencement of all sorts of destruction. That the scandal was a message sent to warn the good and rip up the faithless. I don't know who was more ambitious—the doomsayers or Violet—but it's hard to match the superstitious for great expectations.

Armistice was seven years old the winter Violet disrupted the funeral, and veterans on Seventh Avenue were still wearing their army-issue greatcoats, because nothing they can pay for is as sturdy or hides so well what they had boasted of in 1919. Eight years later, the day before Violet's misbehavior, when the snow comes it sits where it falls on Lexington and Park Avenue too, and waits for horse-drawn wagons to tamp it down when they deliver coal for the furnaces cooling down in the cellars. Up in those big five-story apartment buildings and the narrow wooden houses in between people knock on each other's doors to see if anything is needed or can be had. A piece of soap? A little kerosene? Some fat, chicken or pork, to brace the soup one more time? Whose husband is getting ready to go see if he can find a shop open? Is there time to add turpentine to the list drawn up and handed to him by the wives?

Breathing hurts in weather that cold, but whatever the problems of being winterbound in the City they put up with them because it is worth anything to be on Lenox Avenue safe from fays and the things they think up; where the sidewalks, snow-covered or not, are wider than the main roads of the towns where they were born and perfectly ordinary people can stand at the stop, get on the streetcar, give the man the nickel, and ride anywhere you please, although you don't please to go many places because everything you want is right where you are: the church, the store, the party, the women, the men, the postbox (but no high schools), the furniture store, street newspaper vendors, the bootleg houses (but no banks), the beauty parlors, the barbershops, the juke joints, the ice wagons, the rag collectors, the pool halls, the open food markets, the number runner, and every club, organization, group, order, union, society, brotherhood, sisterhood or association imaginable. The service trails, of course, are worn, and there are paths slick from the forays of members of one group into the territory of another where it is believed something curious or thrilling lies. Some gleaming, cracking, scary stuff. Where you can pop the cork and put the cold glass mouth right up to your own. Where you can find danger or be it; where you can fight till you drop and smile at the knife when it misses and when it doesn't. It makes you wonderful just to see it. And just as wonderful to know that back in one's own building there are lists drawn up by the wives for the husband hunting an open market, and that sheets impossible to hang out in snowfall drape kitchens like the curtains of Abyssinian Sunday-school plays.

The young are not so young here, and there is no such thing as midlife. Sixty years, forty, even, is as much as anybody feels like being bothered with. If they reach that, or get very old, they sit around looking at goings-on as though it were a five-cent triple feature on Saturday. Otherwise they find themselves butting in the business of people whose names they can't even remember and whose business is none of theirs. Just to hear themselves talk and the joy of watching the distressed faces of those listening. I've known a few exceptions. Some old people who didn't slap the children for being slappable; who saved that strength in case it was needed for something important. A last courtship full of smiles and little presents. Or the dedicated care of an old friend who might not make it through without them. Sometimes they concentrated on making sure the person they had shared their long lives with had cheerful company and the necessary things for the night.

But up there on Lenox, in Violet and Joe Trace's apartment, the rooms are like the empty birdcages wrapped in cloth. And a dead girl's face has become a necessary thing for their nights. They each take turns to throw off the bedcovers, rise up from the sagging mattress and tiptoe over cold linoleum into the parlor to gaze at what seems like the only living presence in the house: the photograph of a bold, unsmiling girl staring from the mantelpiece. If the tiptoer is Joe Trace, driven by lone-liness from his wife's side, then the face stares at him without hope or regret and it is the absence of accusation that wakes him from his sleep hungry for her company. No finger points. Her lips don't turn down in judgment. Her face is calm, generous and sweet. But if the tiptoer is Vi-olet the photograph is not that at all. The girl's face looks greedy, haughty and very lazy. The cream-at-the-top-of-the-milkpail face of someone who will never work for anything; someone who picks up things lying on other people's dressers and is not embarrassed when found out. It is the face of a sneak who glides over to your sink to rinse the fork you have laid by her plate. An inward face—whatever it sees is its own self. You are there, it says, because I am looking at you.

Two or three times during the night, as they take turns to go look at that picture, one of them will say her name. Dorcas? Dorcas. The dark rooms grow darker: the parlor needs a struck match to see the face. Be-yond are the dining room, two bedrooms, the kitchen—all situated in the middle of the building so the apartment's windows have no access to the moon or the light of a street lamp. The bathroom has the best light since it juts out past the kitchen and catches the afternoon rays. Vi-olet and Joe have arranged their furnishings in a way that might not re-mind anybody of the rooms in *Modern Homemaker* but it suits the habits of the body, the way a person walks from one room to another without bumping into anything, and what he wants to do when he sits down. You know how some people put a chair or a table in a corner where it looks nice but nobody in the world is ever going to go over to it, let alone sit down there? Violet didn't do that in her place. Everything is put where a person would like to have it, or would use or need it. So the dining room doesn't have a dining table with funeral-parlor chairs. It has big deep-down chairs and a card table by the window covered with jade, dracena and doctor plants until they want to have card games or play tonk between themselves. The kitchen is roomy enough to accommodate four people eating or give a customer plenty legroom while Violet does her hair. The front room, or parlor, is not wasted either, waiting for a wedding reception to be worthy of. It has birdcages and mirrors for the birds to look at themselves in, but now, of course, there are no birds, Violet having let them out on the day she went to Dorcas' funeral with a knife. Now there are just empty cages, the lonely mirrors glancing back at them. As for the rest, it's a sofa, some carved wooden chairs with small tables by them so you can put your coffee cup or a dish of ice cream down in front of you, or if you want to read the paper, you can do it easy without messing up the folds. The mantel over the fireplace used to have shells and pretty-colored stones, but all of that is gone now and only the picture of Dorcas Manfred sits there in a silver frame waking them up all night long.

Such restless nights make them sleep late, and Violet has to hurry to get a meal prepared before getting ready for her round of heads. Having a knack for it, but no supervised training, and therefore no license to do it, Violet can only charge twenty-five or fifty cents anyway, but since that business at Dorcas' funeral, many of her regular customers have found reasons to do their own hair or have a daughter heat up the irons. Violet and Joe Trace didn't use to need that hairdressing pocket change, but now that Joe is skipping workdays Violet carries her tools and her trade more and more into the overheated apartments of women who wake in the afternoon, pour gin in their tea and don't care what she has done. These women always need their hair done, and sometimes pity darkens their shiny eyes and they tip her a whole dollar.

"You need to eat you something," one says to her. "Don't you want to be bigger than your curling iron?"

"Shut your mouth," says Violet.

"I mean it," says the woman. She is still sleepy, and rests her cheek in her left hand while holding her ear with the right. "Men wear you down to a sharp piece of gristle if you let them."

"Women," answers Violet. "Women wear me down. No man ever wore me down to nothing. It's these little hungry girls acting like women. Not content with boys their own age, no, they want somebody old enough to be their father. Switching round with lipstick, see-through stockings, dresses up to their you-know-what . . ."

"That's my ear, girl! You going to press it too?"

"Sorry. I'm sorry. Really, really sorry." And Violet stops to blow her nose and blot tears with the back of her hand.

"Aw, the devil," the woman sighs and takes advantage of the pause to light a cigarette. "Now I reckon you going to tell me some old hateful story about how a young girl messed over you and how *he's* not to blame because *he* was just walking down the street minding *his* own business, when this little twat jumped on his back and dragged him off to her bed. Save your breath. You'll need it on your deathbed."

"I need my breath now." Violet tests the hot comb. It scorches a long brown finger on the newspaper.

"Did he move out? Is he with her?"

"No. We still together. She's dead."

"Dead? Then what's the matter with you?"

"He thinks about her all the time. Nothing on his mind but her. Won't work. Can't sleep. Grieves all day, all night . . ."

"Oh," says the woman. She knocks the fire from her cigarette, pinches the tip and lays the butt carefully into the ashtray. Leaning back in the chair, she presses the rim of her ear with two fingers. "You in trouble," she says, yawning. "Deep, deep trouble. Can't rival the dead for love. Lose every time."

Violet agrees that it must be so; not only is she losing Joe to a dead girl, but she wonders if she isn't falling in love with her too. When she isn't trying to humiliate Joe, she is admiring the dead girl's hair; when she isn't cursing Joe with brand-new cuss words, she is having whispered conversations with the corpse in her head; when she isn't worrying about his loss of appetite, his insomnia, she wonders what color were Dorcas' eyes. Her aunt had said brown; the beauticians said black but Violet had never seen a light-skinned person with coal-black eyes. One thing, for sure, she needed her ends cut. In the photograph and from what Violet could remember from the coffin, the girl needed her ends cut. Hair that long gets fraggely easy. Just a quarter-inch trim would do wonders, Dorcas. Dorcas.

Violet leaves the sleepy woman's house. The slush at the curb is freezing again, and although she has seven icy blocks ahead, she is grateful that the customer who is coming to her kitchen for an appointment is not due until three o'clock, and there is time for a bit of housekeeping before then. Some business that needs doing because it is impossible to have nothing to do, no sequence of errands, list of tasks. She might wave her hands in the air, or tremble if she can't put her hand to something with another chore just around the bend from the one she is doing. She lights the oven to warm up the kitchen. And while she sprinkles the collar of a white shirt her mind is at the bottom of the bed where the leg, broken clean away from the frame, is too split to nail back. When the customer comes and Violet is sudsing the thin gray hair, murmuring "Ha mercy" at appropriate breaks in the old lady's stream of confidences, Violet is resituating the cord that holds the stove door to its hinge and rehearsing the month's plea for three more days to the rent collector. She thinks she longs for rest, a carefree afternoon to decide suddenly to go to the pictures, or just to sit with the birdcages and listen to the children play in snow.

This notion of rest, it's attractive to her, but I don't think she would like it. They are all like that, these women. Waiting for the ease, the space that need not be filled with anything other than the drift of their own thoughts. But they wouldn't like it. They are busy and thinking of ways to be busier because such a space of nothing pressing to do would knock them down. No fields of cowslips will rush into that opening, nor mornings free of flies and heat when the light is shy. No. Not at all. They fill their mind and hands with soap and repair and dicey confrontations because what is waiting for them, in a suddenly idle moment, is the seep of rage. Molten. Thick and slow-moving. Mindful and particular about what in its path it chooses to bury. Or else, into a beat of time, and sideways under their breasts, slips a sorrow they don't know where from. A neighbor returns the spool of thread she borrowed, and not just the thread, but the extra-long needle too, and both of them stand in the door frame a moment while the borrower repeats for the lender a funny conversation she had with the woman on the floor below; it *is* funny and they laugh—one loudly while holding her forehead, the other hard enough to hurt her stomach. The lender closes the door, and later, still smiling, touches the lapel of her sweater to her eye to wipe traces of the laughter away then drops to the arm of the sofa the tears coming so fast she needs two hands to catch them.

So Violet sprinkles the collars and cuffs. Then sudses with all her heart those three or four ounces of gray hair, soft and interesting as a baby's.

Not the kind of baby hair her grandmother had soaped and played with and remembered for forty years. The hair of the little boy who got his name from it. Maybe that is why Violet is a hairdresser—all those years of listening to her rescuing grandmother, True Belle, tell Baltimore stories. The years with Miss Vera Louise in the fine stone house on Edison Street, where the linen was embroidered with blue thread and there was nothing to do but raise and adore the blond boy who ran away from them depriving everybody of his carefully loved hair.

Folks were furious when Violet broke up the funeral, but I can't believe they were surprised. Way, way before that, before Joe ever laid eyes on the girl, Violet sat down in the middle of the street. She didn't stumble nor was she pushed: she just sat down. After a few minutes two men and a woman came to her, but she couldn't make out why or what they said. Someone tried to give her water to drink, but she knocked it away. A policeman knelt in front of her and she rolled over on her side, covering her eyes. He would have taken her in but for the assembling crowd murmuring, "Aw, she's tired. Let her rest." They carried her to the nearest steps. Slowly she came around, dusted off her clothes, and got to her appointment an hour late, which pleased the slow-moving whores, who never hurried anything but love.

It never happened again as far as I know—the street sitting—but quiet as it's kept she did try to steal that baby although there is no way to prove it. What is known is this: the Dumfrey women—mother and daughter—weren't home when Violet arrived. Either they got the date mixed up or had decided to go to a legally licensed parlor—just for the shampoo, probably, because there is no way to get that deepdown hair washing at a bathroom sink. The beauticians have it beat when it comes to that: you get to lie back instead of lean forward; you don't have to press a towel in your eyes to keep the soapy water out because at a proper beauty parlor it drains down the back of your head into the sink.

So, sometimes, even if the legal beautician is not as adept as Violet, a regular customer will sneak to a shop just for the pleasure of a comfy shampoo.

Doing two heads in one place was lucky and Violet looked forward to the eleven-o'clock appointment. When nobody answered the bell, she waited, thinking maybe they'd been held up at the market. She tried the bell again, after some time, and then leaned over the concrete banister to ask a woman leaving the building next door if she knew where the Dumfrey women were. The woman shook her head but came over to help Violet look at the windows and wonder.

"They keep the shades up when they home," she said. "Down when they gone. Should be just the reverse."

"Maybe they want to see out when they home," said Violet.

"See what?" asked the woman. She was instantly angry.

"Daylight," said Violet. "Have some daylight get in there."

"They need to move on back to Memphis then if daylight is what they want."

"Memphis? I thought they were born here."

"That's what they'd have you believe. But they ain't. Not even Memphis. Cottown. Someplace nobody ever heard of."

"I'll be," said Violet. She was very surprised because the Dumfrey women were graceful, citified ladies whose father owned a store on 136th Street, and themselves had nice paper-handling jobs: one took tickets at the Lafayette; the other worked in the counting house.

"They don't like it known," the woman went on.

"Why?" asked Violet.

"Hincty, that's why. Comes from handling money all day. You notice that? How people who handle money for a living get stuck-up? Like it was theirs instead of yours?" She sucked her teeth at the shaded windows. "Daylight my foot."

"Well, I do their hair every other Tuesday and today is Tuesday, right?"

"All day."

"Wonder where they are, then?"

The woman slipped a hand under her skirt to reknot the top of her stocking. "Off somewhere trying to sound like they ain't from Cottown."

"Where you from?" Violet was impressed with the woman's ability to secure her hose with one hand.

"Cottown. Knew both of them from way back. Come up here, the whole family act like they never set eyes on me before. Comes from handling money instead of a broom which I better get to before I lose this no-count job. O Jesus." She sighed heavily. "Leave a note, why don't you? Don't count on me to let them know you was here. We don't speak if we don't have to." She buttoned her coat, then moved her hand in a suit-yourself wave when Violet said she'd wait a bit longer.

Violet sat down on the wide steps nestling her bag of irons and oil and shampoo in the space behind her calves.

When the baby was in her arms, she inched its blanket up around the cheeks against the threat of wind too cool for its honey-sweet, butter-colored face. Its big-eyed noncommittal stare made her smile. Comfort settled itself in her stomach and a kind of skipping, running light traveled her veins.

Joe will love this, she thought. Love it. And quickly her mind raced ahead to their bedroom and what was in there she could use for a crib until she got a real one. There was gentle soap in the sample case already so she could bathe him in the kitchen right away. Him? Was it a him? Violet lifted her head to the sky and laughed with the excitement in store when she got home to look. It was the laugh—loose and loud—that confirmed the theft for some and discredited it for others. Would a sneak-thief woman stealing a baby call attention to herself like that at a corner not a hundred yards away from the wicker carriage she took it from? Would a kindhearted innocent woman take a stroll with an infant she was asked to watch while its older sister ran back in the house, and laugh like that?

The sister was screaming in front of her house, drawing neighbors and passersby to her as she scanned the sidewalk—up and down—shouting "Philly! Philly's gone! She took Philly!" She kept her hands on the baby buggy's push bar, unwilling to run whichever way her gaze landed, as though, if she left the carriage, empty except for the record she dropped in it—the one she had dashed back into the house for and that was now on the pillow where her baby brother used to be—maybe it too would disappear.

"She who?" somebody asked. "Who took him?"

"A woman! I was gone one minute. Not even one! I asked her . . . I said . . . and she said okay . . . !"

"You left a whole live baby with a stranger to go get a record?" The disgust in the man's voice brought tears to the girl's eyes. "I hope your mama tears you up and down."

Opinions, decisions popped through the crowd like struck matches.

"Ain't got the sense of a gnat."

"Who misraised you?"

"Call the cops."

"What for?"

"They can at least look."

"Will you just look at what she left that baby for."

"What is it?"

" 'The Trombone Blues.' "

"Have mercy."

"She'll know more about blues than any trombone when her mama gets home."

The little knot of people, more and more furious at the stupid, irresponsible sister, at the cops, at the record lying where a baby should be, had just about forgotten the kidnapper when a man at the curb said, "That her?" He pointed to Violet at the corner and it was when everybody turned toward where his finger led that Violet, tickled by the pleasure of discovery she was soon to have, threw back her head and laughed out loud.

The proof of her innocence lay in the bag of hairdressing utensils, which remained on the steps where Violet had been waiting.

"Would I leave my bag, with the stuff I make my living with if I was stealing your baby? You think I'm crazy?" Violet's eyes, squinted and smoking with fury, stared right at the sister. "In fact, I would have taken everything. Buggy too, if that's what I was doing."

It sounded true and likely to most of the crowd, especially those who faulted the sister. The woman had left her bag and was merely walking the baby while the older sister—too silly to be minding a child anyway—ran back in her house for a record to play for a friend. And who knew what else was going on in the head of a girl too dumb to watch a baby sleep?

It sounded unlikely and mighty suspicious to a minority. Why would she walk that far, if she was just playing, rocking the baby? Why not pace in front of the house like normal? And what kind of laugh was that? What kind? If she could laugh like that, she could forget not only her bag but the whole world.

The sister, chastised, took baby, buggy, and "Trombone Blues" back up the steps.

Violet, triumphant and angry, snatched her bag, saying, "Last time I do anybody a favor on this block. Watch your own damn babies!" And she thought of it that way ever after, remembering the incident as an outrage to her character. The makeshift crib, the gentle soap left her mind. The memory of the light, however, that had skipped through her veins came back now and then, and once in a while, on an overcast day, when certain corners in the room resisted lamplight; when the red beans in the pot seemed to be taking forever to soften, she imagined a brightness that could be carried in her arms. Distributed, if need be, into places dark as the bottom of a well.

Joe never learned of Violet's public craziness. Stuck, Gistan and other male friends passed word of the incidents to each other, but couldn't bring themselves to say much more to him than "How *is* Violet? Doing okay, is she?" Her private cracks, however, were known to him.

I call them cracks because that is what they were. Not openings or breaks, but dark fissures in the globe light of the day. She wakes up in the morning and sees with perfect clarity a string of small, well-lit scenes. In each one something specific is being done: food things, work things; customers and acquaintances are encountered, places entered. But she does not see herself doing these things. She sees them being done. The globe light holds and bathes each scene, and it can be assumed that at the curve where the light stops is a solid foundation. In truth, there is no foundation at all, but alleyways, crevices one steps across all the time. But the globe light is imperfect too. Closely examined it shows seams, ill-glued cracks and weak places beyond which is anything. Anything at all. Sometimes when Violet isn't paying attention she stumbles onto these cracks, like the time when, instead of putting her left heel forward, she stepped back and folded her legs in order to sit in the street.

She didn't use to be that way. She had been a snappy, determined girl and a hardworking young woman, with the snatch-gossip tongue of a beautician. She liked, and had, to get her way. She had chosen Joe and refused to go back home once she'd seen him taking shape in early light. She had butted their way out of the Tenderloin district into a spacious uptown apartment promised to another family by sitting out the landlord, haunting his doorway. She collected customers by going up to them and describing her services ("I can do your hair better and cheaper, and do it when and where you want"). She argued butchers and wagon vendors into prime and extra ("Put that little end piece in. You weighing the stalks; I'm buying the leaf"). Long before Joe stood in the drugstore watching a girl buy candy, Violet had stumbled into a crack or two. Felt the anything-at-all begin in her mouth. Words connected only to themselves pierced an otherwise normal comment.

"I don't believe an eight has been out this month," she says, thinking about the daily number combinations. "Not one. Bound to come up soon, so I'm hanging an eight on everything."

"That's no way to play," says Joe. "Get you a combo and stay with it."

"No. Eight is due, I know it. Was all over the place in August—all summer, in fact. Now it's ready to come out of hiding."

"Suit yourself." Joe is examining a shipment of Cleopatra products.

"Got a mind to double it with an aught and two or three others just in case who is that pretty girl standing next to you?" She looks up at Joe expecting an answer.

"What?" He frowns. "What you say?"

"Oh." Violet blinks rapidly. "Nothing. I mean . . . nothing."

"Pretty girl?"

"Nothing, Joe. Nothing."

She means nothing can be done about it, but it was something. Something slight, but troublesome. Like the time Miss Haywood asked her what time could she do her granddaughter's hair and Violet said, "Two o'clock if the hearse is out of the way."

Extricating herself from these collapses is not too hard, because nobody presses her. Did they do the same? Maybe. Maybe everybody has a renegade tongue yearning to be on its own. Violet shuts up. Speaks less and less until "uh" or "have mercy" carry almost all of her part of a conversation. Less excusable than a wayward mouth is an independent hand that can find in a parrot's cage a knife lost for weeks. Violet is still as well as silent. Over time her silences annoy her husband, then puzzle him and finally depress him. He is married to a woman who speaks mainly to her birds. One of whom answers back: "I love you."

There she is. No dancing brothers are in this place, nor any breathless girls waiting for the white bulb to be exchanged for the blue. This is an adult party—what goes on goes on in bright light. The illegal liquor is not secret and the secrets are not forbidden. Pay a dollar or two when you enter and what you say is smarter, funnier, than it would be in your own kitchen. Your wit surfaces over and over like the rush of foam to the rim. The laughter is like pealing bells that don't need a hand to pull on the rope; it just goes on and on until you are weak with it. You can drink the safe gin if you like, or stick to beer, but you don't need either because a touch on the knee, accidental or on purpose, alerts the blood like a shot of pre-Pro bourbon or two fingers pinching your nipple. Your spirit lifts to the ceiling where it floats for a bit looking down with pleasure on the dressed-up nakedness below. You know something wicked is going on in a room with a closed door. But there is enough dazzle and mischief here, where partners cling or exchange at the urging of a heartbreaking vocal.

Dorcas is satisfied, content. Two arms clasp her and she is able to rest her cheek on her own shoulder while her wrists cross behind his neck. It's good they don't need much space to dance in because there isn't any. The room is packed. Men groan their satisfaction; women hum anticipation. The music bends, falls to its knees to embrace them all, encourage them all to live a little, why don't you? since this is the it you've been looking for.

Her partner does not whisper in Dorcas' ear. His promises are already clear in the chin he presses into her hair, the fingertips that stay. She stretches up to encircle his neck. He bends to help her do it. They agree on everything above the waist and below: muscle, tendon, bone joint and marrow cooperate. And if the dancers hesitate, have a moment of doubt, the music will solve and dissolve any question.

Dorcas is happy. Happier than she has ever been anytime. No white strands grow in her partner's mustache. He is up and coming. Hawk-eyed, tireless and a little cruel. He has never given her a present or even thought about it. Sometimes he is where he says he will be; sometimes not. Other women want him—badly—and he has been selective. What they want and the prize it is his to give is his savvy self. What could a pair of silk stockings be compared to him? No contest. Dorcas is lucky. Knows it. And is as happy as she has ever been anytime.

"He is coming for me. I know he is because I know how flat his eyes went when I told him not to. And how they raced afterward. I didn't say it nicely, although I meant to. I practiced the points; in front of the mirror I went through them one by one: the sneaking around, and his wife and all. I never said anything about our ages or Acton. Nothing about Acton. But he argued with me so I said, Leave me alone. Just leave me alone. Get away from me. You bring me another bottle of cologne I'll drink it and die you don't leave me alone.

"He said, You can't die from cologne.

"I said, You know what I mean.

"He said, You want me to leave my wife?

"I said, No! I want you to leave *me*. I don't want you inside me. I don't want you beside me. I hate this room. I don't want to be here and don't come looking for me.

"He said, Why?

"I said, Because. Because. Because.

"He said, Because what?

"I said, Because you make me sick.

"Sick? I make you sick?

"Sick of myself and sick of you.

"I didn't mean that part . . . about being sick. He didn't. Make me sick, I mean. What I wanted to let him know was that I had this chance to have Acton and I wanted it and I wanted girlfriends to talk to about it. About where we went and what he did. About things. About stuff. What good are secrets if you can't talk to anybody about them? I sort of hinted about Joe and me to Felice and she laughed before she stared at me and then frowned.

"I couldn't tell him all that because I had practiced the other points and got mixed up.

"But he's coming for me. I know it. He's been looking for me all over. Maybe tomorrow he'll find me. Maybe tonight. Way out here; all the way out here.

"When we got off the streetcar, me and Acton and Felice, I thought he was there in the doorway next to the candy store, but it wasn't him. Not yet. I think I see him everywhere. I know he's looking and now I know he's coming.

"He didn't even care what I looked like. I could be anything, do anything—and it pleased him. Something about that made me mad. I don't know.

"Acton, now, he tells me when he doesn't like the way I fix my hair. Then I do it how he likes it. I never wear glasses when he is with me and I changed my laugh for him to one he likes better. I think he does. I know he didn't like it before. And I play with my food now. Joe liked for me to eat it all up and want more. Acton gives me a quiet look when I ask for seconds. He worries about me that way. Joe never did. Joe didn't care what kind of woman I was. He should have. I cared. I wanted to have a personality and with Acton I'm getting one. I have a look now. What pencil-thin eyebrows do for my face is a dream. All my bracelets are just below my elbow. Sometimes I knot my stockings below, not above, my knees. Three straps are across my instep and at home I have shoes with leather cut out to look like lace.

"He is coming for me. Maybe tonight. Maybe here.

"If he does he will look and see how close me and Acton dance. How I rest my head on my arm holding on to him. The hem of my skirt drapes down in back and taps the calves of my legs while we rock back and forth, then side to side. The whole front of us touches. Nothing can get between us we are so close. Lots of girls here want to be doing this with him. I can see them when I open my eyes to look past his neck. I rub my thumbnail over his nape so the girls will know I know they want him. He doesn't like it and turns his head to make me stop touching his neck that way. I stop.

"Joe wouldn't care. I could rub anywhere on him. He let me draw lipstick pictures in places he had to have a mirror to see."

Anything that happens after this party breaks up is nothing. Everything is now. It's like war. Everyone is handsome, shining just thinking about other people's blood. As though the red wash flying from veins not theirs is facial makeup patented for its glow. Inspiriting. Glamorous. Afterward there will be some chatter and recapitulation of what went on;

nothing though like the action itself and the beat that pumps the heart. In war or at a party everyone is wily, intriguing; goals are set and altered; alliances rearranged. Partners and rivals devastated; new pairings triumphant. The knockout possibilities knock Dorcas out because here— with grown-ups and as in war—people play for keeps.

"He is coming for me. And when he does he will see I'm not his anymore. I'm Acton's and it's Acton I want to please. He expects it. With Joe I pleased myself because he encouraged me to. With Joe I worked the stick of the world, the power in my hand."

Oh, the room—the music—the people leaning in doorways. Silhouettes kiss behind curtains; playful fingers examine and caress. This is the place where things pop. This is the market where gesture is all: a tongue's lightning lick; a thumbnail grazing the split cheeks of a purple plum. Any thrownaway lover in wet unlaced shoes and a buttoned-up sweater under his coat is a foreigner here. This is not the place for old men; this is the place for romance.

"He's here. Oh, look. God. He's crying. Am I falling? Why am I falling? Acton is holding me up but I am falling anyway. Heads are turning to look where I am falling. It's dark and now it's light. I am lying on a bed. Somebody is wiping sweat from my forehead, but I am cold, so cold. I see mouths moving; they are all saying something to me I can't hear. Way out there at the foot of the bed I see Acton. Blood is on his coat jacket and he is dabbing at it with a white handkerchief. Now a woman takes the coat from his shoulders. He is annoyed by the blood. It's my blood, I guess, and it has stained through his jacket to his shirt. The hostess is shouting. Her party is ruined. Acton looks angry; the woman brings his jacket back and it is not clean the way it was before and the way he likes it.

"I can hear them now.

" 'Who? Who did this?'

"I'm tired. Sleepy. I ought to be wide awake because something important is happening.

" 'Who did this, girl? Who did this to you?'

"They want me to say his name. Say it in public at last.

"Acton has taken his shirt off. People are blocking the doorway; some stretch behind them to get a better look. The record playing is over. Somebody they have been waiting for is playing the piano. A woman is singing too. The music is faint but I know the words by heart.

"Felice leans close. Her hand holding mine is too tight. I try to say with my mouth to come nearer. Her eyes are bigger than the light fixture on the ceiling. She asks me was it him.

"They need me to say his name so they can go after him. Take away his sample case with Rochelle and Bernadine and Faye inside. I know his name but Mama won't tell. The world rocked from a stick beneath my hand, Felice. There in that room with the ice sign in the window.

"Felice puts her ear on my lips and I scream it to her. I think I am screaming it. I think I am.

"People are leaving.

"Now it's clear. Through the doorway I see the table. On it is a brown wooden bowl, flat, low like a tray, full to spilling with oranges. I want to sleep, but it is clear now. So clear the dark bowl the pile of oranges. Just oranges. Bright. Listen. I don't know who is that woman singing but I know the words by heart."

COMMENTARY (1997)
JOHN HENRIK CLARKE:
HIS LIFE AND PHILOSOPHY IN HIS OWN WORDS

JOHN HENRIK CLARKE

When he cofounded the Harlem Writers Guild in 1950, Clarke was the only member who had been published. His literary career began in 1948 when he self-published the novel *The Boy Who Painted Christ Black*. His nonliterary career included being a golf caddy and an NBC page in Rockefeller Center. Nonetheless, he was totally consumed with a passion for learning and teaching. He understood the political importance of the work of black scholars, artists, and writers. He spent half his time, as he said, "living in libraries. I would read *all* the books in a library. Then I would read the library itself. By that I mean I wanted to thoroughly understand the system and the people who were in charge of this information. After doing this, I'd move on to another library while thinking and writing about what I had read."

Though he was a fierce and unrelenting proponent of Pan-Africanism, he was known to criticize and sometimes make good-natured fun of some of those involved in it. For instance, when he was asked to comment on the fact that a group of black students at Cornell, where he was teaching, had taken over a dining hall, Clarke quipped, "Well, I certainly hope that this time they improve the food that's served there." After going completely blind, he wrote and edited his last four books and authored scores of articles. Dr. Clarke gave this excerpt to the Harlem Writers Guild as an introduction to its online creative writing course. Later, it became a portion of his obituary, which he had written years before his death. It now also serves as the keynote of this section of the anthology.

I was born January 1, 1915 in Union Springs, Alabama. I remember when I was three years old, I fell off of something. From that unhappy incident, I think somehow my life changed. They tell me that the fall appeared to knock something *into* rather than *out of* me.

In those days, little black Alabama boys were not licensed to imagine themselves as conduits of political and social change. But from the moment that my Uncle Henry put some cool water on my head and I began to heal and mend, I seemed to become a different sort.

Let's face it . . . I was stubborn and fixed upon reinventing myself. While my family called me Bubba, I changed my Christian name. I decided to add an "e" to the family name Clark and I changed the spelling of my middle name Henry to Henrik, in honor of the Scandinavian rebel playwright, Henrik Ibsen, whom I admired for his pure spunk and for addressing great social issues in his play *A Doll's House*.

My father wanted me to become a farmer; feel the smoothness of Alabama clay beneath my feet and become one of the first blacks in our town to own land. But I was worried about my history being caked with southern clay and I subscribed to a different kind of learning and teaching in my bones and in my spirit. It was something vastly different than I would have ever found in the segregated schools of my town in that time. None of the public schools for black people went beyond the tenth grade. I was also displeased with the fact that many, many black people were still being lynched and hung from trees in that same Alabama soil my father so desperately wanted me to own.

I am a Nationalist and Pan-Africanist, first and foremost. I was well grounded in history long before I ever took a history course. The love of the subject was something that I guess was knocked into me when I was three.

In fact I did not spend much time in school—I had to work. One of the things I did to help my family survive was caddying (for white golfers, of course . . . no black "Tigers" in the golfing "woods" then). I caddied for Dwight D. Eisenhower and Omar Bradley long before they were even one-star generals. Bradley was a much better tipper than the future president, by the way.

It was my third-grade teacher, Mrs. Harris, who first told me that I should combine writing with my love of history. I heard her and I agreed. But I knew I had to leave the racist South if I was ever to make much of myself. I could not go around with "Georgia on My Mind" the way my life-long friend Ray Charles could do.

But where to go? That was the question.

In the books that I could garner from what white-only libraries threw away, I read about fantastic places abroad, such as Timbuktu. But I soon settled for a last-class trip on a slow-moving train to New York City.

I selected Harlem and the great libraries of New York City as the laboratory and the academic resources of my mission. And what was my "Mission"? It was to use my will to carve a career of scholarship and activism out of virtually nothing.

Organizations were the keys to this path of struggle. Some of the early ones I helped to found were: the Harlem Writers Guild (1950), Freedomways (1954), the African Heritage Studies Association (1958), and the National Council of Black Studies (1962).

These, as well as every other organization that I was associated with, had one basic principle:

WHEN EUROPEANS EMERGED IN THE WORLD IN THE FIFTEENTH AND SIXTEENTH CENTURIES, THEY NOT ONLY COLONIZED MOST OF THE TERRITORY OF THE WORLD, THEY COLONIZED INFORMATION ABOUT EVERYTHING IN THE WORLD, INCLUDING EVEN THE IMAGE OF GOD!

The last point bothered me to no end for many years. That is probably why I wrote and published *The Boy Who Painted Christ Black* in 1948. It was the first published work of fiction by anyone associated with the Guild. After that came about two hundred short stories, as well as my writing and editing of about sixty works of political and historical nonfiction. Along the way I've held professorships at Cornell and Hunter College. But all that is much less important than the fact that my quest for knowledge and for the uplift of all oppressed people was a *response* to injustice.

That is what every writer has to look for: a chance to change the world through creative struggle and through the best possible use of your thoughts and your oh-so-precious words.

But while I must make this physical departure, spiritually I will not leave you and God will take care of you. When you feel a cool breeze blow across your face every now and then, just know that it comes from the deep reservoir of love that I hold for you. Oh, by the way, Christ *is* black; I see him walking only a short distance away with Nkruma. I think they are coming to greet me.

And let me leave with these words that always guided my steps in the world you still occupy:

MY FEET HAVE FELT THE MANY SANDS
OF MANY NATIONS,

I HAVE DRUNK THE WATER
OF MANY SPRINGS,
I AM OLD,
OLDER THAN THE PYRAMIDS,
I AM OLDER THAN THE RACE
THAT OPPRESSES ME.
I WILL LIVE ON . . .
I WILL OUTLIVE OPPRESSION
I WILL OUTLIVE OPPRESSORS.

"DETERMINATION"

Thank You,
John Henrik Clarke

FROM SOWA'S RED BEANS AND GRAVY (2002)

DIANE RICHARDS

Richards has been a member of the Harlem Writers Guild since 1996. The magazine *Black Issues in Higher Education* put her at the forefront of powerful and thoughtful new writers. Her *Sowa's Red Beans and Gravy* smacks of an earthy yet urban Zora Neale Hurston–influenced confection.

STORY FOURTEEN: HARLEM

Folks in Harlem got more sense than any folk in the world. They holler, they cuss, they fight and when they love you, they really love you. If you're on the outside looking in yah may think folk unhappy, but they ain't. They just pondering or minding their own business. That's what.

I love Harlem cause that's where I live and what I know, right up there on 122nd and Manhattan Avenue. White folks live right across the street too. They are Harlem folk, that's right. You don't have to be black to be Harlem folk. Don't worry me none that old color thang you folks always talking about. Anyway, when I go out in Harlem I change myself to be younger you know cause folks be rushing back and fro and at 110, I can't be bothered moving that fast and don't have to neither. Shoot I done done everythang I want to anyway. I ain't in a hurry to get nowhere no how.

Folks are worried about comin' to Harlem and they betta. There's some funky spirits up here just waiting for you to start trouble. You see Harlem is a village and the village is full of spirits. Most folks look at it like it's part of New York, but it ain't and I'm here to tell you so. Up here on 125th Street folks are real and if they're happy, you'll know it, and if they evil, you'll find that out too. On 57th Street everythang look like it's just doing fine, but underneath that funky ground you got evil, angry thangs stirring up trouble every which away, just waiting, just waiting for yah to come uptown.

Now I don't know if you and Harlem gon get along. That's for you to see. But if you don't know where yah going, it might be betta to stay at home.

STORY FIFTEEN: ONCE UPON A TIME AN EVIL, EVIL FAIRY . . .

Once an evil, evil fairy had it out for me and what I did was bound that evilness. Yes I did. I got me the blackest candle I could find and had a long talk with my will. Every time that thing uttered something evil about me she drew one last breath until she breathed no more. Now, had the man left me alone, he would be alive and well today. I asked the man to stop being so evil to me, but he said that was his natural state of mind, evil. But he didn't know that I created that state of mind.

Don't mess with me.

STORY SIXTEEN: THE CAT MAIN

At first you might think the cat main is a man obsessed with pussycats. He's a man entrapped by the shapes, sizes and scents of the cat. He plots, plans and daydreams about how he can git the common as well as the rare variety of that mysterious creature, the cat.

But, I gots a different story.

Now there was a man who had only a picture of a cat, his cat, in his house, hanging on the wall. The cat's name was Sheldon. I'm telling yah the truth.

The man's name was Marty and he was a strange child. Now there was a woman desperate to be married so she thought Marty was strange but there was a possibility of finding a husband in this strange man. So what is strange she thought to herself. When she called the man, Sheldon, the man's cat talked to her over the phone. I kid yah not. Now that should a sent the girl packing (She was strange too? Don't you think?). But nawh—she wanted more proof that he wasn't stone crazy!

So anyway she got together with the man and he started to kiss and lick her face, and her whole body from head to toe like a cat. Lord child! The girl went crazy. When she asked the man where he learnt it from, he just smiled. He had a worried face but when he was licking, he looks like a little boy.

Well, she never got proof that he wasn't stone crazy cause love is blind, and the cat put a spell on her. She fell in love with the strangest, white cat you ever did see. She married the man, but the cat is her husband. Now you figure it out.

STORY SEVENTEEN: SAD AND LONELY

Ain't no end to being sad and lonely while you alive, so just get over it and start living that's what. No matter how life seems to be going, it's gon be hard for you to stay in the moment and know that everythang is fine right now . . . and now is all you have. But you're human and humans like to worry. You worry worry. You worry about what you want and how you gon get it rather than letting things be. Worrying about worry ain't nothing to get worked up about cause that's what most folks do most of the time—worry. But, if you can let things happen, sit through your nerves showing out, things work themselves out. You can't control folk, but if they standing on your foot, betta tell them to get off it! That's all and that's what. If you want something from somebody, ask 'em, then see what they do.

Husbands leave and mothers die. That's life. Sad and lonely . . . sometimes.

If you have a hard time letting folks know what you feel, you might try getting honest with yoself. What are you afraid of? That they don't want to be with you? Find out now rather than later, that's what.

Everybody, even the evilest somebody want to be loved. Folks want love and that's all there is to it. If somebody is showing their behind, they want love. And, don't let nobody fool you, folks don't want to share their loved ones. Everybody's jealous. Some folks just know how to hide it.

Now just beware of what your loved one's folks were like cause they gon be acting much like their mama and daddy. So if their daddy is contrary, the boy gon be too and if the mama sweet, the girl gon be too.

Sometimes the boy acts like his mama and the girl like her father. Just keep those eyes open before you fling open the doors to your heart. Heed my word now.

Don't use your nature as a tool or something to bargain with or you gon get used. When you try to control somebody, you end up being controlled. So if you want to be free, let your partner be free. Sex and love are two different thangs. Remember that and you'll always know what to do when you have a question on whether you love somebody or not.

Womenfolk don't sleep with no man without a commitment. He must want to commit; you can't make him want to. That commitment will come from his heart otherwise, if it come from somewhere else, like his lying lips, it don't mean nothang.

Men seek love through sex cause they don't know no betta. They bond like women but even deeper if the woman gives him mother love and high nature. This is what they are hunting for anyway. Most women give too much mother love and not enough nature love to satisfy a man. You got to have both. They won't say it, but menfolk want to marry a woman just like their mamas. On a good day it's another way of going home.

STORY EIGHTEEN: MRS. FANNIE MAE GOLDSTEIN

Now, I inherited my altar and my apartment from an old, wise crone who lived 30 years in this apartment at 122nd and Manhattan Avenue. She was a high yella, pass for white gal, and knowed somethang from the day she was born. I figured wasn't no need for me to clean this place of evil spirits cause the evilest spirit in that house was her husband. She killed him off after she found out he was sleeping with another woman. That man got the strangest disease that no doctor could name and then he died begging her forgiveness. Fannie Mae Goldstein. She was black, Jewish, and proud too. That's right. You see in those days mixed folks had a level of respect they don't have today. Near white women marrying black men was an asset to the colored race cause they made light and bright, colored chillun. Any black man in his right mind marrying a light and bright woman was sho smitten and he shonuff had to have some money. That money let him do what the hell he wanted to do while folks were flapping their mouths. Of course his folks wondered why he couldn't settle down with a black woman, but that's another story.

Mrs. Fannie Mae Goldstein was a mess and being colored and Jewish was a heavy burden to carry. Colored, female and Jewish. Says it all, doesn't it? My Gawd that woman had to be strong. That's why she had to go kill that husband off with those herbs from Jamaica. The Negro bought her a synthetic diamond ring and she thought it was a diamond for 20 years. When she found out it was fake, she went off in a huff and wouldn't speak to the poor man for a whole year. The following year she found out that he was sleeping with a white woman. She was through then and that's when she slipped the deadly herbs to him in a Jamaican curry dish.

Seeing that she was Jewish that man wasn't on his job no how cause she was suppose to be a kept woman and she had to cook, iron and clean. Then when he lost his job, she had to wuk. What he do that for? She worked in a school in Harlem with poor chillun. Her heart was in the work, but her pride made her miserable.

Now Fannie Mae's father, Harry Goldstein, didn't give a hoot 'bout what folks said and after he made him a whole lots of money bootlegging he married Nell, the blackest gal he could find and had him three daughters. Nell was the Goldstein's housekeeper's daughter.

Everything after that is history. Harry and Nell had three children, all big boned, fine featured, good haired gals. They all married the blackest men they could find. Fannie Mae Goldstein was one of those girls. However, she was cheated out of her Jewish Princess heritage when Harry died cause in those days her mama, Nell, had no rights cause she was black. So when Harry died the Goldstein family swooped down on the money and disowned the children. But I tell you what, had Fannie Mae decided to pass for white and study that good book Torah, she could a been a Jewish Princess for sure.

STORY NINETEEN: SEX

You womenfolk give the store away when you have sex with a man without no commitment. Then you get mad at men when you don't get hitched. Some of yaw don't care about no commitment either cause you want to run loose like a buck stallion.

Now what you do is your business and ain't no need for me to meddle. But most of you just misery, that's what you are. You high natured and fast and think that if you give way to your nature like men you gon be betta off. But you finding it don't work out that way and it ain't in your favor. If you want to be happy you got to respect yoself and stop giving your nature away like it's every man's business to own. That's what. These days menfolk can knock on every door and it open. No wonder they just acting like fools and when a good woman comes along they say so what and walk on down the street to the flossie waving her behind around. Why should men get a yes every time they ask? For what? If you want somebody to value you, you can't just be standing there waiting to be picked up. That's cheap . . . that's just what I said gal.

All this fussing and fighting between men and women would be over if you women just kept your knees together long enough to get a ring on your finger. And another thang, all this equal power is hog mess cause the minute chillun start sucking on your breast, ain't no equality nowhere to be found.

Now if you mad about mother nature, don't worry none cause when you can't have no more babies, the man can't be making them like he use to either. He may think he Casanova but the young women he trying to woo gon know the truth as well as you.

In love matters don't worry about what the man won't do. Just worry 'bout what you gon do when he get sure of you cause that's when men show their behind. Don't make the mistake and make that man Gawd. If you do, you gon be in more trouble than you can get out of. Remember a man don't pay no mind to what you say, it's what you do that stay on his mind.

A new man gon ask you a question three times . . . you know the question I'm talking about.

It is best if you answer No, No and No if you want more from the man than sex.

STORY TWENTY: EVIL BY NATURE

Some folks just evil by nature. That's what they come here to do, keep up a whole lot of mess. Head doctors say all kind of thangs about folk like depressed, psychotic, chemically imbalanced, schizophrenic, alcoholic, and co-dependent when all a fool is, is just plain old country, low down evil.

Evil folks can't help themselves. They were born that way. You ever seent a baby not even one year old spitting at folks, hupping and hollering in the cradle and biting his mama's titty on purpose? And then have the nerve to smile up in her face spit just a drooling all over. And, every single Sunday just as the preacher start the sermon in church, at the same time, the child start showing out like he's evil and done sat down to dinner with Satan and his court.

You think I'm kidding? It's true chillun if you seen a day.

Just like the good lord sit down and have coffee and blueberry corn muffins, the devil sit down and have tea and biscuits. Evil folks got a right to live in the world just like Christian folk but don't nobody want to believe that evil folks carrying on just like they want to.

Well I'm here to tell you evil folk ain't studding good-hearted folk and they're in hiding cause they don't plan for good folks to take over the world. Evil is ready to party now so look out folks, here they come.

And, if you think I'm lying, if the pope won't bless Madonna's baby what is wrong with the world? And, where does evil live? What does that foolishness mean?

Last thang, if evil sneak up on you, walk wide-legged toward it like you carrying 16 inches of it. Squeeze your eyes up and say, "Were you looking for evil? Here I am."

Be evil and walk in peace.

THE QUEEN OF HARLEM (2002)

BRIAN KEITH JACKSON

Jackson's third novel, *The Queen of Harlem,* showcases the Harlem of
buppies, university students, high rents, and chic parties. But it is also
as soulful and heartfelt as any Harlem classic. Jackson currently lives in
Harlem and has won a host of literary awards and fellowships.

3

*The sign in the window on Malcolm X Boulevard read, Free Ear Piercing. That
seemed rather clear. Argue free. No Thailand haggling. "So it's free." "Yes, the
piercing is free, but the studs are ten dollars." "Then it isn't free." "The piercing is free." "No it's not." "The studs cost ten dollars. The piercing is free."
"Okay. Fine. I only want one, so that's five dollars." "No. You have to buy the
pair." "But I only want one." "I can't separate the pair." "But . . ." "Look, you
either want the shit or you don't." I think that's what they call Harlem clarity.
"All right. I'll take one in each ear. But you should change the sign. I can see the
studs being free and the piercing being ten dollars. The piercing is a service,
but—ouch . . ."*

This wasn't the life my mother had planned for me. Much to her dismay, I'd deferred a year from law school. I loved the law, its rhetoric and
usage of ironic gentility, something I'd nurtured while growing up in the
South. I just wasn't sure I was ready to start a life based on tort and fine
print.

"Then tell me, Mason, why did we pay for that trip around the
world? As far as I know, Stanford is in Palo Alto, not New York," she'd
said over the phone, forgetting the mileage she'd gotten out of telling
everyone I was "traveling abroad." But none of that mattered now. I was
heading to Harlem.

When I got to the town house on move-in day, there was a limousine parked outside. I nodded at the driver as I climbed the steps and
pulled out the Tiffany key chain I'd gotten for graduation. I got a rush

as I stuck in the key, wondering if it would work, and when the lock turned, I looked back at the driver, letting him know I was home.

When I walked in, two suitcases were in the hallway, which made me think she'd taken on another housemate. I started feeling like a child not wanting to share. My duffel bag suddenly felt heavier and made my shoulders sink.

". . . a spectacular meal. Spectacular. I got the caterer's name. The table setting, the flowers. Everything." It was a woman's voice, but I was certain it wasn't Carmen's. Her voice had stayed with me for the last five days. This wasn't chocolate mocha. It was lime sorbet.

"The salad, oh, Carmen, the salad was so fresh you could still smell the Mexicans."

Then there was a laugh. I remembered that laugh.

"Wassup?" I said, standing in the doorjamb of the parlor. A woman was sitting in the room with Carmen. Her hair and face were perfectly done as though she'd just come from the salon.

"Oh, hello," said Carmen. "You've made it. Malik, this is Judith Steinman."

"Hello," said Judith Steinman.

"Wassup?"

"Malik is a southerner. From Mississippi," said Carmen.

"Oh, how wonderful," said Judith Steinman. "I've always liked southerners. Not the women, though. Bitches. All of them. You've definitely got to hide your pearls around those girls. Pure evil. Walking around like a bowl of sugar, but if you dig deep enough you're sure to find a saltine."

"Now, Judith, don't frighten the boy," said Carmen.

"It would take more than that," I said.

"That's good to know," said Carmen. "We were just about to leave. Judith has invited me on a girls' getaway."

"Yes, I can always depend on Carmen to be up for a getaway."

"I hear ya. She's been there in a pinch for me too," I said, trying to hide my disappointment. I had been waiting for my reunion with Carmen and already she was about to leave. I had to remind myself that her ad had read, Rarely home.

"Where are the rest of your things?" asked Carmen.

"This is it. I travel light."

"How I envy you," chimed in Judith Steinman. "Try as I may, I still have so much luggage."

"Malik, why don't you join us for a drink before we go?" said Carmen, extending her hand, signaling for me to come into the parlor.

"I-ight," I said, putting down my duffel bag.

"Sit," said Judith Steinman, patting the sofa next to her. She downed the rest of her drink.

"More wine, Judith?" asked Carmen.

"Well, maybe just half a glass."

"I'll get it," I said. I quickly stood up, taking Judith Steinman's wineglass, but I was moving too fast and as I walked by I hit my shin on the coffee table.

"Ah," I said, trying to hold it in.

"Are you okay?" asked Carmen.

"That's got to hurt," said Judith Steinman.

"Uh-huh. Fine."

"Good. Would you get me a bit more too?" said Carmen, handing me her cocktail glass.

"What's your poison?" I asked.

"Ice cubes," she said, then added, "floating in Jack Daniel's."

"So I see you've already made the switch to brown," said Judith Steinman suggestively. I looked over and she was looking at me.

"Yes, the brown liquors are dangerous," Carmen said. "But I love them, so what can I do? It's the season. So finish telling me what happened."

"Oh, yes. Yes. Divine . . ." To take my mind off my shin I focused on the drinks and their conversation. "We'd just walked in from the dinner party and the phone rang. I answer it and it's Daniel Cumming, you know, the novelist, and he says he's in the neighborhood and has a 'friend' with him. I should have known something was suspicious."

I walked over with the drinks. I gave Carmen hers first. She looked up at me and touched my hand as she took the glass. I walked over to Judith Steinman and gave her the wine. "Thank you," she said, again patting the sofa next to her. "Nothing for you?"

"Nah, I'm cool."

"This is more than half a glass," she said, taking a sip. "That's probably best. Save us all some steps." She turned her attention from her glass and back to Carmen. "I should have just come right out and told him it was late and he couldn't come by, but when a prize-winning novelist calls, you can't just turn him away. Let's face it, you can lunch on that for at least a week, particularly if he's drunk and depressed, which with him is usually the case."

"And how else are you going to end up in one of his books?" said Carmen, shaking the ice in her Jack Daniel's.

"Exactly," said Judith Steinman, raising her glass. "So he comes up and has this handsome young man with him. Just delicious." Judith Steinman looked over at me like I was hanging on a hook in a meat locker. "Completely yummy. I knew he had to be a hustler, or I think they call them escorts now. Who cares? A whore is a whore no matter what you call them." I looked over at Carmen and she met my gaze, took another sip of her drink and then looked back at Judith Steinman. "But I knew he had to be one because Daniel, bless his heart, can write his foreskin off, but I've seen boils better looking than he is, so no boy like this one could possibly be interested in him unless there was some monetary exchange. But I'm not one to judge. Oh, that's a lie. I do judge. That's my job." Judith Steinman let out a shrill laugh, then continued, "Daniel started telling me all the gossip, hardly gossip at all, really. Just a rehash of the same tired stories he's told me a thousand times, but they get better each time, so at least it's entertaining. The hustler, *Johnnie*, for one seventy-five an hour, you'd think he could come up with something more original than that. Well, *Johnnie* is just sitting there smiling, adding nothing to the conversation but looking around the room, being appropriately doe-eyed and attentive, so David—David's my husband," she said to me, touching my biceps and giving it a slight squeeze—"David says to the hustler, 'Let me show you around the apartment.' So Daniel and I stay in the living room and we're chatting having a good laugh and two drinks later I realized that David and the hustler weren't back, and our apartment ain't that god-damn big."

Judith Steinman chugged the last of her wine.

"Can I get you some more?" I asked, looking for any reason to get up.

"No, that's plenty," she said. "We've got to be going," then after a thought, "Maybe just half a glass." I looked over at Carmen and she put her hand over the top of her glass, letting me know she was fine. I got up, my shin reminding me to watch the coffee table, and walked back over to the drinks cabinet. I couldn't believe how easy it was for Judith Steinman to tell her story in front of me, a stranger, but it almost seemed like she enjoyed the added ear. I didn't mind because I knew once she stopped, Carmen was going to leave.

"So I go storming through the apartment and I hear this groaning in our bedroom. Thank you," she said without missing a beat as I handed her the glass. "I opened the door and there they were going at it. It was as though the Discovery Channel had come to East Seventy-ninth Street. I was completely taken aback."

"Yeah, I'd think catching your husband in bed with another man would be surprising," I said, trying to add to the conversation. Relax.

"Oh, who cares about that?" she said with a flip of the hand. "Everybody knows David swings both ways. What surprised me was the look of excitement on his face. I hadn't seen that look since his last prostate exam." She took another drink of her wine.

"So you kicked the hustler out?" asked Carmen.

"Oh, no. He was already paid for so I had no choice but to have a turn myself."

The driver came in and took Carmen's suitcase to the car, then escorted Judith Steinman, who had managed to "half" her way through an entire bottle of white wine, down the steps.

"I shouldn't be gone more than a week," whispered Carmen. *A week?* "You were perfect in there. Make yourself at home." She kissed me on the cheek, then rubbed the lipstick away, but her scent stayed with me as she made her way down the steps to the car. When she slid into the backseat she waved, then I heard laughter.

Limousines and laughter.

Transition is exhausting. I'd planned on just taking a nap, but the sun shining through the curtains and the blue fluorescent numbers on my night table made it clear that a new day was donned.

The coolness of the season made me hug the duvet and I smiled as I looked at my little room. I stretched my body, balancing on my stomach like a baby too young to know stiffness.

I wanted to chill in the warmth of the duvet, but my bladder forced me up. I walked into the bathroom off my bedroom and stared at the mirror over the basin, angling my head in different directions, looking for the most alluring pose. I imagined Carmen standing next to me at some exclusive event, giving over for yet another photo. I could see the caption: Socialite Carmen England and unidentified young friend at . . ."

I rubbed some conditioner and hair food in my palms and ran them over my growing twists. I rotated the studs in my ears. I looked at myself and smiled. It was a big smile and I didn't think Mr. Joe would mind. It was a private smile, a smile that offended no one.

4

In Harlem, Prep was played so the clothes I was used to wearing weren't going to cut it if I wanted to fit in. I'd hit 125th Street, the epicenter of Harlem. Merchandise from stores, and a few cars, spilled out onto the sidewalk, urging and prompting the power of the black green, and I had worked my way up to three shopping bags of baggy jeans, shirts, hooded sweatshirts and a bubble coat.

"What about kicks?" asked the salesman as I started walking out with my bags, the Notorious B.I.G. blaring from the speakers, adding a bop to my stride.

"Yeah, I been kicking it," I said, feeling particularly down.

His "nigga please" look showed he wasn't buying it. "Nah, man. Kicks."

I followed him downstairs and he swept out his hand and before my eyes appeared a whorehouse of shoes, each fighting for my aesthetic attention.

"What size?"

"Twelve."

There was only one shoe of each pair on display, but most of those were chained down, which I guess was to prevent fashionable amputee shoplifters.

The salesman came back with several boxes and pulled out a pair of construction boots.

"New to the city, huh?"

"Yeah," I said, lacing the boots. "Came up from down South."

"Yeah, then you gonna need some good shoes. Niggas be walking.

These are the bomb," he said, tapping the steel toe. I stood up, looked in the mirror. I put my hands deep into the pockets of my new baggy jeans, slouched a bit and angled to my side.

I looked good.

"Yo, G!" said a teenager, touching the shoe on the wall next to the mirror. "Check out these new Pumas. Damn."

"Yeah, Jimmy's been kicking those," said his friend. "Natasha bought 'em for his ass."

"That nigga be having all those ho's buying him shit. I need to find me a honey like Natasha."

"How you sound?" his friend asked, then looked around at the rest of us. "Ever since they got them new uniforms at Micky D's, this nigger think he all that."

"I-ight. I-ight," said the other guy. "At least I got a job, nigga. And I'ma remember that shit the next time you come in looking for a hookup on the food."

"You know I'm just playing with you. I been looking for a job. I even went down to the unemployment office to fill out an application, but them niggas wasn't hiring either."

The two guys started laughing, then butted fists. All forgiven, they rolled back upstairs.

"I'll take the boots," I said, still wearing them and walking over to the tennis shoes the guys were looking at. "These are pretty cool. I mean, they're the bomb."

"Yeah, they the bomb," said the salesman, reassuring me. "You'd be stepping style in those."

"I'll take them."

"You wanna put these on your credit card too?"

"And you know it."

Loving Harlem. Had lunch at this great restaurant; a diner really. M&G. Soul food. Today's special was oxtails. Wasn't feeling that adventurous. Had eggs over easy. Sat at the counter and when the waitress came over she asked, "How you feel?" I love that. How you feel? . . .

A woman came in, sat next to me. "How you feel?" "Girl, my head hurts." "You want a BC?" "It ain't a headache, my head just hurts. Needs time to heal. I can't afford the real deal so I had to settle on the ghetto face-lift. Cornrows.

That girl did them so tight I can barely move my head. When I got in the chair she was arguing with one of the other girls and talking that French. They do good hair, but all I have to say is don't let no angry Haitian get up in your head." And that's how she felt . . .

Carmen was out of the house more than a father who owed child support and I had no choice but to start getting to know the hood.

The vibe in Harlem ran through me and I started to feel at ease, stepping out, cruising in my new urban wear. Seeing all the black faces was like a needed shot, but it left a reaction. I was no longer the only black person around, but even in that I felt like a curious traveler, flipping through a guidebook for direction.

During the day the streets were swarming with activity: the young guys rolling dice and pitching coins or the older men playing the bones, framing the double-five in hand until the right time to slam it down on the makeshift table with the joyful and needed cry of "twenty-five." But like a small town, once darkness set in, the workday done, pedestrians retired to their homes, and few of them were town houses.

On Sunday, fresh from service, the lovely women in their pinned hats, crowns, really, with Bibles under arm demanded my attention. In Harlem, churches and beautiful people were much the same: it was impossible to take ten steps without seeing one.

Mount Olivet, 1907. St. Martin's, 1888. Bethelite Community, formerly the Harlem Club, 1889. St. Andrew's, 1891. St. Ambrose, originally the Church of the Puritans, 1875. Greater Bethel, originally the Harlem Free Library, 1892. Metropolitan Baptist, originally New York Presbyterian, 1884. St. Philip's, 1911, an effort of two black architects, one of which, Vertner W. Tandy, was the first black to receive an architectural registration in New York State. Abyssinian, where Adam Clayton Powell Jr's spirit still thrives, 1923.

Many of the other buildings lining the streets were like corpses waiting to be identified by more than just posters for albums, concerts and malt liquor. But the churches remained a presence, almost screaming, *I shall not be moved.*

The Studio Museum in Harlem became my Metropolitan Museum, and when I walked along 125th Street, the music pumping from stores and cars made me think of the Savoy dance hall, "the Home of Happy

Feet," where race didn't matter, but your moves did. It was a sole thing, a swing thing, a dream thing.

As I walked by the Apollo Theater, in a blink I was back in the Renaissance, back when black was the beginning of all true things and definitions were redefined.

In everything I could see the determination in Jacob Lawrence's colorful migration and over "The Walls of Jericho" I could feel "The Weary Blues" of Langston Hughes as Bessie Smith's voice spilled out onto the dapper streets.

I thought of Zora Neale Hurston, a southerner true. I imagined a hearty laugh coming up from her toes, where a real laugh roots. From the first time I read her work, I'd longed to be her man; longed to be back there to assure her her words were appreciated, long before they stopped blooming from her fingers and mouth.

I walked for hours, drawn by the power found in lore, and when I got back to the town house the past was replaced with the present. Carmen wasn't home and I was back, in my solitude.

CHANGES (2003)

WALTER DEAN MYERS

Myers joined the Harlem Writers Guild in 1968. His early work included the publication of short stories in pioneering journals like *Freedomways* and *Liberator* magazine. His first novel for young adults was published in 1978. Since then, he has written and published eighty more such books, in addition to authoring best-selling and critically acclaimed nonfiction. Myers also plays the saxophone and has been a jazz lover most of his life. Keeping this in mind, he's created an original story about a reunion of aging musicians who go in search of one of their own and find both more and less than they expected. Born in West Virginia, Myers now resides with his family in Jersey City, New Jersey.

I was sitting in Ellie's Lounge, off 125th Street, nursing a beer, when BJ came in. He sat in the corner and leaned against the wall while he waited for Carl to bring him his usual two glasses of whiskey and soda. He downed the first as soon as it had been brought to him, made a face as it went down, and then took a little sip of the second. He looked down the bar, spotted me, and nodded. I nodded back and lifted my glass to him.

"You see that piece about Little Willie in the news?" he asked.

"Little Willie?"

BJ told Carl to show me the article. As Carl started looking for it, I started thinking about Little Willie. If you lived in Harlem, you didn't want to read anything about your friends in the paper. Little Willie had to be in his seventies, probably closer to eighty-something, and I hadn't seen him around for four or five years. BJ didn't say anything more, and I just hoped Little Willie wasn't dead.

Carl handed me the paper. I checked the date and saw that it was two weeks old. The article wasn't really about Little Willie—it was about the closing of the Renaissance Nursing Home. The article dealt with how few places there were for older black folk and how sad it was that this one was closing down. Somebody had marked off a paragraph that mentioned that, among the old folks at the home, was William Jennings, noted jazz guitarist.

"Anybody been up to see him?" I asked.

"Leon went up," BJ said. "He said Little Willie was doing real poor. I been meaning to go up, but I ain't had the chance. Really don't want to see him looking like that."

I knew what BJ meant. Me, him, and Little Willie went back a long way. We had played together when all the clubs had live entertainment back in the fifties and had really done well when all the white kids got into the music in the sixties. Now that we all had some real age on us, we were peeping around corners watching ourselves growing old.

"How old is Little Willie?" Carl asked. He put another beer in front of me.

"Old," BJ answered, which put it where it was supposed to be.

Me and Little Willie hadn't never really been that close, but we were okay with each other. Him playing guitar and me blowing sax kept us from bumping heads and we had us a good playing time, which is all you can ask from music. Little Willie could play with anybody and make them sound good. If you had a little riff you liked to play, he would remember it and lead you into it so sweet it would make you feel like you had it written out somewhere instead of pulling it up from how you felt that day. We made a few records when Atlantic was hot and that brought us a nice little bit of attention. Three months after the first record came out, we got a gig in London, which was the first time any of us had been overseas, except for BJ, who had fought in Korea back in the day.

I don't know what made me decide to go up to the nursing home to see Little Willie, but I did. I guess it was just thinking about how much fun we had together and thinking how it would be to talk about the old times. But when I found the place and saw how rundown it was, I thought to myself that they needed to have closed it down a long time ago.

Little Willie did not look good. His face was drawn and ashy looking, and even from where I stood I could see he was missing some teeth.

"I ain't got no AIDS," he said.

"I didn't say you did," I said.

"How you doing, Earl?"

He had recognized me right away and asked me how I was and how

Marva was. Marva was my wife and I had to tell Little Willie that she had gone to Newark, over in New Jersey, to live with her daughter from a previous marriage.

"We didn't break up or nothing," I said. "She just decided to go live with her daughter."

"Well, you know how women is," Little Willie said.

We talked here and there about old times the way I thought we would and he said he was rundown most of the time.

"What the doctor say?"

"Say I got this and that," he said. "He said I need to get out more and take some walks. But just sitting here thinking on it can tire me out. You know what I feel like?"

"What?"

"You ever be playing a tune and then one day it just don't sound right?" Little Willie was looking at me out the side of his eyes. "It don't sound right and there ain't nothing you can do about it even though you playing all the right changes?"

"Yeah, that happens."

"That's where I am."

"Ain't like it used to be," I said.

"Yeah, you can run that by again."

"You need anything?" I asked.

Little Willie made a gesture with his hand like he was going to say something, but then just looked away. I thought about his last wife. He had been married at least three times. She was the last one I knew about. I wondered if she was still alive. Him being in a nursing home I figured she wasn't, so I didn't ask.

The room was small and there wasn't much in it to see. There was a bed, a dresser with that small television on it, and a closet. One door to the closet was open and I saw what looked like the bottom of a guitar case.

"See you still got your Gibson," I said.

"Yeah, she stays around steady," he said. "You playing?"

Little Willie's question caught me off guard. Funny thing was that I almost said yes. I thought of myself as a player, even though I hadn't really jammed in over four years.

"I pick it up once in a while," I said. "Nothing serious."

"We ought to play," Little Willie said. "Get together, have a few drinks, and see what we can do."

"You want to do that?"

"Yeah, I do," Willie said. "I surely do."

There had been a time when playing was just a joy for me. I thought I just about owned Harlem. We'd get together with some good players and always find something we could deal with. We'd work for our groove, I mean really work! And when we hit it dead on it was a righteous feeling. But that had been so long ago. I still took the horn out once in a while and blew into it. I could still imagine the sound I wanted, but I couldn't get it regular anymore. Not like I used to.

"You think you can get something going?" Little Willie asked. He turned away and coughed into a dirty handkerchief.

"I'll see if I can get some people together," I said.

"You know, John Scott still live on 145th Street," Little Willie said. "Him and his wife. You remember that little yellow gal he used to go with?"

"Yeah, she looked like she was kind of fast, but nobody couldn't get near her," I said.

"That's her," Little Willie said. "She and John Scott got hitched up and they steady in the church. He plays drums in the church band."

"He could always play them skins," I said.

Willie went through his drawer and found a little address book. He went through it and found John Scott's address and had me copy it down. He asked me if BJ was still alive and I told him I had just seen him.

"BJ was always okay in my book," Little Willie said. "He couldn't deal with a whole lot of heavy chords, but he was steady."

"That's BJ for you," I said.

I told Little Willie I had to leave to go downtown. Before I left, he told me to ask the receptionist to bring him in some clean towels.

I didn't get back to Ellie's for a few days. When I did I found BJ and told him about my talk with Little Willie.

"You know I'm ready for some playing," BJ said. "When you want to get together?"

It was the 13th of June and I said if it was all right with everybody, we could get together on the 27th. BJ's enthusiasm surprised me. He was really down for the idea and wanted me to know it.

"That should give me enough time to get everybody together," I said.

BJ didn't have no steady number, but I got the number of the barber shop near where he stayed and he said he would check his messages every day.

Next I hooked up with John Scott. That wasn't no trouble, just found his church and asked for him. He was looking good and prosperous. He had retired from the Transit Authority and spent most of his time working around the church him and his wife attended. When I saw him and told him about Little Willie, he told me that his wife had seen the piece in the paper and spoke on it, but they hadn't done nothing about going to the nursing home to see him.

"You know, that's a shame," John said. "And us calling ourselves good Christians."

His wife was still pretty, and hadn't gotten a bit heavier than she was when I knowed her before. She said it was a shame people had to get old and then she asked John if he remembered the man who wanted him to play up on 142nd Street.

"It's supposed to be a combination art gallery and jazz club designed for the new Negroes who think they don't stink when they fart," John said. "No big money in it, just something to do and show the young people. You want me to give him a call?"

"Why you want to play in a club?" I asked. "We ain't played no club in all these years."

"Make it seem like old times," John said.

I said okay, but in a way, my heart wasn't in it. John had been playing church music, which isn't that far from the blues. I didn't know if BJ was doing any playing, or even Little Willie, for that matter. I did know I didn't want to be the only one to come up short.

My Social Security check came on Wednesday, so I had a few extra dollars. I contacted Little Willie, told him about the club, and he was all for it. It seemed to perk him up.

My horn is an Olds I had bought from a guy who had played with Johnny Hodges back in the seventies. It had a sweet sound for a tenor, even when you used a softer reed. I put two new reeds in a glass of water, and looked through some lead sheets while they were soaking. The next thing I started thinking about was Marva. She used to like to come to the sessions and I remember making up a little signature riff just for her. I'd play it when I saw her sitting at a table in a club or in the audience if we were doing a theater gig. We were close then, and had things to talk about. I didn't have a whole lot of patience and sometimes the talking would lead to an argument, but it was still talking.

My hands were shaking when I put the reed in the mouthpiece and tightened it up.

What you nervous about? I asked myself. You just play with some old men you've played with a hundred times or more.

I eased my way through a few bars of "Sophisticated Lady," thought it sounded good, and jumped right into "Harlem Nocturne." I didn't get through eight bars before I was squeaking like some high school kid taking his first lessons.

The lead sheets I stood up between the butter dish and a ketchup bottle were yellow and curled at the edges. Ellington. The Duke was good when you were down, but too sober to start feeling sorry for yourself. As I played I thought about Little Willie sitting up in the nursing home, BJ getting his messages at the barber shop, and me sitting in my kitchen, watching roaches scurrying along the top of the stove, searching for a sound that got away. Only John Scott was still hooked up.

I practiced for at least an hour every day. The sound smoothed out as my lip firmed, and by the time the day came for the set I was feeling enough confidence to give Marva a call. I asked her how she was doing and she said okay, except for the hip that was giving her a little trouble.

"Me and some of the boys are going to play tonight," I said. "Little club they just opened."

"Get out of here!"

"Yeah, we are," I went on. "Me, BJ, John Scott, and Little Willie. Just wondering if you wanted to come by and hear us?"

"Oh Lord, I can't tonight," she said. "I promised my daughter I'd baby-sit for her. She's going to school for her nursing license."

I said maybe she could come some other time and we chitchatted a bit more before we said good-bye. I was disappointed, but I didn't want to lay that on Marva.

The rain against the windows of the cab as it headed uptown softened the neon lights and took the edge off my jitters. I was the last one to show and John Scott introduced me to the manager, a thin, nervous man who said he had heard my records. From what he was saying, I knew he was talking about somebody else, but I didn't say anything. He asked us to just play three numbers, and I knew he was disappointed in the way we looked. I couldn't blame him.

John Scott was dressed all right, but BJ had on a ratty-looking sweater and Little Willie was wearing a suit that looked three or four sizes too big for him. My suit wasn't nothing special, but it fit and it was pressed. I downed a stiff drink and then another before we got on the stand.

We had decided to start with "Satin Doll," mostly because it's a hard piece to mess up. BJ had said that the piano was in tune, which was good, and he started us off with a good beat on the intro. It took us most of the tune to get ourselves situated around the changes, but we got there and the small audience gave us a hand.

Little Willie said he wanted the first solo on "Round Midnight" and I was glad to let him have it. We got into the piece easy and I could feel how comfortable everybody was getting. When it was time for Little Willie to get into his solo, I looked at BJ and hoped he would be ready to cover if Little Willie couldn't swing it. But then Little Willie started playing and I had to look around to see if it was really him, that's how good he was sounding. I had forgotten how tough Little Willie could be when he was on. He just picked the piece up and made it sing. Hunched over his guitar, as brown as the wood he cradled in his lap, he looked like he was making love to something sweet and tender.

Little Willie playing like that had picked BJ up, and I could hear he was following Little Willie's chords as he played. I didn't know if I was going to front my horn or not, but then the right chords started coming, and I was out there, pushing sound into the darkness, riding on the easy rhythm John was laying down, reaching for the magic I used to call mine. And I got caught up, Lord, I got caught up, and the music was right, and Harlem was Harlem again, young and saucy and sweet and black and as pure as the notes lifting their way into the dark night. Amen, it was good!

John Scott was feeling frisky and wanted to play "Take Five" for our last tune, but I didn't want to play it because the time was too hard to work with, so we eased out of the set with a laid-back version of "God Bless the Child."

We played with joy, and afterward the manager asked us if we wanted to play on a regular basis. BJ agreed right away and the rest of us said we'd think about it. We all wanted to hang out for a while, to keep the time going. But John didn't drink, and Little Willie started coughing, so we broke it up. It had been a good night for all of us, though, and we all hugged before putting Little Willie into a cab to end the night.

When I got home, I called Marva, but her daughter answered and said she was asleep. I told her not to wake her, that it wasn't important.

Two days later I got a call from the nursing home. Little Willie had died and they had found my name and telephone number on his night table.

"We need somebody to make arrangements," the caller said. "Are you family?"

I didn't know how to answer the question. Me, John Scott, and BJ were all Little Willie had. Did that make us family? I guessed it did and I said I would make the arrangements if they wanted me to. They said that would be fine with them.

The club manager found a young group to play on a regular basis, but said we could play from time to time if we found another guitar player. We all said yes, but we never did.

PART FOUR

NEW STORIES: NEW VOICES REFLECT,

RECOUNT, AND REINVENT

<<<<<<<<<<<<<<<<<<<<<<<<<<<<

As Harlem undergoes its reinvention as a racially and economically diverse neighborhood, young writers, educated about its past and familiar with its most recent tides, are adding to the plethora of work that has defined it as a cultural mecca.

Tracy Grant's "Puddin'head Barnes" revisits a Harlem where radios crackled with Brooklyn Dodgers' play-by-plays and jazz floated out of smoky bars, while Karen Robinson channels Chester Himes with her blending of Harlem's illustrious past with the gritty realism of modern Harlem streets in her detective novel 8 *Times a Week*.

Harlem, with its ever-evolving face, continues to rouse the creative ambitions of not just writers, but also musicians, visual artists, and politicians. It has survived riots, poverty, protest, and blackouts, to somehow always reemerge culturally influential, relevant, beautiful, and inspirational.

DREAMING IN HARLEM (2002)

ROSEMARIE ROBOTHAM

Rosemarie Robotham moved to New York City from her native Kingston, Jamaica, to attend Barnard College and later, Columbia University's School of Journalism. She is the author of the novel *Zachary's Wings,* coauthor of *Spirits of the Passage: The Transatlantic Slave Trade in the Seventeenth Century,* and editor of two collections, *The Bluelight Corner: Black Women Writing on Passion, Sex and Romantic Love* and *Mending the World: Stories of Family by Contemporary Black Writers.*

Her story "Dreaming in Harlem" is taken from a novel in progress. "I wanted to write about souls on the very margin of society," she says, "people we turn away from and try not to see. I am hoping to tell the story of four such people in a way that allows us to care about them and root for more than their survival." Robotham lives in New York City with her husband and two children and is senior editor-at-large for *Essence* magazine.

Ti Jean's shift ended at midnight, and he caught the subway home, a clutch of anxiety in his stomach. Would she be there, he wondered, even as he denied to himself just how much it mattered to him that Frances keep her word. She had said she would meet him outside his apartment at half past twelve, that she would wait for him there. She would come alone, she had decided—she wouldn't take Ruby into a situation that might turn out not to be what it seemed, and so for tonight at least, her daughter would sleep at Samaritan House, and they would risk missing curfew at the armory, and having to begin the whole housing process all over again.

Did Ti Jean understand, Frances had queried intently, just how much she had at stake, that she was giving up more than eight weeks of following the rules on the strength of a stranger's promise? Did he see how much she was trusting him, trusting her instincts about him, how much she would be sacrificing in the way of a stable future for herself and her daughter should she turn out to be wrong?

Maybe, just maybe, if Ti Jean's proposal was something other than he said, the city housing office would let them slip by, keeping them in the rehousing program, creeping slowly up the list. But more likely, they would simply strike Frances and Ruby from the rolls, make them start over from scratch, registering at the armory again, getting a new shelter assignment, having to redo the whole tedious process.

Earlier, as Frances grilled and lectured him, Ti Jean had been seized with an odd giddiness at the fact that what he promised was just what he would deliver—a place to stay, sleep, recover, strike out anew, with no expectation or danger from him at all. He knew, because he knew himself, that he would not take advantage of Frances or her daughter. He might be a common street hustler in some people's eyes, but his mama had raised him to have morals, and he'd never force his attention on anyone—man, woman, or child. Besides, Frances could be his mother. Or at least an older sister, though she seemed ageless in the way of dark-complexioned women. He knew she had to be nearing forty, a good fifteen or so years older than him. So why was he thinking now, on the subway home, about the slope of her cheekbones, the restrained sway of her softly rounded hips, the smoky sultriness of her eyes.

He shook his head to make the vision of her as whore-seductress go away. No, this offer of his home wasn't about sex, he reminded himself. It was about decency, generosity, feeling righteous for a change. It was a kind of proxy, too, a hedge against his guilt at not sending for his mother and sister in Haiti, even though he had accumulated the money to do so, even though he had found a space large enough for them all to live. Even now, he had made no overtures, or even inquiries, about bringing them to New York. Instead, he had left them to make do in picturesque Cap Haitien with the few hundred American dollars he sent them each month.

He exited the subway at 116th Street and Seventh and walked the two blocks south to his apartment building. The streets were deserted at this hour, the storefronts shuttered, the sidewalks littered with wrappers and beer cans that might not be picked up for days. As he approached his building, he kept his eyes peeled for her, and wondered if it had been wise to allow her to wait for him on the dark street. He reminded himself that she knew how to survive the streets better than he did, knew how to spot trouble and move along. His heart sank a little as he scanned the empty sidewalk, and he began to prepare himself for her absence. Then, as he crossed the last street before home, he noticed a figure a few feet down on the side street, in the shadow of a fire escape, and he knew it was her. She saw him, but didn't move, just followed him with her eyes as he approached, waiting for him to come to a stop in front of her.

"You're here," he said.

"Second thoughts?"

"No, no. Come," he said.

He reached into his pocket, extracting his keys as she picked up her shopping bag. She followed him into the building, the wary expression back in her eyes. He saw her take note of everything, the bulletproof-paned front door, the cracked stoop, the graffiti on the stone columns framing the entrance. Inside, she surveyed the dirty, mosaic-tiled lobby floor, the once-grand staircase sweeping into the darkness of the landing above, the broken light fixtures, the humid stench of urine in the elevator. Ti Jean, looking through her eyes, saw that it didn't look like much, even to a woman who had spent the last several months living nowhere. But he knew her feelings would change once she got inside his apartment. Silently, he inserted his key into the lock of his front door, and pushed it open. He felt a rush of satisfaction as Frances stepped across the threshold—and gasped.

"Lord!" she breathed. "It's huge."

She rested her shopping bag by the door and just stood there, dwarfed by the broad passageway that seemed to stretch for miles. The hardwood floor, distinctly canted to the left, glowed under the warm light of bell-shaped sconces along the length of the wall. There were doors to rooms off the hall, which at the far end bent in a backward L-shape, leading, Frances supposed, to more rooms. Ti Jean moved along the hallway, opening doors. The first one, directly opposite the front door, led to the kitchen, a makeshift affair with just a sink, a refrigerator, a narrow gas-burning stove, and a metal cabinet, the kind you buy for $19.99 in the hardware store. There was no counter, just a scarred, red-painted table in the middle of the room, and the floor was covered with gray linoleum tiles, some of which were missing, leaving a patchy relief of glue going greenish with age.

"I haven't worked on the kitchen yet," Ti Jean said. "It gets better from here."

Frances didn't look at him. "It's a kitchen," she said. "And with a fridge, too. Anything in there?"

"Of course," Ti Jean said.

Frances moved down the hall to the first room, which contained a blue couch and two director's chairs, one green, one cabana-striped blue. A black trunk was set in front of the couch, on top of a plain beige rug. There was an almost empty bookshelf against one wall, and a television set sat on a small plastic table opposite the couch. It was a simple room, plainly furnished, an embroidered cloth covering the trunk and a jam jar of freshly cut carnations the only touches of grace. Intuitively, Frances knew that Ti Jean had put the flowers out on the trunk for her benefit. Maybe the embroidered cloth had only come out of some closet or store today, as well. Frances was moved, all at once, by the effort Ti Jean had made, this ridiculous young person who was barely a man, who preened and hustled for a living, yet would offer a homeless whore and her daughter refuge in his home.

Frances could see, walking into the rest of the rooms, that Ti Jean had taken great care with this place, that it was his pride and perhaps his vanity. The walls were meticulously plastered and painted in neutral beige; the new light fixtures were neatly installed, almost elegant. He was also obviously a skilled carpenter: The refinished floors were pristine, the built-in shelves and cabinets carefully cut and sanded and smoothly varnished. Only the freestanding furniture was uninspired, mismatched pieces picked up on the street or in consignment shops, with no special flair or design, as if Ti Jean hadn't yet decided his taste and so brought in pieces that were merely functional and unobtrusive, holding space for what might come later, when life had molded him more.

All this Frances was thinking when she opened the last door, around the L-shaped bend in the hallway, past Ti Jean's bedroom with its neat brass bed and high-tech entertainment system sitting on the floor, past the empty living room with the French doors, past the bathroom with its narrow, frosted-glass window and obviously new fixtures. This last room was on the corner, large and square, with bay windows set into right-angled walls, offering an expansive view of the avenue. Frances realized at once that this room was to be theirs, hers and Ruby's. There were two parallel cots, both covered by matching pink-and-green comforters, both with fat, new-looking pillows. A four-drawer plasterboard dresser stood between the beds, and against the opposite wall was a small desk and straight-backed chair. An oblong rug, peach-colored and fuzzy, like a bathroom rug, was on the floor between the beds, the plastic tab that once held its tag still attached. It was the newness and inappropriateness of the rug, more than anything, that told Frances that Ti Jean had spent the morning bringing in pieces that he thought would be essential to their comfort. The dresser was cheap but serviceable. The beds, gently made. The new pillows and the desk—the desk. Tears welled in Frances's eyes, and she turned away from Ti Jean, who was standing expectantly at the door. The desk. A place for Ruby to do homework. Ti Jean had even thought of that.

"This is your room," Ti Jean said so softly Frances almost didn't hear him. When she looked back at him, he was still watching her carefully, and Frances thought she caught a shadow of disappointment in his eyes. She knew it was because she hadn't acknowledged his effort on their behalf. And yet, she couldn't thank him right then. There was that habitual voice in her head, saying there had to be a wrinkle here somewhere, something she wasn't seeing, because life always extracted payment for its gifts. Surely, surely, Ti Jean's offer couldn't be as innocent and openhanded as it appeared.

And so what? she suddenly decided.

So what if he wanted favors? This apartment, these clean, open rooms, these wide windows, this gleaming floor and carefully made bed just might be worth it. So long as this boy knew not to touch her child, she could do this. She would do this, whatever this turned out to be. She would give him whatever it was that he wanted, because this, God knew, was better by far than the shelter, far better than the street, certainly better than all those groping strangers inside the Playhouse.

"It's nice," she said at last. "I'm tired now."

She wanted to say more as Ti Jean turned out the door with a small, dejected nod. His shoulders drooped a little as he disappeared 'round the bend in the hallway, heading, Frances guessed, toward his own room. She wanted to reach out and stop him—he was so very young! She wanted to put her hands on those muscular shoulders and draw him in, much as his own mother might. She wanted to kiss the top of his close-shaven head and maybe even let him show her what he wanted. She would have done that, she would certainly have done that, but when he turned away from her, not forcing the issue, not saying another word, she thought that for tonight, at least, she'd lie alone in this clean, soft bed, turn her cheek into the plump new pillow, and maybe even dream.

FROM 8 TIMES A WEEK (2003)

KAREN ROBINSON

Karen Robinson enjoys writing about show business and is delighted to be a member of the Harlem Writers Guild, Screen Actors Guild, American Federation of Television and Radio Artists, and Actors' Equity Association.

8 Times a Week is her mystery novel that weaves its way through the lives of black Broadway. After Broadway dancer Francine Bower is found dead in her Harlem apartment, handsome detective Alex Barnes is assigned to Francine's case and meets up with the sassy Mrs. Janie James.

Since Detective Barnes couldn't get a word in with Claudette, he decided to go back to the scene of the murder to get a feel for the building and surrounding area. He already saw the way Francine had lived, but was interested in what the neighbors had to say. Maybe something would click, perhaps lead him to the killer.

At 116th Street, he stood outside the black iron gates of Graham Court, wondering how he was going to gain entry. There was no doorman or security guard on duty, so he waited until someone came out. An old man taking his dog for an evening stroll approached the gate and Barnes flashed his badge. The old man nodded and held the gate open.

Once inside, Barnes took the stairs to the second floor and knocked on the door adjacent to Francine's apartment. The door was still marked as restricted because it was part of the crime scene. He knocked again on the neighbor's door and listened in silence to the turn of the top lock. The door opened an inch and he was able to make out a frail woman.

"Hello, Miss James. I'm Detective Barnes. I have a few questions to ask you about Francine Bower."

He heard the unclasping of the lock and sliding back of the chains. She turned the doorknob. They were looking eye to eye. She wore a pink flowered housedress with matching pink fuzzy slippers, her hair piled high and tinted blue.

"Miss James, here's my badge. I'm Detective Barnes, assigned to the Francine Bowers case."

"That's Mrs.!" she snapped. "Mrs. Janie James! I don't know anything about that girl." She squinted her eyes, which indicated to Barnes that she knew plenty.

"Well, may I come in so we can talk? I won't stay long, Mrs. James."

When Barnes got on the other side of Fort Knox, he smiled.

"Mrs. James, I see you're well protected."

She had a dead bolt lock, the bar and stick in the floor, and three sets of chains on the door.

"A girl has to protect herself, you know . . . but you charmed your way in. Well, come on and have a seat Detective Barnes. It is Barnes, isn't it?" She gestured to a chair covered with beige hand-crocheted armrests. Then she looked him over.

He glanced around the apartment. He saw showgirl feathers and plumes, and black-and-white photos of black men with conked hair, wavy hair, brim hats, pleated pants, and white starched shirts. There was also a chorus line of light tan beauties with pointed features, wide smiles, and men's arms draped around them. Harlem in its heyday.

"That's you, Mrs. James?" He pointed to one of the five-by-sevens over the fireplace. She had been a living doll. But now her light skin showed how time changed everything.

"Yes, indeed that's me," she sighed. "Aging sure is a son of a gun."

He knew he was in for story time. She had been a Cotton Club dancer and her late husband had owned the Jimmy James Grill on Lenox Avenue just off 125th Street.

"That's right, Detective. Folks came from all over Harlem for some of Jimmy's hotcakes, chicken in a basket, fried fish, and grits and gravy . . . not to mention his famous punch delight. Yes, Jimmy really made a name for himself. Harlem was a great place to be back then." She settled on a rose-colored divan facing him.

"I came up here from Virginia and it was like magic. I had never seen so many high-falutin' colored folks in my life. I was a country girl coming from dirt roads to paved streets. I remember all that, you know. I partied with the best. Me and my sweet Jimmy. All the stars used to stop by Jimmy's grill. It was something else, I tell you. I helped him make that punch recipe and the gravy that my mama taught me how to make."

She smiled, thinking of the good times.

"I sure miss him, though. He was a wonderful man. His smile could light up a room. He had his business at the grill and I had my job shaking my tan thing over at the club."

Her husband's photo on the mantel resembled early Duke Ellington. Several other photos showed a happy couple. "We had a good life, Detective, a good life." An hour later, after she had filled Barnes in from 1930 to the present, he was ready to finally get some answers. But then she went on about the history of the building, how the L-shaped fish tanks were in the windows on the Seventh Avenue side of the building, where people gathered and watched the goldfish as they promenaded along the avenue. Where porters wore brown uniforms with gold buttons, and dogs would drink water from the curbside. He didn't have the heart to cut the old girl off because she seemed to come alive reminiscing about Harlem. Besides, he was enjoying the stories.

"Would you like some tea, Detective Barnes? I can also fix a little tuna salad, if you'd like?"

He could tell she was lonely for company.

"Oh, no thank you, Mrs. James. I ate something just before coming here."

"Well, what do you want to ask me?"

"Tell me a little about Francine Bower."

"That's easy. Men. She liked her some men. And what a stream of them she had. You know, back in my day you were called 'loose' . . . 'scoundrel' . . . now, I'm not saying that that's what it is, or that's what it was . . . but the way I see it, there were whores then and there are whores now. She had a blazing trail from here to Mississippi!"

Barnes had to hold back laughter. Mrs. James became so animated telling her story that her eyes widened and her little frail fingers with pink frosted polish seemed to flutter. She had warmed up to Barnes, and was ready to pour out her heart. He had put her at ease by listening and looking at her photos. She now trusted him.

She whispered and leaned forward in her seat.

"You never give out all your candy, if you know what I mean . . . you save some Lucky Charms for yourself." She winked at Barnes. He nodded in agreement and found himself lowering his voice with his next question.

"Did any particular man stay around for long? Did you ever hear anything, or see anything unusual going on?"

"These walls are so thick—you know, postwar building—you don't hear nothing, honey, and I mean it. I did see her with a black eye once. I was taking out the garbage. She was crying . . . bawling hard. Tried to cover it up with sunglasses like that fooled somebody. I might be old as dirt, but I get my eyes checked. I tried to get her to talk, but she didn't want to say, so I let her alone."

"Was this recent?"

"Noooo. This was a while back because I had Pedee then."

"Who's Pedee?"

"My ever-loving mutt."

Barnes knew there was a story and a photo to go with Pedee. He braced himself.

"That day Pedee started barking out of control like he knew who socked her in the eye. I told Pedee to settle down, but he wouldn't stop. He just kept barking and barking and barking. I quickly walked back into my apartment. 'Come on in here, Pedee,' I said. You know, Pedee had one bad eye and a bad heart. He'd bump into walls every now and then, but guess that's what happens when you get old and start falling apart. Ahhh . . . anyway, when I got in, I needed something for my nerves so I had a little brandy and Pedee got some dog treats I used to keep for him over there in the corner."

She pointed toward the kitchen. She still had Pedee's green bowl. Barnes listened patiently, but needed to find out more. This man in question could have done more than just hit Francine Bower.

"If he wanted a punching bag, he should meet me down on Twenty-third Street at Danny's gym with the real brothers." Barnes hated when women got beat up on, a common occurrence in his line of work.

"At any rate, Mrs. James, do you remember what he looked like? Any description?"

"No, cause I never saw him. I told you, she had lots of men. To tell you the truth, she had scooped up my nephew a few weeks earlier when he came to visit. She didn't waste no time."

"Your nephew? She was involved with him?"

"Yes, my great-nephew Earl. He works for Airborne, you know that mail company, he was enroute and just stopped by . . . yeah . . . he used to check up on me to see if the old girl was still alive and kicking. That's my sister's boy's third son. My sister had two more after him. Where was I . . . aaahhh. . . . Oh yes, that girl was coming in from one of her jobs. I could tell because she always had that big dancer bag on her shoulder, look like she was always moving all the time, and bags under her eyes. Maybe the girl had allergies, I don't know." Mrs. James hunched her shoulders. "She didn't have too many girlfriends from what I could see. Some women are just that way, you know."

"Well, where is your nephew, excuse me, great-nephew now?"

She shook her head vigorously.

"No need thinking it was him because he met one of those girls that worked with him at the company and transferred to Denver where her people are from. They just had a baby. They are doing fine." She dropped her head and clasped her hands tightly. "Sure would like to see the little baby, though."

"I understand. You have more great-nephews?"

She waved her hand in disgust and sucked her teeth.

"Turkeys . . . they want nothing to do with a rusty gal like me. To them I'm old. I mean, real old. Hey, as you can see from those pictures, I lived my life, and I bet they'll be looking for something when I kick the bucket. Well, I got plans for their lazy behinds."

Barnes moved back in the chair and shook his head. Mrs. James looked down at her fuzzy slippers, shrugged her thin shoulders, and gazed at Barnes.

"Sometimes you don't know what makes people tick. I declare that girl was searching for something . . . you never know what's running through someone's head."

Barnes knew that this was just the beginning. If these were the things people were saying about Francine and the answers he was getting, he didn't know what else to expect.

"Mrs. James, thank you for your time. You've been very helpful. Here is my card."

"Why are you giving me this?"

"Well, I just want you to have it in case you remember something else, that's all. Thanks for the Harlem history."

"Anytime, Detective Barnes. Trust me, I got more stories inside of me than you know. I didn't get to this age for nothing."

As Barnes walked toward the steps, he made a few notes on his pad, thinking this was going to be a long, long case.

PUDD'NHEAD BARNES (2004)

TRACY GRANT

Grant burst on the literary scene in 2000 with his hip, funny, and fast-paced novel *Hellified*. He wrote a special story for this collection, which relies on thoughtful characterization and true-to-life dialogue to capture bar life in mid-twentieth-century Harlem.

Every Saturday afternoon, from April to September, the men from 132nd Street did the same thing. They weren't in the barbershop, they weren't in church, and they weren't on the corner. Whatever had to be done was finished by one o'clock. Unless they were working, the husbands, fathers, and keepers of their Harlem neighborhood were in one place—Darlene's Lounge on Seventh Avenue for the Brooklyn Dodgers game. The owner of Darlene's, Elden "Pudd'nhead" Barnes, had the biggest radio in town, so the men gathered there to hear the broadcast good and loud, their way of simulating the game live from Ebbets Field. And after every game, the same argument would erupt.

"You crazy, Milton! Ain't no way in hell Jackie Robinson is better than Campanella. Campy hit three-twelve last year, forty-one homers and one hundred forty-two RBIs!"

"So what. That was last year."

"Jackie ain't beat it!"

"Just shows how ignorant you are, Fleetwood. Jackie broke the color line. He made history. Wasn't for Jackie, Campy wouldn't even be on the Dodgers!"

"Yes sir," another patron chimed in. "That's right," added another. But Fleetwood, so named for his beloved car, was not moved.

"See, that Nu Nile done got in your brains, Milton." The other men howled with laughter. "History ain't got shit to do with home runs and RBIs. Jackie's day was back in the Negro Leagues, and even then he couldn't hit the curveball. Campy, now *that's* a ball player. We just turned off the game and Campy done saved the Dodgers again. Ain't no better hitter in baseball."

Milton waved his hand in Fleetwood's direction, dismissing what he'd just heard. "What you think, Pudd'nhead?"

"Leave me out, boys, I ain't in this."

"Aw, come on!" the men in the bar angrily protested, refusing to let Pudd'nhead exclude himself.

"Well, uh, you both make a point. You right, Milton, by Jackie breaking the color line in baseball, he's one of the greatest."

"Of course he's the greatest," Milton quipped.

"Campy's having a helluva year, though."

"Will you tell that fool?" Fleetwood asked.

"Stop stalling, dammit," Milton snapped. "Who's the best? Jackie or Campy?"

The bar fell silent as everyone waited for an answer. Pudd'nhead frowned, forming more wrinkles on his face than usual. Finally he sighed.

"I gotta go with Campy." Fleetwood and several other men cheered. Milton was livid.

"Hell with y'all," he barked as he marched out. "They can't beat the Yankees anyway."

Fleetwood and the others were laughing long after Milton left. Many of the men left the bar after the game, some to return home, some to prepare for night jobs. There were many janitors, porters, chauffeurs, and doormen on the block, but no job was considered menial where they lived. All that mattered was that they were breadwinners.

When the game was over, Pudd'nhead changed the radio station. Before long, Dinah Washington's voice could be heard singing "I've Got You Under My Skin." Late afternoon was the closest thing to downtime for Pudd'nhead. He stocked the bar for the evening crowd, cleared glasses and, if asked, prepared a burger, grilled cheese, or fish sandwich on the grill, all while tending bar for Fleetwood and his other regulars. He placed a plastic rack of dirty glasses on one end of the bar and called his one employee.

"Percy! Percy!" he called. "Come clear this rack." A few of the customers chuckled as Percy Barnes, Pudd'nhead's son, emerged from the back room to pick up the rack. Percy lifted the rack and had trouble holding it. Percy scowled at the other men and his father.

"This ain't right, Pop. I got things to do today."

"Don't nobody care what you gotta do. Do it later." Percy shuffled along with the rack of glasses. He was a taller, more handsome version of his father, and he had the confidence to go with his good looks. Except, of course, in his father's presence. Pudd'nhead looked at Fleetwood with a grin. "Sixteen and he got things to do. What he gotta do that he can't do here? I tell him to bring his girlfriends in here."

Fleetwood chuckled. "Who wants to be around they daddy with they girlfriend?"

"He's probably scared he'll lose his girl in here."

"And well he should be." Fleetwood laughed. Then his smile faded. "He's gotta grow up sometime, Pudd'n."

"Here you go. The biggest kid I know."

"Yeah, okay. Why don't you take a break?"

"No time. Evening rush is in a few hours."

"The doctor said slow down. And that evening rush ain't that big."

Pudd'nhead looked at his friend and saw that he would not let it go. "All right, fine. I brought me a ham sandwich." The proprietor took his time as he came around the bar, armed with a paper bag. Pudd'nhead was nearly two hundred fifty pounds, five foot eight and bow-legged. His walk was more of a waddle, slow and labored, and his fleshy, bald head seemed to sink into the rest of his body. The crevice on the side of his head earned him his nickname. From the bag he retrieved a thick ham sandwich, a can of Rheingold beer, and a copy of *Jet* magazine.

"Listen to this, y'all," he announced.

"Do we have a choice?" Fleetwood asked.

"There's a Negro postal inspector," Pudd'nhead read, ignoring his friend. "A.C. Young, fifty-two years old, making fifty-two hundred dollars per year."

"So what?"

"So things are happening, that's what! Here's another one. They say they're getting ready to integrate the D.C. fire department and the Ohio state police."

"Tell you right now, that won't work," Fleetwood announced.

"Why not?"

"Are you kiddin'? If they let niggers in the fire department, they only gonna let 'em fight fire in niggers' houses. And the police? Sheeeeit. I been to Ohio. Won't be no Negro cops out there." A few other patrons nodded and mumbled in agreement. Pudd'nhead looked at his friend with disgust.

"You about the dumbest man I ever seen. Only fightin' fire in niggers' houses. You should be ashamed to open your mouth. It's right here in the magazine."

Two hours later, Pudd'nhead and Fleetwood were in the same place along with a few regulars. Percy was behind the bar, sulking as he poured drinks for whoever came in. Pudd'nhead could tell his son was ready to go, and he thought Fleetwood might even be right. He was almost grown, and who said he wanted to run a bar? The question was on Pudd'nhead's mind when a clean-cut man in a dark suit entered the bar. Pudd'nhead smiled.

"Hey, Walter!"

"Evening, Pudd'n, Fleetwood." Walter waved to the other customers, all of whom called him by name. Percy brought him a glass of beer.

"So how are things at the Theresa?"

"Just fine, Pudd'n. You know you're always welcome to come run our bar."

"No thanks. Too fancy. Besides, I'd have to sell this place," he added, looking at Percy, who ignored the comment. "How's your daughter?"

"Pudd'n, I'm so proud of Gladys I can't stand it. She's going to New York University."

"No kidding! Congratulations!"

"Thank you. She'll be the first in the family. She's got some scholarships, but we have to come up with the rest."

"You'll come up with it."

"You better believe I will," he affirmed.

"Great news," Fleetwood added. "How 'bout a drink on me?"

Fleetwood signaled Percy, who promptly set three snifters in front of the men and poured them each a shot of brandy. Walter told Pudd'nhead and Fleetwood all about how hard Gladys worked and his family's preparations for her. Pudd'nhead was especially interested.

"That's all right, man," he told his friend. It was then that an attractive young girl entered the bar.

"Hey, Daddy."

"Hey, girl," Pudd'nhead called back. As soon as she came in, Pudd'nhead's eyes shot around the bar. The men all looked down or stared straight ahead, though many of them spoke to her. It was understood that if Pudd'nhead caught a man staring at his daughter, swift punishment would follow. He had hospitalized a few men in the last couple of years for ogling Darlene.

Darlene, named after her mother, was easily the prettiest girl in the neighborhood. She was shapely and always wearing a skirt and high heels, fashionable beyond her eighteen years. Today was no different; she wore a maroon, form-fitting dress with matching high heels and nylons, the fancy kind with lines along the back of her caramel legs. She greeted her father and Fleetwood each with a peck on the cheek. Walter Scott was careful not to look too happy.

"Hi, Mr. Scott."

"Darlene, you look more and more like your mama every day."

"Don't she?" Pudd'nhead agreed. "I thought you were going to Blumstein's."

"I went, but wasn't nothing in there. They'll have a new sale next week."

"So where you off to now?"

"To dinner and the movies with Charles, like I told you."

"Where is he?"

"Outside in the car."

"Get him in here."

"Daddy . . ."

"You better bring that boy in here," Fleetwood told her.

"He's all right, Pop. He's my main man," Percy added.

"Just put them glasses up," Pudd'nhead ordered. "Grown folks is talking. Darlene, bring the boy in here or you ain't going."

"Oh, Daddy." Darlene stomped out and no one at the bar reacted. Pudd'nhead turned to Walter. "You lucky, you won't be going through this no more."

"No, but I'll have those slick college boys to worry about."

"You ain't lying," Fleetwood added. "Them boys'll charm the drawers off a snake."

Darlene returned with a tall, sharply dressed, handsome young man. Pudd'nhead's face was full of alarm.

"Daddy, I'd like you to meet—"

"How old are you?" he interrupted. The young man grinned.

"Twenty-four, sir."

"Ain't you a little old for her?"

"Daddy!" Darlene protested. "Charles, this is my father and these are his friends."

Charles offered his hand but he was only greeted with mumbling. He saw Percy behind the bar. Percy had a strange look on his face, as if he were nervous about seeing Charles.

"Percy, what was the number?" Charles asked. The men all looked to Percy. Fleetwood looked down at his shoes. Pudd'nhead looked at his son with absolute shock.

"Five two three," he said sheepishly. A collective groan came from a couple of booths. Whoever had hit the number wasn't in Darlene's.

"Why the hell he asking you what the number was?"

"Take it easy, Pop."

"I ain't gonna ask you again." Pudd'nhead's chest was heaving.

"Pudd'n, calm down," Fleetwood advised.

"Stay out of this!" he shot back.

"Mr. Barnes, I'm sorry," Charles offered.

"Mind your goddamn business," he barked. A few customers moved out of the way. Pudd'nhead cornered Percy. "You a number man?"

Percy didn't answer. Pudd'nhead looked around at his friends and his daughter. Their calm infuriated him more.

"Look like you put one over on me, don't it? You a number man? Huh?"

"Yeah, Pop."

Pudd'nhead hit him so hard it looked like his head might come off. Percy's head rolled back and the rest of him followed, knocking over bottles as he reeled to the floor. Darlene wailed and more customers stood and backed away. Fleetwood jumped over the bar and struggled to hold Pudd'nhead, who was looking to further punish his son.

"Pudd'n, that's enough! Pudd'n!" Fleetwood was fit, but it took all of his strength to hold his friend back. "Darlene, get that boy out of here!"

Darlene was crying hysterically. Walter put a dollar on the bar before leading Darlene and Charles out. "Come on," he advised.

"I'm sorry, sir," Charles apologized. "I didn't know."

"We all play, boy," Walter told him. "Just not around here. Darlene, be back here at nine."

"Mr. Scott, we'll have to leave the movie early!"

"Nine, Darlene."

Back in the bar, everyone watched the spectacle of Percy, unconscious, being carried upstairs to Pudd'nhead's apartment by a couple of regulars. Pudd'nhead was still fuming.

"Pudd'n, you're gonna mess around and have a heart attack. You've got to watch that temper!"

"How I'm supposed to watch my temper if my boy's a number man? Huh?" Fleetwood had no answer for him. "You knew, didn't you? You knew about it and didn't say shit."

"He begged me not to tell you," Fleetwood said. "He ain't stupid. He knew you'd knock his ass out. He promised to tell you real soon. I told him if he didn't, I would."

"You're full of shit. You wasn't gonna say nothin'."

"It wouldn't be a secret forever, Pudd'n. Eventually somebody was gonna ask him 'bout the number, and eventually he'll have to make a payoff."

Pudd'nhead slammed his fist on the bar, shaking all the drinks that rested on it. "You shoulda *told* him, then. If he wanna talk to you, you shoulda told him."

"I would have told him years ago. You always want to shelter him."

"I'm trying to protect him! So he don't catch the hell we caught in the street! Well, he gonna learn now. He gonna know the whippings I took to hold on to this place. Goddamn numbers men ran every bar in Harlem. First numbers, then protection money, before you know it, you outta business. Minozzi's boys still around, y'know."

"I know, Pudd'n."

"Yeah, but ain't nobody stood up no' more. Huh? 'Cause they made an example of me. Do Percy know that, why them *ey*-talians broke my leg? Why half his daddy's head is smashed in? All that so my kids could have a shot and he wanna run numbers? Boy can do any goddamn thing he want, but not that. Not that, Fleetwood. I done paid the price for him to be free of that. I fought for this bar, bled for it. Ain't no numbers men growing old or living a quiet life. Percy ain't tough. He ain't made for that life . . . them numbers gonna bring us all down, man, I'm tellin' you."

Fleetwood saw angry tears in his friend's eyes. "Pudd'n, the boy's got ears. He done heard the stories. He grew up right here in this bar, remember? It took time to realize that it was you they was talking about, but once he did . . . ain't nobody he digs more than you."

"Sheeeit."

"It's true. You're his hero, I don't care what he say or how he act. He loves you. And hearing his mama talk about you made him love you more."

"Well, I'll tell you one thing. This the first time since she been gone I'm glad she ain't around, 'cause she woulda killed him."

After a moment, they both chuckled. Fleetwood put his hand on Pudd'nhead's massive shoulder. Pudd'nhead stared at himself and Fleetwood in the wall mirror behind the bar.

"Ain't no telling where he gonna end up."

"He'll be all right. He's sharp, like his daddy," Fleetwood said.

"I wish he'd learn from his daddy. Might be too late for him. Like you said, he done been in this bar all his life. But if I don't do nothin' else, I gotta keep the girl straight. That's all her mama wanted. Lord knows, that's all . . . " Pudd'nhead's voice trailed off and he looked straight ahead. Fleetwood clapped him on the back.

"It's okay, Pudd'n," he told him. "It's okay, we all miss her."

"It's been over a year Fleetwood, but it just seem like—"

"I know, brother. Just ain't the same around here without Big Darlene, not even the ball games. But you got to hold on. Not just for them kids, either. For all of us."

"I ain't gonna make it much longer."

"Yes you are. You just got to take care. Cut down on the liquor, go on a diet like the doctor said."

"You right. Just gets hard sometimes. Me and Darlene was together at fifteen."

"I remember."

"Remember when Congressman Powell came in here and cracked on her? Congressman Powell! And she told his high-yellow ass she was spoken for. Yes she did, God bless her." Pudd'nhead laughed as a tear streaked down his face. Fleetwood was choked up himself.

"She was a helluva woman."

"Yes she was."

Fleetwood caught himself and brightened his expression. "Hey, how about Café Society next week? Best shake dancers in town."

"No thanks, man."

"Damn, Pudd'n, no shake dancers? I know you old, but you ain't dead!"

Pudd'nhead cracked a smile. "Just ain't thinkin' 'bout that now."

"Look here," Fleetwood advised. "Laly Patrick's bosoms so big, she got a pigeon coop in between 'em. She let the pigeons out every night in her show. Let's buy some bird seed and go."

"Some other time. Fleetwood, I might sell this place."

"Sell it and do what?"

"What me and Darlene always talked about. Maybe move out to Queens or Westchester, you know, take it easy. Maybe you and me can open a new bar."

"I really don't see myself moving, Pudd'n," his friend confessed. "But I know things are different now. We still got the Theresa, still got the Savoy and Smalls, but it ain't the same, it don't really jump like when we were coming up. But I'll tell you something. I know everybody on the block, and you can't put a price on that."

"Maybe not," Pudd'nhead admitted. "Maybe not."

That night, Darlene's Lounge was jumping with music and laughter, as it did every Saturday. Cigar smoke wafted above, the beer tap was flowing, and shots of liquor were tossed back at the bar. The "Stars in Jazz" program was on the radio, which got people dancing. Pudd'nhead worked the bar and laughed at all the neighborhood stories—Joe the undertaker shooting his wife for cheating on him, then hiding her in his funeral home, or Eula Mae beating her daughter in the street for wanting to be a shake dancer. At nine o'clock, Pudd'nhead got a phone call. Then he went outside to find his daughter's date dropping her off in a shiny 1954 Buick. When he saw Pudd'nhead in the doorway, Charles kept a polite distance from Darlene, to her dismay. Puddn'head returned to the bar and whooped with his regulars, tapping his foot to rhythm and blues from King Pleasure, Big Joe Turner, and other well-known singers of the day.

At about twelve-thirty, Percy came in and pushed his way through the crowd, wearing a nice suit. The entire left side of his face was swollen. He and his father saw each other, but neither spoke. Percy found a customer and gave him a folded stack of cash. A celebration was happening at his table because he'd hit the number. Pudd'nhead longed to tell his son something, but he couldn't think of what to say. Percy turned around and left, staring at his father, but never once coming near the bar. Pudd'nhead made his way to the door as fast as he could, hoping to catch his son before he got too far. Percy was almost around the corner when Pudd'nhead came out.

"Percy! Percy!"

The young man turned and looked for a moment before finally returning up the street. Pudd'nhead could see he was still angry as he approached. The swelling of Percy's face gave Pudd'nhead a twinge of guilt.

"Son, I just got upset when—"

"It's all right, Pop."

Pudd'nhead looked around, hoping the words would come to him. He finally focused on Percy, wearing his best suit, looking every bit like a local hustler.

"You and the girl all I got left."

"You got us, your friends, the bar, and a lifetime of memories, Pop."

"Yeah. When you . . . when you get back, we'll sit down and I'll tell you about the Minozzis. You need to know about them."

"Okay."

"I gotta stash for emergencies. Also, there's a twenty-two."

"In the back of the cabinet above the sink, I know."

"Know how to use it?"

"Yeah. But hopefully I won't need to. I just take numbers on the block. Nowhere else."

"You say that now, but—"

"I'm stayin' in the neighborhood, Pop. That way I can watch over everything that's important."

Pudd'nhead nodded. He saw the anger had faded from Percy's face, despite his best effort. He patted his son's shoulder.

"Be careful."

Percy turned and ventured into the night. Pudd'nhead stood on the block, which was quiet except for the Seventh Avenue traffic and the ruckus of Darlene's Lounge in the distance.

THE COMMUTE (2004)

CARMEN SCHEIDEL

Scheidel is a recent graduate of the MFA program at New School University. She lives in Brooklyn, but as you'll see, she dreams of Harlem, and has written a compelling, emotionally loaded story about a white woman's journey across Harlem streets with her lover.

The train droned on as Elias and I made our way home from work. This train, on the Metro-North Railroad from Stamford into New York, had punctuated our lives over the last two years, beginning when we met two summers ago at work, at our jobs in a displaced Wall Street firm that was headquartered in Connecticut.

We saw each other in the halls and at the coffee bar break area, but first spoke amid the train's unforgiving light as empty plastic bottles rolled into our ankles and thin streams of spilled coffee dampened our shoes's soles. Over time, we managed to cozy up in the tight seats, laugh about the day at work, and fly forward on the train's momentum toward the city's white light. We lived in separate boroughs, but held the hope that our separate lives could some day merge into one.

Today on our evening commute home, we sat with our knees pressed up and into the seats in front of us like we were at the movies.

"You know what I can't stand?" Elias was saying. "I can't stand when these guys from the neighborhood make it big and then come back flashing their big cars and gold." Someone had left a copy of the *Post* on the seat next to Elias and he couldn't resist leafing through it.

"You don't think money changes a person?" I said. "Look who we work with. These guys are all from like Indiana and now they have money, so they think they're hot shit."

Elias had gotten his start at the firm as a mail clerk, but over the years had been promoted so that now he oversaw the security detail, where mail was scanned for suspicious packages. I worked in HR, where I could access salary figures for everyone in the firm, some of them were outlandish—three million dollars in a year—and I shared this informa-tion with Elias, who in turn told the entire Spanish-speaking cadre in the mailroom so they knew the exact social strata of the men they carried packages to.

"Yeah, but at least the guys at work aren't flashy," Elias said. "So many guys I know from the neighborhood are just concerned with mak-ing the big bucks, no matter what. They'll do anything for it."

"These guys are no different," I said and remembered that many of the other passengers could hear me.

Outside the train window it was gray, mid-August, and unseason-ably balmy with the threat of rain. The after-work murmur of the train seemed to lull everyone around us: marketing executives from Clairol, Inc., and hedge fund managers from the Greenwich investment bou-tiques were asleep with their heads tilted back against the fluorescent light. The train's electricity flashed through copper wires. Steel drifted fluidly over steel, and there was the occasional shriek of metal against metal, all of it seducing the passengers into dreams, or calm, or submis-sion.

I, on the other hand, felt aggressive. All day I sat in on exit inter-views as individuals became part of the firm's overall head-count reduc-tion. Lives and careers halted in their tracks. My role as an HR person was to sit in on the firings and smile soberly as the boss did the talking. They placed me there in the room in case anyone became irate and Le-gal needed a witness. I wasn't supposed to say a word.

My forced passivity during the meetings made me want to scream, and by the third meeting that morning I decided that *today* would be the day I would tell Elias what I had been avoiding telling him for the past thirty days. I simply had to come clean during our regular after-work stroll through Harlem, where the physical movement and the fresh air coincided to loosen our joints at the end of the day, clear our heads, and, hopefully, in this case, loosen my tongue, which had been constricted for far too long.

The fact was that I had cheated on Elias with Bobby McFadden, a short, balding fireman from Queens, whom I met at my friend Doris's pub crawl. I hated parties like that, but Doris was turning forty and had been there years earlier through my whole divorce. She had in fact brought me biscuits and cheese on several nights so that there would be dinner. I knew that the least I could do was go to the party and have a good time, so I went with it and brought along a bag of cheap party favors—noisemakers, Groucho Marx glasses, and one plastic rhinoceros snout, which I kept on for most of the night. I ordered black and tans. At first, I drank one as a joking ode to myself and Elias, who was attending his night class and couldn't be there. I saluted our differences with the foamy, bicolored beverage until I couldn't see straight. By the time I brought Bobby back to my apartment, waking my roommate Lonn and accidentally blowing a fuse when I tried to turn on a fan, I knew what I was doing. I needed certainty in the relationship, and Bobby, in that moment, helped define what I had been feeling.

I was also mad at Elias for letting his ex-wife, Ruthie, show up unannounced at his apartment and stay for the whole day, as he cooked her plantains and fried Dominican cheese like they were a little family again, even though the woman regularly went months without seeing her son or even phoning him. Still, he allowed her to visit, chat, and make conversation. When it was time for Ruthie to go, she asked Elias for cab fare. All he had on him was a couple of ones and a new fifty-dollar bill set aside for a textbook he needed later in the week, and he gave her the fifty. Elias told me all of this.

"You okay?" he asked.

"Yeah," I said.

He continued reading and leaned his shoulder into mine. Outside the train window, Connecticut's deciduous forest flashed by us. In time the green streaks dulled into streams of white suburban New York houses followed by brown flashes of Bronx buildings.

We got off at 125th Street, Harlem Station. Harlem was just a place midway for Elias and me, where we went each night after work to walk slowly, continue conversation, and aim ourselves at subway trains going in different directions. Elias lived with his eight-year-old son in Washington Heights, Manhattan's little Santo Domingo, where women new to the States often pushed around metal shopping carts on warm days to peddle homemade fast foods: yucca fritters, meat-filled *pastelitos,* and *habichuela con dulce,* a sugary drink made of red beans, coconut cream, and cinnamon. I lived with a roommate I hardly knew in a sixth-floor walk-up in Park Slope, Brooklyn's pluralistic enclave for mixed-race families, experimental writers and filmmakers, food co-op volunteers, vegan lesbians, and Democratic Senator Chuck Schumer.

We were on the street now. The humid air was actually a nice change from the air-conditioned train car, which rumbled above our heads as it departed on the elevated tracks. Behind us in the distance, the sharp steel cut-out of the Triborough Bridge, a hulking mass of industrial fortitude, connected Manhattan, Queens, and the Bronx. That bridge always made me think of islands, that Elias grew up in the West Indies on an island called Hispaniola, with its conjoined twins Haiti and the Dominican Republic, and that on any given day Elias and I could walk the width of our own populous mass of bedrock in North America because we lived in a world that brought us together.

We crossed Park Avenue and began the stroll down 125th Street. I knew I needed to blurt out my little announcement before I lost my nerve. But Elias, on this particular evening, was in a talkative mood. His night class, called Caribbean Experience, was a social history of the African diaspora among the islands, and he was formulating ideas for a paper about Spanish soap operas compared to the American ones.

"For one thing," Elias said, slowing down his stride and turning toward me, "the Spanish soaps all have the same story. There's always a young lady and she's a maid for the super-rich family. And she's an orphan or something, so she has a sad life. But the son in the rich family falls in love with her because she's totally irresistible."

"Men love the maid outfits!" I interrupted. "Did you ever notice on Halloween how many French maids there are?"

He laughed. He always laughed in a way that gave away his foreign rearing: It was high-pitched, girlish, and unrestrained.

"No . . . no . . . ." he said, "but on the Spanish channel, for real, there's always something getting in the way of the love between the rich guy and the poor maid because they can't make it *so* easy or no one would care—and believe me, the people watching it care! So, okay, the maid always has to have a rival—some witch of a lady, who is the daughter of another rich family or something, and she wants to get the rich son for herself."

"Okay, so . . . " I said.

"So the rival tries to poison or stab or maybe suffocate the maid so that she can have him to herself. But the maid survives, because maids are like that! Then the guy's family threatens to disown him and take away his inheritance if he marries the maid, who by the way is now unemployed and sadder than ever. But the guy still does it, he marries her. So they finally get together and when they do, they discover that the rich family's money was actually *the maid's* inheritance from her dead parents! So in the end she gets the man and the fortune, and everyone else goes to jail. End of story. It's all about landing a jackpot without really doing anything to earn it."

I liked him when he was like this. I could see Elias beaming. "Isn't that the same as American soap operas?" I said.

"Oh, on those, everybody's a doctor or a lawyer, so they all have their own money!"

We walked quickly now, reenergized. The sidewalk seemed to open up and a middle-aged man with pointy black shoes strode toward us. He had the look of a down-home preacher: proud face, short, graying Afro. "Now *that's* what I call a good-looking couple!" he hollered as he passed. We must have looked cute together, or happy, like we were out having fun in our office khakis and glasses. Elias pulled me close, reached up to my face, and kissed me slowly. I felt a little dizzy when it was over, and we continued to stroll.

Outside Guinea Hair, a trio of women shouted offers to braid my short blonde frizz. Elias and I declined and kept ambling forward until we reached the intersection of 125th and Madison. It was humid outside and his face was shiny, smiling softly.

"I like looking at you," he said. "No matter how long I've known you, I'm still amazed that we're together." He gazed my way with expressive eyes that surprised me by how much they looked like the almond-shaped, brown eyes of my father's Bavarian family. The sky behind him was silvery and pale as if the light wanted to break through but couldn't. He was wearing a violet-colored business shirt. (He was the kind of man who could pull off a violet-colored business shirt.) Elias's face, the color of toasted almonds and tea with honey, looked beautiful in the diffused light.

"I wish I could take your picture right now," I said. I couldn't imagine losing him; or maybe that's precisely what I was imagining and wanted to hold onto the moment for a while longer. He smiled back at me.

On our first walk through Harlem, two summers ago, I remember falling in love with the details of his face and the tint of his lips.

"They're silver," I told him. "Your lips."

"Silver?"

"Yes. Silver."

A silvery blue, actually, and smooth. I wanted to trace them with my fingertip, but I didn't dare. We were still new to each other, so we turned forward and simply kept walking. A mural next to us, painted onto some construction scaffolding, proclaimed, "Impossibilities are merely things which we have not yet learned."

When I met Elias, he talked a lot about being Dominican, but said he didn't consider himself black. "You don't?" I had asked. I never imagined that he wasn't. "I'm Latin," he said earnestly, looking at me with black eyes, dark skin, a narrow nose, and high cheekbones.

I was from rural Ohio and wasn't accustomed to all of the racial and ethnic nuances that New York had to offer. He didn't see himself as black, but I did.

Still, I often never thought about it. Other things mattered more. I loved the way he looked at me, and the way his warm skin felt next to mine. But sometimes, when we were resting in bed, I would look down at our hands intertwined and be surprised by the stark difference.

Elias pulled my arm and pointed up the street to one of our favorite vendors, a man dressed in African prints twirling a three-foot machete, who was only out sporadically. Tonight he was dressed in full regalia, cutting up coconuts and waving the giant knife in the air like an African freedom fighter who had toned down only for the sake of commerce.

"I have to tell you something," I said.

"Yes, Mofongo," he replied. When he was in a good mood—nearly always—he called me by the names of Dominican foods. Mofongo, a favorite of his, was a comforting mash of salted plantains and roasted pork.

"No. I'm serious," I said.

"Okay," he sidled up beside me and put his arm around me as if I was about to tell him something grave and he wanted to offer comfort. He was always like that, very tender. He would stop off and buy me a sweet potato pie every night that I lingered in front of Wimp's Southern Bakery, even though he was generally low on cash and always had responsibilities waiting.

We waited for the light and then crossed the street to make our way toward the coconut seller.

"I'm not the greatest person," I told him.

"Oh, come on, that's not true. You want some coconut? Come on!"

We picked out a coconut that looked like a fuzzy infant's head and then admired the man's chopping skills as he carved it into bite-size pieces. He handed us white cakes of meat still damp from the milk inside and we were on our way.

"You're not still worked up about your mom's friend, what's his name, are you?" He began to suck on a piece of coconut.

I had brought up that subject again last night. Before Elias, I had never dated someone black. My mother had. So had my sister and my best friend in Ohio. They all seemed to be doing it at the same time. It was the 1980s. My mom was reeling from divorce, and she described the man she was seeing as being like a pair of warm slippers—comforting, good, kind. He was large and muscular. His tremendous upper body controlled an air hammer during the day. By evening he came over and threw a softball with me in the backyard and made soft conversation, asked about school. Despite the man's kindness, I hated him. I was fourteen and hated him for the embarrassment he caused at school in my rural town, where there were no blacks and only one or two families who were not Polish or Dutch or, like my own family, German. I hated my mother for seeing him. Hated division, divorce. Hated myself for being a part of it all.

Around the same time, my best friend and older sister were in the midst of teenage rebellion, acting out by dating bad-boy black boys from Cleveland. Boys who weren't into school and who could get us pot and drive around my sister's huge Buick, going eighty miles an hour on those country roads, blaring cassette dubs of Curtis Blow, Prince, whatever we could get our hands on. It was a stage for them, a stage they were happy to discard in a year. I knew that my reasons for being with Elias were different. But it bothered me that some people might think I was with him to prove something or as a sort of experiment.

When we talked about race, Elias told me he didn't understand why some people in his culture saw dating a white woman as a status symbol. When he said this, I couldn't help but wonder if subconsciously he did associate some cultural cachet with me, a trophy wife of the Washington Heights variety. For that matter, I did wonder sometimes if I was drawn to him in the same way. He was, after all, what Doris called "a man of the islands," and when she said it, she always wiggled her fingers in the air for voodoo effect. Without him I certainly wouldn't be hopscotching through Harlem each night, eating pie with a plastic fork, and laughing with the rest of the block at the loud zoot suits in the windows of one particular men's shop.

"Here," he said, handing me some coconut. "Eat this. And just remember this: You were young then. Don't beat yourself up over it."

We continued to walk west along 125th Street, past the men with the Nation of Islam brochures spread out on card tables and incense burning in steady streams of smoke. Packs of kids in school uniforms yelled and tackled each other as they swarmed the crosswalk. Blinking yellow traffic lights flashed behind them, and a trail of shoppers swung grocery bags. There were people everywhere and horns honking. It felt like the whole movement of the city had converged into this one spot, the epicenter, and over Elias's shoulder a red sign flashed outside the fish store: WORLD'S BEST FRESH CATCH.

"It's all too complicated," I managed to say. "You've got your life, your son." I knew he was willing to make huge changes for me. He had dropped everything for me, changed his entire life to make it amenable to me—moved out of his sister's house, got an apartment of his own with his son, enrolled in night classes, got As on his first three tests.

Still, I worried. It was hard to picture myself in his world. He had grown up in a third-world country, had lived in a house with a dirt floor until he was ten, and he carried the poverty with him. Mostly it showed itself in a generosity of spirit, a humbleness toward mankind, but it also made him afraid to demand things for himself. It made him quiet around my friends and the managers at work, and it made him indulgent toward his American son. The son whom I pitied. The son who was prone to fits, who had every right to be angry over not having a real mother. A son who was lost in the daily maze of Head Start, public school, after-school tutoring, and finally a late fast-food dinner with his dad.

Every time I imagined moving into their home, I saw myself becoming taciturn and sour: The bitter, dull white woman ripping the Nintendo out of the wall and hanging up the phone on the ex-wife. I imagined my quiet disapproval of their ways drying out my core, my emotions shriveling up so that there was nothing left but bitterness. Sometimes I wondered if Elias saw this, too. After all, I did spend very little time at their apartment. It was something we worked around.

"I just have to say," I said, "I have a hard time seeing how this can all pan out."

"It's not a question of how it can work," he said, "but of the fact that it is working. What are you questioning here?"

Actually, I wasn't sure. Maybe my age was the real problem. I heard it repeated in news magazines, gynecological brochures, and even on NPR. Thirty-five was the threshold. The changeover from hopefulness to desperation. From bright future to raising a child with brain damage. Thirty-five! I wasn't even sure I wanted a baby, let alone a husband. But that was the problem. I craved certainty. And of everything Elias could offer, certainty and ease weren't part of the equation.

"Look," I said. I was frustrated now and had become cold. "I've had my doubts for a while now, and I've gotten frustrated with the whole thing. Christ, my eyes are open, that's all I'm saying."

"I don't think you need to curse," he said, his voice quieting, his body veering away slightly, opening up the gap between us. We were both silent, and we walked. We continued west up 125th Street toward Frederick Douglass Boulevard. People rushed past us to get home.

"I haven't been completely honest with you," I said without looking at him.

"Okay . . ."

"I just have this thing I want to tell you and I hope by talking about it we can figure things out between us."

He listened and watched me.

"This isn't meant to hurt you, but I think it's a symptom of some of the questions I've been having." I was nervous and trying to talk my way through it.

"You can just say it," he said.

"It's not like I've been seeing someone, but . . . I had a date a while ago and I haven't felt right about it since then . . . I wanted to tell you."

"Oh, not this again!" he said. "I'm really not up for this! I really don't want to know this. Things have been going so well!"

We walked more quickly now, keeping pace with each other and not saying anything. The humidity in the air was beginning to feel oppressive and I found it hard to breathe.

"It's okay," he finally said. His face was somber, gravely calm. "It's okay because I don't know if I can do what you want. It's been on my mind, too."

"I'm sure it has."

"And I don't know if I have the energy. I'm just not so sure about being around someone, subjecting my son to someone, who every time we argue becomes so enraged that she loses all control."

"I wouldn't do that in front of him!" But I knew that I couldn't be sure. "Why would you say that!" I said. I was a capable person. I just got easily overwhelmed. He wouldn't know, I thought, because it was easy for him to let things go. To sit back and cuddle with his son and visit his sister and tune out the demands of the world! I had been under stress, it was true. I was trying to open a business. To make my fifteen years of corporate work mean something, to make my life mean something. Couldn't he understand this?

I was growing furious.

"You know what I think it is," I said. "The world expects nothing from you, so anything you do is a major achievement. Except in this relationship, it hasn't been enough for me, but rather than admitting that, you ignore it and act like you're doing a bang-up job!"

Elias stopped. He stood there on the busy sidewalk as an immovable object. "That's enough," he said. "I think that's enough. I'm not doing this," he said. "I don't want this." His face was trembling. "I'm leaving. Maybe you can find someone else to escort you the rest of the way." He walked past me.

I stood at St. Nicholas and 125th alone and watched him walk away. He had told me before, when he was speaking about Ruthie, that he was not the kind to look back. As I watched his solid figure walk away, he didn't hesitate or change direction. He only picked up speed and after a while I couldn't distinguish him from the streetlights and flashes of people.

I could not believe this. I stood still. A middle-aged man in an Adidas suit walked toward me. "Oh, baby, it's okay," he said with a little laugh. My face looked so miserable it was drawing attention. I began to walk again. The humid air had grown cool. I could feel it against my face. The night had grown dark. I felt out of place. Pushing past two women with shopping bags, I stumbled into them, knocking a bag from the older woman's hand. "Sorry," I called behind her, and the younger of the women swung a bag at me and yelled, "You better be sorry! Knocking into an old woman like that!"

I wandered down subway steps. I caught the number 1 train heading downtown and found a seat. I sat down without anything to do for the first time since seven that morning. I took a deep breath. I couldn't believe this. A tiny, black man sitting next to me smiled. I smiled back, but turned away.

"How you doing?" he asked. He looked like someone's tiny Puerto Rican uncle in a starched shirt.

"Good," I said. I was clearly miserable. "How are *you?*" I asked in return.

"I'd be better if I was with a nice woman like you!"

"Ha!" I snorted. There was so much bottled up, so much racing inside.

"Are you married?" he asked.

"No," I said.

"Are you in *love?*"

"Yes."

"I mean, really, *really* in love."

"Yehhhhhhhs."

I turned forward, away from him, and could see the other passengers looking, wondering perhaps why I was encouraging this little game of intimacy. I put my head back and closed my eyes. I took a deep breath and my mind began to wander.

"I can't do it!" I had screamed into Elias's face more than once in the past year, "I can't take on everything you've let go to shit your whole life." I had flattered myself that I could save him from himself, that I would make him a better person. In fact, that he needed me.

Later that night I would dream about Elias's son. I hugged and kissed the boy in the dream and his skin felt like his father's. "Is this what it's like to have kids with someone?" I would wonder out loud. For the moment, I would envision the love of one transferring and subdividing into the love of another.

I soon got off at my stop in Park Slope. Many of my neighbors were right along with me, single people alone in the world, walking home just like me. I made my way up the subway stairs and into the fresh air. It was misting outside now, and the light water cooled my face. I turned my head down toward the sidewalk and let it lead me home.

SUDAN WASHINGTON (2004)

FUNMI OSABA

Born in Nigeria and educated in England, Osaba is an attorney and documentary filmmaker. Her new character, Sudan Washington, is strong, smart, and no-nonsense enough to make readers want to forget about other literary legal eagles.

"Counsel?"

"Ready for trial, Your Honor," she stated emphatically.

Sudan was a tall, attractive, dark-skinned African-American woman in her late thirties. She wore her long braids pulled severely back from her face.

"Pick your jury, Counsel."

And so yet another trial was about to begin. Sudan sat down behind the defense table while the clerk began to call out the names of potential jurors who had now filled the courtroom. A familiar tingle of excitement coursed down her spine and played with the edges of her lips so that she appeared to be smiling. She bowed her head, and when she looked up, the smile was gone.

Her expression was now the practiced deadpan which gave nothing away. She glanced briefly at the defendant, whose life she literally held in her hands. He was sitting beside her, turned to his left to get a better view of the potential jurors, whom, as their names were called, came up to fill the juror chairs in the well of the courtroom. His brow was wrinkled with concern; he stared at each juror intently, almost as if he was trying to read their minds as they made their way up to the jurors' enclosure.

She glanced over at the prosecutor's table and was not sure what she felt.

For fourteen years, Sudan had worked in the New York County District Attorney's Office as a prosecutor. She reflected now that a year ago, she would have been sitting at that other table as a top litigator in the Homicide Bureau. She would have been advocating for a victim who often could not be in the courtroom, usually because of their untimely deaths, and very often at the hands of the defendant who would be sitting across from her.

Two years ago, Sudan had started to feel the lethargy that is the telltale sign of burnout. It had become harder to prepare, to stay on the case. She was getting more tired than she cared to admit. The burning enthusiasm, which had previously marked the start of a trial, was missing.

It was time to go.

Sudan briefly played with the idea of changing careers altogether. But she never seriously entertained the idea of doing anything else.

She was a litigator at heart.

The courtroom felt like her home. The jurors, members of her extended family.

Besides, she had a secret weapon, which had made her a top trial attorney: her ability to win jurors over to her side. She had developed an almost uncanny, instinctive ability to connect with jurors both individually and as a group. She had not yet been before a jury that did not like her. And that was often enough to sway their decision in her favor.

Three months after leaving the district attorney's office, she opened an office on 145th Street and announced to the world that Sudan Washington was back in business.

Things were slow at first.

Sudan might have been a maverick in the DA's office, but to the rest of the world, she was just another struggling black lawyer in a city full of lawyers.

Her office was often so quiet, she questioned why she had a receptionist. When the bell would ring, indicating that someone had entered her office, it was usually tourists, winos, or deadbeats looking for free legal service. Paying clients were thin on the ground.

In order to pay the rent, she took on cases in housing court, which she felt demeaned her. She took on cases in family court, which she felt demeaned the children. She dabbled in contested matrimonial cases, which she felt demeaned everyone.

And then Mrs. MacDonald walked into her office.

It was a hot day in July. The air conditioners were going at full blast, but it still felt hot. In order to give herself something to do, Sudan was arranging her filing cabinet alphabetically by client last name, when Tracy, her receptionist, came into her office and told her she had a potential client.

"Did you find out what she wanted?" Sudan asked, her attention on whether Williams came before Winston.

Tracy closed the door and walked farther into the office. She was an attractive Latina who loved the job because Sudan was easygoing and allowed her to spend most of the day on the phone talking to her boyfriends.

Tracy shook her head. "She says she has to talk to you."

Sudan switched her attention from her filing cabinets to Tracy.

"Give me a moment to clear up, then bring her in."

"I'm sorry to bother you, miss," the woman started apologetically.

Like the best litigators, Sudan had begun studying the woman the minute she walked through the door.

Mrs. MacDonald was in her mid-sixties. She wore an ill-fitting, dark-colored wig and carried a tattered plastic handbag. Her shoes—dirty, scuffed, and worn at the heels—looked as if she had worn them her whole life. Her clothes were dull and nondescript. She had the tired look of a woman who had sacrificed her life for her family and received nothing back in return. When she spoke, she had the familiar musical lilt of the Jamaicans.

"That's why I'm here, ma'am. I love to be bothered. Take a sit."

Mrs. MacDonald sat sluggishly, clutching her bag to her breast.

"What can I do for you?" Sudan asked gently, thinking, Definitely not a tourist, not a wino, possibly a deadbeat.

"I don't know if you can help me . . ." she began,

Sudan nodded. She was now sitting behind her desk, wondering where this was all leading. And then Mrs. MacDonald got Sudan's attention by her next statement.

"They said he killed a woman," she blurted, "but I know he didn't do it. He's my husband. He could never do anything like that."

Definitely a deadbeat wanting free legal services, Sudan thought.

She picked up a pencil and fingered it thoughtfully, and then she leaned forward.

"Before you go any further, I must ask you, are you or your husband able to retain an attorney?"

At Mrs. MacDonald's puzzled expression, Sudan clarified by saying, "Pay for an attorney?"

Mrs. MacDonald nodded, relieved. "I don't know how much it costs. You see, I have never had to have a lawyer before. But my husband told me to get money out of the house." She opened her purse and pulled out some money. "I can get more if it is not enough," she said urgently as she pushed the bundles toward Sudan.

Sudan stared at the money and then at the little old lady sitting across from her who looked as if she had not bought a single item of clothing in twenty years.

"How much is this?" she asked.

"Fifty thousand. I can get more. When I sell the house. . . . "

Sudan took it in, swallowed, and then nodded. "I believe I can help you," she said.

They had finished picking their jurors. The jury consisted of five women and seven men; four blacks, two Latinos, and six whites. The two alternates were black. A good jury, Sudan thought. She knew from their suspicious stares that she had not yet won them over, but it was early.

Steven Lloyd was the lead prosecutor. A graying white man in his mid-fifties, he had trained Sudan when she first entered the Homicide Bureau.

Steven Lloyd stood up to address the jury and he told them how he would prove that "this man"—he stabbed a finger in the air in the direction of the defendant—"how this man and this man alone, had killed a harmless, defenseless woman in cold blood. How this man was responsible for the murder of a loving mother who never harmed anyone. A woman who worked as a nurse, who was a responsible member of society, who belonged to her local Baptist church and regularly helped to feed the homeless, how this woman had been killed by this man with malice and vengeance and malevolence," again the finger stabbing, "by this man who was an evil predator, pure and simple."

The finger stabbing went on for a while longer.

The jurors, fresh and ready to do their civic duty, listened intently, occasionally stealing a glance to look past the finger at the defendant, their expressions marked with curiosity.

Mr. MacDonald looked nothing like the evil predator that the prosecutor was describing. In fact, he looked quite the opposite. He was a small man with an ingratiating manner. At sixty-nine, he was older than most murder defendants. He wore a crumpled brown suit, which made him look like the blue-collar worker that he was. He was bald, and occasionally would rub the palm of his hand over his head, producing a dry rustling sound like the crackling of dried leaves in autumn. He had harsh, dark little eyes, set like pieces of flint into an unremarkable face.

Sudan walked over to address the jury. She told the defendant to rise and then asked, "Does he look like a cold-hearted, evil predator?" She fixed her eyes on each of the jurors in turn and allowed them to take in the little old man who stood behind the defense table, slightly hunched, staring alternately at the jurors and then at the top of the table. "No, he does not." Sudan answered her own question. "I will tell you why he does not look like a cold-hearted, evil predator." Sudan said, now standing less than two feet from the first row of jurors. "Because he is not. In this trial, I will ask of you one thing, and one thing only. Will you do one thing for me, Ms. Brown, Mr. Johnson, Ms. Weatherspoon. . . . " Sudan asked earnestly, fixing her eyes again on each of the jurors in turn as she called out their names. This elicited nods. Sudan nodded once in approval, paused, and continued.

"All I ask is that you make these people"—Sudan now used the familiar finger-pointing routine, but this time it was directed at her mentor—"I ask that you make these people do what the law requires them to do." Her voice was now a few octaves higher. "Make them prove, beyond a reasonable doubt, that my client in fact was responsible for this heinous crime."

"Good opening, Counsel."

Steven Lloyd caught up with Sudan in the corridor during the afternoon adjournment.

"Think he did it?"

Sudan shook her head. "The question never even entered my mind."

"Oh, I forgot, you're now a defense attorney." Steve made it sound like an accusation.

"What's that supposed to mean?" Sudan asked indignantly, knowing quite well. Prosecutors often saw themselves as being on the right side, the side of truth, fairness, and justice. They were the good guys, the ones society entrusted with the task of keeping the criminals off the streets and ensuring the safety of the public.

Steven smiled confidently. "We have the murder weapon. Save yourself the trouble. Take the offer."

Sudan shook her head. "At his age, that's a death sentence."

"So be it, Counsel."

Steven strode down the corridor and out of sight. Sudan remained standing in the corridor staring after him. She thought about what he had said. Not only did they have the murder weapon, but they also had her client at the scene of the crime.

What bothered her was that she did not yet have a theory to explain her client's innocence to the jury. Litigation was all about storytelling, Sudan had learned. Whoever told the most believable story was likely to come out victorious.

It just had to be believable and long years of practice had told her that there was a believable story for just about everything that happened. The challenge was to find it. This was on Sudan's mind as she made her way to the jails on the ninth floor.

"They want to settle, second degree murder, ten years."

Mr. MacDonald rubbed the palm of his hand over his head again. Sudan heard the faint sound of rustling leaves in autumn. He had removed his jacket, which lay carelessly across the rough wooden table. He had rolled up the sleeves to his shirt and removed his tie. He shook his head, his expression worried.

"But I did not do nothing. I swear, I did not kill that woman." Even as he protested his innocence, his little eyes still remained like hard pieces of flint.

"I have to inform you of any offer they make. But it is up to you to accept or reject it."

"Ten years." He mulled. "I'd likely be dead by then." He shook his head. "Can you get me off?" He stared hard at Sudan.

"I can try." Sudan paused thoughtfully and stared at her legal pad, as if looking for the answer between the lines on the yellow pad. "You know what our main problem is."

Mr. MacDonald nodded. "How come I was in the house when she was killed and I heard nothing."

Mr. MacDonald rubbed his forehead with his left hand and stared at the rough cement floor. Sudan wondered how his hand got to be so badly wrinkled.

Somewhere, someone screamed, keys jangled, a radio played.

When he next spoke, he seemed suddenly tired.

"I guess I'll just have to see it through." His voice was now barely a whisper. "Tell my wife to get me my pills." He began to massage his chest.

Mrs. MacDonald came to court every day, and every day she sat patiently in the courtroom, listening to the evidence. She would arrive before the courts opened, join the long line of defendants, witnesses, and now attorneys waiting outside the court to walk through the metal detectors, then she would make her way up to the sixth floor. Often she arrived before the courtroom opened and she would sit patiently on a bench outside the courtroom. Many times, Sudan would meet her there.

Mrs. MacDonald never asked questions. She never made small talk. She never expressed anything she was feeling. She puzzled Sudan.

The trial proceeded and Sudan thought that things were going well. The prosecution was relying heavily on circumstantial evidence at this stage and Sudan knew that as long as there were no unpleasant surprises, the case was still wide open.

And then the prosecution called their last witness.

Cray Donovan was a young nurse who worked in the emergency room of the hospital in which Mrs. Forrester, the deceased, had worked. As he loped over to the stand, Sudan leaned over to Mr. MacDonald.

"What will he say?" she asked.

Mr. MacDonald shrugged. "They worked together. That was all," he whispered back sharply.

But that was not all Cray Donovan had to say.

"So it is your testimony here today that you and Mrs. Forrester were lovers," Steven asked.

Beside her, Sudan felt Mr. MacDonald stiffen.

"Why did you lie to me?" Sudan asked.

They were sitting in a small interview room on the ninth floor. It was the end of the day, and the trial was adjourned. Prisoners were about to be transported back to Rikers for the night.

Mr. MacDonald looked at Sudan and began to protest.

"Cut the crap!" Sudan said forcefully. She pulled herself forward in her chair so that her face was only inches from Mr. MacDonald's. "Do you know what we're up against?"

Mr. MacDonald seemed hurt. He shook his head and was about to defend himself when she moved even closer. He could see beads of sweat on her broad forehead, her eyes red with fury.

"You think you're smart, don't you?" She stared hard at him. "They have the unlimited funds to prosecute a case. They have trained detectives. They have crime labs. They have everything. All you have is me. How am I supposed to come up against all that and defend you effectively if you lie to me?"

Mr. MacDonald did not say anything.

"She was your girlfriend, not your cousin."

Now Mr. MacDonald looked embarrassed. He dropped his eyes and Sudan got her answer.

Sudan pulled herself back and stood up from the chair. She walked toward the door and stared through the bars into the corridor. A correction officer who was sitting by the main door looked up and nodded at her. She nodded back.

Behind her, Mr. MacDonald spoke. "How did you know?"

"Because of the way you reacted when Clay Donovan revealed that he and Mrs. Forrester were lovers," Sudan responded. For a moment there was silence.

"So why did you lie?" Sudan turned to face Mr. MacDonald.

"Because I did not think it would help my case if you knew," Mr. MacDonald explained apologetically.

"Don't you think I could have found a way to present it to the jury if I'd known? All along you've maintained that you were cousins. What do you think the prosecution will do when they get you on the stand?"

Mr. MacDonald was silent.

"Did your wife know?"

"No." Mr. MacDonald shook his head emphatically. "She thought we were cousins."

"Mrs. MacDonald, I have to ask you some questions."

They were sitting in the corridor of the Supreme Court, outside the courtroom. It was late and the court had emptied of people. A cleaner pushed his mop down the corridor.

"Did your husband ever cheat on you?" Sudan asked, watching Mrs. MacDonald closely.

For a while Mrs. MacDonald said nothing but continued to stare straight ahead. When Sudan began to think she would not get an answer, Mrs. MacDonald moved her head very slightly. "No," she said. "No, never."

Sudan was now back at the office, it was late but not yet dark. Tracy always stayed until Sudan returned from court. She was never in a hurry to leave. That was the one thing Sudan liked best about her.

Sudan had bought some ribs from the soul food kitchen on 125th Street. Tracy began to eat eagerly but Sudan took a rib, took a bite, and tossed it back in the plate. She realized she had no appetite.

"How did it go in court today?" Tracy asked.

"Not good." Sudan shook her head.

More than catching her client in a lie, the prosecution had managed to do something that was very damaging to her case. They had prepared the ground to present the jury with a motive for murder. Sudan stayed in her office until very late, wondering how she could rehabilitate her client in the eyes of the jury. It seemed an impossible task.

After the prosecution rested, the defense began their case.

Sudan had debated putting Mr. MacDonald on the witness stand. She was not sure if he would make a good witness, if he could with-

stand the rigors of cross-examination. More than anything, she was unsure if she could rehabilitate him on the witness stand. Juries did not like
men who cheated on their wives, it made them look dishonest and unsympathetic. Sudan knew that in order to compensate for the damage
done by the prosecution case she would have to show that the prosecution case was still only circumstantial, that even though Mr. MacDonald
was an adulterer he was not a murderer. She prepped Mr. MacDonald
the evening before and again the morning before he had to take the
stand. With some apprehension, she let him take the stand.

The jurors watched with a mixture of suspicion and curiosity as Mr.
MacDonald rose to take the witness stand. He walked to the witness box
with a hesitant halting manner, and as he sat, he rubbed his head with
the palm of his hand and looked at the jurors as if expecting them to ask
him questions.

"Mr. MacDonald, was Mrs. Forrester your cousin?" Sudan asked.

"No."

"Then why did you tell the police she was your cousin?"

"To protect my wife." He nodded in Mrs. MacDonald's direction.

"You mean your wife believed she was your cousin."

"Yes."

"But Mrs. Forrester was not your cousin, she was, in fact, your girlfriend."

"Yes."

Mrs. MacDonald got up and left the courtroom.

Sudan's tactic was to reveal the damaging information first to mini-
mize the impact it would have on the jury when the prosecution
brought it up.

"Did you kill Angel Forrester?" Sudan asked.

"No, miss, I did not."

Sudan turned to look at the jury and then nodded to the judge.

"Your witness, Counsel."

Sudan walked back to her desk and Steven stood up. He buttoned
his jacket and unbuttoned it, all the time, staring intently at Mr. Mac-
Donald. He moved smoothly from behind the prosecution table and
walked toward the defendant. He stopped when he was halfway between the prosecution table and the witness stand. Sudan watched him

with some apprehension; he reminded Sudan of a predator with the smell of blood in his nostrils.

"Did you kill Angel Forrester?" Steven asked.

"No, I did not."

"Then do you have any idea how she ended up dead?"

"Objection." Sudan rose to her feet with such force she almost toppled her chair.

"Sustained."

Steven looked at Sudan with a mischievous smile, and then turned his attention back to Mr. MacDonald.

"Where were you when Mrs. Forrester was killed?"

"I was asleep."

"Where?"

"In the front bedroom."

"In order to get to the room where Mrs. Forrester was killed, the killer would have had to climb the stairs and walk past the bedroom in which you claim you were asleep. Right?"

"I don't know," Mr. MacDonald replied. He nervously rubbed his head with his hand and in the silence that hung in the courtroom rose the sounds of dried leaves rustling in an autumn breeze.

"Did you tell the police that Mrs. Forrester was your cousin?"

"Yes."

"That was, in fact, a lie."

"Yes, I—"

Steven cut him off before he could continue.

"Did you also tell the police that you were asleep while Mrs. Forrester was savagely attacked."

"Yes."

"Let me see now. A stranger breaks into a house, climbs the stairs, sees you sleeping in a front room, moves on to the back room. Finds a woman there, begins to savagely attack her. Stabs her again, and again and again. We must assume during this time that Mrs. Forrester was fighting for her life, as one would, naturally. She would also very likely have been screaming at the top of her lungs. Am I to understand that it is your testimony here today that you slept while all this was going on?" Steven yelled incredulously.

In the silence the jurors frowned and stared at Mr. MacDonald with distaste.

Steven knew that the jury was his, and moved closer to Mr. Mac-Donald.

"Is that not, in fact, another lie, Mr. MacDonald?"

Mr. MacDonald stammered something. The stenographer asked him to repeat it. Mr. MacDonald opened his mouth, but no words came out. He rubbed his head, which by now was clammy. He rubbed his head again and again, all the time shaking his head.

Steven moved in for the kill.

Stabbing the air before Mr. MacDonald, but positioning himself so that he could see both the jury and the defendant, Steven forcefully bellowed, "I put it to you that you killed Mrs. Forrester in a fit of jealous rage." Steven's voice thundered around the courtroom. "When you found out that she was seeing a much younger man, cheating on you, you became enraged. That morning you had words with her, maybe she taunted you. You got mad, enraged, and you killed her. That's the truth isn't it, isn't it?" And then the unthinkable happened and a hush fell over the court.

Steven froze in midstep.

The jurors gasped.

Sudan leapt to her feet. The court officer reached Mr. MacDonald first as he toppled over.

And as pandemonium broke out in the court, the judge banged his gavel and cleared the courtroom.

The jurors were removed.

Nobody noticed that Mrs. MacDonald had quietly returned, she sat in the back of the courtroom, embraced in stillness amidst all the commotion.

The paramedics arrived and tried to resuscitate Mr. MacDonald. He was rushed to the nearest hospital where he was pronounced dead on arrival. Death was from a massive heart attack.

And so the trial came to an abrupt and inconclusive end.

The judge declared a mistrial and the jury was excused.

Weeks after Mr. MacDonald was laid to rest, Tracy announced the return of a client.

Mrs. MacDonald, looking nothing like the Mrs. MacDonald Sudan had come to know, entered her office.

"I just wanted to thank you for your help," Mrs. MacDonald said with a smile.

Sudan noticed that Mrs. MacDonald now wore a nicely tailored orange suit. Gone was the cheap wig; her hair was straightened, curled, and pulled back in a stylish bun. Gone was the tattered handbag and the dingy shoes. Here before her stood an attractive, self-confident woman with everything to live for. Sudan thought she would not have recognized her if she had passed by her on the street.

Sudan had stood up to welcome Mrs. MacDonald into her office, but the smile was now frozen on her face. She watched Mrs. MacDonald confidently make her way into her office, and with no encouragement choose a chair and make herself comfortable. She arranged herself in the chair, crossed her legs, and then smiled at Sudan.

"I think I owe you some money," she said, opening her designer handbag.

Sudan moved from around her desk.

"You knew," she said softly.

"Excuse me?" Mrs. MacDonald asked.

"You knew all along that she was his mistress."

Mrs. MacDonald brought out a bundle of money. "I think this should settle my account."

"Yet you paid for his defense. Why, why do anything? After all, you were his wife. You could have divorced him and taken most of what he had," Sudan asked.

Mrs. MacDonald gazed at Sudan curiously for a moment and then shook her head. "He always referred to me as his wife, we had been together for so long, but he never married me. I begged him to, many times. Then I found out recently that he had married, he married a woman back home in Jamaica, not long ago."

She left the money on the desk, stood up, and made her way to the door.

"So what did you do?" Sudan asked following her. "Get him to give you power of attorney while he was in jail?"

"He thought it was his idea. When he signed the papers, he said, 'Only take out enough money to pay my lawyer.' He never liked for me to have anything. He was mean that way. I figured if I could take some,

I might as well take all, so I sold the houses. He would not have liked that." Mrs. MacDonald smiled as if at a private joke, then she moved closer to Sudan as if to confide in her.

"He had two brownstones in Harlem. I encouraged him to buy them thirty years ago, I even helped pay for them. He said he couldn't put my name on the deeds because of tax problems. I believed him."

As she was about to exit, Sudan stopped her.

"I have a question for you, Mrs. MacDonald," Sudan said, moving toward the door. "Did you kill Angel Forrester? Was that part of the plan to get control or did you just profit from her death?"

"You are too good a lawyer to expect an answer to that question, Counsel."

Mrs. MacDonald left the office, leaving the scent of expensive perfume in her wake.

It was another balmy afternoon in Harlem. Anything was possible.

MIGDALIA (2004)

RACHEL DE ARAGON

Rachel is a first-generation born-and-bred New Yorker who writes, works, and believes in the city. She also believes that history is best exemplified by those whose stories are not told; those are the people who matter most to her and whose stories she chooses to tell.

"Migdalia," excerpted from her yet-to-be-published novel *The Hole in the Sky,* provides a glimpse of Harlem through the eyes of the recently arrived. Anecdotal and multigenerational, the novel explores what is lost and what can be reclaimed in the process of the "Americanization" of a Puerto Rican family. Rachel has happily been a member of the Harlem Writers Guild for five years.

IN THE VOICE OF LUIS HERRERA, SR.

Migdalia Cruz is the name of a woman who I knew when I first came to New York. She was the one who saved me from the dirty, small room I had rented on the advice of a friend of my brother Fernando. She was the one who taught me how to find something better for less money. I lived with her for more or less two years. Because of Migdalia, I was able to earn enough to bring my family. I was working, washing dishes, and then at the factory, preparing for Luz and Luis to arrive.

She was my girlfriend, but it was not something that was meant to last forever. She was preparing to bring her parents to the mainland. And she also had a fiancé in the army. Her life was planned, as was mine. But it is not easy to be alone. The aloneness in a strange country is a terrible feeling.

I came to New York with nothing except the ticket, and a promise for a job in a factory. Where I lived I simply followed the steps of the other men who had come with me. We came on the night flight together, the cheap one, thinking that we might not ever see the sun again. I was a young man, few things frightened me, because, if I tell you the truth, young men are stupid enough to get on a plane that crashes all the time and think, It can't kill me. Deep down we knew about the planes that didn't make it—the unscheduled ones. Those were planes that they got from who knows where, ones that shook and made the black sky feel like it was paved with stones.

But of course, the night flights were cheaper, and every dollar mattered to us. In those times they didn't bother to inspect the planes they sent to the island, the ones that brought us here. The boat was no better! The boat they had coming from San Juan was a troop transport ship, left over from the war. Since my brother Alberto had burned to death on a ship that took a torpedo during the war, I wasn't about to take that boat.

To be honest, if I had told my mother I was getting into a "Marine Tiger," she would not have given one cent for the fare. She gave me money from the sale of the farm, what was left after the debt was paid.

It was easy to get work as a farm laborer on the mainland. There was one woman from my town who did that, but that was not for me. My idea was to earn money to buy back the farm, to become something more than a day worker. Because Fernando had written from Chicago about factory jobs for Puerto Ricans in New York, I came. Look, my family had never worked for others. We had always owned our land. My idea was to buy it all back. A friend of Fernando from the army had a factory job, and that was where I was going to work. But by the time I got there, they weren't hiring, so I worked washing dishes.

Of the men I came with, two of them have remained my friends for life. Jorge Ruiz and Juan Gonzalez. Jorge went back to Rio Piedras years ago. Believe it or not, now he is an old man who sits on his porch and rocks in his chair. When I went to the wedding of my brother Paco's granddaughter, I went to visit him. But at the time when we first met, in the years right after the war, many people were changing their lives, and Jorge was one of them. He was a man older than the rest of us, but he was built like a rock, with enormous muscles that he got from loading ships with sacks of sugar. To lift a hundred pounds over his head was nothing to Jorge. He was a bear, a giant. He could have been a heavyweight fighter, that's how he was made.

Look, most Puerto Ricans are not so gigantic. We are strong people, but not so tall (although my son-in-law is of a gigantic size). But mostly, North Americans are bigger. I've seen some of them that can't fit in a doorway!

What I know is that many such huge men do not make good use of their size. They are like pumpkins. But Jorge was not that type. He got me a job once as a stevedore, you know, loading ships. Juan and me, we are average-size men, and the work was not suited to us, but at the time, we had no choice.

We lived in a rooming house right next to *el tren,* all together at first, although to tell you the truth, living with Jorge was not so easy. First of all, to keep himself, he ate more than an average amount, and drank beer like water. Secondly, he was always chasing women. This was his business, naturally. But since Juan and me could think of nothing but sleep, and would fall onto our beds as soon as we came in after a day with all that lifting, the habits that Jorge kept were not easy to live with.

After some months, Juan and me got jobs in a factory, so we were able to move to another floor. Then Juan's cousin and his wife arrived. Listen, we were living four in one room.

Being crowded together and yet being alone is how the new person here lives. It was that way for me. No one understands what you need, and I understood nothing of what was going on. I was like a baby bumping into everything. I was fired from one job, and then went to another dishwasher job. That's the way it went for me and Juan. We tried keeping more than one job, and kept saving money.

Now, since then, there are many people in New York who speak Spanish. But then, believe me, it was not so common. Where we lived uptown, in Harlem, in El Barrio, there were Cubans and Puerto Ricans, but when you took the bus, *coño,* not one person could understand us!

Because of this it was easy to get cheated. English-speaking people took advantage of our ignorance, and Spanish-speaking people took advantage because they knew we had to go to them. The rooms we had were owned by a Cuban *chulo* who had lived in this country many years, a man who claimed he had a featherweight title, a champion that couldn't remember the date he'd won. He himself paid rent to another man, a North American, a fat one, pale as straw. We paid fifteen dollars a month, no heat, no hot water. By the money today, that sounds cheap! Later, when I met Migdalia, together we paid fourteen dollars a month for a whole apartment, although we did not have heat or hot water; we boiled the pot. That was my first cold winter. I knew nothing about steam heat. But we were young and preparing for the future! But listen, that little rooster had charged fifteen dollars for the three of us, then when Juan and me moved upstairs—he called it a bargain to charge us ten dollars, and ten dollars to Jorge. He acted like we were cheating him!

Of course, we continued to also help Jorge, because it was a shock to him to be left with so much to pay. Jorge moved in another fellow to help with the cost, but the landlord put another five dollars onto the rent. Then when Juan's family came, up went the rent again! Twenty dollars for less space! In his mind he was a very generous landlord. In our minds, *coño!* We were paying through the nose to sleep four people on the floor with the roaches and the sound of the trains shaking us like the vengeance of God. But truly, we slept only because we could not stay awake.

I bring up money because, at the time, money was what I concerned myself with most of the time. I made ten dollars a week, more or less. The money then was different, you have to understand. A good salary, like a policeman, was maybe fifty dollars a week. Understand? No matter what, I was saving five dollars a week, like a squirrel, *una ardilla*. In fact, at that time that's how I was called, Ardilla, not Luis. Juan still calls me Ardi. But of course I still call him Abé. People assume that his name is Ibrahim, but in truth it's for *abeja*, a bee. Those were our names and our ways.

Juan was very busy, having three jobs and walking all over the city. He tried to find work in his trade—a brickmason—but no one would hire him. That winter he had a hat, which he bought somewhere for fifty cents. A wool hat with yellow and black squares and earmuffs attached, the sort that is meant for a boy. And with those huge black eyes of his, and his round heavy eyebrows, hear me, he looked exactly like a bee!

Juan is a man of dignity and honor. All his money was sent back home, to his mother, to his family. He worked eighteen hours a day, every day. Sometimes the only rest he had was on the subway. He sent all the money back. That is his nature. Unlike myself, who is a younger brother, Juan is the eldest. His father was dead; he was the man of his family, with one brother and four little sisters. At that time, they were all children. Today they are married and have their own families. In fact, with two brothers-in-law, Juan now owns a small hardware store in East Harlem.

Of the men I know now, of my friends and relatives, Juan is the only one who knew Migdalia. Naturally, he has never spoken about that part of my life to any of my family. Just as I carry his secrets, he carries mine. We are true friends.

Alone in New York, one has no friends, because everyone is a stranger. I grew up on a farm, in a town with barely one street. Everyone was known, their ways and their natures. When someone new arrived in the area, it was noticed. Like when Fortuno, my father-in-law, pulled up in his truck. Everyone was curious. Some people were suspicious and kept a distance, and others got to know him very good. I was one who was attracted to his manner of life.

And, of course, his beautiful daughter caught my eye. What a head of hair she had! Heavy hair, which she tied up, but it always escaped into tiny curls going everywhere, the color of new copper pennies in the sun. Skin, as creamy and brown as caramel. And a ripe figure, like a mango where the juice will spill out the minute you touch it. I'm not exaggerating: My wife was the best-looking girl in the whole area, and she still is, although she is no longer fifteen.

She was an extraordinary girl! A girl who could do accounts and drive a truck, but who could also sew and cook and sing like an angel. Compared to her, I always felt that I would fail, disappoint her with my country ways, although my father-in-law assured me that I was man enough for his daughter.

Migdalia was a different type of woman completely, a dark, skinny girl, with a sharp tongue and a great deal of ambition. She had black hair, very long and straight, which she wore high in a comb. She had a gold tooth, which shone so bright when she laughed, it made you laugh. Migdalia was often laughing. I had twenty-two, twenty-three years then, and although I was in love with Luz, I was alone in a city of strangers.

Migdalia was a few years older than me. She had been here some years and spoke English. Not as good as my wife learned to speak it later, you understand, but at the time it was much more than me. But she knew things about this country, like where to get a cheap apartment, and where to buy food cheap. She knew how to read the job notices in the Spanish and also the English paper. She knew how to read the map of the trains, which believe me, is not easy! I had never seen a map before, except the one my wife showed me in a book she had, a map of the whole world.

Look, Migdalia had an account at the bank, and got one started for me. Migdalia understood about the laws of this country, like wages and hours, so that she was not so often cheated. These things now seem simple, but at the time I knew nothing. Migdalia Cruz is the reason I found the good job at the factory, soldering wires, and also why I moved downtown where she found a cheaper rent. Because of her, I put my money in the bank, and got extra, because at that time the banks paid you a lot to use your money, like a loan to them. Believe me, it was Migdalia that helped me, and if it wasn't for her, I wouldn't be here today.

Don't laugh, but when I first got on the subway train, I was scared to death. The moment it arrives, at that moment thousands of people are running in and out. I felt like I would be trampled. Look, the worst thing is, you can't see where you are going. It is not like a normal bus or a truck. I wondered how I was supposed to know when to get out. Jorge had the advantage of at least being in Ponce for some time and San Juan. But myself, I had only been on the bus to San Juan once, and that was for me a long trip, to take the midnight plane here.

On my first subway ride, I got on in a station high above ground, which is higher than standing on the roof at home, which was the highest I had ever been in the open. I was to go to Brooklyn for a job. Naturally, I had seen these high trains from the street where I lived, and was used to them above me. They went by my window like a hurricane every few minutes. So they stopped alarming me after a while.

For several miles, I rode along, looking down at the people below in the street, and it was interesting. Then suddenly, we were in darkness. My first thought was of a blackout. I had heard of this in the cities during the war, from Fernando. Sweat was on my forehead. I thought of bombs falling on me. But the English-speaking people around me were not disturbed. Nowhere did I see someone to ask. Everyone was calm, holding their newspapers, sitting like that, with no emotion. I could not see their faces clearly, because it was so dark. Then, I remembered that, of course, as my brother Fernando had told me, North Americans don't demonstrate much feeling, so I sat quietly, too, waiting to die. Suddenly, it was bright again! But not outside. The lights were on only in the train. I leaned over to see out of the window, hoping to find where I was, but another man was taking the window for himself, and to be frank, he was not going to give me an inch. For what I thought was many miles, I could make out only blackness, strange lights, and long caverns. As the train made one of its stops, I decided it was time to escape because I could not remain in such an unpredictable vehicle all the way to Brooklyn. As soon as I got up to go to the door, millions of people came pushing me back, others were behind me pushing me out. Everyone was pushing and running, so it was clear that there was desperation in that place and I ran, too. Then a woman bangs right into me, going the other way.

"*Hombre, cuidao!*" she scolded me at the top of her voice.

"*Coño!*" I replied without politeness.

"Where do you think you're going?" she asks me, as if I had purposely pushed her.

"*Ai, muchacha,* I'm only running with everyone else!"

Just as I was going to apologize, and thinking that since she spoke to me in Spanish I could ask her something about how to escape, a man with a huge suitcase hits me in the knee. "They are evacuating the train," I began to explain. "It is causing a panic."

But when I looked up, I could see that she was laughing, strong laughter with tears in her eyes.

"*Jíbaro! Hombre!* This is Grand Central Station!" She tossed her head back; she had such a laugh.

I nodded. And she repeated, "Grand Central Station" in English.

"Yes, of course," I said, trying to be a man who knows.

But again, she was laughing. "You will get accustomed to the crowds," she said.

That was Migdalia, who fished me from the river of people and became my guide. A real woman, a girl only a few years older than me, who helped me and became my friend.

PHYSICIAN OF THE MIND
AND HEART (2004)

OLUBANSILE ABBAS MIMIKO, M.D.

Born in Nigeria, Dr. Mimiko is a physician at Harlem Hospital. He has
created a story based on his work experience with the community that
he serves. He has been a member of the Harlem Writers Guild since
1995, and lives with his family in Brooklyn, New York.

The haunted realm often visited by the suicidal mind had never ceased
to fire Malik's imagination in the five years of his work as an emergency
psychiatrist. He was Malik Niles, M.D., assistant professor of psychiatry,
diplomate of the American Board of Psychiatry and Neurology, rising
star, tall and good-looking, and at thirty-five, the youngest-ever chief of
Psychiatric Emergency and Consultation Services at the famed Harlem
Medical Center. He was the author of multiple publications in the fields
of suicidology and psychotrauma, community activist, mentor, and,
perhaps, husband-to-be.

Still, for him, just like K. R. Jamison would say, with every new act
of suicide, night fell fast.

He dashed out of the lobby of the D Pavilion, where his office was
located, and headed for the M Building, whose first floor housed the
hospital's massive ER, with all its glitz and grind. His customarily long
strides made him a difficult person to keep pace with, but tonight he was
walking alone. Malik had just received a page regarding a near-fatal suicide attempt by a woman in her twenties.

He glanced at his old, scratched Seiko. It was 7:00 P.M. and rather
cold and windy for November 29th. He gathered the lapels of his faded,
gray blazer, his favorite, around himself. One more hour and his tour for
the night would be completed. He was gifted with keen senses and a
deep appreciation for nature—factors that kept him sane over the years
of his turbulent adolescence, and had served him well in his adult life to
relax his mind and keep things in perspective.

Malik took in the cool wind that greeted his close-cropped scalp and brown, clean-shaven face in the open walkway. He listened for the music in the rustling of the golden autumn leaves on the oak trees that lined the paved concrete. He sought to comprehend what vicissitudes of life made tonight's victim conclude that every door of hope was sealed off for good, on the particular day when people gave thanks.

He mused about the fact that many of his colleagues regarded him as being a little loony and smiled to himself. Why would a chief of service schedule himself for call every holiday instead of rotating the several psychiatrists under his watch?

But this was the kind of stuff that made him Malik. What did most of these pampered-through-life guys know regarding the floods of psyche-ache that came to millions of people on anniversaries and holidays, other than what they've read in their medical texts? Who among them had a parent put a bullet through his own skull on a day marked for joyful celebration?

Malik's father had committed suicide on Christmas when he was only fourteen. The memories were sharper than the fangs of a cobra.

He'd told Mom that he would be arriving late for Thanksgiving dinner this evening. It was the same story last year, and so would it be for the next. He found it unbelievable that the year 2002, full of events for him, was almost gone. Uncle Ron, his father's only brother, was in town from San Francisco with his ageless wife, Lora. Aunt Ella-Mae, the eighty-year-old matriarch of Mama's family, flew in yesterday from Atlanta, as well.

These past few weeks, Mama had become persistent that he bring Trisha home and introduce her to the family, accusing him of developing "fool's cold feet over the woman of his destiny." Going by the pressures of the past few weeks, he was sure the shrewd mother hen had something up her colorful feathers with this family reunion.

It was cold feet, all right, but regardless, he still had fog to clear from his mind. He had to figure out if he was still going to be with Trisha before going to face the old foxes of the family and announcing a wedding date. Z had continued to loom larger in his heart by the day since he learned about her impending divorce six months ago. His total devotion to Trisha these past three years was well known to friends and foes alike, so if he decided to do the unthinkable and ditch Trish for Z, hell was certain to arrive at his doorstep.

Mama might come around eventually and accept Z after she'd gotten to know how sweet she was, too. She might even miss her only son after the long exile and allow him back under her roof once again.

And then there was Sue. He'd invited her out just after seeing her perform a Ghanaian dance with the Indigo dance troop at the Apollo last week. Sue broke it down like she was the real deal, like she was a princess from the homeland.

What spirits on God's earth have seized control of his mind? Mama would literally smother him if she saw him with his brand-new blonde, African dance or no African dance. Sue would score straight Fs for being the exact opposite of everything Mama loved in Trish, who was about the same height as herself: five foot six and dark chocolate-colored, full features. Mama described Trish as "having some decent meat to cover them bones like a real woman."

Being a fine arts teacher who had turned Mama's place into a mini-gallery for her best paintings hadn't hurt Trish's standing, either. To make matters worse, Trish was now twenty-eight, the exact age at which Mama married his father.

With this on his mind, Malik burst through the automated doors of the urgent care section of the ER and right into specialist Dr. Giovanni, who yelled, "Hey, Niles, the page was mine. I need a one-to-one observation order for bed three!"

Greg Giovanni, at thirty-eight, looked like a clown and acted like one—about five foot three, moon-faced, completely balding and pot-bellied, never serious and never anxious. Ever so often Greg reminded him of Danny DeVito in scrubs.

"So what's up with bed three?" he asked in a measured tone to temper Greg. Greg moved in closer, placed an arm on Malik's towering shoulder, and whispered up to him, "Man, you need to see this babe. She is the bomb. How could she ever have thought of taking her own life? I'll kill myself in her place one hundred times over . . . "

"Greg!" Malik cut him short, flabbergasted.

"Okay, okay, at least nobody can deny this babe's got style. She left her fiancé a suicide note in gold crust. Now beat that, Freud."

Malik snatched the gold-embossed index card Greg trumped up from in between his chubby fingers. To him, this was indeed gold being trivialized by crazy Greg. The note read:

Mike, you know how much I love you,
But I could never have let you do this to yourself.
   Forever your Grace

Dr. Hutchinson, the anesthesiologist, walked over briskly to join them. Malik raised his head from the suicide note momentarily and nodded to acknowledge Z's presence. Zola flashed him a broad smile in return. Malik pretended to ponder the note in his hands. It was of course difficult to focus on the golden letters after beholding Z yet again. She looked crushingly beautiful in her sea-blue scrubs and fashionable white pumps.

Malik had lived with his overpowering feelings for her over the past nine years, since he'd first came to Harlem Medical Center to commence his residency training in 1992. She was just as mind-blowing a sister then—five feet nine, with golden-yellow skin, full lips, and locks worn at shoulder length. But for her having been taken at the time, he would have proposed to her on day one! At twenty-four, she had already graduated from SUNY Downstate Medical School in Brooklyn, was at the Harlem Center for her one-year transitional studies in preparation for subsequent training in anesthesiology, and, painfully, already married to a professor of English at Medgar Evers.

Z was now thirty-three and a separated mother of a six-year-old. To Malik, Z had lost nothing of her charms. In fact, she had matured into a black woman in full bloom.

Greg jarred Malik back from dreamland by saying, "I've never seen you so agitated about a patient, Z!"

Zola fired back, obviously in no mood for fooling around. "Look, this poor woman slashed both wrists and tried to drown herself in her own bathtub instead of going to Thanksgiving dinner with her in-laws-to-be. How much worse could it get?"

"Yeah, and let's not forget about her man," Greg said. "I'm sayin', how the hell does a fiancé deal with driving to his girl's apartment, only to meet her in that state!?!"

"I'm not about to lose this sister!" With that, Zola grabbed Greg by his arm and began pulling him back with her to bed three. Malik broke into a long stride, right on their heels.

"Easy, Z. She's stable. May not even need a blood transfusion. Can't a man enjoy a decent five minutes' relaxation when the ER isn't boiling over?" Greg protested, trying to keep pace with Zola. The cardiac monitors beeping all around added a rhythm that made Greg's tiptoeing look like the dance steps of a grub of a son sentenced by his parents to ballet class. Malik fought the urge to crack up.

"Agreed, Greg. She doesn't need intubation, either—thank goodness. Now get back to the work of maintaining that stability!" said Zola.

"Z, all that's left is putting her on one-to-one, and Malik can help order that."

Zola let go of Greg, turned to Malik, and whispered, "Malik, would you like to say a word to Grace? She isn't saying much to us."

He nodded again. Z gave Malik more details about their newest patient.

Malik marveled at Zola's hypnotic powers over him. Part of him had always enjoyed Z's subtle flirtation with him all these years. When they had first gotten acquainted nine years back, even though she'd recently been married, she would bat her eyes at him rather seductively and call him "Doctor Handsome, Doctor the Greatest," and the like.

In those early days at the Medical Center, Z's mere presence was enough to drive his blood to the boiling point—and indeed, he suspected the feeling was mutual—but he was a man of great restraint, and struggled through the years with the heartache of having fallen so deeply in love with another man's wife.

But with the demise of Zola's nine-year-old marriage, he had found himself struggling once again with a resurgence of his old passions for Z, despite his relationship with Trish. He loved Trish, without a doubt, and she had been his loyal girl for three whole years, but at the moment, he was no longer a stranger to the claim that tender feelings never really die.

In a few minutes, Zola proceeded to introduce him to patient Grace Williams.

"Hello, I'm Dr. Niles, the chief of Emergency Psychiatry," Malik announced softly as he reached out to hold Grace's trembling hands. "Your ER physicians called me because they thought you might want to talk to someone." He deliberately didn't focus on her bandaged wrists.

Zola and Greg quietly withdrew from within the drawn screen to allow Malik to do his thing.

Grace looked pitiful behind the white hospital sheets. In spite of her blood-shot eyes, Malik was instantly struck by her beauty. She was a Halle Berry carved out of flawless ebony.

"Life sucks, Doctor . . . darkness all around me . . . it's a shotgun I need, not a shrink," she finally managed, with fresh tears streaming down her eyes.

Malik pulled up a chair and offered her tissues from his breast pocket. He sighed.

"I can't even pretend and tell you I know what you're going through right now, but if you would be kind enough to help me to begin to understand . . . "

With the spasms of her sobbing relenting a bit, Grace groaned, "Why? Why do I have to tell you anything, Doctor. I don't know anything about you."

"Follow your feelings, Grace. It seems to me your feelings tell you that I genuinely care, that I'm not sitting here for any other purpose than to listen and walk this difficult road with you."

She looked at him for what seemed like an eternity, dabbing at the tears that continued to well up in her eyes.

"Doctor, Mike and I were supposed to be announcing our wedding date before his family tonight, but I just couldn't go through with it. Not anymore . . . " Her voice was drowned by her sobs again.

Malik waited, holding and gently stroking her hand, his face subdued.

"I'm dying, Doctor—of AIDS. But who, other than Mike, is going to believe that I was in the dark regarding this until three days ago? It's not Mike's fault, and so I can't do this to him . . . can't let him do it to himself."

Malik's brow furrowed.

"I'm so sorry, Grace. This must have been a particularly difficult piece of news to hear, especially at this time in your life. But your doctors told me you're infected with the HIV virus. They didn't say you have full-blown AIDS . . . "

"But I can't live with the virus, Doctor. I'm better off forgotten so that Mike can move on with his life."

"Have you told Mike? Anyone?"

Grace nodded, biting her lower lip. "Mike knows. We went together to receive the results. I turned my man's world upside down overnight and he sucks it up like all is well. That's what makes this so unbearable.

Swears on his mother's grave that he still loves me and will never let me go. Says he doesn't judge or blame me."

Malik leaned forward in his seat with heightened attention.

Grace found the strength to continue. "He forced his way with me, that bastard."

Malik gave her a confused look.

"I'm talking about Cleo, the wide receiver. He was the star of our college football team. NFL-bound. I was dumb. He forced his way with me—without a condom. That was my first . . . " She put her hands to her mouth.

"He date-raped you."

"I should have stopped him, done something, screamed, but I let him hold me down there and have his way. I can still smell that animal . . . I was too ashamed to tell anyone . . . didn't want to be the laughingstock of everyone on campus."

"I imagine you must have been scared, too, being that he was the star . . . "

"Scared out of my wits. He reminded me that the university's dream of a championship rested on him, said a whole mob would be waiting to impale me if I as much as caused a stir."

"So you shook off the dust . . . "

"Tried to move on with what was left of the ruins of my life, poured my whole self into academics, all the way through my doctorate. Did my best not to look back. It was the only way I fought off the impulses to slash my wrists. Never dated or slept with anyone again."

"You protected yourself all those years the way you best knew how."

"Yes, till I met Mike. And good Lord, was he persistent." Grace swallowed hard and shut tight her eyes to fight back the tears pooling again. Malik waited.

"I was twenty-eight when Mike came along. Ten years had passed. I thought I had finally shaken off the ghost of Cleo . . . "

"Then . . . ?"

"Mike proposed two weeks ago and we both thought it was a good idea that we underwent some tests to be sure we would both be safe with each other without protection. We've always used condoms . . . then this. How could I pretend with Mike that everything is ever going to be all right again? I could never let him go through with tonight's plan."

"So . . . ?"

"I told him to allow us time so we could think this over, but he was adamant. I watched him so closely, hoping to pick up even a slight change in him, but he didn't waver a bit. He remained as excited about us as ever. . . . It was the most painful thing to see how much he cared. . . . "

"And tonight . . . ?"

"Tonight was when I died. I couldn't bear myself anymore. I asked, Why should I continue living like this? and just wept and wept. . . . Then I left Mike the note . . . "

"And . . . ?"

"I changed into my black silk robe—Mike's special gift on my last birthday, said a prayer to the Lord to forgive me, and bring peace to Mom, Dad, and Mike after . . . after I'm gone."

Grace became totally submerged in her torrent of tears and Malik held her hand until the violent quaking of her emotions quieted into intermittent spasms. Then he began.

"At some point, Grace, every woman or man who's suffered a heart-rending experience like yours will have to be bold enough to begin to take little steps into the future. Yes, you were the victim, and that animal did you wrong. But you don't have to remain a victim. And once you've allowed yourself to cross that difficult bridge from self-blame, you will begin to understand why Mike hasn't loved you any less during the past three days of your painful discovery. For now, we—your doctors and nurses—are so thankful, like I'm sure Mike is, that you are alive, as upsetting as the experience of having survived might be for you."

Grace stared at Malik again. He didn't let go of her hand.

At 8:15 P.M., Malik had completed writing his findings and recommendations on Grace in the consultation form. He ordered her to be placed on one-to-one special observation for suicide, which meant she would have a nurse stay within arm's length of her twenty-four hours of the day. He would have to call Grace's parents in Florida. They, along with that great fiancé of hers, would cast a protective web of unconditional love around her so she could begin the crucial process of recommitting to life.

Mike was anxiously waiting in the lobby to see his beloved. As Malik approached the center aisle to begin making his calls, his own life story began to unfold before him. Mike could have cut and run when he found out that his girl had HIV, yet he stood by her. And here he was, wavering about Trish. Trisha, the sweetest girl ever to be put on mother earth by God, his closest friend and the clear choice of his mother, a wise woman who'd suffered immeasurable heartaches to raise him into who he was now. Yet, here he was, wavering, simply because he was letting an old flame, long tamed, begin to burn out of control again.

He felt ashamed that he even went so far as to ask Sue out, but that he could fix. But he wasn't as sure about how to deal with his feelings for Z. He wondered what Grace would have thought of him if she knew of his situation with Trish, as he sat there, playing God's very angel of piety. He slumped into a chair and held his head in his hands. Greg and Zola spotted him and walked over to join him.

He saw them and said, "Need to make a couple of calls to her folks and I'll be done. When she's medically cleared, please transfer her over to the psych floor. How's her fiancé doing?"

"Let's call him Knight in Golden Armor. I'm assuming we can send him over to the psych unit, after you talk to him, of course. And by the way, I'm still waiting to get a guy like Knight for Z, since she is now officially available but thinks I'm too cute to qualify," Greg chuckled.

After the vintage Greg moment, Malik looked at Zola and her eyes locked into his. He suddenly realized that she'd had her dreamy eyes focused on him all along. She was achingly beautiful, standing there, her gaze glowing with intense fire and tenderness. They were having a dialogue that needed no words.

By 8:40, Malik rolled out leisurely from Lenox Terrace onto 135th street. He had just squeezed in a quick shower—didn't want Mama to say he smelled like hospital when he arrived at her place.

Bob Marley's lyrics, "I wanna love you . . ." drifted from his car stereo. He turned right on Fifth Avenue, heading toward 116th Street where Mama lived. He had been eyeing some brownstones in the neighborhood, with input from Trish, but pulled back recently in order to get his love life sorted out first.

Harlem, sweet Harlem, he thought. He didn't know what the neighborhood of his birth would look like in ten years with gentrification encroaching from downtown.

Mama would have her dinner table set now, with Uncle Ron, Aunt Lora, and shrewd Ella-Mae sitting in a circle, plotting strategies concerning another man's life—his.

He loved his mom more than anyone else in the world. The same old Mama, now sixty-one and going strong, who thought she could still beat his behind even at fourteen when he left his homework undone to hang out with the kids that slung drugs. Mama, who would bake him his favorite corn bread to wash down with Kool-Aid as a child when he did right.

Mama would be really pleased if Trisha appeared in front of the family tonight. Her sensing that all was not right between him and Trish of late was perhaps the only reason she hadn't picked up the phone to invite Trish herself.

He flipped on his cell phone and held it to his heart, still feeling a lingering heaviness deep within. He wanted to call Trish.

What is love? And does love always lead to happiness? he asked himself again. Was love the intense warmth that bathed the soul when one watched a graceful dancer, like Sue? Was it the simple, comforting peace shared over soul food with a caring and dependable friend, like Trisha? Or was it the fireworks that literally crackle up inside the mind when one stood before the object of one's intense desire, like Zola? Even for a physician of the mind, these were hard questions, questions he knew he could not escape for long.

He decided to turn off his cell. For now, he would go home to his mama and the rest of his family and stuff his face with turkey and homemade gravy and everything else that the good women in his life had cooked up. Then he would retire inside himself in the quiet of the night to draw inspiration from the soul-stirring stories of the Mikes and Graces of the world.

MY FATHER'S FIRST BRA (2004)

AYESHA RANDOLPH

Randolph describes herself as a Harlem-born, raised, and educated teacher. She still lives in Harlem and tends to write very funny and moving stories about what she's seen and remembers. Her recollections often have the reader laughing even before they start. "My Father's First Bra," a true story, is but one example.

On Saturdays, it was always just my dad and me. Sundays we would go to my grandmother's house with the rest of our family and spend the day. Monday through Friday it would be school, baby-sitter, then home to eat and sleep. But Saturdays was just my dad and me, ever since my mom died ten years ago.

We bicycled around Central Park, went to Steak n' Take on 116th Street, washed clothes, went to the movies, visited the Schomburg, went on the Museum Mile, shopped on 125th Street, and walked around Woolworth to see what was new, or just stayed at home to watch cartoons, read to each other, and play fight. We don't spend that many Saturdays together now, more by mutual consent, but I will never forget those special days.

One Saturday, years later, my dad and I had lunch over at Native's on 118th Street and he laughingly told the tale of one very eventful day. Dad and I always played rough. As a child I would try and hit him with everything I had, and he would show me the correct way to hit, kick, and give a good sucker punch. I had won many a fistfight because of what he taught me.

Most of the time the fight would end with my father holding me back with one hand on my chest, until I got tired. On this particular day, my dad and I were play fighting, and I got a good stomach punch in. His hand shot at me as I ran in for a second blow. I don't recall the pain that flared in my chest, but I do remember sobbing on the floor. I must have been twelve years old. Not knowing what to do, he called my grand-mother.

My grandmother, Christalyia Agatha Stevens Randolph, is the type of woman that finds something wrong with you even if your name is Mother Theresa. She is eighty-four years old going on 380. If there is a problem, she must have a say. She is the judge and jury among my rela-tives. The sheep in my family follow her decisions submissively. Don't get me wrong, I love and cherish my grandmother, just not when I'm around her.

My dad presumes she is always right. (I think he takes the term "honor thy mother" a little too seriously.) But on this occasion, she helped out (which was rare). She said, "That girl is getting older. She needs a bra."

Not making the connection, Dad said, "What are you talking about?"

"She is growing breasts. You know, becoming a woman. It is natural that she is a little sore."

"Are you sure?"

"Of course I'm sure! What do you take me for, an idiot?! Just do what I say!"

My father said, "Oh . . . all right," and hung up the phone. He sat back and started to cry, "Oh God, why me?" He picked me up as he con-tinued with, "Ayesha, get dressed. We're going shopping."

"What for, Daddy?"

He looked at me puzzled, as if unsure of my identity, and said, "Just get dressed." He put his slacks and T-shirt on. He then began to comb and brush that patch of grayish black hair that hung on the back of his head for about twenty minutes. He dressed me in a T-shirt and rainbow pants and did my hair the way he normally did, in three pigtails. Those pants and pigtails were two of the main reasons why I got in so many fights when I was in school.

Not soon after, we stood in front of Lerner's department store on 125th Street, between Frederick Douglass Boulevard and Adam Clayton Powell, Jr., Avenue. I held his hand as he looked down at me and said, "It's not that difficult." I remember not understanding what he meant back then, but I smiled anyway and nodded my head. When we finally went inside, my father gave my hand a squeeze. As we walked around the store, I pointed to the solid-color pants they had on display.

"Daddy, can I have one?"

My father didn't answer, he led me straight to the stairs, he stopped and mumbled to himself, "It's not that difficult." We went down the spiral stairs hand in hand. We hit the bottom and looked around. We saw teddies, bras, panties, garter belts, stockings, and pantyhose. The assortment was mind-boggling: small, large, XL, and the colors. Oh my God, the colors: pink, blue, red, green, and wine. It looked like a lingerie rainbow. And they were all as far as the eye could see. My dad grunted as he took it all in and said, "It's not that difficult."

"Dad, what's this?"

He glanced at what I was holding and mumbled, "It's a garter— What are— Put that down!!" He snatched it out of my hand and threw it behind him. He took my hand firmly and guided me down the many aisles. We finally stopped in front of a display of young adult wear.

My father, in his anxiety, looked around and made sure the women in the store were not looking our way. He grabbed the first plain white bra his hand touched. He looked at me with a grin and said, "It's not that difficult."

As we turned around, a cherub of a woman came up to us and said, "Can I help you, sir?

"Hum, er, no, thank you."

"Are you sure, sir? I saw you over here, and you looked kind of lost."

"No, no I don't need any help." As he said this, he dropped the bra, pushed me behind him, and started walking backward toward the stairs.

"I can help you pick a bra for your daughter." The saleswoman picked up the bra and started to walk toward us.

My father said, "No, that's all right!" I started to go up, but I guess I didn't move fast enough, because the next thing I knew his arm was around my waist picking me up. He went up the stairs two at a time. As soon as I turned my head we were once again standing in front of Lerner's department store.

He took me over to the side and said, "Here is what we're going to do. You are going back downstairs to that lady I was talking to, and tell her you need two bras. Got that?"

I nodded my head.

"Good, get two of them. Here is fifteen dollars. Now get going. I'll be right here." He gave me a little push to send me on my way.

I went inside and told the lady what I needed. She helped me out while chuckling and shaking her head. When I was being rung up the woman told me that I didn't have enough money. She then asked where my father was. "He's standing outside," I said. The cashier and the saleswoman started to laugh. She then grabbed my hand and the bag of bras, and started for the door.

My father jumped when the woman said, "Excuse me, sir."

"Yes, what is it?" he said, as he looked around.

"You're fifty cents short, sir. So I just thought I'd—" That is as far as she got because my dad dug into his pants and threw some money at her. He grabbed me and the bag in the blink of an eye. He was off down the street and made a left, going past the newsstand. Then my father stopped and handed me the bag, smiling at me. He took a deep breath and said, "That wasn't so difficult."

PERMISSIONS

From *The Autobiography of an Ex-Colored Man* by James Weldon Johnson, reprinted by permission from Dr. Sondra Kathryn Wilson.

"The Negro's Gift to Mankind" by W.E.B. Du Bois, reprinted by permission of David G. Du Bois.

From *Dark Princess* by W.E.B. Du Bois, copyright © 1928 by W.E.B. Du Bois, reprinted by permission of David G. Du Bois.

Selections from *Nigger Heaven*, originally published by Alfred A. Knopf, Inc., 1926, are reprinted from the University of Illinois Press paperback edition, 2000, by permission of the Carl Van Vechten Trust, and may not be further reprinted without written authorization.

From *Home to Harlem* by Claude McKay, copyright © Claude McKay, 1928, © Hope McKay Virtue, 1955, courtesy of the Literary Representative for the Works of Claude McKay, Schomburg Center for Research in Black Culture, The New York Public Library, Astor, Lenox and Tilden Foundations.

"Negro Life in New York's Harlem" by Wallace Thurman; originally published as an article in the October–November–December 1927 (vol. 2, no. 1) issue of the *Haldeman-Julius Quarterly*, and then as part of the book *Negro Life in New York's Harlem*.

"Spunk" by Zora Neale Hurston, reprinted by permission of the National Urban League.

"Art and Such," written by Zora Neale Hurston for the Federal Writers' Project, 1938.

Excerpt from the Negro Version of *Macbeth* by William Shakespeare and Orson Welles; originally staged in 1936.

Excerpt from *Drums at Dusk* by Arna Bontemps. Hardcover edition originally published in 1939.

From *The Richer, The Poorer* by Dorothy West, copyright © 1995 by Dorothy West. Used by permission of Doubleday, a division of Random House, Inc.

Chapter One from *The Street* by Ann Petry. Copyright © 1946 by Ann Petry. Copyright © Renewed 1974 by Ann Petry. Reprinted by permission of Houghton Mifflin Company. All rights reserved.

From *Go Tell It on the Mountain* by James Baldwin, copyright © 1952, 1953 by James Baldwin. Used by permission of Doubleday; a division of Random House, Inc.

"Spanish Blood" from *Short Stories* by Langston Hughes. Copyright © 1996 by Ramona Bass and Arnold Rampersad. Reprinted by permission of Hill and Wang, a division of Farrar, Straus and Giroux, LLC.

From *Purlie Victorious* by Ossie Davis. Copyright © 1961 by Ossie Davis. Reprinted by permission of Ossie Davis.

Rosa Guy, Chapter 3 from *Bird at My Window*. Copyright © 1965 by Rosa Guy. Reprinted with the permission of Coffee House Press, Minneapolis, Minnesota.

From *dem* by William Melvin Kelley. Copyright © 1967 by William Melvin Kelley. Reprinted by permission of Coffee House Press.

From *This Child's Gonna Live*, copyright © 1969 by Sarah E. Wright, by permission of the Feminist Press at the City University of New York, *www.feministpress.org*.

From *Daddy Was a Number Runner*, copyright © 1970 by Louise Meriwether, by permission of the Feminist Press at the City University of New York, *www.feministpress.org*.

John Oliver Killens, "Yoruba" from *The Cotillion, or One Good Bull is Half the Herd*. Copyright © 2002 by the Estate of John Oliver Killens. Reprinted with the permission of Coffee House Press, Minneapolis, Minnesota.

"Crying for Her Man," by Ann Allen Shockley, reprinted by permission of the author.

John A. Williams, except from *Captain Blackman*. Copyright © 1972 by John A. Williams. Reprinted with the permission of Coffee House Press, Minneapolis, Minnesota.

William H. Banks, Jr., excerpt from *Beloved Harlem*, copyright © 1974, 2002 by William H. Banks, Jr. Reprinted by permission of the author.

From *In the Shadow of the Peacock* by Grace F. Edwards, copyright © 1988 by Grace F. Edwards, reprinted by permission of the author.

"A Christmas Story" by Andrea Broadwater, reprinted by permission of the author.

From Keith Gilyard's *Voices of the Self: A Study of Language Competence*, pp. 15–26, with the permission of Wayne State University Press. Copyright © 1991 by Wayne State University Press, Detroit, Michigan 48201. All rights reserved.

From *Jazz*, reprinted by permission of International Creative Management, Inc. Copyright © 1992 by Toni Morrison.

John Henrik Clarke's commentary reprinted by permission of his estate.

From *Sowa's Red Gravy Stories* by Diane Richards, copyright © 2002 by Diane Richards, reprinted by permission of the author.

From *The Queen of Harlem* by Brian Keith Jackson, copyright © 2002 by Brian Keith Jackson. Used by permission of Doubleday, a division of Random House, Inc.

ABOUT THE EDITOR

WILLIAM H. BANKS, JR., is the executive director of the Harlem Writers Guild. His book *A Love So Fine* was published in 1974 and is widely regarded as the first African-American romance novel. He's also authored *The Black Muslims* and coauthored *Father Behind Bars.*

Banks has worked as a newspaper columnist and correspondent, and won the Award of Excellence in Political Coverage and Service from the United Nations Society of Writers in 1997. He's taught creative writing at New School University and Marymount College and hosts *In Our Own Words,* the only regularly scheduled television program dedicated exclusively to black writing.